The Deluge
VOLUME I

By W. S. KUNICZAK

Novels:
Valedictory
The March
The Thousand Hour Day

Translations:
"The Trilogy" (Henryk Sienkiewicz)
I With Fire and Sword
II The Deluge
III Fire in the Steppe

History:
My Name is Million

Entertainments:
The Sempinski Affair

The Deluge
VOLUME I

Henryk Sienkiewicz

In Modern Translation by
W. S. Kuniczak

COPERNICUS SOCIETY OF AMERICA
with
HIPPOCRENE BOOKS
New York

Published by the Copernicus Society of America, Edward J. Piszek,
president, in its program of modern translations of Polish literary
classics, which begins with "The Trilogy" by Henryk Sienkiewicz that
opened with the publication of *With Fire and Sword* in May, 1991,
and of which this book is the second in the series.

With Fire and Sword, May, 1991 ISBN 0-87052-974-9
The Deluge, October, 1991 ISBN 0-87052-004-0
Fire in the Steppe, May 1992 ISBN 0-87052-005-9

Distributed in the U.S.A. by
Hippocrene Books, Inc.
171 Madison Avenue, New York, NY 10016
Tel. (212) 685-4371

Library of Congress Cataloging-in-Publication Data
Sienkiewicz, Henryk, 1846-1916.
Potop. English
The deluge/Henryk Sienkiewicz;
in modern translation by W.S.Kuniczak —1st ed.
p. cm.
Translation of: *Potop*
ISBN 0-87052-004-0
1. Poland —History —John II Casimir, 1648-1668 —Fiction.
I. Title.

Jacket Illustration: Jozef Brandt, *Ein Gefecht* (det.), Museum Purchase,
1880, in the collection of The Telfair Academy of Arts and Sciences Inc.,
Savannah, Georgia

Designed by Robert L. Pigeon

Endpaper Maps by Eugenia Gore

Printed in the United States of America

For my American and English godchildren: Jack Allen, Adam Kozaczka, and Jackie (Wiesia) Carl — and for my honorary goddaughters Krysia Maciuszko and Rebecca Grey — so that they may love and honor their heritage if they want to — and to the memory of Aloysius A. Mazewski.

—W.S.K.

Acknowledgements

I wish to thank Mark A. Kamienski, Francis Keenan, Jacek Galazka and George Blagowidow, Prof. Lech Ludorowski, Drs. Thomas Napierkowski, Marion Moore Coleman and Stanley Kozaczka, and the indefatigable Mrs. Anna Chrypinska for their hard work, encouragement, assistance or advice

W. S. Kuniczak
Editor-in-Chief

Introduction

In 1905, partly on the basis of his "Trilogy," (*With Fire and Sword*, 1883-84; *The Deluge*, 1884-86; and *Colonel Wolodyjowski*, 1887-88), Henryk Sienkiewicz was awarded the Nobel Prize for Literature. The citation of award focused on the Polish author's "outstanding merits as an epic writer." Elaborating on the decision of the Swedish Academy, C.D. af. Wirsen describes Sienkiewicz as "one of those rare geniuses who concentrate in themselves the spirit of a nation" and who portray the character of their people in the eyes of the world. "If one surveys Sienkiewicz's achievement," he continues in his presentation address, "it appears gigantic and vast and at every point noble and controlled. As for his epic style, it is of absolute artistic perfection."

Having withstood all the tests of time—as James A. Michener notes in his foreword to W. S. Kuniczak's translation of *With Fire and Sword*—Sienkiewicz's great, multi-volume masterwork "remains the soaring prototype of the national epic." Furthermore, *The Deluge* here presented, is arguably the best of "The Trilogy's" three interrelated novels.

For people who have the eyes to see into the true human meaning of historical events, "The Trilogy" is not only "a mirror of a nation's soul" as so many critics recognize today, but a compendium of all those racial memories and feelings that make history a living entity rather than just a listing of facts, dates and figures. Indeed, it is a great deal more than even that. In the profundity of its analysis and its depth of vision it borders upon the prophetic, and that is nowhere clearer than in *The Deluge* which is "The Trilogy's" structural and thematic heart.

Here for all to see is a definition of the Polish national

character and historical experience, in both their worthy and unworthy aspects, that offers and almost point-by-point foreshadowing of all those spiritual and political forces which came together so dramatically in Poland within this decade, shattered the grip of communism throughout Central Europe, helped to restore political and economic freedom to half a dozen nations, and rewrote the dark pages of Soviet domination which cast such a gigantic shadow on the world since 1945. Unthinkable for more than two generations, this astounding bloodless revolution which began with Solidarity in Poland appears almost obvious in Sienkiewicz's brilliant "Trilogy," written almost a hundred years earlier. This monumental epic clearly documents that indomitable national will to live which makes the Poles so committed to their independence that they've been described as "an authoritarian's despair." There is no doubt that this great work, written to "uplift the hearts" in 1883, inspired that nation in its modern struggle to reestablish political pluralism, rebuild their democratic institutions and return to a free economy. Now it is here in English, to teach and inspire others.

On this prophetic or philosophic level "The Trilogy" is a leap across the centuries into our own time, specifically into the agony that gripped the Polish people since 1939. "The more things change," the reader says in wonder, "the more they are the same." Invaders come and go. Victories become disasters. One ruthless enemy replaces another. But the Nation lives, the people survive deep within themselves and eventually triumph, and the road to these immemorial Polish resurrections is always the same. We read *The Deluge* as if it were a Seventeenth Century allegory of our times, recounting all that happened to the Poles and Poland since the Second World War in 1939 and the forced imposition of a Soviet-style system which began in 1944. We experience similar defeats, disasters, treasons and betrayals, the ruthless foreign domination, the resistance focused around charismatic leaders and spiritual forces, Solidarity, martial law and everything that followed, all told in human, personal terms in a work of literary fiction whose author never knew an independent Poland. Indeed, for him as for all his countrymen for more than a century, that Poland lived merely in their hearts.

On its most accessible level, *The Deluge* sweeps even the most jaded reader into an adventure filled with relentless action, centered around the two universal themes of love and war, and involving an unforgettable cast of fictional and historical characters who are developed and portrayed with far more depth than is usual in works of epic fiction. The end result is gripping suspense and reader fascination. *The Deluge* is, in fact, the impassioned tale of two simultaneous struggles: the doomed yet triumphant love of Andrzej Kmicic for his beloved Olenka (or 'Andrei Kmita,' as simplified in this translation for the English reader), and a patriotic struggle against an onslaught by Sweden, Russia, resurgent Cossacks, and a stirring Prussia which savaged the Polish-Lithuanian Commonwealth in the second half of the Seventeenth Century. Both these motifs are marked with rivalry, alienation, separation, courage and treachery, dangers and escapes, disguises and assumed names, betrayal and redemption, plots, battles, tactics, tragic failures and eventual reunion in love and in victory; and both acquire brilliant clarity in one powerful intuitive moment when the confused and misled Andrei Kmita, lost in despair on a personal cross-roads of his own, identifies Olenka with his country, finds his way again, and plunges into his patriotic duty with a devotion that only love can give.

On another level, *The Deluge* excels as a historical novel in which Sienkiewicz brings to life the people, movements, events and the spirit of a turbulent past age where not just individuals but entire cultures stand in open conflict. Like a true master of the epic genre, he fills this vast historical arena with fully-fleshed fictional characters who take active part in the sweep of the history around them, interact with actual historical figures, and fulfill their destinies in the context of the universal whole. So powerfully drawn that it is impossible to think of them as merely invented, these characters give expression to the impact which history has upon the living, and produce a picture of the age in real and human terms.

Two men—Sir Walter Scott and Alexandre Dumas—are generally recognized in Western European literatures as the masters of this genre; the first producing powerful "costume pieces," while the second concentrates on adventure "recounted with gusto and careless responsibility." Sienkiewicz strives for both effects at once and achieves immeasurably more. In the words of one American critic, Sienkiewicz "seizes the outer aspect of an age with all the broad grasp of Scott, and peoples it with characters as vivid, virile, keen-witted and heroic as those of Dumas;"but where those two great predecessors halt, content to stay within the limits of historical adventure, that's where Sienkiewicz's true artistry begins. Going beyond both of them, Sienkiewicz "strikes below the surface events which concern his heroines and heroes to the deeper issues." He throws his imagination upon an epic canvas, and brings to life the mind, soul and character of the Polish nation; and nowhere is that spirit better shown than here in *The Deluge*.

It is well established that Sienkiewicz paid his debt of serious scholarship to the facts of the age being recreated. Despite this, he was occasionally accused of romanticizing some aspects of his work; and even though historians have long viewed the successful defense of Czestochowa in the winter of 1655 as the turning point in the last great Swedish invasion of Poland, his portrayal of that miracle has disturbed some critics.

Polish chronicles of the period wax eloquent on this point; and Sienkiewicz gives a scrupulous, almost word-for-word reflection of those contemporary accounts. Moreover, if we look at that great, heroic act of faith and courage through or own modern eyes, and use it as a palimpsest for the behavior of the Polish people within the last ten years, Sienkiewicz's vision is wholly justified. In this century as in the Seventeenth, Poland lay devastated by war, abandoned by allies, and betrayed into the hands of a ruthless enemy who turned the country into an exploited colony. Then unexpectedly, as during the Swedish deluge that overwhelmed the country, the nation was lifted to new life by a "miracle:" the election of the first Slavic Pope in history. Directed by the exhortations of that Polish priest and spurred by an unquenched love of liberty to yet another monumental effort, an exhausted people "lifted up their hearts," found new resources of courage and endurance, and brought about an astounding bloodless revolution. That is the theme and substance of *The Deluge*, although of course *that* story is full of blood and fire spilled across an enormous stage.

On a purely literary level, "The Trilogy" is the paramount example of the literary epic, fulfilling all requirements of that difficult and demanding genre which so few writers are even able to attempt. This may not be the moment to examine examples of the epic, so let this much suffice: in theme and structure "The Trilogy" deals with episodes crucial to the history of the nation and the people it describes. It does so in strict compliance to a literary tradition that goes back all the way to Homer. Indeed, one commentator goes out of his way to point out that these warriors of the Polish-Lithuanian Commonwealth "fight, love, hate, embrace each other, laugh, weep in each other's arms, and give each other wise advice with a truly Homeric simplicity. They are deeply versed in stratagems of love and war.... They have their Nestor, Agamemnon and Achilles sulking in his tent." And just like Homer, this Nineteenth Century Polish storyteller offers carefully crafted "hyperbolic descriptions" and focuses on personal duels within battle scenes.

The setting in ample, embracing a vast geographic area. The heroes, both historical and invented, play roles of national importance. The actions sometimes border on the superhuman; and although the gods take no part in the story, the Christian faith, the Black Madonna, and other spiritual forces are essential to the people who live in these novels. It is even possible to detect conventions such as epic catalogs and epic similes.

Other criteria of the epic require that the author "use words in a very distinguished way" and that he treat "many sides and a wide range of life;" and among Sienkiewicz's greatest achievements in "The Trilogy" are his descriptions of nature and events, his amazing richness of vocabulary, his wonderful command of dialogue, and his excellent reproduction of the era's everyday speech as used by the full spectrum of the population. Moreover, few writers of any era deal so successfully with such a vast mosaic of different kinds of people within a single work, or speak on behalf of an entire nation, which is the final classical condition for an epic. In that regard, Sienkiewicz himself is our foremost witness. "Nations are represented by their poets and their writers," he said in response to the Nobel Prize. "Consequently, the award of this prize glorifies not only the author but the People whose son he is. It has been said that Poland is dead, exhausted and enslaved. But here is proof of her life and triumph."

However it was the Polish people themselves who best confirmed this point at a delayed fiftieth birthday celebration for their beloved spokesman when they presented him with a small estate, bought through a nation-wide subscription fund, and who continue to buy out every edition of "The Trilogy"as soon as it appears.

Here then is one of the great epics of the modern age which has been "lost" for more than three quarters of a century for those of us who read and think in English. Scholars have long recognized the virtual impossibility of "transplanting" the epic. In the case of "The Trilogy," the problem was deepened by vast cultural differences between West and East, and an astounding Western ignorance of (and indifference to) the histories, cultures and civilizations of many nations at the "wrong" end of Europe.

All that, however, was changed on May 3 this year with the appearance of W.S. Kuniczak's modern translation of *With Fire and Sword*, and now with this truly splendid edition of *The Deluge*. Kuniczak is superbly suited to this task. Indeed, he may well be the only modern writer capable of carrying it out to a successful end. Himself an author of a modern epic—an honored trilogy of the Polish national experience in the Second World War—he is a bilingual, Polish-born, British-trained American novelist whose passion for "The Trilogy" of Henryk Sienkiewicz led him to suspend his own literary career, abandon his own writing, and sacrifice more than eight years to this gigantic task.

The task has been well worth the enormous effort. Kuniczak mirrors Sienkiewicz's imagery, recreates his language within another culture, and bridges the gaps in readers' understanding of those distant and unknown historical events. *The Deluge* comes to life as never before in English, and English-speaking readers throughout the world can now appreciate the impassioned power which Henryk Sienkiewicz exerted over his own countrymen for a hundred years. As Dr. Jerzy Maciuszko notes in his review of this great achievement in *World Literature Today*: "We are dealing here with two masterpieces. The original is the greatest prose epic of Polish literature, the other a masterpiece of translation."

Thomas Napierkowski, PhD.
University of Colorado

The Deluge
(Potop)

VOLUME I

" ... to uplift the hearts."

—Sienkiewicz

Author's Prologue

In the part of the old Grand Duchy of Lithuania that was known as Zmudya, and which antedated the times of recorded history, there lived an ancient family named Billevitch, widely connected with many other houses of Lithuanian gentry, and respected more than any other in the Rosyen region. None of the Billevitches ever held any great public office in the Commonwealth, rising no higher than county stewardships in the Polish-Lithuanian republic of the gentry which emerged from the union of Poland and Lithuania in 1569, but they served their country well in every generation for which they were richly rewarded under various rulers. Their family seat, known as Billevitche, exists to this day, but they had many other properties near Rosyen, Krakinov, throughout the Lauda region, and along the Shoya and Nevyezh rivers as far east as Ponevyezh, so that in time they split into several branches that seldom saw each other. Some of them got together now and then when the Zmudyan gentry gathered for the annual military census near Rosyen on a plain called Stany; sometimes they met in the Lithuanian regiments of the Commonwealth and at the local diets; and because they were wealthy, well-connected and influential with the lesser gentry, even the all-powerful Radzivills of Birjhe had to take them into account.

Their patriarch in the times of King Yan Casimir was Pan Heracles Billevitch, a colonel of Lithuanian Light Horse who also held the office of Steward of Upita under the Radzivills, but who didn't make his home in the family seat. That was held by his cousin Thomas, the *Myetchnik* or Constable of Rosyen. Pan Heracles resided in the villages of Vodokty, Lubitch and Mitruny in the Lauda region, surrounded by the lands of the minor

Laudanian gentry like tranquil islands of learning and enlighten-
ment in the sea of that hardworking, patient and devout
Zmudyan farmer-gentry that traced its own lineage back to the
pagan days before their Duke Yagiello married a Queen of
Poland.

Elsewhere in the country families took their names from their
properties, or the properties were named after the clans that held
them, but it was different with the Laudanians. The Stakyan
clan lived in the village of Morozy which King Stefan Batory
gave them for their valor in the Battle of Pskov; the dour,
heavy-handed Butryms, who were physically the biggest and the
strongest men among the Laudanians, and who stood like an
unbreakable, silent wall in war or in the time of the diets and
smaller local conflicts, made their homes in Volmontov; the rich
lands around Drohjeykany and Mozgi were tilled by the numerous Domashevitch clan, known as skilled foresters and hunters
who tracked the wild game through the Zyelonka Forests all the
way to Vilkomir and beyond. The Gashtovts, famous for the
beauty of their women, lived in Patzunel; the Sollohubs raised
horses and prime cattle in their own woodland clearings; and the
Gosyevitches made pitch and tar in the woods around their
village of Goshtchuny.

There were other clans and families in those territories—or
neighborhoods as they were known among the lesser gentry—but
history took its toll of them as it did in all the other regions of
the Commonwealth. Wars, raids and local turbulence turned
many settlements to ruin, the villages were seldom rebuilt in the
same place where they stood before, and some men called
themselves by other names in the course of time. In these times,
however, at the midpoint of the Seventeenth Century, Old
Lauda was still what it used to be, and the Laudanian gentry
reached the height of its fame and warlike reputation in the
Cossack Wars under the banners of Yanush Radzivill.

Tradition ruled that all of them should serve in the regiment
of Heracles Billevitch. The wealthier among them enlisted as
full-fledged members of the serving gentry—or *companions of the
first rank* as the term was known—bringing an armed and
mounted man-at-arms to fight in the second rank behind them,
and with a string of remounts and a troops of servants. The less

wealthy came alone with just one horse and weapons. The poorest of them, unable to afford a horse or armor of their own, enlisted as common men-at-arms and fought as bravely as their richer brethren. But they were less experienced in public affairs such as national politics, the great issues of their time, the parliament and their local diets. They knew that the King was in Warsaw, that a Radzivill was master of Zmudya and Lithuania, that Pan Hlebovitch was the Radzivills' right-hand-man in the Lauda country, and that Pan Billevitch did all the thinking that had to be done in Vodokty and along the Lauda. That was enough for them and they cast their votes as their old colonel taught them, convinced that he carried out the will of the Radzivills who, in turn spoke for the King in the Lithuanian countries, while the King was the protector of the Commonwealth and father of all the gentry.

As it happened, they weren't that far wrong. Pan Billevitch was more a friend than a client of the powerful autocrats of Birjhe, particularly since he had a thousand votes and a thousand Laudanian sabers at his beck and call. And in those days no one could ignore sabers in such hands as those of the Stakyans, the Butryms, the Domashevitches or the Gashtovts.

All that changed later for the Laudanian gentry, especially when Pan Heracles Billevitch was no longer there to guide them and advise them, and they missed him the most in the memorable year of 1654. A terrible war blazed that year along the whole eastern border of the Commonwealth with an invasion by the Russians and their Cossack allies, and Radzivill himself was disastrously beaten at the Battle of Shklov in which the Laudanian regiment was destroyed almost to a man in an attack on a brigade of French mercenaries.

Pan Heracles was too old and deaf to go to that war—the Lauda men were led by a younger colonel appointed by Radzivill—and when he heard the news of the Shklov disaster he suffered a stroke and died.

The news was first brought to Vodokty by Radzivill's young colonel, one Michal Volodyovski, but it soon seeped through all of the countryside as the shattered remnants of the Laudanians drifted home.

Like the rest of the ruined Lithuanian army they complained

about their Grand Hetman, the brooding Radzivill, who was so sure of his invincibility that he attacked a Russian army ten times more powerful than his own, and so doomed his men and the entire country. Not one voice, however, was raised against the young colonel who led the Laudanians. On the contrary, those who escaped from the disaster praised him to high heavens. Their only consolations were the great deeds they'd done under his command and how brilliantly he led them even in the catastrophe at Shklov. They told how they had cut through the Russian hordes in their first attack, how they crushed and scattered the first regiment of the French brigade whose colonel was sabered by Pan Volodyovski himself, and then, when they were surrounded and under fire from all sides, how they saved themselves by charging through the enemy with the last of their depleted strength.

But the main business of the Laudanians after their return was the funeral of their old commander and the reading of his will in which, to their surprise, they discovered that they were all named as the guardians of his heiress, his granddaughter Aleksandra. All of the Billevitch fortune was to go to her with one notable exception and it was this remarkable codicil that created the greatest commotion and curiosity in the countryside; the village and lands of Lubitch were irrevocably granted to a young man whom none of them knew, one Andrei Kmita who came from the Orsha region in the Smolensk country, and who was also designated as Aleksandra's husband.

Let it be known then, the old man had written, *that it is by my will, and also by that of Pan Andrei's father, the Myetchnik of Orsha who is my lifelong friend, that these two young people join their lives together to God's greater glory, and for the good of our beloved country, unless—and may God forbid such a thing to happen!—the aforesaid young man should dishonor his good name. And should he lose his fortune through enemy encroachments, which is a likely thing these days in the Orsha region, I grant him the estates and properties of Lubitch for his own.*

Furthermore, he wrote, *should my Granddaughter Aleksandra find this marriage unsuitable for any moral or patriotic reason, she may be free to seek consolation in a monastic life, in which all my beloved friends of the Laudanian gentry are charged to assist her, since God's service must always take precedence over the affairs of men.*

The times and customs being what they were none of this was particularly surprising to anyone. Young Aleksandra, or Olenka as she was known since childhood, knew long before what was waiting for her, and all the Laudanians heard for years about the long friendship between the Kmitas and the Billevitches. But young Andrei Kmita was another matter.

Who was he, other than a source of endless speculation in the Lauda region? This much was known: he had the reputation of a restless whirlwind, a spirited young soldier of great fame and courage who led his own private dragoon regiment and Orsha volunteers in the Shklov disaster, but who vanished later so that some people thought he might have been killed. Most of the Laudanians didn't think it likely because the death of such a famous cavalier would have found some echo even in those chaotic times, but trustworthy news about anyone was hard to come by in those violent days. The Orsha region, the home of the Kmita fortunes, was a flaming battleground, as was all of the Smolensk Palatinate in which those rich lands and properties lay for generations, and none of that was expected to belong to the Commonwealth much longer. Whole territories emptied, counties disappeared, and towns, villages and estates turned into smoking ruins. Yanush Radzivill's defeat left the land defenseless. His deputy commander, Field Hetman Gosyevski, had no men or money to raise new regiments of his own, and no help could come from the Polish side of the Commonwealth whose dwindling armies were barely holding on in the Ukraine against the Russians and the Zaporohjans. To look for one young man in the firestorm that engulfed all the eastern territories seemed like an act of folly.

But because the war had not yet reached the *Starostvo* or County of Zmudya, and because the Laudanian gentry soon recovered from the shock of the Shklov defeat, the *neighborhoods* began to come together to decide what everyone should do both in connection with public affairs and in private matters. The Butryms, always the most warlike, began to mutter that it was time to join up with Hetman Gosyevski and to avenge the humiliation they suffered at Shklov; the Domashevitch hunters traversed the forests all the way to the pickets of the enemy and brought back valuable military information; and the Gosyevitch smoke-houses worked day and night to stockpile provisions for a new campaign.

Closer to home concerns, the Laudanians decided to send well-traveled and experienced men in search of Andrei Kmita. They felt immensely flattered by the trust placed in them by their old mentor and commander, and competed with each other in looking after the young heiress in Vodokty whom they swore to protect as if she were their own.

But while violence and turmoil convulsed all the other wide-spread territories of the old Grand Duchy, life went on flowing in a comparatively quiet and peaceful manner in the Lauda country. No one made any claims on the properties of young Aleksandra to whom all the Laudanians referred as "Our Young Lady." No one plowed into her fields, encroached on her pastures, or dared to cut down the notched pines that marked the borders of her woods. On the contrary, every Laudanian village sent whatever produce it could spare to help her even though she didn't lack for anything of her own. And so the riverside Stakyans supplied salted fish, the gruff Butryms sent wagon loads of wheat, while the Gashtovts dispatched hay, straw and cattle-fodder. Smoked venison came from the Domashevitch hunters and barrels of pitch and tar from the Gosyevitch clearings in the forests.

And then, as Winter settled on the land and the year ended, came word of a General Levy that summoned all this simple, hardworking, rural Lithuanian gentry to the defense of the country, and the loyal Laudanians began to stir once more. Whichever youth had grown that year into manhood, and whatever older man was still unbowed by age, prepared to ride to war. The grim Butryms were the first to leave, in silence as always. The Gashtovts who hated to be separated from their beautiful young women were the last to set out for Grodno where King Yan Casimir himself arrived to enforce the mobilization order. The gentry from other and more distant regions of the country were slow to respond to the Diet's summons, and did so in small numbers, but the honest and God-fearing Laudanians reported to a man.

They left, however, without their young colonel. Pan Volodyovski couldn't go. First of all, he was a regular officer, serving under Radzivill's command, and so he had to wait for orders from his Hetman. In the second place, he had fallen ill. Some of his old wounds had opened up again, a blow he'd taken in an earlier battle temporarily paralyzed his arm, so he remained in Pátzunel in the caring hands of the Gashtovt beauties. But the rest of the *neighborhoods* emptied of their able-bodied men. Only bowed old men and young boys sat in the evenings among the women by the firesides and everyone from Ponevyezh to Upita waited for some news.

Aleksandra also waited, closed in by Winter in her Vodokty manor, and seeing no one other than her servants and her Laudanian guardians.

Part One

Chapter One

THE NEW YEAR came in the midst of a cold, dry Winter that covered all of Zmudya with a deep white quilt. The trees bent and crackled under the weight of snow that blinded the eyes of passersby in daylight. At night, by moonlight, the fields and pastures sparkled with pinpoint lights as if the moon had tossed a multitude of spangles on the frozen soil. The forest animals drew closer to human dwellings, and small grey birds, as homeless and as hungry as a flock of orphans, tapped with their beaks on the frosted windows etched with intricate patterns of flowers and ferns.

The evening, the first of 1655, began quietly in the Vodokty manor where Aleksandra sat among her maids in the spinning room. It was an old Billevitch custom to spend the evenings with the servants when there were no guests or visitors in the house so that some notion of manners and good breeding could come to these young women, most of whom were daughters of the poorer gentry, whose own home lives were little better than those of the peasants. They worked as hard as any other servants, learning in exchange how to behave in polite company and how to speak in a cultivated way, although there were also some simple peasant girls in that room that night. These differed from the others mostly in their language since few peasants in Lithuania or elsewhere in the Commonwealth spoke the gentry's Polish.

Aleksandra sat in the center of their circle next to an elderly maiden aunt, Panna Kulvyetzovna. The girls spread to the right and left of her. All of them were spinning and singing soft,

3

gentle songs, mostly of a religious nature, while a gruff old Zmudyan, shaggy as a bear, worked a grinding mill in the shadowed recess by the door, and a young lad tossed fresh kindling on the fire in the great stone hearth with its overhanging copper mantel. Whenever the flames leaped higher among the pine logs in the fireplace, the light revealed the dark, wooden walls of a spacious room which seemed all the longer because of the unusually low beamed ceiling that crouched overhead. Small multicolored stars made out of baked wafers hung from these blackened logs and turned and twisted in the heated air, while long pale braids of combed hemp drooped on both sides of the beams all along the ceiling as if they were captured Turkish standards made of horses' tails. The walls themselves gleamed with reflected firelight that danced among the pewter bowls and platters on the dark oak shelves.

It was a quiet moment, calling for reflection, and Aleksandra seemed far away in her own wandering thoughts as she let the beads of a Rosary slip between her fingers. The spinners shot quick glances at each other, as if wondering when their Lady might call a halt to the work and start a new song for them to sing, but they didn't stop spinning even for a moment. The sharp eyes of Panna Kulvyetzovna hurried them along. The firelight fell on their fresh young faces and the round arms they raised to the spinning wheels; the wheels whirred and hummed and the pale hemp threads gathered on their spools; and the old shaggy Zmudyan kept up a steady droning in the corner with his mill and bellows.

Once in a while the muttering Zmudyan hit a snag in his grinding-mill and growled a thick curse, and Aleksandra looked up from her dreaming thoughts, her musing interrupted, and then the warm firelight bathed her upraised face, her delicately sculpted features, her soft hemp-colored hair, and her sky-blue eyes that looked out seriously but kindly from under her black brows. Her mourning dress added to a natural dignity, unusual even in that age of serious-minded women, and her far-off thoughts seemed to reflect this important moment in her life.

Her grandfather's will destined her to marry a man she saw only once when she was ten years old, and that was almost ten years ago, so all she had was a child's impression of some gangling, restless adolescent, who spent more time running

about the marshes with a bird-gun in hand during that old visit
to Vodokty he made with his father, than in showing any interest
in her.

'*Where is he now and what is he like?*' were the questions that
occupied her thinking. What she knew of him as a man came
from the stories told by Pan Heracles who paid a visit to the
Kmitas in Orsha four years earlier. '*A wonderfully spirited young
man,*' was the way the old man described him, '*though he's a bit
of a whirlwind and awfully quick to act.*'

But time and maturity took care of things like that, Aleksandra knew. The hot-blooded and high-handed young men of her
time settled down soon enough to steadiness and dependability
although he certainly hadn't been very quick to come calling on
her. According to the marriage contract agreed upon by old Pan
Heracles and the older Kmita, the young man was supposed to
come at once to Vodokty to win her approval, but the times
themselves got in the lovers' way. First came the terrible two-
year war of the Cossack Rebellion in the south, and her promised husband went off to the battlefield of Berestetchko where
the Cossacks were finally beaten down and driven from the
borders, although the peace that followed was doomed from the
start. Shot and wounded there, Pan Andrei took some time to
come back to health and then he spent more time nursing his
dying father. Then came the new Russian war, new turbulence
and disasters, and so four years went by and Andrei seemed to
have disappeared into the unknown.

'*Where is he now?*' she had to ask herself. '*And will I ever see
him?*'

And there were other questions, no less pressing for that quiet
and serious-minded young woman. '*Will he love me,*' she wondered. '*And will I be able to love him?*'

She knew that she was ready to love a man just because she
had never given her love to anyone before; all she needed was
a spark of real and honest affection to turn her quiet longing into
a blaze as bright and steady as the never-dying fires lighted in
pagan times for the ancient Lithuanian Gods. So she asked
herself over and over whether he'd want her of his own free
will, not as part of a marriage arranged by their families, and if
he'd be ready to meet her love with one of his own. There was
nothing unusual in the idea of an arranged marriage; it was an

everyday occurrence in her times, and most young people kept the bargain even after the death of their parents. But the children's duty to parental will didn't necessarily go hand-in-hand with their own desires, and so some deep and troubling thoughts bowed her head that night and sent her mind soaring.

'*Who are you now?*' she seemed to cry out across the vast open distances that separated her from that unknown young man who was supposed to share her life and who filled her mind with so many questions. '*What have you become? Are you near or far away somewhere?*' And finally the question that troubled her most of all: '*Are you still alive or did you fall already in some battle somewhere?*'

She saw her own heart like an open door flung wide to receive a welcome guest and sending out a beckoning light across the dark, snowy miles of fields and woods and distant places hidden in the night.

'*Come to me, then,*' cried all her thoughts, fluttering down upon her like a flock of sparrows that settle on a lone young tree in an empty plain. '*Come... because there's nothing worse than this uncertainty and waiting.*'

★　★　★

And suddenly, as if in reply to her silent summons, she heard the sound of a sleigh bell jingling in the distance—jingling and nearing and growing louder in those dark, night-shrouded winter spaces across which she sent her own anxious thoughts.

She came awake, brought back from her wondering by the persistent little sound, and then she remembered that the Gashtovt girls sent someone almost every night for medicines for the young colonel they were nursing, and Aunt Kulvyetzovna quickly confirmed that notion.

"That'll be from the Gashtovts," she said. "They'll want some more herbs from the medicine chest, I expect."

The uneven sound of the sleigh bell jerking about on the traces grew louder and clearer and then it was silent; someone had come and halted before the door.

"See who's out there," Panna Kulvyetzovna ordered the shaggy Zmudyan.

He left the room for only a short while. Back again, he

turned to his mill and muttered in his own slow, phlegmatic dialect: *"Panas Kmitas."*

"And the word became flesh!" cried Panna Kulvyetzovna.

The spinning girls leaped to their feet, their spools and wheels clattering on the floor around them, and Aleksandra also rose and turned towards the hearth to hide a flood of powerful conflicting emotions. Her heart was beating like a hammer in her breast and a bright flush spread across her pale cheeks.

And then the door flew open, and a tall young man, dressed in a sable cap and rich traveling robes, was standing in the door, throwing sharp glances around the spinning room, and a strong young voice rang out with a question:

"Hey! And where's your lady?"

"Here I am," Aleksandra said. She spoke quietly in what she hoped was a steady voice that would both hide and master her sudden onrush of feeling.

The young man stepped firmly into the room, slammed the door behind him, whipped the fur cap off his head and threw it on the floor.

"I'm Andrei Kmita," he said and bowed deeply.

She looked up, caught a swift glimpse of tumbled hair as pale as her own, a dark windswept skin, a dark mustache, sharp grey eyes staring brightly out of a young and carefree face that seemed to brim with good-humored confidence and laughter, and then her own eyes fell and fixed themselves on the floor between them.

Meanwhile he cocked one hand at the hip, twisted the ends of his mustache upward with the other, and said:

"I haven't even been to Lubitch yet. I've come here straight from the camp, just as fast as the horses could bring me, to pay my respects. The wind couldn't have brought me faster! Let's hope you'll think that it's a lucky wind, one that brings you something that'll please you."

"So you knew about... grandfather's death?" she asked in a calm, measured tone that she hoped masked her own excitement and confusion.

"Not till those little local greybacks of yours found me and told me about it," he said with quick pride, some sadness, and the careless, off-hand impatience with which the highborn gentry dismissed their inferiors. "But once they told me, I shed

some honest tears for him, my good benefactor! He was a real
friend to us, almost a brother to my own dead father, God rest
both their souls. You probably know that he came to see us four
years ago? That's when he promised you to me and showed me
your picture which was enough to keep me sighing for a lot of
nights. Hey, my girl, I'd have come here sooner but war's not
a mother. Funeral drums are more to her liking than a wedding
party."

His sharp directness, clear and to the point, confused her for
a moment and she looked for another subject and a safer one.

"So... you haven't seen your Lubitch yet?"

"There's lots of time for that." His easy, cheerful tone dismissed his new estate to relative unimportance. "My first duty
is here and so's a much sweeter legacy for me to see! Only you
keep turning into those shadows so I can't get a good look at
you. Turn around, will you? That's the way! And I'll come
around from the fireside and... That's it! Now I've got you!"

And the laughing young soldier caught Olenka's hands,
whirled her towards the firelight and peered into her averted
face.

"As God's my witness," he cried out. "What a gift you are!
I'll buy a hundred masses for the peace of my benefactor's soul!
So when's the wedding?"

"Oh, not yet," she said, trying to free her hands. "Not yet for
a while."

"Well it can't be soon enough for me even if I've got to set
this house on fire to get things warmed up! Dear God, but you
are really something special! I thought your pretty miniature
might've been faked a little, the way some of them are, but I can
see the artist aimed too high for his meager talents. A hundred
lashes for a bungling amateur like him! He'd do better painting
a barn door than trying to picture all those rare beauties I'm
feasting my eyes on right now. As God's my witness, what a
legacy to get!"

Out of breath, Olenka finally freed her fingers from his eager
grasp and took a step backward.

"Grandfather was right when he called you something of a
whirlwind," she said and smiled warmly despite all her training.
She knew that all the customary proprieties were slipping from

her grasp but somehow that didn't seem to matter a great deal just then.

"We're all like that out in the Smolensk country," he cried out. "Not like your mumbling Zmudyans. It's everything or nothing with us, and it's got to be the way we want it right away or somebody dies."

She smiled again, surer now and more in command of herself, getting the measure of this human windstorm.

"It sounds as if you have Tartars living with you over there," she said.

"Who cares who's there since you and I are here?" he shot back, grinning with delight. "You're mine, that's what matters, and not just because my father and your grandfather wanted us together but from my heart too, with all my own wishes and affections!"

"Well... that we still have to see about. I mean about the heart and the affections..."

"The Devil we do! If I can't have your love, freely felt and given, then I'll just put a bullet in my head and that will be that. Having seen you once I'd be a fool to try living anywhere without you!"

She looked at him and heard him and she was hardly able to believe what she saw and heard. But his strong young voice rang with such sincerity, and his quick straightforward speech and his easy manner carried such a glow of honesty about them, that her own heart lifted towards him in a flood of pleasure and affection. And then she remembered that they were still in the spinning room, among the awestruck gawking servant girls, and a new flush spread across her face because she'd quite forgotten the simplest rules of hospitality.

"But we're still in the servants' quarters... Let's go into the reception rooms." She gestured to the servant boy, ordering a light. "Perhaps you'd like a supper after your long journey..."

And then she turned to the old maiden lady. "You'll come with us, auntie?"

The young officer snapped a quick look at the older woman who seemed just as wide-eyed, staring and out of breath as all the maids around her.

"Auntie?" he asked. "Whose auntie?"

"Mine," Olenka said and introduced the flustered old woman.
"Panna Kulvyetzovna."

"Then she's my auntie too," the young man said at once and
seized the old maid's hands and began to kiss them. "By God,
I've a comrade in the regiment whose name is also Kulvyetz.
His family crest and calling is *Hippocentaurus*. Is he some relation?"

"It's the same branch!" the breathless old lady bobbed a little
courtsey.

"A good man," Kmita said and then shrugged and added: "But
just as much of a hothead as I am myself."

                                ★   ★   ★

Meanwhile the servant boy came running with a lantern and
they passed into the hall where Pan Andrei threw off his traveling robes. And then they walked into the main rooms and
reception chambers of the manor house.

Left alone, the young servant girls gathered in a tight, excited
little huddle, chattering like magpies. The handsome and richly
dressed young man made a powerful impression among them
and they showered him with exaggerated praise.

"It's like there's a glow around him," one of them squealed
and giggled. "I thought it was some kind of a prince when he
first came in."

"And did you see his eyes? Like a lynx!" said another.
"There's no way to say No to a man like that."

"That's the worst thing to do with that kind," said a third. "I
mean to say No."

"And he whirled our lady around like she was a twig! You
could tell at once she'd caught his heart. But then whose heart
wouldn't she be able to catch?"

"And what about him? If you'd catch one like him you'd run
after him all the way to Orsha, though people say that's at the
end of the world."

"Our young lady's lucky!"

"The rich always have it better. Ey, that's pure gold, that
young knight."

"The Gashtovt girls were saying that the young colonel
they're nursing is also a good-looker."

"I never saw him but I bet he's nothing next to this Pan Kmita! There can't be another like him in the world!"

"*Padlas!*" the old Zmudyan cursed suddenly in the corner where his mill had jammed.

"And will you keep quiet, you shaggy old thing?" the young women shouted. "A person can't think with all that muttering and cursing! Yes, yes, I bet you wouldn't find a better catch than Pan Kmita even in Keydany among the Radzivills."

"Or in a dream," said another.

"You should have such dreams."

★ ★ ★

That's how the serving gentlewomen discussed the new arrival in the spinning room while other servants rushed to set the table in the dining hall. Aunt Kulvyetzovna bustled in the kitchens, supervising supper, and the two young people were left alone in the reception chamber.

Pan Andrei hardly took his eyes off Olenka and the more he stared at her the brighter his own eyes seemed to shine. At last he said:

"What a treasure you are! There are people who love money more than anything, others live for war and loot and horses, but I wouldn't trade you for anything! The more I look at you the better I like the idea of marriage, and the sooner the better. By God, how about tomorrow? Ah, but those eyebrows of yours, those lashes, they're so black and even you've got to be touching them up with burned cork or something."

"I've heard that some women do that," she said. "But I don't."

"And those eyes! They must've fallen clear out of the sky. I tell you, I'm quite lost for words."

"You're not lost for many," she murmured, feeling her own heart racing in her breast. "In fact I wish you'd lose a few more of them, because this is all happening far too quickly and I'm starting to feel very strange about it."

"That's how it is with us in the Smolensk country!" Pan Andrei laughed merrily and slapped one strong fist into another. "With women as in battle, you've got to charge straight into the fire. You'll have to get used to it, my queen, because that's the way it's going to be with us from now on."

"And you'll have to change some of these ideas," she cautioned, out of breath. "Because it can't be like that at all."

"Change?" He laughed. "Well, why not? I've never taken a back seat to anyone anywhere but, Devil take me, I'll try even that if that's what you want. I tell you, my sweet lady, I'd pull down the sky for you if I could. If I've got to change my ways then I'll change them for you. I know well enough that I'm a rough, crude soldier, a lot more at home in a bivouac than in manor chambers. I am what I am and I never had a reason to be any different."

"That doesn't matter," she said at once, smiling at him with so much undisguised affection that he felt as if he were turning into melted wax. "Grandfather was also a soldier but he was a good, kind and decent man none the less. Still, I thank you for your good intentions."

"Ey,"—and Pan Andrei couldn't quite believe just then what was happening to him nor what he was saying—"I think you'll lead me about on a thread... Or like a bear with a ring through his nose."

"You don't look like the kind who is lead anywhere he doesn't want to go," she said and laughed softly. "You'd have to settle down a bit more for that."

"How's that, then?" Kmita showed his white teeth in a wolfish grin. "You mean I'm not settled down enough? Didn't the good Fathers break enough canes on my back in school? Didn't they pound enough wise and pious maxims into my thick skull?"

"And which maxim do you remember best?"

"*When you're in love, go straight for the knees,*" Kmita shot back at once, flung himself down on his knees before her and threw his arms around her own.

"Get up!" she cried at once. "You didn't learn that from any good Fathers! Get up or I'll get angry with you... and auntie will be here any minute...!"

But he stayed where he was, laughing up into her eyes, and she had to smile and laugh at him in return.

"Let a whole armored regiment of aunties come galloping in here," he cried, grinning from ear to ear, "and it won't hold me back!"

"Get up!" she cried, laughing.

"I'm up," he said and sprung to his feet.

"Sit down!"

"I'm sitting."

"You can't be trusted," she accused, badly out of breath. "You're a real Judas."

"That's not true," he said and seized her hands and kissed them. "Because my kisses are honest and sincere. D'you want to find out?"

"Don't even think about it!"

But she was laughing as she said it, delighted with that handsome, fiery young man who seemed to burn with youth, health, strength, courage and affection.

"Ay, what eyes, what lips," he murmured. "Help me, good saints, to hold still."

"You don't need the saints for that," she pointed out. "You've kept your distance for four years, and never even thought of dropping in to see me, so now keep it longer."

"I've been a damn fool, that's what," he said. "I admit it freely! But all I'd seen of you was that little portrait your grandfather showed us. I tell you, I'll have that painter tarred and feathered and whipped through the marketplace in Upita if I get hold of him! Look, I'll confess. Forgive me if you want. If not, I'll cut my throat. I looked at that picture and I said: '*Hmm. A good-looking little thing but there's a lot of pretty girls running about the world. I've time.*' My poor old father, God rest his soul, nagged at me day and night to run and get married but it was always the same thing with me. '*I've time. Weddings don't sprout wings and fly away just because they're delayed a little. Brides don't go to war and nobody puts a bullet in them.*' It's not that I was going altogether against my father's will, as God is my witness; I just thought I'd try a taste of war before settling down. Now I see what a damn fool I was because I could've gone to war anyway, married or not, and look what I missed here in the meantime! Thank God I've managed to get back in one piece and it's not too late. So how about a few more kisses, if you'll let me?"

"I think it'll be better if I don't," she said.

"Then I won't ask," he said. "I'll take them Orsha fashion.

We've a saying back home, '*if you can't get it when you ask for it, then take it without asking.*'"

And the young man seized Olenka's hands again and began to kiss them, and she didn't put up too much of a struggle because, as she was quick to tell herself, she didn't want to seem stand-offish and unfriendly.

Aunt Kulvyetzovna entered the room just then, took one look at the young pair, and raised her eyes piously to the ceiling as if calling on all the saints to witness her disapproval. But she didn't say anything except to invite them to the supper table and they followed her arm-in-arm into the dining hall.

Chapter Two

THEY WENT TOGETHER, arm-in-arm like brother and sister, into the large and handsomely furnished room, where a variety of dishes waited on the table along with a mossy crock of a fine old wine. Olenka had already eaten that evening so Kmita sat down to the meal alone, eating and drinking with the same exuberance with which he'd been speaking, and she looked at him quietly from the side, glad to see him so at home at her table.

"So you're not coming directly from Orsha?" she asked after he satisfied the worst of his hunger.

"Who knows where I've come from?" He laughed and showed his strong white teeth in a cheerful smile but there was a serious note in his voice as well. "Seems like I've been dodging back and forth all over the country and never spending two days in the same place. I've been living like a wolf, tearing at the enemy whenever I could, and slipping away before they could trap me."

"But how did you manage to keep fighting against such great odds that even the Grand Hetman had to give way before them?"

"How did I manage? I just did it, that's all. That's my nature. Act first and think about it later if it's worth thinking about at all."

"Grandfather did say that you were ready for anything. Thank God you've escaped unharmed."

"Oh, they were after me, alright!" Kmita laughed again. "You'd think I was a bird, the way they tried to catch me! But I'd just dart away and nip them somewhere else. I made such a

15

nuisance of myself that the Russians put a price on my head. Hey, but this is a wonderfully tasty roast!"

"Dear God!" Olenka cried out, pleased and astonished at the same time by this carefree young man who could talk in the same breath about a stuffed roast goose and a dead-or-alive bounty on his head. "But you must have had a strong force of your own?"

"I had two hundred good dragoons but they got whittled away in a month. Then I picked up what volunteers I could, from whatever corner of earth or Hell they came from, making sure I didn't ask too many questions. They're good fighters, all of them, but they'll end up dancing on a gibbet if the enemy doesn't get them first."

Laughing, and helping himself to more wine, Pan Andrei shook his head.

"You haven't seen such a collection of ruffians in all your life, my lady. Even my officers, all of whom are wellborn gentry known throughout our part of the country, have some kind of verdict hanging over their heads. I've packed them off to Lubitch because, to tell you the truth, I wouldn't know what to do with them in a peaceful countryside. But to the Devil with them, anyway. We've better things to talk about, you and I."

"So you've come to us with your whole regiment?" she asked.

"That's right. The Muscovites locked themselves in the cities for the Winter because the weather's really fierce out there in the east, and my own men and horses are also on their last legs. We're as worn out as an old broom with all the sweeping we've been doing. So the Grand Hetman assigned us winter quarters in Ponevyezh and not a moment too soon."

"Please have some more to eat," she invited.

"I'd eat poison for you!" he burst out and loaded his platter with another helping. "Yes, well... so I left some of my cutthroats in Ponevyezh and some in Upita and I've invited the more worthy ones to stay with me in Lubitch. I'll have them over here in a day or two to pay their respects."

"I know some of the Laudanian gentry went to look for you," she said. "Where did they find you, then?"

"They found me when I was already on the road to Ponevyezh," Pan Kmita said, indifferent. "I'd have come here without them."

"Please help yourself to more wine," she said.

"I'd drink poison for you!"

"So it was the Laudanians who told you about grandfather's death and his testament?"

"About the death, yes. The testament I knew about before, God rest my benefactor's soul! Was it you who sent those people after me?"

"No, I did not," she said and flushed again. "It was entirely their idea. All I had on my mind were prayers and mourning."

"That's what they said too. Hmm. A snotty bunch of little greybacks they were, I must say. I wanted to give them something for their trouble and they got their backs up right away. '*Maybe the Orshan gentry takes tips like lackeys,*' they said to me. '*But not the Laudanians!*' So I thought, well, if they won't take money, maybe I'll give them a hundred lashes each to teach them some manners."

"*Jezus Maria!*" Aleksandra sprung to her feet and stared at him in horror. "And is that what happened?"

"No... it didn't." Kmita stared at her with astonishment. "Hey! Don't look so afraid. I let them off, even though my guts heave at the sight of such bareback clodhoppers who think themselves our equals. But I thought they'd raise an uproar all over the country, slander me unjustly for a violent man, and maybe even manage to turn you against me."

"Thank God you showed restraint!" It took a long moment for Olenka to regain control over her rapid breathing. "Otherwise I'd never be able to look at you again."

"And why's that?"

"It's a minor gentry, and closer to the soil than the greater houses, but it's an ancient and famous one none the less," Olenka explained. "Grandfather always loved them. They served in many wars together, and he welcomed them to our house in peacetime. It's an old friendship which you have to honor."

She pressed her hands together as if in a prayer and a slight tremor slipped into her voice as she looked down at his darkening face.

"You have a heart, after all," she murmured. "And you wouldn't want to spoil that mutual respect and affection that we've all had for each other here for so long."

"Good God, I didn't know anything about that!"he cried out. "May they chop me into mincemeat if I did!"

Then he shrugged and a wry, contemptuous grimace passed across his lips.

"I've got to admit that this barefoot gentry doesn't fit my ideas of who and what we are," he said. "I mean, back home a peasant is a peasant and the nobility is established well enough so that two of them don't have to ride on the same mare together. This homespun, plow-pushing collection of grey-backs has no more in common with families like the Kmitas and the Billevitches than perch have with sturgeon, even though both have the right to call themselves fish."

"Grandfather used to say that possessions don't count for anything beside decency and goodness,"she offered. "And those are decent people. Otherwise he'd never have appointed them my guardians."

"Them?" Pan Andrei's eyes grew wide with amazement. "He made them your guardians? All of the Laudanian gentry?"

"That's right. Don't frown like that because his wishes are as holy to me as the scriptures. I'm surprised,"—and now her voice took a wondering note—"that the men who found you didn't tell you anything about it?"

"I'd have...!" And the astonished Orshan struggled to control his anger. "I can't believe this! There must be a dozen greyback villages around here... D'you mean to say that all these furrow-jumpers sit in council over you? And that they're going to be holding diets over me as well, scratching their heads about whether I'm to their liking? Ey, my girl! Don't make jokes like that because my blood is starting to boil!"

* * *

And he did, indeed, look as if a sudden rush of blood would burst out from between his steel-grey eyes, so Aleksandra did her best to speak in her gentlest manner even though she left no doubt that she meant everything she said.

"I'm not joking, Andrei! I'm telling you the God's honest truth. They won't sit in any judgment over you, that isn't their way. And if you try to be a father to them, like grandfather did, if you don't push them away and treat them with contempt, you'll win not only their lifelong affection and respect but my own as well.

"Believe me,"—and the anxious tremor returned to her voice—"I'll be grateful to you as long as I live if you'll just show them friendship."

Her gentle tone took on the character of a mother pleading with a child, but his face remained dark with challenged pride, and flashes of anger shot across it like lightnings through a clouded sky.

"That's something I didn't expect," he said coldly. "I'm willing to respect a dead man's wishes and I can see how Pan Heracles could've left you in their care until my arrival. But once I've set foot in this place that's the end of all guardianships but my own! Not just those puddle-jumpers but the Radzivills themselves have nothing to say here!"

Aleksandra grew thoughtful as she listened to him and it took her a moment to find a reply.

"You're wrong to let your pride sweep you away like that," she said as firmly as she could without seeming harsh. "Grand-father's wishes must be carried out to the letter and in their entirety or not at all; I see no way to pick and choose among them... But you'll soon see that the Laudanians don't push themselves where they aren't wanted. They are all serious and self-respecting people and they've a pride and dignity of their own so you don't have to worry that they'd ever interfere without cause."

"They'd better do the worrying about that," he snapped. "Not I."

"I doubt that it would ever happen," she assured him gently. "If there was ever any grave problem between you and me... something that would set us against each other... well, then I expect they might say something..."

"God help them if they do," he muttered.

"But I believe that everything will go smoothly for us here," she went on in a softer voice and with a warm and hopeful brightness in her eyes. "So that this guardianship of theirs will seem as if it weren't there at all."

He thought about this for a while then nodded and shrugged.

"You're right," he said. "Our wedding will put an end to all that anyway. But let them just sit quietly like rabbits in their burrows and keep their noses out of my private business because, as God's my witness, I don't let anybody blow into my soup! I think the best thing for you to do is set our wedding date right away and that'll take care of everything."

"I can't do that until the mourning is over," she reminded him.

"Ay, that's right! I forgot about that. So how long do I have to wait?"

"Grandfather himself wrote it shouldn't last longer than six months."

"I'll dry up like a splinter in that time! But let's not have any harsh words between us. You've started to look at me as if I was some kind of miscreant and, as God's my witness, that's the last thing I'd ever deserve from you. Hey there, my sweet queen, is it my fault I've a nature that lives on extremes? If someone angers me I'd tear him to pieces, but just as soon as the anger's past I'd stitch him together with gold threads."

"You'll be a frightening man to live with," Olenka said smiling.

★ ★ ★

But he was also smiling, and looking at her fondly, so that the angry moment was quickly forgotten.

"Your health, my sweet," he said and raised his goblet to her. "This is a first class vintage, and with me good wine and a sharp saber are just about all that matters. Why should I be frightening? You'll turn me into a lapdog and lead me around on a silk thread, I've no doubt about it!"

Then he laughed again and shook his head with another unbelieving smile.

"... Me, who could never bear to take anybody's orders! Even now I preferred to raise my own troops and go my own way rather than bow and scrape before the King's Hetmans... But if there's something about me that doesn't sit quite right with you, something you don't like, then try to forgive it because I learned my manners on horseback, not in ladies' chambers, and it'll take a while for me to turn into some kind of courtier."

"Grandfather taught me to value brave, straightforward men," Olenka said quietly.

"And he was right to do it," Kmita said. "There's not much time for fancy talk out east where I come from. It's a hard land out there, blood flows like water everywhere you look, and a quick saber counts for a lot more than cultivated phrases. Yes, that's how it is, so even if somebody runs afoul of the law, even if he's got the tribunals breathing down his neck, people still honor and respect him as long as he's got a man's heart beating in his chest. You'll see it for yourself when you meet my good comrades and companions, all of whom would be rotting in some dungeon in more settled times. They're a rough lot, yet in their own way they're worthwhile men."

"They must be or they wouldn't be your friends," Olenka said softly.

"We are what our times make us," Pan Andrei said and shrugged with something like regret. "Even the women in our territories wear riding boots, carry a saber and lead their own troops. Like the late Lady Kokosinska, aunt of my second in command, who died a soldier's death leading her own company. Her nephew's been declared an outlaw just because he burned down a neighbor's manor and carried off his daughter, but now he rides with me and avenges his aunt as best he can even though he didn't give two hoots about her when she was alive."

He paused, frowned and shook his head.

"That's how we are," he said. "How could we be different? Where are we to learn smooth talk and courtly manners, even the best of us? Where we come from, my love, it's enough to know that in war we fight, at the diets we argue, and when the tongue fails to make our point we make it with a saber. That's what your late grandfather saw in me when he came to Orsha, and that's the kind of man that he chose for you."

"I've always honored his wishes," Olenka said softly and lowered her eyes.

"So give me those hands again, sweet girl," he cried out. "As God's my witness, you've really gone straight to my heart! I'm so blinded by you that I don't know how I'll find the way to that Lubitch that I've yet to see."

"I'll give you a guide," she offered.

"Eh,"—and his careless laughter rang out again, as clear and cheerful as a crystal bell—"I can do without one. I've a lad from

Ponevyezh along with me and he'll know the way. Besides, I'm used to rattling about strange highways after dark."

Midnight began to strike in the tall Gdansk clock that stood in the corner of the dining hall.

"Time to go," Kmita said and sighed. "Ah, how quickly it passed in your sweet company... It seems like I just got here, doesn't it?"

"Yes. It does." She nodded.

"Tell me, though, d'you feel anything for me? D'you love me at all?"

"I'll tell you at another time," she said and felt her heart beating swiftly in her breast. "You'll be coming to see me often, won't you?"

"Every day!" he cried. "Unless the earth should open up under my boots and swallow me horse and all!"

"Well then, there'll be time for us to say many things to each other."

"And now it's time to go."

Pan Andrei rose and they went out together, arm-in-arm as before, into the entrance hall where he put on his thick traveling robes again. It was cold there, a freezing wind blew in from the porch outside where his sleigh and horses were harnessed and waiting, and he urged her to go back into the warm rooms they left.

"Sleep well," he said at last. "I know that I won't close a single eye tonight, thinking about your beauty."

"As long as you don't think of something you shouldn't be thinking," she murmured. "We have time, remember? But hadn't I better give you a man with a lantern after all? It's a long way to Lubitch through the woods, and we have wolves around Volmontov this time of the year."

He laughed again, a clear joyful sound that seemed to fill the cold anteroom with warmth.

"Ey, my sweet," he said. "What am I, a goat that I should be scared of wolves? A wolf is a soldier's friend because he often feeds on what a soldier leaves him. Besides, I've a brace of pistols in the sleigh. So good night, my dearest. Good night!"

"Go with God," she murmured.

★   ★   ★

She stepped back into the warmth of the house and he went out onto the porch. He saw that the door to the servants' hall had been left ajar, and he caught sight of several pairs of girls' eyes peering out at him, and he sent them a kiss through the cold night air.

Then the sleigh bell jingled—loud at first, then dwindling in the distance—and then there was silence.

A soft, still night settled on the Vodokty manor house, so quiet after the young man's visit that Aleksandra could hardly believe he had been there at all. But she could still hear Pan Andrei's welcome words, she listened to his open, clear laughter, and she could see that tall, youthful figure which seemed to be able to create a whirlwind of excitement and gaiety everywhere around him. She went on listening for the sound of the little bell until long after it was gone, swallowed in the darkness, and she was quite sure then that she had never felt more lonely or alone.

She took a candle and went slowly to her own rooms where she knelt to say her evening prayers but she had to begin them anew five times before they came out as mindfully as they had to be. Her thoughts flew to that sleigh speeding across the snow and to the young man in it. She saw the dark forest on one side of the track and another dark wall of trees on the other. She saw the broad glittering strip of snow winding through the darkness, and then she seemed to be looking once more at that tumbled, corn-colored hair, that laughing mouth, and those white teeth gleaming like a strong young dog's.

Brought up to seriousness and dignity, and conscious of her role and place in the country and within the civilization of her times, she found it hard to deny that she was greatly taken with that wild young soldier. He had alarmed her, true. He'd even frightened her a little with his untamed passions. But how appealing he was with just that straightforward, devil-may-care honesty and confidence in himself. Even that moment of overweening pride when he jerked up his head, like a spirited young mustang, at the mention of her Laudanian guardians, made him seem extraordinary and attractive.

'... *Not even the Radzivills have anything to say to me here,*' he'd said, snorting like a Turkish thoroughbred.

"That is a man," Olenka told herself. "That's not some milksop or a spoiled weakling who doesn't know what he wants or what to do to get it."

Her grandfather had loved strong and decisive men like that, she thought.

"... And," she murmured, "he was right to do so."

Caught up in restless thoughts which seemed to dart like startled birds between deep joy, a great inner peace and anxious excitement, she hardly heard her old maiden aunt knocking on her door.

"You sat there an awfully long time," the old lady grumbled, coming in with her own night candle in her hands. "I left the two of you alone this first time, longer than I should have, so that you'd have a chance to talk and get to know each other. So what do you think of him? Hmm? He seems like a fine young man to me."

Olenka ran to her and put her head on the old woman's chest.

"Oh auntie," she whispered.

"Oho," the old woman muttered. "So that's how things are."

And she raised her knowing eyes and her candle towards the shadows that danced on the ceiling.

Chapter Three

ALL THE WINDOWS of the Lubitch manor house were ablaze with light when Pan Andrei's sleigh drew up before the porch in the snowy courtyard, and he listened with a wry grin to the roar of voices that spilled out of his house in raucous celebration. It didn't take his boon companions long to find the wine cellar, he thought in amusement, but the least they could have done was to come out to greet him.

Then he shrugged, grinned again and leaped out into the snow. If he knew anything about them, they'd have been at the table for hours already; they probably never even heard the soft jingling of the sleigh bell amid the clink and clatter of goblets and flagons and through their howls of laughter. The manor servants were pouring out of the house to meet their new master, bowing to clutch his coat-tails, kiss his hands and clasp their arms around his knees, and he could see that they were both curious and uneasy about him because a change of an estate's ownership usually meant great changes in the lives of the house servants and the villagers alike. Old Znikis, the village headman and overseer of the manor holdings, stood bowing halfway to the ground in the entrance hall, holding the traditional bread and salt on a silver tray, and Pan Andrei tossed him a purse of silver coins to share among the lackeys, grooms, stable-hands, serving girls, and the thick press of curious staring peasants who'd run up from the village.

He pushed into the house, amused at the thought that his picked followers made themselves so at home in Lubitch while he was away, and promising himself to curb some of their more

outrageous behavior, but all his good intentions disappeared at
the sight of them. They greeted him with a roar of joy. All of
them staggered to their feet just as soon as he appeared in the
doorway, and marched towards him with cups and goblets held
high in the air, pacing with the unsteady, solemn dignity of
drinkers who were long past being merely three sheets to the
wind, and bellowing their greetings.

"Our host is here!" they cried. "Our good shepherd! Our
friend and benefactor!"

He laughed at them, pleased that they had managed so well
for themselves in his absence, and he laughed all the harder as he
watched them lurching drunkenly towards him, tripping on the
litter of bottles underfoot, stumbling across the furniture and
knocking over the stools and the benches.

"*Haeres! Haeres* is here!" they cried, dipping into the Latin
classics of their erudition which, like the curved, open-guarded
karabela sabers that swung on silk cords from their belts and
sashes, was the mark of their station as gentlemen and nobles.

"Long life to him! *Vivat!*"

First in this staggering crowd came the gigantic Pan Yaromir
Kokosinski, a young man not much older than Kmita himself,
whose reputation as both a ruthless soldier and a savage brawler
had given him a notoriety feared across the country. His thick,
red face was disfigured by a saber slash that ran diagonally from
across his forehead, split the right eye and cheek, and clipped
one side of his mustache shorter than the other. Condemned to
death and confiscation of his properties in the Smolensk region
for arson, murder and the abduction of a young gentlewoman,
this 'worthy good companion' now served as Pan Andrei's
friend and first lieutenant, protected from the hangman by
Kmita's influence and wealth, and by the fact that the tribunals
were powerless in wartime and most court verdicts were held in
abeyance.

Close at his heels came Pan Ranitzki, a deadly young duelist
and murderer, outlawed in the Palatinate of Mstislav for sabering
one powerful landholder in a drunken quarrel and shooting
another out of a roadside ambush. He was a highborn noble
descended from a long line of senators and statesmen, but he'd
have been hanged a dozen times over if it weren't for Pan
Andrei's protection and the chaos that rendered the courts

impotent in wartime. Staggering after him came skinny little Pan Rekutz-Leliva, whose hands were stained only with Russian and Cossack blood, but who had drunk and gambled away his whole inheritance some three years earlier and who attached himself to Kmita ever since.

Fourth in this line of staggering and cheering young notables was the ruthless and quick-tempered Pan Uhlik, also a gentleman of the Smolensk province, who'd been condemned to death for breaking up and scattering a tribunal that had been called to judge him, and whom Pan Andrei protected largely because he had a sweet singing voice and played beautifully on the flute.

Next came the huge and none too bright Pan Kulvyetz-Hippocentaurus, a man as tall and thickset as Kokosinski, who could stun a horse with one blow of his fist or break a man's back in a single bearhug, and who snapped iron horseshoes with the fingers of one hand.

Last came Pan Zendt, a man of uncertain origins although he called himself a Livonian noble, who had no property of his own and earned his pay by training Kmita's horses. His chief distinction in that fearsome company was that he could imitate to perfection any animal or bird.

★ ★ ★

These, then, were Kmita's chosen friends, officers, mentors and companions. Now they surrounded the laughing Pan Andrei while Kokosinski raised his double-handled goblet and sang, off-key and hoarsely:

"Drink with us, gentle host,
While the wine is flowing...
So that you an' we may drink
E'en in our going..."

The others joined in the chorus and Kokosinski handed Pan Andrei his own quart-sized goblet, full to the brim with an aged *Dembnyak* mead, while Zendt immediately handed him another.

"Here's to my girl!" Pan Andrei shouted.

"*Vivat!*" roared the others while the mullioned windows shook and shivered in their thick lead frames. "*Vivat!* We'll have ourselves a wedding to beat all weddings! Long life to the happy couple! *Vivat! Vivat!*"

And then their questions came tumbling out like grain from a split sack.

"So what's she like? Hey, Andy, is she good to look at? Is she like you hoped? Are there any like her in the Orsha country?"

"In Orsha?" Carried away by the merriment around him, by the warm anticipation of his wedding day, and by his memory of his first evening with Olenka, Kmita drained his goblet and cried out: "To the Devil with Orsha! You can use our Orshan girls to stuff kitchen chimneys in comparison with her! There just isn't another like her in the whole wide world!"

"That's what we wanted for you!" Pan Ranitzki said. "So when's the wedding then?"

"As soon as the mourning's over."

"To Hell with mourning! Babies are swaddled in white cloth, not in funeral shrouds! Just as soon as the wedding bells start ringing that's the end of mourning! Get at it right away, Andy, right away!"

"Right away!" chorused all the others.

"Think of all those little Kmitas anxious to be born!" Kokosinski shouted. "Don't keep the poor things waiting up there in heaven! Let them start trotting about the earth, the poor little beggars!"

"Don't keep them waiting!" the drunken chorus chanted. "Be kind to them! Have mercy!"

"Hey, hey, gentlemen!" Rekutz squealed and giggled in his spiraling thin voice. "We'll get drunk at that wedding like nobody's ever been drunk before...!"

★ ★ ★

Pan Andrei laughed and drank with them, feeling closer to them with each passing minute, until it seemed to him that all the hardships, violence and bloodshed that marked his life up to that joyful moment of meeting Olenka were slipping away, and that only goodness and happiness waited for him ahead. The fierce flushed faces of his war companions bobbed around him in the heated air like a dim, barely recalled reminder of past cruelties and dangers, and he let them clutch at him, embrace him and grasp him by the shoulders as they pulled him towards the heaped platters, bottles and flagons on the table.

"Listen, my dear lambs," he said at last. "Ease up a little, will you? Let me catch a breath! Or to put it in another way, go to Devil and leave me alone, alright? Let me take a look around my new house."

"What's your hurry?" Uhlik asked. "Time for all that tomorrow! Right now let's get back to the table, eh? There's still a few good fat-bellied jugs waiting to be cracked."

"We've already looked over your property, Andy," Ranitzki added. "It's pure gold, this Lubitch."

"Great stables!" shouted Zendt. "There're two Turkish racers, two first class war horses, a pair of Zmudyan trotters and a pair of Kalmuks. Everything here comes two-by-two like in Noah's Ark. We'll take a look at the breeding stock tomorrow."

And then he neighed so exactly like a stallion that everyone else burst out laughing.

Kmita was delighted.

"So it's all in such good order around here, then?"

"And wait till you see the cellar!" Rekutz squeaked. "Rows and rows of crocks and jugs, all sealed with pitch and mossy with old age, lined up like regiments on parade."

"God be praised then," Pan Andrei said. "Let's get to the table and drink to our good fortune."

But they had hardly staggered back to the benches and refilled their goblets when Ranitzki leaped up with another toast.

"Here's to the health of Pan Billevitch!" he shouted.

"Idiot!" Kmita said. "You're drinking to the good health of a corpse?"

"Idiot!" the others chorused. "Let's drink to Andy! Long life to our host!"

"And to you!" said Kmita.

"May we have good times in these hospitable chambers!"

Pan Kmita threw a quick glance around the aged mahogany walls of the dining hall and saw a row of dark, disapproving eyes fixed on him harshly out of the old ancestral portraits of Billevitch patriarchs that hung at eye level along the length of the low-ceilinged chamber. Lining all the four walls above them were rows of ancient hunting trophies, the skulls of bison, elk and deer, some black with age and others gleaming with unstained yellow bone, and with horns and antlers wreathed about them like barbaric crowns.

"There must be good hunting around here," he said, nodding at the trophies.

"We'll try it out tomorrow," Kokosinski said. "Or maybe the day after. After all, what's the hurry? We're home, aren't we? Hey, you're a happy man, Andy, that you've got a good roof over your head!"

"Not like us," moaned Ranitzki.

"Let's drink to forget our misery," Rekutz hiccoughed sadly.

"No, not to forget," the gigantic Pan Kulvyetz bellowed solemnly, wagging a huge finger. "But once more to the health of our Andy, our beloved commander! It's he, gentlemen, who's given refuge in this fine Lubitch of his to us poor unfortunate exiles, am I right?"

"Kulvyetz's right!" all the others shouted. "He's not as stupid as he looks!"

"Ey, it's a hard life for us homeless orphans," Rekutz went on squealing and sniffed with sentimental tears. "You're our only hope, Andy! Don't drive us poor innocents out into the storm...!"

"Hey, give it up, will you?" Pan Andrei said at once. "Nobody's driving you anywhere, for God's sake. What's mine is yours, you know that."

But they were all on their feet then, lurching and staggering around him, and taking turns to throw their arms about him and to press their flushed sweated cheeks against his, while thick tears wrung out of them by drunken self-pity flowed down their savage faces.

"There's no hope for us except you!" Kokosinski went on with maudlin affection but there was also a cold sly gleam in his cruel eyes. "Don't turn us away! Let us rest our poor heads in some quiet corner... we don't ask for more than a few corn husks and a pile of straw...!"

"Have mercy!" Rekutz squealed.

"Hey, come on, give it up!" Kmita said again. "What's come over you?"

But they were too caught up in their own vision of themselves as the innocent, misunderstood and abused victims of envy and injustice to pay attention to anything he said.

"Don't chase us out, naked and unwanted anywhere, into the cruel world!" Uhlik moaned. "Look what they've done to us already... us, nobles of property and position... robbing us of all our substance and good name as well!"

"For God's sake!" Kmita cried. "Who's chasing you anywhere? Eat, drink, sleep... do whatever you damn well like here! What more do you want?"

"No, don't deny it, Andy," Ranitzki went on thickly, while round livid splotches, always a sign of violent emotions ready to erupt in this unbridled man, appeared on his sallow face like the spots of a lynx. "Don't deny it. We're lost without you... doomed..."

And here he paused as if confused by his own drunken rhetoric and cocked a wobbling finger like a pistol aimed at his own head. Then, peering around with glazed eyes, he stammered with owl-eyed solemnity:

"Unless... our l-luck turns or f-fortune takes a different c-course..."

"Why shouldn't it?" all the others bellowed. "Sure it will! It's bound to!"

"We'll pay them back for all our misery!"

"And we'll get rich again!"

"And we'll return to our high honors and positions! God blesses the innocent! Good for us, gentlemen! Everything's bound to go well for us again if we stick together!"

"To your good luck and happiness!" Kmita shouted as the mead started roaring in his head.

"You couldn't have said it better, Andy, if you were a saint," Kokosinski boomed and threw his huge arms around Pan Andrei. "Things will get good for us again 'cause they've got to, and it all starts with you!"

★ ★ ★

Toasts followed one another, casks and flagons emptied, everyone talked at the same time to everybody else but no one heard or listened to anyone but himself.

Pan Andrei drifted into a hazy no man's land of memory and dim recollections, in which he was no longer sure where he was, whose house they had invaded, nor how they had got there. Rekutz let his head droop towards his chest and began to snore. Kokosinski started gurgling out a song and Uhlik joined him with the flute he drew from inside his surcoat. Ranitzki, who

had a well-earned reputation as a deadly swordsman, was fighting a bare-handed duel with an invisible antagonist, cutting and
slashing at the steamy air.

"You thrust an' I parry," he muttered drunkenly into his own
visions. "You cut an' I slash. One... two... three... An' you're
finished."

The huge Kulvyetz-Hippocentaurus stared at him dumbly for
a while with his bulging eyes, then shrugged and said: "You're
a fool, Ranitzki. Flap your arms all you want but Kmita could
lay you out in three blows anytime he wanted."

"That's because he could lay out anyone," Ranitzki shot back.
"But you come and try me!"

"You're good with a saber, I'll give you that much," Kulvyetz
growled. "But I'd beat you with pistols anytime."

"D'you want to bet on that? A ducat a shot!"

"You've just lost a ducat." The giant's swollen face split in a
yellow grin. "What are we shooting at?"

Ranitzki let his dulled eyes sweep around the room and then
jerked his head at the hunting trophies hanging along the walls.

"There! Right between the horns! A gold-piece for a hit?"

"Make it two! Three!" the others started placing bets and
arguing with each other and Kmita shook himself out of his own
alcoholic stupor.

"What's the bet?" he asked, peering around as if through a fog.

"A ducat a shot between the horns!"

"Why not?" He grinned, shook his head and struggled to his
feet. "Do it!" he shouted. "Three ducats a shot. Zendt, get the
pistols!"

The horse-breaker lurched out of the room while the others
shouted, argued and pounded on the table but he was back
almost at once with an armful of pistols, a pouch of lead balls and
a powder horn.

"Is this thing loaded?" Ranitzki seized and cocked a flintlock
handgun.

"It's loaded!" Zendt croaked.

"Four, five, six ducats!" Kmita yelled, just as drunk and oblivious of everything that was happening around him as all of the
others.

"Quiet! Hey, you'll miss, Ranitzki!"

"No I won't!" The pistol wobbled wildly in the drunken

young man's outstretched and unsteady hand. It swept in a wide blind circle towards the massive skull of a forest elk that hung closest to him. "There... that one, right between the horns... One, two..."

"Three!" Kmita howled.

The shot crashed out. The room filled with black acrid smoke.

"He's missed!" Kmita shouted and pointed at the yellow scar that the bullet gouged in the dark, aged paneling of the wooden wall.

"Best out of two!" cried Ranitzki.

"No! My turn!" Kulvyetz yelled.

Just then a crowd of manor servants, alarmed by the shooting, burst into the room.

"Out! Get out!" Kmita roared and counted for Kulvyetz. "One... two... fire!"

Another shot thundered in the room and this time shards of bone flew out of the shattered skull.

"Pistols for everybody!" all the others shouted, leaped to their feet, and started to pound and pummel the terrified grooms and lackeys with their fists. "Run and get our pistols! Move it! Jump to it!"

"On... two... fire!" Kmita howled.

★ ★ ★

Within a quarter of an hour the long, low-ceilinged room sounded and looked like a battlefield. Pistol shots crashed and thundered like cannon in the enclosed space. Red muzzle blasts licked like tongues of fire through the thick black smoke that smothered the candlelight and turned the shooters into threatening shadows who lost all idea of why they were shooting or what they were supposed to shoot at. Zendt's voice accompanied the cannonade croaking like a raven, squealing like a falcon, howling like a wolf and roaring like a bear. White shards of bone showered down on the yelling pistoleers from the shattered skulls, and long yellow splinters flew about like shrapnel out of the gouged walls and ruined portrait frames. Several of the Billevitch ancestors were shot to pieces in the chaos, and the blood-mad Ranitzki fell into one of his murderous furies and hacked the rest of them to shreds with his saber.

The terrified servants stared with bulging eyes at this wild entertainment which looked more like a Tartar raid than anything they ever saw or imagined in this peaceful manor. The frightened dogs began to bark and howl outside while groups of villagers ran up to the main house and clustered in the courtyard. The manor maids crowded outside the windows, flattening their noses against the fogged frosted glass, and peered inside to see what was happening.

Zendt spotted them at last. He uttered such a shrill and high-pitched whistle that even Ranitzki dropped his saber and covered his ears.

"Birds, gentlemen!" Zendt cried out. "There're birds outside and pecking at the windows!"

"Hey hey! Get the birdies!"

"Let's have a little dancing!" howled the drunken voices and the entire savage company poured out of the house.

They were so far gone in their intoxication that even the bitter Winter frost failed to sweep the fumes of wine and mead out of their steaming heads and put a damper on their mad excitement. The manor girls ran about screaming and protesting as Pan Kmita's drunken company chased them through the courtyard, caught them among the stables and outbuildings, and dragged them back into the manor house where, in another moment, a grotesque parody of a dance began.

The revelers paced and leaped about in the thick, acrid smoke, amid the wreckage of the portraits and the hunting trophies, whirling their squealing partners round and round the table on which spilled wine and mead formed a crimson lake, and that was how Pan Andrei Kmita and his boon companions celebrated their first night in Lubitch.

Chapter Four

DURING THE NEXT FEW DAYS Pan Andrei made daily visits to Vodokty and each night that he returned to Lubitch and his roistering friends he declared himself more in love with his adored Olenka. Each day that he saw her he discovered something new about her. Every visit to her filled him with amazement as he watched the growth of her affection for him. He sat with her for hours—sure that he had never met anyone as warm and loving but, at the same time, as wise beyond her years—and he knew as he listened to her thoughtful words that he could become an entirely different man with her as his teacher. Each night that he left her for the long ride to Lubitch he was more in awe of her gentleness, nobility and wisdom, and ever more grateful for that astonishing stroke of luck that picked him for her husband.

Then one day he said to his boon companions:

"Listen, my little lambs. You're going to pay your respects to her today. We've made arrangements, she and I, to take a sleigh ride to Mitruny so as to have a gallop through the woods and look over that third property of hers. She's going to receive us there formally so make sure you behave yourselves or I'll slice you all into goulash. Understood?"

"We hear you," they chorused, went off to get themselves dressed in their finest clothes, and shortly afterwards four harnessed sleighs carried the richly uniformed and equipped young men towards Vodokty.

Pan Andrei sat with Kokosinski in the leading sleigh, a Russian *troika* built in the shape of a silvery bear and drawn by three

spirited Kalmuk horses, whose bridles and headgear were decorated in the Smolensk fashion with peacock plumes and broad
multicolored ribbons. A lad held the traces in the neck of the
bear and the two passengers sprawled in the broad back seat
under thick fur robes. Pan Kmita was resplendent in green
velvets lined with sables and hooked with golden loops, and in
a sable cap with a heron's plume streaming past his ear. He was
excited and happy about the day's adventure but also ill-at-ease
about the wild excesses of their nights in Lubitch.

"Listen, Kokoshka," he said at last to his traveling companion.
"We've gone too far in our amusements these past few evenings,
especially on that first night when the skulls and portraits got
knocked about. And those girls! That's the worst thing of the
lot. That damned Zendt always gets these wild ideas and then
I've got to foot the bill. I'm worried about people gossiping
about all that, you know what I mean? It's a matter of my
reputation here."

"Hang yourself on your reputation," Kokosinski said, shrug-
ging with indifference. "That's about all it's good for, like
everything else about us."

"And who's to blame for that? Even people back home
looked at me as if I was some kind of a scoundrel because of you
lot."

"Is that so?" Kokosinski laughed. "And who had Pan Tumgrat stripped naked and then dragged him on a rope's end in the
snow? Who cut down that uppity Warsaw noble who asked if
people in Orsha walked on two legs or still on all fours? Who
chopped up the two Vyzinskis, both father and son? Who
scattered the last provincial diet to the four winds?"

"That thing with the diet was in our Orsha country, not here,
and there's nothing unusual about it anyway. It's done all the
time. Pan Tumgrat forgave me on his death bed. As for the rest,
don't make a point of it, because a challenge and a sword fight
can happen to anyone."

"And did I mention everything? How about those two military courts-martial for looting and public disorder that are waiting for you at the Hetman's headquarters?"

"Not for me but for all you cut-throats!" Pan Andrei snapped
back. "All I'm guilty of is letting you loose among private
citizens. But no matter. Just make sure, Kokoshka, that you

keep your mouth shut, you hear? Especially about those portraits and those girls! If Olenka finds out about them I'll put all the blame on you where it belongs. I've already told the maids and the manor servants that if they breathe one word about all that I'll skin them alive."

"Get yourself shoed like a horse, Andy," Kokosinski said and laughed into Kmita's face. "You've turned into a proper little gelding. I can see that this girl's going to put a ring in your nose and have you dancing about like a tame bear to any tune she plays. I tell you, if people back home in Orsha could see you now nobody would believe that you're the same man."

"And you're a fool, Kokoshka!" Pan Andrei said coldly. "If I've changed at all it's only for the better. As for Olenka, you'll see for yourself that there's no joking around with her. She has a mind of her own, and it's a lot sharper and sees things a lot clearer than any man you've ever known, that's certain. Her grandfather raised her to look at things as they really are, to come to her own judgments and to make decisions, and she doesn't put up with any wrongdoing. If you want to show off in front of her about what a devil-may-care and rough and ready fellow you are, she'll have you hanging your head down like an errant schoolboy with just one cold look. You tell her how you laugh at the law whenever you feel like it, and she'll tell you right off that a real nobleman doesn't behave like that, because that hurts the country. She'll say it straight into your face and you'll feel as if somebody kicked you in the teeth, and then you'll wonder why you couldn't see that for yourself before..."

He paused, spat into the snow, and slammed one angry fist into the palm of the other.

"*Tfui!*" he snarled. "It's pure shame what we've been doing around here. We've raised Hell wherever we've been and now we've got to account for it, standing in shame like convicts, on trial before decency and goodness! Ah, but those manor wenches! That's the worst thing yet!"

"I didn't think they were bad at all," Kokosinski drawled, grinning from ear to ear. "Fact is I thought they were pretty good, ha ha. I hear there are some awfully pretty girls in some of these greyback villages around here. And that they don't mind a bit of slap and tickle."

"Who told you that?" Kmita asked at once.

"Who? And who if not Zendt? He always sniffs out the best looking birds. He took a ride yesterday out towards Volmontov and he saw a whole lot of them coming home from vespers. '*I thought I'd fall off my horse,*' he said, '*they were so neat and pretty!*' And right away, every time he looked at one, she showed him all her teeth. And no wonder! With all their own men gone into the army the birds have got to be feeling a bit lonely."

"Hey!" And Kmita jabbed his elbow into Kokosinski's side. "What if we take a ride some evening? Eh? As if, you know, we lost our way or something?"

"And what about your precious reputation?" Kokosinski laughed.

"Ay, that's right, goddamit! Shut up about it, then. Go by yourselves or, better yet, forget the whole thing. You wouldn't be able to get through the night without some kind of brawl and I want to live in peace with this local gentry. Olenka's grandfather, God rest his soul, made them all her guardians."

"Yes, you've mentioned that," Kokosinski said. "But I just can't believe it. How come he got to be so close with those puddle-jumpers?"

"Ah... He served with them in a lot of wars." Pan Andrei shrugged and grimaced with distaste. "But to tell you the whole truth, Kokoshka, I didn't like the idea myself the first time I heard it. It was like he'd set them over me, you know what I mean?"

"That's right, Andy." Kokosinski grinned at Kmita with a sly, goading show of contempt and pity. "That's how it's going to be from now on for you, my lad. You'll have to be nice and gentle with those piddling little greybacks and lick their greasy boots."

"The plague will squeeze the life out of them first!" Kmita snarled, immediately enraged. "Shut your mouth about it or I'll shut it for you! They'll take my orders and be glad to do it, just like you!"

"Oh yes?"

"Yes, goddamit! We've got six hundred men ready for anything, remember? There isn't another regiment like it in the country!"

"Seems like their colonel's going to be wearing skirts from now on," Kokosinski drawled again, amused, and shrugged in his turn. "People say there's another colonel living around here somewhere. I forget the name... Volodyovski, was it? He's the one who led the Laudanians at Shklov. They're supposed to have put up a good fight there even though they lost an awful lot of people."

"I've heard of him," Kmita said, then peered eagerly ahead. "There! There's the Vodokty manor. Hey, driver, crack your whip! Let them know we're coming!"

★ ★ ★

The driver standing in the neck of the bear whirled his long whip around and snapped it skillfully in the frozen air; the other sleigh-drivers followed his example, firing off salutes like a volley of pistol shots; and they pulled up at the manor house as jauntily and smartly as if they were a wedding party coming for the bride.

Pan Kmita led them through a broad, unpainted entrance hall into the dining chamber where, as in Lubitch, rows of hunting trophies stared at them whitely off the walls, and here the young men stopped, shooting swift, curious glances at the door through which Panna Aleksandra was to appear among them. Meanwhile, mindful of their commander's threats, they talked among themselves as softly as if they were in church.

"You've got a way with words," Pan Uhlik whispered to Kokosinski. "You greet her from us all."

"I was composing my address on the way," Kokosinski answered, somewhat ill-at-ease. "Only Andy kept interrupting my train of thought so I'm not sure how smooth it'll come out."

"Just make it bold, that's what! Let it come out any way it wants to as long as it makes us seem like a dignified bunch who know our way around in polite society."

"And here she comes now."

Aleksandra did come in at that moment and stopped in the doorway as if surprised by so many visitors, and Pan Andrei felt as if his heart were about to leap out of his chest. He was used to seeing her at night, by the light of candles, and the crisp white daylight seemed to bring out her natural dignity and beauty even more powerfully than before. Her eyes had the clear, blue glow of mountain stream; her dark brows seemed like ebony arches against her smooth white forehead; and her pale gold hair shined above it like a coronet.

She stood looking quietly and gravely at her company, as poised and stately as a great lady receiving welcome visitors in her own house, and her finely sculpted face seemed all the brighter and loftier because of the black silks, edged with ermine, in which she was dressed.

Kmita's roughnecks gaped at her, dumbstruck and astonished, as if she was a vision that had stepped out of one of those classical foreign paintings that hang in the halls of great lords, and they didn't know what to do with their hands and feet. They were, Pan Andrei knew, used to an entirely different kind of women; a lady, in the full meaning of the word, was totally beyond their experience. He hid his grin by lifting his hand to his mustache, hardly able to keep a straight face at the sight of their stiff, clumsy bows, open mouths and wide staring eyes.

"I've brought you my comrades," he said at last and kissed Olenka's hands. "They're a fine, worthy lot, my love, as I've already told you, even though they seem to have lost their tongues on the way."

"It's a high honor for me," Aleksandra said, "to receive such distinguished cavaliers in my house."

Her courtsey could have done honor to the Radzivills themselves, Pan Andrei thought proudly and bit down on his mustache, delighted that his girl should show such courtly poise. Meanwhile his 'distinguished cavaliers' were elbowing Kokosinski in the ribs and pushing him forward.

"Get out there, will you?" Ranitzki hissed. "Do your stuff."

Pan Kokosinski took a step forward, cleared his throat importantly, took up a rhetor's stance and prepared to launch into an oration.

"Most highly exalted and illustrious lady," he began.

"Most noble lady will do," Pan Andrei corrected.

"Most... ah... noble lady," Pan Yaromir tried again, thrown off stride by the interruption. "And our... ah... benefactress. Forgive me if I've got a bit mixed up in the correct form of address..."

"It does no harm," Aleksandra said. "And it casts no aspersions on such a gallant gentleman."

"Hmm. Ah. Yes. Well, anyway." Kokosinski threw despairing glances at his comrades who ground their teeth and hissed at him with fury. "Most noble lady and our benefactress..."

Striking a lofty pose and searching desperately for the proper classical allusions, Pan Kokosinski had begun to flounder and Kmita could hardly keep himself from laughing.

"I... ah... don't know what I ought to praise the most in the name of all the Orshan gentry,"Kokosinski struggled. "Whether it's your ladyship's great beauty and evident virtues... Or the unbelievable luck and happiness of Pan Andrei Kmita, our dear friend and beloved commander... Because even if I should ascend to the clouds, even if I should reach the... ah... clouds, as I said... even if my words should soar to the clouds..."

"Will you get out of those damn clouds!"Kmita shouted.

The officers and gentlemen spluttered with wild laughter and then, recalling their commander's stern warning about their behavior, they clapped their hands across their mouths and tugged at their whiskers.

"D-do your own greetings, then, you heathen dogs," Pan Yaromir stammered at them, as red as a boiled beetroot.

But Aleksandra herself came to his rescue.

"I couldn't equal your erudition, gentlemen,"she said, "I am sure. This is only a simple country house, not the great halls to which you must be accustomed. But I am quite certain that I don't deserve such homage from such a gallant and distinguished company."

She raised the edge of her dress slightly with the tips of her fingers, and courtseyed again with that profound inner dignity and grace that seemed to elevate everything around her, while the fierce young Orshans didn't know what to do with their own clumsy hands and stared wildly at each other and the floor. They wanted to appear well-mannered and polite in the presence of such a courtly lady but they had no idea how to go about it so they started to growl and mutter, tug their mustache ends and slap at their sabers.

"We've come here to escort you in style to Mitruny," Pan Andrei said at last. "It's fine weather for a sleigh ride, we couldn't ask for better. The snow is hard and crisp and God has given us a beautiful clear day."

"Thank you,"she said. "I'd like that. I've already sent Aunt Kulvyetzovna to Mitruny to prepare a supper for us there. If you'll just excuse me for a moment I'll put on something warmer for the ride."

She smiled again at them all, turned and left the room, and Kmita grinned in triumph at his dazed companions.

"So what did I tell you?" he cried out. "Eh? Isn't she a princess? What do you say now, Kokoshka? So she's put a ring in my nose, has she? And didn't she make you look like a mumbling schoolboy? Did you ever see a girl like her anywhere, any of you?"

"You didn't have to make a clown out of me," Kokosinski growled. "But I admit I didn't expect such a highborn lady."

"She'd hold her own anywhere!" Kmita went on proudly. "Her grandfather, God rest his soul, spent more time with her in Keydany among the Radzivills than he did here in the countryside. And what a beauty, eh? She had you all gaping at her as bug-eyed as carp in a fishpond!"

"We ended up looking like a bunch of clods," Ranitzki snarled with rage. "But Kokosinski is the biggest jackass of us all."

"So now it's Kokosinski, eh?" Pan Yaromir snarled in his own turn. "And who elbowed me forward to do all the talking? You should've stuck your own spotted mug out there if you're such a courtier!"

"Settle down, lambkins," Kmita ordered. "Settle down, you hear? You can be as amazed as you like but let's not have any quarrels here."

"I'd leap into fire for her!" Rekutz squealed. "Chop my head off if you want to, Andy, but that's the God's truth!"

★ ★ ★

But Pan Andrei was far from thinking about duels just then. On the contrary, he was pleased to see the effect that his Olenka had on these hard-bitten, ruthless and often uncontrollable and cruel reprobates, whose fierce pride was equal only to their murderous rages. They were, as he had told her, a product of their violent and desperate times, and he knew that he hadn't been much better in their common past; but he was starting to suspect that he had far less in common with them than he had supposed.

Meanwhile Olenka returned, dressed in otter furs which made

her bright face seem even brighter than before, and they stepped outside.

"Is that our sleigh?" she asked and pointed at the silver bear.

"Yes, that's for us. Do you like it?"

"I haven't seen one of that kind before," she said, as pleased as a child. "Where does it come from?"

"Moscow, for all I know," he said and laughed easily. "It's part of the booty I took from the Russians. And it's just right for you and me to ride in because my coat-of-arms includes a lady carried by a bear. There are other Kmitas whose crest and seal is a pair of crossed banners, but they are descended from Filon Kmita of Tchernopyl, in the Ukraine, and it's a lesser house than mine."

"And when did you capture this pretty little bear, then?"

"I really can't remember. Sometime in this last war. Our own lands and possessions are lost in the east and I doubt that any of us will see them again. All we have these days is what we take from the Russian boyars. And because I've served Lady War as faithfully as I could, she's rewarded me with quite a fair fortune."

"I would wish us all a better benefactress," Aleksandra said seriously and sadly. "War may reward one man now and then but she also wrings bitter tears out of the whole nation."

"God and the Hetmans will change all that," he answered.

As he spoke, he wrapped her against the frost in a rich sleigh robe of close-weaved white linen, lined throughout with the thick white fur of Siberian wolves. Then he dropped down beside her and shouted to the driver:

"Crack that whip, lad! Let's get going, then!"

The sleigh driver cracked his whip, uttered a short piercing whistle, and the horses leaped at once into a full gallop. The cold air whipped against Kmita's and Olenka's faces and robbed them of breath so that they rode in silence, listening to the hiss of ice and snow under the sleigh's runners, to the thunder of the horses' hooves pounding the snow ahead, and to the cries of the driver.

★ ★ ★

At last Pan Andrei bowed towards Olenka.

"Are you happy?" he asked.

"Yes," she said and raised the otter muff towards her lips to block the swift flow of the icy air.

The sleigh flew like the wind.

The day was bright with the glare of snow and crackling with frost that glittered everywhere around them like a shower of multicolored spangles. The white roofs of the wayside dwellings they passed in the village looked like round mounds of snow out of which columns of reddening smoke seeped into the air. Dense flocks of crows and blackbirds wheeled above them with a raucous cry, lifting out of the leafless trees that bordered the highway.

Two miles beyond Vodokty they galloped into a silent forest where the air was so dark and still that the ancient trees seemed to be asleep. The gnarled old oaks and venerable birches closed tightly around them and flowed past them as if in a dream, slipping away so swiftly that they could barely catch a glimpse of their brooding stillness, and they flashed among them, fast as shooting stars, as if their horses had grown wings.

Such speed dazzles the mind and overwhelms the senses, and Aleksandra felt as if invisible wings of her own had lifted her into the freezing air. Thrown back against the furs that lined the sleigh, she closed her eyes and gave herself entirely to this silent flight. She felt a strange lassitude, both precious and alarming, flowing over her, as if her young Orshan lover had swept her up into those glittering Winter skies by some sort of magic, and carried her off into a world she had never known except in her dreams and her imagination.

She felt a pair of strong arms tightening around her, and then her chilled lips were suddenly hot and burning as if a firm but gentle seal had been pressed against them, but her closed eyes defied her commands and refused to open.

The dream-flight continued.

On and on they flew.

And then a voice was murmuring in her ears.

"Do you love me?"

"With all my heart and soul," she said.

"And I for life or death!"

And again Kmita's sable cap bowed over the soft white otter fur that framed Olenka's face.

* * *

She didn't know the exact source of the mysterious glow that inflamed her senses, whether it was the pressure of his hungry kisses or the wild speed of that magic journey, and she didn't care.

'*Let it go on forever,*' she murmured to herself. '*Let it never end.*'

The forest sped past them like an endless vision of icy walls and fairy-tale spires. The horses snorted. The pounded snow sent booming echoes into the wall of trees, and there seemed to be no limit that either she or anyone else could set on their happiness and joy.

"I'd like this ride to take us to the end of the world!" Kmita shouted, full of love and laughter, and she began to recover her dazed mind and her stolen senses, her consciousness of time and place and of herself as a product of all her traditions, and of the rules that her upbringing and her civilization had imposed upon her.

"What are we doing?" she whispered.

"Loving each other!" he cried out and pressed his lips to hers once again.

"But this is a sin..."

"What kind of sin can it be when we love each other?"

"Enough," she murmured. "Mitruny lies just around the corner."

"This corner or another," he cried out. "Who cares? They'll all be the same from now on."

And standing up in the speeding sleigh he raised both his arms and began to shout, laughing and crying out into the snowy tree crowns, as if his joy was too immense for even his broad chest.

"Hey ha! Hey ha!"

"Hey hey!" the young men called out from the sleighs that flew in their own glittering clouds of snow behind the silvery bear. "Hey hey! Ha!"

"What's all this shouting about, then?" she asked, laughing in her turn.

"Happiness!" he cried. "Joy! Love of life! Why don't you give a shout yourself?"

"Hey ha!" Olenka's clear young voice rang through the frosted air.

"My God, how I love you!" he cried and threw his arms about her.

Then, falling back, he raised his face to the speeding sky and began to sing.

> *"Hey, mother dear,' the young girl cries,*
> *At the break of day.*
> *'There's knights acomin' from the woods,*
> *They'll steal me away."*

"And what does her mother say to that?" Olenka asked, laughing, and Pan Andrei sang the second verse.

> *"Don't look at them, daughter,*
> *Run and bar the door.*
> *Or your heart will leap out of your breast*
> *And follow them to war."*

"Who taught you such pretty songs?" she asked. "And where did you learn them?"

"War did the teaching, love. On cold lonely nights. That's what we sang around the bivouac fires to keep ourselves remembering what life is about."

★ ★ ★

But suddenly loud, urgent cries behind them were calling on them to pull up and halt and Pan Andrei spun around, angry and surprised that his companions would dare to intrude on these precious moments with Olenka. And then he spotted a lone horseman galloping a few dozen paces behind them as quickly as his weary horse could take him, and he recognized the breathless messenger at once.

"God's truth!" he cried out, immediately alert. "That's my sergeant, Soroka. Something must've happened in Upita. Pull up, driver! Pull up!"

"Wait! Wait! Pull up there!" the others shouted in the sleighs behind them and hurried their own drivers and horses to catch up with Kmita.

The silver bear sloughed to a halt, the horses sliding stiff-legged across the icy highway, and then the sergeant was pulling up his own foam-spattered animal beside them, and gasping out of breath.

"Your Excellency..."

"What is it, Soroka? Speak up, man! What's the matter?"

"Trouble, sir! Upita's on fire! We've got a real fight on our hands there, colonel!"

"Jezus Maria!" Olenka cried out.

"Don't be alarmed, my lady," Pan Andrei said at once and turned again to the gasping sergeant. "Who's doing the fighting, then?"

"Soldiers and burghers, Your Honor." The old sergeant's chest was heaving as he fought for breath. "The town square's burning. The townsfolk barricaded themselves in their council house and sent for help to the garrison in Ponevyezh. I made it here, to Your Excellency, as fast as I could!"

While the old sergeant was making his report the other sleighs came galloping up and sliding to a halt, and Kokosinski, the gigantic Kulvyetz, the angry Ranitzki, Uhlik, Rekutz and the breathless Zendt leaped out and ran to surround Pan Andrei and Olenka.

"But what's it all about?" Pan Kmita demanded.

"The burghers wouldn't feed the men or the horses, colonel." The sergeant struggled to control his breathing. "It's like we didn't have no proper requisitions for rations and fodder, or script from the Hetman..."

"So the men started taking it on their own?" Pan Andrei asked coldly.

"That's right, Excellency. We laid a proper siege to the burgomaster in the town square where they put up a barricade against us. Then somebody started shooting so we set fire to a couple of buildings... Now there's a real fight going on and the townsfolk got all the church bells ringing for alarm..."

Kmita's eyes began to glint with anger.

"Hey, gentlemen! *Sukurs!*" Kokosinski shouted. "Let's get there right away and give our lads a hand!"

"The damned bean-counters refuse to feed the soldiers?" Ranitzki's wind-reddened, sallow face was now wholly covered with the telltale livid splotches of his murderous fury. "Cut and thrust, gentlemen! Cut and thrust! Let's teach them a lesson!"

Zendt laughed, a mad shrill sound so exactly like the scream of a screech-owl that the horses panicked and began to kick against the traces, while Rekutz lifted his pale watery eyes to the sky and squealed out: "Kill 'em! Cut 'em down! Send 'em up in smoke!'

"Silence!" Pan Kmita shouted, so loud in that still forest air that the echoes boomed like cannon among the trees, and Zendt reeled and staggered back as if he'd been struck in the chest with a blacksmith's hammer.

"You're not needed there!" Kmita snapped at his gaping officers. "We don't need to spill any more blood than has been shed already, understand? I want all of you to get into one pair of sleighs and ride back to Lubitch. You're to sit there and wait until I send for you."

"What do you mean...*sit?*" Ranitzki leaned forward, mad eyes narrowed, and his hand clutching at his saber as if he was about to fight anyone who'd dare to give him an order. "What do you mean...*wait?*"

But Pan Andrei looked into his eyes so coldly that he backed away.

"You heard me," Kmita hissed and drew the edge of his open palm along Ranitzki's throat. "One more word from any of you and it'll be your last."

All of them grew still and silent then, clearly afraid of their commander, even though in the course of their daily lives they might treat him with the careless give-and-take of their own rough and ready kind, and he turned to Aleksandra in the silver sleigh.

"Well, that's the end of our sleigh ride, my dear," he said. "Go back to Vodokty. Or take the sleigh and pick up your aunt in Mitruny, whichever's best for you..."

"And you?" she asked quickly.

"Ah,"—and he made a swift, bitter gesture as if an angry memory had returned to haunt him—"I might've know that those jailbirds of mine wouldn't sit still for long. But don't worry, I'll soon settle them down. All they need is a few heads lopped off and then they'll be quiet."

"God look after you and guide your hand in justice and mercy," Aleksandra said.

"Be well and don't worry," Pan Andrei said and kissed her hands again and pressed them to his chest and wrapped her once more in the wolfskin robe. "I'll be back quickly, you can count on that, because I've something really worthwhile to come back to now."

Then he jumped into another sleigh and ordered the driver to take him to Upita.

Chapter Five

SEVERAL DAYS PASSED without a word from Pan Andrei and they were anxious days for Panna Aleksandra even though she was certain that he would pacify his unruly soldiers, restore peace and order, and treat the victims with justice and understanding. But, in the meantime, three of the Laudanian gentry came to visit her.

The first to come calling was old Pakosh Gashtovt of Patzunel, the patriarch of his clan, famous for his supposed riches and six lovely daughters, three of whom were married to the neighboring Butryms while the three youngest were still at home and nursing the injured Pan Volodyovski. The second to arrive that day was Kasyan Butrym, the oldest man alive in the Lauda country, a tough old warrior who could still remember the times of King Stefan Batory and his victorious wars on the Tsars of Moscow. Last to come was Yozva Butrym, a son-in-law of Pakosh, who was known among the neighborhoods as 'Yozva the Peg-leg,' and who was one of the most feared men in the Lauda region.

Aleksandra was particularly curious and surprised when she saw him stamping up the porch steps to the manor door because she knew him for a bitterly unforgiving man, as hard on himself as he was on everybody else, even though his harsh judgments were never unfair. He was a huge dour man, as heavy-shouldered and sinewy as all the other Butryms, but although he was barely fifty years old and strong as a bear, he hadn't gone with the rest of the Laudanians to enlist in the new Lithuanian army that was gathering in Rosyen. He stayed at home that Winter because an old war injury crippled him in cold weather; a

50

Cossack cannon ball had carried off one of his feet in the war of the Hmyelnitzki Rebellion, and made him even more irritable, angry and judgmental than he was before. Now he tramped in on his wooden leg, as cold and silent as a granite tomb, and she knew instinctively that nothing good would come from his visit.

But she received them with all the courtesy to which they were accustomed in the Billevitch manor, guessing at once that the two clan patriarchs had come to check with her on Pan Andrei and to find out what she thought of him.

"We had in mind to pay him our respects," old Pakosh began in his usual gentle and paternal manner. "But we hear he's still not back from Upita. So we thought we'd come over and ask you, little sweetheart, when the best time might be for a trip to Lubitch?"

"I should think he'd be home almost any time," she assured them warmly. "And he'll be pleased to see you, I am sure, because he's heard so many good things about you as my chosen guardians, first from my late grandfather and then from me as well."

"Just as long as he doesn't treat us like he did the Domashevitches when they brought him news of the old colonel's death," growled the dour Yozva.

But Aleksandra heard the muttered comment and replied at once politely but firmly.

"Don't hold that against him. Perhaps he didn't receive them quite as hospitably as he should have done but that's all in the past. He didn't know our customs and what we've all meant to each other here. He's not from our country. But now he's quite ready to make amends and live with everyone in peace, respect and friendship. And don't forget that he came fresh from the war which took so much from him. Soldiers are alike that, aren't they? Their tempers are sometimes as sharp and quick as their sabers."

Old Pakosh Gashtovt, who wanted nothing more than just to live in peace with the entire world, nodded and said:

"That's why we didn't think all that much about it. One wild boar will snort at another when they come across each other unexpected like. So why shouldn't people? We'll go to Lubitch like we used to do, and pay our respects to Pan Kmita as we did with the old colonel, may he rest in peace. Yes, that's what

we'll do so that your young man will know that he's welcome
here, and that we're ready to look up to him like we did to your
grandfather, sweetheart."

"Tell us though, little one," the bowed old Kasyan murmured.
"D'you like him, or not? Because that's also our duty to ask, as
you know."

"God will repay your caring," Aleksandra said and went on
carefully so as not to hurt the Laudanians' feelings. "Pan Kmita
is a fine man. But you understand, that even if I saw something
in him that I didn't care for, it would be wrong for me to talk
to anyone about it."

"Ah, but you didn't see anything like that, sweet soul?" the
old man persisted.

"Nothing!" she said firmly. "In any case, nobody here has the
right to judge him or, God forbid, look at him with suspicion!
We'd do better to give our thanks to God that he has come
among us!"

"What's there to be so thankful for?" the harsh Yozva muttered dourly, as gloomy and as cautious as a real Zmudyan. "If
we find something for which to be thankful, then we will be
thankful. If we don't, we won't."

"And did you talk about the wedding?" Kasyan asked.

"Pan Kmita wants it as soon as possible," Olenka said and
suddenly dropped her glance, overcome by shyness.

"That's no surprise," Yozva grunted coldly. "Did you ever
hear about a bear that wasn't in a hurry to get at the honey? But
why don't you speak up, Father Kasyan, and tell us what's
itching on your tongue, instead of nodding over there like a
sleepy hare in the noonday sun?"

"I'm not sleeping," the ancient man said softly. "I'm just
looking into my own head to find the best way for saying what's
in there. It's like the Lord Jesus told us, you've got to do to
others as they do to you. We don't mean any harm to Pan Kmita
just as long as he doesn't do any to us. Which God forbid,
amen."

"We have our own ways here," Yozva Butrym muttered.
"And everybody's got to fit into them or things will go badly."

But this was just a little more than the proud young heiress
was willing to hear. Her dark brows narrowed and her voice
became tinged with a touch of loftiness and disdain.

"We're not discussing a servant," she said shortly. "Remember that he will be the master here and that it's his will, not ours, that's going to matter. And he will also take your place in guarding my interests."

"So we're to mind our own business, eh?" the gloomy Yozva grunted.

"What I mean is that I want you to be his friends, just as he wants to be yours," Aleksandra said with a certain desperation in her anxious voice. "But doesn't he have a right to live in his own house as he pleases? Isn't that everybody's right? Tell me if I'm wrong, Father Pakosh."

"That's God's own truth," the Patzunel patriarch murmured but Yozva Butrym turned again to the nodding elder of his own family and clan.

"Don't keep dreaming there, Father Kasyan!" he reminded.

"I'm not dreaming, lad. No, I'm not dreaming. Just looking into my own head..."

"And what do you see there?"

"What do I see? Hmm. Pan Kmita is a great lord, a real highborn noble, and we're just poor folks who work our own soil. And he's a great soldier too, famous in the army, who fought the Russian enemy all alone when everybody else gave way to despair. God give us more like him, that's what I say. But his company... ah... that's another matter..."

And here the old man turned to the other patriarch and gestured to him to take up the tale.

"Tell us, neighbor Pakosh," he murmured. "Tell us what you heard from the Domashevitches! That those friends and officers of Pan Kmita are all evil men, condemned by the courts, stripped of their names and fortunes, and ready for hanging! Oh they were hard on the enemy, there's no denying it, but they were just as hard and cruel to their own people out there where they came from! They burned and looted and pillaged and murdered, that's what they were doing! There's not one of them that doesn't have innocent blood on his hands! That's the kind of friends Pan Kmita brought among us!"

He paused for breath, his wrinkled old face red with indignation, and Aleksandra felt his pain and grief in her own breast and understood his bitterness and anger.

"Ey," he resumed. "If it was just a sword fight here and

there... Or a raid or two, like after a quarrel... that can happen to the best of us. But they live like Tartars! They'd have rotted behind prison bars years ago, if it wasn't for Pan Kmita who loves them and protects them! And now they've barely shown their faces here and it's already common knowledge who and what they are! On their first night in Lubitch they shot their pistols at the portraits of your own Billevitch ancestors, and cut them to shreds, which Pan Kmita ought not to have allowed because they're his benefactors too."

Olenka covered her eyes with both her hands feeling as if her world had begun to shift under her feet.

"That can't be!" she cried. "That couldn't have happened!"

"It could because it did!" The old man shook with disgust and anger. "He let them profane the blood that he's about to join with his own in marriage! And then they dragged the manor wenches into the house for their ugly pleasures! Tfui!"—and the quivering Butrym elder barely held himself from spitting on the floor—"That's beyond forgiving! That's something we never had around here before! From their first day among us they started off with debauchery and violence and pistols! From the very first day!"

And here old Kasyan became truly angry and started pounding the floor with his walking stave while Olenka felt her face darkening with shame.

"And those troops of his?" Yozva Butrym muttered bitterly. "Those soldiers he left in Upita? They're no better than their officers, that's certain. Who ran off Pan Sollohub's cattle herd? Pan Kmita's people, that's who. Who beat up the peasants on the highway when they were taking their pitch to the market? Again Kmita's men! Pan Sollohub's gone for justice to Keydany and now there's a new riot in Upita! We used to live in peace here as nowhere in the country, but these days nobody goes to sleep without a loaded musket close to hand and guards at the windows. And why? Because Pan Kmita is among us with his worthless friends."

"Don't say such things, Father Yozva," Olenka pleaded, offended but ashamed. "Please don't speak like that!"

"And what am I to say, then? If Pan Kmita's innocent then why is he keeping such people around him? You tell him, sweetheart, to turn them out or hand them to the hangman or we'll never have any peace again. Their ways are a danger and an insult to every decent man and woman living in the Lauda. The whole countryside is in an uproar about them."

"What am I to do?" Olenka didn't know how to face their bitterness and anger. "Perhaps they are as you say... evil, worthless people... but they're his war comrades. Will he get rid of them just because I ask it?"

"If he doesn't," grim Yozva Butrym grunted so low that she barely heard him. "Then he's the same kind."

* * *

Numb with shock, Aleksandra stared at them with horror but her own pride had risen up in anger. Her consciousness of her own worth as a woman challenged whatever understanding she might have tried to find for those murderous libertines and wastrels, who had hung themselves like millstones around Pan Andrei's neck, and ruined his good name.

And wasn't his name to be her own as well?

"Alright, then!" she cried. "Let things be as they may! He has to drive them off. He'll have to choose between them and me. If what you say is true, and I'll know the truth of it today, then I won't forgive them! No, neither the shooting in Lubitch nor the drunken rioting! I may be a woman all alone here, and they're an armed horde, but I won't give way!"

"We'll help you all we can," Yozva said.

"Dear God!" she cried, feeling her own anger boiling up inside her. "Let them do what they want but not here! Not in Lubitch! Let them be whatever suits them, that's their own concern and they'll pay for it with their own necks! But when they drag Pan Andrei into their own mire... when they corrupt him with their debauchery... that's my business too!"

"That's what we were thinking," the Butrym patriarch nodded slowly and looked at Aleksandra with sorrow and pity. "A young man's like a wild colt, easily led astray, and the more spirit that he has the greater the danger."

But Aleksandra's sense of shame and anger was turning against herself and her eyes started to fill with tears.

"My God, the shame of it," she whispered. "It's... beyond contempt. I thought that they were just crude, clumsy soldiers, but they're far worse than that. They've not only covered themselves with infamy, but they've spilled their own debauchery and filth on Pan Kmita as well! Ah,"—and her eyes darkened with a sudden unforgiving fury —"I should have known it from the start! God, but I was stupid! Thank you, good friends, for opening my eyes to those lying traitors. I know what I have to do about them now."

"That's just it, my dear," old Kasyan murmured gently. "That's it, my sweet child. Goodness speaks through you. Goodness and all the old virtues that let people live in decency and kindness, as God meant them to. And we'll help."

"But,"—and her hot, bitter tears were now close to spilling—"don't blame Pan Kmita for everything they do. He may not have acted wisely where they are concerned, but he is so young and... and... so full of life... And they push him into evil and temptation..."

"We don't blame him, dear heart," old Pakosh whispered sadly. "We know who's to blame."

And now Olenka felt a new emotion flooding through her body. Loathing replaced the shame and contempt and anger. Disgust gave way to determination to rid Pan Andrei of his profligate companions who seemed to her no more than common looters who were pillaging everything she had begun to love and care about. She'd placed all her warmest hopes and feelings in Pan Kmita's keeping, looking to him as the man whose love would transform her life and make her unique, and now she knew herself to be deeply wounded in her childlike openness and trust, and bitterly insulted in her own self-image as a woman. She was ashamed for him and for herself as well, and this shame and anger searched, above all, for someone else to blame.

"As long as I'm alive," she swore to herself. "They... won't remain here. They're the guilty ones and they'll have to go. Not just from Lubitch, you can be sure of that, but out of our whole country!"

The three Laudanians looked at her with pride and affection, pleased to see that strength, maturity, courage and conviction with which their young heiress was about to challenge the

Orshan invaders, but they were also anxious to soothe her wounded feelings.

"It's like our good neighbor Pakosh said," old Kasyan Butrym murmured. "It's not Pan Kmita who's all at fault here. It's not him we blame but those cut-throats who've attached themselves to him like burrs to a hound's tail. We know he's young. We know he'll change if he gets the chance. Pan Hlebovitch, the King's *Starosta* for all the Lauda country, also did some stupid things when he was a boy. And now he governs all of us with wisdom and justice and who remembers what a wild young fool he was years ago?"

"Take a young dog," the gentle Patzunel patriarch quavered in a voice that seemed as close to breaking with emotion as Olenka's own. "You take him out into the woods and all he does is play, pull on your coat-tails, won't go for the deer... But give him time and he'll learn to do what he has to."

Olenka wanted to say something more, but the hot sudden tears which she fought to hold back from the start, burst out of her and choked her and poured down her cheeks.

"Don't cry," Yozva Butrym asked, stern and dour as always, but as shamed and angry by what he'd had to do as she was herself.

"Don't cry, don't cry," the two old men begged her.

But she was too deeply hurt to listen to their pleading. She could find no consolation in their love and pity no matter what they said or did after that.

★ ★ ★

After they left she felt quite drained and empty. Dark thoughts settled upon her like a flock of crows on a barren field, cawing and pecking and tearing at her peace of mind. She could hardly find a quiet and comfortable corner for herself in her entire house where she could get away from that onrush of anxiety and anger.

'*How could they,*' she murmured over and over to herself, no longer sure at whom to direct her bitterness and contempt. '*How could he?*'

She didn't want to leap to hasty judgments, she wanted to be fair, and she began to feel an odd gnawing sense of distaste,

almost of ill-will, against her Laudanian guardians and Pan
Andrei as well.

What hurt her pride more than anything, she knew, was the
need to defend him, to explain, and to find excuses for his
mindless folly. How could he have put her in such a degrading
position? Ah... and that company of his!

Her small fists clenched in rage at the thought of those vile,
leering creatures and, at once, their cruel faces rose up to mock
her in her memory. She saw them as they were, not as she
wished to see them despite her best instincts, and she couldn't
understand why she failed to recognize at first sight all those
gross telltale signs of vicious self-indulgence, and that vulgar
greed, debauchery and corruption that stamped their coarse
features.

"... Kokosinski, Uhlik, Zendt, Kulvyetz," she found herself
reciting their names like a litany of evil. "And the others..."

They were, she thought, men without a conscience. Without
human feelings.

She couldn't even think of them as cruel caricatures of the
warrior gentry, or as grotesque imitations which had been
warped by their own selfish passions beyond anything that
resembled manhood.

"Scum,"she whispered. "Garbage!"

Hatred was wholly foreign to her. Never before had she
experienced that ugly and corrosive feeling. But now it flooded
over her and burned her like acid and it began to gnaw at her
image of Pan Andrei as well.

"Shame!"she whispered through lips that felt as dry as parchment. "Shame! How could he! He'd leave me here every night
to go back to kitchen maids..."

She knew that she had never been humiliated as badly and as
cruelly before in her entire life.

Time passed unnoticed, the day darkened further, and Aleksandra went on pacing through room after room, but she could
find no peace anywhere inside her. It wasn't in her nature to
bow helplessly to fate, to endure indignity without a struggle, or
to accept humiliations as if they were part and parcel of her life,
although that was the lot of many women in those heartless
times. She knew her own worth and understood the fierce,
proud stock that bred her. Her poise and manner and the

courtly graces that went with her station were like a soft, thin coverlet of snow that covered an ancient river whose powerful vitality and dangerous currents only a fool would question. She wanted to spill all that channeled fury against those mocking evil spirits at once! Immediately! She wanted to smash them, overwhelm them, and sweep them away into whatever darkness had created them.

But what were her weapons?

"Tears," she whispered, bitterly resentful and, for the first time, she hated that weak, subservient image of a child that even the most enlightened civilizations of her time imposed on a woman. "Tears and pleading..."

And what, she thought, if Kmita refused to get rid of his foul companions?

"*Ah... if he refuses...*"

But she wouldn't let herself think just then of what would have to happen if her weapons failed.

★ ★ ★

And suddenly her oppressive thoughts scattered, interrupted. A servant boy came into the room carrying an armful of pine logs and kindling to set a new fire in the open hearth. She watched as he began to rake the few remaining live coals, that still glowed dully under last night's ashes, and a new decision leaped to life inside her.

"Kostek!" she ordered quickly. "Saddle a horse and go at once to Lubitch. If the master is back then ask him to come to see me straight away. If he's still gone from home then get old Znikis, the estate foreman, to mount up behind you and bring him here to me. Jump to it, lad!"

The boy took a moment longer to lay and light the fire and ran to do as he had been commanded. Bright flames began to roar high into the chimney. Sparks snapped and crackled as the frozen sap burst and split the firewood and Olenka's spirits started to lift as well.

'*Perhaps God will change things after all,*' she thought. '*Perhaps it wasn't all as bad as the guardians said it.*'

"We'll see," she said firmly and turned towards the spinning room where, once again, she could lose herself in the ages-old Billevitch ritual of supervising her young household charges, listening to Winter tales, and singing songs of praise. "We'll see."

★ ★ ★

The next two hours seemed to take for ever. Hope and anxiety struggled with each other until she thought that her poor aching head was about to burst. The fire hissed and crackled, the flames were booming in the chimney, and the wind outside had risen to a melancholy howl. She strained her ears for the sound of hoof beats which the wind would have muffled anyway; and then, without warning, young Kostek was back, covered with frost and shivering in the doorway; and she was up on her feet and looking down at him while her own breath seemed to die away.

"Well?" she said at last.

"Zni-k-kis is in the h-hall," the boy stammered, his teeth chattering with the cold. "The m-master's still away."

She was out of the room and standing before the old Lubitch estate overseer so swiftly that she had no idea how she had got there, and watched him bowing to the ground, cap clutched to his chest, as he went through the clumsy peasant ritual of greetings for the lady of the manor to which he belonged. She motioned him to follow her into the privacy of the dining chamber, but he didn't dare to step across the threshold and halted beyond the door.

"What's new in Lubitch?" she asked to get him started.

The peasant shrugged, made a helpless gesture.

"Eh... The master's gone..."

"Yes, I know he is in Upita. But how are things in the manor?"

"Eh..." And again the hopeless shrug and the helpless motion of a gnarled old hand.

"Listen to me, Znikis," Olenka said firmly. "Speak up. Tell me what I'm asking and don't be afraid. Nothing will happen to you, understand?"

"Yessum," he mumbled deep into his beard, but his thick, work-worn hands went on twisting the shabby old fur cap anyway, and he kept his worried old eyes fixed on the floor between his cracked bast boots.

"I hear that the master's a good, decent man," she said to

encourage him. "But his company... makes trouble. Is that true?"

"Ey, lady," the old peasant muttered. "If they was only trouble..."

"Speak up," she urged him. "Tell me everything."

"Can't, m'lady," he muttered. "I'm afraid. I been told to keep my mouth shut, see..."

"Who told you that?"

"The master..."

"Ah, is that so?"

"Yessum..."

"We'll see about that!"

There was a long, cold moment of silence as she paced swiftly up and down the room, while the old peasant's eyes followed her uneasily.

"Listen to me," she said at last as she stopped before him. "Where do you belong?"

"I'm a Billevitch man. From Vodokty. I don't come from Lubitch."

"Alright, then. You don't have to go back to Lubitch any more. You can stay with me. Now I'm your Mistress and I'm ordering you to tell me everything you know."

She didn't know what she expected him to do, or what he would tell her, but the old peasant threw himself down on his knees before her, his aged eyes brimming over, and his dark gnarled hands raised up to her as if in a prayer.

"Sweet lady!" he cried. "I don' ever want to see that place again! It's like Judgment Day over there! Them people, ma'am... God help me... they're like thugs and bandits, nothin' else! A man can't tell if he'll live through the day with them around!"

Aleksandra twisted and spun in place as if she had been struck and pierced by a Tartar arrow. She felt all the blood draining from her face, but when she spoke again, her voice was calm and even.

"Is it true that they shot up the portraits?"

"Didn't they just! An' they dragged the girls aroun' the house! An' it's the same thing every day! There's nothin' in the village except tears an' terror... An' in the manor it's like Sodom and Gomorrah. The oxen go on the spit, the sheep herd goes into the pot! The people are squeezed dry. Last night they cut down a stable groom for nothin' at all...!"

"They killed a groom?"

"Ay, didn't they!" The old manor foreman was close to tears of his own. "But it's worse for the girls, m'lady... The manor girls ain't enough for them no more. Now they're huntin' for 'em in the village too..."

There was another chilly silence then but Olenka's face seemed to be on fire. A bright crimson flush crept out to stain her pale cheeks and remained there from then on.

"I see," she said at last. "I see. And... when do they expect the master's return?"

"They don't know, m'lady. But I heard them talkin' like they'd better go to Upita tomorrow. They ordered the horses ready for the morning. Way I heard it, they're supposed to stop by here on the way to ask for some armed lads an' gunpowder from the stores. Like it'll be needed in Upita..."

"They're to stop by here?"

"Yessum. That's what I heard them sayin'."

"Good," Aleksandra said, calm and cold as ice. Then she nodded kindly to the kneeling peasant. "Thank you, Znikis. Go to the kitchen now and get yourself some supper. You won't be going back to Lubitch again."

"God bless you, ma'am!" the old peasant cried. "God give you luck an' happiness! God save you an' keep you!"

Left alone, Aleksandra stared for a long, quiet moment into the cold ashes of the great stone fireplace in the dining chamber. The tall mahogany clock ticked out the minutes as the night grew deeper. Her thoughts were calm and ordered and she was at peace; she knew now what she had to do and how to go about it.

Chapter Six

THE NEXT DAY was a Sunday. Early, even before the Vodokty ladies set out for Mass at the Mitruny church that served the whole Laudanian parish, the manor courtyard filled with Pan Kmita's officers, mounted and equipped as if for a campaign, with a troop of Lubitch grooms clattering behind them.

Aleksandra met them in the entrance hall but she seemed an entirely different person from the courteous and considerate girl who tried to put them all at ease only four days earlier. She didn't invite them into the inner rooms, or offer them refreshments, and if they had been as worldly-wise and canny as they thought they were, they'd have known at once that they had stepped into unfriendly country. She was pale but calm, unsmiling and severe. Her aloof nod barely acknowledged their profuse salutations, but they took this cold reception for no more than caution due to Kmita's absence.

Pan Yaromir, braver now than he was the first time in her presence, stepped forward with another exaggerated bow.

"Most noble lady," he began. "We've stopped by here on our way to Upita to pay our respects to you, our gentle benefactress, and to ask for a little neighborly *auxilium* from your stores. Like... ah... maybe a horn or two of gunpowder, and some firearms for those Lubitch men we've brought? And to ask your illustrious ladyship to lend us a few of your own armed retainers too. Our beloved Andy may be in a spot of trouble, so we thought we'd better get up there and help. Nothing quietens down a bunch of noisy burghers faster than a bit of bleeding."

"I'm surprised," she said, cold as ice, "that you're breaking your commander's orders."

"Orders?" Kokosinski gaped at her, amazed. "What orders?"

"Didn't I hear Pan Kmita tell you to sit tight in Lubitch? It seems to me that if that's his wish, that's what you should be doing."

"Eh? Hmm? What's that? Do my ears deceive me?"

"You heard me well enough," she said with contempt.

The Orshans peered at each other, astonished, their eyes wide with shock and their mouths ajar. Zendt whistled like a startled bird. Kokosinski's scarred face twisted in surprise and he began to stroke the top of his head with an uncertain hand as broad as a shovel.

"One would think you were talking to Pan Kmita's stable hands, m'lady," he growled, thrown off stride and quivering with anger. "Hmm. Yes. It's true we were supposed to wait for him at home. But since he's been gone four days without a word, we decided that there's got to be something serious going on up there, and that our sabers would come handy for him. So that's why we're going."

"Nobody needs your sabers anywhere," Aleksandra said. "Pan Kmita didn't go to Upita to fight the enemy. He went to punish lawlessness, and to discipline disobedient and unruly soldiers. Which, it seems to me, is just what might happen to you too if you break his orders. Besides,"—and now her scathing voice sharpened with disdain—"your presence in Upita is far more likely to cause that trouble you claim to be concerned about, than if you stayed away!"

"Ah... Ah... Is that so..."

Open bewilderment crept out on all their faces, as if they were unable to believe their ears, and rage began to glint in their narrowed eyes.

"Yes it is!" she said.

"It's... ah... hard to argue with you, lady."

Still hardly able to believe what was happening here, Kokosinski was finding it almost impossible to control his own rising anger.

"Now's not the time for chitchat," he grated out from between clenched teeth. "So we'll just... ah... take what we've come for, the muskets and the powder and whatever people you can spare, and be on our way."

"Yes you will," she said and nodded coldly. "But you will get neither powder nor men from me, is that clear to you?"

"Is it... clear?"

It was becoming clear. The look on their faces mirrored the amazement that anyone would dare to deny them something that they wanted.

"You mean you won't help us, m'lady? You won't give us a hand in rescuing our Andy? You'd rather something evil happened to him up there?"

"The worst thing that can happen to him anywhere is your company!" she said and stepped towards them, eyes blazing with anger, while they fell back as if a sudden chasm had opened up in the ground before them.

"Hey! By God's wounds!" Kokosinski cried out. "Hey, comrades, are you hearing this? What is this? Are we dreaming? Are we asleep or what?"

"Leave at once!" she ordered and pointed an imperious hand towards the door. "Get out! Do you hear?"

"This can't be happening!" Ranitzki hissed out between bloodless lips while the dark leopard spots of fury spread across his face.

Pale with rage, the lawless company stood as still as statues, staring at each other with disbelieving eyes, but none of them could find a word to stammer in reply. Only their teeth began to glint under their trembling whiskers, and their fists clutched the handles of their swords and daggers.

It was a dangerous moment, Olenka could tell. They had done murder for far less than that. They and their ruthless kind would burn down a manor and put whole villages to the torch for one tenth of the opposition they were facing here, but all they did now—all that they could do—was glare at her with eyes that had gone dim with shock.

She sensed the sharp animal fear and the instinct of self-preservation that flickered like a warning light behind their furious eyes and held them in check. This house, they knew, was under Kmita's powerful protection. Those galling insults came from his wife-to-be. So they bit back their rage, staring at her with all the hatred of their terrible frustration, and she went on pointing to the door, her eyes as hard and chilling as the spears of ice hanging outside the windows.

A long moment passed before Kokosinski got a grip on his own boiling fury.

"Since... we've had such a courteous reception here," he ground out in thick, clotted phrases. "Since we've been... ah... so politely treated in this house... there's nothing left for us but to thank our charming hostess for her hospitality... and take our leave."

He swept her a deep, tight-lipped bow, full of such elaborate and threatening irony that Aleksandra felt all the blood draining from her face, and the others stepped forward one by one to follow his example.

"... Such graciousness," they grated out between clenched teeth, dusting the floor before her with the hawk and eagle feathers in their jeweled caps, and then striding out without a backward glance.

"... Such... immeasurable kindness."

When the doors slammed behind them and she was finally alone in the icy hall, Olenka fell back into a chair, trembling throughout and hardly able to breathe.

She closed her eyes to hold back the hot, bitter tears that seemed to scorch her eyelids. She was exhausted and drained of all her strength, because even her strong young body couldn't match her fortitude and courage, or meet the needs of her determination.

★ ★ ★

Outside, gathered around their horses in the freezing court-yard, Kmita's boon companions stared glumly at each other—still not quite able to believe their abrupt dismissal, and wondering what to do—but none of them wanted to be the first to speak.

"Well?" Kokosinski finally broke the silence.

"Well what?"

"Are you happy, lambkins?"

"Are you?"

"Ey, if only Kmita didn't have anything to do with this place,"

Ranitzki snarled and twisted his clenched fists in a convulsive gesture. "If she wasn't Kmita's..."

"But she is Kmita's!" Rekutz shrilled. "Go and tread on his coat-tails and see what happens to you."

But by now, Ranitzki's face had turned entirely into a spotted mask, narrow as a lynx, and trembling with fury.

"I'll stand up to him anytime," he snarled. "And you too, you squeaky piece of carrion!"

"Try it!" Rekutz screeched.

Both seized their sabers, but before either could draw a blade, the gigantic Kulvyetz-Hippocentaurus rolled between them like a mountain boulder.

"By this fist!" he bellowed, shaking a huge hand the size of a bread loaf. "By this fist, I swear, I'll brain the first one who gets his steel clear!"

His red oxlike eyes swept from one of the would-be duelists to the other, glaring like a mad bull about to charge a strip of red bunting, and they quietened down at once. They knew what those rocklike fists could do.

"Kulvyetz is right!" Kokosinski said. "We need to stick together now more than ever, lambkins. I'd say we ought to get to Kmita as fast as we can, or she'll paint us blacker than the Devil the moment she sees him."

"Not if we get to see him first!" Uhlik piped up.

"It's a good thing none of you snapped at her," Kokosinski grunted. "Though I admit, I had a real itch in my tongue and my fist as well. But let's get to Kmita, eh? What d'you say? If she's going to try to turn him against us, let's get our licks in first. God help us if he ever turns his back on us... They'd hunt us down around here like a pack of wolves!"

"The Hell with them!" Ranitzki snarled. "What can they do? It's wartime, isn't it? Aren't there enough desperados hanging around the highways? We'll just gather ourselves a troop and laugh at every judge under the sun! Here Rekutz, let's have your hand. I'll let you off this time."

"You'll let me off?" Rekutz grinned and giggled. "I'd have cut off your ears! But alright, let's drop it. The little bitch insulted all of us, none more than another."

"Imagine it," Kokosinski said, shaking his head with wonder. "To tell such men as us to get out as if we were peasants!"

"And me," Ranitzki said. "Me! With the blood of senators running in my veins!"

"Us!" they cried, "Nobles! Men of stature!"

"War heroes!"

"Exiles! Innocent orphans, victims of injustice!"

But Kulvyetz interrupted this litany of anger and self-pity by stamping his huge boots in the snow and snapping his chilled fingers.

"What're we standing around here for like beggars at a church door?" he growled. "It's cold! My feet are freezing! And you can bet your boots nobody's going to bring us out a nice, hot stirrup cup. Let's mount up and get out of here!"

"Alright, let's get going then," Pan Yaromir ordered. "Send those Lubitch lackeys back where they come from because they're useless to us without guns and powder and let's get on our way."

"To Upita!" Zendt cried and hooted like an owl.

"To our good friend Andy! We'll tell him how they've mistreated us here!"

"Just so's we don't pass him on the way..." Uhlik warned.

"We won't. There's just the one highway. Mount up! Let's get started."

They climbed into their saddles and rode out of the courtyard at a straggling walk, still chewing on their anger and humiliation. Ranitzki, whose murderous rages choked him unless he could drown them in spilled blood, turned at the gate to shake his fist at the manor house.

"Blood!" he groaned thickly. "I need blood!"

"If only there'd be a falling out between her and Kmita," Kokosinski muttered. "We'd come calling on her ladyship again but in our own way."

"With a few flints and torches, eh?" Rekutz giggled shrilly.

"God grant it," Uhlik said, raising his eyes piously to the clouds.

"That heathen bitch," they snarled. "That snotty little screech owl."

Cursing the Billevitch heiress and snapping at each other, they reached the woods where a vast flock of crows soared out of the trees and whirled above them in a somber cloud. Zendt started cawing at them exactly like a raven and a thousand raucous voices answered him at once.

"Shut your mouth!" Ranitzki snarled at Zendt. "You'll bring bad luck down on us with that graveyard croaking! Those damn birds are screeching over us as if we were carrion!"

But the others laughed, amused, and Zendt went on cawing. Fools! What would they know about prophecies? The great black flock swooped over them, so low that the massed beating of their wings startled the horses with its swift surging sound, and they rode on into the dark wood.

★ ★ ★

Beyond the woods they caught a glimpse of the squat thick-timbered barns and houses of Volmontov, the home of the Butryms, and they spurred towards them at a trot. They were chilled to the bone, even the air seemed frozen in their lungs, and they still had a long way to go. But in the settlement itself they had to slow down because the broad track was full of sleighs and people coming back from church and from the pre-Lenten fair in Mitruny. The huge, bearlike Butrym men glanced coldly at the passing riders, half guessing who they were; but the young women who sat huddled in the sleighs had heard all about the wild doings in Lubitch, and they stared at Pan Kmita's friends with undisguised curiosity.

They, in turn, struck proud military poses, riding as stiffly as if on parade on their snorting thoroughbreds, dressed in the oriental finery they'd stripped off Russian boyars or looted from their camps, and looking out with hard contemptuous eyes from under their cocked fur caps.

They rode in line abreast, their heads held high and their fists resting at the hip, giving way to no one.

"Out of the way there," one of another of them shouted now and then, and the grim Butryms stepped aside, giving way with darkly hooded glances, and the young cavaliers rode on chatting with each other.

"Take a look at these people, gentlemen," Kokosinski noted. "Every man's got a pair of shoulders like a barn door and eyes like a wolf."

"If it wasn't for those long black sabers you'd think they were peasants," Uhlik said.

Ranitzki stared with professional curiosity at the Butryms' old-fashioned weapons in plain iron scabbards. "You could spit a whole ox on a thing like that! Not quite your usual run-of-the-mill greybacks, eh? I'd like to try my hand with a few of them."

And the famous duelist began to fence in the air, thrusting and chopping with his bare hand.

"He'd go like this and I'd go like that. He'd cut and I'd parry. Then cut, slash, thrust and that'd be the end."

"You'd have no trouble finding a quarrel here," Rekutz hinted. "They don't need much, I hear."

"I'd rather try my hand with those girls of theirs," Zendt said suddenly and neighed like a stallion.

"Look at them!" Rekutz cried and whistled with enthusiasm. "Straight as a candle, every one of them!"

"A candle? Keep your candles! They look more like pine trees! And look at those plump round grinning faces, will you! Those bright eyes! Cheeks as red as if they'd painted them with beet juice!"

"Ay... ay! It's hard to stay squirming on a horse with a sight like that."

* * *

Then the homes of the Butrym settlement fell away behind them, they were in open country, and they put their horses into a trot again.

In half an hour they came within sight of a tavern halfway between Volmontov and Mitruny where, as was the Sunday custom in that neighborhood, the farming gentry stopped on their way from church to rest and warm themselves on cold Winter days. Riding up to the low, barnlike building, the Orshans noted more than a dozen padded one-horse sleighs, and several saddled horses tied to the rails outside.

"Let's get a drink," Kokosinski said. "I could use some *go-jhalka* in my belly. It's cold enough out here to freeze the air in the guts."

"No harm in a dram!" all the others chorused. "Let's get our whiskers wet!"

They dismounted, tied their horses to the uprights under the overhanging roof, and entered the single dark and cavernous room, where they found a thick crowd clustered around the kegs behind the serving counter, and along the plain deal benches that lined the low walls.

All the men were sipping mulled ale or hot-brewed, buttered *Krupnik* made of millet, vodka, spices and fermented honey. All of them were Butryms: large, gloomy men dressed alike in black tallowed boots and grey homespun coats, lined with woolly sheepskin or padded with coarse ticking. They said so little to each other that there was hardly more than a low growling mutter running through the inn. Their look-alike size and clothing gave them the uniform appearance of soldiers, all the more pronounced because of their broad untanned leather belts and the long plain heavy-hilted saber that each of them wore in a black iron scabbard.

But their ages told a different story since all the Laudanians of military age, that is to say every able-bodied man between sixteen and sixty, had left for the army. Most of the Butryms gathered here were gnarled old men, well on the way into their seventies, or barefaced youths in their earlier teens who had stayed home for the Winter threshing.

Now, seeing the splendid, richly-dressed Orshan cavaliers pushing in among them, they moved a step or two away from the counter, and eyed them in curious though not unfriendly silence. The new arrivals' fierce glances, martial bearing, and polished equipment, would appeal to this warlike rural gentry, and the young cavaliers put on an extra swagger as they strode to the serving counter.

The Butryms murmured and nudged each other, watching them with interest. Now and then a low, muttered question fell as abruptly as a stone among them and the replies were just as brief and to the point.

"That's the Lubitch lot?"

"That's them."

"Pan Kmita's people?"

"Who else."

Meanwhile the Orshan cavaliers pushed their way to the trestled pine planks that served as a counter and dipped their whiskers in tankards of *gojhalka*. The clear, harsh corn liquor distilled from burned millet made their eyes water and reddened their faces, and then Kokosinski began to sniff the air like a wolfhound who had caught the scent of much better prey, and put down his tankard.

"*Krupnik*," he said. "By God, I smell *Krupnik*."

"Let's have some!" Rekutz squealed.

"Hmm. Why not?" Kokosinski's cruelly disfigured face was alight with pleasure. "That's far more to the taste of a noble's palate than this peasant hogwash."

"True," Rekutz grinned and giggled. "*Gojhalka* is good enough to take the chill off the bones, but a noble liquor calls for serious drinking."

"Ah... But do we have time?"

"We've time," said Ranitzki.

"Upita won't burn down in an hour," Pan Uhlik observed.

"And we deserve some consolation after the cold-hearted cruel way we were treated in Vodokty."

"So to the table, gentlemen!"

"To the table!"

They ordered a flagon.

★ ★ ★

Seated around a plain deal table with a steaming flagon of sweet-smelling *Krupnik* to improve their humors, the Orshans began to feel somewhat better about their humiliation in Vodokty. The powerful, aged liquor spread its warming glow. They drank and smacked their lips, sighing with pleasure and peering through the gloom at the watchful Butryms, but there wasn't very much to see. The room was dark. Thick snow caked the narrow little windows, screening the cold sunless light that seeped from outside; and whatever light leaked out of the fire, was blocked by a dozen dim figures, unrecognizable in the gloom, who crouched before the hearth with their broad backs turned towards the room.

Zendt cawed again. The cavaliers laughed. The harsh croaking call was so lifelike and so real, that all eyes in the room turned towards their table, and the huge young Butryms started edging up towards them with broad grins spreading on their curious faces. The dim figures by the fireplace also stirred and twisted around to see what was happening, and Rekutz was the first to notice that they were women.

"Birds, gentlemen!" he squealed. "Titmice, by God, seated by the fire!"

"So I see," Kokosinski grinned.

Zendt crowed and cawed. And suddenly the low dark room filled with the shrill squealing of a rabbit shaken by a dog. The rabbit's agonized sobbing weakened, turned into the final strangled scream of death, and then a rutting stag bellowed out his challenge. The Butryms stared, amazed.

"Birds!" Rekutz said again.

"So they are!" said Uhlik. "What d'you suppose they are doing here?"

"Maybe there's dancing here and they come to dance."

"Wait and I'll ask them," Kokosinski said and called out cheerfully: "Hey there, good ladies, what are you doing there by the fire?"

"Getting our feet warm!" thin voices piped back from beside the hearth.

"You are, eh? Ha Ha! How about letting us warm them for you?"

And the young gentlemen rose, left their table, and strode towards the fireplace, where a dozen girls and women sat on a long deal bench, with their bare feet thrust out and resting on a log rolled before the hearth. Their wet boots steamed drying beyond the log.

"So you're warming your pretty little legs, are you?" Kokosinski asked.

"And a nice set of trotters they are too," Rekutz squeaked, bending towards the log.

"Get away there!" one of the girls giggled.

"I'd rather get closer than away, ha ha!" Rekutz giggled back. "Particularly since I've got a surefire system for warming chilled feet, and that's a quick whirl around the dance floor! So what do you say?"

"Leave us be!" the girls cried and laughed.

"No harm in it, is there?" Kokosinski shouted.

"If we're to dance then let's dance!" Uhlik cried and reached for the flute that he wore in its own small scabbard dangling beside his saber. "We've even brought the music!"

He piped out a jittery little dance-tune, the cavaliers bobbed and weaved before the girls, dragging them off the bench, and the young women squealed and cried out in half-hearted protest, and made a mildly angry pretense of pushing off the ardent cavaliers.

"Hoo-Ha!" Rekutz squealed.

Who knows how the day might have ended if they were different men and if no one knew them or their reputations? This was an era when people did what seemed natural to them, and the time was right to relax the rules before the seriousness of Lent, and the young women weren't all that averse to a little dancing with the highborn Orshan cavaliers. But then a huge dour form loomed out of the shadows and Yozva Butrym appeared in the firelight.

"You want a dance?" he growled into Pan Kulvyetz's face and caught him by the shirtfront. "How about with me, then?"

"With you? Hmm. Maybe later, eh?" Kulvyetz's mustache twitched while his dull red eyes narrowed in speculation. "Right now I'd rather take a turn with some of your women."

"Hey, what's wrong?" Rekutz challenged, sniffing the air for trouble, while the telltale wildcat spots began to spread and darken on Ranitzki's face. "What's the matter with a harmless little dance after church on Sunday? It's not like it's Lent, is it?"

"Maybe not," Yozva muttered grimly. "But we've heard about you. We know what you are. So you go and do your dancing somewhere else."

"What's that?" Rekutz shrilled. "What was that you said?"

Uhlik stopped playing. Zendt laughed like a loon. Ranitzki stepped up, clutching at his saber.

"We'll dance with whoever we damn well please!" he shouted. "You want to try to stop us?"

"Gather round, lambkins!" Kokosinski shouted. "Gather round! Looks like we're going to get a little exercise!"

They drew together, forming up behind him, but a crowd of tall, broad-shouldered oldsters and massive young Butryms rose from the dark corners, and assembled behind Yozva like a wall.

"You want trouble?" Kokosinski asked.

"Who do you think you're talking to anyway?" Ranitzki demanded.

"To Hell with talking," Yozva growled. "We don't want you here. Get out of our tavern!"

Ranitzki, whose livid face was now alight with fury, and

whose one concern was never to miss a fight, unsheathed his saber with lightning speed and struck Yozva in the chest with its iron hilt.

"Kill!" he screamed out. "Blood!"

Swords and sabers leaped out of their scabbards. Steel clashed together. Women screamed and shouted. Powdered dry mud and sawdust boiled up under the stamping boots and obscured the fighters. But suddenly the gigantic Yozva Butrym backed out of the battle, seized a huge, rough-hewn bench as lightly as if it were a reed, whirled it over his head and tramped back into the melee.

"Room!" he shouted. "Give me room to swing!"

And soon the groans of terribly injured men began to seep and drift out of the swirling dust cloud.

Chapter Seven

ON THAT SAME EVENING Pan Kmita rode into Vodokty at the head of several hundred men whom he brought from Upita so that he could turn them over to the Grand Hetman in Keydany for provisioning and quarters. Upita was too small for so many extra mouths to feed. It was obvious to him that any soldiers trying to make ends meet in winter quarters, especially the kind of soldiers that he was forced to lead, wouldn't stay out of trouble for long in such a small town, and that after eating the luckless townsfolk out of house and home they'd have to resort to robbery and pillage.

One look at his command was enough to confirm his judgment. In fact he didn't think that a worse kind of human refuse could be found in the entire Commonwealth. But where was he to look for better men? With Yanush Radzivill defeated at Shklov, the Russians and their Cossack allies flooded the best part of the country. The remnants of the Lithuanian regulars pulled back to the hereditary Radzivill possessions around Keydany and Birjhe to refit for a new campaign. The gentry of the overrun palatinates either followed the Radzivill army or looked for shelter in territories that had so far escaped the ravages of invasion. The best of them were gathering in Grodno under Field Hetman Gosyevski, which is what the royal manifestos ordered all citizens to do in this emergency. But even those few who listened and obeyed, did so at such a snail's pace and in such small numbers that Kmita was, indeed, the only man who showed the Russians any opposition.

He didn't ask himself why he was driven to do it. Patriotism

76

may have had something to do with his private war: the loss of Smolensk, Vitebsk and the Orsha country filled him with special hatred for the despised Muscovite invaders whom Polish armies always crushed before without any trouble. But the main reason might have been that he was a ruthless and impatient man, unable to stand any challenge to his pride and his personal liberties, and that he needed turmoil and excitement to feel alive and free.

The men he gathered around himself were just as wild as he. Unable to draw on gentry and disciplined soldiers, he picked up whoever came his way, wherever he found them: homeless vagabonds with nothing to lose, men without name or substance who had no sense of duty to their country but needed a banner under which to ride, runaway grooms, fugitive manor servants and army deserters, small-town apprentices who'd rather rob peasants and loot lonely manors than serve a merchant master, and condemned criminals in flight from the law. They flocked to him because he offered them protection and pillage. In his harsh hands, which could be merciless in punishing infractions, they turned into fierce fighters, ready for anything, and he loved them for it. But they soon earned themselves a terrible reputation in the countryside, especially when he wasn't with them to keep an eye on their worst excesses and they were led by Kokosinski, Kulvyetz, Uhlik, Zendt and the murderous Ranitzki.

Had he been a steadier man himself, these irregular marauders could have become real soldiers and true defenders of the Commonwealth, earning forgiveness for their crimes by devoted service. But four years of constant raids, hit-and-run attacks, ambushes and bloodshed, turned his own willful and impulsive nature into reckless fury, so that his volunteer detachments were more like beasts of prey. The Russians took care to stay behind strong walls in whatever district he picked for himself, but his savage raiders were just as hard on their own countrymen as they were on the invaders, and he usually let them take whatever they wanted from the unfortunate civilian populations they were supposed to defend and protect.

Being a volunteer himself, and serving without the authority of a regular commission that might allow him to requisition the supplies he needed, he had no other way to arm them, feed them and get them their horses. If he couldn't wrest his supplies from the enemy, he took them by force wherever he found them, and the grim rules that governed partisan warfare could make some allowances for that.

But being also the sort of man that he had become, one whose own natural pride, high spirits and courage were warped by years of living like a wolf, he had gone farther than that. He saw no harm in anything that his men might do in order to survive, and neither tears, pleading, laws nor simple justice could curb his unrestrained and unbridled will.

That's who he was and those were the kind of men he led on that memorable evening; and if his defenders could find excuses for him at the Hetman's court, pointing out that he fought the Moscow hordes of Trubetzkoy and Hovansky when everyone else had given up the struggle, he knew that he'd begun to slip into that deadly, shadowy no man's land beyond either justification or forgiveness, where cruelty, brutality and simple lack of mercy obscured whatever finer motives he might have.

He also knew that the only reins that still restrained those dark unfettered passions that boiled in his soul, were his new feelings for Olenka and what she represented, and he was determined to keep her no matter what it cost him. Now, riding up to her door, he could still see himself as the knight and soldier he had always been in his imagination, and thought of the murderous troop that clattered into the snowy courtyard after him as the brave and loyal defenders of their country that they could have been.

*   *   *

One look at them, however, was enough to shake even Olenka's great courage and determination. '*These are... common brigands,*' she thought in dismay.

Each of them wore whatever he wanted: spiked Russian helmets, Cossack sheepskins, shaggy furs and hoods, faded brocades and metal-studded coats of coarse, untanned leather. Each of them carried whatever weapon best suited his fancy: muskets, Cossack pikes, Mongol horn bows, pole axes and spears, riding gaunt horses dressed in a wild variety of Polish, Russian and Turkish gear.

"*Dear God,*" she thought in pain. "*And he calls them soldiers?*"

Her disgust and fear subsided only when Pan Andrei ran into the room, as high-spirited, confident and carefree as ever, and started kissing her hands with all the enthusiasm of his animated nature. She had planned to receive him with some severity and distance but her heart was beating far too fast, she was too pleased to see him, and she couldn't hide the sudden joy caused by his arrival. Besides, she reasoned, if she was to tell him how she'd driven his boon companions from her house, perhaps she had better put him in a receptive frame of mind. Moreover, she knew that no matter what she thought and planned, her feelings dictated their own courses, and his love for her was so crystal clear that all her disappointment in him started to melt like snow around an open flame.

'*He really loves me,*' she thought. '*There's no doubt about it.*'

"God, how I've missed you!" he said in his turn. "I was ready to set that whole damn town on fire just to get here quicker!"

"I was getting worried that the trouble might get out of hand," she told him. "Thank God you've come back."

"Trouble?" Laughing, he made a quick careless gesture. "There wasn't much to it. The soldiers started roughing up a few feather-merchants and that's about all."

"But you've quietened things down again?"

"Yes I did." He shrugged and glanced away. "In a manner of speaking... Ah, I'll tell you all about it in a minute, sweetheart. Just let me sit down for a bit because I'm awfully tired. Ey, it's good to be here, in this warm Vodokty of yours. Paradise couldn't be any better, I should think. A man could spend a lifetime sitting here and just staring into those beautiful, loving eyes, I swear... But I wouldn't mind something hot to drink, if you'd be so good, because the frost outside is a real killer."

"I'll get some spiced mulled wine with whipped eggs and cream ready for you at once," she said, happy to be looking after him.

"And could you have some small keg of *gojhalka* rolled out for my roughnecks? It would help if you'd tell your people to let them into the cattle barns so that they might get warmed up a bit near the animals. We've ridden hard in that icy wind and they're frozen stiff."

"I won't deny them anything," she said and smiled at Kmita. "Since they are your soldiers."

She smiled at him again with such warmth and caring that his own eyes brightened, brimming with affection, and then she slipped out of the room as softly as a kitten.

"I won't be a moment..."

"Even a moment," he called out after her, "will feel like lifetime!"

★ ★ ★

Left alone, Pan Andrei began to pace up and down the room, stroking his head and tugging at his mustache, and wondering how to tell her everything that happened in Upita.

"I've got to tell her the full truth," he muttered, grim and ill-at-ease. "There's no help for it. Even if Kokosinski and the others laugh at me for acting like a dancing bear."

He went on pacing and pulling at his hair and then he started to get impatient that the girl was gone from the room so long.

'*What the Devil*,' he thought. '*She's a soldier's daughter. She ought to know how things are now and then.*'

A serving lad edged into the room with a candelabrum full of lighted candles, bowed deeply and left, and then the young lady of the manor was back again. She carried a polished pewter tray, and on the tray a steaming stonewear jug fragrant with Hungarian wine, and a cut-crystal goblet with the Kmitas' coat-of-arms engraved on its facets which Pan Andrei's father had given to Pan Heracles in his time.

"Hey!" the young man cried out and took a leap towards her. "You've got both hands full, have you? Now's my chance to steal a little kiss!"

And he leaned towards her through the sweet-smelling steam and she tried to turn her laughing face away.

"You're cheating!" she cried. "That's not fair! Stop it or I'll drop the tray..."

"Go ahead! What's a little spilled wine? There's more in the cellar. But a man could lose his mind from the rarities I'm sampling!"

"You've lost yours a long time ago... Will you sit down? Sit!"

He did as he was told and she filled the goblet.

"So tell me now how you resolved things in Upita," she said.

"How I resolved things? Like Solomon."

"God be praised for that!" her voice rang with gratitude and joy. "I really want everyone in the county to think of you as a wise and fair man. How did it go, then?"

Kmita took a deep drink.

"I'd better tell it all from the beginning," he said. "What happened was that the burghers and their mayor wanted requisition scripts from either the Grand Hetman or from Pan Gosyevski. *'You gentlemen are irregulars,'* they told my men. *'You don't have the right to free food and quarters. We'll give you shelter out of the goodness of our hearts but if you want provisions we've got to know that we'll be paid for them.'"*

"They were right in that, weren't they?"

"Sure, according to the law. But my men had sabers. And the way it works in war is that men with sabers are usually more in the right than the men without. *'We'll carve the requisitions on your skins!'* they told the bean peddlers and then all hell broke loose. The mayor and his rabble barricaded themselves in the town square and my boys went after them. There was some shooting. The poor lads set fire to a few barns, just to put the fear of God into those money-grubbing skinflints, and they quietened down a few of them..."

"They quietened them down? How? What do you mean by that?"

"A saber blade across the head will quieten down most people," Kmita shrugged and said.

"But dear God, that's murder!"

"It's at that point that I got there. Right away the soldiers came running to me with complaints about the way they're forced to live and how they've been mistreated. *'What are we to do,'* they said, *'about our empty bellies?'* I sent for the mayor. He took his good old time deciding what to do but finally showed up along with three others, and all of them started howling and wailing straight away. *'Alright, we'll feed them without requisitions,'* they said at last. *'But why are they killing people? Why are they burning down the town? We'd share the little that we have for no more than a word of thanks, but they want fatback, smoked meats, vintage mead! And we're poor people around here, we don't have such things!'"*

"That's right," Alexandra said. "Upita isn't a rich town."

"Rich or not they should've known better than to threaten

me," Pan Andrei muttered. *"The law's on our side,'* they said. *'And you, sir, will answer for your men before a tribunal!"*

"God will bless you if you gave them justice!" Olenka cried out.

"If I gave them justice?"

And here Pan Andrei grimaced like a shamefaced schoolboy caught in a transgression and began to tug again at his tumbled hair.

"Ey, my queen!" he called out in a mournful voice. "Ey, my sweet jewel...! Don't be angry with me..."

"What did you do, then?" she asked anxiously.

"I had them flogged," he recited with a single breath. "A hundred strokes each for the mayor and his aldermen."

Olenka said nothing. She gripped her knees with both hands and stared down in silence. But he had more to say.

"Cut me down if you want!" he cried. "Take my head, just don't be angry with me! I haven't told you everything that happened..."

"There's more?" she groaned softly.

"They sent for help to Ponevyezh, you see. So a hundred town guards came tramping in with a few officers. I scattered the louts to the four winds, as anyone would expect, and as for the officers... Ah, sweetheart, don't be angry, for God's sake..."

"What about the officers?" Alexandra whispered.

"... I had them stripped naked and chased through the snow with whips," Kmita blurted out. "Like I did one time in Orsha to Pan Tumgrat."

She raised her head then. Her pale face had grown hard with judgment, shame flooded her cheeks, and her eyes were alight with anger.

"You've no decency!" she said. "No conscience!"

Startled and surprised, because his confession didn't seem to him much more than a piece of pardonable mischief, Pan Andrei sat staring at her in silence for a moment.

"What is this?" he asked at last in an altered voice. "Is this some sort of game? Or do you really mean what you're saying to me?"

"I mean that what you've done is unforgivable!" she cried out. "That's something that a wild beast might do, not a man of honor! I mean that I care about your good name, even if you don't, and I am ashamed that you've no sooner come into our country than the entire neighborhood has cause to point at you as a heartless ruffian!"

Angered, Kmita's lips twisted into a sneer.

"What do I care about your petty neighborhoods? One dog guards ten hovels and he's not overworked doing it."

"But there is no stain on those simple people! There is no disgrace attached to anybody's name! No one except you is going to be answering to the law!"

"Don't you worry your pretty head about the law," Kmita laughed and shrugged. "Everybody is his own master in this good Commonwealth of ours as long as he's got a sharp saber in his hand and knows how to get a good troop together. What will they do to me around here? Whom do I have to fear?"

"If you're so fearless... so without remorse... then you had better know that I *do* fear something!" Aleksandra told him. "I fear God's anger. I fear the sight of poor people's tears and suffering and I hate injustice. I may be just a woman to you... just a wife-to-be... but I'm as conscious of my own good name as any so-called gentleman, and I don't want to share anyone's infamy as my marriage portion!"

"Ey there," he snarled, feeling his anger boiling up into a trembling fury. "Ey, there! Don't you threaten me with rejection, my lady. Maybe you don't know me yet as well as you should...!"

"Perhaps I don't!" she said at once, distraught but unshaken. "And perhaps grandfather didn't know you either!"

Kmita leaped up, his eyes ablaze with rage, but her own proud Billevitch blood had surged to life inside her.

"Scowl all you want!" she challenged him, as fearless and contemptuous as anyone he had ever faced. "Go on, grind your teeth! I may be *just a woman*," she stressed with mock disdain, "while you have a whole regiment of murderers behind you, but you won't frighten me into silence! Don't you think I know what your men are doing every night in Lubitch? How they desecrated my family's portraits and debauch the girls in the village? It's *you* who doesn't know *me* if you believe I'll swallow such humiliations without a word of protest! I don't ask for much from you but I want decency and goodness in my life, and that's a condition to my marriage that no one's testament can forbid. Indeed, it was my grandfather's wish that I should marry only a worthy and honorable man."

Kmita, who was really ashamed of the Lubitch misdeeds, lowered his head and muttered:

"Who told you about those portraits?"

"All the gentry in the county is talking about it."

"I'll pay those tinpot nobles for all their goodwill," he growled in a gloomy, threatening tone. "That shooting... that happened after drinking... among friends. No one was thinking clearly. As for those girls, I didn't have anything to with them."

"I know," she said, so anxious to believe in his innocence that she clutched at every word that might make it seem as real as she wished it was. "I know it's those shameless, vicious creatures around you who cause all the trouble... Those traitors and bandits..."

"They're my officers," he said. "Not bandits."

"And I told those officers of yours to get out of my house!" she said.

★ ★ ★

She expected rage and braced for an explosion. Instead, astonished, she saw that Kmita seemed quite unconcerned about her announcement; indeed, her news appeared to amuse him and put him into better humor.

"You threw them out of here?" he asked.

"I did!"

"And they went?"

"Yes!"

He laughed and shook his head with wonder.

"By God, you've a lot of spirit! I like that! You took a real chance, you know, because they're a dangerous bunch and a lot of people have paid a stiff price for taking them lightly..."

Then he grinned and a sly, self-satisfied look spread across his face.

"But they know better than to pick a fight with me, don't you see? They slunk out of here as humbly as whipped dogs, didn't they, and d'you know why? Because I've got them shaking in their boots!"

He laughed, pleased with himself, and started twisting the ends of his mustache upward, but this sly vanity and that sudden switch into careless good humor stripped the last of her remaining patience.

"You have to choose between them and me," she said coldly. "And that's all there's to it."

But Kmita didn't seem to notice her determination or to grasp the importance of what she was saying.

"What's to choose?" he asked so lightly that her heart constricted. "I've got you and I've got them as well, don't I? There's no choice to make. You don't want them here? That's fine, they don't have to come here. You're free to do whatever you like in your own house, but why should I turn them out if they didn't give you any real trouble?

"Hey, my sweet,"— and now his voice became warm and sentimental and oblivious of everything but himself—"you don't know what it's like to fight side-by-side with someone in a war... There's no kinship that binds men closer than sharing common dangers. You have to understand that they saved my life at least a thousand times, just like I saved theirs! And now because they happen to be homeless and hounded by the law that's all the more reason to take care of them.

"Besides,"—and once again his laughter was so careless and so unconcerned, that she felt as if she was speaking to a child who simply couldn't grasp what she was trying to tell him—"every one of them is a highborn noble, except Zendt whose origins are a little hazy, but even he has some worthwhile virtues. You've never seen such a horse-breaker in you life, and if you ever hear him imitating birds and animals you'll get fond of him yourself."

And here Pan Andrei grinned as naturally and simply as if there had never been a moment of anger or conflict between them, and Aleksandra felt a pang of hopelessness as if she was trying to clutch a real whirlwind that would always slip between her fingers.

Nothing she said struck home.

All her concerns about his good name and public opinion, as well as all she tried to tell him about the need for gentle and mature judgment, seemed to bounce and slide off him like blunted arrows from a suit of armor. His unawakened conscience had no way to understand her outrage or to grasp the criminality of his lawlessness.

How was she to appeal to him, she wondered in despair.
What could she say to be understood?

"Let God's will be done,"she said at last, resigned. "Since you
renounce me, then go your own way. God will look after me
as He has always done."

But Kmita couldn't have been more dumbfounded.

"I? Renounce you?" he asked, astonished. "Whatever gave
you that idea?"

"You did!" she cried, despairing and close to tears. "If not
with words then with what you do! Can't you see that I can't
give myself to a man who is stained with innocent blood and
tears, who has become a byword for lawlessness and violence,
and who is known everywhere he goes as an outlaw, a criminal
and a traitor?"

But even then Kmita failed to grasp what she was trying to tell
him.

"What do you mean *a traitor*?"

Rage and bewilderment flashed across his features like the
alternating light of a magic lantern.

"Don't drive me mad or I'll do something I'll have to regret!"
he shouted. "May lightning strike me, may the Devil rip the
hide off my back right now, if I ever did anything but fight for
our Motherland while everybody else gave up in despair!"

"You fight for her, yes," she said. "But you do to her just
what the worst of her enemies are doing, because you trample
her, and torment her people, and you pay no attention to either
her laws or those of God himself!"

Her eyes were full of tears. She could hardly see. But she
fought to keep her voice as firm and steady and as resonant as if
none of her terrible accusations could touch her own soul or
wound her as deeply as they did.

"I tell you," she said at last, near the end of her strength but
resolved to continue no matter what happened. "Even if my
heart is to tear itself to pieces... I won't take you if that's how
you are. No! I don't want you like that! I don't want you!"

"Don't talk to me about rejections or I'll go mad!"he shouted,
losing all control. "Holy angels, help me! I'll have you whether
you want me or not! I'll take you if all your fleabitten guardians
and Radzivill and the King and all the demons of Hell jump up

to bar my way! Even if I've got to give my soul to Satan for you!"

"Don't call on Evil or you'll be heard!" she cried, blind with terror and holding her hands before her.

"For God's sake!" he cried, numb with a sudden incomprehensible fear of his own. "What do you want from me?"

"Decency...!" she said.

Both became silent then.

★ ★ ★

The silence spread, interrupted only by Pan Andrei's heavy, gasping breath, but Olenka's final words managed to pierce that thick callus of selfishness and profligate indifference that sheathed Kmita's conscience. He felt humbled, rather than humiliated, and he had no idea why he was ashamed. He didn't know how to answer her or what to do in his own defense. He started to pace fiercely up and down the room while she sat as still as if all life was drained out of her body. Anger, regret and pain hung over them like a poisoned cloud and the long silence became impossible to bear.

"Good-bye!" Kmita said suddenly.

"Go your way then," she said. "And may God show you a different path."

"Oh I'll go! I'll go! It's been a bitter meal that you've served me here!"

"And how do you think I feel?" she asked in a voice thick and choked with tears.

"Good-bye then!"

"Good-bye..."

Kmita took a few strides towards the door then turned as suddenly as if he had been stabbed and leaped back towards her.

"In God's name!" he cried and seized both her hands. "D'you want me to drop dead or what?"

She burst into tears. He threw his arms around her, feeling her whole body trembling with pain and sorrow. "Kill me, whoever still believes in God!" he grated out through tight-clenched teeth. "Strike, don't show pity!"

And finally a cry of vast shame and sorrow burst out of him as well.

"Don't cry, Olenka! For God's sake, stop crying! What did

I do to bring all this about? Alright, I'll do what you want. I'll
send my friends away. I'll set things straight in Upita. I'll live
differently because I love you and I don't want to lose you. For
God's sake, I'll cut myself to pieces for you, I'll do anything!
Only please stop crying and keep loving me..."

And so they clung together for a long time until her tears
ended.

* * *

The moon was already hanging high above the snowy countryside before Pan Andrei set out for Lubitch, with his hangdog
soldiers slouching after him on the highway like a weary, peni-
tent procession. They didn't take the forest road towards Volmontov but took a shortcut right across the swamps which were
frozen solid under the ice and snow. Sergeant Soroka edged up
to Pan Andrei and asked where to bivouac the troops once they
got to Lubitch, but the young commander snarled at him and he
retreated hastily into the ranks behind him.

Kmita rode in silence.

Anger and regret clawed at his vanity and pride. A rising
sense of disgust with himself gnawed at his stubborn vanity, and
at all his glib rationalizations. Never before had he made this
kind of an accounting of who he was and what he'd truly done,
and his conscience seemed suddenly as heavy and oppressive as
an iron helmet. He could find no excuses for what he had
become.

'*My God*,' he thought, '*what's the matter with me? I've brought
my stained and tattered reputation out of the bloody chaos in the East
and what have I done to mend it?*'

He knew that he was just as much to blame for the debauch-
eries in Lubitch as if they were his own idea in the first place;
he let his hell-bent roistering companions run wild on their first
night there and he closed his eyes to all their dissipations from
then on.

And what about Upita? His soldiers ravaged and abused the
townsfolk and all he did was to compound their viciousness with
his own. And he'd done worse than that! He'd thrown himself
on the Ponevyezh garrison, killed or wounded perhaps a dozen
men, and flogged their naked officers through the snow. A
tribunal and a guilty verdict were a foregone conclusion.

He cursed himself.

He gnawed his knuckles in impotent shame and fury. What kind of way was that to start his new life?

Even if he escaped the hangman's noose somehow, he'd be sure to forfeit his privileges and titles. Neither could he do any longer what he did so many times before: gather a troop of marauders around himself, put himself beyond the reach of justice, and laugh at the law. How could he do that now? He was about to marry, to settle down in Vodokty, wasn't he? He wanted to be done with his freebooting ways, to ask for a regular commission in the Hetmans' army, and to serve with honor like every other patriotic soldier. And even if he managed to avoid any punishment under Radzivill's protection how could he face Olenka? He thought that there was something ugly and contemptible about his crimes, something degrading for a real noble. He felt besmirched and contaminated by his entire life.

'*Maybe there's some way to make amends,*' he thought. '*Some restitution for all those acts of savagery and folly... But what about people's memory?*'

No matter what he did from now on he'd always be remembered for what he had done before, and neither his own conscience nor Olenka's disappointment in him would ever let him find that image of himself that he had always wanted.

But now, with the picture of Olenka's sorrow so fresh in his mind, he saw a spark of hope. She hadn't yet rejected him entirely! He was sure that he saw forgiveness in her eyes just before they parted and he rode away. How good she was, how kind! An angel couldn't be more forbearing and forgiving! And how right she was in everything she told him!

He wanted to turn his horse around and gallop back to her at once. No, not tomorrow. Not the day after. But immediately. To throw himself down at her feet, and beg her to forget his past, and to kiss all those tears off her loving face... He wanted to burst into tears of his own at the thought of how hurt she'd been by his wild stupidity.

"By God's sweet Mother," he cried out in torment. "I'll do what she wants. I'll see to it that my companions are well taken care of, and then I'll ship them off to the ends of the earth if that's necessary, because it's true that they draw the worst out of me."

And here he was suddenly quite sure that when he got to
Lubitch he'd find them all roaring drunk, abusing the servants
or dragging the luckless village women through his rooms, and
a wild rage, as sudden and as overwhelming as all his impulses,
seized him by the neck and shook him like a dog. He was
gripped by such a mindless fury that he wanted to hurl himself
on anyone at all, even on those cut-throat marauders who
straggled in their long winding lines behind him, and saber them
without mercy.

"I'll show them orgies," he snarled. "They've never seen me
as they're going to!"

Infuriated, he started to kick his horse and to tear spasmodically at the reins so that the animal went wild in its own turn,
and Soroka muttered to the men behind him:

"Watch out. The colonel's got the Devil in 'im. Don't come
near 'im if you want to live."

Chapter Eight

OLD SERGEANT SOROKA could never be accused of being a prophet but he was right that night: Pan Andrei did indeed have a demon in him.

A deep peaceful silence was spreading through the night around him. The moon was bright and clear, the sky glittered with a myriad stars, there wasn't even a breath of wind to nudge the snowy branches overhead, but a violent storm was raging in his heart.

The road to Lubitch seemed longer to him than it had ever been. Some kind of fearful doubt, never encountered anywhere before, reached out towards him from the spangled darkness, out of the depths of the forest and from the moonlit fields. Weariness settled on him like a boulder, all the more crushing because he'd spent the whole previous night in Upita in drunken celebration.

He wanted to shake himself free of this sudden stupor, to wear out his exhausted mind with fresh physical exertion, and to let the wind of a violent gallop clear those gloomy clouds out of his pounding head.

"Ride!" he commanded, turning to his soldiers, and spurred his horse forward.

He shot into the darkness like an arrow, his troopers followed at a thundering gallop, and they flew among the gaunt wintry trees and through the empty fields like one of those ghostly cavalcades of Teutonic Knights that people in the Zmudyan countryside talked about on cold Winter nights: cursed demons, sprung from Hell, who whirled through the air under a full moon to signal the coming of fresh war, or to serve as portents of some terrible disasters. The thunder of their hoof-beats flew ahead of them and trailed behind them, their horses' labored breath boiled about them in streamers of white mist, and they didn't slow down their headlong rush until the snow-covered roofs of Lubitch showed beyond the bend.

The gates to the courtyard stood wide open in the lifeless silence.

Surprised, Pan Kmita peered around for someone to come out of the house as soon as the wide enclosure among the manor buildings filled with his men and horses. But no one appeared to welcome him or even to ask who he was. He expected to find every window ablaze with torchlight, to hear the shrill piping of Pan Uhlik's flute and the screech of fiddles, and the raucous shouts and laughter of his reveling companions; instead, only the two tall windows of the dining hall showed a flickering light, as pale and uncertain as a guttering candle. The rest of the house was as dark and silent as if it was abandoned.

Sergeant Soroka was the first to leap off his horse and hurried forward to hold his commander's stirrup.

"You'd better turn in," Kmita told him. "Find whatever room you can for the men in the servants' quarters. Bed down the rest in the stables. The horses can go into the cow sheds and the barns."

"By your order, sir!" Soroka, an old soldier who had served the Kmitas for years, touched his wolfskin cap. "I hear and obey!"

Kmita climbed wearily off his horse. The doors into the entrance hall gaped open and the hall itself was as cold and frosted as the night outside.

"Hey there!" he shouted. "Where is everybody?"

But no answer came out of the silent house.

"Hey there!" he shouted once more, angry to be ignored on his own threshold, but the dark silence continued as before. "What's the matter here?"

He pushed his way into the soundless house.

"They're drunk again," he muttered and, at once, his irritation gave way to savage rage. Riding home he was blind with anger at the thought that he'd find another drunken orgy in his house

but now this cold grim silence goaded him into a fresh bout of
fury.

He threw open the doors of the dining chamber. The dim
red light of a tallow candle swayed and sputtered on the massive
table so that, at first, Pan Andrei could see nothing in the silent
gloom; and it was only when he slammed the door, and the rush
of cold air from the hallway died down behind him, that the
wavering light steadied enough to show the row of bodies laid
out along the wall.

"Are they dead drunk, or what?" he muttered, suddenly uneasy, and leaned over the nearest of them. The prone man's face
was hidden in the shadow but Kmita recognized him by his
white leather belt and the little sheath in which he carried his
ever-present flute.

"Wake up, Uhlik!" he shouted and began to prod the man
angrily with the toe of his boot. "Get up you soused hogs! On
your feet!"

But Pan Uhlik lay quite still, with his arms limp along his
body, and beyond him lay all the others in an even row. Not
one of them stirred or yawned or flipped open a bleary eye or
even muttered an irritated curse, and suddenly Kmita noticed
that all of them sprawled on their backs in the same position,
with their stiff booted legs flung out before them and their heads
lined evenly against the shadowed wall, and an icy premonition
tightened in his chest.

He leaped towards the table, seized the candle holder with a
trembling hand and carried the light down to those hidden faces
and then the hair stirred in horror on his head.

He could recognize Uhlik only by his belt. The face and head
were a shapeless, bloody mass without a mouth or nose or a trace
of eyes or any other features, and only a stiff bloodstained
mustache protruded from that crimson pulp to show that this
had once been the face of a man. Next to him lay Zendt with
bared teeth glinting in a frozen grin and with a glaze of terror in
his bulging eyes. Ranitzki's livid death-mask, dotted with
round red stab-wounds among its pale leopard spots, was the
next in line.

Pan Andrei moved from one of them to another.

He was numb with horror.

The weak flame that trembled on the tallow wick cast a dull

reddish glow on their smashed heads and massacred faces, but Kokosinski—dearest to Kmita of them all because the two of them were boyhood friends and neighbors—seemed to be merely sleeping. His bloodless face was set in lines of peaceful and untroubled calmness, and only a single dark wound in the side of his neck showed that his sleep was a lasting one. The gigantic Kulvyetz was fifth in that ghastly line, huge as a slaughtered bear, with his clothing slashed to ribbons across his massive chest and his whole head and face cut and chopped to pieces by a dozen sabers.

Pan Kmita brought his candle close to each of these bloody masks, peering less for some sign of life than to assure himself that he wasn't dreaming. But it was only when he let the wavering light slant into the wide, staring eyes of Rekutz, the last of the fallen, that he thought he saw a tremor pass across the eyelids.

He put the spluttering candle on the floor and shook the man gently.

"Rekutz!" he called out softly. "Rekutz! It's me... Kmita!"

The dimmed eyes closed and opened and then closed once more. The pale lips quivered and the mouth moved softly without a sound.

"It's me," Kmita cried again.

The dying man's eyes opened for a moment and filled with recognition. The weak voice bubbled out almost without a breath.

"... Andy," he murmured. "Get... a priest..."

"Who did this to you?" Kmita screamed and caught himself in fury by the hair.

"Bu...tryms," Rekutz whispered, his lips barely moving. Then his body jerked in a single spasm. He stiffened. His eyes fixed whitely on the ceiling and he died.

★ ★ ★

Kmita made his way to the table as if he'd suddenly aged by half a century. He set down the light with trembling hands and slumped in his chair, rubbing his fists across his face like a man waking from a nightmare who is still unsure if the scenes around him belonged to real life or if they were just a continuation of his abandoned dream. The sight of those still, dead bodies, half-hidden in the gloom, forced an icy sweat to burst out on his forehead. His hair felt as if it was standing stiff and erect all over his head.

And suddenly he screamed out, so loudly that the windows shivered in their frames:

"Come here everyone! Here! Here!"

The soldiers who were making up their bedrolls in the servants' hall next door dropped what they were doing and burst into the room and Kmita pointed to the row of corpses.

"... Dead, all of them!" he snarled in a dull croaking voice. "Killed... murdered...!"

They crowded in, staring in amazement. Some of them carried burning bundles of pine and pitch-covered torches that cast a lurid light into the flat dead eyes ranked along the wall. Their first dumbstruck astonishment gave way to anger and excitement. Coarse, threatening shouts and questions clashed in the violent air, as word of the massacre spread to the men who found more distant quarters in the barns and stables, and who now came running to the manor house, scenting blood and trouble.

The manor blazed with light in every room. It filled with shouting men, a turbulence of cries, calls, questions, threats and curses, in which only the dead showed an unnatural calmness. They were as indifferent to everything around them as if none of that frenzied turmoil had anything to do with them, and as peaceful as they had never been in their restless lives. Their souls were gone, Pan Andrei thought numbly; neither battle cries nor the clash of goblets would wake them again.

Meanwhile the thick, uncertain roar of the soldiers' voices turned to shouts of fury and demands for vengeance, and Kmita shook himself free of the leaden dullness that seemed to have fallen on him like a wall.

"To horse!" he howled madly, leaping to his feet as if blind fury lifted him by the hair. "Mount up!"

The soldiers rushed to the door, pushing and shoving and trampling each other, and in less than half an hour, more than a hundred riders were galloping at break-neck speed along the broad, snowy highway, as if all the devils in Hell were breathing down their necks.

And leading them—wild-eyed and bareheaded, and with his naked saber gleaming in his hand—rode Andrei Kmita like a man who had given up his soul.

"Kill! Murder...!"

Their battle cries echoed among the trees and shattered the night's quiet.

* * *

Elsewhere in the countryside the night was as still and silent as a frozen dream. The pale white moon had already risen to its highest point in that lone lunar trek towards a scarlet dawn, when suddenly that journey seemed accelerated, the silvery light became suffused with a crimson glow that looked as if it were seeping from the icy earth, and the night watchmen in the distant settlements of the Laudanian gentry wondered if they had fallen asleep on guard and if a new day had crept up on them unaware.

The angry red light deepened in the sky and began to spread as if sunrise were about to burst out of the midnight forests, until at last the whole sky trembled with that lurid glow, and then there was no longer any doubt about what was happening. A sea of fire swirled above the homesteads of the luckless Butryms, where Kmita's savage soldiery were slaughtering the terrified population amid raw clouds of smoke, while pillars of flame, flying sparks, and whirling sheets of fire roared into the sky.

Torn from their sleep, the people of the nearest settlements clustered outside their homes and stared into that distant glow with muttered speculations.

"A fire, or what?"

"It's got to be some fire..."

"Out towards Volmontov, isn't it?"

"Looks that way."

Crowds of Gosyevitches gathered outside their homes and workshops in Goshtchuny. The Sollohubs left their wintering herds in their forest clearings and spilled into the highways. The streets of Drohjeykany, Mozgi, Patzunel and Morozy began to fill with bands of Gashtovts, Domashevitches and Stakyans who peered uneasily into that crimson sky, wondering what had happened and what they should do.

"That's not just an ordinary fire," they told each other with a rising sharpness. "The enemy must've got through the forests to Volmontov and is murdering the Butryms!"

The distant crash and rattle of gunfire confirmed their suppositions and then the churchbells of Krakinov and Upita began to clang in the traditional signal of alarm.

"That's it then!" the gathering Laudanians shouted to each other. "It's a raid. Let's go help the Butryms! Let's not leave our brothers to perish alone!"

And as the bowed, aged patriarchs of the clans discussed the event, wondering how invaders could have come through their deep Winter forests undetected, all the youths and adolescent youngsters who had stayed at home for the Winter threshing ran to prime their muskets and their fowling pieces, and buckle on their sabers and saddle their horses.

★ ★ ★

Soon afterwards, in the sleeping manor of Vodokty, a quiet but persistent knocking wakened Aleksandra from her own troubled dreams.

"Wake up, Olenka!" Aunt Kulvyetzovna called outside her door. "Get up, dear, get up!"

"Come in, auntie!" she answered sleepily. She was exhausted by her earlier tears and the emotional turmoil of the evening. "What's the matter?"

"Volmontov is burning!"

"In the name of God the Father, the Son and the Holy Ghost!" she cried out, wide awake at once, and leaped from her bed.

"You can hear the shooting all the way out here," the breathless old woman reported in a shaking voice. "There's a battle going on... God have mercy on us!"

Olenka's cry sounded terrible even to her own ears. She began to dress in trembling haste, pale as a ghost and hardly able to grasp the hooks and buttons that slipped through her fingers. Her whole body quivered as if in a fever. She alone among her frightened household had no doubt about the identity of the enemy who fell that night on the luckless Butryms, and she felt as if a part of her own soul had been torn out of her shaking body.

In moments her room filled with all her maids and servants who stumbled in with tears pouring down their faces, and with wails of terror, and she threw herself down on her knees before a holy painting.

"God have mercy on them," she recited, struggling to control her own tears and to divert the terror of the other women into a litany for the dead and dying. "Holy Mother, have mercy on them. Light of salvation, have mercy."

"Have mercy," the girls and women prayed on their knees, following her example.

"Have mercy... Have mercy..."

They were about halfway through the prayer when a violent pounding shook the outer doors. The serving women leaped to their feet, wide-eyed with a fresh wave of terror, and a single shout lifted from their breasts.

"Don't open up! Don't open!"

But the pounding went on with doubled force as if the invisible intruder was about to batter down the doors, and Kostek, the young servant lad, ran into the inner room among the clustered women.

"M'lady!" he cried out. "There's a man outside beating on the door! Should I let 'im in or not?"

"Is he alone?" she asked.

"Yes... Alone..."

"Then open the door."

The boy ran to obey.

Aleksandra seized a lighted candle and passed into the ceremonial dining room followed by Miss Kulvyetzovna and all her maids and spinners. An icy calm—colder and more profound than all the snows piled so deeply and widely outside—had fallen on her mind and gripped all her feelings. But she barely managed to position the candlestick firmly on the table, gathering all her women behind her and turning to face the entrance, when the outer doors creaked and rattled open, the iron bars clattered along the hallway floor, and Kmita appeared before them.

"... Olenka," he whispered.

He looked, she thought, like a demon or an evil spirit. He was unkempt and tattered, black with powder smoke and streaked and splashed with wet and drying blood. He stood swaying wildly as if the floor was buckling under him, gasping out of breath and with a mad, lost light wandering in his eyes.

"My horse fell in the woods," he gasped. "They're after me...!"

"You burned Volmontov?" she demanded coldly.

"Yes... yes. I..."

He wanted to say something more, but in that moment she heard shouts and cries nearing at great speed on the road outside, and the frantic drumming of many horses's hooves on the highway leading from the woods.

"... The devils!" he cried out in a cracked, rasping voice as if his head was on fire with fever. "Coming for my soul... So be it!"

But Alexandra no longer looked at him. She turned to her maids and women who were staring at that terrifying bloody apparition as if he were, indeed, a lost soul escaped from hellfire.

"You saw nothing here," she commanded, cold and aloof and stern as they had never seen her. "Am I understood? If you're asked about this... about him... you'll say that he was never here, is that clear? And now back to the servants' hall, all of you! And bring me more light!"

They trooped out, still fearful but barely even whispering to each other, and Alexandra fixed her steely eyes on Kmita's own.

"And you," she said and pointed to the door of a neighboring chamber. "In there!"

★ ★ ★

Meanwhile armed, mounted men crowded into the court-yard, leaped out of their saddles and burst into the house. She knew them all by name—each of the Butrym boys, all of the aged Gashtovts and every Domashevitch—but she had never seen them as they appeared just then: disheveled, stained with blood and powder, and lusting for vengeance.

"What is it? What are you doing here?" she demanded calmly, barring the way through the dining hall, while they glared about and pushed forward around her with naked sabers gleaming in their hands.

"Kmita burned down Volmontov!" they shouted in chorus. "He's murdered everyone... men, women children! That's what he's done!"

"We've crushed all his vermin," Yozva Butrym thundered. "And now we want his head!"

"Blood!" howled the others.

"We want his blood!" they shouted, oblivious of where they were or anything else around them. "Kill the murderer! Cut him down!"

"Then go after him!" she cried out, meeting their furious glances with a cold stare of her own. "Chase him! Why are you standing here?"

"But isn't he here? We found his horse foundered in the woods..."

She never lied. Indeed, dishonesty in thought as in deed was totally foreign to the upbringing of the Polish Lithuanian gentry who were raised from childhood to always tell the truth. The Laudanians would know all about that, she knew very well, and she prayed that they'd take her flushed cheeks and her uncertain voice for no more than anger and disgust.

"He isn't here," she told them. "The house was locked and barred for the night. Why don't you try the stables and the cattle barns?"

"He must've skipped into the woods!" some Laudanian shouted. "After him, good brothers!"

"Wait! Silence!"

"What? What?"

"Keep still!" Yozva Butrym's deep voice boomed like a cannon in that enclosed space. Then he stepped up to Olenka with a cold light in his narrowed eyes.

"Don't hide him, my lady," he said, harsh as death and grim as retribution. "Don't try to protect him. That is a doomed, cursed man."

"I curse him right along with you!" she said bitterly, and raised both her hands, along with the candle she was holding in them, towards the ceiling and to the Holy Icon in the room behind her.

"Amen!" the Laudanians chorused. "Let's search the outbuildings and then into the woods! After him! We'll find him! After the murderer! Let's go!"

"Let's go!" they shouted, pushing from the room and spilling into the courtyard and the night outside. "Don't let him get away!"

Yozva Butrym stood for a moment longer, staring coldly into Olenka's own chilled eyes, while the stamp and rattle of running boots and the gleam of naked weapons filled the entrance hall, and then all the hunters were gone after their prey. Some of them ran with lighted torches to spread among the barns, and to search through all the scattered workshops, sheds, silos and haylofts, while the rest mounted their horses and galloped into the woods. Soon all of them were gone, their voices died down among the trees, and the drumming of their horses' hooves dwindled in the distance.

She stood, still as a statue, listening to the silence, and then she knocked feverishly on the door of the inner room where she had hidden Kmita.

"They're gone!" she called out. "You can come out now!"

Pan Andrei staggered out of his hiding place as if he were drunk.

"Olenka..." he started.

But she shook her head, as forbidding as a wrathful angel on Judgment Day, and her long, loosened hair rose and flew behind her shoulders like a cloak.

"No more," she said coldly.

"I..." he tried again.

"I don't know you," she said as distantly as if not one moment of nearness or a spark of warmth had ever glowed between them.

"Listen..."

"Not one word! I don't want to see you anywhere again. Take a horse from the stables and leave here at once!"

"Olenka," he groaned, stretching his hands towards her, but she took a swift, horrified step away from him, as if he was a serpent coiled in her path and ready to strike.

"Your hands are as bloody as Cain's!" she cried out. "Go and don't come back!"

Chapter Nine

THE NEW DAY SEEMED as pale as a corpse, throwing a grey light on the piles of rubble which were all that remained of Volmontov after Kmita's raid. Dead men and horses lay thrown about among the gutted ruins of homes, barns and byres, where scattered groups of weeping and distraught survivors searched for the bodies of their kin in the coals and ashes.

All of the Lauda country was in shock and mourning. True, the populous local gentry inflicted a staggering defeat on Kmita's marauders, but at a heavy price. Beside the Butryms, who suffered the most, there wasn't a single settlement in which widows weren't mourning dead husbands, children didn't cry for their missing fathers, or parents weren't weeping over fallen sons. The Laudanians' victory was won all the harder because all their fighters were either too bowed down by age, or too close to childhood, to have left in answer to their country's call. The King's proclamation of a General Levy throughout Lithuania had stripped the countryside of its best and fittest fighting men, but Kmita's followers were slaughtered to a man. Some met their deaths in the ruins of Volmontov, defending themselves so fiercely that even the wounded went on fighting to the end, while the rest were hunted down the next day in the woods and killed without mercy.

Kmita himself, however, vanished without a trace. No one could suggest how he'd got away or what happened to him. The Laudanians searched for him in Lubitch, supposing that he might make a stand against them there, but to no effect. Others believed that he found his way to the Zyelonka Forests and then, making his way further east, stumbled upon some hideout in the impenetrable Wilderness of Rogov, where only the Domashevitches would have been able to find him. Yet others said that he ran off to join Hovansky and that he'd come back, in time, with the Russian hordes.

Meanwhile the surviving Butryms gathered around Panna Aleksandra so that the Billevitch estate looked for some days like a besieged encampment. The manor house filled with women and children. Whoever couldn't find shelter in Vodokty went to the neighboring Mitruny which Aleksandra deeded over to the ruined Butryms as their new possession. Moreover, a hundred armed men, supplied by each of the Laudanian clans in turn, camped permanently around her home in expectation that Kmita wouldn't give up so easily and that he might come back after the young heiress. The more important families in the region, such as the Schyllings and the Sollohubs, sent troops of armed lackeys and manor Cossacks to reinforce Aleksandra's protecting garrison, so that Vodokty took on the appearance of an armed camp on the eve of an attack or enemy invasion.

Panna Aleksandra walked among these crowds of distraught women and armed men, seeing the human misery caused by her violent lover and listening to the bitter curses hurled at Kmita's name, and each of these was like a sword thrust through her own heart.

She couldn't help thinking that she was the cause of all this suffering around her. It was because of her that this wild, unbridled man came to the Lauda country, ruined so many lives, destroyed their peace, burned down their quiet villages and townships, trampled on the laws, and left such a bloody memory behind him.

She found it almost impossible to believe that one human being could do so much harm in so little time, especially since he wasn't a totally evil and corrupted man. She was closer to him, and knew him better than anyone else in the countryside, and so she also knew that a vast gulf of difference lay between Kmita's true character and his savage acts; and it was this knowledge that brought her the most pain. She had no doubt that this turbulent young man, whom she'd begun to love with all the strength and power of her freshly wakened feelings, could be vastly different! That he had qualities which could have made him an example of what a knight and neighbor ought to be, earning affection, respect and admiration instead of those curses.

It seemed to her at times that it was some doomed, evil spirit—some vast, unclean power!—that seized him and hurled him into all his acts of unpremeditated violence, and then she felt a profound sense of grief and an enormous pity for this wretched man whose loving words were still ringing in her ears.

Meanwhile a hundred law suits were brought against him in the courts, a hundred protests were lodged with the authorities, and Pan Hlebovitch, the King's *Starosta* for the Lauda County, posted him as a miscreant and an outlaw, to be hunted down and killed on sight if there was no way to bring him to the bar of justice.

* * *

But the law's verdicts were one thing, and their execution was another, because the Commonwealth was sinking deeper into chaos every day. A terrible new war hung over the country and came closer to Zmudya step by bloody step. The powerful Yanush Radzivill of Birjhe, who alone had the armed might to enforce the edicts throughout Lithuania, was too absorbed in power politics, and too engrossed in plans to raise his own family above all the others even at the price of the public good. Other magnates also thought more about their own advantage than the country's needs, as the great structure of the Commonwealth, weakened and undermined by the Cossack Wars, cracked all around them and began to topple.

More and more with each passing day, this rich and populous nation, filled as it was with a gallant knighthood, was turning into mere loot and booty for rapacious neighbors, while laws were either flouted or ignored, concern for public welfare went into abeyance, and selfishness and greed triumphed everywhere. Each man's security began to lie only in his own saber, and everyone knew that he could depend only on himself, so that while filing their lawsuits and protests against Kmita, the Laudanians kept their weapons handy.

But a month went by without a sign of Kmita. The Laudanians began to breathe a little easier. The wealthier nobles called off the armed retainers they'd sent to Vodokty;   the minor gentry started drifting home, anxious to get back to work, to their Spring plowing and to their peaceful firesides; and the less that everyone thought about armed resistance the more they pressed for retribution in the courts against the absent Kmita.

True, he was out of reach but his Lubitch was there as a rich and plentiful source for settlement. Some of the Laudanian elders wanted to seize that prosperous former Billevitch estate and turn it over to the ruined Butryms, but Aleksandra advised them against it. She not only took part in their deliberations but steered their thinking into peaceful courses, urging them to pursue the matter in the courts.

"Don't compound his violence with your own," she said. "Let all the innocence be on your side. He is a rich and well-connected man and he'll find backers to support his case. Give him cause for complaint and you'll only damage your own chances before the law. Let your claims be so clear and unblemished that any court in the land would have to give you justice even if his own brothers were sitting on the bench.

"Tell the Butryms to take nothing from him," she counseled with such clear-headed logic that the oldest and most experienced of the Laudanian leaders wondered at her wisdom. "I will give them whatever they need for now, and Mitruny is a far richer property than Volmontov ever was. And if Pan Kmita should show up here again let them leave him in peace until the case is settled. Remember that you can seek judgment against him only as long as he is alive."

They listened to her arguments, quick to see the logic of her counsel, and few of them noticed that such delays could benefit Pan Kmita as well. If nothing else, they guaranteed his life.

And what if she did try to safeguard the wretched, hunted man from some misadventure? No one thought anything of it or said much about it. The simple country gentry listened to her as if to the gospels, accustomed over generations to taking their cue from the Billevitches, and the Lubitch lands remained untroubled and untouched. Indeed, if Pan Andrei appeared there in that time he'd have been able to live in peace until the courts decreed what to do with him.

* * *

But he did not appear. Instead, about a month and a half later, a strange-looking man whom no one ever saw before in the Lauda country, brought Aleksandra a letter from Kmita.

'*Dearest, beloved Olenka whose loss I mourn with all my heart,*' Pan Andrei began, and then went on with sorrow and regret: '*All creatures, and especially men, have it in them to avenge themselves and to pay with evil for whatever evil might come their way from others. I offer no excuses for what I did to that stiff-necked Laudanian gentry but I do beg for your understanding. It wasn't done out of cruelty, or without a cause, but because they murdered my friends and dear companions with such brutality, and with such disregard for their youth and station, that even the Tartars or the Cossacks couldn't have treated them any worse than that. Neither will I deny that rage destroyed my judgment, but who can question anger when it wells up out of the spilled blood of one's closest friends? It seemed to me that the spirits of the late-lamented Kokosinski, Ranitzki, Uhlik, Kulvyetz, Rekutz and Zendt called out to me for vengeance just in the moment when I thought only of living in peace and friendship with all the Laudanians, wanting to change my life according to your loving counsel and advice.*

'*So as you listen to the complaints against me, hear also a little of my side,*' he begged her, '*and judge me with fairness.*

'*I'm full of pity for those unfortunate people in Volmontov, because the innocent suffered there along with the guilty, but a soldier who avenges his brothers' blood can't tell the difference between innocence and guilt and so he spares no one…*

'*I wish to God that none of it had happened, along with everything else that damaged me in your loving eyes,*' he wrote, pleading for her compassion and her understanding. '*The loss of you is my heaviest penance for the sins of others, and for my own just anger as well, since I can't forget either you or your love for me.*

'*May the tribunals judge me,*' he asserted. '*May the diets confirm the most cruel verdict, may I be stripped of my good name and substance, may the earth open at my feet and swallow me alive, if that is what it takes to make amends! I'll bear it all if only you don't throw me out of your heart altogether! I'll do everything they want. I'll give up Lubitch. I'll give up all my Orshan possessions once the war is won and the enemy is driven back into his own borders. I'll gladly give them all the captured treasure I've buried in the forests, if only you tell me that you'll keep faith with me as your late grandfather commands from the other world…*

'*You saved my life*,' Aleksandra read through her own tears of pity. '*Won't you now save my soul?*'

Nor could she doubt the pain and sincerity in his final plea.

'*... Let me make restitution for the injuries I caused, and give me a chance to change my life for the better, because I can see it clearly now that if you turn your back on me then God will also abandon me, and sheer desperation will drive me to even worse excesses than those which already stain me.*'

She wouldn't have been who and what she was if she was unable to respond with pity to this passionate appeal. She was one of those women who love only once. Her love for him, she knew, may have been like a woodland seed carried by the winds before it found its soil, but once it rooted and became a tree it could be torn out of her only along with her heart. But how could she forget everything that happened even if, in time, she could forgive it all?

His regret may have been heartfelt and genuine, she knew, but his spirit remained as wild and willful as it had ever been; and his untamed nature couldn't have changed so completely in such a short time that she'd be able to think about a future at his side without doubt or fear.

She needed him to show her deeds, not words.

Without such deeds, how could she say to this man who drowned the countryside in blood, and whose name was mentioned throughout the Lauda region only along with curses: "Come to me! Everything is forgiven! In exchange for the blood you've shed, and for the tears and misery that you've caused, I give you my heart and my hand as well...?"

So she wrote something different in reply.

'*I told you that I don't want to see you, or to know you, and I'll stand by that even if it should tear my heart apart. What you've done to the people here isn't made right with money or possessions because material things don't resurrect the dead. Neither is it possessions that you've lost but your name and honor. I will forgive you when your victims have forgiven you. I'll welcome you when they have welcomed you. Let them plead for you and I will listen to them. But since that can never happen, look for your happiness elsewhere and beg God's forgiveness rather than my own, because that is what you need the most.*'

She wept over each word of this letter, sealing it with the

Billevitch signet ring, and took it out herself to the waiting messenger.

"Where are you from?" she asked, looking curiously at this strange emissary who seemed less like anybody's servant, or even like a normal human being, than a wild, shaggy creature sprung out of the forests.

"From the woods, lady."

"And where is your master?"

"I'm not allowed to say. But he's far from here. It took me five days to get here, riding hard..."

She nodded. "Here's a gold piece for you. Is your master well?"

"He's in good health. Strong as a bear, he is."

"Is he poor or hungry?"

"Him? Hungry?" The man laughed. "He's rich like a King!"

"Go with God, then" she said.

The man bowed to the ground.

"Wait," she added. "Tell him... tell him... I wish him God's mercy."

★　★　★

The man went away and again weeks passed without news of Kmita. But everyone's minds were soon absorbed by public concerns, each flash of news being more desperate and urgent than the one before.

Hovansky's Russian armies flooded ever greater portions of the Commonwealth. Not counting the Ukrainian territories torn away after the Cossack wars, and looking only at the Lithuanian provinces of the old Grand Duchy, the Russians swarmed over the palatinates of Polotzk, Smolensk, Vitebsk, Mstzislav, Minsk and Novgorod. Only the territories of Trotzk, Brest-Litovsk, a part of the overrun Palatinate of Vilna and Zmudya itself, were still able to draw a free breath, but even there the people expected unwelcome visitors any day.

It seemed as if the Commonwealth had fallen to the lowest rung of helplessness, unable to defend herself against an enemy whom she always treated with contempt and whom she crushed at will in countless other wars.

True, these were no longer the backward, primitive Muscovite boyars and corrupted *Streltsi* who had been little more than tax-collectors for the Tartar Khans. Moscow was bursting out-ward. Its divided petty principalities and dukedoms were on the road to becoming the Russian Empire under the first few of the Romanovs, and of the powerful Hovanskys who were its real rulers, aided by the still turbulent Cossacks of Hmyelnitzki who were a seeping wound that drained the Commonwealth's best blood and resources.

But despite this threatening transformation of Muscovy into a hungry and ambitious Russia, and the continuing eruptions of Cossack unrest, soldiers and statesmen alike continued to believe that the Grand Duchy was not only able to repel this invasion by itself, without help from the Polish Hetmans who were fighting for their own lives in the Ukraine, Ruthenia and Podo-lia, but that it could hurl the Russians back into their own country and fix its own victorious banners once more on the Kremlin walls.

It could but it didn't. Disunity, private quarrels and preoccu-pations with personal advancement among the magnates and the wealthier gentry, made this great organism impotent to defend itself, so that even those citizens who were ready to sacrifice their all for the common cause found themselves paralyzed and unable to act.

Meanwhile the territories which were still unoccupied by the enemy filled with thousands of refugees, both commoners and gentry. The local populations couldn't feed and shelter all those displaced masses so that the towns and villages of Zmudya became cauldrons of misery, hunger and despair which often burst into violence, robbery, fighting and fresh chaos.

* * *

Spring drew near at last. The Winter had been fierce beyond all reckoning and the snows still lay in thick, forbidding layers not merely on the forests but on the fields as well. Famine, the grim brother of War, loomed over the country when the old year's food stores were finally used up and fresh supplies had not yet sprouted from the frozen soil. A traveler no sooner left his home when he came across unburied corpses scattered in the fields and littering the roadside. Frozen and gnawed by preda-tors, these victims of hunger fed countless packs of wolves which multiplied in numbers never seen before, and which became so bold that they left the forests and invaded small towns and villages, where their grim howling blended with human pleas for mercy or pity.

The long Winter nights gleamed with flickering bonfires in the woods, in the fields, and at village boundaries where destitute masses huddled in their rags, running after every passerby with pleading, threats and curses. A superstitious terror gripped the entire country. Many people started saying that all these lost campaigns and unparalleled disasters were connected with the name of King Yan Casimir, and that the letters J. C. R. engraved on the coinage stood not just for '*Joannes Casimirus Rex*' but for '*Initium Calamitatis Regni*,' or the beginning of the end for the Commonwealth. And if such fear and chaos ruled the territories that were still untouched by war and invasion, Hell itself seemed to burst free in the provinces lost to the enemy.

All constants disappeared. There was nothing left for the people to believe. All of the Commonwealth seemed racked by a mindless fever, sinking into the hopelessness of an incurable disease like a man on the point of dying, and torn apart by quarrels and accusations. Prophecies of new wars and rebellions fanned the flames of bitterness and fear, while various powerful families, seized by a storm of jealousy and self-interest, glared at each other like hostile independent states rather than members of the same nation who shared common dangers, carrying whole counties and provinces behind them.

That's how it was that Spring in Lithuania where the bitter quarrels of Yanush Radzivill, the *Voyevode* of Vilna and Grand Hetman of the Lithuanians, and his rival, Field Hetman Gosyevski, reached their boiling point and threatened to explode into open warfare. The rich and well-connected Sapiehas of Vitebsk, who had long envied the power of the Radzivills, backed Hetman Gosyevski while their supporters heaped mountains of abuse on the grim Radzivill. They charged him with such an unbridled appetite for glory that he threw away the flower of the army on the field of Shklov, rendering the whole country helpless before the enemy. They spread the malicious tales that he thought less about the welfare of the Commonwealth than about the rights of his own House to sit in the councils of the German Empire, that he dreamed of an independent kingdom for himself, and that, as the leading Protestant of the region, he advanced the careers of his co-religionists over the Catholics.

It even came to pitched battles that Winter and Spring between the partisans of both sides, while their wealthy patrons, pretending that they knew nothing about this fratricidal bloodshed, sent complaints about each other to Warsaw, further dividing the discordant Diets and letting loose an unbridled lawlessness at home. All that a man like Kmita had to do to escape justice in that kind of setting was to take one side or the other, throwing his lot with either of these magnates, and place himself beyond the reach of any retribution.

★ ★ ★

Meanwhile the enemy pressed on, stopped here and there by castles and fortified places, but for the most part finding little or no resistance. Under these circumstances nobody in the Lauda country stirred far from their weapons especially since both the Hetmans were away. The Hetmans did what they could against Hovansky's and Trubetzkoy's eighty thousand fighters, raiding and snapping at their flanks, but this did little more than impede their progress. Yanush Radzivill, a famous commander whose name alone used to be a threat until the Shklov disaster, even won a few considerable successes, while Gosyevski took turns in either fighting or negotiating brief delays in the enemy advance. Pawel Sapieha also offered some resistance of his own. All of them gathered whatever fighting men they could, knowing that the invasion would resume with full force in Spring, but they had few trained soldiers, the Grand Duchy's treasury was empty, and the gentry of the occupied provinces could no longer reach them.

"There was time to plan for things like that before the Shklov defeat," the Gosyevski partisans complained with good reason. "But it's too late now."

And it was, indeed, too late for a serious effort by the Lithuanians. The Polish troops of the Commonwealth couldn't come to help because they were all in the Ukraine, fighting against Hmyelnitzki, Sheremet and Buturlin. The news of their heroic battles, epic marches and successful sieges did seep north now and then to encourage the most disheartened doubters; the names of the two Crown Hetmans rang with new-won glory and, next to them, the name of Stefan Tcharnyetzki, the great *husaria* leader, helped to awaken a new spirit of resistance. But no one's fame, no matter how inspiring, was a substitute for armed help, and so the two Lithuanian Hetmans retreated slowly westward, quarreling with each other each step of the way.

At last Radzivill pitched his camps in Zmudya and a semblance of peace returned to the Laudanians. True, there was fresh trouble from local Protestants who felt bolder now that their leader stood once more among them, and who attacked some Catholic churches in their towns, but the countless raiders who ravaged the countryside in the name of one or another of their powerful patrons, hid in the forests, dismissed their marauders, and the country people could draw an easier breath.

And since almost anything will serve to inspire new hope in the midst of profound despair, a better spirit spread throughout the Lauda. Aleksandra lived peacefully in Vodokty as before. Pan Volodyovski, who just then started to come back to health in Patzunel under the loving care of the Gashtovt beauties, spread the word that the King would come north in Spring with an army of newly raised or hired regiments, after which the war would take a better turn.

Thus encouraged, the farming gentry started taking their plows into the fields where the snows had melted and the first buds of Spring appeared in the windrows. The days were brighter under clearing skies and everyone started to feel better about the times to come.

Then something happened.

The peaceful interlude ended for the Laudanians, never to return, and the name of Kmita rang among them with new dread and hatred.

Part Two

Chapter Ten

PAN VOLODYOVSKI, who was so slight in build that he scarcely came up to Yozva Butrym's shoulder, was still a young man despite his many years of experience as a soldier, and as far as the Laudanians were concerned he was their most valued asset in those troubled times.

Who was he and where did he come from? This much they knew: his home was somewhere in the *kresy*, as the eastern borders of the Commonwealth were known; he was the best swordsman they had ever seen among the Polish, Lithuanian and Ruthenian gentry; he spent all his youth in the service of the late Prince Yeremi Vishnovyetzki, the hero of the Cossack Wars, whose lost Transdnieper Country had been a bulwark against Tartar and Russian encroachments until it fell away from the Commonwealth some thirteen years earlier; and he took service with Yanush Radzivill when Prince Yeremi's famous soldiers scattered throughout the country after their leader's untimely death in poverty and oblivion.

Other than that he was a pleasant, cheerful, easy-going young man who took life as it came, serving his country as best as he could, although his small size along with a warm and sentimental nature made him unusually susceptible to beautiful but unattainable women.

Ever since he returned from the Shklov campaign, the little colonel stayed at the home of old Pakosh Gashtovt, the patriarch of the Patzunel Laudanians, who took some pride in his reputation as the wealthiest man in the Lauda country. The old man gave a hundred silver dollars to each of his three daughters who had married Butryms, beside such sumptuous supply of linens, clothing and household inventory that few young gentlewomen in the old Grand Duchy had a better dowry. His three younger daughters were still unmarried and living at home and it was this trio of lively, good-hearted and gentle young beauties that watched over Pan Volodyovski whose right hand, numbed by old wounds and the fierce Winter weather, gradually regained feeling as the Spring came nearer.

All the Laudanians who'd watched that hand at work at the battles of Shklov and Sepyelev were quite sure that a better one couldn't be found in all of Lithuania, and so the neighborhoods competed with each other in their respectful attentions to the little colonel. The Gashtovts, Domashevitches, Gosyevitches and Stakyans sent him regular wagon loads of fresh fish, dried mushrooms, smoked venison, pitch and hay, so that neither he nor his grooms and horses would lack anything, and whenever he felt a twinge of pain in that all-important hand they raced each other to Ponevyezh for the local surgeon. Old Pakosh also felt immensely honored to have such a famous house guest, and practically swept the dust before him as he walked, so that Pan Volodyovski couldn't have had it better if he was convalescing in Keydany under Radzivill's own roof.

In fact the only thing that worried the Laudanians that Spring was the sad awareness that, sooner or later, their distinguished young guest would tire of country living and go to Keydany. They racked their heads for some plan to keep him among them and the best idea they came up with was to have him marry Panna Aleksandra.

"Why should we search the world for a husband for her?" the canny clan elders decided at a special meeting where they looked into both these matters.

"Since that traitor Kmita stained himself with such infamy," they agreed, "that only a hangman would have any use for him, it stands to reason that our young lady must also have thrown him out of her heart by now. So let Pan Volodyovski marry her instead! Since we're her guardians according to the old colonel's testament we can give permission to substitute a good man for a bad one, can't we? That way she'd have a decent husband and we'd gain a fine young cavalier, along with a good neighbor in Lubitch, and a first class commander for our regiment as well!"

Having come to this unanimous decision, the elders went first to pan Volodyovski who agreed without giving it a thought one way or the other, and then to Aleksandra who needed even less time to give them her decisive 'No.'

"Only my late grandfather had the right to dispose of Lubitch," she told them. "And only the courts can take it away from Pan Kmita. As for my marriage, don't even think about it. There's still far too much pain in me for anything like that. Yes, I've turned my back on that other man, the one whom we've all cursed here, and that is enough. So don't bring another man to Vodokty, no matter how worthy he might be, because I won't even receive him in my house."

★ ★ ★

There was nothing more to say after such a firm refusal, and the troubled elders made their way home with their noses somewhat out of joint.

Pan Volodyovski was far less troubled when he heard about it and the three Gashtovt girls were troubled least of all. In fact they were delighted. Each of them was head-over-heels in love with the young knight and he was very fond of them as well, especially of the younger Maryska and Zonia because the oldest of them, Terka, complained too much about male treachery.

They were the prettiest girls in Patzunel, he thought—tall, straight-backed and pink-cheeked, with eyes as blue as cornflowers and hair as pale as hemp—and when he watched them cross a meadow on their way to church they brought to mind a row of Spring blooms opening in a field. Old Gashtovt also took some pains over their education. The church organist from Mitruny taught them to read and trained them in church music and Terka even mastered the art of the lute.

It was small wonder, then, that the warm-hearted little soldier would rather mend his health in Patzunel, under their loving care, than in the sumptuous courts of the Radzivills in Keydany or Birjhe.

He was particularly fond of those long Winter evenings, after old Pakosh Gashtovt climbed into bed with his jug of hot, honey-smelling *Krupnik*, when he sat by the fireside with his three beautiful young nurses. Suspicious Terka worked her spinning wheel, sweet-faced Maryska played with a tuft of hemp, Zonia's slim, strong fingers wound bright threads of wool, and he told stories about old campaigns or about the wonders he'd seen in various magnates' houses. All work would stop then, the girls stared at him as if he were a rainbow, and one or another of them cried out: "Ah, can that be? Are there really such miracles in this world? I won't close an eye all night!"

One evening at the end of March, after their twilight meal, he and the girls gathered by the hearth whose bright light spilled across the whole length of the low-ceilinged, darkly paneled room, and got ready to spend their usual hours of tales and stories. Old Gashtovt was snoring behind the stove and Pan Volodyovski was in a specially happy and light-hearted mood because his hand was almost well enough to wield his saber with its normal skill.

"What shall it be tonight, then?" he asked, pleased with the world around him. "Songs or stories?"

"Stories!" the girls cried out.

But the little soldier felt like teasing them for a little longer and asked Terka to sing for them and play on her lute.

"You sing one," she answered and pushed away the instrument which he held out towards her. "I've got work to do. You must've learned some songs in all your travels."

"Of course I've learned some. But I'll sing one only if you sing another. Your work will be there when you've finished singing, won't it? It won't go away. Hey, if a woman asked you for a song, my girl, you'd oblige her soon enough but you always say 'No' to a man!"

"Because they deserve it."

"All of them?"

"All!"

"Do you feel that way about me as well?"

"And what if I don't? Stop teasing! Why don't you start singing?"

Pan Volodyovski struck the lute, made a comic face and intoned in a high falsetto:

> *"Seems I've come to such a place*
> *Where no lady likes my face..."*

"Ey, that's not right, not fair!" Maryska cried out, turning as red as a ripening plum.

"That's just a soldiers' song that we used to sing in winter

quarters, hoping that some sweet soul would take mercy on us,"
Pan Volodyovski said.

"I'd take mercy on you..."

"Thank you, my dear! But if that's so then there's no point
in finishing that song. So let the lute pass into better hands."

This time Terka didn't push the instrument away. Instead she
formed her mouth into the obligatory rosebud as the Mitruny
organist had taught her, struck a chord on her lute and sang:

> *"Don't go near the boys in May*
> *And don't believe a word they say*
> *'Cause every boy's a cunning snake*
> *An' all their loving is a fake."*

"Well I'll be damned!" Pan Volodyovski shouted and burst out
with laughter. "Are all the lads such traitors, then? And what
about the soldiers?"

Terka narrowed her small mouth even further and sang with
doubled energy and conviction:

> *"They're worst of the lot,*
> *They're worst of the lot!"*

"Don't pay her no mind," Maryska said at once. "Terka's
always like that."

"How am I to pay her no mind," Pan Volodyovski teased,
"when she puts such a mean label on my whole profession that
I don't know where to hide in shame?"

"There you are!" cried the pouting Terka. "First you want me
to sing and then you make fun of it! That's just like a man!"

★ ★ ★

But the songs led to what the girls wanted to hear in the first
place and Pan Volodyovski found himself telling another story.

"Truth to tell, Miss Terka," the little soldier said, "you've such
a lovely voice that all we'd need to do is dress you in breeches
and you'd be able to sing in Warsaw in St. John's Cathedral
which is where their Majesties themselves come for Sunday
worship."

"And why should we dress her in breeches?" asked the youngest, Zonia, who was always curious about anything to do with
royalty and Warsaw.

"Because women don't sing in the choir at St. John's. Just
men and boys. I heard them there often when we came with

our late-lamented Prince Yeremi, the *Voyevode* of Ruthenia, to take part in the election of our present King. Some of them roar deeper than an auroch and others squeak higher than a fiddle. It's a real wonder! There's a whole mess of musicians and singers in that place and when they all let go together you'd think you were listening to the Seraphim in Heaven."

"Oh how I'd love to hear that!" Maryska cried out, pressing her hands together as if in a prayer.

"And did you see the King often?" Zonia asked.

"I talked with him as often as with you. After the battle of Berestetchko, where we beat Hmyelnitzki to end his first rebellion, he pressed my head to his chest in thanks. He's a great man and so merciful that once you've seen him you just have to love him."

"We love him without even seeing him!" the girls cried out, enthralled. "And does he wear his crown every day?"

"That would be really something!" Volodyovski laughed. "He'd need an iron head for that, that crown's not made of feathers! No, the crown rests in the church, where it gathers dignity, and His Majesty walks about in a black hat with ostrich plumes and diamonds which are so bright that they light up the entire castle."

"Ah, who'd imagine that! Though people do say that the King's castle is even more splendid than the Radzivills' in Keydany..."

"Keydany? That's like a chicken coop next to the King's castle! The royal palace is a great big building, made of brick and stone, and you won't see a piece of wood anywhere in there. There are two rows of chambers and galleries on each side of it and each one's richer than the next. That's where you'll see famous wars and victories painted on the walls, such as those of Sigismund III and Vladyslav IV. There's no way to see it all in a week of staring, and it's all so lifelike that you wonder why you can't see the men and horses move and hear all the shouting, but I don't suppose there's a painter who's able to make moving pictures."

"I should say not!" cried the girls. "And what else do you see there?"

"Well, there are rooms paneled from floor to ceiling in gold leaf, and the chairs and benches are covered in cloth-of-gold and damask and brocades, and the tables are made of marble and alabaster. And as for the vases, boxes, ornaments and clocks that tell the time day and night you wouldn't be able to list them all on a sheet the size of an oxhide."

"Fancy that! An oxhide! And the King and Queen walk through all those rooms and count all their goods?"

"And at night they have a theater to amuse them," Pan Volodyovski said.

"Fancy that! A theater! What's a theater?"

"Hmm... how am I to tell you. It's a place where they show all kinds of comedies and you can see Italian dancers leaping about higher than a goat. It's a kind of room, bigger than most churches, all lined with tall columns. Those who want to amuse themselves sit on one side of it, and the other side has scenery and stages that go up and down, or turn every which way on big screws. So sometimes you see darkness full of clouds, and at other times you see pleasant brightness. On top there might be a sky full of stars or sunlight and at the bottom there's a dreadful Hell full of fire and devils..."

"*O Jezu!*" the girls cried.

"That's right," Pan Volodyovski said. "Full of devils. And sometimes you see a great sea with ships and mermaids. And some figures come down from the sky and others rise up out of the earth..."

"The one thing I wouldn't want to see is that Hell!" Zonia cried. "How come the people don't run away at such an awful sight?"

"Because it isn't real. The Devil has nothing to do with it and it doesn't vanish at the sign of the cross. It's all made by human ingenuity and people clap their hands with pleasure when they see it. Even the bishops come there with their Majesties, along with all kinds of dignitaries and important people, and afterwards they all sit down to a banquet with the King."

* * *

Some hours had passed, it was getting late, and it was time to bring the evening to an end, but the girls wanted to know more about the royal doings.

"And what do they do in the morning and throughout the day?"

"That depends on what they feel like doing," the small knight informed them. "In the morning they might take a bath. They've a room there that doesn't have a floor. Instead there's a big hole with a tin bottom shining as bright as silver and there's water in it."

"Water in a room!" the girls cried out in wonder and amazement. "Did you ever hear of such a thing?"

"That's right. That's how it is. And it falls or rises, as you want, and it can be either hot or cold because it comes out of different pipes that carry either one kind or the other. You twist a fancy little tap and in it comes, so deep that you can swim in it like fish in a pond. No monarch anywhere has a castle as fine as our Most Merciful Sovereign, everybody knows that, and all the foreign ambassadors are the first to say it. Just like no other King rules over a nation as worthy as ours. There are all kinds of fine and decent nationalities in this world and yet God has seen fit to bless ours with His special mercy."

"Our King is lucky," Terka sighed with feeling. "What a happy man!"

"He'd be a lot happier if it wasn't for all these awful wars that flog the Commonwealth for our sins and tear at it for our inability to live together in friendship and respect. He carries that whole burden on his shoulders and the diets don't make it any easier for him. We do the sinning and he gets all the blame. But is it his fault that nobody wants to listen to him?"

"And why won't they listen?" Maryska's bright blue eyes were filling with tears while Pan Volodyovski sighed and his pointed little mustache moved sadly up and down.

"Hard times have fallen on our Commonwealth," he said. "So hard that all our history has never seen the like and it's our own fault. The most trivial enemies treat us with contempt. Us, mind you, who held all the Turks and Russians and Tartars at bay for more than a century! But that's how God punishes pride, you see. Thanks be to Him, at least, that my hand is better, because it's high time to remind the enemy of who and what we were. It's a sin to sit here, doing nothing, while our country is living through such awful times."

"Ah," the girls cried out. "Don't talk about leaving!"

"How else can it be? I'm happy here with you, my dears, but the happier I am the worse I feel about it. Let the politicians argue at the diets but a soldier's business is out in the field. While there's life there's service. People say that we've lost all our ancient virtues and that's why God's judgment has come down on us."

Maryska started sniffing and her tears spilled over on her cheeks.

"Yes, you'll go," she sniffled. "You'll forget about us. And we'll dry up or something, all alone... Who's going to defend us here if you go away?"

"I won't forget you ever," the little soldier said. "I'll always be grateful. But who is it that you're so afraid of? Is it still that Kmita?"

"Who else? The women use him to scare children with in these parts, as if he was a werewolf or an evil spirit."

"He won't come back," Pan Volodyovski said. "And even if he did, he wouldn't have those other ruffians with him who, as people say, were a lot worse than he. Ay, it's a real pity that such a good soldier should've stained his honor so badly and lost his good name along with a fortune."

"And the Lady, too."

"Yes, and the young lady. People say a lot of good things about her."

"She weeps all day, they say, the poor thing..."

"But surely not for Kmita?"

"Who knows?" sniffed Marysia.

"Hmm... All the worse for her then," the little colonel sighed. "Because he won't dare to show up here any more. The Grand Hetman disbanded most of the Laudanians because he can't feed them, so that we've plenty of good men here now, enough to resist anybody. Kmita must know they're back and that we'd chop him to pieces without any trials. He'd have to be a fool to stick his nose into these parts again so be at ease about him. He may be a mad, fearless devil but he's not an idiot."

"Still," Terka said. "Our men will leave again quite soon. They've been sent home only for a while."

"Ah!"—and now Pan Volodyovski's voice grew heavy with disgust and anger—"The country needs an army and the Hetman disbands the few good men he has because he has no money! It's enough to drive a man mad, I tell you! But maybe we'd better say good

night. It's late and time to sleep... Only make sure you don't
dream about Kmita with his fiery sword...."

★   ★   ★

He got off the bench and turned towards the inner door but
he barely took one step towards the guest room when a sudden
uproar burst out in the hall and a frantic voice began to yell
outside:

"Open up! For God's sake! Faster! Faster!"

The girls squealed in terror, the little knight ran to get his
saber, but Terka jumped forward and unbarred the door, and
some unknown man stumbled into the room and threw himself
on his knees before Volodyovski.

"Help, Excellency...!" he gasped, out of breath. "The lady's
been taken...!"

"What lady!"

"From Vodokty..."

"Kmita!" Volodyovski shouted.

"Kmita!" shrilled the girls.

"Kmita," the man said.

"Who are you?" Volodyovski asked.

"I'm the Vodokty foreman..."

"We know him," Terka said. "He used to bring the medicines
for you."

Just then sleepy old Pakosh Gashtovt climbed out from behind the stove, while two of Pan Volodyovski's servants ran into
the room to see what all the shouting was about.

"Saddle up!" Volodyovski ordered. "One of you ride and get
the Butryms! The other get my horse!"

"I've been over to the Butryms already," the foreman said.
"'Cause that's real close by. It's them that sent me here to Your
Excellency."

"When did he take the lady?" Volodyovski asked.

"Just now, seems like... They're still murdering the household
people there... I grabbed a horse..."

Old Gashtovt stood open-mouthed, rubbing the sleep out of
his eyes.

"What's that?" he babbled out. "What? The Lady's been
taken?"

"Kmita is back!" Volodyovski said. "We're going to the rescue!"

Then, turning to his servants, he ordered one of them to ride to the Domashevitch settlement. "Tell them to bring all the hunting guns they've got!"

But the old man was now wide-awake and roaring at his daughters.

"And you too, lambkins! Out with you! Awake the whole village! Get all the gentry here with their sabers! Quick! Ah, so Kmita took the Lady, did he? Eh? God help us all! Oh, the scoundrel..."

"Let's ride and get the people up ourselves," Volodyovski said and ran to the door. "It'll be quicker that way."

Then all of them spilled out of the house and ran to rouse the village.

Chapter Eleven

A FEW MOMENTS LATER old Gashtovt and Volodyovski were galloping down the broad street between the homesteads, along with the little colonel's grooms and the old man's daughters, pounding on doors and windows and shouting with all the air in their lungs: "To arms! To arms! Kmita's back! The Lady's taken in Vodokty!"

The uproar shattered the night's peaceful quiet while half-dressed men and bundled, huddling women appeared in the doors of their huts and houses. Sleepy, gaping youngsters and disheveled men ran out into the street to see what was happening and then, grasping at last what all the yelling was about, started to howl in their own turn: "*Kmita's back! The Lady's been taken!*" And then, still bellowing as if they were being skinned alive, they threw themselves pell-mell towards their stables to saddle their horses, or darted back under their thatched roofs to grope along the walls for their family sabers.

In moments the whole village echoed with shouts of "Kmita's loose again!"

Armed men began to pour out of the squat, whitewashed little homesteads. Pale tallow lights started flickering behind the frosted windows, dogs barked, women wept and wailed, and the whole sleepy little settlement took on the appearance of a seething anthill stirred with a stick and bursting with frenzy. At last the village gentry massed in the open street, some mounted and some on foot, with sabers, muskets, hunting guns, lances, pikes, pole axes and even iron pitchforks gleaming in the darkness above their heads.

It was then about ten o'clock at night.

Pan Volodyovski set them all in order, sent a small mounted troop ahead to guard against surprises, and led the rest towards the ruins of Volmontov where the Butryms had begun to rebuild their burned homes and homesteads. There they would link up with the rest of the Laudanian gentry, he told the gathered Gashtovts. Then he formed all the mounted men at the head of the column and ordered those who didn't have horses of their own to follow close behind.

The moon had barely risen, but the snow that still lay scattered in the fields reflected the starlight, and lighted the road ahead. Those of the gentry whom the Grand Hetman sent home from the army, immediately formed tight military ranks and rode in disciplined and watchful silence, while the others, straggling on foot behind them, yawned, chatted, made a noisy clatter with their weapons, and hurled loud curses at the absent Kmita who robbed them of their sleep.

At last they came to the rebuilt outskirts of Volmontov where a large, armed detachment barred their way.

"Who's there?" hard voices called out to them. "Who's that coming up?"

"Gashtovts! And who are you?"

"We're the Butryms! The Domashevitches are with us!"

"Who's your commander?" Volodyovski asked.

"Yozva the Peg-leg, colonel." The grim, one-legged Butrym rode up to the small knight. "At your service, sir."

"What's the latest news?"

"He took her to Lubitch. They went across the swamps so as to bypass Volmontov..."

"Lubitch?" Volodyovski paused, surprised. "What's he intend to do against us there? Lubitch is no fortress."

"He must think he's too strong for us," Yozva offered. "Couldn't have heard about our people coming home on leave. He's got about two hundred men, along with a whole wagon train of carts and pack horses, so he probably came to help himself to the goods in Lubitch."

"Good!" the small knight rubbed his hands. "We've got him then! How many muskets do you have?"

"We Butryms have about thirty pieces but the Domashevitches have twice that many with them."

"Good. Take fifty men with muskets to guard the swamp
crossings. Quickly now! The rest fall in behind me. And don't
forget your axes!"

"By your orders, colonel!"

★ ★ ★

The column split at once and a small detachment trotted off
towards the swamp behind Yozva Butrym. Meanwhile another
dozen Butryms, who had ridden earlier to alert other settlements, arrived on the scene.

"Are the Gosyevitches anywhere in sight?" Pan Volodyovski
asked them.

"Ah, is that you, colonel? God be blessed!" the new arrivals
shouted. "The Gosyevitches are on their way, you can already
hear them coming through the woods. But does Your Worship
know that he's taken the Lady to Lubitch?"

"I know it. And that's as far as he's going to take her."

Pan Volodyovski didn't doubt for a single moment that the
Orshan ruffian was trapped and as good as taken. It was clear to
him that Kmita hadn't reckoned with the deadliest danger that
faced his expedition: he could have no idea that so many
Laudanians were home from the army. Sure of himself and
confident in his strength, he believed that the neighborhoods
were as drained of able-bodied fighting men as they were on his
first visit to the Lauda country. But in reality—counting the
Gosyevitches who would soon be there, but not including the
more distant Stakyans who couldn't possibly reach Lubitch in
time for the battle—the little knight could bring three hundred
trained and disciplined men against him.

Indeed, more armed gentry poured into Volmontov with each
passing minute, and finally the Gosyevitches were also there in
their full clan strength. Pan Volodyovski mustered them on the
road, delighted to see the speed and precision with which they
formed and dressed their ranks. One glance was enough to tell
him that these were trained soldiers, not the usual mob of
bickering petty nobles to whom every order had to be explained. The little colonel was all the more pleased because he
was looking forward to the time when he would lead this tough,
dangerous and determined farmer-gentry against a real enemy,

as he would as soon as the Grand Hetman could afford new levies.

Midnight was long past when they set out through that still, dark forest which Kmita used to traverse so happily every day while he was courting Olenka in Vodokty.

They moved at a brisk military pace, silently and swiftly. A full moon was hanging in the starry sky, throwing white beams of light on the woods, the road and the advancing warriors, and striking cold sparks off their bared sabers.

As they rode, they talked quietly to each other, sharing news and speculation about the event.

"There were a lot of strangers around here in the last few weeks," one of the Domashevitches murmured. "We thought they were vagabonds, or deserters from the Hetmans' armies, but they must've been Kmita's spies."

"Sure to have been," said another. "Seems like there were new beggars every day knocking on the doors in Vodokty and asking for alms."

"And what kind of men does Kmita have with him?" Pan Volodyovski asked. "Do any of you know?"

"The grooms who got away from Vodokty say they're Cossacks. Kmita must've joined up with Zoltarenko or Hovansky. He was just a bandit up to now but this makes him a traitor."

"Cossacks?" asked one of the Domashevitch hunters. "How could he bring Cossacks all the way out here?"

"That's right," said a Gashtovt. "It'd be hard to slip by unseen with a big troop like that. Any of our regiments would've stopped them on the way."

"Not necessarily! He could've made his way through the forests, couldn't he? And then again, how many great lords ride around the country with their own household Cossacks? And who can tell the difference between them and the other kind? If anybody challenged them they'd have called themselves some magnate's private escort and that'd be that."

"Ay, he'll fight hard in Lubitch," one of the Gosyevitches suggested. "He's a stubborn and determined man, to give the Devil his due. But our colonel will be more than enough for him."

"The Butryms all took an oath that they'd get him this time

even if every one of them gets killed in the process. They want him dead worse than anyone."

"Huh! And how will we get our just dues out of him if he's dead? It'd be better to take him alive and hold him for the courts."

"What courts?" a Butrym snorted.

"That's right," said a Gashtovt. "Who thinks about courts nowadays when nobody can be sure of what will happen tomorrow? Did any of you hear the rumors about a new war with the Swedes?"

"God forbid such a thing! Don't we have our hands full enough with Moscow and Hmyelnitzki? All we need now are Swedes and that'd be the end of the Commonwealth for sure!"

But suddenly Pan Volodyovski turned around and ordered total silence. The moonlit roofs of Lubitch lay in sight before them.

"Not a sound out of any one of you now," he warned. "And muzzle your horses."

★ ★ ★

The disciplined ranks fell silent at once. The column stole forward as softly as a shadow and in a quarter of an hour the Laudanians were within a short gallop's reach of the manor and its broad enclosure.

All the windows in the main house were ablaze with light which spilled out into the courtyard, illuminating a mass of armed men and horses, but there wasn't a sentry in sight anywhere. Either Kmita was too confident of his strength, Pan Volodyovski thought, or the guards had left their posts to join in the looting. One sharp glance revealed them as Cossacks whom the little knight fought for so many years under the great Yeremi Vishnovyetzki, and then more recently under Radzivill, and a wry grin curled the lip under his pointed mustache.

"If these aren't local Cossacks," he muttered to himself, "then this scoundrel's gone too far this time."

He signaled his men to halt and watched the crowded courtyard for a little longer. Some of the Cossacks stood holding lighted torches. Others lurched and scurried in every direction, carrying crates and bundles out of the house and stuffing them into wagons and hurrying back inside. Yet others led the horses from the manor stables or drove the cattle out of the barns and byres. The glow of burning brands cast a sharp light over a busy scene that resembled a hasty moving day.

Kristof Domashevitch, the patriarch of his clan, edged up to Pan Volodyovski then. "Looks to me, Your Honor, like they're trying to carry off the whole manor," he said.

"They won't carry it far," Volodyovski murmured. "And that goes for their own skins as well. But I'm surprised at Kmita. Such an experienced soldier and he didn't post sentries anywhere?"

"Why should he when he's got a powerful mob like that one? I'd say there's more than three hundred men out there. If our lads hadn't got back from the army when they did he'd have been able to drive those carts right through every settlement in the county."

"All the better," Volodyovski said. "Is this the only road to the manor?"

"Yessir. There's nothing but lakes and swamps behind."

"Very good. Dismount, gentlemen!"

The well-trained warrior gentry leaped out of their saddles, formed a long skirmish line and started to surround the manor and its outer buildings without a need for orders, while Volodyovski led his main detachment straight towards the gates.

"Wait for my command," he murmured. "Pass the word. No shooting before that."

Some forty paces separated them from the fenced enclosure before they were noticed, and a few dozen Cossacks ran to the palisade, leaned over the fencing, and peered into the darkness.

"*Hey, shto za lude?*" fierce voices called out in the Ruthenian dialect. "Who's that coming out there?"

"Halt!" Volodyovski shouted. "Fire!"

Every firearm that the gentry carried blazed out at once but their echoes were still rattling among the outbuildings when Pan Volodyovski cried again: "At a run... forward!"

"Strike and spare none!" the Laudanians replied with the ancient Polish battlecry. "*Bij, zabij!*"

And they threw themselves forward at a run.

* * *

The Cossacks fired off a hasty volley at the charging men but they didn't have the time to reload their muskets before a dense crowd of armed gentry rushed the gates, hurled them down, and fell upon the milling and surprised defenders. A fierce hand-to-hand fight broke out immediately among the piled crates, the half loaded wagons, and the terrified horses that shrilled in alarm.

The Butryms, always the most dangerous in hand-to-hand encounters and the most thirsty for vengeance on Kmita, pressed forward like a silent wall, although the image that came to mind was one of forest boars sweeping through freshly sprouted undergrowth, breaking and trampling everything before them and slashing with their sharp, white tusks at anything that moved. The Domashevitches, Gosyevitches and Gashtovts weren't far behind them.

Kmita's Cossacks defended themselves with the grim ferocity of their kind from behind the wagons, crates and bales piled about the courtyard, and musket fire rattled off the roof and out of all the windows, but there was little shooting once the lighted torches were thrown down and trampled underfoot. Plunged into sudden darkness, the combatants grappled with each other hardly able to tell an enemy from a friend. But once the Cossacks were driven from the courtyard, and started barricading themselves in the house and stables, the musketry burst out anew with fresh intensity. Every window bristled with musket barrels and a hail of lead rattled along the cobbles.

"Attack the doors!" Volodyovski shouted. "Get under the walls!"

The Laudanians crowded against the manor walls and pressed into doorways which offered some shelter from direct musket fire but their situation wasn't very much improved. They couldn't storm the house through the windows where the Cossacks hurled fire and lead right into their faces, so Pan Volodyovski ordered them to chop through the thick wooden doors with axes. But even that was easier to order than accomplish. The main doors of the manor were built along the lines of an old-fashioned castle gate out of overlapping oak planks, generously studded with massive iron nails, which blunted the axe blades and turned them aside. The strongest men threw themselves in vain against those massive portals. Held fast inside with heavy bolts and bars, and further reinforced with logs jammed against their inner surfaces, the doors resisted every effort to batter them down. The Butryms hacked at the main door in grim, silent rage while the Gashtovts and the Domashevitches attacked the side doors that led to the kitchens and the estate strong-room.

Fresh men relieved the attackers after a fruitless hour. Some of the huge iron bosses fell out of the main door, to be replaced at once with musket barrels thrust out by the Cossacks, and gunshots crackled out again. Two more Butryms fell, shot through the chest, but the rest went on hacking the thick oak planks with an added fury. And then, just as it seemed as if the besieged Cossacks would escape their vengeance, safe behind that unbreachable barricade, the Laudanians heard new shouts coming from the road behind them.

"The Stakyans!" someone cried. "The Stakyans are here!"

And the long-delayed Stakyans, who had marched and ridden all night to get to the fighting, spilled out of the shadows, with a great mob of armed Vodokty peasants running behind them to help their young mistress.

★ ★ ★

These reinforcements must have caused dismay among the defenders because, at once, a strong young voice thundered behind the door: "Hold it! Stop that battering! Listen, damn you all! Let's talk!"

Volodyovski ordered a pause in the attack. "Who's speaking there?" he asked.

"Kmita, the Seneshal of Orsha! And who are you?"

"Michal Volodyovski, colonel of the Grand Hetman's Laudanian Regiment, and a serving officer of the *Voyevode* of Vilna."

"I'm honored," said the voice behind the door.

"Never mind the civilized formalities," Pan Volodyovski snapped back. "What are you doing here?"

"I'd be more justified in asking what you are doing here," Pan Kmita replied. "We've never met, you and I. We don't know each other. So why are you attacking me in my own house?"

"Enough of this, you traitor!" Pan Michal shouted back. "These men with me are Laudanian gentry who have a few accounts to settle with you! They charge you with banditry and murder, and they want satisfaction for the innocent blood you've spilled, and now you've added abduction to your record! And do you know the penalty for crimes against women? You'll pay with your head for that!"

There was a moment of silence behind the scarred portals and then Kmita's calm voice sounded out again.

"You wouldn't call me a traitor again if it wasn't for these doors that keep us apart."

"So open them! Who's stopping you?"

"A lot of your Laudanian mongrels will turn belly-up before that happens here," Kmita laughed. "You won't take me alive!"

"Then we'll drag your dead carcass out of there by your heels. It's all one to us, whichever you choose."

"Is it? Well, here's a piece of news for you. I've a powder barrel right here beside me and the fuse is lit. If you don't leave me alone and get out of here I'll blow up the house, myself and all of us inside, so help me God! You hear that? Now try to come and take me!"

★ ★ ★

The silence that fell then was even longer than before. Pan Volodyovski wondered how to answer. The gathered Laudanians stared in horror at each other. There was no doubt in anybody's mind that Kmita was reckless enough to do as he said: one angry impulse on his part would rob them of vengeance, shatter all their hopes for legal compensation, and Panna Aleksandra would be lost beyond any possibility of rescue.

"God help us!" one of the Butryms muttered. "That Devil's mad enough to do it!"

But Pan Volodyovski gave some thought to what he knew of Kmita; the young ruffian's own self-confidence and pride, he believed, might offer a better solution.

"There's another way!" he cried out. "Come out here, you traitor, and fight me man to man! If you win you'll go free!"

This time the silence was so deep that the little knight thought he could hear the hearts pounding in all the chests around him.

"A sword fight?" Kmita asked at last. "Yes, that could solve the problem..."

"It will unless you're a coward!"

"Don't worry about that. But do I have your word as a gentleman that I'll go free?"

"You have it."

"Never!" fierce voices shouted among the Butryms.

"Quiet, damn you!" Volodyovski thundered at them. "I'm in charge here! Either keep quiet or let him blast himself and every one of you to kingdom come!"

The Butryms quietened down at once and, after a moment, one of them muttered: "Ay... what choice do we have? It'll be as you want it, sir..."

"What now, then?" Kmita jeered. "Will your clodhoppers go along with that?

"They'll swear to it if you want."

"On what? Are they carrying crucifixes with them nowadays?"

"On the crosspiece of their sabers, what else?"

"Let them swear!"

"Gather around gentlemen! Gather 'round!" Pan Volodyovski called out to the Laudanians who stood spread out against the wall all around the house. "I take you all as witnesses that I challenged Pan Kmita, the Seneshal of Orsha, to single combat, and that I swore to him that he'll go free if he comes out the winner. I also pledge to him that none of you will interfere with his leaving which is something all of you must swear on God and His cross..."

"But wait a minute!" Kmita interrupted. "All my men and the young lady will be free to go with me as well!"

"The lady stays here," Volodyovski said at once. "And your men will become the property of this gentry."

"Out of the question!"

"Then go ahead and blow yourself up!" Pan Volodyovski shouted, annoyed and in no mood for haggling. "We've already wept over that poor young woman you've abducted. And as for you, the quicker you're in Hell the better!"

There was another moment of protracted silence while Kmita thought it over, and everyone else waited, hardly able to breathe in their anxiety.

"Alright then," Kmita said, agreeing. "Let it be as you want for now. If I don't carry her off today I'll do it next month. There's no way that you'll keep her from me! Now get on with the swearing!"

"Swear!" Pan Volodyovski ordered.

"We swear it," the massed Laudanians chorused. "By God and His cross. Amen!"

And then the iron bars that held the portals closed from the inside began to grate open.

★ ★ ★

Pan Volodyovski stepped back to give Kmita room, and the massed Laudanians followed his example. The doors opened and Kmita came out. The little knight saw a tall young man, as slim and lithe as a linden tree, and bursting with health, strength, and power. He stood in the pale new light of a returning day, which brushed across his haughty features and his harsh, set face, looking at his enemies almost with indifference.

"Well, I take you at your word," Kmita said at last. "God only knows if I should but it's too late to worry about that. Which one of you is Pan Volodyovski?"

The little knight stepped forward. "I am," he said.

"You? Hmm." Kmita seemed amused. "I can't say you're exactly a Colossus, eh? I expected someone of more substantial stature though I'll admit that you're a damn good soldier."

"Well, I can't say the same about a commander who forgets to post his guards," the little colonel shrugged. "If you're as good with a saber as you are at elementary tactics I won't work up a sweat with you this morning."

"Where do you want to fight?" Kmita asked, annoyed.

"Right here will do. The courtyard's as flat as a table top."

"Good enough. Get ready to die, then."

"Are you that sure you'll win?"

"I see you've never been to the Orsha country if you've any doubts about that!" Kmita snapped abruptly, then softened his tone. "I'm even feeling a little sorry for you, because I've heard of you as a first-rate soldier. That's why I'm telling you once more and for the last time: leave me alone and forget about this. We don't know each other, so why are you getting in my way?"

"You know why!"

"The girl is mine by her grandfather's will," Kmita said and shrugged. "And so's this property. So I'm taking only what belongs to me..."

Then he stared boldly at the Laudanians as if daring them to voice a contradiction, shrugged again, and his voice took on a note that bordered on regret.

"It's true I raided those people in Volmontov, but let God judge who struck the first blow. Maybe my officers were a rough and self-willed lot, and maybe they weren't, but that's not the point. What matters is that they did no harm to anyone around here, but they were slaughtered like wild dogs just because they wanted to dance with some girls in a tavern. Blood calls for blood, doesn't it? And what about the rest of my soldiers? I'll swear on God's wounds that I didn't come to these parts with any bad intentions, and how was I received...?

"Still,"— and he shrugged again—"let one injury pay for the other and let's call it quits. I'll even add something of my own, like a neighbor, to pay for the damage. I'd rather do it that way than any other..."

"And where did you get these Cossacks you've brought here this time?" Volodyovski broke in.

"That's my affair." The haughty tone returned at once to Kmita's harsh voice. "But I didn't hire them against our country, if that's what you're thinking. They're here on my business."

"Is that so?" Cold scorn gripped Pan Volodyovski's voice. "You get help from the enemy to settle your personal affairs, eh? And how will you pay for that help if not with new treason? No, laddie, this won't wash! I wouldn't interfere with any kind of peace you might make with this gentry, but calling in the enemy is another matter. You won't weasel your way out of that one, fellow! So enough of this talking! Take your position right now and get on with it, because I know you're starting to shake in your boots, even though you call yourself an Orshan fencing master."

"So be it," Kmita said grimly, shrugged with contempt, and took up his stance.

But Pan Volodyovski was suddenly in no hurry to begin the duel. He didn't draw his saber. Instead he looked up at the sky where a blue-grey dawn had begun to spread, while the first golden ribbon of the rising sun streaked the dark horizon in the east. The bright glow deepened as he watched, the night crept away, but the courtyard was still sheathed in shadows near the manor house which seemed crouched in darkness.

"Looks like a fine morning," Pan Volodyovski remarked in a pleasant tone, and drew his saber almost as an afterthought. "But it's still some time before we have full daylight. Would you like some torches so you can see better?"

"It's all one to me," Kmita said.

"Hey, gentlemen!" Pan Volodyovski called out to the Laudanians. "How about getting us a few lights for this Orshan dance?"

His lighthearted tone put a new spirit in the uneasy gentry who set off to the kitchens after firewood, while others picked up the torches trampled in the fighting, and in a short time fifty scarlet flames leaped up in the courtyard.

"Looks like a real funeral procession, doesn't it," Pan Volodyovski murmured, pointing with the end of his saber to the red glitter in the murky twilight.

"They're burying their colonel," Kmita said at once. "So why shouldn't there be a show?"

"Quite a dragon, aren't you. A real fire-eater."

Meanwhile the gentry backed away to form a silent circle around the two knights. All the torches lifted high into the air; the crowd peered across each other's shoulders, curious to see two expert swordsmen at work against each other, and uneasy that Kmita might get away; and the duelists watched each other with cool, measuring eyes.

Pan Volodyovski seemed as merry as a lark on a sunny morning.

Kmita was still as death.

The silence was so absolute that the watchers heard the hiss of the torches as clearly as if they were burning right next to their ears.

"Begin!" Kmita said.

Chapter Twelve

THE FIRST CLASH of the sabers seemed to strike an echo in the heart of each man who crowded to watch the duel. Pan Volodyovski struck a light blow, as if he didn't care about it one way or another. Pan Kmita parried easily and struck in his own turn, the little knight turned the blow aside, and then the dry clatter of the sword blades picked up speed and purpose.

Kmita attacked with fury, as if he wished to dazzle and overwhelm his small antagonist with sheer dash and power, but Pan Volodyovski seemed almost asleep. He thrust his left hand behind his back and stood as quietly and as unconcerned as if nothing of any great importance was happening around him. His right hand hardly moved, making small, barely noticeable gestures as if he only wanted to protect himself from the hurricane of blows that flashed around his head.

The watching gentry held its breath, fascinated by that untroubled calmness, and it was quickly clear to them all that their little colonel was merely testing his dangerous opponent. Once in a while he took a small step backwards. Sometimes he stepped forward. His saber seemed to move by its own volition. Kmita struck with passion that bordered on anger but Pan Volodyovski was as cool as a teacher instructing a student, and as the duel heated up he only grew calmer.

At last, to the astonishment of the Laudanians, he began to chat quietly with the exasperated Kmita.

"A little conversation might pass the time," he said. "This won't be quite as boring. Aha, so that's the Orshan method? Looks like you Smolensk gentry must do your own threshing because you're better suited to waving a flail than a saber. Are you really the best among the Orshans? Hmm... That stroke is in fashion only among court bailiffs. That one's from Courland, not bad for scaring mongrels with a cudgel. Watch the end of your saber, mister. Don't bend your wrist like that or you'll see a little game called 'Pick-it-up.' You're not listening! Watch it! Now... pick it up!"

The last phrase came with particular insistence as Pan Volodyovski made a swift, half-circular motion with his hand, drew his weapon sharply back towards him, and before anyone grasped what he was saying, Kmita's saber flew out of his fingers like a piece of thread whisked out of a needle, whirled in the air above Volodyovski's head and clattered on the cobble stones behind him.

"That's called saber-plucking," he said.

Kmita stood swaying like a drunken man, pale as a sheet with humiliation, and staring at the little soldier with disbelieving eyes. Meanwhile Volodyovski stepped aside, pointed to Kmita's fallen sword, and said once more:

"Pick it up!"

It looked for a moment as if Kmita would throw himself barehanded on his small tormentor. He was already poised to leap, and Pan Volodyovski brought his saber-hilt against his own chest to point the curved blade towards the maddened Orshan, but Kmita hurled himself at his fallen weapon, seized it and charged his unruffled opponent.

The Laudanians were as used to sword fights as any other gentry but none of them ever saw anything like this anywhere before. Loud murmurs swelled among them. Their watching circle tightened and thickened with fresh ranks of amazed observers as newcomers crowded up behind them, including Kmita's Cossacks who pushed their heads in among the gentry as if all of them had lived in perfect harmony all their lives.

Spontaneous cries burst out of them now and then as they recognized a master swordsman of truly legendary dimensions. Sometimes they gave vent to a shout of nervous, uncontrollable laughter as he toyed with the shamed and humiliated Kmita, paying him even less attention than a bored cat might give to a trapped rodent that had lost its flavor.

His saber strokes seemed so indifferent as to be contemptuous.

He thrust his left hand carelessly into the pocket of his breeches, not even bothering to keep a swordsman's stance, while Kmita gasped in shame and snarled in helpless fury with flecks of spittle foaming on his mouth.

At last a thick, grating sound strained out of his whitened, tightly-clenched lips.

"Finish it," he muttered. "Spare me... the shame!"

"As you wish," Volodyovski said.

There was a sudden, swift hiss of steel through the air along with a quick half-strangled cry, and then Kmita threw his arms as wide as if they were nailed to a cross, the saber tumbled from his hand, and he fell facedown at the feet of the little colonel.

"He's still alive," Pan Volodyovski observed dispassionately. "Or he'd have fallen on his back."

Then he stooped and started to clean his saber blade on Kmita's coat-tails.

* * *

The gentry bellowed with a single shout of joy and amazement, but suddenly other fierce cries boomed out among the Butryms who rushed out of the circle with drawn sabers raised above their heads.

"Finish him off, the traitor! Kill him! Cut him into pieces!"

And then the Laudanians saw something even more astonishing than the surprising duel. Their little colonel seemed to spring upward, and to grow to a size that towered above them all; the saber of the nearest Butrym flew out of his fist in just the same way that Kmita's had done only moments earlier; and Pan Volodyovski's voice lashed at them like a thunderbolt.

"Keep away!" he roared while a strange, deadly light glittered in his eyes. "Back off! He's mine now, not yours, you hear? Back away!"

The huge Butryms, cowed by the small knight's anger, stood at once as if they were rooted in the soil, and he went on in the breathless silence: "I don't need any butchery here! You men are gentry! You ought to understand that gentlemen don't finish off a wounded opponent. One doesn't do that even to an enemy, not to mention someone wounded in a duel."

"He's a traitor!" grunted one of the sullen Butryms. "That kind deserves killing."

"If he's a traitor then he should be handed over for justice to the Hetman so that his punishment may be a warning to others of his kind. Anyway, he's mine now, not yours, and I decide what to do with him. If he licks himself back to health you can get at him through the courts and you'll get a lot more out of him that way than if he was dead. Understood? Alright then, who's the best field-surgeon among you?"

"Kris Domashevitch," the Laudanians chorused. "He's been patching up everybody in the Lauda for years."

"Good. Let him dress his wound. Then get him on a bed inside while I go to console that unfortunate young woman."

* * *

Having said his piece, Pan Volodyovski sheathed his saber and pushed into the house through the battered portals. The gentry at once began hunting down and roping Kmita's disarmed Cossacks, who would become their servants, serfs and plowmen from now on. Only a few of these tried to get away, jumping out of the rear windows and bolting for the woods, but there they ran into the waiting Stakyans. The rest surrendered without much resistance. Meanwhile the victorious Laudanians set about looting the packed wagons where they found rich booty. Some of them wanted to pillage the house as well, but they were held back by the recollection of Pan Volodyovski's anger and the awareness that this used to be Billevitch property, and that Aleksandra was somewhere inside.

In the meantime the little knight searched for the girl throughout the entire building and finally found her in the manor strong-room, behind a thick, narrow door off the sleeping chamber in the far corner of the house. This was a small square cubicle with heavily barred windows no wider than loopholes, enclosed by stone walls of such depth and thickness that—as Pan Volodyovski could tell at a glance—it would have escaped any damage in the suicidal explosion that Kmita had threatened.

'Hmm, he thought at once. *'So he's not quite as bad as I thought he was. At least he wouldn't have taken his poor captive with him.'*

She meanwhile, this poor captive he had come to rescue, sat on a large, iron-bound money chest not far from the door, keeping her head lowered in what seemed like the utmost hopelessness and grief, and her face quite hidden by her long, loosened hair.

She gave no sign that she heard his entrance and he supposed at once that she took him for one of Kmita's men, or perhaps her fallen abductor himself. So he stood by the narrow little door, not quite knowing how to announce himself, and feeling more foolish with each passing minute.

"My lady," he tried at last. "You're free."

He was expecting an outburst of joy, perhaps an outpouring of grateful thanks as well, but the unnerving sky-blue eyes that lifted towards him from under that mass of tumbled pale hair showed no comprehension, and the beautiful face at which he stared, dumbstruck with amazement, was as still and lifeless and empty of feeling as the stone walls around her.

"You're free," he tried again. "Try to understand. God took mercy on your innocence. You can go back to Vodokty any time you wish."

This time Billevitchovna seemed to understand him. She rose, brushed her hair aside with a steadier hand, and asked: "Who are you, sir?"

"Michal Volodyovski," he introduced himself. "Colonel of Dragoons in the service of the *Voyevode* of Vilna."

"I heard battle sounds... gunfire?" Her voice was gradually returning to normal. "What happened?"

"We came to your rescue."

And now the young woman returned to full awareness of everything around her.

"Thank you!" she murmured rapidly in a quiet voice in which the little knight could hear a note of anxiety and fear. "And that other man...? What happened to him...?"

"Kmita? Don't worry, m'lady. He's stretched out in the courtyard. And by my own hand, I might add."

The little soldier said this with a touch of vanity, hoping to see a gleam of admiration in those sky-blue eyes, but he was sorely disappointed by what he saw instead. The young woman didn't say a word in reply. Instead she swayed as if struck a painful and violent blow, started to grope behind her for something firm to lean on, and finally sat heavily back on the chest from which she had risen.

Volodyovski leaped at once towards her. "What's wrong, m'lady? Are you ill?"

"It's... nothing. Nothing." He saw that she was struggling for composure. "Give me a moment, sir... Permit me... So Pan Kmita is dead?"

"To the Devil with Kmita!" he cried out, interrupting. "It's you I'm worried about just now!"

But these words seemed to restore all her strength and courage. She rose again, stared straight into his eyes and cried out in a voice full of anger, impatience and despair: "For God's sake tell me! Is he dead?"

"Pan Kmita is wounded," the little soldier muttered in surprise.

"He's alive?"

"Yes. He's alive."

"Good," she murmured. "Thank you!" And then she took a few uncertain steps towards the door and the main rooms of the house beyond it.

Pan Volodyovski waited a moment longer, shaking his head in bewilderment, and moving his pointed little whiskers up and down as he tried to understand the young woman's strange response to news of her rescue.

"Is she thanking me for wounding Kmita?" he muttered and scratched his head, surprised and confused. "Or for not killing him...?"

And then he followed the young woman into the main house.

* * *

He found her standing as still as if she'd turned to stone in the middle of the adjoining bed chamber, while four Laudanians were carrying in the unconscious Kmita. The first two edged in sideways through the narrow door, cradling the wounded man's back and shoulders in their arms, while his head dangled lifelessly between them with both eyes closed and dark clots of blood in his matted hair.

"Slowly now!" Kristof Domashevitch urged, moving up behind them. "Easy across that threshold! And hold up his head, one of you, will you?"

"How are we to do that with both arms busy?" they grumbled but, in that moment, Aleksandra stepped forward, just as pale as

Kmita, and placed both her hands like a cradle under his hanging head.

"Ah, is that you, milady?" Kris Domashevitch asked. "Is everything alright with you?"

"Yes," she said in such a quiet voice that it seemed little more than a mere whisper. "Carefully now..."

Pan Volodyovski peered sharply at all this, sensing something odd hidden within this scene that he simply didn't understand, and he moved his little mustache fiercely up and down, which is what he always did whenever he was stirred, puzzled, bewildered or annoyed.

Meanwhile Kmita was lowered to the bed. Kris Domashevitch started to wash the blood out of his hair and then bandaged a ready poultice to the wound.

"That ought to do," he muttered. "All he needs now is to keep still and quiet... Ey, but that's an iron head, and no mistake. You'd think a blow like that would split it in half, wouldn't you? But he's young, maybe he'll recover. Still, that was some blow!"

Then he turned anxiously to the pale Olenka.

"Let me wash your hands, sweetheart, eh?" he offered. "Here, there's some water... But you've got a real merciful heart to get yourself all bloodied up over a man like that."

Talking to her in gentle, soothing tones, the old man started to mop the blood off Olenka's hands, while she flushed and grew deathly white in turn, torn between a variety of conflicting feelings.

"There's nothing more for you to do here, m'lady," Pan Volodyovski said firmly and moved towards her as if to step between her and the wounded Kmita. "You've shown your Christian charity to an enemy and now go back home!"

And he trotted forward with an expectant smile, offering her his arm, so that the two of them could walk out of the house together. But she never even glanced at him. Instead, turning to the Domashevitch patriarch, she asked him in a low, hushed voice to lead her outside.

They left the room with the little knight trailing disconsolately in their wake, puzzled and somewhat out of sorts and wondering what he'd done to make her so upset.

"You'd think I was the miscreant and abductor here," he grumbled to himself. "Not the rescuer. Why is she so angry?"

The massed farmer-gentry greeted them with cheers, saluting their young heiress along with their colonel, but she walked through their ranks with a cold, angry fire in her eyes, swaying unsteadily as if about to fall, and with her pale lips pressed tightly into a bitter line.

Chapter Thirteen

AN HOUR LATER Pan Volodyovski rode back towards the settlements at the head of his victorious Laudanians. The sun had climbed high into the sky. The fresh Spring morning was as bright and cheerful as if it were Summer. The Laudanians trailed behind him in a loose, carefree crowd spread without order all over the highway, chatting about the events of the night and singing the praises of their little colonel, but he sat on his saddle without a word.

He couldn't shake himself free of his remembered image of those bright blue eyes looking up at him out of that mass of fallen, gleaming hair, and the quiet, imposing dignity of that tall, slim figure.

"Amazing how beautiful she is," he muttered to himself. "A real princess... Hmm. I saved her life, that's certain, and perhaps her innocence as well, because even if that strong-room held together in the blast she'd have died of fright. She ought to be grateful, oughtn't she? Instead she glared at me as if I was some kind of stable groom when I offered her my arm. Was it just pride? Could be. Or was she still confused? Ah, who can make out what goes on in a woman's head..."

Such thoughts and others like them kept the puzzled young man awake through the night and troubled him all morning. He remembered that the Laudanians wanted to marry her to him and the idea was suddenly terribly attractive. True, she had turned him down that last time without a moment's thought, but that was before she knew anything about him. Now, however, everything was different! He had torn her out of the hands of an abductor, facing swords and bullets in the process, so that she was, in effect, like a fortress he had stormed and captured.

Who had more right to her?

So why not try again?

Folk tales were full of legends about rescued maidens giving their hearts and hands to the knights who saved them, and who could tell if her gratitude wouldn't turn, in time, into a powerful attraction? And if, for some reason he didn't understand, she didn't seem all that fond of him at first sight it was all the more important to try to win her over.

But then another thought intruded. What if she still loves and thinks about that other fellow?

"No, that can't be," Pan Michal reassured himself. "If she hadn't sent him packing in the first place, he wouldn't have tried to carry her off by force."

She's young, he argued with himself. Unprotected. It's time she got married. All kinds of gallants would be pestering her from now on, that only stood to reason. Some will have an eye on her property, others will be drawn by her stunning beauty, yet others will be sniffing after a connection with her family. She should be pleased to have a defender who has already proved what he can do!

"Ey, and it's high time for you too, my lad, to settle down a bit," Pan Michal told himself. "You're still young but the years run quickly. You won't earn your fortune in the service, that's certain, and old wounds make poor companions when the hair turns grey. Besides, there's even more to this marriage business. Once you've tied the knot, you'll be able to get all those other girls out of your mind as well!"

And here Pan Volodyovski heaved a sigh, remembering a whole procession of pretty young women whom he pursued fervently but unsuccessfully all his turbulent young life. There were some real beauties among them, connected with great houses of truly ancient lineage, but none of them seemed dearer to him just then, or better born and worthy, than Panna Aleksandra.

He felt that he had stumbled across a stroke of quite amazing luck that wasn't likely to repeat itself, especially since he'd also managed to render this remarkable young woman such an extraordinary service.

"So why wait?" he mused. "Why put it off? Am I going to get a better chance than this? Where? When? How? Great fortunes smile only once so let's go courting and be done with it."

But one other thought got in the way of this perfect vision of his well-earned happiness and ease. A new war was coming any day. It isn't right, he thought, for a knight to play the gallant lover while his threatened country cried out for his services in the field. Pan Michal was a soldier to the bone, and although he spent all his life in harness, starting off when he was still practically a lad and fighting in every war that broke out in his times, he knew what he owed to the land which he called his own and never thought about rest or comfort for himself.

On the other hand, the same awareness told him that since he served his country honestly and with all his heart, asking for nothing and expecting little more than wounds, hunger and lean times, his conscience was clear. He didn't have to question his motives, as some others might. He'd proved his selflessness, patriotism and fidelity, and this reminder filled him with fresh confidence and a powerful sense of his own worth and value.

'*Others had their good times and pulled strings on their own behalf,*' he thought. '*I fought. Surely that means something. The good Lord is sure to help me out and reward me now.*'

He also reasoned that since there was no time for protracted courtships he had to act quickly. All he had left, so to speak, was one throw of the dice: go to Vodokty, propose on the spot, and then either marry right away or get the gate and forget about it.

"I've got the gate before, I can get it again," he muttered over and over, and twitched his little yellow mustache like a beetle feeling his way through familiar air. "What harm will it do me?"

But, he worried, won't this sudden courtship, coming so soon after his rescue of the beautiful young heiress, seem like the badgering of a money-lender who wants his debts paid in full and with interest as fast as he can?

"Maybe that's not a gentlemanly thing to do," he mused and racked his head for some more honorable solution. Would she think it vulgar?

"But how can one expect gratitude and goodwill unless there was some service to begin with?" he reasoned. And if his precipitous proposal seems a bit distasteful to the girl, if she feels slighted by it, he'd always be able to say: *'My lady, I'd gladly spend a year coming over to court you, but I'm a soldier and the war is calling!'*

"So why not? I'll do it!" Pan Volodyovski told himself. "I'll ride right over there and do it!"

But, after a moment, another doubt presented itself, because what would happen if she said to him: *'Go to your war then, Mister Soldier. And after you've come back you can take your time and do your courting like it should be done, because I won't give my heart and hand to a man I don't even know.'*

If she said that, he knew, all chance would be gone. Delay would be fatal. The war might take years. Some other man might sweep the girl off her feet while he was away. But the greatest threat to his hopes, he knew, would lie in himself. He knew better than to trust his own constancy in matters of the heart. Love blazed up in him as hot and quick as fire in dry straw and died just as swiftly, and he knew that unless he had a wife to come home to, one to whom he would give all his loyalty and faith, he'd keep on wandering all his life from camp to camp, from battle to battle and from one pair of bright little eyes to another, without a warm roof over his head and no nearer to some dear, loving soul than he had ever been!

In the end Pan Volodyovski didn't know what to do about this, what to decide or which course to follow, especially since he'd never been much for pondering and thinking.

★ ★ ★

Because all this head-scratching was giving him a headache, and because there seemed to be no air left to breathe in his pleasant Patzunel retreat, Pan Volodyovski jammed a cap on his head and went outside to fill his lungs with some fresh May air. But on the threshold of the little manor he came across one of Kmita's raiders who had been turned over to old Pakosh Gash-tovt as his share of the Lubitch booty. The Cossack was sunning himself on the porch and picking a few glum notes out of the triangular eight-string Ruthenian mandolin that all young Cossacks learned to play as part of their courting.

"What are you doing here?" Pan Volodyovski asked.

"Picking a few tunes, master," the Cossack sighed in answer, lifting a worn young face which seemed as gaunt and harrowed as a beggar's.

"Where are you from?" Pan Michal went on, not really caring one way or another but glad to have an excuse to interrupt his musing.

"From far off, master. Far..."

"So why didn't you run off like the rest of your captured comrades? What a bunch of ingrates you men turned out to be! The gentry spared your lives in Lubitch so that they'd have someone to work their soil and you bolted just as soon as your ropes were off!"

"Not me, master," the young Cossack said. "I'll stay put here till I'm dead."

"You like it here so much, then?"

"Who's better off in the Steppe, let him run. I'm better off here. I had a bullet through my leg, and this young lady, one of the old man's daughters, wrapped it up for me and said a kind word too. I've never seen a better-looking girl, or a kinder one, in all my born days. So why should I leave?"

"Which one of them was it?"

"Maryska."

"And it's for her you're staying? Are you hoping to earn her from old Pakosh with your work?"

"Who can tell."

"He'd sooner put a bullet in a Steppe buck like you than give him his daughter."

"I've got gold buried in the woods," the Cossack said quietly. "Enough to fill my cap a couple of times over."

"From what? Banditry?"

"If that's what people call it."

"Well, even if you had a whole sack of gold it wouldn't do you any good with Pakosh." Pan Michal yawned and shrugged. "He's gentry and you're a peasant."

"I come from petty boyars."

"Well, if you're from the small Ruthenian gentry then you're worse than a peasant because you're a traitor. How could you fight for the enemy against the Commonwealth?"

"I didn't," the young Cossack said.

"So where did Kmita get all you men if it wasn't from Zoltarenko and Trubetzkoy?"

"From the highway, master. I served with the Field Hetman till the regiment fell apart 'cause there wasn't anything to eat. I couldn't go home because it's long gone. Burned, looted, who knows. Others went robbing on the highways so I went there too."

Pan Volodyovski stared at him in surprise because, like everyone else in the Lauda country, he thought that Kmita seized Olenka with raiders borrowed from the Russians.

"You mean Kmita didn't get you from Trubetzkoy?"

"Most of my lot rode with Trubetzkoy or Hovansky before they took off robbing on the highways. But Pan Kmita got us on the road."

"So why did you enlist with him?"

"'Cause he's a famous ataman, and a great war leader."

"So are a lot of others. So why did you pick him?"

"People say that signing up with him is as good as getting a bagful of silver. That's why we joined him. But God didn't give us any luck."

Pan Volodyovski shook his head in wonder, thinking that perhaps Kmita wasn't quite as bad as everyone supposed, and then he stared thoughtfully down at the pale young boyar and shook his head again.

"And you really love that girl so much that you'd stay here, working like a dog, just so you can be near her?"

"That's how it is, master."

* * *

Pan Volodyovski walked away, thinking that this was a stubborn and determined fellow and that it was determination that always won the day.

"He doesn't rack his head about what to do," he muttered in gloom. "He fell in love and he's staying put and that's all there's to it as far as he's concerned! That's the best kind of man, the steadiest and most loyal. If he really comes from the petty boyars then he's the same kind as our farmer-gentry. Once he digs out his pot of gold old Pakosh might relent and give him his daughter. And why? Because he didn't waste time scratching his head about this and that but dug in his heels and went after her! Well, I can dig in my heels just as well!"

Thinking and muttering to himself in this fashion, Pan Volodyovski walked on along the sunlit track, stopping now and then to stare at the ground or to raise his eyes into the brilliant sky, and then he caught sight of a flight of wild ducks passing overhead and started counting them in search of an omen.

"I'll go... I won't go... I'll go..."

The count came out in favor of going.

"Alright! So I'll go!"

And the little knight turned back towards the house. But, on the way, he stopped at the stables where his two grooms, Ogarek and Syrutz, were sitting in the sun and throwing dice to amuse themselves.

"Syrutz," Pan Michal said. "Did you plait Basior's mane today?"

"I did, colonel." The young servant lad scrambled to his feet. "Why, sir? Are we going somewhere?"

"Hmm. Maybe. I'll see."

Pan Volodyovski went into the stable. His horse caught his scent and neighed softly at him from beside the manger and the little knight drew near, patted the stallion's side, and started counting the plaits on Basior's neck.

"Go... stay... go..."

And again the count came out in favor of riding to Vodokty.

"Saddle the horses!" Pan Volodyovski ordered the two grooms, coming out into the sunlight with his mind finally made up. "And get dressed decently yourselves!"

Then he marched swiftly into the Gashtovt house and started hunting for his best uniform and his richest-looking accouterments and equipment. He picked out his best pair of long, Swedish boots of bright yellow leather with wide, ornamental flaps pulled up high on the thigh, and with gilded spurs screwed into the heels, and put on a brand new scarlet coat and breeches. Across his shoulder he hung a handsome leather baldric into which he slipped a rapier in a polished steel scabbard with some gold wire threads worked into the guard and, across his upper chest and neck, he buckled a half-cuirass burnished as bright as silver. He also owned a new lynx-fur cap with a fine heron feather but since that went better with a Polish costume he donned a rimmed Swedish helmet, the kind known as a Morion, with a sharp, round crest curving along the top and with up-swept narrow points in the front and rear.

Thus dressed, he went out onto the porch where old Pakosh Gashtovt eyed him with curiosity.

"Ah, and where is Your Excellency off to, then?" he asked.

"Where am I off to? Hmm." Pan Michal cleared his throat and twisted the waxed points of his yellow mustache. "I thought I'd... ah... ride over to Vodokty. It's only right I should ask after your young lady's health, as good manners call for, or she might take me for some kind of oaf."

"Hee hee," the old man giggled. "It's like there's a glow coming from Your Honor... All those colors! A robin could hardly find brighter red feathers for himself. Our lady would have to be as blind as a fencepost not to fall in love straight away... Hee hee!"

The two younger Gashtovt girls came back just then from their morning milking, each carrying a filled wooden pitcher, but at the sight of Pan Volodyovski both stood as still with astonishment as a pair of startled forest does.

"Is that a King?" Zonia asked, her bright blue eyes wide open with amazement.

"You're dressed as if you were going to a wedding," Maryska whispered with worshipful admiration.

"Could be!" the old man chortled. "There could be a wedding out of it! Because he's going to Vodokty, calling on our lady."

At once the milk pitcher slipped out of Maryska's hand, bounced on the ground before her, and spilled its contents almost as far as Pan Volodyovski's boots.

"Be careful there, you silly young goat!" the old man roared at her. "Watch what you are doing!"

Maryska said nothing. She picked up the wooden pitcher and walked quietly away.

Pan Volodyovski mounted his horse, his two grooms formed up behind him, and the three of them trotted off in the direction of Vodokty. The day, he thought, couldn't have been more promising. The soft May sunlight played on the little knight's polished cuirass and helmet as if another, smaller sun was moving among the birches planted by the road, and he wondered, somewhat nervously, what the result of this expedition would be.

"Am I going to come back with a ring in my hand or a burr

in my tail?" he asked himself aloud and Syrutz hurried forward to ask what he said.

"That you're a fool!" he snapped.

The lad fell back, confused.

"Well, if I get the gate, it won't be the first time," Pan Volodyovski answered his own question, and got a sudden burst of confidence out of it, because there was some reassurance to be found, in love as in war, in something familiar.

Chapter Fourteen

ALEKSANDRA DIDN'T RECOGNIZE Pan Volodyovski when he rode into Vodokty and he had to introduce himself all over again. But once she heard his name she received him with the courtesy any wellborn caller could expect. If she was pale, withdrawn and somewhat distracted he took it for a natural consequence of her recent shock and thought no more about it. He was no courtier but neither was he a stranger to polite behavior so he put on a creditable performance as he bowed with a deep flourish, his hand on his heart, and launched into his speech.

"I came to ask after your ladyship's health," he began formally then added: "I should have come over sooner, perhaps the next day, but I didn't want to make a nuisance of myself."

She answered him in kind, as distant and polite as the usage of the time demanded of a young woman in her circumstances. "It's kind of you, sir, that having rescued me from such a peril you're still concerned about me. Sit down, won't you? You're always welcome here."

"My dear lady!" Pan Michal said in turn. "If I forgot about you I'd be unworthy of that grace and mercy that God sent my way by allowing me to come to your rescue."

He thought it quite a graceful little speech and cocked his ears for some responding signal but Aleksandra remained troubled and remote.

"No, it's I who should be thanking God," she answered politely. "And you too soon after..."

Pan Volodyovski hoped for a better opening but he would take whatever came his way. He thought that courting wasn't all that different from that Chinese game of strategy called 'chess' which the Persians and the Mongols brought from the East a hundred years earlier; young officers used chessboards to study the elements of tactics on which the classic Polish battlefield formations were based.

"Ah, if that's so then let's both thank Him. Together, as it were. Because I ask for nothing better than to defend you from now on whenever you need me."

Pleased with this bold gambit which moved the game right into the heart of the matter, Pan Volodyovski patted himself mentally on the back and started twitching the points of his upturned little whiskers which thrust into the air higher than the end of his uptilted nose. She, in turn, sat in silence and in some confusion. A pale flush appeared on her cheeks and her lowered lashes threw a line of shadow.

'*Hmm... That's a good sign,*' Pan Volodyovski thought, and clearing his throat in a manner he hoped might make him sound more dignified and profound, he advanced another cautious pawn. "You know, of course, my lady, that I was the commander of the Laudanians after your grandfather?"

"Indeed I do," she said quietly. "Grandfather was too ill to go on the last campaign but he was terribly pleased to hear whom the Prince-Palatine of Vilna entrusted with his regiment. He said that he knew you by your reputation as a famous soldier."

"He did, did he? Hmm."

"I heard him myself. He thought the world of you. And the Laudanians said the same thing later on."

Still young enough for flattery, no matter how sincerely spoken and well-earned, Pan Volodyovski liked praise as much as anyone. But he thought that he had better steer the conversation into an area where he could tell Aleksandra more about his background.

"I'm just a soldier," he shrugged and said simply. "Not worth much more notice than most of my kind. But I'm glad that you've heard a little about me because now I won't seem like some unknown guest that nobody ever heard of and whom the wind blew in from God knows where. It's always good to know with whom one is dealing, don't you think? There are a lot of men wandering around these days who claim high birth and offices for themselves and some of them aren't even gentry."

"No one would think that of you," Olenka said at once. "Because we have gentry of the same name here in Lithuania."

This gave the little knight the opening he hoped for.

"It's a different clan."

* * *

He explained that his full family name was Kortchak-Volody-ovski, that his ancestors came from Hungary, descending from one of Attila's nobles who was obliged to run for his life and who took an oath that he'd become a Christian if the Holy Mother helped him to save himself.

"Which he did," the little knight concluded. "After he put three rivers between himself and his enemies. And now you'll find those three rivers in my coat-of-arms."

"So you're not from these parts by birth?" Olenka asked quietly.

"No, my lady. I'm one of the Ruthenian Volodyovskis, from the Ukraine, and I own a little village there to this day even though it's long been taken over by the enemy. But I never paid much attention to it anyway, being less concerned about property than the dangers that threatened our country from its various neighbors, and serving as a soldier since I was a boy. I served first under our late-lamented Prince Yeremi, the *Voyevode* of Ruthenia, under whom I fought at Mahnovka and at Konstantinov and in the siege of Zbarajh in the Cossack Wars, and after the battle of Berestetchko His Majesty himself singled me out for praise. God is my witness that I didn't come here to boast or blow my own trumpet. I'm saying all this just so you'll know I'm not some fair-weather soldier who handles a soup spoon better than a saber, and that I've spent my life in honest service, ready to spill my blood whenever it was needed, and that I kept my name as clean as anyone."

"... If only everyone was like you," Aleksandra murmured.

"Are you thinking about that scoundrel who tried to carry you off by force?" Pan Volodyovski asked, a little surprised.

But she said nothing, staring at the floor.

"Hmm. Well. He was paid off well enough for what he tried to do," Pan Michal resumed, then went on in his straightforward, honest manner, remembering what he'd heard from Maryska's Cossack and willing to be fair. "People say that he'll recover but that won't save him from punishment by the law. He's not quite as bad as he's been painted, by the way, because he didn't get his Cossacks from the enemy but off the public highways."

"What?" Olenka asked swiftly, fixing her eyes in quick anxiety on Pan Volodyovski's face. "How do you know that?"

"From one of his men. He's a strange fellow, this Kmita, I've got to admit it. I called him a traitor to his face just before the duel and he didn't say one word to defend himself. He must be as proud as the Devil."

"But he is not a traitor?"

"No. It seems he isn't."

"And is this what you're telling everyone about him now?"

"I haven't told anyone yet because I didn't know it myself until today, but I will from now on. That kind of slander is too harsh even for a man's worst enemy. And he has quite enough to answer for without it."

Olenka's eyes, he noted, were resting on him once more with gratitude and respect.

"What a wonderfully decent man you are," she murmured, as if unable to believe that honesty, sincerity and goodness were still possible in a world where selfishness and violence seemed to be the rule. "So decent that it's rare..."

And Pan Volodyovski, pleased with himself and thinking that everything was going just as he hoped it would, started moving his mustache up and down again.

★ ★ ★

'Hmm. *I've struck the right chord somewhere,*' he mused, encouraged by the sudden warmth and gratitude in her eyes, and went on aloud: "I'll say even more! Pan Kmita's way of going about things has to be condemned, particularly where his violence against you is concerned, but it can't be much of a surprise to anyone who has one good eye in his head. Sheer desperation must've pushed him into going after you like that! But what else could he do when he thought he'd lost you?"

She was nodding then, her eyes fixed on him as if he was telling her exactly what she had to hear, and he told himself that he had better make his move, stick closer to the point, and bring the conversation back to his proposal.

"Yes. Desperation. And it'll probably push him in again because you are so beautiful that Venus herself could take lessons from you..."

He paused then, because she made a pained, impatient gesture as if any mention of her beauty was offensive to her after what had happened to the Butryms, but once launched into his own declaration he couldn't turn back.

"How can you stay safe unprotected, looking as you do?" he cried out. "There are more Kmitas in this world, you'll awaken more passions of this kind, and there're sure to be other attempts against you...

"God gave me the chance to save you once," he said earnestly. "But the war horns are already sounding, and who'll protect you after I am gone? My dear lady, soldiers have a somewhat restless reputation in matters of the heart, I know, but that's not quite fair... we aren't all alike!"

And here the little knight threw himself suddenly on his knees before the astonished and frightened Olenka.

"My own heart isn't made out of a rock," he pleaded. "I couldn't stay indifferent to such rare beauty any more than Kmita! I inherited your grandfather's regiment, God rest his soul, let me inherit his right to protect you as well! Allow me to look after you, to taste the sweetness of mutual affection, and take me for your permanent defender! Do that and you'll live safe and unmolested because even if I should go to war my name will be enough to serve as your shield!"

But she had jumped to her feet and was staring at him as if he was a creature of a kind she never saw before, and he went on, still on his knees and missing the effect of his impassioned words on the distressed and angered Aleksandra: "I don't have much in the way of material things but I'm a noble and an honest man. And I can swear to you that you won't find a single stain on either my coat-of-arms or my conscience."

★ ★ ★

Out of breath, and finally noticing that things weren't going quite as he intended, he assumed that it was just a matter of too much thrown at her too quickly and he cast about for some way to put her more at ease.

"I realize I may be... ah... a bit precipitous in my declaration but time is short, you see. I know you'll understand that duty must come first... and that I won't turn a deaf ear to our country's call even for you... So tell me, won't you, that I can at least have a little hope."

"You're asking the impossible!" she cried out, pale as a ghost and trembling with such powerful emotions that the little knight stared up at her in sudden open-mouthed amazement of his own. "Dear God! That's out of the question!"

"Out of the question?" he asked at last, feeling as if she had thrown a bucket of iced water over him, but still not quite able to believe her anger. "Why should it be out of the question? I'd think you could find an answer without a lot of trouble..."

"And that's why I'll tell you straight off: No!"

"No?

"No!"

And the proud young woman's brow furrowed in such shock, pain, impatience and revulsion that it seemed to twist into a mask of horror.

"I owe you a great deal, sir," she said, clasping her arms around herself as if in need of protection against an icy chill. "I won't deny my debt! And I'm quite ready to give you anything you ask except myself. That... I can't!"

But Pan Volodyovski had finally got the point and rose slowly back to his feet.

"You don't want me, eh?" he asked. "Is that it?"

"I can't!"

"And is that your last word on the subject?"

"Last and irrevocable!" she cried.

"But maybe it's only my hurry that's not to your liking? Can't you give me at least a little hope?"

"I can't! I can't, I tell you!"

"Hmm... Yes. I see," the little soldier sounded bitter even to himself. "So I find no more luck or happiness here than I've found elsewhere. So be it."

Hurt pride and disappointment brushed his voice with a quick anger of his own.

"But don't offer me payment for my services, my lady," he snapped out. "That's not what I came for. I didn't ask for your hand to collect a debt but because I felt a great affection for you... Indeed, let me tell you, if you said you'd take me because you felt you had to I'd have to bow out...

"But,"—and here he shrugged, more in contempt for his own failure than for her rejection—"if you won't, you won't, and that's all there's to it. This isn't the first time I've had my nose put out of joint and it's likely not to be the last. It looks like that's what's written for me, always to ask and always to be refused. Well, that's God's will. Don't worry, I won't bother you again. If you don't want me that's fine with me too. I hope you'll find someone who's more to your fancy, even if it's that Kmita who came after you like a Tartar..."

And here a sudden thought occurred to Pan Michal and he cursed himself for failing to guess it before.

"Ah! Maybe that's what makes you so annoyed? Eh? The fact that I pushed my saber between the two of you? Is that what it is?" Angry contempt edged his voice with cruelty and disdain. "But if you can think that his kind is better than mine then I really came to the wrong place!"

Olenka turned away, bowed into her own hands, and cried out "God...! God...! God...!" in such pain and sorrow that it would have melted a cast-iron heart, but Pan Volodyovski was now too upset to pay much attention.

He went out, jumped on his horse without another word and rode away at once.

"I won't set foot in this place again," he told himself out loud.

Syrutz rode up at once to ask what his master said.

"That you're a fool!" Pan Volodyovski snapped.

"That's what Your Honor told me coming the other way," the puzzled lad offered and pulled back his horse to ride beside Ogarek.

* ★ *

Pan Volodyovski was a man of action rather than a thinker: a plain and simple soldier, as he called himself, who took things as they came rather than rack his brain uselessly about them. But he didn't understand Olenka's attitude and his pride was hurt.

"That wasn't exactly a sweet reception I got in that place," he muttered like a small, disappointed bear who had reached out for a honeycomb and got stung instead. "I offered honest feelings and she sent me packing. Ah, it looks like I'll be single as long as I live. What's written is written. To the Devil with that kind of fate, there's just no justice in this world! But what was it about me that she didn't like?"

He furrowed his brow, trying to unravel the unfathomable riddle, and suddenly slapped his thigh.

"I've got it!" he cried out. "She still loves that other fellow! It can't be anything else."

But this illumination didn't clear the clouds off his gloomy face.

"So much the worse for her," he growled after a moment. "Because if she can love him after everything that's happened then she'll always love him. He's already done the worst that he can. Now he'll go to war, earn new respect, mend his reputation, and it would be wrong for any man to interfere with that. In fact an honest man should do his best to help him because it'll all come out to the country's profit in the end...

"That's how it has to be," he muttered glumly after another silence. "He's too good a soldier to abandon in these dangerous times. The country can use a man like that. But what is that special quality that he has? What's his secret? What did he do to win her like that, heart and soul? Some men have that luck. All they do is give a girl a glance and she's all set to jump into fire after them..."

But no amount of thinking solved the mystery for the little soldier and he heaved another deep sigh of bitterness and regret.

"Ah, if there was a way to find out how they do it. Even a clue might help. Then maybe I'd also manage something for myself because it's certain that sheer merit never got anyone very far with women. Pan Zagloba was right to say that a vixen and a woman are the world's most ungrateful and untrustworthy creatures... Ay, it's a real shame that there's nothing for me with that Billevitch beauty, another chance like this one isn't going to come around tomorrow... I wonder, though, will she marry that Kmita or not? She loves him, that's certain, but she's been cruelly disappointed in him, so who knows what she'll end up doing? She might give up the idea of marriage altogether, poor thing, and what a waste that would be! Ay, it's a bitter pill for me to swallow but I've a feeling that things are a lot harder for her just now."

And here the sentimental little knight gave way to sympathy

for the unfortunate young woman, shaking his head sadly and smacking his lips in pity.

"May God look after her!" he sighed. "I don't hold anything against her. Why should I? Getting the gate is nothing new for me, I've been here before, but this is her first taste of suffering, poor girl, and she couldn't ask for a harsher one!"

And then Pan Michal felt a pang of conscience.

"Dammit, but I've acted like a real clown!" he burst out, disgusted with himself. "There she was, hardly able to breathe with all her pain and grief, and I had to stick pins in her about Kmita's failings! May the Devil take me if that was a gentlemanly thing to do! I'll write her a letter straight away, asking her forgiveness, and after that I'll help her the best way I can."

★　★　★

Further reflections of that kind had to be put aside because Syrutz trotted up just then and drew Pan Volodyovski's attention to a pair of riders who appeared on the wooded slope ahead.

"Looks like Pan Kharlamp, master, along with some other man," he said.

"Where?"

"Up there, master. On that hill."

Pan Volodyovski looked up, noted the two riders, and wagged his head in doubt.

"I see two men, that's true. But Pan Kharlamp is with the Grand Hetman. What makes you think that's him?"

"I know him by that big dappled mare he's riding. The whole army knows that mare."

"You're right, that does look like her. But it could be another."

"No way master. She's got a gait like no other horse I've ever seen. Look how she paces, sir."

The horse was, indeed, a pacer rather than a trotter, a rarity in their times, so Pan Volodyovski and his grooms spurred their own animals forward in a gallop and in a few more moments the little knight recognized Pan Kharlamp, an old Radzivill soldier with whom he almost fought a duel at one time, but who had since become one of his best friends.

"How are you, Nosey?" he cried out, throwing his arms around the fierce-looking Lithuanian Light Horse officer whose most outstanding physical characteristics were a nose as long as a double-barreled pistol and a pair of whiskers that dangled to his chest. "What are you doing in these parts?"

"Looking for you! With orders and money."

"From whom? And what for?"

"From our Hetman, the Prince-Palatine of Vilna. He sends you a commission to raise a new regiment, and I've another one for Pan Kmita too if you can help me find him. He's supposed to be around here somewhere."

"Kmita as well? Yes, he's in these parts. But how are we to recruit two regiments in the same district?"

"He's to go to Troki and you'll stay in the Lauda."

"But how did you know where to look for me?"

"Oh that was easy. The Hetman himself was asking about you until those Laudanians who are still in service told him where to find you. You've no idea how highly he regards you! I heard him say myself, many times, that he never expected to inherit anything from the Palatine of Ruthenia but, instead, he got the greatest knight that Prince Yeremi had."

"Let's hope God also gives him Prince Yeremi's good fortunes in war," Pan Volodyovski said seriously, then smiled with quick pleasure. "Well, this is quite an honor for me, to get this commission. I'll get to the recruiting right away. There's never a shortage of good men around here if only someone can provide the money for horses and equipment. How much did you bring me?"

"You can count it when we get back to Patzunel," Pan Kharlamp said.

"Patzunel, eh?" Pan Volodyovski laughed, his defeat in Vodokty completely forgotten. "So you've already sniffed your way in there, have you? Be careful, Nosey! Because there're more pretty girls in that place than poppies in a garden."

"Which is why you enjoyed your stay there, I expect." Pan Kharlamp grinned and nudged the little soldier. "But wait a minute, I've another letter for you from the Hetman. And this one is private."

"Hand it over, then!"

Chapter Fifteen

THE GRAND HETMAN'S LETTER was brief and to the point although it was couched in terms better suited to an independent monarch than to an officer of the Commonwealth who, at least in theory, was no better than any other noble. Yanush Radzivill wrote in the first person plural. He stressed the need for urgency and speed, reminding Volodyovski in the gentry's Latin that there was *periculum in mora*, or danger in delay.

'*If you wish to please Us then see to it that your new regiment is ready to march by the end of July or by mid-August at the latest,*' he ordered.

Nor did he miss an opportunity to vent his spleen at Hetman Gosyevski who, as the treasurer of Lithuania, disbursed the Grand Duchy's funds.

'*We're worried about horses for your men because we've little money we can send you, being as usual at loggerheads with the Gosyevski faction, who'd rather see the country go down to disaster than support Our measures.*'

Then he charged Pan Volodyovski with responsibility for Kmita's commission.

'*Give half that money to Pan Kmita, for whom Pan Kharlamp has another order for recruitment, because we'll have a sore need for men of spirit in the times ahead. But since we've heard about his misbehavior in the Upita district it'll be up to you to judge and decide whether he should have it. If, in your view, he stained himself beyond redemption by truly serious misdeeds then withhold his commission and turn him over to the civil courts because We don't want to give Our ill-wishers, such as Pan Gosyevski and the Voyevode of Vitebsk, any new cause for stirring public discontent against Us, which they'd be sure to do if We entrusted such important functions to unworthy persons. But if you judge that his transgressions don't amount to much then give him this chance to clear his name by faithful and energetic service. In that event he is to ignore all summonses against him because, as Our officer, he'll pass to Our hetmanic jurisdiction and We will judge him, not the civil courts, after his term of service.'*

Radzivill ended by pointing out to Pan Volodyovski that this additional duty was *'a measure of Our confidence in your loyalty and judgment,'* and signed it with his hereditary Lithuanian titles as Prince of Birjhe and Dubinki, as well as *Voyevode* of Vilna which, along with his Grand Hetmancy, was his principal office under the Commonwealth.

"The Hetman is terribly worried about horses for you," Pan Kharlamp said when the little soldier finished with the letter.

"And so he should be. The petty gentry in these parts will flock to the colors at the first call but all they have are little Zmudyan ponies. Every one of them will have to be re-mounted."

"I know those ponies," Kharlamp said. "They're wonderfully tough and nimble."

"Bah, but what do they look like? The people around here are as big as oaks. You put them on little animals like that and you'd think you've got a regiment riding on a pack of dogs!"

Pan Kharlamp laughed, amused, but the little colonel wasn't making jokes.

"This is no laughing matter, Nosey. It's a real problem. But I'll get to work right away and we'll come up with something. Oh, and leave Pan Kmita's commission with me as well, will you? I'll take care of it. He couldn't have got it at a better time."

"And how's that?"

"Because he behaved like a real Tartar around here, seizing girls by force. He has more summonses hanging over his head than he has hair on it! It's only been a week since I dueled with him."

"If you dueled with him then he's flat on his back," Pan Kharlamp observed.

"But he's getting better. Another week or two and he'll be on his feet."

★ ★ ★

Then, because he spent so much time in the provinces, cut off from contact with public affairs, the little knight asked for the latest news.

"Ah, it's the same old thing," Kharlamp sighed. "Pan Gosyevski snipes at our Hetman every chance he gets and you know what it's like when our top commanders disagree. Everything's going to the dogs. It looked for a while as if we were getting the upper hand over the Russians, and we'd surely ride their necks back into their own country if only we could all unite in a common cause. Hetman Gosyevski is to blame for it all."

"But others blame Radzivill."

"Traitors, that's who they are. The *Voyevode* of Vitebsk spreads that kind of tale but what can you expect? The Sapyehas threw their lot behind Gosyevski a long time ago."

"The *Voyevode* of Vitebsk is a decent man," Pan Michal observed.

"Are you another Sapyeha partisan, then? Taking their side against the Radzivills?"

"I take the side of our country, which is what all of us ought to do. As for Sapyeha being a decent man, I'd say it to Prince Yanush himself, even though I serve under him."

"All kinds of worthy people tried to make peace between them," Kharlamp shrugged and sniffed. "But it's all gone for nothing. The King is sending whole flocks of messengers to our Prince these days. There are all kinds of rumors about great events shaping up around us but no one knows anything for sure. We expected the King to join us with the General Levy this Spring but nobody came. People say the new forces might be needed elsewhere."

"Must be the Ukraine again."

"Who knows? Lieutenant Brohvitch was on guard one day at the Prince's chambers when Tyzenhaus arrived from His Majesty for a private meeting with our Prince. Brohvitch tried to listen at the door but all he heard was what the Hetman said when they were coming out. '*This could lead to another war,*' the Prince-Palatine said according to Brohvitch, but none of us could figure out what it meant."

"He probably misheard. What kind of new war could there

be? The German Emperor wishes us well these days, a lot better than he does the Russians who are getting far too strong for anybody's good. Our treaty with the Swedes is good for another six years. And the Tartars are helping us in the Ukraine for a change which they wouldn't do without the Turks' consent."

"Like I said," Pan Kharlamp noted. "None of us could get to the bottom of it."

"It must be just a rumor. But I am really glad to have fresh work to do because I started getting too comfortable and settled without a new campaign."

★   ★   ★

Then their talk shifted once more to Kmita. "So you want to take his commission to him on your own?" Kharlamp asked.

"Yes. Didn't I tell you? That's what the Hetman orders. I ought to look in on him anyway, just to be polite, and the Hetman's letters make a good excuse. Whether or not to give him that commission also needs some thought but I don't know what I'll do about that."

"Well, that suits me fine," Pan Kharlamp looked pleased. "This is only the start of my mission and I'm anxious to get on my way. I've recruiting orders for Pan Stankevitch too. Then I've to go to Keydany to wait for the artillery that's to gather there. And then to Birjhe to see if the castle defenses are in good condition."

"To Birjhe too? All the way on the Courland border?"

"That's right."

"That's a bit odd." Pan Michal was surprised. "Why does Birjhe need protecting? And from whom? The Russians didn't win any new victories lately and they're far from Birjhe. The Courlanders can't be thinking of a war with us. Those Letts, Latvians and Estonians up there make very good soldiers but they're few in numbers; Radzivill alone could snuff them out with one hand if he had a mind to. And since I see that we're raising new regiments all over the place then we'll soon have enough troops to defend even those provinces that the Russians have already taken. So what's it all about?"

"I'm just as surprised as you are," Kharlamp shrugged. "Especially since I've been told to hurry. And if I find that Birjhe needs new fortifications I'm to get in touch with Prince Boguslav Radzivill, the Grand Hetman's nephew, who is to send that foreign engineer, Peterson, at once."

"I can't say I like the sound of that," Pan Volodyovski muttered. "I hope it doesn't mean some kind of a rebellion or a civil war. God keep us from anything like that! But once Prince Boguslav takes a hand in something you can be sure the Devil will be happy."

"Don't slander him," Kharlamp warned and frowned. "That's a valiant lord."

"I don't deny his valor. But he's more of a German or some kind of Frenchman than a Pole, that's certain. The Radzivill House is all he cares about and if he ever gives a thought to the Commonwealth it's just to see how he can use it to elevate his own family."

Pan Kharlamp, who served under the Radzivills all his life and who revered his Hetman in just the same way that Pan Michal loved the late Prince Yeremi, was glaring at the little soldier across his huge nose, but Pan Volodyovski hardly seemed to notice.

"It's Prince Boguslav who feeds our Hetman's pride," the little colonel said. "Which, as God knows, is great enough without it. And all those quarrels with the Sapyehas and Gosyevski are also his doing."

"I see you've turned into quite a statesman," Pan Kharlamp's voice began to drip with sarcasm. "You ought to get yourself married, my small friend, so that such mighty brains might be passed on through the generations."

Stung where he smarted most, Pan Volodyovski threw his friend a careful glance, wondering how much he'd heard. "Married, did you say?"

"The quicker the better!" Then the bewhiskered Light Cavalryman took note of Pan Michal's glittering finery. "Ey, it looks like you're fishing for a bride already in these parts, the way you're dressed up!"

"That's best not talked about," Pan Volodyovski muttered.

"Ho ho! So that's the way the winds blow around here! Come on, admit it. D'you have your eye on some local girl?"

"Everyone has to swing on his own gate," Pan Volodyovski grunted, flushing as red as a boiled beet. "So don't ask about another man's rejections because you've been given enough of your own. Do you think I've time to think about getting married when I've a regiment to raise?"

"So be it then." Pan Kharlamp grinned through his fearsome whiskers. "Will you be ready by July?"

"The end of July. Yes. And thank God for sending me this job or I'd have died of boredom. God knows where I'll get those horses, though..."

★ ★ ★

The Grand Hetman's commission and the prospects of hard work went far to lift Pan Volodyovski's spirits so that by the time that he and Kharlamp rode into Patzunel he quite forgot his debacle in Vodokty.

News about the regiment that he was to raise flew across the settlement with lightning speed. The gentry flocked to old Pakosh's house to ask if it was true and responded enthusiastically when their little colonel told them that it was. There was some grumbling that they'd have to leave in July, before harvest time, but no one questioned the need for every man to go. Pan Volodyovski sent messengers galloping throughout the Lauda country, and to some of the estates of the wealthier gentry, and several dozen Stakyans, Domashevitches and Butryms arrived that evening for a consultation. Then it was time for boasting, threats hurled at the enemy, and an exchange of speculations about future victories. Only the Butryms sat and listened in their gloomy silence but no one took their wordlessness against them because everyone knew that they'd report for duty to the last man when the moment came.

The next day all the settlements buzzed with excitement like so many beehives at swarming time. No one talked about Pan Kmita and their lady anymore; the coming campaign was the only topic of Laudanian curiosity and comment. Pan Volodyovski also let his momentary bitterness against Olenka change into understanding and forgiveness, thinking that her refusal, like his sudden ardor, were bound to repeat themselves elsewhere anyway. But he gave quite a bit of thought to what he should do with Kmita's new commission.

There then began days of hard work for the little soldier. He traveled back and forth across the whole region, sent letters throughout the county, and drafted manifestos. He moved to

Upita where he set up his recruiting office, and the hard-work-
ing, patriotic farmer-gentry responded to his call just as readily
as the wealthier landowners for whom, at least, he didn't have
to find and buy the horses. The gentry came all the more
eagerly because his stature as a knight and soldier was just as
great among them as his indefatigable little body was insignificant. Most of his new soldiers, however, were the Laudanians
whose brisk little ponies made them look like bears mounted on
a pack of greyhounds, and for whom regular cavalry horses had
to be found somewhere. Pan Michal threw himself into his
work with all the furious energy of a trout tossed into boiling
water, but because he was both tireless and inventive, his new
regiment took shape efficiently and swiftly.

                              *   *   *

He also found time to pay a visit to Kmita in Lubitch, hearing
that the young raider was coming back to health although he was
still confined to his bed.

Pan Andrei recognized him at once and grew even more pale
than he was to start with, while his hand jerked by reflex towards
the saber that hung above his bed. But seeing his visitor's
reassuring smile he stretched out his hand to him instead.

"Thanks for coming to see me," he said. "That's very decent
of you."

"I came to ask if you hold any grudge against me," Pan
Volodyovski answered.

"I hold no grudges because I've been fairly beaten, and by a
first-rate player. I hardly made it past your first few strokes."

"And how's your health?"

"You're probably surprised that I managed to squeeze
through alive from under your saber. I must say that I'm
surprised myself." Then Pan Andrei shook his head and smiled
with wry admiration. "Well, nothing's lost. You'll be able to
finish me off anytime you want."

"That's the last thing I've in mind," Pan Volodyovski said.

"You've got to be some kind of a Devil," Pan Kmita said in
wonder. "As God's my witness, I'm far from boasting because
I've just barely clawed my way back from the next world, but I
always thought that if I wasn't the best swordsman in the
Commonwealth then I must be the second. Instead, what hap-

pened? I wouldn't have been able to parry your first stroke if that's what you wanted. Where on earth did you learn so much?"

"There is a little bit of a natural talent, I suppose," Pan Michal admitted. "And my father trained me from my earliest years. He used to tell me: '*God gave you the stature of a gnat so learn to sting like one. Because if people aren't afraid to look you in the eye they'll laugh in your face.*' Then, later, serving under the *Voyevode* of Ruthenia, I picked up the rest. There were several men in Prince Yeremi's service who could face me without any trouble."

"Good God, is that possible?"

"Certainly. There was Pan Podbipyenta, a Lithuanian noble of an ancient family, who was killed at Zbarajh, God rest his gentle soul. He was a man of such immense strength that it was impossible to parry his blows because he could slice right through the blade and the man behind it. And then there was Pan Skshetuski, my dearest confidant and friend, of whom you must have heard."

"Of course I've heard of him! Who hasn't! He's the one who went across the Cossack lines at Zbarajh, isn't he? And saved the whole army? So you're from that pack, are you? And a Zbarajh hero? Well, no wonder then... But wait a minute, I've heard about you too, I think. Is your first name Michal?"

"Actually I'm George Michal, named for both St. George and St. Michael in that order, but since all George ever did was trample a dragon, while Michael commands all the Hosts of Heaven, I picked St. Michael for my patron saint. So yes, I am called Michal."

"There's no question that St. Michael is the better choice," Pan Andrei observed. "So you must be that Volodyovski who made mincemeat out of the famous Bohun?"

"I'm the man."

"Well! It's no shame to get whacked over the head by that kind of saber!" Pan Andrei laughed. "I wish we could be friends."

Then his pale, handsome face twisted suddenly as if a shard of pain pierced him through the body.

"It's true that you called me a traitor," he grunted at last, "but you were wrong there."

"I know that now," Pan Volodyovski said. "Some of your Cossacks told me. And I might as well tell you that if they hadn't told me where you got them, and if I thought like everybody else that you'd run off to the Russians and teamed up with Hovansky, I'd never have come here today."

"Oh, the people around here have been honing their tongues on me, that's for sure," Kmita said bitterly. "But I no longer care. I admit I've some heavy debts to pay but it's also true that the locals received me very badly."

"You've done yourself the most harm with burning Volmontov and this latest raid."

"That's why they're hounding me with lawsuits. I've a dozen summonses lying here already and I can expect a lot more as soon as I'm better. It's true I burned down Volmontov and cut up some people. Let God judge me, though, if I did it out of sheer savagery or blood-lust. That same night, just before that burning, I took a vow to live in peace with everyone, win over all these local greybacks, and even make full restitution to the counter-jumpers in Upita where I really let things get out of hand. But what did I find at home? My good companions butchered like sides of beef and laid out on the floor. When I found out who did it, it was as if the Devil took possession of me... Can you believe why the Butryms murdered them? Because they wanted to dance a little with some of their women! Who wouldn't want vengeance for something like that?"

"My dear fellow!" Pan Volodyovski answered. "I grant you that your comrades were treated too harshly. But they were killed less by the local gentry than by their own evil reputations. No one would mind them dancing with anyone if they were decent men."

Kmita, however, was deep in his own memory and following his own trend of thought.

"Poor lads," he murmured. "Their ghosts came in here every night when I was lying in a fever. Right through that door. I saw them as clearly as if they were still alive, all grey and bloody, and moaning *'Andy! Pay for a Mass for us, because we're in torment!'* I tell you, all my hair stood on end because the smell of brimstone was so strong. I bought a Mass to ease their souls a little..."

He paused, then shrugged helplessly and went on: "As for

that abduction... well, no one could've told you this but she saved my life when the locals were after me, and then she ordered me never to come back. So what else was left for me to do?"

"Even so," Volodyovski said. "That's a Tartar's way."

"You can't know what love is all about," Kmita muttered. "Nor what it means when a man loses everything he cares for."

"I don't know about love?" the little soldier shouted in anger and amazement. "I've been in love since I was hardly taller than my saber! True, the object of my affections may have changed from time to time..."

"What kind of love is it when the object changes?" Kmita interrupted.

"Then I'll tell you about someone else. It's something I watched with my own eyes. At the time of Hmyelnitzki's first rebellion, Bohun, who is now the most revered leader among the Zaporohjan Cossacks, carried off Skshetuski's girl, the Princess Helen Kurtzevitchovna, whom my poor friend loved above everything! That was a love! I tell you, the whole army wept to see Skshetuski's suffering. His beard turned white in his early twenties. He was like a dead man. But what do you think he did about his tragedy?"

"How the Devil am I to know?" Kmita asked, annoyed. "I wasn't there, was I?"

"Then listen and learn! Because our Motherland was in danger and humiliated as never before, and because she needed every one of us, he didn't go off searching for the girl although it tore his soul to shreds to be able to do nothing for her! He turned his private tragedy into an offering to God, dedicated himself to our country's service, and fought in every battle under Prince Yeremi until, at Zbarajh, he covered himself with such fame and glory that everyone now speaks his name with admiration and respect. Compare his deeds with yours and recognize the difference."

Kmita said nothing, biting on his mustache, while Pan Volodyovski went on:

"And that's why God rewarded Skshetuski and gave him back his girl. They married right after the relief of Zbarajh and they've already had three fine boys although he's still in harness, commanding the King's Own armored regiment in the Ukraine.

And what did you do? How did you behave? Causing turmoil and disorder in wartime is as good as helping the enemy, not to mention the fact that you almost lost your life a few weeks ago. And you also came close to losing your girl altogether in the last few days."

"I did?" Kmita tried to sit up in his bed. "What happened to her, then?"

"Nothing happened to her. Only a certain gentleman asked for her hand in marriage."

Rage glinted in Kmita's caved-in eyes, his face lost all color, and he tried to struggle out of bed but he was still too weak to stand on his feet.

"Who was it?" he shouted. "Tell me, for God's sake!"

"It was I, myself," Pan Volodyovski said.

"You?" Kmita stared, astonished. "You? How can that be?"

"Quite simply," Volodyovski shrugged. "I asked and she replied and that's all there was to it."

"You damned sly snake!" Kmita grated out. "You won't get away with it, I swear! If I can't get you with a saber I'll shoot you out of ambush! But what did she say? Quick, tell me the worst! Did she accept you, then?"

"She sent me packing without a second thought," Pan Volodyovski said.

*   *   *

Another deep, protracted silence followed while Kmita fixed his fevered eyes on the little soldier. He, in the meantime, looked at the wounded raider with something like pity.

"Why do you call me a snake?" he asked. "Am I your brother or one of your own kind? Did I break faith with you? I beat you in a fair fight and I was free to do whatever I wanted."

"Even so, one of us would've died for that," Kmita muttered. "If I couldn't reach you with a saber I'd have put a musket ball through your head, and to Hell with my soul after that."

"You'd have had to shoot me, then. Because if she'd accepted me I'd have refused to meet you in another sword fight. Why would I want to bother? Hah, but d'you know why I got the gate?"

"Why?" Kmita's voice was as dull and lifeless as a distant echo.

"Because she still loves you."

This was more than the wounded man could bear. His head fell back on the tumbled pillows, a thick oily sweat burst out on his forehead, and for a long moment he couldn't find a word to say.

"I feel weak all of a sudden," he murmured at last. "But how... do you know... that she loves me still?"

"Because I've eyes to see with and a mind to add up what I'm seeing," Pan Volodyovski shrugged. "It's all quite clear now that she refused me. First of all, when I told her right in this house, after that abduction, that I cut you down and she was free to go, she looked close to fainting and instead of thanking me, like I expected, she treated me as if I'd committed some kind of a crime. Then, when the Domashevitches were carrying you into the house, she lifted and supported your head with her own hands like a loving mother. And finally, when I proposed to her, she gave me an answer like a kick in the teeth. And if that's not enough proof for you, it must be because you got cracked across the head and your brains got scrambled in your skull."

"Ah... If that was true," Kmita murmured weakly. "If I could believe it... They've been putting all kinds of balsams on me here but your words are the best remedy of all."

"Is it a damned sly snake, then, who brings you that kind of remedy?" Pan Volodyovski smiled.

"Forgive me. I spoke without thinking. But I just can't believe that she could still want me."

"I said she loved you, not that she wanted you. That's quite a different matter."

"If she won't marry me then I'll just smash my head against this wall and be done with it," Kmita said. "And that'll be that."

"It doesn't have to be like that at all," Pan Michal observed quietly. "It all depends on how sincere you are in wanting to make amends. We're at war, you can serve your country. You can win new glory and mend your reputation. What man is free of sin? Which of us doesn't have something on his conscience? But the road to penance and forgiveness is open to everyone in our Commonwealth. If you sinned by selfishness start serving selflessly. If you hurt your country with turmoil in wartime, start working to save it. If you've injured people out of arrogance and pride, help to heal their wounds with humility and affection. That's a far better road for you to take then smashing your head against a wall."

Kmita stared at the little knight as if each of his words was a new discovery. "You're speaking to me as if you were my most devoted friend," he said finally.

"I'm not your friend but, to tell the truth, I'm not your enemy either," Pan Michal replied. "And I'm also sorry for that girl of yours. I owe her something for a few harsh words I told her on parting. Getting the gate is nothing new for me and I'm not going to hang myself because she refused me. Neither do I bother wasting time on grudges. But if I can point you towards a good path it'll help our country because you're a good and experienced soldier."

"But isn't it too late? There are so many tribunals waiting for me... I'll have to go to court as soon as I can get out of this bed. I could escape and run for it, I suppose, but I don't want to live like that anymore... Ah, there are so many trials ahead. So many! And each is certain to bring a guilty verdict."

"Hmm. It looks as if I might have a remedy for that as well," Pan Volodyovski said and pulled the Grand Hetman's letters from inside his coat.

"What's that?" Kmita cried, catching sight of the Radzivill seal. "A Hetman's commission? For whom?"

"For you. Once you have a military function to perform in wartime you pass under the Grand Hetman's jurisdiction and you don't have to answer any civil summons. Listen then, to what the Prince-Palatine writes to me about you."

Then the little colonel read out Radzivill's private letter of instruction, took a deep breath, moved his pointed whiskers up and down, and said: "So you see it's up to me whether to give you this commission or not."

"And what have you decided?" Kmita asked in a low, trembling voice, almost beyond hope.

"That you ought to have it," Pan Volodyovski said.

* * *

Kmita lay as still on his pillows as if his heart had stopped beating in the interval between his question and Pan Michal's answer, and for a long time afterward he didn't seem to have anything to say. Then tears appeared like unexpected visitors in his cold, grey eyes.

"Let me be torn apart by wild horses if I ever met a more decent man than you," he murmured at last. "If Olenka refused you because of me, if she really loves me, then you've all the more reason to drag me down and to trample me into the mud. Any other man would look for revenge and do his best to bury me even deeper in infamy and despair. But you offer me your hand instead and pull me from the grave."

"Our country's needs come first," Pan Michal said simply. "But I'll tell you this much. If you had borrowed those Cossacks from the Russians I'd have let you rot."

"What an example you are to everyone!" Kmita cried. "Let me shake your hand! God willing, I'll find a way to repay you because I'll owe you the remainder of my life!"

"There'll be time to talk about that when the war is over," Pan Michal said and smiled. "But now listen carefully. Forget all those summonses and get to work, you hear? Serve the Commonwealth with all your heart and even the Laudanians will forgive you because they're very conscious of our country's honor. You've still time to clean your slate, earn everyone's respect, and end your days in glory brighter than the sun. And I can think of one young woman who'll be happy to reward you warmly in your lifetime."

Pan Michal tried to leave immediately after that, anxious to get back to his own recruiting, but Kmita wouldn't let him go, ordering wine for his guest and calling for his clothes with an eagerness and enthusiasm that made Volodyovski smile with satisfaction.

It was close to evening before the little knight could finally break away, ride out of Lubitch and take the forest road that led to Upita. It was the same road, running past Vodokty, on which Kmita and Olenka took their final sleigh ride.

"Best thing I can do to make amends for my hard words," the little soldier mused, "is to tell the Billevitch girl that Kmita is not only getting back to health but that he's rising out of his ill-repute as well. He's not all that bad. There's a lot of good in him, that's clear. He's just a hothead who needs to mature and cool down in service. I think she'll be pleased to hear all this and maybe I'll get a kinder reception from her this time than I did the last time."

Here the sentimental little knight heaved another sigh, wondering aloud if there was some gentle, loving soul somewhere on this earth who would respond in kind to his unrequited yearnings.

Plunged in such thoughts he finally reached Vodokty where a shaggy Zmudyan shambled out to open the gate to the courtyard, showing no hurry to admit a guest.

"The Lady's not to home," he mumbled in the slow, phlegmatic manner of his kind.

"Ah, she's gone somewhere?"

"She's gone."

"Where to?"

"Who knows?"

"And when will she be back?"

"Who can tell?"

"Come on now," Pan Volodyovski snapped. "Get your thick, lazy tongue working like a human being! When did she say she'll return?"

"Maybe never." The Zmudyan shrugged, unhurried and unconcerned. "Took all her things and carts, she did. Looks like she's gone far. And for long."

"Hmm. Is that so?" Pan Michal muttered gruffly to himself. "Well, I really made a mess of it this time, didn't I."

And he took the slow, winding road back to Upita and the coming war.

Part Three

Chapter Sixteen

IN NORMAL SPRINGTIMES, when the first warm sunbeams pierced the thick coverlet of grey Winter clouds, and green shoots burst out of the soil in the fallow wheat fields, new hope would also quicken in the hearts of the people. But the Spring of 1655 failed to lift the spirits in the troubled Commonwealth. All of the eastern borderlands, from the Baltic in the north to the southern Wild Lands along the Black Sea, were gripped in a vise of fire that engulfed ever wider territories despite the Spring downpours.

Moreover, the sky filled with frightening omens which promised even greater catastrophes and disasters. Time and again the clouds formed soaring towers and great fortress walls which toppled with a roar of thunder. Lightning lashed the thawing, snowbound earth; pine woods turned yellow; and the branches of leaf-bearing trees became gnarled and twisted as if they were stricken by the same malignancy that started killing woodland animals and birds.

Anxious observers saw unusual markings on the sun showing an apple clutched by a dark hand, a pierced heart and a falling cross, and a terrible restlessness and alarm spread throughout the country while the monks and scholars searched their books in vain for an explanation of these signs and portents.

There was talk of new wars and then suddenly, coming from God knew where, rumors of an invasion by the Swedes flew through every town and village in the Commonwealth. There didn't seem to be anything to confirm these fears, especially since the armistice with Sweden still had six years to run, and yet this new danger was discussed even in the diet which King

Yan Casimir Vasa, a Catholic descendant of the Lutheran royal house of Sweden, called in Warsaw on the nineteenth of May.

More and more nervous eyes turned west towards Swedish Pomerania and the territories of Great Poland, or Vyelkopolska, which lay nearest to it and on which any new storm would be the first to burst. Special embassies followed one another to King Charles Gustav II in Stockholm, but instead of calming the general uneasiness they merely excited worried speculation.

People asked apprehensively: "Why would so many important senators go on these urgent missions unless there was a real threat of war?"

Others looked for their peace-of-mind in logic.

"The Commonwealth has done nothing to provoke invasion. The armistice is in full effect. The Swedes can't have forgotten the drubbing they suffered at our hands the last time we fought them. Why, even their great Gustaphus Adolphus, who had no peer in all the states of Europe, was twice defeated by Pan Konyetzpolski. They'd hardly risk their hard-won military reputations against a nation that always triumphed over them before. True, the Commonwealth is weakened and worn-out by the eastern wars but we still have untouched resources in Prussia and Great Poland, don't we? There won't be any war!"

"Then why are the western borders being fortified?" the pessimists and the fearful wondered in reply. "Why does the diet vote new taxes and enlist new soldiers?"

And so the arguments swayed back and forth that Spring between hope and doubting until, at last, the manifesto of Boguslav Leshtchynski, the principal military convocator for Vyelkopolska, put an end to all this speculation. He declared a 'state of peril and emergency' in the western territories, called out the nobles and provincial gentry of all the palatinates and counties that made up Great Poland, and summoned all able-bodied squires and landholders of the Vyelkopolian regions to the defense of the borders against an invasion by the Swedes.

All doubts vanished then.

The cry of "War!" rang through Vyelkopolska and echoed in every other territory of the Commonwealth. And it wasn't just an ordinary war but a new one added to two others. Hmyelnitzki, aided by Buturlin's Muscovites, was raging like a plague on the eastern and southeastern borders; Hovansky's and

Trubetzkoy's Russians were ravaging the northern and north-eastern country; and now the Swedes were marching from the west. The fiery vise was turning into a hoop of flames and the country became like an encircled war camp under siege.

That camp, however, was in deep trouble of its own. One traitor, the venal Radeyovski who felt himself slighted by King Yan Casimir, was already in the tents of the new invaders, ready to advise them, guide them to all the weak points in the Commonwealth's defenses, and ease their way to victory. Nor was there any shortage of private bickerings and quarrels; no dearth of powerful magnates looking at each other with dislike or envy and ready to sacrifice the good of the country for personal advancement; no lack of influential courtiers angry at the King for failing to invest them with some rich promotion and plotting against him; no sparseness of religious dissidents to whom the Protestant Swedes offered a promise of sectarian triumphs; and, finally, there was no scarcity of self-willed troublemakers, puffed-up political buffoons, greedy and self-centered materialists in love with their possessions, or men who were simply lazy and indifferent.

On the credit side, the rich and fruitful Vyelkopolska country proved generous with its money. The towns and cities supplied their full required complement of musketeers and pikemen. The village squires were in no hurry to leave their comfortable manors but they were prompt to send their conscripted peasants, each landowner furnishing one able-bodied serf for each ten furrows tilled on his estate. This Furrow Infantry, led by experienced captains appointed by the local petty diets, and uniformed in bright territorial colors, marched into camp many weeks before the gentry, castellans, palatines, and other noble holders of Crown offices could make their appearance. They assembled in three localities along the Notetz River, building entrenchments all day long at the fords and crossings near the market towns of Pila, Uistye and Vyelen, and peering anxiously behind them for some sign of the mounted gentry which had been called to arms in the General Levy.

★ ★ ★

Meanwhile the first of the dignitaries arrived in the Uistye earthworks. He was Pan Andrei Grudjinski, the *Voyevode* of

Kalish, who moved into the burgomaster's house along with a
large suite of servants, courtiers and retainers dressed in blue and
white. He was expecting all the Kalish gentry to flock to him
at once, but when no one showed up to greet him he sent for
one of the captains of peasant infantry who were building walls
along the river.

"Where are all my people?" he demanded.

The captain, Pan Stanislav Skshetuski, a cousin of the famous
Yan Skshetuski who saved the army at the siege of Zbarajh,
smiled with a mixture of bitterness and pain.

"What people?" he asked.

"The General Levy of the Palatinate of Kalish!"

"Illustrious *Voyevode*," Pan Stanislav's voice rang heavily with
contempt. "This is sheep-shearing time and the brokers in
Gdansk won't pay for unwashed wool. All of our country
squires are standing knee-deep in their sluicing ponds or watching their scales, and thinking, quite correctly, that the Swedes
will get here in their own good time, so there is no point to
hurrying out to meet them."

"What?" The *Voyevode* looked troubled. "Did nobody come,
then?"

"Not a living soul, other than the foot soldiers. After all,
harvest-time is near and a good squire doesn't leave his home
before his crops are in."

"What are you telling me?" The territorial magnate's mouth
dropped open in astonishment.

"That the Swedes will get here soon enough," the captain
repeated.

"What do I care about the Swedes?" The *Voyevode's* pockmarked face was suddenly crimson. "What about my shame
before the other territorial magnates? How can I face them if
I'm the only one here from the Kalish region?"

Skshetuski's smile was no less bitter than before.

"You'll forgive me, sir, but it's facing the Swedes that we
ought to be more concerned about. Anyway, you won't have
to feel your shame alone because no gentry has reported from
any territories, not just from your own."

"They must be mad!" Pan Grudjinski muttered.

"No sir. They're just quite sure that if they don't hurry here to welcome the Swedes, the Swedes will come calling on them on their own."

"We'll see about that!" the *Voyevode* snapped.

Then he called for ink, paper and goose quills, and sat down to write. After a half hour he sprinkled sand on the paper to dry the ink and struck it with his fist.

"I'm sending a final summons, calling on everyone to report for service no later than the twenty-seventh of the month!" he said. "I don't think they'll want to ignore that. Now, tell me, do you have any news about the enemy?"

"We have. Wittemberg is mustering his army near Stettin in Swedish Pomerania."

"Is there a lot of them?"

"Some reports list them at seventeen thousand. Others say there are more than that."

"Hmm." The *Voyevode's* flushed, fleshy face grew somber with thought. "We won't muster that many here on our own... What do you think of our chances against them?"

"If the gentry doesn't come as ordered then there's no point in even talking about it."

"They'll come, don't worry. It's a normal thing for the General Levy to drag their feet. But will we manage to hold the Swedes once the gentry gets here?"

"No sir," Pan Stanislav said calmly, then went on to explain: "We don't have any soldiers."

"What? What do you mean *no soldiers*? Of course we've got soldiers!"

"Your Excellency knows as well as I that whatever trained, regular soldiers the Commonwealth still has are all in the Ukraine. We haven't received a single regiment although God only knows which of these invasions is the bigger threat."

"But our territorial infantry? Our provincial gentry?"

"For every twenty peasants there is maybe one who ever smelled gunpowder. They'll be good soldiers after their first campaign, but not now. As for the provincials, Your Excellency should ask any experienced commander if the General Levy could ever face regulars in the field. And especially the kind of regulars that Wittemberg is bringing. They're all disciplined professionals, thirty-year veterans of the German wars, and as used to bloodshed as our country squires are to their good times and comforts."

"So you value the Swedes so highly above your own people?

"No sir, I don't place a higher value on them because if we had fifteen thousand troops of the kind who fought Hmyelnitzki at Zbarajh, regulars and heavy cavalry, I wouldn't be concerned. But God help us to make any kind of showing with what we have here."

The *Voyevode* leaned forward, his hands on his knees, and peered carefully into Pan Stanislav's face as if trying to decipher some hidden meaning in his words.

"Why did we come here, then?" he asked. "Wouldn't you think it wiser to surrender?"

Pan Stanislav flushed crimson at these words.

"If such a thought ever occurred to me I'd ask Your Excellency to have me impaled!" he said. "If you ask if I believe in victory then I'll tell you frankly, like a soldier: No! But why we came here is another matter. We're here to hurt the enemy as much as we can, to buy time for the rest of the country to get itself ready, and to block the invasion with our bodies for as long as one of us is still alive."

"Praiseworthy sentiments," the *Voyevode* grimaced with distaste. "But it's easier for you soldiers to talk about dying than for us who'll bear the responsibility for such useless bloodshed among our brother gentry."

"That's what the gentry's blood is for!" Pan Stanislav answered. "That's why they are gentry!"

"Yes, yes." The *Voyevode* seemed distracted. He made a careless and impatient gesture, as if what the captain had just said scarcely deserved a comment. "We are all ready to die if we must, of course, which is the easiest thing to do in any event. But we, whom Providence made into the nation's leaders, have a higher duty. We have to weigh the usefulness of what we do, not merely hunt for glory. It's true the war has almost started but, after all, Charles Gustav is a relative of our King and ought to show us some consideration. That's why we should try some negotiations because, at times, a good word can be more effective than the sword."

"That's not my business," Pan Stanislav said in a dry, clipped voice.

The same thought must have occurred in that moment to the *Voyevode* because he nodded coldly, grunted, and dismissed the captain.

★ ★ ★

Skshetuski was only half right in what he said about the gentry's leisurely response to the country's danger. It was true that hardly anyone appeared until after the sheep-shearing season, but by June 27, or the final date set for the assembly, quite numerous crowds began to arrive in the main walled camp on the plain between the small towns of Pila and Uistye.

Each day, thick clouds of dust billowed above the dry, sun-drenched roads, announcing some new territorial cohort. The gentry came in a vast, noisy throng, in carriages and on horseback, trailed by baggage carts and wagons that creaked under the weight of provisions and supplies. Each of these warriors surrounded himself with a swarm of cooks, lackeys, grooms and body servants. Some of them carried enough weapons to equip three men. They wore every kind of armor and cuirass, carrying ancient lances, musketoons, horse-pistols, sabers, broadswords and even maces used in former times for cracking armorplate, so that the few experienced soldiers in the camp could tell at a glance that none of them knew anything about war.

The truth was that of all the gentry in the Commonwealth the Vyelkopolians were the most unwarlike. No Tartars, Turks or Cossacks ever set foot in their peaceful counties. Their long tranquility was like a deeply soothing and disarming dream, hardly interrupted since the Fourteenth Century wars with the Teutonic Knights, so that none of them could even imagine what war was about. If any one of them ever felt some stirring of a martial spirit he enlisted in the regular forces of the Crown and fought as well as any other soldier. But most of them preferred to stay among their fleshpots, enjoying their comforts, and flooding the commercial towns of Prussia with their wheat and wool, so that it was difficult to believe they were the same breed of men as the fierce warrior gentry of the eastern borders. And now that the approaching Swedish storm pulled them away so rudely from their peaceful pastimes, they thought that no one could arm himself enough, or carry enough provisions and equipment, or bring enough servants to watch over their masters' goods and care for their bodies.

They made strange soldiers, as their captains were soon to discover. One or another of these country cavaliers would take his place in the ranks with a nineteen-foot wooden tilting lance, and with plate armor strapped around his chest, but wearing a straw hat so that he might feel cooler in the sun. Others talked so loudly to each other that nobody could hear the officers' commands; or they stood yawning, eating and drinking in formation, complaining about the heat and calling for their servants. All of them viewed military discipline as an affront to their dignity and argued about every order that seemed like an abridgment of their liberties. Nor did they pay attention to any Articles of War.

A real ball-and-chain that dragged behind this army was a vast train of baggage carts and wagons, spare mounts, hunting dogs and horses, the herds of cattle earmarked for each warrior's table, and the uncountable mobs of servants who guarded their masters' tents, animals, arsenals, wine casks and provisions, and who fought and quarreled with each other at every opportunity. It was against such an assembly of accidental warriors that the redoubtable Arvid Wittemberg, an old commander who spent his youth in the campaigns of the Thirty Years' War, led seventeen thousand disciplined Swedish veterans from the direction of Stettin and the Oder River.

Who, as the thoughtful men in the Polish camp asked themselves that Summer, could doubt the outcome? On one side lay the chaos of the Polish camp, full of noisy arguments, quarrels, grumbling and disputes; and a force composed of docile farmhands, harmless artisans, and good-natured peasants who were turned into infantry by decree, or of country squires freshly pulled away from shearing their sheep. On the other side marched grim battalion squares which responded to a leader's order like silent machines, gleaming with ordered rows of pikes and muskets and moving like a single sword in their General's hand. These were true craftsmen, bred to war, and acknowledged as the century's masters of their trade, as cold and ruthless in the practice of their terrible profession as only years of experience and discipline could make them.

★ ★ ★

But the gentry kept on gathering in ever greater numbers, along with all the Vyelkopolian dignitaries and magnates who arrived with their own private household troops and retinues of servants.

Soon after Pan Grudjinski, the camp at Pila witnessed the imposing entry of Kristof Opalinski, the powerful *Voyevode* of Poznan. Three hundred musketeers dressed in red and yellow marched before his carriage, a great suite of courtiers and retainers surrounded his person, and a troop of heavy cavalry, armed and equipped in Western European fashion and wearing the same colors as the musketeers, closed the cavalcade. Sitting beside him in Opalinski's coach was his jester, Stah Ostrozka, whose job it was to amuse the *Voyevode* on his tedious journey and ease the burdens on his furrowed brow.

The arrival of this distinguished personage heartened everyone. His kingly bearing, lofty forehead, grave thoughtful eyes and his reputation for diplomacy and wisdom, made it impossible for anyone to believe that he could ever suffer some stroke of misfortune. For people accustomed to respect the trappings of high office, and to honor noble birth and conduct, it seemed as if the Swedes themselves would hardly dare to raise a sacrilegious hand against such a magnate.

His passage through the crowded street brought booming cheers of joy, deep bows, and a cloud of caps hurled into the air. Those who were somewhat tremulous about their future military prospects felt new hope and courage surging through their bodies as the cortege wound slowly to the burgomaster's house. It was as if the majesty and glory of the Commonwealth herself had come to spread her sheltering wings over her defenders.

Opalinski was perhaps better known in his time as an orator and writer, a highly cultivated satirist who played the role of Cato in the senate, denouncing frivolity, selfishness and greed. He saw himself as a defender of the public good, and as the scourge of private interests, but he was also an ambitious rival of the exiled sub-chancellor Radeyovski.

Everyone knew that he was deeply wounded when the King didn't name him to the post vacated by the traitor, who was rumored to be a lover of the Queen, and whom the King stripped of his public office. His finely featured aristocratic face, glimpsed through the carriage window, seemed like probity itself. Seated beside him, and dressed in a miniature copy of his somber clothing, Ostrozka mimicked all the grave, restrained bows and gestures with which this most magnificent of the Vyelkopolian nobles acknowledged the crowd's ecstatic acclamations.

Nor was he alone to arrive that day. The dust had barely settled in the street behind him when heralds galloped in to announce the coming of his cousin, Pyotr Opalinski, the *Voyevode* of Podlasye, with his brother-in-law, Yakub Rozdrazevski, who was the Palatine of Inovrotzlav. Each of them brought one hundred and fifty armed men as well as a retinue of courtiers, servants and other retainers.

Others followed swiftly. Hardly a day passed thereafter without the entrance of some potentate. All seemed to be related by birth or by marriage. The little town became so packed with dignitaries that they ran out of houses for their suites of courtiers, while the surrounding meadows bloomed with the tents and pavilions of bivouacking gentry. It was as if all the brightest and most fantastically colored birds in the Commonwealth had come to roost in Pila, glowing in all the shades of red, green, blue and yellow on a variety of plumage, since every magnate's followers sported his own colors, and the Furrow Soldiers wore the multicolored hues of every township and locality in the ten palatinates that made up Great Poland. The mobilized provincial gentry wore, of course, whatever they pleased, and the richer the better.

On the heels of these warriors and commanders came a swarm of peddlers and shopkeepers who couldn't find room for their stalls in the market square and so set up long rows of sheds on the outskirts of the little town. Here they sold every kind of military gear and equipment, from arms to clothing, along with food and drink. Field kitchens smoked and steamed there night and day, spreading the thick aroma of *bigos*, meat-and-cabbage stews, and spiced soups and ox roasts, while the warrior gentry, armed with soup spoons as well as their sabers, milled about outside, eating and drinking, trading gleeful gossip, speculating about the absent enemy, and making pointed comments about their gathering leaders.

The jester Ostrozka moved among them in his patchwork costume of multicolored squares, waving a clown's scepter festooned with little bells, and looking for all the world like the fool he was supposed to be. The gentry flocked around him eagerly wherever he appeared.

"Who's this?" he asked and then recited a set of witty couplets that satirized one magnate or another. "And who's this now?"

And the gentry roared with laughter, guessing his riddles, and laughing all the louder when the rhymes proved especially spiteful or malicious.

★ ★ ★

One afternoon the *Voyevode* of Poznan himself appeared among them. He mingled freely with the country squires, tossing a kind word here and a smile there, and complaining mildly about the King for failing to send at least a few regular regiments to help them.

"They don't think about us in Warsaw, gentlemen," he murmured. "They don't care about us. They say that the Hetmans don't have enough soldiers to cope with Hmyelnitzki in the Ukraine so they can't spare any for us here in Vyelkopolska. Hah, what can I say? It seems that the Ukraine is more important to them than we are... We're in disfavor, gentlemen, if you can believe it! It's almost as if they sent us out here to be killed for nothing."

"And who's to blame for that?" asked some other noble.

"Who is to blame for all the misfortunes that plague the Commonwealth?" the *Voyevode* replied. "It can't be we, dear brothers, since we're here to shield and defend her with our bare breasts!"

The listening country squires were immensely flattered that this powerful, highborn, rich and well-connected noble—'the Count of Benin and Opalenitza,' as he styled himself—should call them his *dear brothers*, and view them as his equals, so one of them cried out at once:

"Illustrious Palatine! If there were more advisors like you near the King we wouldn't have been marked like sheep for slaughter here! But the way it is in Warsaw nowadays, the lower you bow and scrape the higher you rise! True merit has no value!"

194

The Deluge

"Thanks for your kind words, dear brother," Opalinski beamed on the flatterer. "But whose fault is that? The fault lies with him who takes bad advice. Yes, yes, dear brothers, our freedoms are like salt in their eyes in Warsaw. The more of our gentry that dies, you see, the easier it'll be to impose royal absolutism on the rest of us."

"Are we to die here, then, so that our children will groan in oppression?"

The strange commander, who had such a peculiar way of heartening and inspiring his soldiers, said nothing in reply and the dumbfounded squires began to gape and stare at each other in open-mouthed amazement.

"So that's what it's all about?" many voices shouted. "Is that why we're here? Sure! We can believe it! It isn't just today that the idea of *absolutum dominium* has occurred in Warsaw! But if that's what they're up to now we can give some thought to it ourselves!"

"And to our children!"

"And to our possessions which the enemy is going to loot and ravage!"

The *Voyevode* continued to listen in silence as if he had no encouraging words for his troubled soldiers and more and more of them started shouting that King Yan Casimir was to blame for all the national disasters of their time.

"And do you remember the times of King Yan Olbracht, gentlemen?" the *Voyevode* murmured.

"*In King Olbracht's reign, the Gentry died in vain!*" the assembly roared, quoting an ancient proverb, and angry voices cried out: "Treason, brothers! Treason!"

"The King's a traitor!" some enraged voice bellowed in the crowd.

And the *Voyevode* kept his mournful silence.

★ ★ ★

But suddenly Ostrozka, who trotted all this while through the crowds at his master's side, crowed like a rooster, flapped his arms and cried out so loudly that all eyes turned to him at once.

"Gentlemen!" he shouted. "Sweet brothers! Listen to my riddle!"

As volatile and changeable as the weather, the milling provincials immediately lost their sense of public outrage and crowded about the jester, eager to hear his latest witticisms and ready for amusement.

"We're listening!" several dozen voices shouted. "We're listening!"

The clown began to blink his eyes, mimicking a well-known mannerism of King Yan Casimir, and squealed out in a high-pitched voice:

> *"He took his brother's crown for better or worse,*
> *But let his brother's fame be buried with his corpse.*
> *He sent his former chancellor running for his life,*
> *And plays the 'Undersecretary' along with his wife."*

"The King! The King! That's Yan Casimir, as I live and breathe!" the gentry bellowed from everywhere around and a huge burst of laughter thundered in the gathering. "May the Devil take him, how cleverly he put it!"

The *Voyevode* laughed as heartily as everybody else, but when the noise died down a little he took a serious tone.

"Ah, but even that messy love affair is something for which we'll have to pay with our own blood," he sighed sadly. "That's what we have come to! But here, Ostrozka, take a gold piece for your clever rhyme."

"Chris! Chris, my dear!" the jester cried out with the familiarity allowed to his kind. "Why do you attack others for keeping fools around them when you not only keep me at your side but even pay me extra for a riddle? But I've another for you..."

"As good as the other?"

"Better. Only longer. But where's my gold piece, then?"

"Here!" Opalinski said, laughing in advance.

"All right then, gentlemen," the jester shrilled, crowed again and flapped his arms like the wings of a barnyard rooster. "Listen! And can you guess his name?"

> *"He played the role of Cato, flaying at the greedy.*
> *His weapon was a goose-quill, defending the needy.*
> *To a traitor's job he had some aspirations*
> *And now he's become the Conscience of the Nation.*
> *Pity he knows so little about fighting*
> *Because the Swedes won't panic at his writing,*
> *And because wars aren't won with rhetoric and reason*
> *He's all set to follow a traitor into treason."*

Everyone seemed to guess this riddle as quickly as the other but this time no one dared to laugh. A choked guffaw or two sounded here and there, followed by a silence, while all eyes turned to Opalinski whose suddenly scarlet face flushed a deeper crimson.

Meanwhile the jester peered about expectantly and asked with his most innocent expression: "Well? Who's the rascal? Can't anybody guess?"

And when the hushed silence went on he turned blandly to the *Voyevode*. "How about you, Chris? Can't you name that scoundrel? No? Then pay me another ducat as a forfeit!"

"Take it!" Pan Opalinski said, suddenly out of sorts, tossing him a coin.

"God bless you, Chris! But tell me one more thing, will you, eh? Didn't you try for the sub-chancellorship after Radey-ovski?"

"I've no time for silly badinage just now!" the flushed Opalin-ski snapped and lifted his hat in farewell to the gathered gentry. "Goodbye for now, gentlemen! I must attend a meeting of the War Council."

"You mean a 'family council,' don't you Chris?" Ostrozka reminded. "Because you're all related to each other there and the safety of your own skins is your main concern."

Then he turned to the crowd of gentry and, imitating the *Voyevode's* courtly bow, he added: "Which is just along your line of thinking, gentlemen, isn't it."

With this, the jester trotted after his retreating master but they had barely taken a few dozen paces when a huge bellow of convulsive laughter burst from the crowd behind them. It boomed and echoed for a long time, long after the *Voyevode* vanished from everybody's sight, until it dwindled and dissipated in the ordinary noises of the camp.

Chapter Seventeen

THE WAR COUNCIL at which Pan Kristof Opalinski presided that day was all the more unusual because none of the gathered Vyelkopolian magnates knew anything about military service.

Unlike the Lithuanian and Ruthenian 'kinglets,' who were as much at home in the flames of battle as salamanders were said to be in fire, whose bodies bore the permanent imprint of armor driven into their flesh, and whose entire lives passed in the unending raids, battles and campaigns that swept across the Steppes and the eastern forests, these were all civil dignitaries holding administrative offices and positions, and although they mustered in wartime along with all the other gentry called out in a national emergency, they never occupied high command positions. Centuries of peace softened their martial spirit and changed them into statesmen, scholars and literary men who bore no relation to that great Vyelkopolian knighthood from which they were descended, and which once held the might of the Teutonic Knights at bay for generations.

Now, gathered to decide how to defend their territories from invasion, they peered at each other with uncertain eyes, unwilling to be the first to say anything. They waited for their 'Agamemnon,' the most resplendent and respected magnifico among them, to give them their cue.

But 'Agamemnon' himself didn't quite know what to do in a Council of War, having no idea of either strategy or tactics, so he launched into another list of complaints against the King, citing his lethargy and ingratitude, and the heartlessness with which Vyelkopolska had been left unaided to its own devices.

If, however, he didn't know what to say, his listeners were enthralled by the way he said it. Even the experienced Stanislav Skshetuski, who was summoned there with the other captains to give whatever professional advice might be necessary, fell under the spell of his eloquence. His poise and gestures brought to mind the great orators of the Roman Senate. His head was high. His coal-black eyes seemed to be hurling lightnings. His lips expelled thunderbolts of rhetoric, and his silver beard trembled with emotion as he described the cataclysm that was about to overwhelm the country.

"What is the true source of a nation's suffering?" he demanded in tones as clear and polished as the brightest crystal. "The fate of its sons. And we here will be the first to suffer. It's across our lands and our possessions, won for us by our ancestors, that the enemy will spill like a hurricane rolling from the sea…"

Arms spread in appeal for reason and justice, like an image hanged upon a cross, he poised the questions that troubled all his gathered relatives and kinsmen.

"And why are we to suffer? What have we done that we should have our herds seized and taken, our wheat fields trampled into dust, and our villages, brought to prosperity with our own hard labor, set on fire and burned?

"Were we the ones who injured Radeyovski?" he went on, eyes raised to the ceiling. "Did we bear false witness against him and then drove him like a hounded criminal to seek protection overseas…?

"No!" he cried. "Neither do we insist that the empty title of 'King of Sweden,' which cost our Motherland so much blood already, should remain in Yan Casimir's signature! Two wars are scorching our borders! Was it necessary to provoke a third one…?

"Let God and the nation judge the guilty one," he thundered and went on in the same injured, judgmental and supplicatory tone for another hour. "But we are not to blame! Let us, then, wash our hands of this innocent blood which is going to be spilled for nothing because it's not our doing!"

No one could equal Kristof Opalinski's speeches. He was the most gifted orator in the senate of his time. His classical and literary allusions were unsurpassed on any public rostrum either in prose or in poetic couplets. But when it came to the needed military dispositions, he had nothing to say, and the Council turned for counsel to the Furrow captains. One of them in particular, Pan Vladyslav Skorashevski, was a knight of such profound experience and such wide renown that even regular commanders welcomed his advice. Now he proposed the construction of three separate camps, one at each of the main river crossings, but at such close distance to each other that each could aid the others. He also urged fortification of the entire riverline in the arc of the camps so that the defenders could make a strong stand wherever the enemy appeared.

"Once we know which way Wittemberg is heading," he advised, "we'll concentrate all our forces there and give him a warm welcome. I, in the meantime, with Your Excellencies' permission, will take a small party west to Tchaplinek. It's a lost position and I'll pull back in time but it's a good place from which to watch the enemy and send word about them."

That, then, was the decision and first thing next morning the gathering army got to work in a slightly more determined spirit. The assembled gentry finally mustered about fifteen thousand men and the peasant soldiers entrenched them in a walled arc of more than six miles.

The camp at Uistye, being the strongest one, was placed under the command of the *Voyevode* of Poznan, while other magnates sent their men to garrison the smaller earthworks in Vyelen and Pila. Pan Skorashevski left for the little border town of Tchaplinek and the Vyelkopolians settled down to await the Swedes.

★ ★ ★

June ended in this fashion and July began. Not a single cloud marred the open sky and the heat of the Summer sun beat down on the plains like a glowing furnace, driving the sweltering gentry for shelter among the trees. The days and nights proved to be so torrid that many of these grumbling and reluctant warriors abandoned the camps altogether and had their tents pitched in the shaded groves where they settled down to a round of boisterous feasts and noisy celebrations.

But these raucous banquets were like serenity itself beside the squalling clamor of their grooms and servants who fought each other for access to the river each time it came to watering the horses. They drove several thousand animals to water three times a day so that, from a distance, it sounded as if three battles raged each morning, noon and night on the riverbanks.

The army's spirit, however, seemed good at the start, no matter how much cold water Opalinski threw on their enthusiasm, and the outlook didn't seem as poor as some of the experienced men believed at the outset. If Wittemberg had come in the first days of July he might have found determined resistance which, as often happened with such volunteer soldiers, could have changed into a dogged ferocity as the embattled squires caught fire in the heat of combat. Officers like Pan Skshetuski and other Furrow captains had seen that before, and thought that another Yeremi Vishnovyetzki could have turned the camp at Uistye into a second Zbarajh, and write another epic of heroic struggle into the pages of their country's history. But, as it happened, the *Voyevode* of Poznan could merely write, not fight or inspire others.

They thought it possible that Wittemberg moved slowly on purpose. The old Swedish fox was not only a master of warfare but he also knew how men behaved on a battlefield. Years of experience taught him that fresh recruits were the most dangerous when their eagerness was still burning high. That's when newly drafted, untrained citizen-soldiers could charge the oldest regiments, scattering them like chaff, because they fought with the red-hot passion of an unblooded weapon, freshly come from under a blacksmith's hammer, tasting their first battle fury and oblivious of unexperienced danger. But once such passions were allowed to cool, the same men turned into heavy, sluggish and lethargic creatures who were as spiritless and lifeless as slabs of pig-iron piled outside a forge.

It wasn't courage that this army lacked, the captains agreed. But what they sorely needed was a soldier's patience and the ability to wait with that stubborn and disciplined endurance that veterans acquired only by long practice.

Weeks passed, following each other in aimless succession of boredom and waiting, and the unruly Vyelkopolian army began to fall apart.

The sun burned down on them hotter than before.

The listless and lackadaisical gentry refused to drill, complaining that the horseflies made their horses restless and that the

mosquitoes, swarming in tens of thousands in that marshy landscape, made them too uncomfortable in the open. Their lackeys
fought each other more fiercely than ever, competing for the
coolest woodland spots for their masters' bivouacs, which caused
some saber fights among the irritable provincials as well.

It began to happen that one or another of these sullen warriors, riding down to the river at sunset to water his horse, turned
the animal's head homeward, vanished in the night, and was
never seen in the camp again.

★ ★ ★

Nor did their leaders act as good role models. Pan Skorashevski barely sent word from Tchaplinek that the Swedes
were nearing, and that they would be across the border in less
than a week, when the War Council agreed to give a leave of
absence to Pan Zygmunt Grudjinski, the son of the *Starosta* of
Grudno and a nephew of the *Voyevode* of Kalish.

Pan Andrei Grudjinski was especially eloquent and insistent
in his nephew's cause, pleading that "if I am to lay my head on
this battlefield then, at least, let my nephew live to inherit my
fame and carry my name into future generations." He eulogized
the young man's virtues, pointed out that he was barely in the
first flush of manhood, and praised his noble spirit "in as much
as he gave one hundred good foot soldiers to the Commonwealth's defense," and the Council agreed to send him home on
the eve of battle.

Next morning, early on July 16, the young magnate rode
openly out of the earthworks, surrounded by a dozen servants,
while crowds of jeering gentry, goaded by Ostrozka, followed
him to the outskirts of the camp.

"My lord!" the jester shouted at him from a distance. "I grant
you a new motto for your coat-of-arms and a new addition to
your family name! '*Deest*' or Deserter!"

"Long live Deest-Grudjinski!" the gentry howled, flinging
lumps of parched earth after the red-faced, angry young nobleman who kicked his horse forward in fury and impatience.
"Run to your burrow, rabbit! Run! Hop hop!"

"And don't weep too hard for your uncle either!" Ostrozka
went on calling. "His contempt for the Swedes is just as great

as yours, and he'll turn his back on them just as quick as you, as soon as they appear!"

The uproar became so general that the *Voyevode* of Poznan himself came running with several Furrow captains to explain that the young lordling was only taking a week's leave for some pressing business and that he'd be back in camp in time for the battle.

* * *

But this bad example from above had its effect, and that night some hundred rural gentry followed young Grudjinski, thinking, no doubt, that they were just as good as he, although they left the camp with greater discretion and with fewer servants. Pan Stanislav Skshetuski, the captain of the Kalish infantry, clawed at his hair in anger and despair because his own men also began to seep into the night taking their cue from their master-gentry.

The *Voyevodes* called another meeting of the council in which the masses of the gentry demanded to be heard and the night passed in chaos of quarreling and shouting. Everyone suspected everyone else of trying to desert and the cry of "Either everyone or no one!" flew from man to man. Rumors that the *Voyevodes* themselves were leaving the camp swept through the raging crowds and the harassed magnates had to show themselves over and over to the howling mob as the night went on. Some twelve thousand men sat on horseback until dawn, ready to gallop off at the first sign of their leaders' panic, and the *Voyevode* of Poznan himself rode among them with his hat in hand, and with his lofty brow naked in the starlight like a Roman Tribune's, assuring everyone that he would "either die with them or live among them."

"Gentlemen!" he cried, carried away by the greatness of his moment. "Brothers! Our fates are the same! It's either life or death for all of us together!"

The mobs responded with either cheers or jeers, and he came back to the council meeting—hoarse, weary and intoxicated by his own great words—and quite convinced that he had rendered a remarkable service that night to his country.

But he had less to say at the council table, tugging at his beard and forelock with despair and muttering: "Decide what you wish, my lords, if any of you can. I wash my hands of what is sure to happen because it isn't possible to do anything with this kind of army..."

"Excellency!" Pan Skshetuski said. "The enemy himself will restore order here. Let the guns start firing, let the siege begin, and the gentry will fight on the walls like lions just to save their necks rather than raising all these riots in the camp. There's nothing new in this, believe me. It's all happened many times before."

"But what will we fight with? All the artillery we have are a few signal pop-guns, good enough for shooting off at banquets, but useless for battle!"

"At Zbarajh Hmyelnitzki had seventy carronades and Long Toms while Prince Yeremi had just a dozen field guns and half a dozen mortars."

"But he had regulars, not this provincial rabble! He had his own incomparable regiments, famous throughout the world, not a market-day gathering of country sheep-clippers and gentleman farmers!"

"Send for Skorashevski!" advised Pan Tcharnkovski, the castellan of Poznan and a brother-in-law of the despairing Kristof Opalinski. "Make him the Camp Constable. The gentry respect him. He'll hold them together if anybody can."

"That's right! Send for Skorashevski," urged the *Voyevode* of Kalish, far less eloquent that night than when he was pleading for his nephew's discharge. "We need him here much more than in Tchaplinek or wherever he is."

"That makes sense! Good idea! Do it!" cried a dozen others. "Let him take care of it!"

That was the War Council's only decision that night and the sole measure the Vyelkopolian magnates took to prepare for the coming siege. The rest of the meeting passed in complaints against the King and his French-born wife, and in denouncing the lack of regular reinforcements which left the Commonwealth's most prosperous provinces defenseless before the Swedes.

★ ★ ★

The next morning neither calmed the camp nor restored the gentry's sagging spirits. On the contrary, the chaos burst out with new force and spread even wider as someone launched the rumor that the Protestants among them, and especially the Calvinists who had many converts in the western districts, sided with the Swedes, and that they were ready to go over to the enemy at a moment's notice. Moreover several respected patriotic Protestants, such as Pan Shlyhting and the Kurnatovski brothers, confirmed these suspicions and pointed out the leader of this budding treason. The dissidents, they said, comprised a secret circle under Pan Rey, a well-known rioter and troublemaker, who had served in the German wars as a Lutheran volunteer and formed a great admiration for the Swedes.

This news no sooner started sweeping through the earthworks when ten thousand sabers glittered in the air and a true firestorm threatened to burst above the camp.

"Treason!" howled the gentry. "We're harboring traitors in our midst! Ingrates conspiring against their own Mother! Vipers ready to strike us in the back!"

"Death to them! Stamp them out! Let's have them here and now!"

"It's the worst kind of treason, gentlemen!" they harangued each other. "And the most insidious! Let's burn out this plague before it overwhelms us all!"

The *Voyevodes* and the captains had to run again among the roiled masses, soothing their rage and trying to defuse an explosion of fratricidal bloodshed, but they found this even harder to accomplish than the night before.

No one, least of all the officers, had any doubt that Pan Rey stood ready to betray his country. He had adopted so many foreign ways, and he was so contemptuous of anything Polish, that only his native language distinguished him from Germans. The riot began to dissipate only when the Council decided to order him out of the camp, but even then the shouts of "Treason! Treason! Kill them all!" echoed for many hours.

Finally the camp quieted down and a strange, withdrawn lassitude fell upon the discouraged and distracted gentry. Some of them stumbled along the walls as if half asleep, peering with dull eyes across the plains on which the Swedes were expected any day. Others turned to prayer, losing all interest in material matters. Yet others threw themselves into an orgy of eating and drinking and a sort of desperate, devil-may-care gaiety in which death itself seemed like some grotesque and macabre joke.

No one in that vast assembly of troubled human beings gave a thought to victory because no one could believe in anything but defeat. And yet the enemy they expected was not much more powerful than they. In numbers, in fact, the Vyelkopolians had a small advantage. The Swedes' sole superiority lay in their trained and disciplined battalions, better artillery, and a commander who knew how to fight a war.

* * *

So while at one edge of the Vyelkopolian plain the Polish earthworks hummed, boiled, roared, feasted and filled with sounds of fury, and then quietened down, subdued into apathy, like a sea whipped by contrary winds—and as the mobilized provincials held noisy meetings to debate each order as if they'd come together to elect a King—the other edge, greening among the broad meadows of the Oder River, darkened with the calm and steady regiments of the Swedes.

First in the line of march was the King's Guards Brigade, led by Benedict Horn, a grim soldier whose name was still whispered throughout Germany with terror. Marching behind him were two thousand picked, broad-shouldered men, matched for height and weight, armed with new wheel-lock muskets and long Swedish rapiers, and dressed alike in deep Spanish-style helmets and yellow leather coats. They were renowned for their iron discipline, indifference to death, and unemotional coldness under fire.

Karl Schedding, a famous German mercenary commander, led the Goteborg or West Gothland Brigade, consisting of two regiments of infantry and one of mounted *Reiters* or armored dragoons. Half the infantry carried muskets and the other half bristled with long, slim pikes which were used as a hedge against cavalry. In the times of Sigismond III, one of the earlier Vasa kings of Poland, one regiment of armored winged *husaria*, the traditional battering ram of the Polish armies, shattered this brigade in a single charge, and now it was composed in most part of Germans.

The two Smalland brigades were led by the famous Irwin who lost his right hand in the German wars while defending a regimental battle flag. He had the reputation of a murderous religious fanatic and a grim, singleminded soldier, just as hard on himself as he was on his men, and caring for nothing except war and bloodshed. While other great captains of the Religious Wars that devastated Europe between the Oder and the Rhine evolved in time into cold, matter-of-fact professionals, looking at warfare as no more than their chosen trade, he retained the same fierce Calvinist fanaticism with which he began, singing psalms and quoting from the Scriptures while slaughtering men without a thought of mercy.

The Vastmanland Brigade marched behind Dragenborg while the world-famous sharpshooters of the Halsingborg Brigade were led by Gustav Oxenstern, a nephew of Charles Gustav's famous Chancellor who guided the policies of Sweden ever since the reign of Gustavus Adolphus. The Ostergotland or East Gothland Brigade advanced under Fersen, and Wittemberg himself commanded the two Varmland brigades while, at the same time, acting as Field Marshal of the entire army.

Seventy-two heavy guns gouged deep black furrows in the sandy soil of the Oder plains that unfolded behind this human engine of destruction which devastated all of Germany, and which, especially in its superb Swedish infantry, could find its match only among the Royal Guards of the Kings of France.

They marched in battle order, ready to form their lines and columns at a single sign, and looking from a distance like a land-born fleet of advancing castles with the square towers of their pikes rising above the hard-edged rectangles of musketeers around them. Soaring aloft from these towers of pikes, and flowing above a sea of heads, helmets and plumed hats towards the Polish border, were the skyblue banners with white and yellow crosses which had waved victoriously above the century's every battlefield between the Baltic and the Rhine.

Each day, mile after mile, the distance between the two armies narrowed.

And finally, on July 21, while passing through the dark, broad stretch of pine woods near the village of Heinrichsdorf, the approaching Swedes saw their first Polish border post. A vast single cry of joy rang out at this sight, bursting from those grim and silent ranks in which marched the looters of half a continent.

All the drums and trumpets thundered in salute, and all the banners snapped open in the sudden breeze.

Wittemberg himself rode forward, surrounded by a glittering staff of officers and nobles, to watch his regiments march past him across that invisible woodland line which would begin his new campaign of conquest.

He watched them coldly, saluting with his hat, while his battalions passed in parade review. All the regimental battle flags dipped before him; thirty-thousand boots beat out a single rhythm like a giant heart; ten thousand hardened fists slapped the hardwood stocks of their muskets in presenting arms; and seventeen thousand of Europe's finest warriors advanced into Poland.

The cavalry rode past with rapiers drawn. The gunners marched with lighted matches beside their rumbling cannon. The sun stood in the middle of the sky to mark the noon hour of a brilliant day, and the woodland air was rich with the smell of pine sap and fresh pitch.

Chapter Eighteen

THEY CAME OUT of the woods—one steel rank after another, one grimly silent regiment followed by the next— and another great, joyful shout tore out of their chests.

A landscape such as they'd never seen before lay spread out below them.

The grey country track, flooded with Summer sunshine, dwindled and disappeared across the horizon. The quietly cheerful countryside around them lay open to the gaze like arms thrown wide in welcome. The rich, fragrant soil seemed to be smiling, beckoning, glowing with nodding grains, dotted with cool, shaded oak groves and green with pastureland wherever they looked.

The smoke of hidden homesteads, rising softly from behind the trees as far as they could see, hung in the sunlit air, pale with distance and stilled with the untroubled tranquility of centuries. White flocks of sheep grazed peacefully in the meadows and long-legged storks paced with stilted dignity where the green of the meadows gave way to gleaming wetlands.

A soft, warm silence spread across it all. There was a sense of sweetness in the sparkling air, and a hospitable richness pulsing from the soil, and it seemed to the astonished, staring Scandinavian warriors that they were entering that legendary and idyllic Promised Land, flowing with milk and honey, which waited for them with open arms as if they were God-sent guests, not an invading army, and their fierce, joyful shout shattered the silent air.

Used as they were to the infertile, rocky soil of their native country, and to the winter darkness of their northern forests, the land-starved, hungry hearts of these ruthless conquerors and rapacious looters filled with an overwhelming longing to possess it all. A wild-eyed enthusiasm seized the advancing ranks that spilled out of the dark, pine-scented border woods into that unexpected treasure house that opened before them.

But there was something else, a grim sobering thought that glinted darkly behind their glowing eyes. They were professionals, forged in the brutal fires of half a continent that they devastated in the Thirty Years' War, and they expected a hard and bitter fight before they grasped those riches for themselves. They knew the dangerous reputation of the people who lived in these fortune-laden spaces, and they were sure that the price of conquest would be high. The terrible disaster of Kirkholm, where three thousand Polish horsemen under Hodkevitch wiped eighteen thousand of Sweden's best soldiers off the face of the earth, was still alive in Swedish memories. Tales of those irresistible winged riders, related in awed whispers as if they were giants out of a Nordic Saga, still echoed in the dark Winter huts along their windswept shores. Nor were the wars of Gustavus Adolphus entirely forgotten. Drilled as they were in the invincible traditions of that swooping Scandinavian eagle, they knew that the fierce resistance they expected here blunted his talons not just once but twice.

So their harsh outburst of possessive joy was tempered with foreboding, a kind of wondering caution and uneasiness, and their commander seemed to share their thoughtfulness and concern. He watched the passing regiments of infantry and armored heavy Reiters with the cold, ruminating eyes of a shepherd calculating the worth and value of his flock, and then turned to a corpulent, red-faced man who sat on a horse beside him.

"Your Excellency is sure, then, that these forces are enough to crush the troops assembled at Uistye?" he asked.

The heavy, thick-lipped man stroked the curled blond wig that fell to his shoulders from under a plumed cavalier hat and turned his small moist eyes on the Swedish marshal.

"Your Excellency may depend on it," he drawled with assurance. "If we had one of the Hetmans waiting for us there, along with some of the Crown regular contingent, then I'd advise waiting until His Majesty himself can join us with the bulk of the army. But what we have here is more than enough to deal with those Vyelkopolian lords and their provincial levy."

"But won't the Hetmans send them reinforcements?"

"No. They won't."

"How can you be so certain?"

"Two reasons. One,"—and the flushed, fleshy man lifted a thick, ringed finger—"whatever troops they have, and they don't have many to begin with, are all tied up in Lithuania and the Ukraine."

"We know that," the Swedish marshal said. "What's the other reason?"

Smiling with cold amusement, Wittemberg's advisor lifted another finger.

"The second reason, and the most important, is that neither Yan Casimir, nor his ministers, nor the diet in Warsaw believe to this minute that His Majesty King Charles Gustav would ignore the armistice, the embassies, and their willingness to negotiate our differences, and begin a war! They still hope for a last minute peace, ha ha ha!"

Here the squat, red-faced man took off his broad-brimmed hat, wiped the sweat off his glistening forehead and added with grim satisfaction: "Trubetzkoy and Dolghoruki are in Lithuania. Hmyelnitzki's in the Ukraine. And now we're entering Vyelkopolska. That's what the rule of Yan Casimir has brought about!"

Wittemberg glanced at him curiously. "And this pleases you?"

"What pleases me is that I'll have justice! I'll have revenge for all the indignities I've suffered! And furthermore, I can see as clearly as if it were written in the palm of my hand, that my advice and Your Excellency's sword will place the world's richest and most splendid crown on King Charles Gustav's head."

Wittemberg let his eyes range far ahead, spanning the broad woods, the timberlands, the yellow sweep of wheat fields heavy with rich grain, and the green fecundity of pasture lands and meadows.

"Yes, it's a beautiful and productive country," he said after a moment. "And Your Excellency can be sure that after the war

His Majesty won't think of anyone but you to be his viceroy here."

The fleshy man lifted his hat once more and raised his small, embittered eyes to the cloudless sky.

"Nor do I want to serve any other master," he said in a thick, fervent voice that trembled with a mixture of suppressed emotions.

As superstitious as any other soldier, Wittemberg glanced quickly at the clear blue canopy that spread silent and untroubled overhead, as if he expected a sign of God's anger to manifest itself in a flash of fire.

But no thunder rumbled there at those words. No bolt of lightning came down to strike the thickset, red-faced speaker who was surrendering his own country—already spent and groaning under the onslaught of two other enemies—into the hands of a third invader. His name was Hyeronimus Radeyovski, a former favorite of King Yan Casimir and vice-chancellor of Poland in the united Polish-Lithuanian Kingdom, and now the most faithful and devoted servant of the Swedes.

The Swedish general and the Polish traitor sat for a while longer in quiet, contemplative silence while the last two infantry brigades marched out of the woods, and then the long black stream of jolting cannon and creaking baggage carts rolled into the sunlight.

The boom and rattle of regimental drums drowned out the measured tread of the soldiers' boots on the country highway and the blare of trumpets rang across the woods with harsh, threatening echoes.

★ ★ ★

Finally the staff moved forward as well. Radeyovski rode beside Wittemberg ahead of the others.

"Oxenstern is a long time coming back," Wittemberg observed. "I hope nothing's happened to him. I'm not sure it was a good idea to send him to Uistye. Do you think they'll see through his disguise?"

"Why should they? One trumpeter looks much like another. And it was a good idea to send him there with Your Excellency's letters. He'll be able to inspect the defenses, look over the leaders, and judge what they're thinking. An ordinary messenger wouldn't manage that."

"But what if someone recognizes him?"

"Only Pan Rey knows him over there and he's ours, body and soul. But even if they do catch on to who and what he is, what of it? They won't harm him. On the contrary, they'll go out of their way to make him feel at home."

Radeyovski laughed quietly, shaking his head with wonder and amusement.

"I know my Poles," he said, smiling with contempt. "After all, I am one of them. We'll do anything just so that foreigners will think well of us. It's one of our great failings that we'll always ignore everything said by the best of us, but we'll turn ourselves inside out to be praised by strangers. So don't worry about Oxenstern, Your Excellency. Set your mind at rest, nothing will happen to him. He just hasn't had enough time to get back, that's all."

"And what effect will our letters have there, do you think?"

Now Radeyovski burst into open laughter.

"If Your Excellency will let me play the prophet I'll tell you exactly what is going to happen! The *Voyevode* of Poznan is a well-read and civilized man, so he'll reply in a well-read and civilized manner. But since he also likes to see himself as something of an ancient Roman, his reply will be written with an eye to history. He'll say that he'd rather spill his last drop of blood than surrender, that he'd rather face death than dishonor, and that his great love for his Motherland commands him to fall in defense of her borders."

"And do you think he's likely to do that?"

"He?" Radeyovski's whole, thickset body quivered with amusement. "It's true that he'd spill his last drop of blood for his country, but since he keeps it in his inkpot rather than his veins it isn't likely to harm anybody, least of all himself. I'm sure that after that Roman declaration there'll be polite inquiries about our health, good wishes for the future, and finally a plea for our consideration where his and his relatives' property is concerned. For which he and all his relatives will be quite properly and politely grateful."

"And what does Your Excellency think will be the end result of all that?"

"The end result?" And again Radeyovski gave way to a paroxysm of cold, contemptuous laughter. "The end result will be that they'll lose whatever heart they have, that they'll start trying to negotiate, and that we'll occupy all of Vyelkopolska without a single shot fired at anybody."

"I hope that Your Excellency is a real prophet," Wittemberg observed.

"I'm sure of it," Radeyovski said. "I know these men. And I have friends and supporters in high places all over this country so I know exactly how to move against it. My mistreatment by Yan Casimir, as well as my devotion to His Swedish Majesty, can assure Your Excellency that I won't miss a trick!"

Then Radeyovski nodded quietly, staring with thoughtful eyes at the rich landscapes that unfolded in their soft and beguiling colors before the marching Swedes.

"Times have changed in this Commonwealth," he added and shrugged briefly. "And people are different. Everyone's more concerned about his own bailiwick than the country as a whole. All these territories, for example, that we'll be passing over in the next few days belong to the Opalinskis and Tcharnkovskis and Grudjinskis, and since they're the very same magnates who command at Uistye they'll be as soft as butter in their negotiations."

"Your Excellency's knowledge of this country is of inestimable value to His Majesty," Wittemberg remarked. "I'm sure it'll be rewarded just as generously."

"I know my own kind," Radeyovski shrugged again, as open about his own accession to the Swedes as he was indifferent to his country's welfare. "As for the lesser, ordinary gentry, they're never a problem. Just guarantee their freedom to squabble with each other in their petty diets and they'll go along with their *Voyevodes*."

"So judging by what Your Excellency tells me, I presume that I can think of these territories as already ours?"

"You can, Excellency!" Radeyovski answered eagerly. "Yes you can! You can!"

"In that case I claim all these lands in the name of his Illustrious Majesty, Charles Gustav of Sweden," Wittemberg said gravely.

★ ★ ★

Two days earlier, before the Swedish forces marched onto
Vyelkopolian soil, a Swedish Army trumpeter arrived at the
main Polish camp with letters for the *Voyevodes* from Wittemberg and Radeyovski.

Pan Skorashevski himself led him to Kristof Opalinski's quarters while the provincial gentry gaped at him as the first Swede
they had ever seen. They made admiring comments about his
proud bearing, his well-bred manly features, his upturned yellow mustache combed out at the ends into a pair of stiff outspread military brushes, and his lordly manner. A curious crowd
trailed him to the house occupied by the *Voyevode*, calling out
to acquaintances spotted on the way, and pointing at the Swede
with excited fingers.

"Look at those boots!" some of the gentry laughed. "If they
were any longer he'd be wearing them around his neck. And
look at that long straight rapier he's got hanging there."

"That's a rapier? Looks more like a roasting-spit, ha ha ha!"

"That's a nice bit of silver embroidery on that pendant,
though."

The Swede, in turn, peered around with equal curiosity,
tossing sharp, careful glances at everything from under his tall-
crowned, broad-brimmed military hat as if he was counting the
men and inspecting their fortifications. He seemed to stare with
a particularly undisguised curiosity at the swarming mobs of
provincial gentry whose eastern-style dress was, apparently, a
novelty for him. Pan Skorashevski suspected that this might be
a disguised officer, sent as a spy rather than an envoy, but when
he raised the question with the *Voyevodes* he was told that it
made no difference.

"No, you will not arrest him!" Pan Opalinski told him. "He
came with correspondence. Even if he was Wittemberg himself
we have to take him at face value. Indeed, I'll even give him
ten ducats for his trouble."

The War Council met to read and discuss the letters while the
trumpeter was placed in the hospitable hands of Pan Kristof's
courtiers who, in turn, turned him over to the curious gentry.
They, as fascinated by him as if he was a visitor from another
planet, took him at once to the liquor stalls and started drinking

with him *na umor*, in the Cossack manner, as if guzzling liquor until they were senseless was the best solution to all and every problem.

Drinking, they talked. The Swede had some pigeon German which the Vyelkopolian country squires understood from their commercial dealings with the Prussian cities, and he regaled them with tales of Wittemberg's successes. He babbled about the huge Swedish forces on their way to Uistye and made a point of describing the artillery which, as he put it, was of a quality and caliber never seen in the field before and which could demolish anything before it. In no time at all inflated rumors spread among the tents, growing more threatening with every repetition, so that hardly anyone slept that night in the Polish earthworks.

Near to midnight the detachments quartered in the other camps began to arrive at Uistye. The assembled dignitaries weighed their reply until long past sunrise and the provincials passed their time in excited gossip about the might of the approaching Swedes. They shot anxious questions at the trumpeter about his commanders, about the quality of the troops, their weapons and their battle tactics, and everything he told them flew through the whole camp as soon as he said it. The nearness of the enemy gave every detail a particular importance and no one seemed to notice that these revelations made the Swedes appear quite invincible.

At dawn, Pan Stanislav Skshetuski came in from patrol with news that the Swedes were near Valtz, a day's march away, and the gentry rushed to arms as if the battle was to start at any moment. Most of the horses and servants were out of the encampment, still in their bivouacs and pastures, and they came pouring in with utmost confusion, trampling everything in sight. The various county contingents ran to form their ranks. Troops of provincial gentry buckled on their armor, mounted their horses and pushed into formation. But because the eve of battle is the most terrifying moment for untried and inexperienced soldiers, the chaos threatened to reach the proportions of a panic, and it took the hoarse, sweating captains a good part of the morning to get the army in some sort of order.

The noise and yelling deafened everyone. The shouts drowned out words of command and even the cry of trumpets.

From everywhere around came howls of "Yan! Peter! Onu-
fryi...! Where the devil are you! Where's my horse? What's
happened to my servants? Yan! Peter! Come here, damn your
soul!"

A single cannon shot fired in that moment would have sent
the whole assembly running for their lives in mindless, headlong
panic.

But slowly, step by frantic step, the territorial levies calmed
down and took their places in the battle line. The gentry may
have lacked experience but they were, after all, the traditional
defenders of their country so that by noon the camp looked
quite impressive. The brightly uniformed peasant infantry stood
on the walls, bringing to mind a hedgerow full of flowers; thin
wisps of smoke rose from the gunners' matches in the gun
emplacements; and the plain before the earthworks filled with
the mounted squires, formed into their provincial regiments and
troops, and gripped by sudden passion and impatience to begin
the battle. The shrill snorts and neighing of their restless char-
gers sent warlike echoes ringing through the trees in the nearby
groves and flooded them with ardor.

★ ★ ★

Meanwhile the *Voyevode* of Poznan dispatched the Swedish
trumpeter with his reply to Wittemberg's and Radeyovski's
letters which took the form that Radeyovski had foreseen—in
other words both 'courteous' and 'Roman'—after which he
ordered a strong cavalry patrol to the north bank of the Notetz
in search of prisoners to question.

His cousin Pyotr, the *Voyevode* of Podlasye, was to command
this expedition in person, leading his own household troop of
one hundred and fifty dragoons, while Captains Skorashevski
and Skshetuski were ordered to collect a few more volunteers
from among the gentry so that these untried warriors might
finally get a whiff of gunpowder as well.

They made a brave sight as they rode along the regimental
lines: Pan Stanislaw as dark-skinned as all the Skshetuskis, with
fierce aquiline features decorated by a long white scar left by a
saber stroke, and with his long black beard whipping in the
breeze; and Pan Vladyslav looking a bit less martial with his
plump, kindly face, drooping lower lip, redrimmed eyes and

dangling pale mustache, but well-respected for his wide military skills and universally admired for his personal courage.

"Well gentlemen," they repeated riding along the ranks. "Who wants to try the Swedes? Who wants a sniff of powder? Join us, gentlemen, join us! Who will volunteer?"

They crossed a fair distance with no result before anyone stepped forward. The provincials stood still, blinking at each other and nudging each other, suddenly embarrassed and unwilling to be the first to move, and muttering to their neighbors in the ranks: "I'll go if you will."

"Well, what about it, gentlemen? What about it?" the two captains shouted.

They were beginning to get impatient when suddenly, as they were passing the Poznan contingent, a little man dressed in a jester's multicolored patchwork clothes and riding a child's pony galloped out from behind the ranks.

"Mister provincials!" he shouted. "From now on I'm the volunteer and you are the clowns!"

"Ostrozka! Ostrozka!" the gentry roared, amused and delighted.

"As good a man as any of you, that's certain!" the jester replied.

"Tfui! What the devil!" cried Pan Rosinski, a provincial judge. "Enough of this clowning! I'm volunteering!"

"And I! And I," cried a dozen voices. "One life is enough! I'm going too!"

"Make room for me!" others began to shout. "I'm as good as you! Let's not have anybody push himself ahead of anybody else!"

And just as moments earlier no one stirred, less worried about the Swedes than what their brother-gentry might think of their undignified eagerness, so now they poured out of the ranks from every direction. In moments five hundred horsemen grouped behind the two captains while dozens more came galloping from each county and district contingent, pushing each other, racing to be the first, colliding and quarreling.

"Enough, dear brothers!" Pan Skorashevski cried in his kindly voice and began to laugh. "Enough! We can't all go this time!"

Then he and Skshetuski put their volunteers in order and led them away. The army watched them as they forded the river, broad but quite shallow at this point, and took the highway leading to the border. Their bright coats and weapons caught the light of the afternoon sun at the bends of the road for a while longer and then they were gone.

Half an hour later the *Voyevode* of Poznan sent everyone back to their tents, deciding that it made no sense to keep more than twenty thousand men waiting in the ranks while the enemy was still a whole day's march away. But alert sentries were set to pace the walls, the cavalry's horses were kept within the earthworks, and everyone was warned to mount up and assemble at the first muffled sound of a signal trumpet.

The waiting was over.

And along with that there was a sudden end to all the anxious worrying and doubting and arguments and quarrels; it was just as Pan Skshetuski had foretold: the nearness of the enemy did what all the efforts of the officers failed to accomplish.

Discipline was restored at once.

Sagging spirits lifted.

The first successful engagement might even send it soaring, everyone believed, and the excited gentry looked eagerly for anything that might be taken for a lucky omen.

Chapter Nineteen

AS IT HAPPENED, they didn't have long to wait for a fresh wave of encouragement and enthusiasm.

That evening, just as the setting sun threw a blinding glare along the river and the woods beyond it, the sentries spotted a long trail of dust rising in the north, and then a large group of men and horses moving in the dust cloud. The whole army climbed up on the walls to see what kind of new guests to expect and then one of the Grudjinski dragoons galloped in from an outpost on the riverbank with news that the raiding expedition was coming back again.

"They're coming back! Successfully!" the word flew eagerly from mouth to mouth. "The Swedes didn't devour them after all!"

The raiders, meanwhile, wound slowly through their sunlit dust cloud and then began to ford the river. The gathered gentry peered at them through the reddish glare, shielding their eyes from the sharpening brightness as the air around them turned into gold and purple.

"Ey, am I wrong? Seems to me as if there's more of them coming in then went out," observed Pan Shlyhting, the magistrate of Syeradz.

"Is it prisoners they've got, then?" cried some other squire, who evidently expected only the worst of a meeting with the Swedes and couldn't believe his eyes. "As God's my witness, brothers, they've got prisoners!"

In the meantime the riders drew close enough so that the watching crowds could recognize their faces. Pan Skorashevski rode in front—smiling, nodding his head in his kindly manner, and chatting with Skshetuski—while a large group of horsemen surrounded several dozen disarmed infantrymen behind them. The sight of these downcast, slogging foot soldiers, each of them wearing a hat as broad-brimmed as a wagon wheel, brought a booming cheer from the staring gentry.

"*Vivat* Skorashevski!" they bellowed, leaping off the earthwall and running forward to surround the returning scouting expedition.

"Long live Skshetuski!"

In moments, jubilant dense crowds ringed the entire detachment, gaping at the prisoners and bombarding the escort with excited questions, while others shook their fists at the captured Swedes.

"What do you say now, you sons of bitches? Well? So you wanted a war with the Poles, did you? And what do you think of it now?"

Others shook their sabers in the prisoners faces, threatening to turn them into mincemeat, and asking how they liked the taste of Polish steel.

"Gentlemen, gentlemen," Pan Skorashevski cautioned. "Don't yell like a bunch of schoolboys or the Swedes will think you've never tasted war before. It's a normal thing to take prisoners in wartime."

The volunteers who joined the raiding party now rode as proudly as if they won a war, looking down at their less adventurous companions out of fierce, haughty faces.

"How was it, then?" the questions flew at them from everywhere around them. "Did they give up easy? Or did you have to sweat a little? How do they fight? Eh? Are they good or bad?"

"They're good men," Pan Rosinski answered. "And they put up quite a fight. But they're not made of iron. A saber cuts them like anybody else."

"They couldn't stand up against you, eh?"

"They couldn't take the weight of the charge."

"Hey, gentlemen, d'you hear? They couldn't take the charge. So what did I tell you? The charge's the thing like it's always been!"

★ ★ ★

If someone had sent this gentry into a charge at this very moment they'd probably find more than enough enthusiasm and determination to carry the day. But there was nobody to charge anywhere in sight. Instead, well after sunset, another trumpeter appeared at the outposts with Wittemberg's demand for an unconditional surrender.

The infuriated gentry wanted to massacre the messenger on the spot, but the leadership called another meeting to discuss the letter even though it was couched in such sharp, unequivocal and contemptuous terms that there was really nothing to talk about. The Swedish marshal wrote to inform the magnates that Charles Gustav was sending his own troops to help his cousin Yan Casimir in his war with the Russians and the Cossackry, and called upon the Vyelkopolian gentry to lay down their arms without further trouble or face the consequences. Reading this letter, Pan Grudjinski couldn't control himself with rage and slammed the table with his fist, but the *Voyevode* of Poznan soon took this show of spirit out of him.

"Do you believe we have a chance of victory here?" he asked. "No? Then tell us, how many days can we defend ourselves? Are you ready to take the responsibility for all the useless bloodshed that can begin tomorrow?"

After a long debate, the council decided to ignore the letter and see what happened next. Nor did they have long to wait. The next day, on Saturday, July 24, the outposts sent word that the Swedish army was in sight at Pila. The whole encampment boiled at once with activity like a shaken beehive. The gentry armed themselves once more and mounted their horses. The *Voyevodes* galloped back and forth, giving contradictory orders, until Pan Skorashevski took charge of it all, got everyone positioned where they were supposed to stand, quietened down the shouting and restored a semblance of order.

Then he called for volunteers to try their hand against the enemy in hand-to-hand encounters—the traditional Polish prologue to a battle—and led a few hundred of the braver gentry across the river.

This time the gentry followed him readily enough. The traditional *hartze*—a sort of miniature cavalry encounter in which small groups of horsemen fought each other between the watching armies—was largely a matter of single combat, man to man, and since every country squire was trained in swordsmanship from childhood few of them felt a reason for any kind of fear.

They crossed the river and formed up to wait for the enemy who, in the meantime, spilled across the horizon as if some dark and mysterious forest had pulled up all its roots and was now rolling remorselessly towards them. Foot and horse regiments swung quickly and silently into line, long lines of cannon began to dot the plain, and the sun glittered, cold as ice, on their massed pikes and muskets.

The waiting gentry expected that picked Swedish horsemen, Reiters and dragoons, would gallop out towards them to try their long straight rapiers against the Polish sabers, but they did not appear. Instead, small groups of men and horses halted on a number of hillocks which lay at a distance of a few hundred paces and started busying themselves in place.

Pan Skorashevski threw one quick look at them and commanded: "Columns left, to the rear! Ride!"

But he had barely spoken when long streams of black smoke boiled out of the hillocks, there was a sudden hiss and rumble overhead as if a flock of giant birds had passed above the gentry, and then a thunderous roar shook the air amid the screams of wounded men and horses.

"Hold your line!" Pan Skorashevski shouted. "Stand fast! Dress your ranks!"

But another iron flock whirred towards the gentry, and then came another, and this time the panicked squires scattered in all directions, calling on God and all the saints to help them, and galloped pell-mell back to the encampment.

Pan Skorashevski cursed and raged among them but that didn't stop them.

★ ★ ★

Having brushed the Vyelkopolians aside with so little effort, Wittemberg continued his march until he reached the crossing near Uistye. The earthworks here were defended by the Kalish gentry whose cannon opened fire at once. Streamers of gunsmoke spread in the still air between the two armies but the Swedes paid no attention to this cannonade.

The watching gentry saw the enemy forming their battle line with a chilling calmness as if no one among the Swedes doubted in their victory. The great hard-edged rectangles of musketeers and pikemen swung left and right with the precision of a single body; the mounted Reiters wheeled as if on parade; the engineers set about constructing their revetments, parallels and gabions, and the gunners started to emplace their cannon. The light shot hurled at them from the Polish trenches fell short everywhere; all it did was to throw some sand on the working parties.

Pan Stanislav Skshetuski led two squadrons of Kalish cavalry out of the Polish earthworks, wanting to throw the Swedes into disorder by a quick attack, but the hesitating gentry showed little willingness to charge anyone. Their lines broke at once as the braver men among them attempted to push forward while the more tremulous reined their mounts behind them. Two regiments of armored cuirassiers sent by Wittemberg hit them head-on like an iron fist and, after a brief clash, drove them off the field and chased them all the way to the Polish trenches.

Meanwhile the sun had set.

The Polish *vivatovki*—light field pieces that were little more than an arquebus mounted on two small wheels, and which were used mainly to pop off salutes during feasts and banquets—kept firing until it was too dark to see anything ahead. But they no sooner fell silent when a vast uproar broke out in the camp behind them where several hundred downhearted provincials tried to slip out of the camp under the cover of night.

Others tried to stop them.

Sabers flashed.

Threats thundered through the air, the cry of "Everyone or no one!" swept once more through the encampment, and every passing moment suggested to the captains that it was 'everyone' who was more likely to run off than 'no one.'

The panicked gentry's disillusionment and anger turned also on their inept commanders, but for reasons far more typical of these comfort-loving squires than the fact that their various *Voyevodes* and magnates were quite incompetent and unfit to command an army.

"They're sending us with bare bellies against cannon!" the complainers wailed, and then turned their indignation against Wittemberg.

"We came out for the *hartze* in the best of faith! Like civilized people! He could've sent his own riders against us, couldn't he? But what does he do instead?"

"Imagine shooting guns at us!" they howled. "What kind of people reply to a challenge with artillery?"

"Yes, yes," others muttered. "Everyone does what's best for him, that's reasonable enough. But it's a swinish custom not to go hand-to-hand against a man... That's not playing fair! Ah, is this the kind of war we've been brought here to fight?"

Others lost whatever heart they had and gave up any hope of making a successful stand.

"They'll smoke us out of these earthworks like badgers from a hole," they muttered and then looked for something other than themselves to blame. "The camp is laid out all wrong... The walls aren't strong enough... We shouldn't be here to begin with, some other place would've been better to defend..."

From time to time panicked voices bellowed: "Brothers! Gentlemen! Run! Save yourselves!"

And others shouted: "Treason! Treason! We've been sold out, betrayed! Treason!"

It was a night of chaos, fear, desperation and confusion that grew by the minute.

Nobody listened to any kind of order; the *Voyevodes* didn't know what to do or how to bring their men back under control and, finally, too distraught even to make their usual ringing speeches, they lost their heads altogether and gave way to despair. If Wittemberg had launched a night attack he would have taken the earthworks unopposed.

★ ★ ★

But at last the terrible night wound to its dreary end. Dawn came. The sun rose slowly, as if unwilling to look down at the dispirited, gloomy gathering below, and its pale grey light fell on a wandering, demoralized crowd that trailed aimlessly among the tents and wagons. Most of these so-called soldiers were too drunk by then to care about anything. Others stumbled about, cursing their hopeless fate, or sat plunged in listless gloom lamenting their misfortunes, and all of them were far more ready for shame and disgrace than for any thought of fighting or resistance.

To make matters worse the Swedes used the night to bridge and ford the river farther downstream, getting their infantry and cavalry to the Polish bank under the cover of darkness, and the dawn found them formed for battle on the landward side of the Vyelkopolians' camp where there were few if any entrenchments. What had to be done at once was to get to work, fortify the exposed, open rear of the surrounded earthworks, and barricade that gaping, unsecured back door before it was forced. Skorashevski and Skshetuski begged everyone they could induce to listen not to waste a moment before this was done but no one, either among the leadership or the common gentry, wanted to hear anything about it.

Instead, one word—'negotiations'—was on everybody's lips and envoys were dispatched to the Swedish camp under a flag of truce. In reply, the Swedes sent a splendid embassy, headed by Radeyovski and General Wirtz, who rode in with smiles on their faces, and fresh green branches in their hands as a sign of amity and peace.

They rode towards the house of the *Voyevode* of Poznan but Radeyovski stopped often among the crowds of gentry, bowing to them repeatedly with his plumed Swedish hat and waving his imitation olive-branch, smiling with obvious joy and calling out greetings to his acquaintances among them.

"Gentlemen! Friends! Dearest brothers!" he cried out in a voice that carried through the camp. "Be calm! Don't be afraid! We didn't come here as your enemies! No one is going to harm you! We are here to save you and protect you! It is entirely up to you whether another drop of blood is to be spilled in this place...!

"But,"—and the traitor's rasping voice began to sound like a balm of pure, soothing reason to the leaderless, confused and dispirited gentry—"if you want to preserve all your liberties and freedoms, rather than bowing to a tyrant who wants to impose a *dominium absolutum* on you and your children, and who has brought our dear country to its final ruin... if you, I repeat, would rather live in peace under a good and merciful lord, a truly splendid monarch, and a warrior of such mighty reputation that all of this Commonwealth's enemies will run in panic at the sound of his name... if, as I say, that's what you'd rather have in the place of bloodshed... then place yourselves and all that's dear to you under the benign protection of His Majesty King Charles Gustav of Sweden!

"Here!" And he waved a piece of rolled parchment in the reddening air. "I bring a guarantee of all your ancient privileges and freedoms! Your right to vote! Your rights of discussion! Your freedom of religion! Your salvation, brothers, lies in your own hands!

"Gentlemen! Brothers!" he appealed at last. "Who else but His Most Illustrious Majesty, the King of Sweden, can put an end to the Cossack rebellion and the Russian war? Have mercy on our Motherland, dear brothers, even if you have no mercy on yourselves!"

And here the traitor's voice quavered as if he was choking with tears of patriotic feeling.

The gentry listened, peering at each other in astonishment as if not quite sure whether to believe their ears, and here and there a stray, hesitating voice cried out: "*Vivat* Radeyovski... our chancellor! Long live Radeyovski...!"

And he rode on, bowing and beaming at fresh crowds of listeners, and his stentorian voice echoed in yet another corner of the camp, "Dearest friends...! Good brothers..." until at last he and the Swedish general disappeared through the doorway of Kristof Opalinski's quarters where all the *Voyevodes*, the magnates and the dignitaries waited.

The lesser gentry packed the space outside the meeting house so tightly that a nimble man could have crossed the entire market square by skipping across their heads as if they were cobble stones. All of them, no matter what they thought about it, felt and understood that the decisions made inside that building concerned not only them and what would happen to them but also the fate and future of their entire nation.

Soon afterwards some red-coated servants of the *Voyevode* came out to invite the more notable 'personages' among the provincials inside to the meeting. These hurried in, eager to take part in the deliberations, and a few of the ordinary gentry also managed to squeeze in behind them. The rest, massed in the open air, crowded against the door and the windows to hear any word that might seep outside.

* * *

Not since the first clod of earth was turned in the camp at Uistye had there been such a breathless silence among the Vyelkopolians. Those who stood closer to the windows heard, from time to time, loud voices raised in argument, angry exclamations, and sounds that brought to mind the echoes of a storm. Orators rumbled on and on. Speakers droned. Sharp cries of protest, muffled by the walls, were like occasional angry punctuations. Hours passed. It seemed as if the conference would go on, endlessly, for ever.

But suddenly the outer doors were flung wide, rattling against the walls, and Pan Vladyslav Skorashevski ran out of the meeting.

His face—usually so calm and mild and soothing and kindly that, as the saying went, he might have been used for a healing poultice if pressed against a wound— was twisted now in such a look of stark, disbelieving horror that the assembled gentry fell back in awe and terror. His eyes were bloodshot, glazed with the blank stare of lunacy. His coat and shirt were ripped open on his chest. His fingers clutched his own disordered hair. He fell among the gentry like a thunderbolt, shouting in a shrill, ear-piercing voice:

"Treason! Murder! Shame! We're Swedes now, not Poles! They're murdering our Motherland in there!"

And he began to howl in a spasmodic, helpless fit of weeping, clawing at his hair like a man driven into madness, while a numb, gravelike stillness settled on the crowd as if every chest among them was suddenly robbed of air.

But Skorashevski tore himself out of his mental nightmare and began to run among the gaping country squires, shouting at them in a voice that spiraled with despair: "To arms! To arms, if you believe in God! To arms! To arms!"

A strange, ragged murmur began to rise out of that crowd of thousands. Abrupt, momentary whispers lifted from the silence, hung in the still, breathless air and died down, sharp and interrupted; it was a sound like the first quick rustling of a wind before a hurricane. Hearts and minds wavered, seized by indecision and poised between disbelief and fear, and in this general consternation of troubled minds and souls, that single tragic voice kept calling: "To arms! To arms!"

Two other voices joined him in a moment, those of his cousin Pan Pyotr Skorashevski and Captain Skshetuski, along with that of Pan Klodjinski, a Furrow Infantry captain of the Poznan contingent, who came running up.

More and more gentry massed around them. The hesitant murmurs began to change into a deep and threatening growl, like a thunderstorm gathering in the distance, and anger flashed like lightning across their dark, grim faces.

Meanwhile Pan Skorashevski managed to master his overwrought emotions.

"Listen to me," he started, pointing at the council house. "What they're doing there is selling our country and shaming us all. Understand, if you can, that we don't belong to Poland any more! It wasn't enough for those Judases in there to surrender all of you into the hands of the enemy, along with all our arms, guns and the camp itself, may they squirm in Hell! No, they've done more than that. They've affirmed in your names as well as their own that we're forswearing our faith to our country, that we're renouncing our nation and our King, and that all these lands, all our towns and cities along with ourselves, will belong from now on and forever to Sweden.

"It happens now and then that an army must surrender," he went on. "But who has the right to renounce his country and his King? Who can tear away an entire province, join a foreign country, make himself a part of another nation, and break his allegiance to his own kind?

"Gentlemen!" he cried. "That is shame that goes beyond mere treason! That is simple murder! That is patricide! Save your Motherland, brothers! Come to her assistance! In God's name, whoever calls himself a noble, fight to protect her and defend your Mother! Let's die here to the last man if we must! Let's spill our blood if that's what is needed, but let's refuse to be Swedes! Let's refuse it! Let us remain Polish! May God curse him who won't give his blood right now for his country's freedom to the eternal fires of Hell! Save our Motherland from shame and dishonor!"

"Treason!" a score of voices roared in reply and other dozens shouted: "Treason! Death to traitors!"

"Join us, whoever calls himself a man!" Skshetuski went on shouting.

"Fight the Swedes! Fight!" Pan Klodjinski echoed.

And they pushed through the crowd, going deeper into the encampment and shouting: "Join us! Stand with us! Treason!" while several hundred others followed in their wake with naked sabers glinting in their hands.

But the vast majority remained mute and stood where they were. And even those who started out behind the protesters began to hesitate, to look back, and seeing how few others were willing to join them in resistance to their leaders' treason, began to slow their pace, to edge out of the determined group, and to slip back into the silent crowd.

★ ★ ★

Meanwhile the doors of the meeting house opened again and Kristof Opalinski appeared on the threshold. He was flanked by Wirtz and Radeyovski. Standing behind him were Pan Andrei Grudjinski, the *Voyevode* of Kalish, and the three other most important Vyelkopolian magnates: Maximilian Myaskovski, Pavel Gembitzki and Andrei Slupetzki.

Grasped in Opalinski's hand was a roll of parchment heavy with dangling seals. He held his head high but his face was pale as if drained of blood, and his eyes seemed wandering and uncertain as they swept across the crowds, although he struggled to appear both merry and delighted.

"Gentlemen!" he announced in a hoarse but steady voice. "Today... in this historic moment... We have placed ourselves under the protection of the King of Sweden. *Vivat Carolus Gustavus Rex!* Long live King Charles Gustav!"

A deathly silence met his ringing cry, and then a single voice called out the phrase with which, according to Polish law and the gentry's custom, any member of the voting gentry could overturn all measures agreed in the petty dietines, and in the Chamber of Deputies itself, and ended all further discussion of the subject: "*Veto!* I protest!"

The *Voyevode* swung his dulled, gloomy eyes slowly towards that voice.

"This isn't a diet," he replied. "So a veto is out of order here. And whoever wants to protest what we've done let him go and argue with the Swedish cannon which can turn this whole camp into a heap of rubble in an hour."

The silence continued for some moments longer and then the *Voyevode* demanded: "Who was it who cried *Veto?*"

Nobody replied.

The *Voyevode* began to speak again.

"All the privileges of the nobility and the clergy will be preserved," he said, stressing every word. "Taxes won't be raised without consent and will be assigned and collected in the same manner as before. All property will be safe from looting and no one will suffer illegal sequestrations. The armies of His Swedish Majesty may not be quartered in the possessions of the gentry, nor may they make their requisitions in a different manner than Polish regular contingents."

Here he paused, listening eagerly to the whispers which flew among the gentry, as if trying to judge the effect of his words upon them. Then he gestured briefly and went on:

"Beside that, I've the solemn promise of General Wittemberg, given in the name of His Illustrious Majesty, that if the whole nation follows our example, the Swedish army will march to Lithuania and the Ukraine and that it won't stop fighting until all our lost territories, towns, provinces and castles are won back and returned to the Commonwealth! *Vivat Carolus Gustavus Rex!*"

"*Vivat!* Long live King Charles Gustav!" several hundred voices cried out of the crowd and the cry spread wider with each passing minute. "*Vivat Carolus Gustavus Rex!*" the cheers boomed and echoed throughout the encampment.

And here, in the eyes of the entire gathering, the *Voyevode* of Poznan turned to Radeyovski and the Swedish general and embraced them both. The dignitaries followed his example, and so did the gentry, and their shouts and cheers filled the camp with such a joyful roar that it flew across the abandoned earthworks and spread far into the countryside beyond.

But the *Voyevode* had a few more words to say. He asked his 'brother gentry,' with the friendly courtesy for which he was famous, to grant him just one more moment of silence and attention, and then announced in a voice brimming with sincerity and affection:

"Gentlemen! General Wittemberg invites all of us to a banquet in his camp, so that we might drink to our new brotherhood with a noble nation!"

The last threadbare skeins of doubt, uncertainty or resistance—not to mention patriotism, dignity, humanity and honor—seemed to snap and dissipate at the prospects of eating and drinking, good times and a well-filled belly, and all the massed Vyelkopolian gentry, wherever they were in the camp that morning, bellowed as one man: "*Vivat* Wittemberg! Long life to him! *Vivat! Vivat! Vivat!*"

"And afterwards, gentlemen," the *Voyevode* went on. "We will go home in peace, to begin the harvest, knowing that we have saved our Motherland today."

"History will honor us," Radeyovski added. "And future generations will look at us with love and understanding."

"Amen to that," Kristof Opalinski said.

Then, suddenly, he realized that the eyes of the gentry in the square before him had lifted over his head and that they were staring at something behind and above him.

He turned and saw his jester who had climbed part way up the wall. Now, clinging with one hand to the lintel of the door, Ostrozka was writing something with a piece of charcoal, and the dire biblical words of warning, laden with doom and promises of disaster, appeared one by one, as grim as ghosts, above the darkened doorway:

Mane... Tekel... Fares...

The skies overhead became black with clouds because a storm was coming.

Part Four

Chapter Twenty

IN THE VILLAGE of Buhjetz which lay close to the border of Podlasye in the Lukov country—and which, in those times, belonged to the family of Pan Yan Skshetuski—an old man and two lively little boys enjoyed the last of a golden afternoon in the apple orchard. The children were tanned as dark as little Gypsies, and as full of health and sunshine as a pair of berries, while the broad-backed, powerful old man still seemed as full of strength and energy as one of those bearded aurochs that used to rule the forests in medieval times.

He sat on a shaded bench between the manor and the well-stocked fish pond, peering in drowsy contentment at the carp that leaped in the water, while the two boys, one about five years old and the other just a year younger, were playing at his feet. Age hadn't bowed his wide shoulders; his eyes—or rather one of his eyes, since the other was filmed over with the white of blindness—reflected good health and humor; and his crimson forehead showed the yellow gleam of bare bone peering out of an old scar. Each of the little boys had seized one of his bootstraps and pulled on them in opposite directions but the broad-shouldered corpulent old man was paying more attention to the leaping fish.

"Dance, dance," he muttered. "You'll dance even better in a frying pan after Lent, or when the cook is scraping off your scales." Then he turned with mock ferocity on the little boys. "Let go of my boots, you scamps! If you tear off the bootstraps I'll twist off your ears! What a pair of darned little nuisances you are! I'm not surprised by Longinek, because he's still little, but Yaremka ought to show more sense. Leave me in peace or I'll throw you in the pond!"

But the old man was obviously devoted to the little lads and both of them knew it because neither paid any attention to his threats. In fact Yaremka, the older of the two, began to stamp his feet and pulled even harder.

"I want Grandpa to be Bohun and carry off Longinek!" he insisted.

"Leave me alone, you little pest, I say! What a torment you are, the two of you."

"Want Grandpa to be Bohun!"

"I'll give you Bohun," the old man huffed. "Wait till I call your mother!"

Yaremka shot a quick look at the back door of the manor house, but seeing that it was closed and that his mother was nowhere in sight, he repeated for a third time: "Want Grandpa to be Bohun!"

"They'll drive me to an early grave, these little rascals," the old man complained. "Alright, I'll be Bohun, but just this once, understood? What a trial you are! Remember to leave me alone after this!"

Having said his piece, the old man groaned a bit, swooped up Longinek in his arms and started running with wild cries in the direction of the pond. Longinek, however, had a brave defender in the person of little Yaremka, who became Pan Michal Volodyovski in such instances, and who pursued the fat and wheezing Bohun armed with a linden twig in place of a saber. The little rescuer caught up with the fat abductor and began to whip his legs without mercy. Longinek, playing the role of Mother in this favorite drama, yelled to high heavens, as did both the imitation Bohun and Pan Volodyovski, but courage prevailed over evil in the end. Bohun released his victim and fled back to the shade of the tree where he collapsed on the bench gasping like a bellows.

"What pesky little rascals," he wheezed, mopping his crimson face. "It'll be a miracle if I don't have a stroke right here and now and give up the ghost!"

But his time of torment wasn't over yet because Yaremka stood before him once again. Flushed with health and excitement, tumble-haired and with determination shining brightly in his eyes, the little boy seemed like a persistent fledging hawk as he tugged at the old man's arm.

"Want Grandpa to be Bohun!" he demanded even more insistently than before.

After a great deal of pleading and a solemn promise that this time would be definitely the last, the story repeated itself in every detail after which the three of them settled down on the bench.

"Want Grandpa to say who was the bravest!" Yaremka insisted.

"You! You!" the old man assured him.

"And will I grow up to be a knight?"

"Of course you will. You have a great soldier's blood in your veins, that's why! God grant that you'll be as thoughtful, steady and high-minded as your father when you're grown. You'll be less of a pest that way, understand?"

"Want Grandpa to say again how many bad men my Daddy killed in the war!"

"I must've told you a hundred times! You'd count all the leaves on this tree easier than adding up all the enemies that your father and I sent to the next world between us. If I had that many hairs growing on my head, all the wig-makers in the Lukov country would get to be rich men just out of giving me a trim! I'll be damned if I'm lying!"

Here Pan Zagloba, who was the old gentleman in question, remembered that he shouldn't curse in front of the children. And even though for lack of another audience, he was fond of telling the two little boys about his former military triumphs, he let the moment pass. Instead, he bent another anticipatory glance at the leaping fish.

"We should tell the gardener to set up his nets at sundown," he murmured. "There's a whole mess of carp and catfish just itching for the pot."

* * *

Just then the back doors of the manor house opened to reveal a tall, dark-haired woman, as beautiful as the southern sun of the Steppes in which she was raised, with a deep flush spreading through her cheeks and with black eyes as deep and warm and luminous as velvet. Another little boy, this one merely three years' old, clung to her skirt on the back porch as she shaded her eyes and looked in the direction of the linden tree.

This was Lady Helena Skshetuska, wife of Pan Yan Skshetuski, who had been born a Ruthenian princess in the old rural family and clan of Bulyhov-Kurtzevitch.

"Come here boys!" she called out, catching sight of her two older sons sitting beside Zagloba. "Have you been pestering Grandpa?"

"Not a bit of it!" the fat old knight assured her. "In fact they've been behaving pretty well."

The two boys scampered towards their mother through the herb and vegetable garden at the back of the manor, and she asked the old man what he would like to drink that afternoon.

"Hmm," he mused. "We had pork for dinner so mead would be best."

"I'll have it brought right out. Only you shouldn't be sleeping out in the open air, father. You're sure to catch a chill."

"Ey, it's warm today and there's no breeze. But where did Yan go, daughter?"

"He's gone to the stables."

Pani Skshetuska addressed Pan Zagloba as 'father' and he called her 'daughter' although they weren't related in any way. Her family came from beyond the Dnieper, in the former country of the Vishnovyetzkis, while his ancestry was a total mystery. God only knew where he came from, particularly since his stories differed each time that he told one, but he had rendered her some great services while she was still a young, unmarried girl, saving her life and rescuing her from terrifying dangers, so that both she and her husband honored him as they would a father. Indeed, he was regarded with awe throughout the countryside, both for his sharp wits and the wisdom of his long experience, and for the valor he'd shown in a variety of wars, especially in the War of the Cossack Rebellion. His name was widely known across the Commonwealth and the King himself delighted in his tales and his pithy sayings. As for the local gentry, they accorded him even more respect than they showed to Pan Yan Skshetuski, even though Skshetuski had won immortal glory for himself during the siege of Zbarajh.

A few moments after Pani Skshetuska went back into the

house, a serving lad brought out a mossy demijohn of aged vintage mead, made of spiced and fermented honey, which Pan Zagloba sampled with every sign of pleasure out of a crystal goblet.

"God knew why He created bees,"he muttered and sipped the sweet liquor.

Then he went on sipping it slowly and sighing with contentment, gazing at the glimmering, sun-drenched pond and the deep woods beyond it.   It was perhaps two o'clock in the afternoon and there wasn't a cloud in sight anywhere between the broad horizons. The blooms and flowers of the linden tree above him fluttered to the ground without a sound, and the crown of the tree buzzed with whole choirs of bees which soon began to visit the rim of his glass, gathering the honeyed liquor with their furry legs. Swirling above the broad pond, and rising from the misty banks of reed cane that dwindled in the distance, came flocks of wild ducks and geese, spangling the sky like strings of small black crosses.   Sometimes a flight of cranes darkened the pale blue emptiness above them and belled with raucous cries. Other than that there was a great, peaceful silence all around, the blessed and cheerful quietness of an August day, when the ripe wheat is ready for the harvest and the sun floods the land with the sheen of gold.

The old man's eyes either rose to follow the birds across the sky or sunk in the purple distances of the woods, rising and falling slower and more sleepily as the level of the mead in his demijohn dropped towards the bottom, while the humming of the bees played his lullaby.

"Yes, yes,"he muttered, nodding in somnolent assent. "God gave mankind a beautiful time for the harvest... yes, yes, there's no doubt about it."

His eyelids blinked heavily once or twice. He opened them again just long enough to mutter: "The lads wore me out, bless their little hearts..."

Then his head drooped down across his chest and he began to snore.

★ ★ ★

He slept for quite a long time, nodding in the sun, until a cooler breeze brought him awake again, and then he heard the voices and the footsteps of two men who were coming quickly towards his bench under the linden tree. One of them was Pan Yan Skshetuski, the hero of Zbarajh, who was home on a month's leave from the Ukraine trying to rid himself of a stubborn fever; the other was a stranger whom Pan Zagloba had never seen before but who resembled Pan Yan almost like a twin.

"Let me introduce my first cousin, father," Pan Yan said. "This is Pan Stanislav Skshetuski, of Skshetushev in the Kalish region, and a captain in that county's levy."

"A pleasure, a pleasure!" Pan Zagloba muttered, shaking off the last of his sleepiness. "You're so much like Yan that I'd say straight off *'That's a Skshetuski'* without an introduction. Welcome to our home!"

"It's a great pleasure for me to meet you sir," Pan Stanislav said. "All the more since I've heard so much about you everywhere I've gone. You're an example to us all."

"Ah well," the fat knight said, pleased as ever to be praised and honored. "One did what one could while the strength lasted in the bones. Even now I wouldn't mind another taste of war because it gets into a man's blood, don't you know, with us old campaigners. But why do you two look so worried? Eh? Yan's gone quite pale, I see!"

"Stanislav brings us terrible news, father," Pan Yan said gravely. "The Swedes have marched into Vyelkopolska and occupied it all."

"Eh? What? What's that? What d'you mean they've occupied it all? How could they do that?"

"Quite simply, sir," Pan Stanislav said. "The Palatine of Poznan handed it over to the enemy at Uistye, lock, stock and barrel."

"What? What? What are you saying, man? You mean they surrendered?"

"They not only surrendered but they signed an act of renunciation, forswearing their allegiance to our King and Country! It's supposed to be Sweden over there now, not Poland."

"Dear God! What is this? The end of the world or what? What is this I'm hearing? Just yesterday Yan and I were talking about this danger from the Swedes, because we heard that they might be coming, but we thought it would all blow over as it has before. At most, we thought, His Majesty would give up his Swedish titles and that would be that!"

"Instead we've given up an entire province and God only knows how it'll all end."

"Enough, by God!" Pan Zagloba bellowed, seizing his head in both hands. "Enough or I'll have a stroke! How could that happen? You were at Uistye yourself and saw it all with your own eyes? Has there ever been such an act of treason anywhere before?"

"I was there," Pan Stanislav said and nodded grimly. "I saw it. As for the full extent of the treason you'll be able to judge it when you've heard it all. We were in camp at Uistye, about fifteen thousand territorial infantry and gentry, watching over the crossings on the Notetz. It's true it wasn't much of a force, and you sir, as an experienced military man, know best if the provincial levy can ever take the place of trained regulars. But with a good commander we could have done something. Instead, just as soon as Wittemberg showed up, they got to parleys and negotiating. Then Radeyovski came and talked them into the rest of it, by which I mean a calamity and a shame unknown in all history."

"How's that, then?" The fat old knight looked as if he'd never understand what he was hearing then. "Nobody resisted? Nobody protested? Did they all agree to betray their country and their King?"

"All decency is dying out these days and the Commonwealth is dying right beside it," Pan Stanislav said. "The opposition didn't amount to more than half a dozen men. I thought Pan Skorashevski would go mad. He and I and his brother and a few other officers did what we could to stir up the gentry. We ran through the whole camp, begging the provincials to show a little backbone and pleading for resistance. But what was the use? Our gentry were more anxious to dip their spoons and wet their gullets at Wittemberg's banquet than to try their sabers in any kind of battle. Whoever wouldn't go that far into treason either went home in disgust or headed for Warsaw where the two Skorashevskis carried the news to the King. As for me, having neither a wife nor a family, I headed here to my Cousin Yan, thinking that we'd come up with something to turn the tables on the enemy. It's a good thing that I found you gentlemen at home!"

"So you've come straight from Uistye?"

"That's right. The only rest I took was what my horses needed. As it is, one foundered from exhaustion."

"And where are the Swedes?"

"They must have got to Poznan already by now and from there they'll spread throughout the whole country."

★ ★ ★

Then they were silent. Pan Yan stared at the ground, grim as a brooding storm cloud, with his heavy fists pressed between his knees. Pan Stanislav sighed. Pan Zagloba stared from one to the other of the two Skshetuskis, still unable to come to terms with what he had heard.

"None of this augurs well for the future," Pan Yan said at last. "In the old days we'd have one setback for ten stunning victories, and the whole world stood in awe and wonder at our might and valor. Today we get not only a steady diet of disasters but treason as well. And not just by individuals, which can happen in any society, but by entire provinces...! May God find some mercy for our unhappy country."

"By God," Zagloba said. "I've seen a lot in this world but I still can't believe this."

"What are you thinking of doing, Yan?" Pan Stanislav asked.

"You can be sure I won't stay home even though I'm still shaking with that fever. First I must think of a safe refuge for my wife and children. Pan Stabrovski, a kinsman of mine, is the King's Forester in Byelovyezha Forest and makes his home in the township there. Even if all of the Commonwealth fell into enemy hands they won't find their way into Byelovyezha. My wife and children can go there tomorrow."

"You can't be too careful," Stanislav agreed. "Even though it's a long way from here to Vyelkopolska there's no way to know how far the war will spread."

"We'll have to let our local gentry know about this too," Pan Yan said. "They'll have to get together and start thinking about defense measures of their own."

Then he turned to Zagloba. "And how about you, father?

Will you go with us or would you rather accompany Helen to the forest?"

"I? Will I go with you?" The old knight prepared to launch himself into one of those fierce perorations for which he was famous. "Maybe I wouldn't go if my legs took root in the ground, 'though I'd ask to be uprooted quick enough! I'm as anxious to smell Swedish meat again as a wolf longs for a whiff of mutton! Ha, the scoundrels! The fleas are nipping at them in their droopy drawers so they can't sit still, so they have to fidget and invade somebody! I know them well, with their plumes and stockings, because I served against them the last time they stuck their snouts into the Commonwealth. And if you want to know who it was who knocked down Gustaphus Adolphus and took him prisoner then you'd better ask the late Pan Konyetzpolski! I won't say another word about it!"

Now warmed up and letting his rich imagination suggest that he was the hero of that famous moment when the late Hetman Konyetzpolski stopped the last invasion by the Scandinavians, the old knight assured the two younger men that the Swedes had good reason to remember him.

"They must have heard that Zagloba isn't as young as he used to be," he cried. "That's what it's all about! But we'll soon see about that! I still have a thing or two to show them! Dear God, why did you take down all the fences round the Commonwealth and let all our neighbors' pigs start rooting among us? They've already gobbled up three of our best provinces. And who's to blame for that if not traitors? Eh?"

Pan Yan was used to Pan Zagloba's flamboyant harangues—which, by that time, were purely a matter of habit—whose goal was to assure whoever was listening that the old knight was, or might have been, responsible for every notable incident in recorded history. But Pan Stanislav listened to him with a kind of awe.

"The plague didn't know whom to take so she took decent people and left all the traitors!" Zagloba went on. "I wish she would pay a call on the *Voyevode* of Poznan and the Lord of Kalish—not to mention Radeyovski and all his aunts and uncles! And if God wants to increase the population of Hell he can fill it up with all those who signed that act of capitulation at Uistye!

Ha! So they think Zagloba's getting old, do they? They'll soon know the difference! Yan, let's decide right now where to go and what to do because I can't wait to get back on horseback!"

"Going to the Hetmans in the Ukraine isn't easy these days," Pan Yan said. "The enemy has cut them off from the rest of the Commonwealth and their only connection with the world is through the Crimea. Thank God the Tartars are on our side this time. My thought would be to go to Warsaw and defend His Majesty who must be needing every loyal man he can find."

"If only we get there in time," Pan Stanislav warned. "His Majesty must be pulling together whatever troops he can and he'll be marching on the enemy long before we come in sight of Warsaw. That battle might be taking place at this very moment and we'll be too late."

"That's true too."

"Let's head for Warsaw anyway," Pan Zagloba said. "But listen a minute. I know that our three names are sure to fill the enemy with terror and dismay but we ought to have a few more bodies with us. Why don't we call out some of our local gentry? Even a small troop might help. They'll have to go anyway when the General Levy is called out in this region so they won't be hard to persuade to set out a bit earlier. We can do more with a larger force and we'll be welcomed all the better by the King in Warsaw."

"Don't let my words surprise you, sir," Pan Stanislav said. "But after what I've seen at Uistye I'd rather go to war alone than with a crowd of sheep-clipping country squires who don't know anything about military service."

"Ah well, you don't know our gentry around here! You won't find one who hasn't sampled some campaign before. They're all experienced men and good soldiers too."

"That's different, then."

"I should think so too! But wait a moment longer! Yan already knows that once I put my head to work I'm full of ideas. That's why I lived in such a close and confidential relationship with the late *Voyevode* of Ruthenia, our dear Prince Yeremi. Let Yan tell you how often this greatest war leader of the modern world took my advice on one thing or another and he was never sorry that he did it."

Pan Yan, who disliked lies and had no recollections of that

kind, made a gruff noncommittal gesture somewhere between a headshake and a shrug. He was genuinely fond of the garrulous old noble, and neither stretched the truth to support Pan Zagloba's exaggerated claims nor let himself cast any public doubt on his credibility.

"Just finish what you started saying to us, father," he urged with a shade of worry and impatience in his voice. "We are wasting time."

"What I started saying? Alright, here's what I started saying. It's not the man who clutches at his sovereign's coat-tails who is the best defender of his King and country. He who serves best is he who beats the enemy, and the best way to do that is to serve under a great commander. Why should we go to Warsaw when the King might've already gone to Krakow, Lvov or even to Lithuania? My thought is to join up right away with the forces of the Grand Hetman of the Lithuanians, Prince Yanush Radzivill. That's a warlike lord and a great military leader. So people gossip about him being all puffed up with pride and ambition, but what's wrong with that? At least he'll be too proud to capitulate to the Swedes! That's a real Hetman, a soldier to the bone, not some Vyelkopolian pen-pusher with ink in his veins! True, it'll be a little tight for us over there, what with two wars going on at the same time, but at least we'll get to see Pan Michal Volodyovski who serves now in the Lithuanian corps. We'll be together again like in the old days, Yan! Hmm? Eh? What do you say to that? If this isn't good advice then may the first Swede we meet take me for a hostage!"

"Could be!" Pan Yan agreed, brightening up at once. "That could be just the thing!"

"And we'll get to escort Helen and the children as far as Byelovyezha because that'll be on our way."

"And we'll be serving among real soldiers, thank God," Pan Stanislav added. "Not a bunch of squabbling country bumpkins."

"That's right! We'll be fighting and campaigning, not politicking or eating out all the cheese presses and chicken coops in the countryside!"

"I can see sir," Pan Stanislav said to the fat knight, "that you're just as formidable at a council table as you are in the field."

"Eh?" Pan Zagloba beamed with pleasure. "You think so, hmm? What?"

"It really is the best course to follow," Pan Yan agreed. "Riding with Michal once more will be like the old times. You'll meet the greatest soldier in the Commonwealth," he said to his cousin. "And one, moreover, who's my dearest friend, closer than a brother. But let's go and warn Helen to get ready for the journey."

"Does she know about the war already?" Pan Zagloba asked.

"She knows. Stanislav told his story to us both. She's all in tears, poor thing. But when I told her that I'd have to go she agreed at once."

"I'd like to start out first thing tomorrow morning!" Pan Zagloba cried.

"And so we shall," Pan Yan said.

★ ★ ★

They set out the next day. Pan Yan sent men with teams of relay horses and provision wagons to wait for them in every major habitation all the way to Belsk; and in just five days, not even stopping anywhere for the night, the little expedition came to the outskirts of Europe's largest, deepest and least known virgin forest, which stretched in a dense, dark and largely impenetrable mass all the way to the woody marshlands of Prussia and Mazuria, and flowed into the vast reaches of the Lithuanian forests in the north.

Six days after leaving home, Pan Yan led his family convoy into those dark primeval depths which no invader in history had ever entered to emerge alive.

They made their way through a dim, silent landscape of vast forest giants that blocked out the light five hundred feet and more overhead, riding among hidden chasms and ravines, overgrown mounds of deadfall, and blind contradictory trails that crisscrossed unchanged in this wilderness since prehistoric times and dwindled into nothing within a hundred paces. A lost stranger, wandering without a guide, would never find his way out into civilization, even if he escaped the forest's vast animal populations. The still, breathless nights echoed with the distant roaring of bison, bears and aurochs, the grunting snarls of wildcats crouched in the invisible black branches that roofed every trail, the fierce squeal of boars, and the baying of great packs of timber wolves.

What trails there were, linking scattered settlements of trappers and pitchmakers who spent their whole lives in those deadly shadows, edged past unbridgeable chasms filled with a densely packed, tangled vegetation piled higher than a horseman, uprooted oaks whose toppled sides loomed taller than most rooftops, deep sunken craters that once contained the roots of the fallen giants, sudden black swamps, and seething green lakes hidden in an eternal mist that seemed all the more terrible and threatening in their hungry and indifferent stillness.

The only permanent track that wound through the outer reaches of this naturally inhospitable wilderness was a short, stone highway, known as the Dry Road, that connected the Royal hunting lodge and its supporting settlement with Belsk and the outside world. That is the road that the Kings' court and household used in the hunting seasons, and that is the track that carried Yan Skshetuski's small party to safety.

Pan Stabrovski, the King's chief forester and huntsman, seemed to go mad with joy at the sight of his unexpected visitors, particularly the children whom he kissed and hugged as if they were the most precious creatures he had ever seen. An old bachelor living alone for years at a time, he seldom ventured from the forests unless it was time for his annual rendering of accounts with Pan Gosyevski, the Treasurer of Lithuania. Other than that, the only humans he ever got to see were the trackers, trappers, hunters, tanners, pitchmakers, woodcutters and haulers whose work he directed, and who were sometimes hard to tell from the prowling predators whose skins and furs they wore.

The news of the war was as fresh to him as if it had broken out only the day before but that was no surprise. It happened often that wars, invasions, rebellions and other great human convulsions came and ended elsewhere in the Commonwealth, or that Kings died and new monarchs ascended to the throne, and no word of it ever reached the forest.

"It'll be boring here for you, my dear," he apologized to Helen. "There is nothing to do and nowhere to go. But you'll be safe here, you and the little ones, of that I assure you. No enemy will ever penetrate those forest walls of mine. And if one should try, he'll never escape an ambush by the forest people.

It'd be easier for the Swedes to conquer the entire Commonwealth—which God forbid!—then come in here without an
invitation.

"I've been here twenty years now," he assured Skshetuski,
"and even I can't find my way through more than a fraction of
this wilderness. There are forests within forests here, where no
human being has ever set foot. Only the wild beast creeps along
those trails, and no one knows what kind of creatures, unknown
or forgotten elsewhere in the world, still make their lairs in
there. As for the few people hereabouts, we live in peace as
quietly as God intended when He created Man. We've a chapel
in the settlement and a priest from Belsk calls on us once a year.
Your family will be as safe here, Yan, as if they were in Heaven,
if only the boredom doesn't get them down... But at least we've
never yet run out of firewood in Winter."

Pan Yan was delighted to find such a refuge for his wife and
children but not even Pan Stabrovski's eager hospitality could
delay the rest of the expedition.

The three knights merely rested in the King's Lodge until
daybreak and rode out at sunrise, led straight across the trackless
labyrinth by experienced woodsmen whom Pan Stabrovski
loaned them for the journey.

Chapter Twenty-one

WHEN PAN ZAGLOBA and the two Skshetuskis finally reached Upita, after a difficult journey through the wilderness and the Lithuanian forests, Pan Michal Volodyovski was so overjoyed at seeing his two old friends again that he almost seemed to lose his mind with pleasure. It had been a long time, a matter of some years, since he'd had any news about either of them. As for Pan Yan, whom he loved better than a brother, the little colonel was sure he'd be in the Ukraine, cut off in the southeast with the rest of the Crown Hetmans' army, and not likely ever to see the Commonwealth again.

He hugged and embraced them over and over, and rubbed his hands in anticipation of their good times together, and when they told him that they came to take service under Radzivill it was as if their reunion would go on for ever.

"Thank God we're all getting together again, the old Zbarajh crew," he said. "A man can feel good even about a war when he knows he has good friends around him."

"That was my idea," Zagloba said at once. "Because these other two wanted to go searching for the King. But, as I told them, why shouldn't we sample some of the good old times again with our friend Pan Michal? If God looks as kindly on us here as he did with all those Cossacks and Tartars during the Rebellion, we'll soon have a few Swedes on our conscience, what?"

"I'm surprised, though, that you already knew about the war and the events at Uistye," Pan Yan said. "Stanislav rode his horses into the ground, bringing the news to me. And we pushed just as hard to bring the news here, thinking you wouldn't have had the time to hear about it from anyone else."

"The Jews must have sent word," Pan Zagloba nodded. "They always hear everything first and they've such a close connection with each other that if one of them sneezes in Vyelkopolska in the morning the rest shout 'Gesundheit' in the Ukraine by nightfall."

"I don't know how it happened, but we heard the news two days ago," Pan Michal said. "Everyone's enraged about it now, though not many could believe it the first day. I'll tell you another odd twist to it all: there was still nothing definite said about any war with Sweden, but you'd think that the birds themselves were chattering about it. It was suddenly on everybody's lips and for no good reason. Our Prince must also have guessed something, or he knew what nobody else suspected, because he's been buzzing around like a fly in hot water, and now he's back in Keydany and busier than ever. New recruiting has been going on for two months already, not just by me but also by Stankevitch and a certain Kmita, a young soldier from Orsha, who—as I hear it—already brought his men to Keydany, ready for field service. He got the job done faster than the lot of us."

"How well do you known the Prince *Voyevode* of Vilna?" Pan Yan asked.

"Well enough, I suppose," Pan Michal said. "I've fought in the whole Russian war under his command."

"What's he like? Do you have any idea what he plans to do?"

"He's a first-rate soldier, a real old-time warlord, and probably the best field commander in the Commonwealth now that our late beloved Prince Yeremi has been taken from us. The Russians handed him a bad defeat, that's true, but he had only six thousand men against their eighty thousand. Pan Gosyevski and the *Voyevode* of Vitebsk are really bitter about him because of that, saying he threw away the flower of the army out of sheer pride, taking on such great odds by himself because he didn't want to share his victories with them. God only knows what really happened there. But he fought well himself, and risked his own person a dozen times over, and if he only had enough men and money even now, not a single Russian would get out of this country alive. It seems to me that he'll go for the Swedes with everything he's got, and that we won't just wait for them in Zmudya but go looking for them in their own possessions along the eastern Baltic."

"What makes you think that?"

"Two reasons. One is that he'll want to mend his reputation as a general which is a little shaky after his last campaign. And the second is that he's a real warrior and he loves campaigning."

"That's it exactly!" Zagloba interrupted. "I know him well! He and I were schoolboys together and I used to do his detentions for him. He always loved war, which is why he liked to go around with me because I too paid more attention to my horse and lance than to my Latin grammar."

"Whatever he is," Pan Stanislav said. "He's no Kristof Opalinski! This is a totally different kind of man, God be praised for it!"

Volodyovski started questioning him at once about everything that took place at Uistye, tearing at his hair as he heard the whole shameful story, but when Pan Stanislav finished his account he agreed that nothing of that kind could happen with Radzivill.

"He's as proud as the Devil, that's true," he said. "And he thinks there isn't a family as good as the Radzivills in the entire world. It's also true he can't stand any opposition to his plans and that he has a real feud going with Field Hetman Gosyevski—who, by the way, is a decent and patriotic man—just because Pan Gosyevski won't always dance to Radzivill music. People say he was angry at His Majesty because the Grand Hetmancy of Lithuania didn't come to him as fast as he wanted. I'll admit all that, along with the fact that he persists in his religious errors, that he is filling Lithuania with his fellow heretics, and that he squeezes the Catholics whenever he can. But I'll swear he'd rather spill the last proud drop of that Radzivill blood he values so highly than sign the kind of capitulation that you saw at Uistye. We'll have a real war here, don't worry about that, because we'll have a real warrior as our Hetman, not some kind of scribbler."

"That's what I want to hear!" Zagloba cried out. "Pan Opalinski scribbles with his goose-quills and he soon showed

everybody what that's worth! Ha, let me tell you, those paper
scratchers are the lowest kind of man on earth. They no sooner
pluck a feather out of a goose's rump when they think they've
swallowed all of the world's wisdoms! They're quick to point
out other people's errors, but when it comes to actually doing
something that matters, you won't find them anywhere in sight.
I used to do a bit of rhyming myself in my youth, all the better
to turn women's heads, but luckily I grew out of it and let my
martial nature get the better of me."

"And I'll add this much," Pan Volodyovski said. "When all
the gentry around here finally get together there'll be enough
good men for half a dozen armies. Just as long as the money lasts
because that's the most important thing."

"God save me from any more provincials!" Pan Stanislav cried.
"Yan and Pan Zagloba already know how I feel about it, but I'll
tell you, sir, that I'd rather be a rear rank man-at-arms in a
regular regiment than a Hetman over all the territorials in the
world!"

"The people in this country are made of sterner stuff," Pan
Volodyovski said. "They lack neither courage nor endurance
and they make first-rate soldiers. I've an example of that in my
own new regiment. I simply had no room for everyone who
came hurrying to enlist, and of those I picked there isn't one
who hasn't served in combat. Wait till you see them! If you
didn't know it from me, you'd never guess this wasn't an old
regiment, composed of long-service veterans. They've been
honed and hammered into steel in a dozen fires, and they stand
as steady in their ranks as Roman legionnaires. The Swedes
won't find them as easy to swallow as those Vyelkopolians."

"Let's hope that God will change all that around," Yan Skshetuski said. "People say the Swedes are good fighters but they
could never stand up to our regulars in the field. We beat them
every time we fought them, and we did it when they had the
greatest general in their history."

"Hmm. I must say I'm curious about them," the little colonel
grinned like a greedy cat, moving his pointed little whiskers up
and down. "If we didn't have these two other wars tormenting
our country I wouldn't mind this new one! We've had a taste
of Turks, Tartars, Cossacks and God only knows who else. It's
only right to sample the Swedes as well. The Polish part of the

Commonwealth might have a problem with them, particularly
since all the Crown troops are in the Ukraine, but I can see just
what'll happen here! Radzivill will leave the Russian war in Pan
Gosyevski's hands and turn his whole attention on the Swedes.
It won't be easy, that's true! But with God's help we'll manage."

"Let's go to Keydany right away, then!" Pan Stanislav urged.

"I have orders to put my regiment on alert and to report to
Keydany myself in three days," Pan Volodyovski said. "But let
me show you that last order, gentlemen. It's quite clear from
the tone of it that the Prince-Palatine has been thinking about
the Swedes."

★　★　★

Pan Volodyovski unlocked a small chest that stood on a bench
under the window sill, took out a sheet of paper, straightened it
out and began to read:

*'We note with great joy in your last report that your regiment is fully
mustered and ready to march when needed. Hold it on the alert, because
We are about to witness such times of anguish and turmoil as never
before, and you, yourself, come to Keydany as speedily as possible where
We shall be waiting for you with impatience.'*

"Yes, that seems clear enough," Zagloba interrupted. "None
of this Swedish business is news to the *Voyevode*."

"The next passage is a little less clear," Pan Michal remarked.
"But that could be just the Radzivill manner. Listen to this."

*'Don't believe any rumors until you hear everything from Our own
lips. We shall do what God and Conscience command Us, with no
regard for any calumny that the envy and ill-will of others might throw
on Our name. At the same time, We welcome this time of trial that
will prove beyond any doubt who is a true and loyal friend of Our
House, ready to serve it even in adversity. Kmita, Nevyarovski and
Stankevitch already brought their new regiments here. You should leave
yours in Upita in case it's needed there. It might be that you will march
to Podlasye, to place yourself under the orders of Our Illustrious
Cousin, Prince Boguslav Radzivill, the Grand Equerry of Lithuania,
who commands other of Our forces there. You will hear all this
confirmed and explained to you by Us in person once you have arrived
here. In the meantime We urge you to a speedy execution of your orders
and await you in Keydany.'*

"Then he signs it in his usual manner," Pan Volodyovski said.

"With both his hereditary Lithuanian titles and with his civil and military offices under the Commonwealth."

"Hmm. Yes. It's clear enough from this that we'll have a war," Pan Zagloba said.

"And since the Prince writes that he'll act as God and his conscience order him to do that only means he'll fight the Swedes with everything he has," Pan Stanislav added.

"I just think it odd that he writes about loyalty to his House at a time like this," Pan Yan noted thoughtfully. "Our Motherland is a lot more important than the Radzivills, and needs a lot more help."

"Ah, that's just his manner," Pan Volodyovski shrugged. "You know how it is with these powerful magnates. Though I admit I didn't much care for that part myself since I serve our country, not the Radzivills."

"And when did you get this letter?" Yan asked.

"This morning. I had it in mind to start out later in the afternoon so as to be there sometime tomorrow morning. You should get some rest here after your long journey and I'll be back late tomorrow night. And then we'll take the regiment where we're ordered."

"Maybe to Podlasye, again, eh?" Pan Zagloba queried. "It'll feel good to defend our own dear countryside!"

"To the Prince Equerry," Pan Stanislav added.

"Prince Boguslav is also in Keydany just now," Pan Michal replied. "He's an interesting man, worth a second look if you get a chance. He's said to be a great soldier and an even greater knight, but you won't find a penny's worth of Polishness anywhere about him. He wears only foreign-style clothes, and speaks only in German or in French, so that you can listen to him for an hour without understanding a word he is saying."

"He fought with great courage at Berestetchko," Pan Zagloba said, citing the great battle that put an end to the First Cossack War and the Hmyelnitzki Rebellion several years earlier. "And he raised a splendid regiment of German infantry at his own cost, as I recall."

"Those who know him best praise him somewhat less," Pan Volodyovski offered. "He's quite enamored of everything French or German, which isn't surprising since his mother was a German princess, a daughter of the Elector of Brandenburg.

People say his late father was so anxious to marry the Elector's daughter that he not only waived the dowry, which is hard to squeeze out of those threadbare, penny-pinching German princelings anyway, but actually paid a stiff fee on his own account. But what the Radzivills really want is to increase their standing in the Holy Roman Empire, of which they are princes, and which is what all those German dukes and kinglets call themselves, and that's why they look for German connections whenever they can. I have this from Pan Sakovitch, an old confidant and friend of Prince Boguslav. He and Nevyarovski spent a lot of time with the Prince in many foreign countries and they always served as seconds in his duels."

"He fights so many duels, then?" Pan Zagloba asked.

"As many as he has curls in his perfumed wig! God only knows how many of those foreign counts and princes he has notched all over Western Europe. He's as impulsive as he's fearless and, by all accounts, he'll send out a challenge over anything."

Pan Stanislav, who was sunk in reverie for several silent moments, now shook himself free of thought and said that he had also heard about Prince Boguslav.

"It's not far from where I live to the Elector's borders and Prince Boguslav is almost always there. I remember what my own late father used to say about that Radzivill marriage with the Elector's daughter. People didn't like it. There was a lot of grumbling about such a great House marrying foreigners. But now maybe it'll all turn out for the best."

"And how is mixed breeding ever for the best?" Pan Zagloba challenged. "You cross a barnyard duck with a fighting rooster and you'll get a flea-bitten bird that quacks at the sunrise and drowns in a fishpond."

"Actually it will turn out well for the country now, because being related to the Radzivills, the Elector ought to be more friendly to the Commonwealth, and a lot depends on his good-will nowadays. It's true that if you sold all the Radzivills at a public auction you'd be able to buy the Elector along with his whole duchy, but that proverbial penny-pinching thrift has turned the Brandenburgers into quite a power. Their present *Kurfurst*, Friedrich Wilhelm, has a solid treasury and a very decent army of twenty thousand men with whom he could put a stop to the Swedes without a lot of trouble."

"But will he do it?"

"He ought to. His duchy is a fief of the Commonwealth and he himself is a vassal of the Polish Crown. It would be the blackest ingratitude on his part if he forgot all the kindnesses he and his House have received from us."

"Ah, it's bad business to count on foreign gratitude," Pan Zagloba muttered. "Especially with heretics. I remember this *Kurfurst* of yours from when he was a boy. He was always a glum, glowering little squirt, peering around that long nose of his as if the Devil was whispering in his ears. I told him about it to his face when the late Pan Konyetzpolski and I were pacifying Prussia. He's just as much a Lutheran as the King of Sweden. Let's just hope the two of them don't cook up some mischief for the Commonwealth together."

"D'you know something, Michal?" Pan Yan said suddenly. "I don't feel like resting here today. I'd like to ride with you to Keydany this evening. Nights are good for travel at this time of year, because they are cooler, and I'm anxious to put an end to all these uncertainties. There'll be some time to rest tomorrow, I am sure, since the Prince is unlikely to march out right away."

"Particularly since he ordered my regiment held in Upita," Pan Michal observed.

"That sounds good to me!" Pan Zagloba cried. "I'll come with you, then!"

"Then let's all go together," Pan Stanislav said.

"We'll be in Keydany at daybreak tomorrow," Pan Volodyovski said. "And we can even catch a nap on horseback on our way."

* * *

Two hours later, having refreshed themselves with some cold meats and a good local mead, the four knights set out on their journey, making such good time that they were in Krakinov even before the sunset.

Along the way Pan Michal told the others all about the country through which they were riding, about the famous Laudanian gentry, about Kmita, and about most of the major events that occurred there recently. He even confessed his unsuccessful wooing of the Billevitch heiress which, as he put it, was as ill-starred as every other amorous venture in his life.

"The only good thing about it is that war is near," he said. "Otherwise I'd really be in mourning. I hate to say it but with luck like mine it looks as if I'll end up my days as a bachelor."

"That won't harm you much!" Pan Zagloba stated. "Being single is an honorable condition and pleasing to God. I've also decided to remain unmarried though it's a shame there won't be anyone to carry on my name and inherit all my fame and glory. I love Yan's children as if they were my own but it's not the same. I mean little Skshetuskis aren't Zaglobas, are they."

"Oh you old scoundrel!" Pan Michal exclaimed. "You picked a fine time, didn't you, for renouncing women! You're like the old wolf who pledged to abstain from mutton after he lost his teeth!"

"That's not true!" Zagloba defended himself. "It wasn't all that long ago that you and I were at the Royal elections in Warsaw, remember? And who were all the women looking at if it wasn't me? But if you're that itchy to get married, don't worry, you'll get your turn. Just don't waste your time looking for a woman because that's a sure guarantee of failure. Let them come to you! It's wartime now and good men are getting scarcer every day. Let this Swedish war last a year or two and there won't be any competition left for us at all! The girls will be so anxious to find a good husband we'll be picking them off trees like plum cherries in Summer!"

But Pan Michal's sentimental heart looked for relief in gloomy introspection.

"Maybe I'll die too," he sniffed. "And maybe it's time I did. I'm tired of rattling about the world without a hearth and corner of my own. I'll never be able to tell you gentlemen what a fine and beautiful young woman she is, that Billevitch girl. A man could really love and care for somebody like that! Ah, I really thought I found something this time. But no, the Devil had to bring that Kmita at just the wrong time! How does that man do it? He must have given her some kind of love potion, I am sure, or she wouldn't have chased me off like that. Look over there, just past that hillock, that's the Vodokty manor. That could've been my refuge, a peaceful shelter for my old age. Ah, I tell you, every bear has his cave and every wolf his hole in the ground, but all I've got is this nag plodding under me and this old war saddle on which I am sitting..."

"Ey, I see she really got to you, my lad," Pan Zagloba murmured.

"Yes she did. I tried to knock out this wedge with another, if you know what I mean. Pan Schylling, who is a major landowner around here, has a good-looking daughter, so I thought I'd try my luck there as well. At least that would have got the Billevitch girl out of my head, wouldn't it? But what do you think happened? Old Schylling was away and Miss Kathy thought it was Pan Volodyovski's stable-boy that came calling on her, not Pan Volodyovski himself! I was so bowled over by that humiliation that I never showed my face in that place again!"

Zagloba roared with laughter.

"Poor little Michal! You do have a problem with your puny stature! The thing for you is to find a wife as skimpily constructed as you are, don't you see? Ay... whatever happened to that pesky little creature who used to be lady-in-waiting with Princess Grizelda, back in the Transdnieper days? The one whom our late-lamented friend, Pan Podbipyenta, intended to marry? She was just the right size for you, a real little berry, though her eyes shined brighter than any I've ever seen."

"That's Anusia Krasienska!" Pan Yan said at once. "We were all mad about her at one time in Prince Yeremi's court, Michal as much as any! God only knows what's happened to her now."

But the little knight, whose passions were never as constant as his unrequited longings, had found a new target for his romantic sighs.

"Ah, the poor dear!" he cried. "If only I could find her and console her! Ey, just remembering her makes me warm inside! What a fine girl that was! Yes, yes, those were good times that we enjoyed in Lubnie in Prince Yeremi's country but that's all blown away with the wind. Neither will we ever have a leader like our Prince. A man knew, serving under Yeremi Vishnovyetzki, that every time he faced the enemy he'd ride back with another victory. Radzivill may be a great warrior but it's not the same. You don't serve him with all your heart, he doesn't have that fatherly feeling for his men, nor does he ever let you into his own mind. It's as if he was some kind of a

monarch, always looking down on everybody from a height, and
yet the Radzivills are no better than the Vishnovyetzkis."

"That's all water over the dam, my friend" Pan Yan Skshetuski
said. "Let Radzivill be as distant as he pleases. But since the
salvation of the country is resting in his hands, and since he's
willing to spill his blood in her defense, then let God bless him
for it, and we'll serve him as loyally as we can."

★ ★ ★

The four knights chatted quietly about many matters, riding
through the night along the moonlit highway. They recalled
moments from the past and pondered about the present, wondering how their Commonwealth would manage when three
separate wars, each one terrible enough to topple the strongest
state, were ravaging her all at the same time.

Then they turned to their evening prayers and to the recitation of the litany to the Holy Mother, and then sleep stole upon
them out of the warm, quiet night and they began to nod and
sway, dozing in their saddles. The night was soft as velvet. The
sky glittered with a myriad stars. Their horses plodded steadily
under them as they slept, soothed by the gentle swaying motion
and the warmth of memories, until the dawn started gleaming
below the horizon and Pan Michal shook himself awake.

"Gentlemen!" he cried out. "Wake up! Keydany is in sight!"

"Heh? Hmm? Keydany?" Pan Zagloba muttered. "So soon?
Where?"

"Straight ahead. You can already see the tops of the towers."

"Looks like a very decent sort of town," Pan Stanislav said.

"It's a fine city," Pan Volodyovski told the three newcomers.
"As you'll see for yourselves in daylight."

"Is this a part of the Prince-Palatine's family inheritance?"

"That's right. It used to belong to the Kishka family. The
present Prince's father got it from the Kishkas as part of their
dowry when he married Anne, the daughter of the former
Voyevode of Vitebsk before that title passed to Pan Sapyeha.
Now it's a real jewel among the Radzivill possessions. There
isn't another town like it in all of Zmudya."

"What makes it so unique?"

"The Radzivills don't allow anyone to settle here unless he

has unusual skills and special permission. The town is also famous for its mead."

"Good mead, eh?" Pan Zagloba brightened quite considerably. "That does sound like an interesting city. And what is that great big building up there on a height?"

"That's the new castle, built by the present Prince."

"Is it fortified?"

"No, but it's a magnificent residence. It's not defensive because no enemy has set foot in these parts since the times of the Teutonic Knights three centuries ago. That pointed spire you see in the middle of the town, that's the parish church. The armed monks of the Germanic Order built it back in pagan times, then it was given to the Calvinists, and then, under Prince Kristof Radzivill, Father Kobylinski sued it back into the hands of the Church."

"All the better then!"

★ ★ ★

Chatting and peering about with great curiosity, the new arrivals followed Pan Volodyovski into the cluster of small homes and gardens that made up the suburbs, and then, as the sun burst into the sky and began to climb, into one of the cleanest, neatest and most orderly towns in Lithuania.

"This is known as the Street of the Jews," Pan Michal explained as they rode into the bustling little city. "You might call this the finance center and the heart of the gold and silver smithing trades. Going this way we'll get right to the city square. Look how many people are out and about already! And look at how many horses there are outside the smithies, along with servants in liveries other than the Radzivills! There must be some kind of special congress in Keydany."

"Looks like a very busy town," Pan Stanislav noted.

"It is! It's always full of visiting gentry and great lords, many coming from way beyond the seas, because this is also the Protestant center for all the country south of Swedish Courland. All the heretics in Zmudya practice their spells here, safe under the Radzivills' protection. And here's the market square already! Look at that clock tower. People say you can't find a better one in Gdansk."

"Looks like a lot of churches, too," Pan Zagloba peered around with interest. "But aren't there any inns?"

"They may look like churches but that great building you see over there, the one with four spires, that's the Calvinist Assembly where they get together every Sunday to blaspheme God and the Holy Mother, and that other structure next to it belongs to the Lutherans. As for the inns, you're quite right, there aren't any in this town. If you come here to stay overnight you have to look for a room with friends, although there's always a welcome for visiting gentry in the castle. The guest wings there are so spacious and so richly furnished that some visitors stay for a year or more, eating and drinking all they want at the Prince-Palatine's expense."

"There's something in this air," Pan Zagloba sniffed, "that makes it seem quite foreign."

"You're right in that as well," Pan Volodyovski said. "There are next to no Poles or Lithuanians living here. It's all Scots and Germans, and more Scotsmen than anybody else! They make great infantry, by the way, terribly fierce in a hand to hand attack with their halberds and pole-axes. The *Voyevode* has one regiment of Scottish volunteers recruited right here in Keydany. Ha, look at all these carts and carriages in the square! There really must be some kind of special convocation in this town today!"

"I'm just surprised that no thunderbolt hits that nest of Calvinists," Pan Zagloba muttered, eying the great stone structure they were passing then.

"That did happen once," Pan Volodyovski said. "There used to be a round cupola right between those towers till it was cracked right off by a bolt of lightning. The father of Prince Boguslav is buried in those catacombs, the same Yanush Radzivill for whom the present *Voyevode* is named, the one who belonged to the conspiracy against King Sigismond III. One of his own stable hands split his skull in half and so he died, as miserably and dishonorably as he lived."

"And what's that tall, long building over there?" asked Pan Yan. "The one that looks like a red brick barn?"

"That's the Prince's paper mill. And next to it is the printing factory where they make all the Protestant bibles and tracts in the country."

"To the Devil with all this!" Pan Zagloba snorted and spat in disgust. "Lucifer take this cursed, Godless town where a man has to fill his belly with nothing other than heretic air! Satan, it seems to me, could be ruling here just as easily as a Radzivill!"

"Don't blaspheme against the Radzivills, my friend," the little knight cautioned. "They are what they are. But one of them might soon prove to be the savior of the country."

Chapter Twenty-two

THEY RODE THE REST of the way in silence, looking with great curiosity at the clean, neatly delineated town where every street was either paved or cobbled, which was a rarity in those days anywhere in Europe. Once across the square they turned into Castle Street which rose towards the splendid new residence of Prince Yanush Radzivill that overlooked the town from its height of land. It was a palace rather than a fortress, with two long wings running at right angles out of the main structure, and forming a vast cobbled courtyard closed off on its open end by a tall ornamented railing like a row of spears. A massive stone gate-house and a pair of open portals crouched in the middle of that iron grille, displaying the Radzivill coats of arms along with the black wing and eagle's claw of Keydany, and guarded by a detachment of Scottish halberdiers.

It was still early but the courtyard was already crowded with an assortment of liveried servants, dressed in a variety of uniforms and colors, who were gaping at a regiment of dragoons at drill in front of the main building. The long rank of soldiers, uniformed in sky-blue coats and deep Swedish helmets, stood motionless on horseback with rapiers drawn and slanted at the shoulder, while an officer was saying something to them, and Pan Michal recognized him at one glance.

"By God, that's Kharlamp," he said. "D'you remember him?"

"What?" Pan Zagloba stirred with pleasure. "The same Lithuanian man-eater that you were supposed to duel with in Lipkov during the elections?"

"The same man! But we've been good friends since that time."

"I recognize him by his nose!" Zagloba exclaimed. "It's a good thing that helmet visors aren't in style any more because he'd never be able to close one on that beak. But he probably needs a separate suit of armor for that proboscis anyway."

Meanwhile Pan Kharlamp spotted Volodyovski and trotted towards him.

"How are you, Mickey?" he called out. "I'm really glad you've come here!"

"And I'm glad to see you! But here, d'you remember Pan Zagloba? From that time in Lipkov?" And then the little colonel began to introduce the others: "This is Pan Yan Skshetuski, commander of the Royal Armored Regiment, the hero of Zbarajh..."

"Dear God!" Pan Kharlamp cried. "Do I hear correctly? You, sir, are the greatest knight in the entire Commonwealth!"

"And that's his cousin Stanislav, the captain of Kalish, who comes here straight from Uistye..."

"Ah! Then you witnessed a terrible disgrace... We know already what happened at Uistye."

"That's why I'm here," Pan Stanislav said. "In hopes that nothing of that kind could happen here as well."

"You can be sure of it. Radzivill is no Opalinski."

"That's just what we were saying yesterday," Pan Michal observed.

"Ah!" The long-nosed, bewhiskered Lithuanian dragoon was overjoyed to see them. "Let me welcome you in the name of the Prince-Palatine as well as my own! He'll be delighted to hear that you're here because he really needs such knights as you. Come and visit with me in my quarters where you can change your clothes and refresh yourselves a little. I'll join you in a moment because I've already finished the morning's drill."

With this, Pan Kharlamp spurred his horse back towards his soldiers and ordered: "Left turn to the rear! March!"

Hoofbeats rattled at once on the cobblestones. The long rank split in half, then split again wheeling in formation, and then a long column of fours rode off at a walk towards the barracks hidden behind the palace.

"Good soldiers," Pan Yan said, casting an expert eye at the mechanical movements of the departing dragoons.

"You'll find only small gentry and petty boyars serving in that arm," Pan Michal explained.

"Thank God!" Pan Stanislav cried. "You can see at a glance that these aren't provincials!"

★   ★   ★

A half hour later, the four knights sat with Pan Kharlamp in his bachelor quarters, sharing a large tureen of warmed malt liquor thickly laced with cream, and talking about the various signs that heralded the new war.

"What are people saying around here?" Pan Michal wanted to know.

"Everything and nothing," Pan Kharlamp replied. "No one knows anything for certain so we get different rumors every day. Only the Prince knows what he intends to do and he is keeping it close to his vest. I've never seen him that thoughtful and that closed in on himself, even though he puts on a cheerful air and is as kind to everyone as never before. People say that he paces his rooms all night long, talking to himself, and during the day he locks himself for hours at a time with Harasimovitch."

"Who's this Harasimovitch, then?"

"He's an administrator from Zabludov in Podlasye, not much of a figure. A sly little lick-spittle of a man who looks as if he was nursing a weasel in his shirtsleeves. But he's the Prince's confidant and knows all his thinking. To my mind, all this secret plotting and conniving will result in a terrible, all-or-nothing war against the Swedes, which is what everyone is waiting for impatiently around here."

"But is there some action?"

"Letters, my friends. Letters. Everybody seems to be writing to the *Voyevode* these days. The Prince of Courland, Hovansky, the Elector... it's a real storm of paper, take my word for it. Some people say that the Prince-Palatine is negotiating with the Kremlin to pull the Russians into a league against the Swedes. Others say just the opposite. But the most likely thing, as I said, is an all-out war with everybody, the Swedes and the Russians at the same time. There are more troops coming into Keydany every day. Those of the gentry who are the most loyal to the

Radzivills have all been summoned here. There're armed men everywhere you look. What more can I tell you? Somebody is going to get all this falling on his head, make no mistake about it, and we'll have our arms scarlet to the elbows because when Radzivill goes to war it's no joke."

"That's the spirit!" Pan Zagloba started to rub his hands together with every sign of pleased anticipation. "There aren't many old warriors left who remember me from the last time that we fought the Swedes. But those that still remember will never forget me!"

"Is Prince Boguslav here as well?" Pan Volodyovski asked.

"He is. Moreover, we're expecting some distinguished guests today because the upper chambers have all been made ready and there's to be a great banquet tonight. I doubt, Michal, that you'll get to see the Prince today."

"He ordered me to report to him the first thing on arrival."

"Maybe so. Still, he's awfully busy... I don't know if I should say this to you, even though everyone will know it in another hour, but there are some strange things happening here these days."

"What things? What things?" Zagloba demanded.

"Well... you've all heard of Pan Yuditzki, haven't you? The famous Knight of Malta? He came here a few days ago and Pan Gosyevski arrived soon after him. Everyone was surprised to see the Field Hetman here, knowing how bitterly hostile he is to our Prince, but we took it for a sign of a new unity and friendship between our two commanders, brought about by this new Swedish threat."

"God grant that should happen," Pan Yan said. "Only unity can save our country at a time like this."

"I thought that myself. Well, yesterday the three of them locked themselves in the Prince's chambers for a private conference. All doors were closed and guarded and nobody could hear anything they said. Only Pan Krepshul, who guarded the door to the conference room, told us that they were really shouting at each other. Pan Gosyevski was especially loud..."

"Hmm. Yes. That could be anything," Pan Volodyovski mut-

tered. "The Field Hetman was never much of a Radzivill supporter but he's a decent and patriotic man."

"But afterwards,"—and here Pan Kharlamp began to twist his
shaggy head with astonishment and lowered his voice—"when
the Prince-Palatine took Pan Gosyevski and Pan Yuditzki to
their rooms... they put a guard on their doors."

"What? How can that be?" Volodyovski shouted, leaping to
his feet.

"All I know is that there're Scottish musketeers standing at
both doors, with orders to let no one in or out on pain of death."

The four knights stared at each other with wondering eyes
and Pan Kharlamp seemed no less surprised by his own words
than they. He peered from one of them to another as if hoping
that they might have a reasonable explanation for this unexpected and unusual event.

"Does this mean that Pan Gosyevski is under arrest?" Pan
Zagloba asked. "You mean to say the Grand Hetman has locked
up the next ranking military commander? What's going on
here?"

"How should I know?" Pan Kharlamp worried. "And Pan
Yuditzki too, a great knight like that..."

"But didn't the Prince's officers wonder about that? Didn't
they look for an explanation? And didn't you hear anything that
might give us a clue?"

"I asked Harasimovitch, but all he did was put a finger across
his mouth and said they were traitors."

"What do you mean 'traitors?' How could they be traitors?"
Pan Michal seized his head in both his hands, trying to understand what defied every comprehension. "Neither Pan Gosyevski nor Pan Yuditzki are any kind of traitors! The whole
Commonwealth knows them as decent and devoted men who'd
die for their country!"

"Nobody can be trusted nowadays," Pan Stanislav muttered in
deep gloom. "Didn't Kristof Opalinski play the role of Cato?
Didn't he scourge the greedy and the selfish and the disobedient?
But when it came down to the root of the matter he sold not
just himself to the enemy but his entire province as well."

"I'd give my head in surety for such men as Pan Gosyevski and Yuditzki!" Pan Michal cried out.

"Ey, Michal, don't you pledge your head for anyone," Zagloba advised. "They wouldn't have been arrested without a good reason. They've had to have some dealings with the enemy, and that's all there's to it... How else could it be? So the Grand Hetman is getting ready for war, needing every bit of help he can get... So whom would he arrest if it wasn't people he can't trust? And if these two men really can't be trusted then they should be rotting in the dungeons, not sitting in their chambers! Thank God they've been exposed in time! Ha! The dogs! Imagine conniving with the enemy at a time like this! Imagine turning against their own country and undermining a great warrior's enterprise! By God's Holy Mother, they deserve a lot worse than they've received!"

"Strange things," Pan Kharlamp muttered, twisting his head back and forth. "Strange times. It's more than my head can cope with. Because, consider, these aren't only great men and powerful officials, but they've been jailed without a trial and without approval from the diet which is something that the King himself has no right to do."

"That's right!" Pan Michal cried.

"It looks as if the Prince wants to impose a Roman discipline on us," Pan Stanislav said. "And to act as a dictator in a time of war."

"Let him be a dictator as long as he beats the Swedes!" Pan Zagloba answered. "I'll be the first to vote him dictatorial powers!"

Yan Skshetuski sat silent for a long, thoughtful moment.

"If only he doesn't aspire to be a Lord Protector," he said. "Like that English Cromwell who raised his sacrilegious hand against his own sovereign."

"Bah, Cromwell!" Pan Zagloba shouted. "Cromwell was a heretic!"

"And the Prince-*Voyevode*?" Pan Yan asked him gravely. "What is he?"

★ ★ ★

They sat in a dark and gloomy silence for a while then, looking at each other with uncertain eyes because the future

seemed suddenly inimical and threatening, and only Pan Kharlamp put on a fierce scowl and began to bristle.

"I'm not much younger than the Prince," he growled. "But
I've served under him since he was a lad! He was my troop
leader when he was still a boy. Then he was my captain. Then
he was my Field Hetman and now he's my Grand Hetman and
supreme commander. I've known him a lot longer that any of
you, and I honor him and love him, and that's why I ask you to
watch your words about him. Don't put him on the same level
as a Cromwell or I'll have to say something we'd all be sorry to
hear!"

Here Pan Kharlamp's huge whiskers twitched ferociously and
he started looking at Pan Yan with a threatening air, but Pan
Volodyovski fixed him with one cold glance. '*Don't even think
about it,*' the little soldier's eyes seemed to be hissing out in the
icy silence, and Pan Kharlamp, who admired Pan Michal as
much as he respected his talents as a swordsman, immediately
lost some of his ferocity.

"Yes, he's a Protestant," he resumed in a calmer voice. "But
he was born to it, he didn't renounce the true faith on his own.
He'll never be a Cromwell or a Radeyovski or an Opalinski
even if Keydany were to crumble into dust around us! That's
not in his blood. This is a Radzivill."

"Let him be a horned Devil, if he wants to be!" Pan Zagloba
shouted. "If only he jabs those horns into the Swedes!"

"I just can't get over these arrests," Volodyovski went on,
shaking his head in consternation. "Pan Gosyevski! Pan
Yuditzki! Who'd have thought it possible? Seems like the
Prince isn't showing much regard these days for his invited
guests."

"What are you saying, Michal!" Pan Kharlamp cried out.
"He's as kind and considerate to everyone nowadays as he's
never been in his entire life! He's a real father to the gentry
now! You remember how he used to be before? Always a knot
or furrow in his forehead and just one word on his lips. '*Duty!*'
he'd snap at us all the time. '*Do what you are told!*' And now he
walks among the junior officers and the serving gentry, and asks
about their families, their properties and their children, and he
calls everyone by name, and he wants to know if anyone's
unhappy in the service."

"Are we talking about the same Radzivill?" Pan Volodyovski shook his head in wonder.

"All I know is that this man who thinks himself the equal of any sovereign monarch, now walks about arm-in-arm with a boy like Kmita! It happened only yesterday or the day before. None of us could believe it! I grant you, the Kmitas are an old and well-established family, and Pan Andrei has brought in a regiment like none you've ever seen, but he's barely out of his teens and he's got a whole slew of court cases hanging over his head, which is something you know more about than I."

"Yes. I know." Pan Volodyovski nodded. "Has Kmita been here long?"

"He's away just now. Gone to pick up another infantry regiment for the Prince. No one here is in such high favor nowadays. I heard the Prince saying, as Kmita rode away, that there isn't another man like that in his service. *'He'd hold the Devil by the tail for me, if that's what I ordered,'* he murmured out loud. *'He'd do anything.'* It's true that Kmita's regiment is like none other in the army. The men and the horses both look as fierce as a herd of fire-breathing dragons. But even so..."

"Enough," Pan Michal said. "If the Prince-Palatine is taken with Kmita that's all the better for the Commonwealth these days. That's a fine young soldier and he really is ready for anything."

* * *

Further talk was interrupted by the entrance of a curious and unusual figure: a dry, wriggling little man in his early forties with a tiny face, thin lips, a threadbare mustache, and slightly slanted eyes. He seemed unable to keep still, twisting about nervously like an eel, and with his small beady eyes darting about like sparrows as if trying to see everything at once. Once across the threshold, he bent himself in two, then straightened up as if a spring snapped open in his spine. Then he bowed in another imitation of profound respect, twisting his head as if he'd just hauled it out of his own armpit, and broke into a rapid chatter that sounded much like the creaking of a rusty weather-cock.

"Greetings, Mister Kharlamp, greetings!" he broke into an

obsequious prattle and bobbed a bow to Pan Volodyovski. "My respects, dear colonel. Your servant, sir, your servant."

"Greetings to you Master Harasimovitch," Kharlamp said. "What are you after here?"

"God sent us some distinguished guests, I hear. I came to offer my services and ask who they are."

"Why? Did they come to see you?"

"Oh no, oh no. I'm quite unworthy of such company. But since the Grand Chamberlain is away just now... and I'm, so to speak, acting in his place... I came to extend the greetings of the house."

"You've about as far to go to the Grand Chamberlain's staff as a carp has to a fishing pole, Master Harasimovitch," Pan Kharlamp said sharply.

"And do I deny it? No, no, I'm just a servant of Radzivill servants. A most humble person. But since the Prince himself sent me here to ask who is visiting with you in your quarters, you'll answer me, Mister Kharlamp, and you'll answer at once, even if I was just a lackey and not a court official."

"I'd even tell an ape if it came to me with an order," the long-nosed knight replied. "Listen then, Mister, and jot down the names if they're too much for your memory. This is Pan Skshetuski, the hero of Zbarajh, and that's his cousin Stanislav, come here straight from Uistye."

"My God, what do I hear!" Harasimovitch cried.

"And that's Pan Zagloba."

"My God, what do I hear...!"

"If you're that shaken on hearing my name, just imagine what effect it'll have on the enemy," Pan Zagloba stated.

"And that's Colonel Volodyovski," Kharlamp finished, although Harasimovitch knew him very well.

"Ah! Another famous saber!" the sycophantic steward fawned at the little soldier, "and a Radzivill one at that! His Highness is overwhelmed with work these days but he's sure to find time for such famous company, I'm sure he will! And in the meantime, how can I be of service? The whole palace is at your disposal gentlemen, and so are the cellars."

"We've heard about the famous Keydany meads," Zagloba said quickly.

"Yes, yes!" Harasimovitch bowed again, wriggling about like

a speared eel. "And they're justly famous. I'll send a selection over right away. But may I hope that you'll stay with us longer, gentlemen?"

"That's why we've come," Pan Stanislav said. "To stand at the Prince's side from now on."

"A most praiseworthy sentiment, gentlemen. Most praiseworthy." And here Harasimovitch seemed to shrink into himself so that he appeared at least a foot shorter. "Particularly since awful times are coming."

"Have you heard anything new?" Pan Kharlamp demanded.

"The Prince never closed an eye last night, questioning emissaries. The word is bad and it's getting worse. Charles Gustav has already followed Wittemberg into the Commonwealth, all of Vyelkopolska is now in his hands and Poznan's been taken. Mazovia is about to fall. The Swedes are on the outskirts of Warsaw which our King abandoned without any means of defense and they'll be in the city any day. The news is that King Yan Casimir lost a major battle, that he's thinking of running off to Krakow and then maybe overseas to beg for foreign help. Ay, it's bad everywhere, bad..."

"Then why do you look as if you were pleased about it?" Pan Zagloba thundered.

"Do I look pleased? Well, some people say that it's not so bad, that it could be worse because the Swedes are very well behaved. They cause no harm to anyone. They keep their agreements. They don't levy taxes or make any inroads on our liberties. They don't interfere with the Church. And that's why everyone is glad to accept Charles Gustav's protection... Aye, it's a shame what our Yan Casimir has done to the country. It's all lost for him now. Lost, gone, for ever... A man could weep for the pity of it all..."

But Pan Zagloba had enough.

"Will you stop wriggling about?" he shouted. "Will you tell it straight? I've never heard such bad news told with greater pleasure!"

Harasimovitch pretended not to hear him and went on repeating: "Aye, it's all lost, all gone. The Commonwealth is finished. She can't fight all three wars at once. It's all gone for ever, finished for all time. Well, that's God's will. And only our Prince can save Lithuania."

★ ★ ★

The lurid words still seemed to hang in the gloomy air when Harasimovitch vanished behind the door and the five knights sat bowed around their table as if quite crushed by the terrible weight of the news they heard.

"A man could go stark raving mad!" Volodyovski shouted finally.

"You're quite right there," Pan Stanislav said. "God give us a quick war, and the sooner the better. At least a man in combat has no time to think or to feel despair."

"We'll get to wish for the bad times of Hmyelnitzki's Rebellion, you'll see," Pan Zagloba offered. "We had disasters then as well but we had no traitors."

"Three wars all at once," Pan Stanislav murmured. "When, to tell the truth, we've scarcely the strength to cope with one of them."

"It's not the strength we lack," Pan Yan said and shook his head sadly. "We've lost our will and spirit, that's our greatest trouble. It's our own lack of decency and honor and virtue that's killing our Motherland today. Let's pray that we'll find something different here."

"I won't draw a clean breath until we're in the field," Pan Stanislav said.

"And when are we finally going to see that Prince?" Zagloba demanded.

Chapter Twenty-three

PAN ZAGLOBA'S WISHES came true quicker than he hoped because scarcely an hour went by before Harasimovitch was back in Kharlamp's quarters, bowing even lower, and begging the distinguished guests to follow him to a private audience with Yanush Radzivill.

They went at once.

Harasimovitch led them across the open courtyard which was already full of milling officers and gentry. In places, as they passed, great crowds were arguing about the same news which the five knights heard from their obsequious guide only an hour earlier, and every face seemed alight with flickers of uneasiness or with feverish anticipation and anxiety. Clusters of officers and nobles crowded around wildly gesticulating speakers. Words and phrases spilled out, crisscrossed like sabers in the sullen air, and left behind an even deeper void of worry, uncertainty and fear.

"Vilna is burning!" cried one man. "Vilna's been burned to the ground!" insisted another. "Not even a trace of ashes is left to mark the place!"

"Warsaw has fallen!"

"No, not yet it hasn't!"

"The Swedes are in Galicia... The province of Syeradz will resist them..."

"No, it won't, it'll follow the example of the Vyelkopolians! Treason everywhere! What calamities! God, dear God! Have mercy! A man has no way of knowing what to do with his hands and saber..."

Such cries and whispers, each more fearful than the one before, hovered around the five knights as they pushed their way through the crowd of officers and gentry in the wake of Harasimovitch, and now and then Pan Michal's army friends stopped them to chat with the troubled little colonel.

"How are you, Michal? Ay, we're in a mess of trouble, aren't we! We're as good as dead! Greetings there, colonel, greetings! Who are the guests you're taking to the Prince?"

Pan Michal sidestepped all these anxious queries as quickly as he could, not wanting to delay the audience with Radzivill, and so they made their way to the central block of the sprawling palace, guarded by ceremonial sentries of the Hetman's Janissary Guard, dressed in tall white caps and light, Turkish-style chain-mail and scaled armor.

In the entrance hall, and all along the main staircase which was lined with tubbed orange trees, the press of people was even more dense than in the packed courtyard outside. Here the discussions dealt with the arrest of the Field Hetman and Pan Yuditzki. The matter had seeped out already and both amazed and bewildered everyone. Nobody could get to the bottom of it; no one could imagine what it was all about. There were bursts of anger and words of agreement praising the Prince's foresight, but all heads and eyes turned anxiously to the head of the stairs, and to the great rooms waiting beyond the staircase, as the crowd pressed forward in anticipation of hearing an explanation from the Prince himself.

A river of heads seemed to surround the five officers and to flow upward towards the audience chamber where the Prince-Palatine was to receive his regimental colonels and the most notable of the local gentry.

Scottish halberdiers lined the marble balustrade to keep the crowd moving at a steady pace. "Slower," they murmured all along the stairs. "Slower, gentlemen."

And the crowd flowed on, halting now and then as a halber-dier dropped his weapon across their path so that the group ahead could file into the audience chamber.

At last the starry, sky-blue ceiling that could rival any European throne room, gleamed through the open portals and the five knights entered a great, lighted space. Their first glance caught a broad dais at the far end of the lofty room, with a gleaming suite of officers and nobles dressed in magnificent, multicolored costumes, and others like them crowding about the open aisle in the center.

The Prince's chair was still standing empty in front of his most important officers and courtiers but it seemed to possess a power of its own. Tall-backed like a throne, it carried a carved, gilded princely miter poised upon its summit, with the thick amaranthine folds of a velvet robe trimmed with snowy ermine flowing out of it to the floor.

The Prince was still to enter his reception hall but Harasimovitch wriggled through the crowd with the five knights in tow until he came to a small, concealed door at the side of the dais, and vanished like a ghost behind it.

Then he was back, as suddenly as he'd disappeared, and bowed with even more profound obeisance as he begged the knights to hurry inside because the Prince was waiting.

★ ★ ★

The room they entered wasn't particularly large but it possessed a strange power of its own. It was brightly lighted through a row of mullioned Tudor-style windows, and richly lined with stamped leather paneling into which broad gilded flowers had been pressed.

They saw two men bowed over papers at the far end of the room and speaking with some urgency to each other in low, murmuring voices. One, still quite young and dressed in Western European court clothes—with a long, blond natural-hair wig falling in thick corkscrew curls to his powerful shoulders—was whispering something to an older man who listened to him with deeply furrowed brows, nodding from time to time in thoughtful agreement, and so absorbed by the conversation that he didn't notice the newcomers at first.

He was, as they could see, a huge, powerfully-built man in his middle forties, dressed in a scarlet Polish costume pinned together at the throat and shoulders with costly, jeweled clasps. His face appeared enormous in that glaring light, etched with lines of pride, dignity and power, so that he seemed in part a brooding lion and a raging warrior. It was the face of a stern monarch and a ruthless ruler. His long, drooping mustache gave him a lowering look that was both somber and unsettling with its energy and power; and the entire figure, in all its massive splendor, seemed like a monumental sculpture hewn violently out of solid marble with an iron hammer. His bushy eyebrows were narrowed with attention, but it was easy to imagine what would happen when they rose in anger and he turned the full fury of his rage on anyone who dared to stand in his way.

Watching him, the five knights felt dwarfed in their own eyes and, at the same time, shaken and exalted. This was a man for whom the whole huge castle appeared too narrow and confining, as did the province of Zmudya and the entire Grand Duchy of Lithuania. Here was, they knew without a doubt, the great Yanush Radzivill, hereditary Prince of Birjhe and Dubinki, *Voyevode* of Vilna, the leading oligarch in the Commonwealth and Grand Hetman of the Lithuanians: a man of such vast pride, power and ambition that all his titles and possessions were like nothing for him.

The younger man, the one who looked like an English royalist cavalier, was Prince Boguslav, son of the Hetman's rebellious, murdered uncle, who held the title of King's Equerry, or Master of the Horse, and who was one of the wealthiest magnates in the Commonwealth in his own right.

He whispered for a while longer into the Hetman's ear and then said out loud: "I've signed the document as you see, Your Highness. Now I must be going."

"Leave then, since that's how it has to be," said Yanush. "Although I'd much rather have you here tonight because no one can be sure of what's likely to happen."

"Your Illustrious Highness has thought of everything," Prince Boguslav answered. "But over there, as you know, the matter still needs some special attention. I leave you in God's hands."

"May God protect our entire House and grant it greater glory."

"*Adieu, mon frere.*"

"Adieu."

The two princes pressed each other's hands, after which the Prince-Equerry walked swiftly from the room, and the Grand Hetman could turn to his guests.

★ ★ ★

"Forgive me gentlemen," he addressed them warmly, although

his low, dragging voice was heavy with exhaustion, as if he'd come close to his limits of endurance. "I'm sorry I kept you waiting. But these days are enough to shatter any peace of mind and none of us are free of distraction. I've heard your names already and I'm overjoyed that God should send me such knights in such times. Sit, my dear friends, be as at ease in my rooms as if you were at home. Which of you, then, is Pan Yan Skshetuski?"

"I am he, Your Highness," Pan Yan said. "Gladly at your service."

"Ah, let's see... you're the *Starosta* of... what? The name escapes me..."

"I'm not a *Starosta* of anything, Your Highness," Pan Yan said. "I've no public offices or titles."

"What?" And the massive eyebrows narrowed in displeasure. "They didn't make you at least a *Starosta* for what you did at Zbarajh?"

"I didn't ask for it."

"Because they should've given it to you without any asking! What are you telling me? No one thought to reward you? They forgot about you?"

Then the huge head shook with solemn wonder as if unable to comprehend how such a thing could happen.

"But why should that surprise me?" the slow, thick voice grated out, heavy with contempt. "The only people honored nowadays are those who have spines made out of willow branches, bending at every breeze... So you're not a *Starosta*? Well, be happy that you've finally come to where people have better memories for merit, and where every loyal act is richly rewarded. As,"—and he suddenly turned to Pan Volodyovski—"in your case, colonel."

"I've not yet done anything to merit your attention, Highness," said the little knight.

"Leave such judgments to me. And in the meantime take this document, which is already probated in the courts at Rosyen, giving you the freehold of Dyktyema for life. It's not a bad piece of property and a hundred plows go out to work it in the Spring. Take it for lack of anything better that I can find just

now, and tell Pan Skshetuski that a Radzivill doesn't forget his
friends or those who follow him in service to their country."

"H-highness," Pan Michal stammered. "I'm... I'm overwhelmed..."

"Don't say anything." Radzivill waved his hand as if the rich
gift he'd just made was unworthy of any further comment.
"Indeed, forgive that it's so little. But tell your friends that no
one loses if he throws in his lot with the Radzivills, for good or
for evil. I'm not a King, but if I were then God is my witness I
wouldn't forget about such a man as Yan Skshetuski, or such as
Zagloba..."

"That's me!" Pan Zagloba stepped forward with alacrity, being
more than a little irritated that so much time had passed without
any mention of himself.

"I guessed that much since I was told you were somewhat
advanced in your years."

"I went to school with your illustrious father, Highness," the
fat knight said at once. "And because he loved all the knightly
virtues from his youngest days he honored me with his confidence and friendship."

Pan Stanislav, who knew Zagloba less well than the others,
looked startled at this declaration, since only the day before in
Upita the fat knight claimed a schoolroom friendship with
Yanush Radzivill, not Kristof, his dead father. But that would
have been impossible anyway, since Yanush Radzivill was many
years his junior.

But the Grand Hetman seemed pleased rather than surprised.

"So you're a native of Lithuania, then?" he asked Pan Zagloba.

"Yes. I'm from Lithuania," the fat knight shot back without
hesitation.

"Then I expect that you've also been slighted and ignored
when it came to recognizing merit," Radzivill remarked. "Because we Lithuanians are quite used by now to ingratitude. It's
our steady diet. I tell you, gentlemen, if I were to give you
everything you've earned then I'd be a beggar. But that's our
fate, you see. We give our blood, our lives and our fortunes,
and no one even nods in our direction. Ha! That's how it has
to be! But as they sow, so they shall reap, God will see to that.
And you, sir, aren't you the famous knight who killed the

Cossack Burlay and cut off those three Turkish heads at the siege
of Zbarajh?"

"Burlay was my work, Highness," Pan Zagloba stated with a
lofty glare. "It was said at the time that no living man could
fight him and survive, so I had to show the younger generations
that not all valor had drained out of the Commonwealth. As for
those three heads... well, hmm... that could have happened now
and then in the heat of battle, but somebody else achieved that
feat in Zbarajh."

The Prince was silent for a moment.

"Doesn't it hurt you, gentlemen," he resumed quietly. "To
see the cool treatment that we get in Warsaw?"

"What can one do, Highness?" Zagloba replied. "A man may
not like it much, but that's how things are."

"Be of good cheer though, good friends, because things will
change. I am already in your debt, just for the fact that you've
come to join me. And even though I'm not a ruling monarch
my thanks don't end with an empty promise."

"Your Highness," Pan Yan said quietly with a touch of pride.
"We didn't come here for rewards or fortunes. We came because an enemy attacks our Motherland and we want to fight for
her under a famous warrior. My Cousin Stanislav already witnessed cowardice, anarchy, disgrace and treason at Uistye, but
here, under a great commander and a faithful defender of our
country, we expect to beat the enemy, not to give way before
him. We're here because death waits for the enemy under your
command, not triumphs and victories. That's why we want to
serve you. We're soldiers. We have come to fight."

"If that's what you came for then even that'll be granted to
you," the Prince-Palatine said gravely. "You won't wait long, I
swear it, although there's another enemy to dispose of first. The
ashes of Vilna have to be avenged. The Russians must be driven
back into their own borders. We shall be starting out any day
against them... Ah, but I don't want to detain you any longer.
You must need rest after your long journey and I've so much
work to do that time seems to be burning in my hands."

Then, turning to Pan Volodyovski, he asked him to see to it
that his friends lacked for nothing while they were his guests in
Keydany, and to be sure to bring them to that evening's banquet.

"Master Harasimovitch," he ordered at last. "Tell our friends in the audience room that I can't come out to them today because I've too much on my hands just now. But they'll find out everything they want to know tonight at my table. Goodbye, then, my friends. Be well, and think well of Yanush Radzivill because he's in sore need of your friendship nowadays."

And here this powerful magnate, this mighty oligarch who looked down his nose at all the princes of the German Empire, began to shake the hands of Pan Zagloba, the two Skshetuskis, Kharlamp and Volodyovski, as if he was no better than a simple soldier. His huge, gloomy face glowed with the smile of kindness, and the vast distance which he normally kept between himself and everybody else dwindled into nothing.

★ ★ ★

Outside again, Pan Stanislav couldn't praise him warmly and heartily enough.

"What a leader!" he exclaimed as they pushed their way through the crowds of gentry gathered in the reception hall. "What a warrior!"

"I'd jump into a red-hot fire for him!" Zagloba enthused. "You notice how he knew all my best triumphs by heart? Things are going to get awfully hot for the Swedes when this lion roars and when I add my own voice to his. There's not another great lord like him in the Commonwealth, and of the ones who left us, only Prince Yeremi and old Pan Konyetzpolski could've been his match. Ha! This is no petty little castellan who's the first of his line to sit in a senator's chair. You know the kind! The seat of their breeches still hasn't lost its nap on the council benches, but they already jerk their noses up in the air and look down at the ordinary gentry. First thing they do is have their portraits painted, so they can always have their senatorial dignity in front of their eyes, even if they can't find it anywhere behind them!

"Michal, my friend,"—and here the fat knight turned his beaming face on the little colonel,—"your fortune is as good as made! It looks like it's enough for a man to brush against Yanush Radzivill to have his threadbare jacket turn to cloth-of-gold! Advancement is easier here, as I see, then getting a bagful of rotten apples anywhere else! You can stick your hand blindfolded in this Lithuanian fish pond and come up with a fat, lively trout straight off!

"Yes, yes, that's my idea of a master!" Zagloba went on. "God bless you, Michal, you're in luck at last. You started humming and hawing back there like a bashful bride after the knot's been tied, but no matter! What's the name of that new freehold of yours, anyway? They've some awfully heathen place-names in this Lithuania; every time you hear one it's like throwing a handful of nuts against a wall. But what's the difference how you twist your tongue as long as the rents give you a nice income?"

"I really got a bit surprised back there," Pan Michal admitted. "Because it isn't true about promotions being easy here. I've heard a lot of old soldiers complaining about the Prince's penny-pinching ways. It's only now that everyone's being showered with all this unexpected kindness."

"Is that so? Well, do this much for me. Stick that land grant deed in your belt, and the next time somebody complains about the Prince's lack of gratitude, you just belt him in the snout with it! You hear? You won't find a better argument, my lad."

"It's clear to me that the Prince is going out of his way to win new supporters," Pan Yan said thoughtfully. "He must have some far-reaching plans in mind."

"You've heard his plans!" Pan Zagloba babbled, carried away by his own enthusiasm. "Didn't he tell us that we'll be avenging the ashes of Vilna?"

"Yes, well, that's the Russians. But what about the Swedes?"

"All in good time! Be patient! People have been slandering him for looting some of the Vilna treasures for himself, but he wants to show that he doesn't need anything from anybody else, and that he's willing to spend his own fortune in the common good. You can't fault him for that! I wish all our leaders were cut from the same cloth!"

★ ★ ★

They found themselves at last in the palace courtyard where every moment brought fresh arrivals clattering through the gate. Whether these were mounted troop detachments, dense caval-cades of armed local gentry, or carriages full of local dignitaries with their wives and children, the gate disgorged an endless

procession of color and excitement, and Pan Michal, as curious
in this bustle as any new arrival, dragged his friends to the gate
where they might satisfy their own appetite for news and watch
the passing show.

"Who knows, Michal," Pan Zagloba told him. "This is your
lucky day. Perhaps you'll find a bride for yourself among these
young gentlewomen in some of these coaches. Look over there!
Isn't there something white sitting in the back of that open
carriage?"

But the sharp-eyed little Pan Volodyovski recognized the
white-robed visitor from a distance.

"That's not a would-be bride but rather the man who might
tie the knot," he said. "That's Bishop Partchevski, the head of
the Church in Zmudya. And that's Father Byelozor, the Roman
Catholic archdeacon of Vilna, beside him."

"You mean to say they visit with a Protestant?"

"What choice do they have? If that's what's needed in the
public cause that's what they have to do."

"Dear lord!" Pan Zagloba exclaimed with every sign of pleasure. "How busy it is around here! How much noise there is! I
thought I'd rust back home in the country like an old key stuck
in an unused lock but this is more like the good old days. And
look at all those girls! I'll be damned if I don't do a bit of
courting before the day is over!"

* * *

But whatever else the fat knight had in mind remained unex-
pressed because, at that moment, the soldiers stationed at the
gate poured out of the guard house, formed two ceremonial
ranks, and presented arms to the arriving bishop.

"That's a nice bit of politicking on the Prince's part," Pan
Zagloba said. "I mean to honor the bishop even though he
doesn't recognize the supremacy of the Church. Let's hope this
is the first step towards his conversion."

"You can forget about that." Pan Volodyovski shrugged.
"His first wife did all she could to bring that about but it was all
for nothing. In fact she died of grief and disappointment, as the
story goes. But why are the Scots still on parade? Some other
dignitary must be on his way."

A large detachment of armored cuirassiers clattered through the gateway, surrounding a pair of gilded, ceremonial coaches.

"Those are Ganhof's Reiters," Pan Michal said at once, recognizing the heavy German cavalry which Yanush Radzivill maintained at his own expense, as he did the Scottish musketeers, halberdiers and pikemen. "But who's in those coaches?"

"Whoever it is he's more important than the Bishop of Zmudya," Pan Zagloba offered. "The whole guard is out and lined up for inspection."

Drums rattled out a long ceremonial roll, the guard presented arms, and the gentry crowded forward to catch a glimpse of the new arrivals.

"That's Pan Korf in the first coach!" Volodyovski said, recognizing the *Voyevode* of Wenden, a Latvian province lost to Poland a long time ago when it became part of the Swedish foothold in the eastern Baltic.

"So it is!" Pan Yan cried, pleased to see the old Polish noble. "An old Zbarajh acquaintance of ours."

The northern palatine recognized them too.

"Greetings, old friends and comrades!" he called out, leaning out of the window of his coach in passing and pointing to the coach behind him. "We're bringing some interesting guests!"

"Such as who?"

But the *Voyevode's* coach rattled past before he could answer and the five knights stared curiously at the splendid, gilded vehicle that followed, drawn by four white palfreys, and displaying the Prince's personal coat-of-arms. Seated inside were two equally splendid gentlemen of lordly poise and bearing, dressed all in black in the foreign fashion. They wore tall, broad-brimmed hats with white ostrich plumes and curled blond wigs falling to their shoulders, and wide lace collars that spread across the dark velvet doublets on their chests and shoulders. One of them, a fleshy, soft-skinned man, showed a sharp, pointed beard and an upswept moustache with the ends combed out into stiff, pale brushes; the other, a younger man, had perhaps a slightly less military bearing, but he may have been the more important of the two because he wore some kind of order on a golden collar.

One glance was enough to mark them as foreigners, particularly since they peered with great curiosity at the palace, at the crowds, and at the eastern-style clothes and uniforms around them.

"Who the Devil's that?" Pan Zagloba asked.

"I've never seen them here before," Volodyovski answered, then beckoned to the officer commanding their escort. "Hey, Tokashevitch! Come here a moment, will you?"

"Greetings, colonel!" the young officer replied. "It's good to see you here!"

"Who are these two wig merchants that you've brought along?"

"They're Swedes."

"Swedes? Here?"

"That's so. And an important pair they are too. That fat one is Count Loewenhaupt, and the thinner one is Benedict Shitte, Baron von Duderhof."

"Shitte?" Zagloba said, twisting his head in wonder and sniffing the air. "Duderhof?"

"Don't blame me for it," the young cuirassier shrugged. "They've got some strange names up there in the north."

"And what's their business here?" Pan Volodyovski asked.

"God only knows," the young officer said. "We've been escorting them from Birjhe on the border. They've probably come to negotiate with the Prince because the word in Birjhe is that we're going to scorch their tails up there in Estonia."

"Ha, you scoundrels!" Pan Zagloba shouted after the envoys' carriage which, by that time, had circled the courtyard to stop at the main doors of the central building.

"You invade Vyelkopolska!" he bellowed. "You dispossess our King! And here you've come to bow and scrape before Radzivill just so he won't tickle your Estonia for you! You'll be galloping back to your Duderhofs so fast you'll split your fancy breeches! We'll put some runs in your droopy stockings, just you wait and see! Long live Radzivill!"

"Long life to him!" roared the gentry gathered by the gate.

"*Defensor patriae!*" howled the fat knight. "Protector of the country! Let's get at those Swedes, gentlemen! At them, I tell you, at them!"

* * *

A curious crowd began to gather happily around Pan Zagloba,

while he, seeing himself once more in his favorite role of orator and mentor, climbed up on a protruding buttress of the gate and launched into a fiery harangue.

"Gentlemen, listen to me!" he roared in a voice that carried across the courtyard. "I'll tell those of you who don't know me that I'm an old Zbarajh hand, and that it was this old fist that cut down the Cossack Burlay, the greatest Zaporohjan ataman after Hmyelnitzki himself! Whoever hasn't heard about Zagloba must've spent the years of the first Cossack war shelling peas, or in plucking chickens, which I don't expect in such a gathering as this!"

"Listen to him! Listen!" several voices rose out of the crowd. "That's a famous knight! There isn't a greater warrior in the Commonwealth!"

"Let me tell you, then!" the old knight held forth. "I've earned my peace! My old bones would rather get a little rest! I'd be better off snoring behind a stove, sampling fresh village cheeses and slurping buttermilk, or picking up ripe apples in the orchard. That is if I wasn't standing in the corn fields with my hands folded behind my back, or patting village girls while they're bending over in the furrows... It's a sure thing the enemy would've been delighted to let me vegetate in peace, because both the Swedes and the Cossacks know that I've a heavy hand, and God only grant that my name should be as well known to you as it is to them!"

"Hey!" some new jeering voice shouted in the crowd. "And who's that old rooster that's doing all that crowing over there?"

"Don't interrupt!" other voices shouted.

"Forgive him, gentlemen!" Pan Zagloba cried. "He cackles like a hen in a barnyard because he doesn't know any better. He's just a young cockerel who still doesn't know his cockscomb from his tail!"

The gentry roared with laughter and the luckless heckler started to beat a hasty retreat, pursued by the jokes and jeers of the crowd.

"But back to the matters in hand!" Zagloba resumed. "As I said, I've earned my peace and quiet. But because our Motherland weeps in agony, and because the enemy is trampling on our soil, I'm here, as you see, to fight beside you against these invaders in the name of that one Mother of us all! So hear this!

Whoever fails to stand beside our Mother now, whoever doesn't come to her aid in her hour of need, isn't her true-born son but some misbegotten foundling! I'm an old man, and maybe these new trials and tribulations are too much even for my great strength, but I'll be shouting with my last breath: *'Down with the Swedes! Down with them! Let's get at them, gentlemen and brothers!'* Let's take an oath right now that we won't sheathe our sabers until the last of them is either chased back across the sea or stone-dead and buried!"

"We're ready to do that without any oaths!" many voices cried. "We'll go where our Hetman leads us! We'll fight whom we have to...!"

"That's the spirit, brothers! You saw those two foreign weasels in their golden coach, didn't you? They know what's waiting for them. They know that Radzivill is too tough a nut for their teeth to crack. They'll be trailing after him over there in the palace, shaking in their drawers and kissing his elbows for lack of anything closer to their noses, and begging him for peace. But the Prince, gentlemen, from whose council chamber I have just returned, assured me in the name of the entire country that there won't be any scribbling or negotiating here! No deals! No parlays! We're to have war and nothing but war!"

"Let's have it then!" more and more voices shouted in the crowd. "What are we waiting for? Let's start it!"

"But," the fat knight went on. "Even the greatest general needs to know that his men are with him. So let's go and shout our sentiments under our Hetman's windows! Let's tell him that we're hungry for some Swedish meat! Follow me, gentlemen! Follow me!"

And the fat knight leaped nimbly off the stone buttress on which he'd been standing and dived into the crowd which parted to receive him and then closed behind him. The whole vast gathering surged across the courtyard, sweeping up greater numbers as it flowed towards the tall, lighted windows of the council chambers, and shouting in one great voice: "At the Swedes! Let's have them! At the Swedes!"

* * *

The reaction to this demonstration wasn't quite what Pan Zagloba hoped for or expected, because Pan Korf ran out into the courtyard almost at once with a strange look of worry etched across his face, and with Colonel Ganhof, the Prince's foreign cavalry commander, running close behind him.

Both began to hush and quieten the excited gentry, begging them to disperse and to make less noise.

"Dear God," Pan Korf exclaimed. "The windows are about to shatter with all this commotion! You've no idea, gentlemen, what a bad time you've chosen for this show of feeling. How can you display such a lack of discipline, and insult important foreign envoys in this way? Who started all this?"

"I did!" Zagloba answered. "Tell His Highness, Your Grace, in the name of everybody here, that we're begging him to be hard with that pair of poodles! We'll stand behind him to our last drop of blood!"

"Yes, yes, I thank you gentlemen in the Hetman's name. Thank you, but that's enough. Quieten down, I beg you. Use your heads, will you? Think about what you're doing or you'll place the country in jeopardy beyond imagination. These are really bad times to insult an envoy."

"Who cares about those flea-bitten envoys?" Pan Zagloba roared. "We want to fight, not parlay!"

"Yes, yes..." Pan Korf and Ganhof both looked terribly worried, harassed and embarrassed. "We're glad to see such a fine show of spirit but it's a bit early... The start of the campaign is still a few days off, you see... Why don't you all come in, instead, and have some refreshments? The tables in the public rooms are spread with the best foods and liquors. Come in and enjoy them. You know the old saying, nobody fights well on an empty stomach."

"That's true!" Pan Zagloba agreed immediately.

"Couldn't be more true!" other voices cried. "We've done what we came for! The Prince knows now how we feel about the Swedes so we might as well go in and enjoy ourselves!"

The crowd broke up at once, most of it heading for the public rooms with Pan Zagloba marching at their head, while Pan Korf and Ganhof made their way to the Prince's private council chamber where the Grand Hetman sat with the Swedish envoys, with Bishop Partchevski and the archdeacon of Vilna, and with several other leading dignitaries and officials.

"Who started that riot?" the Prince asked coldly, his heavy face still flushed with anger and displeasure.

"It was that noble who arrived today, that famous Pan Zagloba," Pan Korf said.

"He's a grand old man," the Prince muttered. "But he's starting to throw his weight about too soon around here."

After which he beckoned to Ganhof and began to whisper urgently into the colonel's ear.

★ ★ ★

Meanwhile, greatly pleased with his accomplishment, Pan Zagloba paced in a stately manner towards the public rooms below, flanked by Pan Michal and both the Skshetuskis.

"And what do you say to that, my friends?" he purred with pleasure. "I've no sooner set foot in this territory and I've already inspired all this gentry with love for our country. It'll be easier now for the Prince to send those envoys packing. I imagine that this service won't pass without some reward, although it's always the honor that counts first with me, not any kind of payment. Ah, but what's wrong with you Michal? Why are you suddenly as quiet as a church mouse, and why are you staring so hard at that coach over there?"

"It's she," the small knight groaned.

"Who?"

"The Billevitch girl."

"The one that stuck a burr under your tail?"

"The same one. Look at her, will you, gentlemen? Isn't she enough to make a man wither with grief and mourning?"

"Hmm. Let's take a look," Pan Zagloba murmured. "Let's get a little closer."

The open carriage drew up before the main doors of the palace and the watching gentry caught sight of a corpulent old noble with long dangling whiskers, and with Aleksandra sitting next to him. Pan Michal fixed his mournful eyes on her and swept his hat to the ground before her, but she failed to notice him in the crowd, sitting as quiet and as proud in her regal beauty as she was when she sent him on his way.

Pan Zagloba took in her poise and grace and dignity, heaved a quiet sigh of his own, and said: "Yes, she's a noble's child, there's no mistaking that. But too finely bred for a soldier, my poor friend. I'd rather have the kind of woman who's hard to tell from a siege-gun at first glance."

"Would you know the name of that gentleman who just arrived here?" Pan Michal asked one of the local gentry, and nodded towards Aleksandra's carriage.

"Of course I know," the man answered. "That's Pan Tomasz Billevitch, the Constable of Rosyen. Everybody knows him in this place because he's an old friend and supporter of the Radzivills."

Chapter Twenty-four

YANUSH RADZIVILL didn't show himself to his guests that day, eating his noon meal with the Swedish envoys and with the dignitaries with whom he was conferring. But orders went out early to the regimental colonels to have all the Household Regiments and particularly the foreign-officered infantry standing by on alert in full marching order. The air itself seemed to smell of gunsmoke. Massed troops surrounded the palace grounds as if a battle were about to erupt against its walls. Everyone expected the army to move out no later than next morning, pointing to the uncountable numbers of Radzivill servants who were loading wagons with arms, costly furnitures, and the Prince's treasury. Harasimovitch hinted that the wagons were to go to the Castle of Tykotzin in Podlasye, one of the stronger of the Radzivill fortresses, where the treasury would be more secure than in the indefensible Keydany.

News spread seemingly out of nowhere that the Field Hetman was under house arrest because he had refused to join his forces with those of Radzivill, thus setting the whole campaign in jeopardy, but no one paid much attention to it. The preparations for the march, the movement of troops, the grim rumble of cannon wheeled out of the palace arsenal, and that normal rush and bustle that is part and parcel of an army setting out to war, turned all minds to the certainties of the immediate future rather than the confusions of the recent past.

The mass of gentry dining in the great halls thrown open to the public talked only about the coming war; about the burning of Vilna which had been in flames for ten days, put to the torch by the raiding Russians of Hovansky; of news from Warsaw where the Swedes were expected to enter any day; of their swift advances, and of the Swedes themselves. The gentry was enraged by what they perceived as Swedish treachery, in as much as Charles Gustav broke his armistice with the Commonwealth, and thirsted for vengeance. The news from Vyelkopolska not only failed to dampen their spirits but actually goaded them into greater fury since it was now quite clear to them all why the Swedes had enjoyed such spectacular successes. Quite simply, they were yet to come face to face with real soldiers under a real Commonwealth commander. Radzivill was the first such general that they were to meet, a professional who had spent his lifetime in the flames of battle and one who imbued everyone with absolute confidence in his abilities, particularly since his colonels swore that they could beat the Swedes on the battlefield.

"It can't be otherwise," said the battle-wise, experienced old Michal Stankevitch, who commanded the Radzivill *husaria*. "I remember the Swedes from the other wars. I know that they fight fiercely out of castles, in walled camps and from behind entrenchments, but they've always been afraid of our cavalry in the open field. And with good reason. Every time they stood up to us in the open they were soundly thrashed. It isn't a battlefield success that gave them Vyelkopolska but treason and the ineptitude of provincial levies."

"That's quite right!" Pan Zagloba echoed and gave his own peculiar explanation of Swedes and their country. "They're a wishy-washy lot at best. Their soil is so poor that it won't grow decent wheat which is why they eat pancakes made of ground-up pine cones. Call me a liar if that isn't true! Others among them trot about on the beaches and gulp down whatever the sea tosses out to them. There isn't a more greedy nation on earth, nor has the world seen more rapacious looters, because they live all their lives with an empty belly. Say what you like about the Tartars but they, at least, always have some horsemeat to chew on. A Swede won't see a roast goose in a year, so they're always hungry unless they happen to come across a big catch of fish."

And here Pan Zagloba turned rather grandly to the venerable Colonel Stankevitch.

"And when did you make your first acquaintance with the Swedes?" he asked.

"Under Prince Kristof, the father of our present Hetman. And you, sir?"

"Under Pan Konyetzpolski, father of today's young Constable of the Crown. We gave Gustaphus Adolphus something to think about in Prussia and we took a lot of Swedish prisoners. It's there I got to know them inside out. They were quite a wonder for our lads because, as you ought to know, they're all fantastic divers! And why shouldn't they be? They're always sloshing about in the water, looking for a fish. So we told them to show us how they go about it, tossed a few of them into a hole chopped into the ice, and what do you think happened? Out they popped from another ice hole and every one of them had a herring in his teeth."

"Good God, sir, what nonsense if this you are telling us?"

"May I drop dead if I didn't see that with my own eyes more than a hundred times! And that wasn't all. They got so fat on Prussian bread that they wouldn't go back home at all! Colonel Stankevitch is quite right to say they're mediocre soldiers. Their infantry may be passable but their cavalry? God have mercy! That's because there aren't any horses in their country and they don't learn in childhood how to sit on one."

"I hear, though, that our first order of business is to avenge Vilna," said another noble.

"That's correct," Pan Zagloba said. "That's what I advised the Prince-Palatine when he asked me what he ought to do. The Russians first, I told him. But we'll take care of the Swedes when we've settled our accounts with Hovansky. Those envoys upstairs must be sweating buckets."

"They got a very fine reception," said Pan Zaleski, an influential landed gentleman. "But they won't get much more, the miserable little beggars. And the best sign of that are the marching orders sent out to the army."

"Dear God, dear God," said Pan Tvarkovski, the Justice of Rosyen. "Isn't it strange how the spirit rises in the face of danger? Here we were almost desperate at the hands of one invader, and now we're ready to take on two at once!"

"That's how it always is," Pan Stankevitch said. "You can kick and humiliate a man a long time and finally he has a bellyful of it, and suddenly fresh strength and determination come out of nowhere. Didn't we suffer enough here in Lithuania? Haven't we put up with enough pillage and destruction? We kept looking to the King and the Polish levies, not thinking much about our own resources, until we were left with only one choice! Either we beat both our enemies by ourselves or we go down for good."

"God will help! Enough of all this waiting!"

"They've got us up against the wall with a knife at our throats!"

"So let's tickle theirs! We'll show that Polish gentry what kind of soldiers we've here in Lithuania! There won't be any Uistye among us!"

★　★　★

The wine flowed and the enthusiasm soared, and it was clear to everyone that when you find yourself at the edge of a precipice, with nowhere else to go, then one great final effort often brings salvation. Each man in this great gathering of gentry and soldiers, who only recently turned an indifferent ear to all of Yan Casimir's desperate pleading for universal military service, understood at once that it was a matter of do or die. The time was now or never. All hearts and every mind turned to Radzivill; every mouth repeated his proud and dangerous name which—until recent times—always went hand-in-hand with military triumphs. It was entirely up to him to reach out and seize all those scattered forces, imbue the dulled, despairing minds with a will to victory, and to place himself at the head of armies quite sufficient to win both the wars.

After the midday meal, the Prince summoned each of his most important colonels to a private audience, speaking face-to-face with Mirski who commanded the elite *pantzerni*, with Stankevitch, Ganhof, Kharlamp and Mieleshko of the Radzivill Dragoons, with Oskierka who led the Household Hungarian Infantry, and with Nevyarovski, Sollohub, Volodyovski and several others. Old soldiers wondered at this individual attention rather than a regular war council to which all the commanders would come at the same time, but everyone was pleasantly surprised. Each colonel left his meeting with some sign of the Prince's gratitude and favor. All that Radzivill demanded in return was loyalty and trust, which they were all willing to give him anyway.

They also noted that the Prince was anxious for any news of Kmita and left orders to be told at once of his return.

* * *

It was already evening when Pan Andrei arrived at the palace, where all the halls and chambers blazed with candlelight in expectation of the gathering masses, and he hurried to his quarters in the barracks to change into his finest clothes for the evening's banquet. Nearby in Kharlamp's rooms he found Pan Volodyovski, met the new arrivals, and threw himself into his preparations with his usual energy and enthusiasm.

"It's awfully good to see you," he told the little colonel, pumping his hand so hard that it seemed as if he wanted to tear it off his arm. "It's as if I was seeing a real brother. You can believe me because I always say whatever pops into my head and I don't know how to mask my feelings. It's true that you cut a mean notch into my head but then you pulled me out of the grave, and set me back on my feet, and I'll remember that as long as I live. I tell it everywhere that if it wasn't for you I'd be rattling my chains behind bars somewhere. I wish that kind and decent men like you rained down from the sky. And if anyone feels differently about that then he's a jackass and I'll be glad to trim his ears for him."

"Enough, enough," Pan Michal said, embarrassed.

"I'd go through fire for you, you might as well know it. And I'll fight anyone who thinks I am lying."

Here Pan Andrei shot a sharp glance around the room but no one there saw any reason to take up his challenge. These were Pan Michal's dearest friends who'd known him for years. Besides, every soldier in Radzivill's service liked and respected the little cavalry commander, and only Pan Zagloba had something to say.

"You're a fiery young soldier and no mistake," he grinned up at Kmita. "It seems to me that we'll get along quite well, you and I, since I know better than anyone how much our dear friend Michal is worth."

"More than the rest of us together!" the young soldier cried impulsively. Then he shrugged, made a disarming gesture, and turned to Pan Zagloba and both the Skshetuskis. "I don't want to detract from your own great value, gentlemen, because I know you're all fine men and famous knights as well. So forgive my quick mouth, if you'd be so kind, because I'd dearly like to earn your friendships too."

"There's nothing to forgive," Yan Skshetuski smiled. "What's in the heart is often in the mouth."

"And I'm all for that!" Pan Zagloba cried. "Let me hug you, lad!"

"Gladly! You don't have to say that twice to me."

The young knight and the old one threw their arms around each other and then Kmita shouted: "Hey, but we've got to do some serious drinking tonight on that account!"

"You don't have to say that twice to me," Pan Zagloba echoed.

"We'll slip out of the banquet early, eh? What do you say to that? And I'll make sure there won't be a dry throat among us."

Pan Michal watched the impetuous young soldier with a small sigh of envy, and with some mild resignation in his sentimental heart, and started moving his little whiskers forcefully up and down.

'*You won't feel like slipping out, my lad, when you see who's sitting at that banquet table,*' he mused, eying Kmita.

*   *   *

He was about to open his mouth to tell Pan Andrei that Olenka was in Keydany with her great-uncle Tomasz but, for some strange reason, the words stuck in his throat and he changed the subject.

"And where's your regiment?" he asked.

"Right here in town. Harasimovitch brought orders to my quarters to have my men ready to ride at midnight. I asked if all of us were marching out but he said no. I've no idea what is going on. Some officers have similar orders, others don't. But the foreign infantry is all on alert."

"Some of the troops might leave tonight and others in the morning," Yan Skshetuski offered. "That's not unusual with a corps as large as this one."

"Whatever it is I'll be sure to do some drinking with you for at least an hour. I'll set my men on the road and catch up with them later."

But in that moment Harasimovitch shot into the room as if he'd been fired out of a catapult.

"Illustrious Excellency!" he shrilled from the threshold and bowed before Kmita to the ground.

"Here I am! What's up then? Is something on fire?"

"To the Prince, sir! To the Prince at once!"

"Just let me finish dressing," Pan Andrei snapped and shouted for his servant: "Jump to it, lad! My *kontush* and my sash or you'll lose your ears!"

The boy came running with the rest of Kmita's costume and, in another moment, the young man was dressed and on his way. He seemed to be aglow with youth and energy, gleaming in costly fabrics and jeweled clasps and buttons, and as bright-eyed and joyful as if he was going to his wedding, and Pan Michal heaved another sigh of gentle resignation.

He didn't think that he had ever seen a handsomer young man. His tight-sleeved, knee-length *zhupan* undercoat was made of silver appliqued brocade, thickly stitched with diamonds and pinned at the neck with a single sapphire as large as a pebble, so that lights seemed to shimmer around him as he moved. Thrown across his shoulders was a sky-blue velvet *kontush* coat, with the split sleeves lined with glittering white silk and pinned back at the shoulder, giving the impression of jeweled wings that trailed through the air behind him.

Around his waist he wound a hand-embroidered white silk sash of such intricate and costly workmanship that it could be drawn through a signet ring, although when fully opened, it was as long and wide as a cloak that could cover a mounted man all the way to the ground. A light, silvered saber, sheathed in a jeweled scabbard that blazed with sapphires like a comet's tail, hung on silk cords from beneath his sash where he thrust the ceremonial gilded *buzdygan*, or ridged, short-handled mace of a cavalry commander.

Watching him, the little soldier sighed.

There couldn't have been a better-looking young man in Keydany that night, he thought. '*And what do I look like?*' Another sad sigh escaped him as he shook his head. '*A sparrow*

*beside an eagle, that's what. No wonder the girls take me for my own
errand boy.'*

And when Kmita vanished behind the door he said to Pan
Zagloba: "Nobody could get anywhere with a woman with *that*
as his competition!"

"Just take thirty years off my back and you'd soon see," Pan
Zagloba said.

★ ★ ★

The Prince was already dressed and costumed for the banquet
when Kmita stepped into his private chambers; his Master of the
Wardrobe had left moments earlier with two Negro dressers, and
they were left alone.

"God bless you for hurrying," the Prince said at once.

"I'm at your service, Highness."

"What about your regiment? Is it ready?"

"As you've ordered, Highness."

"Can it be trusted?"

"They'll ride straight through the gates of Hell if that's where
I send them."

"Good. I need men like that. And the kind like you, who're
ready for anything. I'm always saying that I depend on you
more than anyone."

"Highness," Kmita said. "I can't compare my merits with
those of your old soldiers. But if we're to march against the
enemy I won't lag behind."

"I don't deny the merits of the older men." The Prince
shrugged and thought deeply for a moment. "But there may
come a time when the most loyal of them will begin to doubt
me."

"May anyone who fails Your Highness in a time of danger die
like a mangy dog!" the young man burst out, and the Prince gave
him a long, careful stare.

"But you won't turn your back on me, will you?"

"I? Highness..." And the young knight flushed and choked
with a sudden onrush of feeling, so that Radzivill had to prompt
an answer out of him.

"What are you trying to say, my boy?"

"I confessed my worst sins to Your Highness as if to a father.
And there're so many of them that only a father's heart could

find forgiveness for me. But there's one crime of which I've never been guilty, sir, and that's ingratitude."

"Neither have you ever broken your word," Radzivill said kindly. "An oath is sacred to you. You've confessed to me and I've not only given you a father's forgiveness but I've come to love you as if you were the son I never had. So be that son to me and give me your friendship."

The Prince stretched out his hand and the young man seized it and pressed his lips to it in fealty and affection. Time passed as they stared in silence at each other and then the Prince fixed his calculating, distant eyes on Kmita.

"The Billevitch girl is here," he said suddenly. "Did you hear about that?"

Kmita grew pale and stammered out some disjointed phrases which Radzivill dismissed without a word.

"I've sent for her on purpose," the Prince said. "It's time to put an end to that quarrel between the two of you. God knows that my head is splitting with work these days but I found time to have a word with the Constable of Rosyen about you."

Kmita stared at his benefactor with unbelieving eyes. "How will I ever be able to thank Your Highness?" he stammered out at last. "What can I do to repay your kindness?"

"I made it clear to Pan Billevitch that I want the two of you to marry and he won't stand in your way. I also told him to get the girl used to that idea."

"Ah, Your Highness..."

Radzivill waved his hand.

"Oh, not right away. We've time. It all depends on you, just like the rest of your future. I'll be pleased to see your happiness coming to you through my intercession, as so many other rewards are sure to come your way, because you're meant for great things. Yes, you've sinned, but you're young. Young men make mistakes. Look, though, at the reputation you've made for yourself already. You've quite won over the youth of the country, they're ready to go wherever you lead them, and there ought to be no limit to how high you rise. You're meant for something far better, by God, than county offices and titles! D'you know, by the way, that you've a family connection with the Kishkas, which is one of the oldest families in Lithuania, and that I too am linked with them through my mother? So you may think of yourself as my relative as well! All you need is stability, and marriage is the best prescription for that. So take that girl if she's still dear to you and remember who gives her to you now."

"Dear God!" the young man cried. "What do I have to do to show my gratitude? My life is yours, Highness! I'll give all my blood for you! But how else can I serve you? Tell me, sir! I'm wholly at your orders!"

"Repay my goodwill with yours. Have faith in me. Trust me. Believe that what I do is for the public good. Don't turn your back on me when you see others breaking their allegiance. Stand by me even if everyone deserts me... if treason flares everywhere... even if I too..."

"Highness...?" Kmita waited.

But the Prince bit back his last words as if catching himself in time before he said too much and the young man cried out impulsively:

"I swear it! I give you my word, sir, that I'll stand behind you to my dying breath! You are my only leader, father and bene-factor."

Kmita stared at the Hetman with eyes full of loyalty and fire and suddenly caught his breath.

The change that swept across Radzivill's granite features was simply terrifying. His face turned scarlet, thick with blood; the veins swelled into dark, knotted cords on his neck and temples; sweat burst out on his lofty forehead and his eyes burned with an unnatural glow.

"What is it, Highness?" Kmita cried, alarmed. "Are you ill? What is it?"

"It's nothing... nothing!"

Radzivill rose and stepped swiftly towards a small prayer pulpit in the corner where he seized a crucifix, tore it off the wall, and started to gasp in a string of violent, suffocating phrases that he barely managed to control:

"Swear... on this cross... that you'll never leave me! Not while you're alive!"

"Highness..."

Kmita stared. In spite of all his readiness, faith, loyalty and enthusiasm he was dumbfounded by this sudden metamorphosis.

He was stunned by this half-strangled, gasping apparition, and fixed his eyes on the towering figure with utter amazement.

"By Christ's suffering..." Radzivill's rattling breath seemed about to choke him. "Swear it!"

"By Christ's suffering," Kmita said at last and laid his fingers on the crucifix. "I swear it."

"Amen!" the Prince said in a solemn tone.

The echoes under the tall, vaulted ceiling of the chamber repeated the *Amen* and the two men stood in silence for some moments staring at each other. The only sound in that suddenly stilled and thickened air was the harsh, heavy breath that struggled out of Radzivill's massive chest, and Pan Andrei couldn't tear his astonished eyes away from the Hetman.

"Now... you're mine," Radzivill said at last.

"I've always been yours, Highness," the young knight assured him. "But tell me sir, if you would, what is this all about? Why did you doubt me? What is going on? Is something threatening your illustrious person? Has some new treason been uncovered?"

"A time of trial is near," Radzivill said, dark with gloom and heavy with foreboding. "As for my enemies, don't you know that Pan Gosyevski, Pan Yuditzki and the *Voyevode* of Vitebsk would do anything to ruin me and bury me alive? But that's how it is! The enemies of my House are rising everywhere, treason spreads like wildfire, and fresh national calamities are looming all around us. That's why I say to you, the time of trial is coming... It is almost here."

Kmita kept still and silent but the Prince's words cast no new light on the confusion that settled on his mind. What could threaten the powerful Radzivill at this of all times? He had more troops under his command than ever before. Just in Keydany and its neighborhood stood so many new and veteran regiments that if he'd had anything like their numbers before the Shklov disaster the course of the whole Russian war would have been quite different.

So what could it be? Gosyevski and Yuditzki may have stood against him but he had them safely under lock and key. Pan Pawel Sapyeha, the *Voyevode* of Vitebsk, may not like him much but he was far too decent, honest and patriotic to enter into any conspiracies against anyone on the eve of a campaign against the enemy.

"God knows this is all far over my head!" Kmita cried out, bewildered, as he always would be by great affairs that went beyond the simple cut-and-parry solutions of a soldier. "I don't understand any of it, sir!"

"You'll understand everything before this day is over," Radzivill said quietly. He took the young colonel's arm and turned towards the doors. "Now let's join my guests."

★　★　★

They passed through several rooms, corridors and galleries. From far off, from the vast audience hall which took up half a floor in the central building, came the soft sounds of a chamber orchestra led by a French conductor sent by Prince Boguslav. The music was a minuet, in fashion at the French court at this time, and its mild, tinkling notes drifted in quiet counterpoint to the murmur of massed human voices.

Prince Yanush halted and listened briefly outside the final door.

"God grant that these same people whom I'm receiving under my roof tonight won't go over to my enemies tomorrow," he muttered.

"Your Highness," Kmita said at once. "I don't believe there's a Swedish partisan among them."

Radzivill jerked erect as if wakened from his musing by a sudden danger. "What do you mean by that?"

"I mean, sir, that there are only good, honest soldiers behind that door. That's all."

"Let's go in then. Only time will show who is good and honest. And God will judge intentions."

Twelve pages, dressed in plumes and velvets and picked for their beauty, clustered about the great gilded doors to the audience chamber, but at the sight of the approaching Hetman they hurried to form two escorting ranks.

"Did Her Highness enter the hall already?" the Prince asked about his wife.

"Yes, Highness," the boys chorused. "Her Highness has entered."

"And the foreign envoys?"

"They're also there, sire."

"Then open the door!"

Both halves of the tall, ornate doors flew apart at once and a stream of brilliant light poured through them to illuminate the gigantic figure of the Hetman who strode in, followed by Kmita and flanked by his pages, and mounted the dais on which chairs had been set up for the most distinguished guests while several hundred others filled the main floor below.

All eyes turned to him at once and a single, vast cry broke out of the assembled knighthood: "Long live Radzivill! Long live our Hetman and commander! *Vivat! Vivat! Vivat!*"

The Prince bowed his thanks as his principal guests rose to their feet to greet him on the dais, and motioned for everyone else to be at their ease, but their enthusiastic cheers went on unabated. Beside his wife and several ladies of her court, the main table consisted of the two Swedish envoys, the ambassador of Moscow, the *Voyevode* of Wenden, Bishop Partchevski, Father Byelozor, Pan Myezevski who was a former councillor of King Yan Casimir, Pan Komorovski, Pan Hlebovitch who served as the *Starosta* or governor of Zmudya and who was also the Prince's brother-in-law, one young member of the powerful Patz family, Colonel Mirski of the Radzivill household armored regiment, Colonel Ganhof, and Count Weissenhoff, an ambassador of the Prince of Courland.

The Prince greeted each of them in turn and bowed to the assembly whose heartfelt cheers rang among the rafters.

"Long live Radzivill!" they shouted on and on. "Long may he lead us! All power and glory to him!"

It was a moment, Pan Andrei thought, that would live in his memory and his heart for ever.

Chapter Twenty-five

UP ON THE DAIS, the Grand Hetman moved among his most important guests, saying a few kind words to each as hospitality required. He bowed and gestured pleasantly to everyone, greeting several nobles who pressed towards the dais on the floor below, and seated himself in his crowned, high-backed chair under an overhanging baldachin made of crimson velvet trimmed with ermine tails.

Standing half-hidden behind these costly draperies, Pan Andrei peered at the celebrating crowd as eagerly as his master but for a different reason. His heart was pounding in his chest. His eyes skipped from one face to another, seeking that one precious face, that single set of unforgettable, dear features and that special figure, that seemed to be etched into his heart and filling his whole soul.

'She's here,' he told himself over and over. 'I'll see her in a moment... speak to her.' And his eyes searched the room with even greater urgency, more anxious than ever.

'Hey! There! Above the edge of that feathery fan... Those dark, curving brows... That white forehead... That pale golden hair... Is that she?'

... And Kmita held his breath as if afraid that this living portrait would take fright and vanish. The feathers move. The fan snaps shut. The face is exposed... But no, it wasn't Olenka. Not this time. Not yet.

His eyes leaped farther, glided across graceful forms, touched glowing faces as bright with youth and life as flowers come to

304

sudden bloom among the silks and velvets, and stood stock-still again in yet another moment of hope and illusion.

"No, it's not her," he whispered. "It's not she."

And then at last—hey, there in the arch of the window frame—something white and glowing caught his eyes, held them and fixed them, and suddenly darkened everything else around him.

'*Olenka...*'

He found what he was seeking.

The orchestra began to play again but he didn't hear it. He was tuned to another music, the remembered gentleness of her voice, and his heart began to hammer in his chest again. The crowds moved about, swirled, passed back and forth before the dais, bowing to the Hetman and the dignitaries, but the young soldier hardly noticed them.

He couldn't speak, as if he were stricken deaf and dumb. He'd been rendered sightless. All he could see was that one, dear face and it was as if he'd never seen the girl before.

'*...Olenka? Not Olenka?*'

On one hand, she seemed unchanged. The same sweet gentle face and figure he loved in Vodokty. But on the other hand—in that vast, candlelit gathering of uniforms and costumes—she seemed different... smaller... more childlike and appealing.

'*Hey,*' he thought. '*Wouldn't I just hold her to my heart? Wouldn't I hug her, kiss those sweet lips and those long black lashes and that tall white forehead...?*'

And here memory flashed like lightning through Pan Andrei's head.

He saw that spinning room where he had seen her first. He felt the warmth of those quiet little chambers where they sat for hours. He sensed the joy that gripped him on the sleigh ride to Mitruny when he thought that their loving journey would never have an end. It was soon after that unforgettable moment, he remembered, that people started to intrude into their private world, setting her against him.

"*May lightning strike it all!*" he shouted deep within himself where nobody could hear him. "Look what I had and what I've thrown away! She was so close and now—ah, dammit all—she's so far away."

She sat in that framed cavity of mullioned glass and granite, so distant as to seem beyond reach and any possibility of touching, and a vast, raging anger seized him by the hair along with some strange, immeasurable grief and pity that defied expression.

'*Ey you, Olenka!*' he cried out in his soul, unable to force the words through his throat to his dry, twisted lips. '*Ey, you...!*'

He had so many moments of wild rage at himself when he recalled everything he'd done before and after coming to the Lauda country, that he wanted to order his men to stretch him across a wagon wheel and lash his back to ribbons. But he never felt such fury as he did just then when he saw her again after such a long and hopeless separation, seeing her as even more beautiful and desired than she was when they were close and when they loved each other, before he had lost her. Ah, far more beautiful than he remembered in his imagination!

'*A thousand lashes wouldn't be enough,*' he thought bitterly, '*to pay for such folly.*'

He wanted to watch himself on the rack, broken on the wheel. He wanted to feel the hot agony of his own blood flowing under torture. But because he was here, in public among distinguished people, he merely ground his teeth together and bit his lips as if to inflict some pain on himself, and repeated over and over under his breath:

"Serves you right, you jackass! Serves you right."

* * *

Meanwhile the sounds of music dwindled for a moment and he heard the voice of the Hetman at his ear.

"Come with me!"

He shook himself back into awareness of where he was and what he was doing as if a harsh and confusing dream was suddenly interrupted.

The Prince stepped off the dais and began to mingle with the crowd. His face wore a mild and kindly smile that added even more to his majestic bearing. This was the same magnificent lord who astonished French courtiers with his munificence and his regal manner while he was entertaining Queen Marie-Louise in his estates at Nyeporetz; the same fantastic, legendary being of whom Jean Laboureur, the French King's biographer and historian, wrote in such ecstatic terms in his account of his Eastern European journeys. Now he stopped to chat with the more imposing matrons, with the more important and influential gentry and with his officers and colonels, for each of whom he had some special word of praise, astonishing everyone with his memory and winning their hearts in an instant.

All eyes were fixed on him, following him wherever he appeared, and he moved slowly through the great assembly until he stood at last near Pan Tomasz Billevitch.

"I thank you, dear friend," he said, "that you've come to see me. Although to tell the truth I ought to be angry. Your Billevitche are less than a hundred miles from Keydany but you're a real *rara avis* under my roof."

"Your Highness," the old noble answered, bowing with delight. "It's a sin against our Motherland to take up your valuable time these days."

"And here I was thinking that maybe I ought to invade your Billevitche," the Prince joked. "Still, I imagine you'd find a few kind words for your old war companion?"

The old Constable flushed with pleasure, glowing as red as a beetroot on hearing himself singled out for such intimacy, and the Prince went on:

"If only I had the time! There is just never enough of it these days. But I'll be sure to find some when you're giving your young kinswoman in marriage. I owe at least that much to you and to her grandfather, the late Pan Heracles."

"God give the girl her happiness as soon as possible!" the old noble cried.

"And in the meantime I want to introduce Pan Andrei Kmita, the Seneshal of Orsha, who comes from that branch of the Kmitas which is related to the Kishkas and thus, through that maternal connection of mine, to the Radzivills as well. I'm sure his name is familiar to you from Pan Heracles who loved the Kmitas as if they were his brothers."

"Indeed, indeed," the old noble mumbled, somewhat dazzled by the high connections of the young cavalier which Radzivill himself was announcing for everyone to hear.

"My respects to you, sir," the young man said boldly and with a touch of pride. "Colonel Heracles was like a father to me, and my benefactor too. And even though his work didn't see the fruition he wanted, and his good wishes for me fell on bitter times, I've never ceased in my affection for all the Billevitches who are as dear to me as if my own blood was flowing in their veins."

"And in particular," the Prince said, letting his hand rest intimately on the young man's shoulder, "there's one Billevitch lady for whom he never ceased to care, as he confided to me a long time ago."

"And I'll say it straight into anybody's face!" the young man snapped sharply.

"Easy... easy now," the Prince said. "As you see this is a really fiery cavalier which led him into a few excesses you might have heard about. But since he's young, and under my most special protection, I expect that you and I will manage to win some leniency for him if we plead his case before that lovely judge who means so much to him."

"Who can deny anything to Your Highness?" the old noble cried. "The girl must say like that pagan priestess did to Alexander: *Who can stand in your way?*"

"And we, like that great Macedonian, will content ourselves with that prophecy," the Prince answered, laughing. "But enough of this. Take us to your kinswoman because I'm also anxious to see her again. Let's pick up on Heracles' interrupted work and set things right again."

"I'm at Your Highness' service, as always," the flattered old noble replied, hardly believing the honor that the Prince was showing to him and his family. "There she is, sitting by the window under the care of Pani Voynillovitch, a kinswoman of ours. Only I beg Your Highness not to be offended if she seems confused. I've had no time to prepare her for this meeting."

* * *

Pan Tomasz's anxiety seemed to be well-founded although Olenka had caught sight of Kmita, walking beside the Hetman, a few moments earlier. This brief glimpse was enough to help her get a grip on the sudden onrush of conflicting feelings but, even so, she thought that she would faint.

All color left her face.

She was as white as a sheet of untreated canvas or freshly bleached linen. Her legs shuddered under her and she stared at the young knight as if he was a ghost returning from another world.

Could she believe her eyes? She had imagined him as a lost, homeless wanderer eking out a pitiful, hand-to-mouth existence in some distant forest, hounded by justice like a homeless animal, or as a convict sitting in some tower and peering out through iron bars with despairing eyes. God alone knew how she pitied him, how bitterly she wept in her solitude over his cruel but well-earned punishment and disgrace. And here he was, walking beside the Grand Hetman in Keydany—free, proud, resplendent—with a colonel's baton thrust into his sash, holding his head high among the highest personages in the country, and with a hard, commanding look in his steel-grey eyes.

How was it then? Were all her tears for nothing? He didn't need anybody's sympathy and pity when the Grand Hetman, the great Radzivill himself, laid his hand on his shoulder with such easy familiarity. A rush of strange and contradictory emotions swept through her like fire.

Relief came first, as if a great weight was lifted from her shoulders. Then sharp regret over all that useless and unnecessary pain that gnawed at her whenever she thought of his suffering. Then that quick touch of helplessness and futility that any decent human being feels at the sight of lawlessness which goes unpunished, and crime that escapes its proper consequences; and, along with that, a sudden joy and pleasure, a sudden sense of confusion about her own judgments and an almost fearful admiration for this strange, apparently indestructible young man who could lift himself, unscathed, from such a bottomless morass.

Meanwhile the Prince, her great-uncle and Kmita finished their conversation and started to draw near.

The girl closed her eyes and felt her shoulders narrowing and lifting like the wings of a threatened bird that wants to hide its head.

She was quite certain that they were coming to her. She knew, without seeing them at all, that they were coming closer. She could feel their nearness. She even sensed the moment when they stood before her. She was so sure of it that she rose, with her eyes still closed and seeing nothing, and courtseyed deeply before the Grand Hetman.

"Dear God," she heard him speaking. "Now I don't wonder at that young man's passion. What a lovely flower you've become! I welcome you under my roof, my dear, with all my heart, and not just because you're the grandchild of my old friend, Heracles Billevitch. Do you remember me at all?"

"I remember, Highness," she replied.

"But I wouldn't have known you, I admit," Radzivill said kindly. "You were a child when I saw you last, far from the jewel that you've grown to be. But raise those eyes a little, won't you? Let me look at you. By God, I pity the man who'd lose such a treasure. And here is such a man, standing here before you. Do you recognize him as well?"

"I do," she whispered, keeping her eyes fixed on the floor between them.

"He's a great sinner," the Prince said. "And I bring him here to you for confession. Give him whatever penance you think necessary but don't deny him absolution or sheer despair might drive him into worse transgressions."

Then, turning to Pan Tomasz and the chaperoning cousin, he went on: "We should leave these two young people alone, don't you think? It isn't right to eavesdrop on confessions and my own faith forbids it anyway."

With this Radzivill led the others back into the center of the room and Pan Andrei and Olenka were suddenly alone.

Her heart was fluttering like a frightened dove in a hawk's sudden shadow, and he too found himself moved in ways he couldn't imagine. Gone, all at once, was his boldness, his impulsiveness and his self-assurance. He couldn't find a single word to say. They stood in silence for a long time, not looking at each other.

★ ★ ★

When he did, finally, find some words to say, his voice was so subdued that he hardly recognized it as his own.

"You didn't expect to see me then, Olenka?"

"No," she whispered.

"Dear God, if there was a Tartar standing here beside you you'd be less afraid! Don't be afraid of me. Look how many people are around us. Nothing could happen to you here, especially from me. But even if we were alone in this room, with no one else in it, you'd have nothing to be concerned about because I've sworn to treat you with respect. Trust me, that's all I ask."

She looked up at him clearly for a moment.

"How am I to trust you?"

"It's true," he said softly. "I've done terrible things but that's all over now and none of it will happen again. I told myself after that duel with Volodyovski, when I thought I might die, that I'd never be violent with you again. No raids, no fire and sword. '*No*,' I said, '*you'll win her through decency and goodness and earn her forgiveness.*' Ach, I told myself, her heart isn't made of stone! Her thinking can change! '*Let her just see that I'm different now and she'll forget the past.*' So I swore to be a better man and I'll keep my word. And right away God blessed me because Volodyovski brought me my commission. He could've kept it, it was up to him, but he gave it to me anyway. He's such a fine man! But thanks to that I passed under the Hetman's jurisdiction and didn't have to face all those tribunals. I made a clean breast of it all to His Highness, as I'd do to my father, and he not only let it all fall away behind me but promised to help ease the sufferings of others that I hurt. God bless him for his heart! But what I'm saying, Olenka, is that I won't be an outlaw, that I'll make my peace with everyone, that I'll regain my good name in faithful and honorable service to our country, and that I'll make amends for everything I've done... Hey, Olenka, does that mean anything to you? Can't you find one kind word for me?"

"Can I believe you?" the girl asked, speaking as much to him as to herself.

"You can, God help me," Kmita said at once. "You ought to. Look who else believed me. The Grand Hetman, Pan Volodyovski. They knew everything I ever did and yet they could believe me. You see? Why would you be the only one who could never trust me?"

"Because I saw human tears running thanks to you. Because I saw fresh graves."

"Grass will grow on the graves," he said quietly but firmly. "And I'll soothe the tears."

"Do that first, then."

"But give me some hope that I might get you back. It's easy for you to say '*Do it first.*' But what if, in the meantime, you marry someone else? God help me, I'd go mad, I know it! In God's name I beg you, Olenka, give me some assurance that I won't lose you before I've made my peace with that Laudanian gentry. Remember what you wrote me? That they must forgive me? I swear that they will! I carry that letter everywhere I go like a holy icon and I read it to myself every time that I'm down in spirit. All I need is to hear from you again that you'll wait and not marry another."

"You know that I can't do that even if I wished to. Grandfather's will forbids it. My only other choice has to be the convent."

"Oh, and wouldn't that be a fine thing to hear! For God's sake give up that idea because I start shaking at the thought of it. Give it up, Olenka, or I'll throw myself down at your feet, right here in front of everyone, and plead with you never to do that to yourself. I know you turned down Volodyovski because he told me about that himself. In fact it was he who urged me to win you through decency and goodness. But what use would that be if you became a nun?"

Made eloquent by fear and despair—two states of being that were so rare for him that he didn't even understand quite what he was feeling—he let the words spill out of him unchecked.

"You'll tell me that virtue is its own reward? Well, I'll tell you that I love you beyond reason and that is all I want to hear about. When you left Vodokty and I got back on my feet I looked for you everywhere. I had a regiment to raise, I didn't have time to eat or sleep or find a single moment for myself but I kept on searching. That's how it is with me, you see, that I can't find any peace without you! There isn't anything that I can do about it! I finally heard that you were with Pan Tomasz in Billevitche and then I really couldn't find any peace of mind. To go or not, those were my only questions. I'd have done better wrestling with a bear. But then I told myself to wait. Because I still hadn't done anything to show that I'm different now. And so I didn't go.

"But then,"—and he looked towards Radzivill with gratitude and affection—"the Prince, my dearest father, took mercy on me. He sent for you so that I might, at least, fill my eyes with love because very soon now we're leaving for the war. Ey, my dear girl, I don't ask you to marry me tomorrow! I know I must earn you. But let me hear a kind word from you, that's all I want for now. I don't intend to get killed if I can help it but war's an uncertain business, anything might happen, and I'm certainly not going to hide from the dangers! So can't you give me some sign of forgiveness?"

"May God protect you," she said softly and his heart leaped as if touched by fire. "May you come back safely."

"Ay, sweetheart!" he cried out, overjoyed that his words had some effect on her. "Thank you for that much if there can't be more! And you won't be going into any convent?"

"Not yet."

"God bless you for ever!"

★   ★   ★

And then in just the way that ice thaws in Springtime, suspicion began to melt and disappear between them, and each felt closer to the other than just a moment earlier.

Their hearts felt lighter.

Their eyes acquired light, perhaps even laughter.

And yet Olenka knew that she had promised nothing, and Kmita, in his new-found thoughtfulness, was too wise to ask for anything that she couldn't give. She felt it would be wrong to close his door to changes; she thought it would be both uncharitable and beneath her dignity to leave him without hope. She didn't question his sincerity because she knew he was too honest and straightforward to manufacture lies and pretend to what he didn't feel.

But the main reason why she didn't thrust him away again—why she didn't hold back on that hope he needed—was, she knew, that she still loved that proud, impetuous young man who'd captured both her heart and her imagination. An avalanche of bitterness, pain and disappointment may have fallen on that love but it didn't crush it. It was still there, still alive like an ember glowing under ashes, and like all true and honest affections always anxious to trust and forgive.

'He's better than what he does,' she told herself. 'And he's free now of those who led him astray before. Only a sense of hopelessness might drive him to those wild excesses... so let him be free of hopelessness as well.'

And her quiet, gentle heart beat faster with the joy of her own forgiving. Her cheeks flushed as fresh as roses under a morning dew; her eyes shined with life, matching his own look of happiness. It was as if a great light flowed out of both of them so that passing strangers who didn't know them or hadn't heard their story, but who caught a quick glimpse of those two beautiful young people, wondered who they were because there was no one like them in that brilliant gathering of soldiers, gentry and young gentlewomen.

They were all the more striking as a pair because, quite by chance, they had both dressed in matching colors. She too wore a cloth-of-silver gown, clasped closed with sapphires, and with a white-lined *kontush* of blue Venetian velvet thrown across her shoulders.

"Must be a brother and sister," said those who didn't know their names but others pointed out that this was unlikely. "His eyes shine too much when he looks at her," they said.

* * *

Meanwhile the Chamberlain signaled that it was time to go in to dinner and everyone moved quickly to form the procession. Count Loewenhaupt, all in plumes and laces, led the Princess Radzivill whose long train was carried by pages with angelic faces; Baron von Duderhof followed with Madame Hlebovitch, wife of the Radzivill governor of Zmudya, with Bishop Partchevski and Father Byelozor walking worriedly behind them. To those who watched them, the two churchmen looked as sad and stricken as if they were going to their execution, but nobody could understand why they'd feel that way.

Prince Yanush, who as the ruling oligarch and the host, would sit with his wife at the head of the banquet table, but who gave precedence in the procession to his most important guests, led Madame Korf, wife of the *Voyevode* of Wenden who had been visiting in Keydany for more than a week. Behind them wound a glittering serpentine of paired gentlemen and ladies pacing with the stateliness and haughtiness of their kind.

Kmita led Olenka.

She let her arm rest lightly on his own, her head at his

shoulder, and he shot quick sideward glances at her delicately carved and molded features, happy beyond all his expectations, glowing like a torch, and feeling himself to be the greatest magnate of them all since he was so close to the greatest treasure. Pacing to music in that slow, measured, gliding step that the world would know later as the *Polonaise*, the gathering entered the banquet hall which was so tall and spacious that it seemed like a building of its own. A horseshoe table, set for three hundred guests, groaned under the weight of its gold and silver.

Prince Yanush, whose precedence rested on his offices and on his family connection with many kings and princes, sat with his Princess in the place of honor, receiving the low, respectful bows of his foreign and Lithuanian guests who advanced into the room and seated themselves at the table according to their rank.

But something seemed to trouble him that night. Perhaps it was awareness that this was the last peaceful gathering of his friends before a terrible and incalculable war that would decide the fates of four great nations. His smile appeared strained after a time, and his cheerfulness had that forced gaiety that tries to mask distraction, so that he looked like a man burning up with a hidden fever.

A cloud seemed to pass at times across his ominous and intimidating forehead which, as those close to him could see, was thickly beaded with drops of glistening sweat. At other times his quick, questioning eyes darted among his guests, resting uneasily on the faces of some of his colonels, and then his leonine features narrowed as if pierced with pain or swelled with sudden anger. Nor was he alone in that distracted state among the dignitaries. The envoys, the ecclesiastic leaders, Pan Korf and Pan Hlebovitch and all the others with whom the Prince had been conferring for three days, also looked ill-at-ease, uncertain and irresolute. The two long arms of the giant horseshoe were already ringing with the high spirits, joviality and cheerfulness common to celebrations, but the head of the table sat in gloomy silence, occasionally sharing a few hushed, nervous comments and unsettled glances.

But was that so curious? The gathering below them consisted of many officers and colonels for whom the coming war brought the likelihood of death; but it's far easier to die in a war, washed clean of sin by the sacrifice of one's life for others, than to carry the awful burden of responsibility for its success or failure; and that was how the guests at the lower tables explained the Prince's uneasiness to themselves.

"He's always like that before a war," said old Colonel Stankevitch. "But the more gloomy he is at the start, the worse for the enemy it turns out to be. He'll be cheerful enough on the day of battle."

"Even a lion growls and mutters to himself before a fight," Pan Zagloba added. "And that's to work himself up into a greater fury. Every great warrior of antiquity had his own way to prepare for war. Hannibal, I'm told, threw dice by the hour. Scipio Africanus recited poetry. Pan Konyetzpolski talked only about women. As for me, I like to get my head down on a pillow for an hour or so, although good wine in good company is also very useful."

"But look at the bishop, gentlemen," Pan Stanislav said. "He's as white as a sheet of parchment."

"That's because he's at a Calvinist table," Pan Zagloba explained in a low voice. "And he might swallow something unclean without knowing it. Old people say that the Devil can't get into liquor, so that you're safe to drink everything everywhere, but food, and soup especially, is another matter. That's how it was with me in the Crimea where I was a hostage for some years. The Tartar *mullahs*, which is their word for priests, could fix such a fantastic mutton roast with garlic that one bite was enough to make a man renounce his Faith, forswear his salvation, and run to their flea-bitten prophet."

Here Pan Zagloba let his voice drop even lower.

"I don't say this to insult His Highness," he added in a whisper. "But I'd make a sign of the cross over these dishes, gentlemen. God protects him who protects himself."

"What are you telling us, sir?" Pan Stanislav answered. "Whoever says his grace before a meal is safe anywhere. We're up to our necks in Lutherans and Calvinists in Vyelkopolska but I've never heard that they could cast a spell."

"Yes, you've more Lutherans in Vyelkopolska than a fat dog has fleas," the old knight said at once. "And that's why they sniffed their way to the Swedes as fast as they did. If I were the Prince I'd turn my hounds on those envoys over there rather than stuffing their bellies with all these rare dishes. Look at that

Loewenhaupt! He's wolfing down that food as if he was a calf fattening for the market. He'll even fill his pockets with sweet-meats for his wife and children, I wouldn't be surprised. And that other foreign freak... what's his name... by God, I've forgotten. What was it, Yan?"

"Ask Michal, father," Yan Skshetuski said.

★ ★ ★

But Pan Michal didn't hear anything they said. In fact like Kmita earlier in the evening he saw and heard nothing for much the same reason. He sat between two women. On his left was Miss Elzbyeta Syelavska, an unmarried lady in her early forties, and on his right was Olenka Billevitch. Panna Elzbyeta fluttered over him, telling him about something in a very lively manner, and he blinked at her now and then like a startled owl, saying distractedly, '*You don't say*,' and '*Fancy that now*,' while all of his attention focused on the other side. He strained his ear for the murmur of Olenka's voice, he heard the rustle of her gown as she moved beside him, and his whiskers twitched so fiercely in his pity for himself as if he wanted to send Miss Elzbyeta scampering off in panic.

'Ey, what a lovely girl that is,' he groaned deep inside. 'What a rare beauty. Take mercy on my misery, dear Lord, because there can't be a sadder orphan than me anywhere on earth. My whole soul squeaks for some dear woman of my own and every time I see one there's some other soldier quartered there already. What's going to happen to me in the end? I'm sick to death of this lonely wandering...'

"And what do you plan to do after the war?" Panna Elzbyeta asked him just then.

"Take Holy Orders," he snapped with some venom.

"And who's that talking about Holy Orders at a celebration?" Kmita asked merrily, leaning across Olenka. "Hey, that's Pan Volodyovski!"

"I can believe that *you're* not thinking of it," Pan Michal muttered glumly.

And suddenly Olenka's silvery voice was ringing in his ears.

"Neither should you be thinking about it," she said. "God will give you a wife as good and kind as you are yourself."

The sentimental little knight began to melt at once. "If

someone played music right into my ear I wouldn't be more pleased to hear it," he said.

* * *

But by this time the rising roar of voices all along the table broke into the three young people's conversation, because the wine was already flowing by the flagon, and the Prince's colonels began to argue about various points of the campaign ahead.

Pan Zagloba drowned all other voices with his recollections of the Siege of Zbarajh, and his listeners stared at him as if he were an oracle, their faces quite on fire with excitement and their hearts bursting with courage and determination, so that it seemed as if the spirit of the great *Yarema* was hovering above them.

"That was a leader!" the famous Mirski said. "I saw him only once but I'll remember him until my last moment."

"A true Zeus with thunderbolts in his hands!" old Stankevitch shouted. "We wouldn't have come to these extremities if he was still alive."

"D'you remember how he had the forests cut down beyond Romne to open a highway to the enemy for himself?"

"It's thanks to him that we beat Hmyelnitzki at Berestetchko!"

"And God took him from us just when we needed him the most."

"God took him," Pan Yan Skshetuski said in a firm, ringing voice. "But he left a legacy for all future Commonwealth dignitaries and commanders. And that's never to parley with any enemies but to beat them all!"

"No parleys! Beat them down!" roared several dozen voices. "Beat them! Beat them! Beat them!"

"And our own great Hetman will be the executor of that testament!" Mirski said.

* * *

Suddenly the huge clock in the gallery above the hall began to hammer out the hour of midnight and, at the same time, the crash of an artillery salute fired in the courtyard made the walls tremble and rattled all the windows.

All talk died down. There was a heavy silence.

"Bishop Partchevski's fainted!" someone cried farther up the table. "Bring water!"

Men leaped to their feet all around, trying to see what was happening at the head of the table, but the bishop hadn't lost his consciousness entirely, he'd merely slumped weakly in his chair, and now the chamberlain held him up while Madame Korf splashed water in his face.

A second salvo made the windows tremble once again just then, followed by another and another.

"*Vivat Respublicam!*" roared Pan Zagloba, rising to his feet. "Long live the Commonwealth! *Pereant hostes!* May all her enemies perish!"

But more explosions drowned this beginning of his speech and the gathered gentry began to count the salvos.

"Ten... eleven... Twelve..."

The windows moaned mournfully after every thunderous salute and the candle flames dimmed and wavered in the gusting air.

"Thirteen... fourteen!" the banqueters counted. "The bishop's not used to the sound of guns. He's spoiled the whole evening because, look you there, the Prince is all out of sorts himself. Look how he's sitting there, all gloomy and grim... Fifteen, sixteen! They're shooting as if this was a battle! Nineteen... Twenty!"

"Quiet there!" other voices broke out in various corners of the room. "The Prince wants to speak!"

"Silence! Quiet for the Prince!"

All sounds dwindled to nothing in the banquet chamber, and all eyes turned to Radzivill who stood erect and looming like a giant, with a filled goblet in his hand.

But the sight of his face choked the breath out of almost everyone. There was something terrible in the blue-grey hue of his lips that went beyond mere paleness, and in that convulsively twisted mouth that tried to imitate a smile. His short, asthmatic breath seemed even more difficult and painful than at other times; his broad chest heaved under the scarlet velvet and the cloth-of-gold; his eyelids drooped like the hooded gaze of a giant raptor; and his thick, heavy features looked as if they were in the grip of some terrifying vision, or as if they were frozen by that icy rigidity that comes to the face of a dying man.

"What's wrong with the Prince?" anxious whispers flew

around the tables, while an unspeakable premonition, anxiety and fear settled on all faces. "What's going on here?"

He, meanwhile, had begun to speak in short, breathless phrases.

"Gentlemen! Some of you... may well be frightened by this toast... But, whoever trusts in me, whoever truly cares for our country's good... and whoever is a true friend of my House... he'll raise his glass with mine and say: *Vivat Carolus Gustavus Rex*, our King from today on!"

"*Vivat!*" echoed the two Swedish envoys and several dozen of the foreign officers.

But the vast, crowded hall lay plunged in a deathly silence. The colonels and the gentry stared at each other with wide, unbelieving eyes, as if asking whether the Prince had suddenly gone mad, and frightened cries erupted all along the tables.

"What's that? Did we hear right? Is this some joke...? A nightmare...?"

And then a thick dark pall of silence settled on the chamber.

★ ★ ★

An almost inexpressible horror and amazement lay on all the faces, and the astonished eyes turned again towards Radzivill who still loomed before them like a waiting giant. But he was breathing easier now, as if a huge stone weight had rolled off his chest.

Color began to return slowly to his face as he turned to Pan Komorovski, his principal advisor.

"It's time to promulgate the agreement that we've signed today," he said, "so that everyone may know where he stands. Read it out!"

Pan Komorovski rose, unrolled a sheet of parchment that lay before him on the table, and began to read.

"*Unable to do ought else in the present state of chaos and destruction which has gripped our country, and losing all hope of assistance from King Yan Casimir and the Polish territories of the Commonwealth, we, the nobles and the people of the Grand Duchy of Lithuania, forced by the most dire of necessities, hereby place ourselves under the protection of his Illustrious Majesty the King of Sweden on these general conditions.*"

"**One,**" Pan Komorovski read in the stony silence. "*To fight* *together against common enemies, exclusive of the Polish King and the Polish people...* **Two**: *The Grand Duchy of Lithuania will not be joined to Sweden but will remain connected with it in the manner that served it in its relationship with Poland, that is to say: equality in all things between the two separate nations, nobilities and senates...*

"**Three**," the slow, wavering voice went on in that gravelike stillness: "*Freedom of speech and discourse in the Diets will not be abridged...* **Four**: *Freedom of religion will never be threatened...*"

The reader went on in that amazed and horrified silence until he came to the phrase: '*We affirm this act this day with our signatures, for our descendants as well as for ourselves, and we swear to it and guarantee it for all time.*' And then a threatening murmur ran across the room—in part a sigh and in part a mutter—as if the first harsh breath of an approaching storm had rustled through a forest.

But before the storm could burst in all its fury, old Colonel Stankevitch rose to speak and began to plead.

"Highness! We can't believe our ears! By Christ's wounds, sir, is this to be the end of the Commonwealth? How can we abandon our brothers and desert our nation and form a union with an enemy? I beg you, sir, to remember who you are! Think of your years of service to our country! Recall the unblemished glory of your House and tear up that shameful document, hurl it down and trample it underfoot! I know that I speak for every soldier here and for every member of our brother gentry, because small as we are beside you, even we have a right to decide our own fates. Don't do this, Highness! Don't do this! There's still time to come to another decision! Have mercy on yourself and on us all and on our Republic!"

"Don't do this! Have mercy!" hundreds of voices sounded. "Have mercy! Have mercy!"

And all the colonels and commanders leaped to their feet and marched towards the dais, and the venerable white-haired Pan Stankevitch threw himself on his knees in the open space between the two long arms of the horseshoe table, and the roar of protesting voices thundered everywhere.

"Don't do this! Don't do this!"

Radzivill lifted his massive head, a crimson flush swept across his huge, glowering face, and lightnings of anger seemed to flash in his glaring eyes.

"You dare to question me?" he burst out in fury. "Is this an example of your discipline and obedience? You want to be my conscience? You want to teach me how to serve my country? This is no piddling petty dietine and you didn't come here to vote on anything! And as for the ultimate responsibility for all this I take it upon myself!"

He struck his great chest with his fist, fixed his blazing eyes on his protesting soldiers, and suddenly shouted: "Who isn't with me is against me! I know you! I knew what to expect! Know this much then: there is a sword hanging over your heads at this very moment!"

"Don't do this, Highness!" Pan Stankevitch begged. "Show mercy to us and to yourself!"

But further pleas were drowned by the despairing voice of Pan Stanislav Skshetuski, who witnessed the treason of the Vyelkopolians, and who now grasped his hair in both hands as if the darkest pit of Hell had opened up under his feet for the second time.

"Don't beg him!" he cried out. "It won't do any good! He's been nursing that serpent for years, don't you see? God's wrath has fallen on our Commonwealth and on all of us!"

"Two great magnates sell our Motherland on two opposite ends of our country!" Pan Yan Skshetuski shouted. "May God curse this House and all its generations! Shame! Disgrace! God's anger upon you!"

Hearing this, Pan Zagloba shook himself free of his own dumbstruck amazement and started to bellow:

"Ask him how much he took from the Swedes, the traitor! How much did they pay him? Look at him, that's Judas Iscariot himself standing there before us! May you die in despair, you turncoat! May your whole clan crumble into dust! May the Devil drag the soul out of you, you traitor!" And then he howled twice more: "Traitor! Traitor!"

And in that moment, seized by absolute despair, Stankevitch snatched the colonel's *bulava* from his sash and hurled it with a clatter at the Prince's feet.

Mirski hurled the second.

Yozefovitch threw the third one, Colonel Hoshtchitz threw

the fourth, Volodyovski—pale as a ghost—flung the fifth, Oski-erka tossed the sixth, and all these treasured symbols of authority rolled across the floor while more and more voices shouted within that lion's den, crying out into the terrible face of the infuriated lion: "Traitor! Traitor!"

The huge swollen face of the enraged magnate became suffused with blood until it seemed as if a stroke would send him crashing to the floor across his own table.

"Ganhof and Kmita!" he roared in a frightful voice. "To me!"

At once the four double doors leading into the chamber from the halls and the stairways outside, flew open and rattled against the walls, and four companies of Scottish musketeers marched into the room. Ganhof himself led them from the central doors.

"Halt!" the Prince shouted and turned towards the colonels. "Whoever's with me, cross to the right side of the room!"

"I'm a soldier, I follow my Hetman," Kharlamp said and crossed the empty floor.

"I am too," said Myeleshko. "Let God judge the rights and wrongs of this matter."

"I protested as a citizen," said Nevyarovski who had thrown down his *buzdygan* along with the others but who apparently now had second thoughts about defying Yanush Radzivill. "But as a soldier I have to obey."

A few other junior officers and a fair number of the private gentry followed them to the right side of the dining hall but the vast majority, including all the senior colonels along with Pan Zagloba and the two Skshetuskis, remained where they were.

The Scottish infantry surrounded them like a living wall.

* * *

Kmita, who jumped to his feet along with all the others when the Prince raised his toast, stood as if turned to stone, his eyes fixed in a glazed, sightless stare on the air before him, repeating to himself in a strangled voice: "God... God... What have I done?"

A soft, urgent voice was whispering at his ear: "And you, Andrei? And you...?"

He stared like a madman into Olenka's eyes and suddenly seized himself by the hair, remembering his oath upon the crucifix, knowing that his soul's salvation depended upon it, and also knowing he was lost and doomed no matter where he turned.

"I'm cursed for ever!" he shouted. "May the earth devour me!"

The beautiful face of the Billevitch heiress was aflame with anger.

"Shame to all those who stand behind the Hetman!" she cried like an avenging fury. "Choose! Dear God almighty! What are you doing? What are you waiting for? Choose!"

"*Jezu! Jezu!*" he groaned.

This was the moment when the other colonels began to throw their symbols of authority at the Hetman's feet but Kmita didn't move. Nor did he stir when Radzivill summoned him and Ganhof to his side, and when the Scots marched into the chamber. He stood as stiff and livid as a corpse, oblivious to everything about him and torn by his terrible emotions, with madness and despair burning in his eyes.

"Olenka!" he said at last, turning to her and stretching his arms towards her, but she stepped back with horror and disgust etched into her face.

"Traitor!" she hissed into his face. "Get away from me!"

In that instant Ganhof shouted "Forward!" and the Scottish troopers surrounding the prisoners moved towards the doors.

Kmita began to walk behind them, as blindly as if he were walking in his sleep, and as if he no longer cared what would happen to him.

The banquet was over.

Part Five

Part Five

Chapter Twenty-six

THE PRINCE SAT CONFERRING late into the night with Pan Korf and the Swedish emissaries after that fateful banquet in Keydany. The reception given to his announcement disappointed all his expectations and gave him a glimpse of a threatening future.

He had been careful to set the time of the announcement in the middle of a cheerful celebration when minds and thoughts are at their highest pitch of pleasure, amity and agreement; he expected some opposing voices but counted on many more supporters, and the strength and violence of the protest shook some of his vast confidence in himself. Everyone, it seemed—that is to say everyone but a handful of Calvinist gentry and his foreign officers—declared against the treaty with Charles Gustav, or rather with his brother-in-law, Field Marshal Pontus de la Gardie, who commanded the Swedes garrisoned in the northeastern Baltic territories they'd taken from Poland in previous incursions.

The Prince did order the arrest of all protesting senior army officers, but what good would that do? What would the serving gentry in the ranks have to say about it? How would the regulars react? Wouldn't they ask what happened to their colonels? And won't they try to get them back by force?

And if that happened, what would the proud Prince have at his command other than a few regiments of dragoons and his foreign infantry?

Furthermore—and this was the most enraging thought of all—there'd be the whole country to pacify... all that armed and

327

warlike gentry to bring back to obedience. Sapyeha, the most
dangerous enemy of the Radzivills, was quite ready to go to war
with the entire world if that would preserve the Commonwealth.

And what about those colonels whose heads can't be lopped
off, after all, without some kind of trial? They'll join Sapyeha
and he'll find himself at the head of all the Lithuanian armies...

'*What would be left for me?*' Radzivill murmured into his own
dark future. Where would he be without troops, client gentry
and loyal supporters?

"And what will happen then?"

The questions were all the more terrifying because the situation in which he found himself was suddenly appalling. He
understood that in those circumstances even the treaty on which
he worked so hard and so long in secret would lose all its
meaning, and the Swedes would treat him with contempt, or
even with hostility over their disappointment. He may have
given them his Birjhe as a guarantee of his loyalty but that only
made him all the weaker now. Charles Gustav, he knew very
well, would shower him with honors, distinctions and rewards
as long as he was the powerful Radzivill. But he'd have only
scorn for an abandoned Hetman.

... And if—the nightmare thought stirred his hair in horror—if
by some strange incalculable twist of fate Yan Casimir stumbles
upon a victory... if sheer bad luck restores his fallen fortunes...
what will be left for the Radzivills out of all their plotting?

The shadow of a great and immediate peril hung over this
great magnate who only that morning had no equal in the
Commonwealth.

★ ★ ★

Later, after Pan Korf and the Swedish envoys climbed into
their coaches and rattled away, the Prince clasped his throbbing
temples with both hands and began to pace rapidly up and down
his room.

From outside, through the open windows, came the challenges of Scottish halberdiers and the dull rattle of departing
carriage wheels. The gentry's charabancs and coaches sounded
as hurried as if fleeing from a plague and a specter of worrisome

restlessness, concern, alarm and thwarted calculations stalked through the room behind him.

It seemed to him that some other presence followed him about and whispered in his ear: '*Loss of friends and power, poverty and a disgrace to boot.*' Wasn't it true that he, the Grand Hetman and the *Voyevode* of Vilna, was already humbled and humiliated? Who would suppose yesterday that there'd ever be a man who'd dare to shout *Traitor* right into his face?

And yet he heard it with his own ears and the men who shouted this were still alive!

He thought that if he were to go now to that empty banquet hall he'd still hear the echoes among the vaulted arches calling "Traitor! Traitor!"

A terrifying anger seized him by the throat and threatened to strangle the gasping Lithuanian magnate. His nostrils flared, his eyes filled with blood, and the engorged veins swelled dangerously on his forehead.

"How did this happen?" he cried into the mocking shadows. "Who dares to question me, hurl insults to my face and go against my will?"

And then his raging mind filled with sudden visions of punishments and tortures for those protesting rebels who dared to do something other than trail at his heels like a pack of humble and obedient dogs. He saw the blood dripping from the executioners' axes, heard the dry snap and crackling of bones broken on the wheel, and he gorged himself with these bloody landscapes of vengeance and destruction. But then a colder, realistic thought reminded him that a whole army stood behind those rebels, his gnawing anxieties returned, and he heard once more that whispering in his ear.

'... *Abandonment, poverty, a trial and judgment.*'

"How's that, then?" he asked himself astonished. "Is a Radzivill unable to decide the fate of the country, either holding it for Yan Casimir or handing it over to the Swedes?"

Couldn't he give it, sign it over, or deed it to anyone he wanted like his own estates?

Shocked and amazed, the great magnate stared open-mouthed into the void before him.

"So who are the Radzivills, then?" he asked himself.

Who were they yesterday? What did everyone think of them

throughout Lithuania? Or was it all a terrible delusion? But won't Prince Boguslav stand with him with all his regiments? Won't his own uncle, the Elector of Brandenburg and Prussia, also stand behind him? And won't the might of Sweden, which still terrified the memories of the Germans, rank itself victoriously behind the three of them?

"For God's sake," he told himself coldly, dismissing his fears. "All of that Polish Commonwealth is on its knees before this new master! Who could or would oppose us?"

He laughed. It was absurd to anticipate failure and disaster. On one side stood the King of Sweden, the Prussian Elector, all the Radzivills and, if necessary, Hmyelnitzki with all his hosts, along with the *Hospodar* of Valachia and the hungry Rakotchy of Transylvania with his savage Magyars! And on the other side? The *Voyevode* of Vitebsk with Mirski and Stankevitch, with that trio of Podlasyan gentry from the Lukov country, and with a handful of mutinied regiments...

"What is this," Radzivill asked himself. "A comedy? A joke?"

And he burst again into a roar of laughter.

"Let them all go to Sapyeha if they want to!" he shouted. "Or to Hell! It's all one to me!"

*   *   *

But, after a moment, his face sagged with fresh anxiety and gloom.

"Those with power welcome only the powerful as their equal partners," he muttered. "A Radzivill who tosses Lithuania at Charles Gustav's feet will be loved and courted. A Radzivill who asks for help against Lithuania will be despised and dismissed like a helpless beggar."

So what was he to do?

The foreign officers would stand with him but their regiments were comparatively few, and if the Polish-Lithuanian troops went over to Sapyeha it would be he who'd control the fate of the country. Besides, each of those mercenaries will carry out his orders but he'll never serve from love, or from conviction, or back the Radzivill cause with the wholehearted enthusiasm of a true believer. What he needed were men whose names served as a magnet, who could inspire and attract others with their courage, fame, audacity and readiness for anything no matter how dangerous or reckless; he needed someone whom the rest would follow.

And whom did he have?

"Kharlamp's an old, used-up war horse. Good for taking orders and that's all. Nevyarovski has no influence, his own men don't like him. The rest amount to nothing. I don't have anyone who'd capture the allegiance of the army and serve the cause as if it was his own."

Then there was Kmita. Young. Enterprising. Fearless. Widely known and talked about as a skillful soldier and belonging to one of the principal families in the country. Standing at the head of a powerful regiment which he raised largely at his own expense. A man who seemed created to inflame and lead all the restless spirits in Lithuania and beyond, and if that were not enough, full of faith and fire of his own.

"If he attached himself to my cause, he'd grasp it with complete commitment, with the kind of wholehearted devotion that only a young man's trust and love can give. He'd be an apostle. A man like that would mean more than whole regiments of strangers. His faith would sweep up all the young knighthood of the country and fill my camps with others of his kind."

But even he had doubts, it seemed. He didn't throw down his *bulava* along with the others, Radzivill remembered, but neither did he stand beside him against the protesters.

"I can't depend on anyone," the Hetman muttered darkly. "They'll all go to Sapyeha. None of them will want to share what I have to offer."

And what was that? he asked himself in doubt.

'*Shame and disgrace*,' his conscience whispered to him.

'*Lithuania*,' said pride and ambition.

The room grew dark because the candles had begun to gutter and only a pale silvery moonlight seeped into the chamber through the window panes. The Hetman stared into this hypnotic glow and fell into deep thought. Something was stirring in that indefinite light; dim figures rose out of the shadows, massed and swelled in numbers as if a great army was darkening a moonlit plain, coming out of the sky and out of the future. The Prince saw regiments of armored *pantzerni*, troops of the winged *husaria*, squadrons of light cavalry, others... A forest of lances and banners flowed above them along the silver highway painted among the stars...

A man rode at their head, bareheaded like a triumphant conqueror coming back from a victorious war. No sound intruded into that shadowed chamber but the Prince heard clearly the voice of the people and the cheering army: "*Vivat defensor patriae!* Long life to the savior of the country!"

"Who is that man'? he asked.

The army drew near.

Another moment and the face of their commander would be revealed by moonlight. The gold *bulava* in his hand and the three horsetail standards carried at his back showed him to be at least a Grand Hetman. His face looked familiar.

"In the name of the Father, the Son and the Holy Ghost!" the Prince cried. "That's Sapyeha! And where am I? What am I to have?"

And again came the twinned whispers of his pride and conscience.

'*A kingdom*,' said the one.

'*A noose*,' said the other.

*   *   *

The Prince clapped his hands, summoning attendants, and Harasimovitch appeared at once in the doorway, bowing to the floor.

"Bring new lights!" the Prince ordered.

Harasimovitch trimmed the guttering candlewicks then went out and returned at once with new candelabra.

"It's time to rest, Your Highness," he suggested. "We are well past the second cockcrow, sire."

"No," the Prince said. "I dozed off here for a moment and nightmares oppressed me. Is there any news?"

"Some noble brought a letter from your second cousin, Prince Michael Casimir in Nesvyesh, but I didn't dare to come in unsummoned."

"Give it here at once!"

Harasimovitch handed him a sealed package of papers which the Prince ripped open and began to read, but what he read twisted his face with fresh disappointment. His younger cousin Michael Casimir, the Prince of Nesvyesh and Olytza, was the third most powerful Radzivill in the country, second only to Boguslav and himself, and the Hetman counted on his backing. But the patriotic young man didn't want to have anything to do with his Swedish union.

'*God keep Your Highness from such thoughts,*' he wrote. '*I also care for the greatness of our House, and the best proof of that is the work that I've been doing in Vienna to give us a vote in the imperial councils, but I won't betray either our Motherland or our King, and I urge Your Highness to follow the same course.*'

The young prince wrote that he was under siege in his castle by Hovansky's Russians, and didn't know if his letter would ever be delivered, but he begged Yanush Radzivill to turn back to the cause of patriotism and duty.

'*It's still not too late to make amends,*' he wrote, urging contrition and reconsideration. '*Whatever harm's been done can be repaired by faithful and loyal service against the enemy. As for any help from me, I tell you from the start, I'll sooner join my forces with the Voyevode of Vitebsk, which I intend to do with no consideration for our common blood or the welfare of our House and family, than share in your infamy and treason.*'

The Hetman finished reading, let the letter drop across his knees, and sat nodding quietly with a pained smile twisted on his face.

"Even my own flesh and blood deserts me," he muttered. "My own kind turns against me. And why? Because I wanted our House to shine with such glory as it never had before? Ha! Too bad! There's still Boguslav. He will not desert me. And then there's the Elector and the Swedes. Whoever turns away from the planting won't share in the harvest."

"Your Highness will deign to answer?" Harasimovitch asked.

"No. There'll be no reply."

"May I go, then? And send in the valets?"

"Wait... Are the guards well posted everywhere?"

"Yes, Highness."

"What's Kmita doing?"

"He tried to smash his head against a wall, shouting about damnation. He wanted to run after the Billevitches but the sentries stopped him. He went for his saber and they had to tie him up. Now he's quietened down."

"The Constable of Rosyen has left, then?"

"There were no orders to hold him here."

"Damn, I forgot! Too much to do to think of everything... Open the windows, will you? My asthma's choking me. Tell Kharlamp to go to Upita and fetch that regiment that Volodyovski raised there. Give him enough money to pay the men for the first quarter in advance and let them have a good time for a while. Tell him he'll have that property I gave to Volodyovski."

"Yes, Highness."

Harasimovitch bowed repeatedly and prepared to go.

"Wait... Ah, that asthma will be the death of me."

"Yes, Highness."

"Ach... What's Kmita doing?"

"As I told Your Highness, he's quiet now. He's lying down. Tied up in his quarters."

"That's right, so you said. Have him brought here. I need to talk to him. And have them cut his ropes."

"Your Highness!" Harasimovitch looked shocked and frightened at the same time. "Have him untied? That is a madman! He might do anything!"

"Let me worry about that."

Harasimovitch left.

Alone again, the Prince walked over to a Venetian credenza, took out a case of pistols, opened it and placed it close to hand on the table behind which he seated himself.

In fifteen minutes four Scottish halberdiers marched in, escorting Kmita. The young colonel was so deathly pale that all blood appeared to have left his face, and his eyes were fevered, but he seemed calm enough. He even looked resigned. It was, the Hetman thought, the face of a man who had sunk into absolute despair.

The Prince dismissed the soldiers. He and Kmita faced each other alone.

★ ★ ★

Radzivill was the first to break the long silence.

"You swore on the cross that you'd never leave me," he reminded the distraught young soldier.

"I'll be damned to hellfire if I keep that oath," Kmita shrugged and said. "And damned if I don't. So what do I care? It's all one to me."

"Even if I were to... lead you into evil... you won't bear the responsibility for that," Radzivill said quietly.

"Really? A month ago I stood accused of murder. Today it seems as if I was as innocent as a child."

"Before you leave this room you'll feel as blameless as if you've never committed a transgression in your entire life," Radzivill said. Then, changing his tone, he asked with an apparent simplicity, kindliness and friendship: "What do you think I should have done in the face of all those enemies, a hundred times more powerful than I, against whom I can't defend this country?"

"Die!" Kmita said harshly.

"If only I could!"

The Prince laughed abruptly, shaking his heavy head with bitterness and contempt for such simplistic answers.

"I envy you soldiers such easy, straightforward solutions. Of course! Why not? Die! Nothing's simpler. None of you have to think beyond that moment. It does not even enter your heads that if I was to unleash an all-out war and then die without winning a successful peace there wouldn't be one stone left standing on another in this entire country! God forbid that should ever happen! I'd be cursed in the next world as I am in this one. I'd say you're thrice blessed, you who are free to perish. Don't you think that I'm also sick of this burden of living? That I'd much rather shrug it all off and put an end to it? But there's no way for me to turn my back on this cup of gall, I've got to drink it to the bitter end, because who else is there to save this unhappy land? And so I have to bow under this new load and struggle on regardless! Let malice and envy accuse me of pride. Let the jealousy of others tell you that I'm betraying our country just to lift myself to new heights. God knows my thinking. He can judge my motives. I don't have to tell Him that I'd much rather throw it all off my shoulders and find an easy way out for myself! And you, all you who desert me and call me a traitor, find me another highway! Show me how else I am to save us all! Do that and I'll tear up that document right now, at this minute, and lead the army against the enemy before the sun rises!"

Kmita said nothing.

"Well? Speak up!" Radzivill cried out at him. "I'm making

you Grand Hetman and the *Voyevode* of Vilna in my place! What are your solutions? You're to recover and defend all the palatinates taken by the Russians, you're to avenge the ashes of Vilna, defend Zmudya from the Swedes, protect all of the Commonwealth itself, drive out all her enemies everywhere, and you are not to die because that's a cheap trick that anyone can do! Hurl yourself alone against thousands but don't die because you're not entitled to that luxury! Save the whole country no matter what it costs you but you must keep on living!"

"I am not the Hetman nor the *Voyevode* of Vilna," Kmita said and shrugged. "And what's not my responsibility is none of my business. But if it's a matter of going alone against thousands, I'll do it!"

"Listen, then, you soldier. Since that great burden of responsibility is none of your business leave it to me and trust that I know what I'm doing."

"I can't," Kmita grated out through clenched teeth.

Radzivill shook his head.

"I didn't expect much from the others," he said bitterly. "I knew what would happen. But I'm badly disappointed in you. Don't interrupt me! Listen! I gave you a new life, freed you from punishment and justice, and took you to my heart as if you were my son. And do you know why? Because I thought you were ready for great things. I needed men who could see and reach beyond the obvious, I admit that, and there was no one near me who had the courage to stare into the sun and charge it too, if need be. All I had were people with small minds and puny souls, the kind who never dare to take a road that no one ever took before. You point such people in a new direction, one that they and all their forefathers didn't follow through the generations, and they'll peck you to death like a flock of crows! But where did those old roads bring us? Why are we standing now on the edge of an abyss? How did we get here? What's happened to that great Commonwealth of ours that used to tell the whole world what to do?"

And here the huge, heavy-shouldered man, the gigantic Hetman, bowed his head between his great, clenched fists, repeating quietly and with pain: "God...! God...! God...!"

It took another long moment of silence before he could resume.

"We've come to the times of God's anger," he said as if resigned but still willing to struggle against forces far beyond his powers. "Times of such calamities and such a general collapse of all our capabilities and values that the old ways are useless. And what happens when I try to find new ways that might help to save us? Then I'm deserted even by those who swore on Christ's wounds to stand by me no matter what happened."

He stepped back then, looming over Kmita, and stared at him as if trying to assess the depth of the young man's soul, the breadth of his mind, and the outermost limits of his soul and spirit.

"By those wounds!" he cried out.   "By that holy suffering! Do you think I've gone over to Charles Gustav for ever? That I really want to link this country with the Swedes? Or that this treaty we've signed will last longer than a year? Well? Why are you staring at me as if you've seen a ghost? Why are you so astonished? Listen, and you'll hear things that will amaze you beyond all the limits of your imagination! You'll hear such things as will stun you with their depth and scope, because what is really happening here is something that no one suspects even for a moment. Something so vast that it's beyond the reach of an ordinary mind. I'm telling you things that'll terrify you but they'll save the country. So don't pull back! Don't fear them! Because if no one helps me in this great design I'll fall, just as you suggested, and the entire Commonwealth will fall right along with me, and so will all of you for all time! I am the only one who can save our country but for that I need more power than any citizen of the Commonwealth ever had before. I must crush and trample every obstacle, whether it's the *Voyevode* of Vitebsk, Pan Gosyevski, the army or the gentry. Any road is good if it leads to the salvation of the nation! All means are justified and right!"

Out of breath, he paused while his great chest heaved under his clothing and specks of foam appeared in the corners of his mouth.

"Rome used to nominate dictators in times of peril," he resumed more slowly. "But I need even greater, longer-lasting power. It's not just pride that pushes me towards it. Whoever feels himself strong enough let him take it in my place. I'll gladly step aside. But when there's no one else... when I'm the only one able to lift the burden... then I will shoulder it even if these walls were to fall on me and crush me!"

And here the Hetman lifted his thick arms as if he really wanted to keep a crumbling roof from falling down upon them, and there was something so vast and gigantic about him—something so immense—that Kmita opened his eyes wide and stared at him as if he had never looked at him before.

"Where is it then that Your Highness is going?" he asked in a changed, wandering voice. "What is it that you're after?"

"I want... a crown!" Radzivill cried out.

"*Jezus Maria!*" cried Kmita.

★ ★ ★

It was quiet then in the cold quickening air of Radzivill's chamber. The silence seemed solid, like a wall. One could almost touch it. And only the lone, mocking hoot of a screech-owl sent its chilling laughter into the night off the castle tower.

"Listen," the Prince said quietly. "It's time to tell you every-thing. The Commonwealth is dying and there is nothing we can do about it. There is no way to save her. What matters first is to preserve this nearer, dearer Lithuanian Motherland of ours from total destruction, to lift her out of the ashes like a Phoenix, rebuild her and make her live again. I can do this. That crown I want will do it. It will breathe new life into this living grave. No, don't shake! Don't shudder! There's nothing to fear. The earth isn't crumbling away under our feet. Everything stands as it stood before. The only difference is that new times are coming. I gave this country to the Swedes to check the other enemy with Charles Gustav's power, drive Russia from our borders, regain everything we've lost, and dictate a just and lasting peace in Moscow. Are you listening to me?"

Kmita said nothing, staring at the Hetman, and the huge, brooding man went on as if he'd forgotten that he was not alone and as if he were speaking only to himself.

"But there aren't enough people in that rocky Sweden, not enough swords and not enough power, to seize and hold all of this enormous Commonwealth. They can defeat our sol-diers—twice, three times, as often as they want—but they can't master us and keep us in obedience. There are too many of us to control. Our lands are too vast to fill with garrisons for ever.

Charles Gustav knows this very well. He knows he can't take over all the Commonwealth and he doesn't want it. He'll take Polish Prussia, a part of Vyelkopolska at the most, and that will be that. But to hold what he's taken he must break our Lithuanian union with the Polish Crown. What will he do with Lithuania then? Who is going to rule it? If I reject that crown it'll fall into those bloody Russian hands that have already torn so many of our territories away. The last thing that Charles Gustav wants to see is more power in the hands of Moscow but that's what has to happen if I refuse this burden..."

He stopped again then, struggling with his breath, and then resumed haltingly and more slowly.

"So... do I have the right to refuse? Can I allow Moscow to devour us? For the hundreth time I ask: where else is there any hope of salvation? Where? In whose hands...?

"Ah," he cried fiercely. "Let God's will be done! I'll take up this terrifying duty. The Swedes are behind me. The Brandenburg Elector promises to help. I'll free the land of war. The rule of my House will begin with victories and the restoration of all our lands and power. Peace will come back to us. There'll be hope and prosperity again. Hovansky's fires won't be scorching our villages and cities. That's how it will be because that is how it has to be—God and the Holy Cross help me!—because I feel that God-given strength and power in myself, because I want the happiness of this country, and because even that isn't the end of what I have in mind... And I swear by all that's dearest to me, that if I only have sufficient health and strength I'll rebuild this entire falling and collapsing structure and make it mightier than it has ever been!"

A living fire seemed to be burning then in the Prince's eyes and his whole massive body seemed to stand in a halo of an unearthly light.

"Highness!" Kmita cried. "The mind can't grasp all this! The head can't contain it! The eyes are dazzled! They can't look that far ahead without terror!"

"Then... later," Radzivill went on, following his own hidden trend of thought. "Later... ah, the Swedes won't deprive Yan Casimir of everything. Why should they? They'll leave him on the throne in Mazovia, in the territories of Krakow, and in all those old Polish lands in Eastern Galicia. God didn't grant him children. There'll be an election. Whom will the Poles choose as their King if they want to keep their union with the Lithuanians? And how can they hope to save themselves without us? When did the Poles achieve that great power that allowed them to crush the Teutonic Order? Only when the Grand Duke of Lithuania, Vladyslav Yagello, came to rule in Krakow!

"And so it will be again,"the great brooding Hetman nodded grimly and stared down at Kmita. "The Poles can't place their country in any other hands than those that rule here. They can't and they won't, because there won't be enough air for them to breathe between the Germans on one side, and the Turks on the other, and with the Cossack cancer gnawing at their vitals. They'll have no choice! A blind man can see it! And so both our countries will be joined again, this time in my House, and then we'll see if those Scandinavian kinglets can hold on to their stolen goods in Prussia and Vyelkopolska!"

"Highness!" Kmita cried. "This is too much! This is far beyond me. I can't look that far into the future."

"But I can,"Radzivill said. "I see my boot grinding down on those skinny Scandinavian ribs. I see a power such as the world has never seen before. I see our hands carrying fire and sword into the heart of Islam, toppling the minarets and raising Christian crosses, while our own people live in prosperity and peace...

"Dear God!" he cried out suddenly. "Give me men who can grasp a fragment of this vision! Give me their hands to work with because the burden is too great, and the task too vast, for one man alone!"

"Highness!" Kmita cried, dazzled by the landscapes that Radzivill was painting before his staring eyes. "Your Highness!"

"You see me, God!"said Radzivill. "You judge me!"

"Highness!"Kmita cried.

"Go!" the gigantic figure cried to the young soldier. "Leave now! Desert me! Throw your *buzdygan* at my feet along with the others! Break your oath! Call me *Traitor!* May this crown of thorns I wear be complete! Join all those others who'd destroy the country, push it into the abyss, turn their backs on the only hand that can save us all, and then plead your case before God! Look for your judgments there!"

But Kmita had already thrown himself on his knees before his Grand Hetman.

"Highness!" he cried. "I'll follow you to my dying breath! I'll do anything you order. You are the father of us all... The savior of our country!"

Radzivill placed both his hands on the young man's head, and again there was that long interval of unbroken and uninterrupted silence except for the shrill, ominous cackling of the screech-owl in the castle tower.

"You will have everything you've ever wished for or desired," the Prince said solemnly. "Nothing will pass you by. It will be far more than your own parents ever wanted for you or that you may have dreamed of for yourself. You and I are as one. As I rise so do you. So rise up now, future *Voyevode* of Vilna and Grand Hetman of the Lithuanians."

Outside, where the silver moonlight had long given way to a warmer light, dawn had come.

Chapter Twenty-seven

PAN ZAGLOBA HAD MORE than his full measure of wine buzzing in his head when he shouted *Traitor* at the terrifying Hetman—and shouting it not just once but three times—so that an hour later, when some of the fumes of the celebration evaporated out of his bald head, he felt quite put out by his own foolhardy carelessness.

He sat with Pan Michal and the two Skshetuskis in a cellar under Keydany castle, pondering the grim hazards to which he exposed himself and his friends, and wishing that for once he'd kept his mouth shut and his tongue behind his teeth.

"What's going to happen now?" he wondered, peering like a gloomy, one-eyed owl at the little knight, for whom he had an immense respect in tight corners of all kinds.

"May the Devil take it all!" snarled Volodyovski. "I don't care what happens!"

"We'll live long enough to see such infamies as neither the world nor this nation witnessed in their histories," Yan Skshetuski said.

"If only we do live long enough," Pan Zagloba worried. "We'd be able to move a few others by our own example. Make them remember what this Commonwealth used to be about. But will we live long enough? That's the question."

"This is incredible! This goes beyond all reason!" Pan Stanislav swung between fury and despair. "Where did something like this ever happen before? Help me, my friends, because I feel I am going mad! Three wars... including the Cossacks... and treason everywhere like a plague. Radeyovski, Opalinski and now this Radzivill... There can be no more doubt about it, it's the end of the world. Let the earth open up under us, I no longer care. Dear God, I'm losing my mind!"

And, clasping the back of his head in both hands, he began to pace up and down the cellar like a caged animal.

"Should we pray or what?" he asked finally. "Help us God, help us!"

"Get hold of yourself, my friend," Pan Zagloba urged. "This is no time for desperation. Cool heads would serve us better."

But Pan Stanislav had come to the end of his patience and forbearance. "I wish you'd drop dead!" he shouted at Zagloba. "It was your idea to come to this traitor! May God's vengeance crush you both!"

"That's enough, Stanislav," Pan Yan ordered sternly. "No one could have foreseen what would happen here. Suffer if you must, because you're not alone to feel this pain, but remember that this is exactly where we're supposed to be! Here, not on the other side. And if you must call on God, then beg him to have mercy on our country, not on us!"

After that, Pan Stanislav had nothing more to say. He merely wrung his hands so violently that his knuckles cracked, and no one else could think of anything to do.

Pan Michal whistled some shrill, tuneless ditty between his clenched teeth, trying to pretend indifference and contempt for everything that happened, but in reality he suffered a double agony. First, as a decent and honorable man, he grieved for his country; then, as a lifelong soldier, he couldn't bear the thought of mutiny and disobedience to his military superior. For this regular, professional officer for whom discipline was an absolute from his earliest manhood, this breach of his oath was such an unforgivable transgression that he would rather have died a thousand times than do what he had done.

"Stop this whistling, Michal," Pan Zagloba asked.

"Why? What difference does it make?"

"What do you mean, *what difference?* And what's the matter with all of us, come to think of it? Why don't we think of some way out of this? Are we to rot here in this cellar while the country cries for every hand and saber it can get? It's a crime to sit behind these bars when the Commonwealth needs one decent man to counter ten traitors."

"You're right, father!" Yan Skshetuski said.

"Of course I'm right!" Pan Zagloba glared. "Thank God that you at least haven't lost your head. What do you think, then? What does this traitor have in mind for us? He isn't likely to have our throats cut, is he?"

Pan Volodyovski burst suddenly into a peal of shrill ironic laughter.

"And why not, if I may ask?" he demanded. "Isn't he the law? And doesn't he have a hangman and a sword? You must not know Radzivill if you think anything would stop him from taking our heads!"

"But under what statutes would he do it? What are you babbling about? What rights does he have over us?"

"Over me, the articles of war," Pan Volodyovski said. "Over you... his pleasure."

"For which he'd have to account."

"To whom? The King of Sweden?"

"Well, you're a fine consolation, I must say," Pan Zagloba muttered.

"I am not trying to console you because I've nothing to console you with," said the little knight. "I am just telling you how things really are."

★ ★ ★

Then they were quiet again, listening for a time to the measured tread of the Scottish halberdiers outside the cellar door.

"Well, there's nothing for it," Pan Zagloba said. "It's time for me to start using my wits."

And then, because no one answered him, he addressed himself to everyone at large.

"I can't believe he'd sentence us to death. If every noble was to have his neck cropped each time he popped off with some hasty word—and a well-liquored one at that—we'd have a headless population in the Commonwealth. And what about our constitutional guarantee of *nemine captivabimus*, or *habeas corpus* as it's known in some other countries? Doesn't that mean anything anymore?"

"You and we are the best example of what it means here!" Pan Stanislav said.

"But all this happened on an impulse!" Pan Zagloba argued. "A moment of anger! I'm sure the Prince will change his mind when he thinks about it. We're strangers here. He has no kind of jurisdiction over us. He has to keep an eye on public opinion too, doesn't he? He can't afford to antagonize the entire gentry, and twisting the necks of four men like us can't be done on the quiet! No, no, I wouldn't think he'd start things off with an iron hand, setting himself up above the law. Hmm... hmm... the more I look at that the better I like it. Over the military, yes, I agree he does have some authority, but he'll be anxious to placate the army which is sure to ask about its own colonels. And where's your regiment, Michal, by the way?"

"In Upita. And a lot of good they're going to do us there!"

"Maybe, maybe not. Tell me, though, are you sure of them? Will they stand behind you?"

"Who knows?" Pan Michal grew impatient. "They like me well enough, I suppose, but they know that the Hetman's orders have to be obeyed."

Pan Zagloba pondered for another while.

"Give me an order for them anyway, to obey me as they'd obey you, just in case I find myself among them."

"Are you under the impression you are free already?"

"No, no... but it does no harm to be prepared. I've been in one or two tight spots in my time, as you know full well, and God has always come through with something to help me. Why don't you deputize me and both the Skshetuskis to act in your place? That way the first of us that manages to slip away can ride to your regiment and bring help for the others."

"What are you prattling about?" irritated, Pan Michal tossed aside the last of his patience. "It's all a waste of time. How is anybody going to *slip out*, as you put it? And how am I supposed to write these orders for you? Do you have pens, paper or ink somewhere in your pockets? So why don't you come down to earth with the rest of us?"

"Sheer desperation," muttered Pan Zagloba. "Give me your signet ring, at least."

"Here, take it and leave me in peace!" Pan Michal replied.

Pan Zagloba took the ring, squeezed it onto the little finger of one hand, and began to pace up and down, deep in meditation.

★ ★ ★

Meanwhile the sputtering little candle stub gave out altogether and they sunk into complete and unalleviated darkness; only the small, barred window high under the ceiling showed a few stray stars glittering in the sky.

Pan Zagloba couldn't take his eyes off that iron grating. "If our late friend Podbipyenta was still alive and with us," he muttered, "he'd have that grille out of there in a second and we'd be out of Keydany in an hour."

"Why don't you lift me up to that window?" Pan Yan asked.

Zagloba and Pan Stanislav braced against the wall and the powerfully built Pan Yan climbed up on their shoulders and took hold of the bars.

"They're creaking! As I love God, they're creaking!" Zagloba cried out.

"What are you talking about, father?" Pan Yan said. "I haven't even started pulling on them yet."

"Why don't you both get up on my back, you and your cousin both? I'll hold you up somehow. I often poked fun at Michal that he's such a cunning little miniature but now I wish he was even skimpier. He'd slip through like a snake."

But in that moment Yan jumped back to the ground.

"It's no use," he said. "They have Scots standing all around the window."

"I wish they'd turn into pillars of salt, like Lot's wife in the Scriptures," Pan Zagloba cursed and then began to mutter. "The night is so dark you could cut it with a knife. It'll be sunrise soon. I expect they'll bring us a few *alimenta* because not even heretics starve prisoners to death. And maybe the Hetman will start to see reason. Conscience often works better at night when the Devil starts gnawing on a sinner. Hmm... Hmm... Could there be only one entrance to this cellar? We'll have to see by daylight. Ey, my head's getting awfully heavy and nothing good is coming out of it... God will stir up some good ideas in my head tomorrow. And for now, gentlemen, why don't we say our prayers? Let's place ourselves in the hands of the Holy Virgin in this heathen prison."

* * *

After a while they started to recite their prayers and then the litany to the Holy Mother. Pan Michal, Pan Yan and the distraught Stanislav were too badly crushed by the catastrophe to do any talking after that, but Pan Zagloba, as he always did in such situations, went on with a long, muttered monologue like an old dog growling in his sleep.

"The way I see it is that tomorrow they'll give us a choice. '*Go with Radzivill*,' they'll say, '*and all will be forgiven*.' They might even toss in some small reward. Good. I'll go with Radzivill. Only we'll see who's the better cheater. So you'll throw gentry into prison, will you? Without regard for their age and merit? Good enough! Two can play those games. Whoever has the time to feel sorry for himself let him weep about it. In the end the fool will be under the table and the shrewd man on top. I'll make you whatever promise you want, you traitor, but what I'll keep won't be enough to patch a leaky boot. If you break your allegiance to your King and country it's alright to break any promise made to you. But there's no doubt that the Commonwealth is at her last extremity when her highest leaders go over to the enemy. Has such a thing ever happened anywhere before? Are there enough torments in Hell for that kind of treason? What did that damned Radzivill lack anyway? Didn't he get enough of everything out of the King and the Commonwealth so that he has to play the Judas with them? Dear God, you're right to be angry, there's no doubt about it. Just hurry with the punishment, will you? The sooner the better and amen to that. The main thing is to get out of this trap at the first opportunity and then we'll see how much opposition I'll stir up for you, Mister Hetman! We'll see how you like the taste of mutiny and rebellion! I'll let you think of me as a friend, why not, until I'm out of here, but if you don't have any better friends than me, then you'd better keep out of dark places when you go bear hunting."

* * *

Pan Zagloba, as both Pan Michal and Pan Yan knew by long experience, could keep up this kind of muttering monologue for hours; and hours did pass, one after another, until dawn began to flicker in the little window.

Grey streams of light slanted between the bars, brightened the cellar darkness, and found the four glum knights who sat on the soiled prison straw with their backs against the cold stone walls. Volodyovski and the two Skshetuskis nodded in exhaustion, snatching what sleep they could between their restless nightmares and bitter reflections, but when the light grew sharper they heard a rumble of harsh, new military sounds coming from the courtyard: the hard tramp of soldiers, the clatter of weapons, the clicking of horseshoes on the cobblestones, and the strident call of war horns near the gate.

All the three knights leaped to their feet at once, alarmed and disturbed. "The day isn't starting very well for us," Pan Yan observed.

"It's sure to end better!" Pan Zagloba offered. "D'you know, gentlemen, what I thought up last night? Seems to me it's likely they'll offer us our lives if we join Radzivill and help him with his treasons. I say we should do it. Why not? Once we're free we can turn our backs on that heretic Judas and stand by our country."

But Pan Yan wouldn't hear of it.

"God keep me from anything like that!" he snapped. "I won't lend my name to treachery, even as a trick. Because even if I turned against the traitor later on I'd still be tainted with conspiracy and I don't want that kind of heritage for my children. No, that's not for me."

"Or me," Pan Stanislav said.

"And I'm telling you right now that I'm going to do it. Meet one piece of trickery with another and trust God to take care of the rest in His own good time. Nobody who knows me will ever say that I did it out of real commitment, and what do I care about gossip from the rest? Ah, may all the Devils take that damned Radzivill! We'll see who does what to whom before it's all over, and who comes out the winner."

* * *

Meanwhile the threatening sounds coming from the courtyard swelled into a roar that drowned out the gloomy conversation, and the four knights stared at each other with yet another question. They heard fierce voices, thick with demands and anger; and along with them came the quick bark of commands, the sharp snap of orders, the rhythmic tread of large bodies of troops moving in formation, and the dull rumbling of iron wheels as if artillery was being dragged into position.

"What's going on out there?" Zagloba demanded. "My God, maybe it's some kind of help for us?"

"It's nothing normal, that's certain," Pan Volodyovski said. "Why don't you lift me up to the window, eh? I know who's who out there and I'll be able to tell what's going on quicker than anyone."

Pan Yan seized him by the waist and hoisted him up as if he were a child and Pan Michal grasped the bars and peered eagerly outside.

"Ah, ah... I see them," he murmured. "It's Radzivill's own Hungarian Infantry. Oskierka commands them or did before last night. They really loved him in that regiment and he's under arrest just like we. I bet they're demanding his release. By God, now they're forming up in attack formation! I see Lieutenant Stahovitch with them and he's Oskierka's friend."

The fierce shouts outside suddenly gathered strength.

"And what's happening now?" Pan Zagloba cried.

"Ganhof's ridden up to them. He's saying something to Stahovitch. My God, what an uproar! And now Stahovitch and two other officers are walking away. It looks like they're going to the Hetman as a deputation. As God's my witness, the mutiny is spreading through the army! They've rolled out cannon against the Hungarians and there's a Scottish regiment out here in battle order too. Ey, there's more! I see some gentlemen-troopers of the Polish squadrons siding with the Magyars. The Hungarians probably wouldn't do anything without them because the discipline in the infantry is really ferocious."

"That's our salvation, then!" Pan Zagloba cried. "But listen Michal, are there a lot of Polish squadrons hereabouts? Because there's no doubt they'll all mutiny as well!"

"Stankevitch's *husaria* and Mirski's *pantzerni* are two days' march away," Pan Michal replied. "If they were here nobody would dare to arrest their colonels. Let's see, what else is there... Kharlamp and Myeleshko have two dragoon regiments, three hundred men in each, but they're with the Hetman.

Nevyarovski also declared for Radzivill but his troops are far away. Then there are the two Scottish regiments..."

"That's four for the Prince."

"Then there's the artillery under Korf. Two more regiments."

"Oy, that's getting to be a lot!"

"And then there is Kmita."

"Ah, ah! Kmita! And what does he have?"

"One regiment but as big as a brigade. Six hundred picked men."

"And whose side is he on?"

"I don't know."

"What did he do yesterday, did anybody see? Did he throw down his *bulava* or not?"

"Can't say. None of us remember."

"Who's against the Prince, then? What regiments that you know?"

"Well, these Magyars first of all, it seems. Two hundred men. A loose crowd of Mirski's and Stankevitch's people. Some gentry. And Kmita, of course, but he's an unknown quantity just now."

"Ay, ay," Pan Zagloba worried. "That's not much."

"These Hungarian Guards are as good as any two regiments in the army. They're all long-term soldiers, trained and experienced as few others in the service. But wait... they're lighting the fuses at the cannon now! It looks like an all-out battle shaping up!"

The two Skshetuskis said nothing, listening in grim silence, but Pan Zagloba twisted about in excitement as if he had a fever.

"Smash the traitors!" he howled. "Pound those sons of bitches! Ey, Kmita, Kmita... It's all up to him. What kind of a soldier is he anyway?"

"Fiercer than the Devil. He'll do anything."

"He's sure to side with us! He has to!"

But Pan Volodyovski was still overwrought by the idea of breached discipline and soldiers who disobeyed their superior's orders.

"A mutiny in the army!" he cried out bitterly. "That's where our Hetman has led us."

"What mutiny? Who's the rebel here?" Pan Zagloba appealed

to the others. "Is it the army which stands by our country or the Hetman who turns against his King?"

"God will judge. But wait. Something more is happening. Some of Kharlamp's dragoons are breaking ranks and coming over to join the Hungarians! They're all good minor gentry in that regiment. Do you hear the shouting?"

The fierce roar of voices booming in the courtyard echoed in the cellar.

"The colonels! The colonels! Give us our colonels!" the massed soldiers shouted.

"Michal," the fat knight urged. "For God's sake call out to them to send for your regiment and for that heavy cavalry of Mirski and Stankevitch!"

"Quiet! Let me watch!"

But Pan Zagloba started bellowing by himself, oblivious of the fact that not even his stentorian voice could reach the mutineers.

"Send for the rest of the Polish squadrons! Cut down all those traitors!"

"Keep quiet," Pan Michal said.

Suddenly, not out in front in the courtyard but coming from somewhere behind the palace, a short, abrupt musket volley shattered the morning air.

"*Jezus Maria!*" Volodyovski cried.

"What is it, Michal? What is it?"

"They've shot Stahovitch and those two others who went with him in protest to the Hetman," the little knight answered feverishly. "It can't be anything else."

"Dear God in all your suffering and mercy! Then it's clear there's no clemency to be expected here...!"

★ ★ ★

But in that moment the sudden crash of musketry in the courtyard overwhelmed every other sound and drowned out their talking. Pan Michal clutched convulsively at the iron bars and pressed his forehead against the heavy grille, but all he could see at first were the legs of the Scottish infantry massed before the window. The swift, measured musket volleys thundered both sharper and quicker; the dry rattle of lead balls splattering along the wall above the cellar window sounded like a hailstorm;

and then the air lurched as the cannon roared, and the palace walls shook and quivered like a foundering ship hammered by the sea.

"Jump down, Michal!" Pan Yan urged. "You'll get killed up there."

"Not for anything in the world!" the little knight cried out in feverish excitement. "Besides, they won't hit me. The musketry's going high and the cannon are firing the other way."

And Volodyovski squeezed himself into the thick stone casement that framed the little window so that he no longer needed Skshetuski's back to stand on. The space below grew dark immediately because the little soldier, slight though he was in build, filled the window cavity completely, but in exchange the three knights on the cellar floor had a running account of the fight outside.

"I can see them now!" Pan Michal shouted down. "The Hungarians are formed up along the opposite wall and are firing their volleys from there. I was afraid they'd let themselves be crowded into an angle of the walls where the cannon would make short work of them... What soldiers! They know exactly what to do, even without their officers, God guide them! Ah, there's too much smoke again... I can't see anything..."

The rattle of replying of musketry overhead began to grow thinner.

"Dear God!" Pan Zagloba prayed. "Don't delay the moment of retribution!"

"What's happening now, Michal?" Pan Yan asked.

"The Scots are getting ready to attack... They're charging!"

"Damnation! That we should be sitting here!" Pan Stanislav shouted.

"They've got there! The halberdiers have closed with the Hungarians! The Magyars are taking them on with sabers! My God, what soldiers! What a sight this is!"

"Ah... that they should be fighting with each other rather than the enemy!"

"The Magyars are winning! The Scots are falling back on the left, as God is my witness! Myeleshko's dragoons are going over to the Magyars! And now the Scotsmen are fighting back to back, they're caught between two fires! Korf's gunners can't shoot without hitting them... I even see some of Ganhof's men joining the Hungarians..."

"And now? And now?"

"The Magyars are attacking! They're fighting their way to the gate, they want to break out of here! What a sight, I tell you! They're going like a hurricane, everything falls before them!"

"Eh? What? The gate?" Pan Zagloba didn't much like the sound of that. "I'd rather they took the palace."

"That's alright! They know what they're doing! They'll be back tomorrow with Mirski's and Stankevitch's regiments... Hey, Kharlamp's killed! No, he's up. He's wounded. They've reached the gate! But what's going on there? Looks like the Scots in the gatehouse are coming over too, they're opening the portals... Ah, there's a real dust cloud boiling up out there... I see Kmita! Kmita! Kmita's cavalry is charging through the gate!"

"On whose side is he?" Pan Zagloba howled. "On whose side?"

Pan Michal said nothing for one more breathless moment but the clash of weapons, the shots and the shouting seemed to double in intensity.

"They're finished!" Volodyovski cried suddenly in a sick shrill voice. "It's all over!"

"Who? Who's finished?"

"The Hungarians! The cavalry has shattered them, they are smashed, crushed, trampled...! I see their standard in Kmita's hand! It's the end."

With this Pan Michal slipped out of the window, dropped back to the floor, and fell into Yan Skshetuski's arms.

"Kill me!" he shouted. "Take my life because I had that man at my mercy and I let him live! I gave him his commission so that he could raise that regiment of cut-throats, scoundrels and gallows birds with whom he's now going to fight against his country. He knew whom to enlist! He knew where to find his own rotten kind! God, let me live long enough to fight him again! I swear that he won't leave my hands alive the next time..."

Meanwhile the shouts, the shooting, the clash of metal and the clatter of the horses' hooves went on unabated beyond the little window but they began to dwindle in an hour. And then a cold, grim silence returned to the courtyard of Keydany palace. No further sound disturbed it other than the measured tread of the Scottish sentries and barks of command.

"Michal, my friend," Pan Zagloba begged. "Take another look out there, won't you? Tell us what has happened."

"Why bother? Any soldier can guess what happened out there. Besides... I saw the cavalry breaking the Hungarians. Kmita's won."

"May he be torn apart with wild horses!" Pan Zagloba raged. "Oh that hellhound, that devil's spawn, that scoundrel! May he end up as a eunuch in a Turkish harem!"

But the mutiny was over in Keydany. Kmita and Radzivill triumphed.

Chapter Twenty-eight

PAN MICHAL was right. Kmita triumphed. The Hungarians and those of Kharlamp's and Myeleshko's dragoons who joined them were lying dead in the courtyards of Keydany Palace. Only a few dozen of them managed to escape and scattered in the countryside where the cavalry pursued them. Many were hunted down in the next few days, caught and hanged. Others kept running until they reached the camp of Pawel Sapyeha, the *Voyevode* of Vitebsk, to whom they brought the first news of the Hetman's treason, of the resistance of the Polish regiments, and of their colonels' arrest.

Meanwhile Kmita stood before Radzivill—angry, disgusted, mired in blood and dust and holding the Hungarians' regimental standard in his hand—while the Grand Hetman received him with open arms.

"Your Highness," the heartsick young soldier said heavily and coldly. "I don't want to hear any praises for what I've just done. I'd rather have been fighting the enemy then those wretched men whom our country needs so badly now. I feel as if I spilled my own blood."

"And whose fault is it if not the mutineers'?" Radzivill demanded. "I'd rather lead them to Vilna, as I planned, but they preferred to rebel against my authority. Well, what's done is done. They needed an example and they'll get more of them."

"We've taken a few dozen prisoners. What does Your Highness have in mind for them?"

"A bullet in the head for every tenth man and the rest to be scattered among the other regiments. You'll go today with

355

orders to the regiments of Mirski and Stankevitch. I want them disciplined, brought under control and put in marching order. I'm making you a brigadier over both those regiments and over Volodyovski's men as well. Their officers are to obey you in everything. I thought I'd send Kharlamp to the Laudanians but I've changed my mind. He's useless, as he proved today. You will go instead."

"And what if they resist? Those Laudanians of Volodyovski's hate me worse than poison."

"You'll announce that Mirski, Stankevitch and Volodyovski will be shot at the first sign of their men's disobedience."

"Then they'll most likely march on Keydany to get them back by force. Mirski's men are all wellborn and well-connected gentry."

"You'll take a full regiment of Scottish infantry and another one of Germans. First you'll surround them and then give them their orders."

"As Your Highness pleases."

Radzivill let his hands rest on his knees and plunged into deep thought. He had much to think about.

"I'd gladly have Mirski and Stankevitch shot," he mused, "if it wasn't for the fact that they're so respected throughout the whole army. A great many people in the country look up to them as well, they'd take it as an outrage. I don't want a countrywide, out-and-out rebellion, the kind we just witnessed here. Luckily, and thanks to you, we taught the mutineers a sharp lesson and any would-be rebels will think twice from now on before they question my authority. But to get them all in line we have to strike while the iron is still hot, and before the dissidents have time to run off to Sapyeha."

"Your Highness spoke about Mirski and Stankevitch," Pan Andrei said. "But you didn't mention Oskierka and Volody-ovski."

"Oskierka is another I can't touch because he's an important and well-connected man. But Volodyovski comes from Ruthenia, he has no one here. A good soldier, true. I was counting on him. So much the worse for him that I'm disappointed. If the Devil hadn't sent those three stray friends of his, he might've acted differently. But after what has happened he'll get a bullet in the head, just like those two Skshetuskis and that other ox, that fat one who first started yelling *Traitor! Traitor!*"

But at these words Pan Andrei jumped as if he had been scorched with branding iron. "Your Highness! The soldiers say that Volodyovski saved your life at Tzibihov!"

"He did. He did his duty. That's why I wanted to give him an estate for life. Now he's betrayed me and so he'll be shot."

But Kmita's eyes lit up with a sudden, angry fire and his nostrils began to flare and quiver like those of a wild mustang.

"That can't be, Your Highness!" he cried out.

"What do you mean *that can't be?*" Radzivill's thick dark brows narrowed in anger of his own. "Are you questioning my orders?"

"No sir. I beg Your Highness," Kmita said but he wasn't begging. He pleaded and pressed his hands together as though he was praying but his words were quivering with anger, ferocity and determination. His voice was like a pistol pointed at Radzivill.

"Not a single hair must fall off Volodyovski's head. Your Highness will forgive me. I'm pleading. He could've kept my commission in his pocket. Your Highness left it up to him, but he gave it to me! I'd have drowned without that. He pulled me out of quicksand even though we were both after the same girl. I owe him almost as much as I owe Your Highness and I swore I'd pay him back in kind!"

He stood over the seated Prince like a challenged raptor, with the light of danger glowing in his eyes, seized by his own impatient and unbridled nature no matter how diffident and respectful he tried to make his words.

"Your Highness will do that for me!" he insisted. "Neither he nor any of his friends can be allowed to feel your displeasure. Nothing can happen to them and, by God, nothing will as long as I'm alive!"

Radzivill stared at him with a seething fury of his own. His will was law in Lithuania and in those vast Ruthenian territories that were part of the Grand Duchy since the Fourteenth Century. Nothing like this had ever happened to him. No one dared to question his decisions or beg for the life of someone he'd condemned.

"I beg Your Highness!" Kmita cried but, in reality, he was

making a demand that couldn't be refused and Radzivill knew it.

He sensed, right at the start of his venture into treason, that he'd have to give way now and then to the despotism of others, because he'd be dependent on the goodwill of supporters who were far less important to him than this fierce young soldier. He knew that this impulsive, barely-controlled Kmita whom he wanted to turn into a loyal and devoted dog, the kind that would pull down anyone who opposed him, would always be a wild, half-tamed wolf instead, the kind that—if enraged—would savage its own master.

He knew this and his proud, vengeful nature boiled with suppressed rage as he tried to impose his iron will once more on this dangerous supplicant.

"Volodyovski and those other three will die!" he insisted, but that was like throwing gunpowder on an open flame.

"If I hadn't beaten the Hungarians it wouldn't be they who'd be dying now!" Kmita cried.

"How's that, then?" the Hetman's threatening voice turned to a snarl of anger. "Are you breaking your allegiance already?"

"Your Highness!" Kmita's sharp, bitter words were about to sweep him into violence, he knew. "I'm not breaking anything... I'm pleading... I'm begging you as I would a father! But that just can't happen! These men are famous throughout the whole of Poland, you can't have them killed! You can't and you won't! I won't be Volodyovski's Judas. I'll follow you through fire, my lord... to Hell itself if that's what you order... but grant me this one favor."

"And if I don't?"

"Then have me shot! Right now! On the spot! I don't want to live! Let the Devil take me alive into Hell! I don't care one way or another!"

"Control yourself, you wretched man!" Radzivill thundered. "Who do you think you are talking to?"

"Your Highness! Don't push me into madness!"

Radzivill knew that this was as far as he could go with this violent follower. Beyond this point lay incalculable dangers, not just to all his plans, his ambition, and his soaring vision of his family's future, but possibly to himself as well. For now, at least, he had to give this human powder keg what he wanted.

"I might listen to a friend's plea," he said coldly. "But never to a threat."

"I'm pleading... I am begging..."

And here Pan Andrei went down on his knees.

"Let me serve you with all my heart and love rather than from just a sense of duty, Highness!" Kmita cried. "Otherwise I'll go mad!"

★   ★   ★

Radzivill said nothing. Kmita knelt, his strained face changing color with alternating tremors of a deathly pallor and a burning scarlet. It was quite clear to the Prince that he was about to hurl himself into some incalculable and irrevocable act which could well change history.

"Get up!" Radzivill said.

Pan Andrei rose.

"You know how to defend your friends," the Prince said. "That adds to your merit. I've proof that you can defend me too and that you'll never leave me. Just watch yourself. God made you out of wind and fire rather then mere flesh and you'll burn up unless you are careful. But I can't deny you anything, you see? I've in mind to send Mirski, Stankevitch and Oskierka to the Swedes in Birjhe. Let Volodyovski and those other three go with them. The Swedes won't tear their heads off and they can sit out the war in peace, which is even better."

"Thank you, Your Highness!" Pan Andrei cried, as full of gratitude, loyalty and affection as he was of bitterness, rage and murder only a moment earlier. "Once more you treat me like a father!"

"Easy... easy now," the Prince cautioned. "I've honored your promise to yourself now you honor mine. Volodyovski and the two Skshetuskis can live. That's settled. But that other one, that bellowing fat Devil, whatever his name is—the one who was the first to call me a traitor!—he is as good as dead. No, don't argue! I've got his sentence engraved on my soul! He is the one who charged me with corruption, accused me of taking bribes, inflamed all the others, and caused that outburst of protest and disobedience which, most likely, wouldn't have taken place without him!"

Remembering that unforgivable insult Radzivill smashed his fist down on the table top.

"I'd sooner have expected death, or the Last Judgment and the end of the world, than that someone would dare to shout *Traitor* to me! To a Radzivill! And to shout it straight into my face before other people! There is no death that's harsh enough for that kind of crime! No, and neither is there any torment that is too excessive for such a transgression! So don't say anything in his behalf because I won't listen."

But Pan Andrei never stepped back from an undertaking once he'd determined to pursue a given course. He was no longer angry. He no longer threatened or implied demands. On the contrary, he seized the Hetman's hand, kissing it with all the love and fealty of a son, and pleaded with all the sincerity he possessed.

"There is no chain or rope, Your Highness, that would bind me tighter to you than this act of mercy,"he said. "But don't do it by halves. Give it all, as befits your greatness. What that noble said last night is what everybody thought, including myself, until Your Highness had the kindness to explain it to me. May I go straight to Hell if I didn't think it. It's not a man's fault that he's a fool. Besides, that old man was drunk. He believed he was speaking out in defense of his country so how can he be blamed? He cried out what was in his heart even though he must have known that he was placing his head on the block. How could he guess Your Highness' true intentions? He doesn't mean a thing to me, but he's like a brother or even a father to Volodyovski, and it's on his behalf that I'm begging you to spare that old man. I can't help that, Highness. That's just how I am. If I love someone I'd give my soul for him. If someone saved me but killed a friend of mine I'd send him to the Devil for his so-called mercy...

"Your Highness!" he cried out, his voice brimming with such love that even the calculating Radzivill stared at him with a new assessment. "You are my father and my benefactor! Let me serve you and follow you to my last breath... to my last drop of blood... Let me trust your mercy as I trust your vision. Give me that noble's life and I swear that I'll die for you right now if that's what you order!"

Still staring at him, uneasily poised between necessary caution and his need for vengeance, Radzivill bit down on his heavy mustache.

"I swore his death," he said.

"What the *Voyevode* of Vilna and the Grand Hetman of the Lithuanians swore yesterday," Kmita said. "The Grand Duke and the future King of Poland can erase as an act of royal clemency."

Kmita spoke from the heart, saying what he felt, but he couldn't have found a stronger argument to save his friends if he was the most skillful diplomat and courtier. The magnate's dark, proud face lit up as if a row of coronation candles had burst into sudden flame around him. His eyes closed in pleasure as he savored all those lofty titles, which were still not his but which he wanted more than life itself, and when he spoke at last it was as if a warm Spring breeze had suddenly blown across the last ice of a departing Winter.

"I find it impossible to deny you anything," he said. "Let them all go to Birjhe. They can do their penance among the Swedes and then, after what you've just said has finally taken place, you can ask for further mercy for them."

"Oh I'll ask! I'll ask," Kmita cried. "And the sooner God grants it all the better."

"Go then," Radzivill said, still savoring the power of a monarch's mercy. "And take them the good news."

But Kmita shook his head.

"The news is good for me," he said. "They wouldn't think much of it, especially since they weren't expecting the alternatives. I won't tell them, Highness. Or it'll look as if I wanted to boast about my intercession."

"Well, please yourself about that. But since that's all settled, go at once for Mirski's and Stankevitch's men because right after that I've another expedition for you. One that's sure to be closer to your heart."

"And what might that be, Highness?"

"You'll go to Billevitche to invite the old constable and his niece to come to Keydany and live here for the duration of the war. Do you understand?"

But now it was Kmita who lost his composure. "He won't want to do it. He left Keydany in a real fury."

"I expect his fury has evaporated out of him by now. In all events, you'll take some men with you, and if they won't come willingly you'll put them in a coach, surround them with dragoons and bring them here anyway. That old noble was as soft as wax last night. He blushed and simpered like a virgin when I talked to him, but even he took fright when he heard a mention of the Swedes, and scampered off like a Devil splashed with Holy Water. I need him here as much for myself as for you. Understand? I can mold that wax into anything I please. And if not, I'll have him for a hostage. The Billevitches can do a lot in Zmudya. They're related to practically everybody. But they'll think twice about any hostile activity when I've their elder in my hands. Moreover, that whole Laudanian country stands behind him and your girl; it would be an irreparable loss if they went over to the *Voyevode* of Vitebsk who'd be sure to welcome them with open arms! This is a most important matter. In fact I'm wondering if I ought to get that old man here before I do anything else."

"Volodyovski's regiment is full of Laudanians," Pan Andrei reminded.

"Yes. Your girl's guardians. That makes up my mind and your first order of business is to bring her here. But listen to this: I'll convert the old man to our point of view, but the girl is your business, understand? Win her as best you can. Once the old constable sees reason he'll help to turn her around as well. If that happens, all's well and good and I'll give you a wedding without more delays. If not, take her anyway. Once the knot is tied the trouble is over. That's the best way with women. Oh, she'll weep a bit, she'll protest when they drag her to the altar, but the next day she'll think that the Devil isn't as black as he's painted, and the day after that she'll be pleased about it. How did you part yesterday?"

"As if she kicked me in the teeth."

"What did she say?"

"She called me a traitor. I thought I'd drop dead."

"She's that fierce about it? Keep her on short reins after you're her husband, and teach her that a woman's place is at the spinning wheel, not meddling in public affairs."

"You don't know her, Highness. With her everything is either black or white, good or evil, and that's how she judges all people and events. There are few men I know who can match her logic or her powers of reasoning. Whatever it is, she goes right to the heart of the matter."

"Well, she went right into your heart, that's certain. So you do your best to go straight into hers."

"God grant it, Highness. I tried force on her once and I swore I wouldn't do that again. So what Your Highness tells me about forcing a marriage on her isn't what I want to do. My best hope lies in your ability to persuade Pan Tomasz that we aren't traitors and that we have our country's best interests at heart. Once he's convinced, he'll help to convince her, and then she'll look at me with different eyes. I'll go and get them now because I'm terrified that she'll go into some convent, like she's pledged to do. But I'll tell Your Highness, with all sincerity, that I'd rather charge the whole Swedish army then stand before her while she's still unaware of my patriotic motives and thinks me a traitor."

"I'll send someone else, if you want. Kharlamp or Myeleshko..."

"No, Highness. I'll go. Besides, Kharlamp's on his back. He's wounded."

"That's just as well. I wanted to send Kharlamp yesterday to take command of Volodyovski's regiment and force them into line if necessary. But he's a clumsy man. He can't even control his own men. He's no good to me. So go and get the old constable and the girl, bring them here, and then get me those regiments. Have no compunctions about any bloodshed. We must show the Swedes we have the power to crush all rebellions. The colonels will go to Birjhe under escort. Myeleshko can take them. I expect that Pontus de la Gardie will take that as another proof of my sincerity, and the more the better. Ey, it's a hard beginning, harder than I thought. I can see that half of Lithuania will take sides against me."

"That won't mean anything, Highness," Kmita said and believed every word he uttered. "Whoever has a clear conscience has nothing to fear."

"I thought," Yanush Radzivill mused, "that at least all of my

own House would stand with me. Instead, just look at what
Prince Michael Casimir writes to me from Nesvyesh."

And the Hetman passed his cousin's letter to Pan Andrei to
read.

"If I didn't know Your Highness' true intentions,"Kmita said,
returning the letter, "I'd think he's quite right, and that he must
be one of the most honest and high-minded men on earth...
God be good to him. I'm saying what I think."

"Go! Go now!" the Hetman said, feeling irritation, impatience and bitterness returning.

Kmita bowed and left.

Chapter Twenty-nine

BUT KMITA DIDN'T LEAVE that day—no, nor the next day either—because threatening news began to come to Keydany from throughout the country.

A runner galloped in that evening with word that the regiments of Mirski and Stankevitch were marching on the Hetman's residence, ready to take their colonels back by force; that they were enraged by the proposed Lithuanian accession to Sweden; and that they'd already sent delegations to all other regular contingents stationed between Keydany and distant Podlasye, telling them about the Grand Hetman's treason, and summoning them to band together to defend the country. Radzivill didn't find it difficult to imagine that a swarm of gentry would run to join the rebels and create a serious force that might threaten him in his unfortified Keydany. He was even more humiliated and angered when he realized, as the mutiny of his Hungarian Guard had shown him, that he couldn't trust his own private regiments as much as he thought.

This overturned all his calculations and changed all his plans. But instead of frightening or disheartening him, it merely drove him into a determined and implacable conviction that he could depend only on himself. He would take the field in person, march on the mutineers with his loyal Scotsmen, with Ganhof's heavy foreign cavalry, and with all the artillery on hand. He'd crush the mutiny in the womb. He knew that soldiers without their commanders were little more than a clumsy mob that could scatter at the first sound of the Hetman's trumpets.

Nor did he hold back from the thought of bloodshed. He wanted to terrify the army with his ruthlessness. He would cow the gentry. He would stamp all of Lithuania into the ground if need be so that nobody and nothing would have the temerity to stir in his iron grip. He would get everything he wanted and it would all be his by his own hand alone.

Several of his foreign officers left that night for the Elector's Prussia to enlist new regiments and Keydany swarmed with men under arms. The Scottish regiments were mustering for the march along with Ganhof's armored cuirassiers, the tamed dragoons of Kharlamp and Myeleshko, and with the cannoneers of Pan Korf. Troops of armed lackeys, grooms and Keydany burghers reinforced the Prince's gathering division, and—as a final measure of security—the captive colonels were ordered transported to Birjhe. The Prince believed that such a distant exile, to a border fortress which the Swedes must have occupied by now, would discourage the mutineers from trying a rescue. It could even undermine the chief cause of their discontent.

Pan Zagloba, the Skshetuski cousins, and Pan Volodyovski were to share the fate of Mirski, Stankevitch and Oskierka.

It was already evening when an officer entered their cell with a lantern in hand and ordered them to follow him at once.

"Where to?" Zagloba queried in an uneasy voice.

"You'll see. Hurry! Hurry!"

"We're coming."

They walked out of the cell. A squad of Scottish musketeers surrounded them in the corridor and Pan Zagloba grew even more alarmed.

"They wouldn't take us to an execution without a priest, would they?" he whispered anxiously to Volodyovski. "Without a confession?" Then he turned to the escorting officer. "And who are you, sir, if I may ask?"

"And what's that to you, sir?"

"Nothing, nothing I suppose... It's just that I've so many relatives throughout Lithuania, and it's good to know who one is dealing with."

"I am who I am," the officer said as if this was the most profound statement he had ever uttered. "But only a fool is

ashamed of his name. So I'll tell you. I am Roche Kowalski, if
that's useful to you."

"A fine family!" Pan Zagloba intoned at once. "The men are
good soldiers and the women know how to keep their virtue.
My grandmother was a Kowalski, but alas, she died before I was
born... And you, sir, which of the Kowalski branches do you
come from? Is it the *Vyerush* sept or the *Korabs*?"

"What's all this interrogating in the middle of the night?"

The gruff young officer, none too bright by all the evidence
he showed, started to look annoyed.

"It's just that you're probably my kin," Pan Zagloba soothed
him. "I judge that by the similarity in our powerful physiques.
You've thick bones and broad shoulders exactly like mine and I
get all my looks from my grandmother."

"Well, then we'll have time to look into that on the road."

"On the road?"

Pan Zagloba felt as if a huge weight had rolled off his chest
and disappeared behind him. He drew a deep breath, smiled
with satisfaction, and bent once more to Volodyovski's ear.

"Hey, Michal," he whispered. "Didn't I tell you they wouldn't
shorten our necks here?"

★ ★ ★

Meanwhile they came to the castle courtyard. The night was
already deep and dark. Only here and there came the flickering
red glow of torches and the gleam of lanterns, throwing their
weak and uncertain light on clusters of soldiers, both mounted
and on foot. The whole of the vast main courtyard was packed
with troop detachments. The grim swirl of organized, military
activity suggested that a march was imminent. A campaign was
starting. The darkness glinted with the points of pikes and steel
musket barrels reflecting the torches. Iron horseshoes clattered
on the cobblestones. Single riders, officers most likely, darted
among the columns.

Kowalski halted his prisoners and escort near a waiting hay
wagon, with the steep sides fashioned out of ladders, and drawn
by four cart horses.

"Find yourselves some seats in there, gentlemen," he grunted.

"Somebody's sitting here already," Zagloba said, clambering
aboard. "And where are our things?"

"Under the straw," Kowalski said and hurried the others. "Faster! Faster! We don't have all night!"

"And who's that here?" the fat knight inquired, peering into the gloom where he could see several men sitting in the straw.

"Mirski, Stankevitch, Oskierka," the three men replied.

"Volodyovski, Yan Skshetuski, Stanislav Skshetuski, Zagloba!" the four knights answered them in turn.

"Greetings! Greetings!"

"Greetings!" Pan Zagloba settled himself on the straw and looked around with curiosity. "We'll be traveling in good company, I see. But where are they taking us? Does anyone know?"

"You gentlemen are going to Birjhe," Kowalski informed them. Then he barked out an order, an escort of fifty dragoons closed around the wagon, and the convoy lurched and lumbered out into the street.

The prisoners began to talk quietly to each other.

"They'll turn us over to the Swedes," Mirski said. "I expected that."

"I'd rather sit among enemies than traitors," Stankevitch replied.

"And I'd rather get a bullet in the brain," Volodyovski cried out bitterly, "than twiddle my thumbs in wartime."

"Don't blaspheme, Michal," Pan Zagloba cautioned. "You can always slip off a wagon with a bit of luck, or even find some way to escape from Birjhe, but you wouldn't get far with an ounce of lead rattling in your skull. Huh! I knew from the start that this traitor wouldn't dare to shoot us."

"What's that?" Mirski stirred. "Radzivill wouldn't dare? It's clear that you've come from far away, sir, and don't know much about him. Once he's sworn vengeance on someone that man is as good as in his grave. I can't remember one instance when he forgave anyone anything."

"Even so," Zagloba said smugly. "He didn't dare to raise his hand against me. Who knows if you gentlemen don't owe your necks to me."

"And what makes you think that?"

"I think it because the Tartar Khan loves me like a brother. And that's because I once discovered a conspiracy against him when I was a hostage in the Crimea. And our own beloved

King, *Joannes Casimirus*, is also wild about me. It's clear Radzivill didn't want to pick a fight with two such potentates at once or they might come calling on him right here in Lithuania."

"Ah! What are you saying, sir?" Old Pan Stankevitch was singularly unimpressed. "What nonsense! Radzivill feels about the King like Beelzebub feels about Holy Water. He'd be even more deadset against you if he knew you were close to His Majesty."

"And what I think," Oskierka said, "is that he didn't want our blood on his hands just now so as not to bring down public outrage on himself. But I'll swear to it that Kowalski has orders for the Swedes in Birjhe to put us up against a wall the moment we get there."

"Oy!" Pan Zagloba said. "You think so?"

★ ★ ★

They were quiet for a time. In the meanwhile the wagon rolled into the city square. The town was asleep. All windows were dark. Only the dogs locked out for the night barked and bayed fiercely at the passing convoy.

"Well, anyway," Pan Zagloba said, looking for something to be pleased about. "We've gained a little time and that's all to the good. Some lucky chance can come our way or I might come up with a good idea."

Then, turning to the old Radzivill colonels, he tried to stir their optimism and to raise their spirits.

"You gentlemen don't know me very well," he said. "But ask my companions. They'll tell you that I've been in some pretty desperate corners in my time but I've always found my way out of them. But tell me, who's this officer who's leading the convoy? Couldn't we persuade him to break with the traitor and join with us in standing by our country?"

"That's Roche Kowalski of the Korab Kowalskis," Oskierka said. "I know him. You'd have better luck trying to persuade his horse, though it's hard to say which of them is more of a dimwit."

"And they made him an officer, a bonehead like this?"

"He carried the regimental flag in Myeleshko's outfit and you don't need a lot of brains for that. And they made him an officer because he amused the Prince. He used to snap horseshoes with

his fingers and wrestle with kept bears. And he's yet to find a
bear he can't stretch out on his back."

"He's such a muscleman, then?"

"Muscles he might have but if a superior told him to drive his
head through a wall he'd start butting it without another
thought. They ordered him to take us to Birjhe and that's
where he'll take us even if the earth was to split open under
him."

"Well, well," said Zagloba who listened to all this with acute
attention. "Quite a determined sort of fellow, I can see."

"Stupid is more like it. All he does when he has the time is
either eat or sleep. You won't believe this but he once slept
forty-eight hours in the guardhouse and he was still yawning
when they got him up."

"I must say I like this officer," Pan Zagloba murmured. "And,
as I noted earlier, it's useful to know who one's dealing with."

* * *

With this the fat knight turned to Pan Kowalski who was
trotting near the wagon on his horse.

"Come closer for a moment, will you, sir?" he called out in a
somewhat careless and superior manner.

"What do you want, then?" Kowalski asked, pulling up his
mount.

"Do you have anything to drink?"

"I might."

"Then hand it over."

"What do you mean *hand it over*?"

"Well, Master Kowalski," Pan Zagloba said. "If it was forbidden you'd have an order to that effect, wouldn't you? But since
you've no such order then hand it over and be quick about it."

"Eh?" Astonished, Pan Roche pushed back his deep Crom-
wellian lobster-pot so that he could scratch his head. "That's
right enough... I mean about the orders. But what is this, some
kind of a demand?"

"Maybe it is and maybe it isn't. But it's the right thing to do
to help out a kinsman, particularly when he's old enough to be
your father. Which I would've been if I'd married your
mother."

"Kin? You're no kin of mine."

"I might be. There are two kinds of Kowalskis, as you know. There's the *Vyerush* branch, whose crest is a billygoat with a raised hind leg, and then there are the *Korabs* whose seal is that wickerwork canoe in which their ancestor sailed to us from England. And that's my branch because I also use the *Korab* for a seal."

"For God's sake!" Kowalski cried out. "Then you really are my kinsman!"

"Why? Are you a *Korab*?"

"Yes. I'm a *Korab*."

"My own blood, as God's my witness!" Zagloba called out. "It's a good thing we've met because that's why I came to Lithuania in the first place, to meet some Kowalskis, and even though I'm here on this wagon—in bondage so to speak—and you are on horseback, I'd like to give you a good hug because kin is kin and blood's thicker than water."

"What can I do about that?" Pan Roche scratched his head again. "They told me to take you to Birjhe and that's where I'll take you. Blood is blood but duty is duty."

"Call me uncle," Pan Zagloba said. "And what about that drink?"

"Here's some *gojhalka*, uncle," Pan Roche said. "That much I can do."

Zagloba seized the proffered canteen with alacrity, drank deeply, and felt a blissful glow spreading through all his limbs while a bright, optimistic light started shining in his head, and his quick, calculating mind found some new illumination of its own.

"Why don't you climb off that horse for a while?" he suggested. "Sit here with me in the straw and we'll have a talk. I want to hear about the family. I respect your sense of duty but nobody told you to stay off the wagon."

Kowalski pondered this suggestion for a while, then nodded and said: "That's right. Nobody told me." And a moment later he sat with Pan Zagloba—or rather sprawled comfortably in the straw heaped inside the wagon—while the fat knight hugged him with a great deal of feeling.

"And what is happening these days with your old man?" he

asked. "Ah, my memory must be going... I can't recall his first name."

"Also Roche."

"And quite right too. Roche begat a Roche, just like in the Scriptures. You should name your son Roche as well so that every pot should have a proper cover. And are you married yet yourself?"

"Of course I am married! I am Kowalski and this is Mrs. Kowalski, see? I don't want another."

And the young officer raised the hilt of his huge dragoon saber to Zagloba's eyes.

"I don't want any other," he repeated.

"And you couldn't make a better choice," Pan Zagloba told him. "I'm really getting awfully fond of you Roche, son of Roche. A soldier is in good hands with a wife like that. And I'll tell you this much, that she'll be a widow before you're a widower. It's a shame, though, that she won't give you any little Roches because, as I see it, you're a really sharp and resolute cavalier and it'll be a real pity for such a fine bloodline to dry up."

"Why should it? I've six brothers," Pan Kowalski said.

"And all of them Roches?"

"That's right, uncle. Every one of us has Roche either for his first name or his second one because that's our special patron saint."

"Let's drink some more to that, then!"

"Gladly," Pan Roche said.

★ ★ ★

Zagloba tilted back the canteen again but didn't drink much out of it and passed it to the officer, urging him to drain it to the bottom.

"It's a shame I can't get a good look at you," he went on. "The night is as black as coals, a man can't see the end of his nose or tell one set of fingers from another. But tell me, Master Roche, where was that army marching to when we left Keydany?"

"Where else? After the mutineers."

"God only knows who's the rebel here," Zagloba observed. "Them... or you?"

"Me a rebel?" Pan Roche stared, amazed. "How can I be a rebel? I'm doing what my Hetman tells me."

"But the Hetman isn't doing what the King tells him, is he. It's certain he didn't tell him to join up with the Swedes. But wouldn't you rather fight the Swedes than turn over your own kinsman to them?"

"Maybe I would. But orders are orders."

"And Mrs. Kowalski would like it a lot better too, I expect. I know her. Strictly between you and me, the Hetman is the rebel because he's going against our King and country. Don't repeat this to anybody else but that's how it is."

"That's not for me to hear," Pan Kowalski muttered. "The Hetman has his place and I have mine and God would punish me if I went against him. That's an unheard of thing!"

"That's a noble sentiment," Zagloba assured him. "I'd be surprised if you thought any different. But what would happen if you found yourself in the hands of those mutineers? I'd be free and it wouldn't be your fault because, as the proverb has it, '*nec Hercules contra plures*,' or in common parlance, 'even Hercules can't cope with a multitude.' I don't know the whereabouts of those rebel regiments but you're sure to know... so why don't we turn a little towards them?"

"Ay, what are you saying, uncle?" Pan Roche gaped in shock. "By God, I'm going to get out of this wagon and back on my horse! It'll be the Hetman who has you on his conscience anyway, not me. What an idea! Turn towards the rebels? As long as I'm alive that's not going to happen!"

"Well, if you can't, you can't," Pan Zagloba soothed him. "I'm glad you're honest about it, though I was your uncle long before Radzivill was your Hetman. And do you know, Roche, what it means to be an uncle?"

"An uncle is an uncle," Kowalski declared.

"I see you've thought that out very thoroughly," Pan Zagloba mused. "But I'm sure you know what Holy Writ has to say about it, namely that in a father's absence you've got to listen to your uncle. That's like parental authority, Roche, and it's a sin to disobey it... Take note that anybody who gets married might become a father, but an uncle has your mother's blood flowing in his veins. It's true that I'm not your mother's brother but my old grandmother had to be your own granny's aunt, so the

authority of several generations is resting in me. And since
we're all mortal, that authority passes from one to another and
neither the Hetman, nor the King himself, can argue against it.
What's true is holy, Roche! Does the Grand Hetman, or the
Field Hetman for that matter, have the right to order anyone, be
it the lowest camp follower in the army, to harm his father, his
mother, his uncle, his grandfather, or his poor blind granny?
Well Roche? Does he have that right? Answer if you can."

"W-what?" Kowalski murmured in a sleepy voice.

"Your blind old granny!" Zagloba repeated. "Who'd want to
marry and have children if that was all he had to look forward
to? Who'd want to have grandchildren? Answer that too, if you
can."

"I am Kowalski and this is Mrs. Kowalski," the sleepy officer
muttered, sinking into the straw.

"And maybe that's just as well," Zagloba said. "If you have no
children there'll be fewer numbskulls running about the world.
Isn't that so, Roche?"

Pan Zagloba cocked his ear but heard no reply.

"Roche?" he called out softly. "Roche?"

But Pan Roche was snoring like a horse.

"Catching a few winks, are we?" Pan Zagloba murmured.
"Hmm. Let me take that tin pot off your head so you can sleep
better. Your cloak might smother you, I'd better take that too.
What kind of a kinsman would I be not to help you out?"

And here Pan Zagloba's hands began to move skillfully and
lightly about the head and shoulders of the sleeping officer.
Everyone else on the wagon was sound asleep, the soldiers
swayed and nodded sleepily in their saddles, and those who rode
ahead kept themselves awake with softly murmured ballads.

The night was dry.

There was neither mist nor moisture in the air.

But the moonless shadows were so black around them that
they had to keep a sharp watch not to lose sight of the highway
and stray off the track.

* * *

In due time, however, the dragoon who led Kowalski's horse
just behind the wagon, saw his commander slipping to the
ground, with his bright helmet firmly on his head and well

muffled against the night chill in his yellow cloak. The officer motioned for his horse.

"Where are we to halt, sir, to rest and feed the livestock?" the old sergeant asked him, drawing near.

But the officer didn't say a word. He mounted and trotted off, passed the advance guard, and vanished in the darkness. After a while the sound of a swift gallop came to the soldiers' ears.

"The commandant is in a real hurry," they said to each other. "He probably wants to find some inn nearby. It's high time to rest the horses too."

Meanwhile a half hour went by, and then a full hour, but Pan Kowalski seemed to be reconnoitering far ahead because no trace or trail of him was anywhere in sight. The horses were weary, especially the four harnessed to the wagon, and they began to drag their hooves as if they couldn't take another step.

The few pale stars began to disappear and the horizon got a little lighter.

"Go and get the commandant, one of you," the old sergeant said. "Tell him our nags are just about done in and the wagon team is finished altogether."

A soldier spurred ahead but returned alone in another hour.

"There's no sign of the commandant anywhere," he said. "He must be a mile out in front by now."

"It's easy enough for him," the dragoons grumbled to each other. "He slept all day, and he got more sleep on the wagon, and here we're rattling about on our last breath along with the horses."

"There's an inn a couple of furlongs ahead," said the soldier who had ridden forward. "I thought I'd find him there. But no way! I listened, like maybe I'd hear his horse, you know? Still nothing! The Devil only knows where he's got to."

"We'll halt anyway," the sergeant decided. "The nags need a breather."

* * *

They stopped at the inn. The soldiers climbed out of their saddles. Some went to pound on the tavern door. Others started hand-feeding their horses with hay they carried strapped

behind their saddles. The prisoners began to stir as soon as the
wagon stopped rolling.

"Which way are we heading?" old Stankevitch asked, looking
up at the pale stars to judge their direction.

"It's hard to say in darkness," said Volodyovski. "Especially
since we're not going towards Upita."

"Doesn't the Keydany-Birjhe highway go that way?"

"Yes it does. But my regiment is in Upita too. The Prince
must've thought they'd oppose our passage and ordered the
convoy to take a round-about road. We turned towards Dalnov
and Korokov just beyond Keydany so we're probably somewhere on the Saulas highway. It's a bit out of the way but we'll
pass Upita and Ponevyesh on the right. There are no other
troops but mine hereabouts because the Prince had them pulled
nearer to Keydany so that he could keeper a closer eye on them."

"And our Pan Zagloba is snoring happily in the straw instead
of thinking up any good ideas as he promised," Pan Stanislav
said.

"Let him sleep. He must be tired out with talking to that
dimwit commandant. He probably tried to convert him to his
real duty. But what's the use? Whoever won't leave Radzivill
for the sake of his Motherland won't do it for an imaginary
kinsman."

"Are they really related?" Pan Oskierka asked.

"They? They're as related as you and I," Volodyovski said.
"There wasn't a word of truth in all that talk about family crests
and Korabs. Pan Zagloba likes to exercise his tongue and I
know for a fact that he has a different lineage altogether."

"And where's Pan Kowalski?"

"Must be with his men. Or in the inn."

"I'd like to ask him to let me mount one of his troopers'
horses just to stretch my bones," Mirski said.

"He probably won't allow that," Stankevitch observed. "The
night's still pretty dark. It would be easy to spur the nag and
gallop away and nobody would even know which way to pursue
you."

"I'll give him my word of honor that I won't try escaping,"
Mirski said. "Besides, it's almost dawn."

"Hey, trooper!" Volodyovski turned to a dragoon who was
standing near. "And where's your commander?"

"Who can tell with him?" the soldier said and shrugged.

"What do you mean talking back like that! When I tell you to get him you jump to it and get him!"

"Yessir! I would sir!" The dragoon snapped erect in his saddle. "Only we can't rightly say where he's got to, colonel. Once he got off the wagon and galloped away that's the last we saw hide or hair of him."

"Tell him when he comes back that we want a word with him."

"Yessir, colonel! By your orders sir!"

The prisoners grew quiet.

From time to time loud yawns sounded in the wagon. The horses chewed their hay. The soldiers slept, propped against their saddles, or chatted quietly with each other, glad to be on firm ground and not jouncing on a blind journey into the unknown which none of them cared for anyway. Yet others gnawed on whatever field rations they carried in their saddle bags because the little inn was shuttered and abandoned and no one lived there any more.

Meanwhile the stars began to flicker out, one after another. The eastern edge of the black canopy overhead started to turn grey. Another day was coming but it didn't promise anything new to the tired, dozing captives in the wagon.

Chapter Thirty

IN THE NEW blue-grey light of dawn the thatched roof of the little inn looked strangely old and grey and the trees that grew haphazardly beside it became edged with silver. The silhouettes of the men and horses hardened and became more pronounced and clear as if they were all emerging out of shadow, and soon it was possible to recognize the faces. The dragoons' yellow cloaks acquired a new brightness and the fresh reddish light began to streak their helmets.

Pan Volodyovski shook off the last grip of sleep, spread his arms wide and yawned from ear to ear, and glanced at the snoring Pan Zagloba.

Then, suddenly, he leaped to his feet and shouted: "God almighty! What a fox! Look gentlemen, look!"

"What's happened?" the waking colonels asked, rubbing sleep out of their own eyes.

"Look! Look!" Volodyovski shouted, pointing to the sleeping man.

The captives peered where he pointed and their mouths fell open with astonishment. There, snoring under Pan Zagloba's short-coat, and with the fat knight's cap tilted on his head, lay Pan Roche Kowalski while Zagloba wasn't anywhere in sight.

"He's got away, as God is my witness!" said the amazed Mirski, looking everywhere around as if quite unable to believe his eyes.

"What a sly, cunning fellow that is!" Stankevitch echoed him. "Devil take me if I've ever seen anybody like him."

"He took the cloak and helmet off that jackass and got away on the dolt's own horse!"

"It's like he's melted into thin air!"

"He said he'd think of something!"

"And that's the last they'll see of him, I bet."

"Gentlemen!" Volodyovski cried out in high spirits. "You don't know this man! But I'll give my oath right now that he'll find a way to get us out as well! I don't know when or how he'll do it but I'll swear to it!"

"I see it but I don't believe it," Pan Stanislav said, shaking his head as if he'd never seen anything more surprising in his life.

And suddenly the dragoons also realized what happened and came crowding over to the wagon, peering with bulging eyes at their commandant, who slept soundly in the straw, with a jaunty cap made out of a lynx pelt pulled over his eyes, and wearing a sheepskin-lined, camel hair short-coat.

The sergeant started shaking him at once without any regard for rank or military courtesy. "Hey, commandant!" he bellowed. "Commandant!"

"I'm Pan Kowalski," the young officer muttered in his sleep. "And that's Mrs. Kowalski..."

"Commandant, a prisoner's escaped!"

Kowalski sat up groggily in the straw and opened his eyes.

"What's going on?" he asked.

"A prisoner's escaped! That fat noble you were talking with, sir!"

"W-w-what?" The last vestige of sleep ebbed out of the young man's foggy brain. Terror gripped his voice. "How can that be? What happened? What idiot let that happen? How did he get away?"

"In your cloak and helmet, sir. The men thought it was you so nobody stopped him. The night was too dark to see more'n a yard ahead."

"Where's my horse?" Kowalski yelled.

"Gone sir. That's what that fat noble got away on, sir."

"On my horse?"

"Yessir!"

Kowalski clutched his head.

"Jezus of Nazareth," he groaned, swaying from side to side. "King of the Jews..."

Then he howled again. "Where's that dimwit who gave him my horse? Where is he? Get him here!"

"The trooper's not to blame, sir!" the sergeant tried to pacify his overwrought commander. "The night was black as pitch and he had Your Honor's cloak and helmet. He rode right past me and I didn't know him! If Your Honor hadn't got on the wagon with him he wouldn't have pulled this off."

"Kill me! Beat me!" the unfortunate young officer moaned in absolute despair.

"What are we to do, sir?"

"Kill him! Get after him!"

"And how are we to do that? He's got Your Honor's horse and that's the best we had. Ours are worn down so bad they can hardly move and he got away long before first cockcrow. We'll never catch him now."

"You'd have a better chance catching the wind," Stankevitch said, laughing, and Kowalski turned on his prisoners in a rage.

"You men helped him to escape!" he howled and started shaking his huge fist in their faces. "I'll show you...! I'll show you!"

But Mirski put him in his place at once. "Who do you think you're threatening, you ignorant shavetail? Keep quiet and remember who we are!"

Pan Roche quivered all over, torn between rage and his habit of obedience, but his prisoners' high rank made him feel just as futile and insignificant as he truly was. Old Colonel Stankevitch snapped an order at him, and drove the last nail into the coffin of his self esteem.

"Take us where you were told to take us, fellow," he commanded. "But don't raise your voice! Respect our rank, you hear? Because tomorrow you might be taking orders from any one of us!"

Pan Roche snapped to attention. He stared. His mouth fell open but he couldn't find a word to say. In the meantime his prisoners were beginning to enjoy themselves.

"Well, well, Master Roche," Oskierka started laughing. "You've really shown yourself to be a jackass, there's no doubt about it. What you say about us helping him is nonsense because we slept just as soundly as you did, and in the second place, each one of us would've looked to his own escape first and foremost! You're a bonehead, and that's all there's to it. The blame is all yours and I'd be the first to have you shot for it. Imagine an officer snoring like a badger in his burrow and letting a prisoner escape in his cloak and helmet. And on his horse as well! This must be the first time in history that such a thing has happened!"

"An old fox fooled a young one," Mirski said.

"Jesus and Mary!" Kowalski cried out. "I don't have my saber!"

"And don't you think he might find it useful?" Stankevitch said, smiling. "Pan Oskierka is quite right, you're a real jackass. I imagine you had pistols in your holsters too?"

"I did," groaned the stricken Pan Kowalski.

And suddenly he was clutching his head again, almost paralyzed with horror and despair.

"And the Prince's letter to the commandant in Birjhe! That's gone too! What can I do now? I'm lost. I'm finished for ever. I'm as good as dead! There's nothing for me now except a firing squad."

"You're right in that respect," Pan Mirski said gravely. "How can you bring us to Birjhe after this? What'll happen when you turn us over to the Swedes and we, as your superiors in rank and position, tell them it's you who has to be locked up? Whose word, d'you think, they'll take? Do you imagine a Swedish officer would hold men like us just because some piddling Pan Kowalski is asking him to do it? He'll sooner believe us and toss you into a cell."

"I'm lost, I'm lost," Kowalski was moaning.

"A trivial matter," said Volodyovski.

"What should we do, sir?" the old sergeant asked.

"Go to the Devil!" roared Kowalski. "How do I know where to go or what to do? May you get hit by lightning!"

"Go on, go on to Birjhe and you'll see what happens," Mirski said.

"Turn around to Keydany!" Kowalski yelled at the dragoons.

"May I turn into a pig's ear if they don't put you up against a wall and blow your brains out!" Oskierka said. "How are you going to face the Hetman? Tfui! All that's waiting for you there is disgrace and a bullet."

"Because that's all I'm worth!" the wretched young man cried.

"Nonsense, Master Roche," said Oskierka. "We alone can save you. You can believe me when I say that we'd have followed the Hetman to the ends of the world, and died for him if need be. We've served him far longer and better than you, and we've all spilled our blood many times in our country's service. But the Hetman betrayed our Motherland, gave this whole country to the enemy, and turned against our King to whom we've all sworn our oaths of allegiance. Do you think it's easy for soldiers like us to go against our general's authority? Or to break every rule of discipline and refuse to obey the Grand Hetman's orders? But whoever stands with the Hetman these days goes against the nation! Who follows him turns upon the King! Loyalty to the Hetman means treason to the King and the Commonwealth! That's why we threw our *bulavas* at his feet, because that's what our duty, our faith and our honor ordered us to do."

Pan Roche stared, mouth agape and eyes bulging like ripe plums, as Pan Oskierka went on in an even graver and more regretful tone.

"And who was it that did that? Was it just one of us? Think of names like Mirski and Stankevitch and what they represent! And who stayed with the Hetman? Scoundrels, no one else! So why don't you take your example from men who are older, more experienced and wiser than you? Why do you risk infamy, with your name published as a traitor all across the country? Think! Look into yourself and then ask your conscience what you ought to do. Should you stay with Radzivill and treason and so become a traitor? Or should you join us, who are ready to spill the last drop of our blood, and spend our last breath, in serving our Motherland? I wish the earth had swallowed us alive before we refused obedience to our Hetman but, at the same time, I hope our souls will never leave hellfire if we betray our King and our country for the sake of Radzivill's ambition!"

This speech appeared to make a profound impression on the wide-eyed, open-mouthed Kowalski.

"So... what is it then, gentlemen," he asked, "that you want from me?"

"That you go with us to the *Voyevode* of Vitebsk who is sure to stand by his King and country."

"But how can I do that when I've got orders to take you to Birjhe?"

"Try to talk to a man like that," Mirski said, shaking his head in disgust.

"But we are telling you to disobey that order," Oskierka was trying to explain. "We want you to desert the Hetman and go with us, can't you understand?"

"Talk all you want sir," Pan Roche shrugged at last. "It won't make a difference. I'm a soldier. What would I be worth if I desert my Hetman? It's not my place to think. That's his affair. I do what he orders. If he sins he'll be answering for my sin as well, and it's my job to keep my mouth shut and my ears open."

"There's nothing you can do with a fool like that," Mirski shrugged. "You'd do better arguing with his horse if Pan Zagloba hadn't taken it."

"I've already committed a sin just thinking about turning back to Keydany," the wretched Pan Roche mumbled on. "I've orders to go to Birjhe. Only I got confused. My wits got addled talking to that noble. And he's my kinsman, too! But how could a kinsman do such a thing to me? I'd maybe understand it if it was a stranger. But blood kin? He must've driven God out of his heart to steal my nag, rob me of the Prince's kindness, and put my head on the block all at the same time... Some kinsman! As for you, gentlemen, you're going to Birjhe, and I don't care what happens afterwards."

"You're can't make any impression on a fool like that if you quoted Scripture," Pan Michal told Oskierka. "You're just wasting your time."

"Halt, you mongrels!" Kowalski roared at his dragoons. "Turn around! About face! We're going to Birjhe!"

The convoy turned around. Pan Roche ordered one of his dragoons to dismount and take his place in the prisoners' wagon while he climbed on the trooper's horse.

"But that a blood relative could do such a thing," he muttered sadly to himself and shook his puzzled head.

★ ★ ★

Hearing him, the prisoners couldn't stop their laughter no matter how uncertain they were about their future, and finally Volodyovski turned to the disconsolate dragoon.

"Take comfort," he said. "That man has pulled the wool over far sharper eyes than yours. He surpassed Hmyelnitzki himself in shrewdness and cunning. And as for the stratagems he pulls out of his head, nobody can match him."

Kowalski said nothing in reply and merely edged a little farther away from the wagon, fearing further jeers. He was deeply ashamed of himself in front of his prisoners, before his staring troopers, and—most of all—in his own eyes as well. In fact he made such a pitiable spectacle in that cheerful, early morning air, that the captive colonels began to feel a little sorry for him.

Meanwhile they passed the morning talking about Pan Zagloba and his miraculous escape.

"It's really astonishing," Pan Volodyovski said, "but there is no form of desperation in this world from which that man can't save himself. Where he can't win through either strength or courage, he'll slip through on cunning. Any other man might lose hope or commit his soul to God when faced with disaster but that's exactly when his head starts working. He can be a real Achilles when he has to, but he likes the role of Ulysses best of all."

"I'd hate to be his jailer," Stankevitch remarked. "Not just because he'd get away from me but because he's sure to make an utter fool afterwards of anyone who was supposed to guard him."

"That he would!" Pan Volodyovski laughed. "He'll be telling stories about Kowalski and making jokes about him for the rest of his life. I can't think of anything worse than getting caught on the sharp edge of his tongue, because there isn't another like it in the Commonwealth. And when he starts embroidering on the truth a little, the way he likes to do, then people just about burst with laughter."

"But he can swing a saber when he has to?" Stankevitch asked, grinning.

"Can he ever! At Zbarajh, he cut down Burlay himself in front of the whole army."

"Well, well," old Pan Stankevitch wagged his head in wonder. "That's a wholly new kind of man in my experience, I must say."

"He already did us a colossal favor by stealing the Prince's orders for the commandant in Birjhe," Oskierka said quietly.

"And who knows what those orders were? I don't really believe the Swedes would take our word for who and what we are, ignoring Kowalski, because we'll come as prisoners and Kowalski will be there as the convoy commander. But at least they'll have no idea what to do with us. They won't shoot our heads off and that's the main thing."

"Quite right," Mirski said. "I made that suggestion just to confuse Kowalski. But I don't get much comfort from the thought of living. Not these days. Not when it's obvious now there's going to be yet another war—a Civil War—right here in Lithuania... That, surely, will be the final end of everything. Why should an old man like me have to look at things like that at my time of life? I'd rather be dead."

"Or I," Stankevitch added. "My God but I remember different times!"

"You shouldn't talk like that, gentlemen," Oskierka admonished. "You should keep on hoping. God's mercy is more profound than man's capacity for evil and His hand can pull us clear out of the water just when we're sure of drowning."

"Prophetic words, sir," said Pan Yan Skshetuski. "For us, men who served in the regiments of the late Prince Yeremi, life is also a real burden nowadays. We are used to victories. All we want is to keep on serving if only God will give us a real commander, not still another traitor, and if it's someone we can trust with all our hearts and souls."

"A man could fight night and day under a man like that," Volodyovski nodded.

"And that's the crux of this whole desperate business," Mirski said. "That's what makes everyone stumble in the dark, wondering what to do, and weighed down with their own uncertainty. I can't speak for you, gentlemen, but I'll admit to a real horror of fratricidal bloodshed. And when I think that I threw down my *bulava*, and defied the Hetman, and that I'm to blame for starting up a mutiny and resistance, then the last of my grey hairs rise up on my head. But what else could a man do in the face of treason? I tell you, I envy those who didn't ask themselves such questions and ripped their souls apart looking for an answer."

"Dear God, give us a leader," Pan Stankevitch said, eyes raised to the sky.

"People speak awfully well of the *Voyevode* of Vitebsk," Pan Stanislav offered.

"Yes they do!" said Mirski. "He's a great lord but he has no rank or standing in the army. And before the King can give him the authority of a Hetman, he can only act on his own and with his own resources. But it's certain he won't be joining any Swedes!"

"Whom else do we have? The Field Hetman, Pan Gosyevski, is in Radzivill's hands."

"Yes, because he's also a decent, patriotic man," Pan Oskierka said.

★ ★ ★

But Pan Volodyovski grew quiet as the others talked and sat in thought for a little while, pondering a moment he recalled from before the war.

"I was in Warsaw at one time," he offered at last, "and came to call at His Majesty's residence to pay my respects, and being the kind and loving man he is, who never forgets a soldier's loyal service, the King invited me to eat with him that day. During that dinner I saw Pan Tcharnyetzki who, as it turned out, was the guest of honor. The King was very pleased with everything that day. He was in high humor. It was a good banquet and he enjoyed himself. He kept hugging Pan Tcharnyetzki and saying: '*Even if we were living through such disastrous times that everyone deserts me, you'll always be faithful.*' I heard him myself, and even then I felt that I was hearing a hint about the future, like it was a prophecy or something. Pan Tcharnyetzki was so deeply moved that all he could say was '*to my last breath, to my last breath,*' and tears started running down His Majesty's face."

"Who knows if that wasn't a true prophecy?" said Mirski, "seeing that the *dies irae et calamitatis* are already here."

"Pan Tcharnyetzki's a great soldier!" Stankevitch confirmed. "No one I know has earned a finer reputation as a field commander."

"Even the Tartars whom the Khan sent to help Pan Revera Pototzki in the Ukraine are so fond of him that they won't serve anywhere where he isn't present," Yan Skshetuski said.

"I even heard him praised in Keydany," Oskierka threw in. "And right in Radzivill's hearing too, although the Prince wasn't pleased about it."

"Even back then his jealousy and envy were gnawing at his guts."

"Well, it's a known fact that evil can't stand the sound or sight of goodness."

★　★　★

So they chatted, passing the time as their wagon bumped along the highway, but the subject to which they returned time and time again was Pan Zagloba and his astonishing escape. Pan Michal assured them that the old knight would find some means to save them too because he'd never been the kind of man who abandoned his friends in adversity.

"I'm convinced he's heading for Upita," he said. "If my men haven't been already beaten and scattered, or dragged to Keydany by force, he'll bring them to help us. I doubt if they'd refuse to come. The regiment is full of Laudanians and they're very fond of me."

"But," Mirski voiced a doubt. "Haven't they always been Radzivill supporters?"

"They always have. But when they hear about his sellout to the Swedes, and about the imprisonment of Pan Gosyevski and our own arrests, they'll give up their traditional affection for the Hetman, I am sure. They're all decent, honest gentry, the kind we've always seen as the backbone of the country, and we can all be sure that Pan Zagloba won't miss a trick in painting Radzivill blacker than the Devil. He can do that better than any man alive."

"Perhaps," Pan Stanislav said. "But in the meantime we will be in Birjhe."

"I wouldn't be too sure. We're tracking back and forth to go around Upita, which is adding miles to our journey, while the Birjhe highway is as straight as an arrow. They could start out two days from now and still beat us to Birjhe. All they have to do is get ahead of us and block our way."

"That's right," Mirski added. "The road from Upita to Birjhe is not only shorter but much better too. It's paved almost all the way."

"There you have it, then," Pan Michal concluded.   "And we haven't even got to Saulas yet."

Chapter Thirty-one

IT WAS CLOSE to evening before they saw the hill known as Sautuves-Kaunas at whose foot lay Saulas—or Siauliei as it was known in the native dialect which was still used by everyone other than the gentry. But even before they got there they noticed signs of great uneasiness in all the towns and villages they entered.

It seemed that all of Zmudya had already heard about Radzivill's accession to the Swedes. The escort dragoons were bombarded everywhere with questions about whether the Swedes were to take over the entire country. They saw great crowds of peasants fleeing from their villages with their wives, children, cattle and possessions, and hurrying to the forests which spread thickly throughout that territory. In other places, where the peasants took Kowalski's horsemen for Swedish invaders, their glowering truculence was so close to violence that the dragoons had to draw their weapons; while in the rural settlements of the petty gentry, inhabited by men of the same stamp as the Laudanians, armed and angry people barred their way and demanded who they were and where they were going. And when Kowalski ordered them to step aside, instead of giving them a satisfactory answer, their mood grew so threatening that only the dragoons' cocked muskets cleared the way.

The great paved highway that ran north from Kaunas to Saulas, and beyond to Mittau near the Baltic coast, was jammed with charabancs and wagons in which the wives and children of the local gentry, looking for shelter from the dangers of a civil war, traveled to the greater security of their estates in Courland.

Saulas itself was empty of either Radzivill detachments or
regular Polish-Lithuanian soldiers, but it provided a new spectacle: Swedish Reiters surrounded in the market place by curious
Jews and burghers. Pan Michal stared at them with a special
hunger since they were the first Swedish soldiers he had ever
seen.

They turned out to be a twenty-five man cavalry patrol sent
out from Birjhe to check the condition of the countryside, but
they created a sensation in the small Zmudyan city where no
Swedes had ever appeared before. Kowalski found a way to
communicate with their officer, asking him to add his troop to
his own for the greater safety of the convoy, but the Swede
refused. His mission was to go as far south as he could to see
whether these new Swedish acquisitions were tractable and
friendly. But he assured Kowalski that the road to Birjhe was
clear of any dissidents; Swedish cavalry detachments, he reported, combed the entire country, some even going as far as
Keydany.

So, after resting his men and horses until long past midnight,
and catching a few uneasy hours of sleep for himself, Pan Roche
got the convoy on the road again, turning east towards the
parallel highway that connected Upita and Ponevyesh with
Birjhe. It was on this final stretch of their journey that the
captive colonels could expect an attempted rescue.

★ ★ ★

"If Pan Zagloba can do it anywhere he'll probably do it
between here and Birjhe," Volodyovski assured the others
shortly after sunrise. "That's if he's managed to march up there
already."

"Maybe he's already lurking in ambush somewhere," Pan
Stanislav said.

"I had some hopes until I saw the Swedes," Stankevitch
shrugged. "But now I think he probably missed his chance and
we're as good as done for."

"It's up to Zagloba's quick wits to find a way around any
Swedish forces he might come across, or to make fools of them
and talk his way out of any tight spots. And he can do that better
than anyone."

"Hmm. Maybe. If he knew the country."

"The Laudanians know it. I've plenty of men in my regiment who cart pitch, firewood and other products all the way to Riga."

"I expect that the Swedes must have occupied all the small towns around Birjhe by now," Stankevitch put in, and Pan Michal started grinning like a hungry wolf that scents some fresh prey.

"Superb looking soldiers, that troop of Reiters that we saw in Saulas," he said and sighed and smacked his lips with pleasure. "Every man-jack of them as big and broad as a barn door. And did you gentlemen note the size and condition of their horses?"

"Fine mounts," Mirski agreed. "They get them in Latvia and Estonia, which is their fief now although all of it used to be a part of Courland and, as such, an autonomous dependency of the Polish Crown. Our heavy cavalry also gets its remounts up there because our local horses are too light."

"Tell me about the Swedish infantry," Pan Stankevitch said. "Their cavalry looks good on parade but it doesn't stand up to ours in the field. I've known times when one of our armored regiments would go through these dragoon-cuirassiers like a knife through butter."

"Ay, gentlemen, you've already had a taste of them," Pan Michal sighed with envy. "And I still have to lick my chops and wonder what they're like. I tell you, when I saw them in Saulas with those broad backs and those yellow beards, it felt as if ants were running up and down my fingers. I could hardly hold still and sit in this wagon."

★ ★ ★

The colonels grew quiet soon after that exchange, but apparently Pan Volodyovski wasn't the only one who entertained such amicable thoughts about the Swedes. The prisoners soon heard their escort saying much the same.

"Did you see those pagan sons of bitches?" one soldier asked another. "We were supposed to fight them and now we'll be shoveling out their stables and grooming their horses."

"God dammit all to Hell!" snarled another soldier.

"Shut your mouth. The Swedes will teach you how to jump through hoops, you can bet on that."

"Maybe I'll teach them something!"

"Sure you will. There's others, a lot better than you, that tried to go against them. And look at what happened."

"That's right," another said. "We're taking our greatest knights to them, just like feeding delicacies to a dog. You know that you can't even talk to one of them without a Jew to do your talking for you? First thing the commandant had to do in Saulas was look for a Jew."

"May the plague take 'em!"

Here the first trooper lowered his voice somewhat.

"People say that the best soldiers are refusing to join up with them against our own King," he murmured.

"And it's true! Didn't you see those Hungarians in Keydany? And didn't the Prince march out against the resisters? Nobody knows yet which way things will go. A whole bunch of our own men fought beside those Hungarians, remember? And now it looks like they're all going to be shot."

"There's their reward for all those years of faithful service!"

"Ah, to the Devil with it! A man would do better running errands for a Jew."

"Halt!" Pan Roche shouted suddenly, riding ahead of the convoy.

"May a bullet jam itself sideways in your mouth," a nearby dragoon muttered.

"What's going on?" the soldiers asked each other.

"Stand still, damn you all!" the command came again and the wagon and its escort halted.

★ ★ ★

The day, as Pan Volodyovski noted with one quick glance, was clear and bright and the wooded landscape lay open all the way to the horizon everywhere he looked. The sun was high and its sharp morning glare revealed a large dust cloud moving swiftly on the road ahead as if a herd of animals was being driven towards the halted convoy.

But something gleamed and glittered in that cloud of dust; it was as if someone tossed a handful of sparks into that tumbled thickness, or as if the light of innumerable candles was glowing under smoke.

"Those are lance points!" Volodyovski shouted suddenly.

"Must be some soldiers coming."

"It's probably more Swedes trying to make sure the country-side is quiet enough to suit them."

"Can't be. Only their infantry has pikes. This cloud is moving far too fast for infantry. That's cavalry with lances! These are our own people!"

"They're ours!" the dragoons echoed all around.

"Heads up!" Pan Roche ordered. "Fall in around the wagon!"

The dragoons formed a tight circle around the wagon, and Pan Volodyovski became so excited that it looked as if sparks were about to leap out of both his eyes.

"Those are my Laudanians with Zagloba!" he shouted. "It can't be anybody else!"

No more than two furlongs lay now between the wagon and the nearing mass of horsemen hidden by the dust, and this distance narrowed rapidly as the new arrivals came on at a fast trot. At last a powerful body of cavalry spilled out of the dust and advanced swiftly in extended order as if about to charge.

Each moment brought them closer. Pan Michal's sharp, excited little eyes spotted a thickset, commanding man who rode on the right flank of the foremost rank, waving a gold *bulava* as he issued his last-minute orders, under a horsetail standard that denoted the rank of a Hetman.

"That's Pan Zagloba!" he cried out, delighted. "As I love God, Zagloba!"

A quiet, warm smile lighted up the dark, grave features of Pan Yan Skshetuski.

"That's him, alright," he said. "And under a horsetail standard too. He's already made himself a Hetman! I'd recognize him anywhere by his brashness and imagination. That man will march into the hereafter just as glib and cocksure as he was on earth."

"May God give him health and strength," Pan Oskierka said and then, making a trumpet out of his folded hands, he started calling to Pan Roche: "Hey, Master Kowalski! Looks like your kinsman's come to pay you a visit!"

But Pan Roche didn't hear him. He was too busy herding his dragoons into defense formation, and this much had to be said on his behalf, that even though an entire cavalry regiment was coming down upon him he was neither flustered nor dismayed. He drew up his handful of troopers in two ranks in front of the wagon, while his opponents came at him from the front and both flanks at once, riding swiftly in a Tartar crescent. But apparently they wanted to parlay first because someone started waving a white flag among them, and loud shouts called on Kowalski to surrender.

"Halt! Halt! Wait a bit!"

"At a walk, forward... march!" Pan Roche commanded.

"Hold it! Give it up! Surrender!"

"Fire!" Pan Roche shouted.

But nothing happened. Not a single dragoon obeyed him and fired his musket, and the amazed Kowalski fell into a rage.

"Fire, you mongrels!" he roared in a terrifying voice and turned on his own men as if he'd gone mad. One blow of his thick fist sent a trooper tumbling into the dust while the rest backed away, ignoring his order, and finally scattered before his raging fury like a flock of quail.

"I'd have those soldiers shot anyway," Mirski said.

Meanwhile Kowalski saw that all his men had deserted him and wrenched his horse around to face his attackers.

"There's my death!" he shouted in a frightful voice in which the captive colonels could read a strange, deeply longed-for expectation of relief, as well as utter hopelessness and despair, as he charged all his enemies alone.

But he barely managed to cover half the intervening distance when a scatter gun boomed among the Laudanians and a shower of hobnails rustled along the highway. His horse stumbled and plunged nose-first into the dust, pinning down its rider, and Pan Roche was left struggling on the ground. He managed to get back on his feet just as some broad-shouldered soldier spurred like lightning out of the advancing ranks and jerked him up into the air by the back of his neck.

"That's Yozva Butrym!" Pan Volodyovski cried. "That's Yozva the Pegleg!"

Pan Roche grasped the tails of Yozva's coat, ripping them off at once, and they began to struggle with each other with all of their vast strength. Yozva's stirrup cracked and burst apart, throwing him off his horse, but he kept his iron grip on Kowalski's neck and the two of them tumbled along the highway like a giant ball.

Then others came running.

At least ten pairs of hands clutched at Pan Roche who threw himself about like a netted bear, butting and roaring and tossing his tormentors into the air like a wild boar beset by a pack of mastiffs, until at last he grew too weak to struggle anymore. He wanted to die, that was clear to everyone who saw him, but all he heard around him were cries that he was to be taken alive.

★ ★ ★

Meanwhile Pan Zagloba was at the wagon, or rather already clambering up on it—throwing his arms in turn around the two Skshetuskis, the little knight, Mirski, Stankevitch and Oski-erka—and gasping out in a breathless, happy voice:

"Ha! There's still some use for old Zagloba, eh? And aren't we going to pour some salt into Radzivill's soup? Gentlemen! We're free as the birds and we've a whole regiment behind us! Let's raid his possessions! What do you say, eh? Did my wits serve me well or didn't they? If I hadn't got us out this way I'd have thought of something else... Eh? What? Eh? Phew, I'm so out of breath I can hardly talk...! But let's get started on Radzivill's properties! Let's send him to the poorhouse! You may think you know that treacherous devil but you still don't know everything about him! Wait till you hear my story!"

The rest of this breathless outburst had to wait, giving way to the shouting of the overjoyed Laudanians, who ran to the wagon to greet their rescued colonel. A press of Butryms, Go-syevitches, Domashevitches, Stakyans and Gashtovts crowded around their diminutive commander, roaring "*Vivat! Vivat!*" for all they were worth, while he waited for the return of silence so that he could speak.

"Gentlemen," he said at last. "My dearest comrades! Thank you with all my heart for your loyalty and affection. I'm deeply grateful to you. Yes, I know, it's a terrible thing to break our oath and go against our Hetman, but when there's no doubt about his treason there just isn't anything else to do! We won't desert our country and our King! Long live His Most Merciful Majesty, our King Yan Casimir! *Vivat Joannes Casimirus Rex!*"

"*Vivat! Vivat!*"

"Let's raid Radzivill's lands!" Zagloba was howling. "Let's flush out his storehouses and cellars!"

"Get some horses for us!" the little knight ordered, and half a dozen men shot off at once to get him his horses.

But Pan Zagloba was never one to miss a chance for a ceremonial gesture. He assumed a serious stance, as befitted the gravity of the moment, and prepared to hand over his temporary command.

"Sir Michal," he addressed Volodyovski formally and grandly. "I acted as a Hetman to your men, and I must tell you that they're a fine body of troops. My congratulations. It was a pleasure to be their commander. But now that you're free to lead them I place my authority in your hands."

"Why don't you take command, sir?" Pan Michal turned to Mirski. "You're the senior officer among us."

"I wouldn't think of it," Mirski said.

"Then perhaps Colonel Stankevitch..."

"I have my own regiment," Stankevitch said. "I don't need another's. Keep your command, colonel. We don't need to stand on ceremonies here. You know your men better than anyone, and they know you. They'll do best in your hands and that's all that matters."

"Do that, Michal," Pan Yan Skshetuski urged. "It'll work best that way."

"So be it then," the little colonel said.

He took the commander's baton from Zagloba's hands, formed up his regiment in marching order in less time than it would take to say a Hail Mary, and rode out at its head with his freed companions.

"And where will we go now?" Zagloba wished to know.

"To tell you the truth, I don't know," Pan Michal admitted. "I haven't had the time to give it a thought."

"It's worth some serious thinking," Mirski said. "And we ought to get our heads together on it right away. But first let me thank Pan Zagloba in all of our names for remembering us the way he did, and for coming to our aid in such a swift and effective manner."

"Eh? What? Hmm?" Pan Zagloba lifted his head proudly and curled an end of his mustache upward with one hand. "You'd be in Birjhe if it weren't for me, that's certain! It's only simple justice to admit that if something needs to be invented Zagloba's head will do it. Hey, Michal, we've been in worse spots that this one, am I right? Do you remember how I saved you from the Tartars that time we rescued Helen?"

* * *

Pan Michal remembered something altogether different, namely that it was he who saved Pan Zagloba, but he kept quiet while his little mustache moved swiftly up and down. Meanwhile the old knight went on with his peroration.

"Nobody needs to thank me, because if something happens to all of you today it might happen to me just as well tomorrow, and you wouldn't leave me in difficulties either, I expect. I'm so pleased to see you free that it seems as if I've won a real victory. I'm glad to see that neither my hand nor my head have got too old to function as they should."

"So you found your way to Upita straight away?" Pan Michal asked.

"And what else was I supposed to find? The road to Keydany? Did you think I'd climb into a wolf's throat? Of course I went straight to Upita. I ran my horse into the ground getting there too, which is a pity because it was a very decent animal, but I was in Upita first thing yesterday and by noon we were on our way!"

"It's a good thing my men believed you." The little knight kept twisting his head in wonder. "It's a miracle, seeing that none of them knew who you were and only a few saw you with me in my quarters."

"As a matter of fact I had no problems with that whatsoever," the fat knight reported. "I had your ring to start with, and the men had just been told about your arrest and the Hetman's treason. I practically walked in on their meeting with delegates from the regiments of Colonels Mirski and Stankevitch who came to urge them to get together with all loyal soldiers and fight the traitor Hetman. So when I told them that you were all on your way to the Swedes in Birjhe, it was like poking an anthill with a walking stick. Their horses were in the pastures but they sent for them at once and by midday we were on the road. Of course I took command over them! Why not? Isn't that just my natural due?"

"But where did you get that horsetail standard, father, and

that gold *bulava*?" Pan Yan asked. "We thought from a distance
that it was some Hetman."

"What? Hmm? I looked the part, eh? And why not?
Wouldn't I be a good one? But where did I get the standard?
Well, right along with the delegates from the resisting regiments,
came a Radzivill officer with an order for the Laudanians to
march to Keydany, and with a Hetman's horsetail and *bulava* to
give him more authority. I had him arrested on the spot and I
had the standard carried over me to confuse the Swedes."

"Dear God, how cleverly he thought it all out!" Pan Oskierka
cried.

"Solomon wouldn't have done it any better," Stankevitch
agreed while Pan Zagloba swelled and reddened with pleasure
like a well-yeasted pancake on a cooking sheet.

"Let's decide, then, what we ought to do," he advised at last.
"If you've the patience to listen to me for a little longer I'll tell
you what I thought up on the way. In the first place, I wouldn't
plan on making open war on Radzivill, because he's a giant pike
and we're a school of perches. It's best for perches not to face
the pike because that's the surest way of going down his throat.
Let's leave him for now to the Devil, and may Old Nick stick
him on a spit and baste him well with pitch so that he roasts
evenly all over."

"And in the second place?" Mirski asked.

"In the second place," Zagloba replied, "if by some chance he
got his hands on us, he'd give us such a hot welcome that every
magpie in Lithuania would have something to screech about for
years. Take a look at this letter, gentlemen, that Kowalski was
carrying to the Swedish commandant in Birjhe, and get to know
this Hetman if you didn't know him well enough before!"

With this Pan Zagloba unbuttoned his coat, drew out an open
letter, and passed it to Mirski.

"What is this? Swedish? German?" the old colonel asked
peering at the writing. "Which of you gentlemen can read
either language?"

It turned out that only Pan Stanislav Skshetuski knew a little
German, since he often traveled on business to Torun near the
Prussian border, but even he couldn't make sense out of the
letter or recognize the language.

"Then let me tell you what it's all about," Pan Zagloba said.

"I had a little time to spare in Upita when the soldiers sent out for their horses, so I had them find me the smartest Jew in town, and he read it all out and explained it to me as clear as the Gospels. What the Hetman tells the Swedish commandant—for the good of the King of Sweden, I might add—is to send Kowalski and his convoy on their way and then, without wasting another moment, have each of us propped up against a wall and shot. But in such a manner that no news of it would ever get outside."

The liberated colonels began to clap their hands in amazement at Radzivill's treachery and cunning and only old Pan Mirski shook his head as if this was no surprise to him.

"That's the one thing about all this I couldn't understand," he said. "I mean that he'd let us slip out of his hands alive. There must have been some reasons we don't know about as to why he couldn't shoot us openly in Keydany."

"Could be he was concerned about what people would say about it, no?"

"Could be."

"What I can't get over is that implacable vengefulness of his," the little knight confessed. "I'm almost ashamed to mention, it but it's not that long ago that I helped to save his life, along with Ganhof, but that's all forgotten."

"And I served him and his father for more than thirty years!" said Stankevitch.

"A terrible man!" Pan Stanislav murmured.

"So my thought is to keep out of his jaws," Pan Zagloba counseled. "To the Devil with him! Let's avoid a battle with him if we can but, on our way, let's do as much damage as we can to his best possessions. We ought to join up with the *Voyevode* of Vitebsk, just to have the protection of some powerful personage around us, but let's take as much as we can out of Radzivill's larders, cellars, stables, storehouses and byres. I can't wait to get started on that work! Let's also help ourselves to whatever rents have been collected for him on his personal estates, because the more of everything that we bring to the *Voyevode* of Vitebsk the better he'll like us."

"He'll welcome us with open arms as it is," Oskierka remarked. "But the way things are, it's good advice for us to join up with him as soon as we can, and nobody will come up with a better idea just now."

"Everyone will vote for that," Stankevitch nodded quietly.

"That's it, then!" Pan Michal decided. "That's what we shall do! Let Pan Sapyeha be that leader for whom we've been praying."

"Amen," the others chorused.

They rode in silence for a while longer until Pan Michal began to squirm restlessly on his saddle.

"But what if we were to nip a few Swedes if we get the chance?" he blurted out at last, peering anxiously at his older and more staid companions.

"I'd say why not?" Stankevitch agreed. "Radzivill is sure to have assured the Swedes that Lithuania is firmly in his grasp and that everyone in the country would turn on Yan Casimir if he gave the word. Let them see what a lie that is."

"Quite right!" Mirski added. "If some Swedish detachment comes our way we'll ride across their bellies! I also agree that we should sidestep any confrontation with Radzivill himself because we don't stand a chance against him. He's a great commander! But it would be worth our while to spend a few days rummaging around Keydany."

"To raid his estates?" Pan Zagloba queried.

"No, more than that! My regiment and Pan Stankevitch's too can slip off towards us unless Radzivill has already crushed them. And even if that happened, as could be, there're bound to be survivors who will run to join us. Moreover, we can count on a fair number of our gentry coming out as well once they see an organized force to group themselves around. We'll hit Radzivill's pride, where he hurts the most, and we'll bring Pan Sapyeha something he can work with!"

Chapter Thirty-two

THEIR CALCULATIONS about reinforcements proved correct at once, because every one of Kowalski's dragoons immediately asked to join the Laudanians. It was a good omen for the future. The liberated colonels were quite sure that more such men would be found in Radzivill's ranks. Moreover, they thought it likely that the first strong blow struck against the Swedes could cause a general uprising throughout Lithuania.

With this in mind, Pan Volodyovski decided on a night march towards Ponevyesh and Upita, where he'd be able to gather up the rest of the Laudanian gentry, and then to slip into the widespread Rogov Forest where he expected the loyalist survivors to look for refuge from the Hetman's vengeance. In the meantime he called a halt near the overgrown and hidden Lavetch River to rest the men and horses.

They stayed there until nightfall, peering out at the crowded highway, and counting the endless groups of peasants who were heading for the refuge of the woods. Once in a while the pickets would bring in a single, frightened peasant to question about the whereabouts of the Swedes, but few of them knew anything useful. All of them were gripped by superstitious terror, and each of them babbled that the Swedes were just around the corner, but none of them could say anything concrete.

At last, after the sun had set, Volodyovski ordered his men to mount. They trotted out of the riverside reeds and willow groves and, almost at once, each of them heard the ringing of a distant church bell.

"What's that all about?" Pan Zagloba asked. "It's too late for the Angelus, isn't it?"

Pan Volodyovski cocked an ear to the urgent sound.

"That's for alarm," he said.

Then he put his horse into a trot along the column formed up on the road.

"Does any of you know the name of the nearest town or village out in that direction?" he asked.

"That's Klevany, colonel," said one of the Gosyevitches. "We go that way with potash, now and then."

"And do you hear the bells?"

"We hear them! That's nothing normal, sir!"

Pan Michal beckoned to the regimental bugler and soon the soft sounds of a muffled trumpet sounded among the thickets. The regiment moved forward. Every man's eyes strained in the direction of the ringing church bells and soon, much sooner than expected, a red glow bloomed in the darkened sky and started to spread and brighten rapidly.

"A fire!" the whisper ran along the ranks.

Pan Michal edged close to Yan Skshetuski. "Swedes!" he said.

"We'll get a taste of them," Pan Yan answered grimly.

"I'm just surprised that they've set fire to the place. Why would they, if they feel at home here?"

"The local landholder must have put up a fight if they were too demanding with their requisitions, or the peasants moved if they touched the church."

"We'll find out soon enough," Pan Michal said and sighed in satisfaction.

Just then Pan Zagloba clip-clopped towards them.

"Hey, Michal," he said uneasily.

"What is it, my friend?"

"I see you've already got a whiff of Swedish meat. There's going to be a battle, I expect?"

"God grant it! God grant it!"

"And what about the prisoner?"

"What prisoner?"

"Kowalski! What other prisoner do we have? It's most important that he doesn't get away. And do you know why? Because the Hetman still has no idea of what happened to you and the other colonels, and there's no way he can find out just

now unless Kowalski escapes and reports it. Am I right? You
have to leave some dependable people to watch him, because it's
easy to run for it in the confusion of a fight! What if he hits on
some good stratagem and hoofs it?"

"The wagon that he's sitting in is more likely to come up with
stratagems," Pan Michal replied. "But you're right. He does
need to be guarded. D'you want to stay behind and keep an eye
on him?"

"What? And miss the battle? Hmm, it's true that I don't see
too well at night... the firelight blinds me... Ah, nothing would
keep me out of the action if we were taking on these heretics in
daylight, as you know! But now, in darkness, and since the
public good demands it, I suppose I'll have to sacrifice myself."

"Good. I'll leave you five men to help. And if he tries to get
away shoot him on the spot."

"Oh, I'll mold him like a piece of wax, don't worry about
that! Ah, but that fire looks bigger every minute. So where am
I to wait with Kowalski?"

"Wherever you want. I've no time for that now."

And the little knight spurred eagerly ahead.

The glare of the nearing conflagration rose ever higher into
the reddened sky. The freshened breeze brought the frantic
sound of church bells ringing out for help and, along with that,
the flat crack of pistols.

"At a trot... forward!" Pan Michal commanded.

★　★　★

Having come closer to the village, they slowed to a walk and
caught sight of a broad street, so brightly lighted by the flames
that burst out of the peasant dwellings which burned on either
side, that one could look for spilled pins all along the highway,
while sheets of fire leaped from one thatched roof to the next.

A sharp breeze tossed bright swarms of glittering red sparks
high into the sky, and flung entire sheaves of burning straw
along adjoining rooftops, casting a fierce, crimson light on the
strip of roadway where groups of people, perceived only dimly
from a distance, ran about as if in a fever. Wails of terror
blended desperately with the bells of a church hidden behind a
clump of trees, with the bellowing of cattle, the barking of dogs
and occasional gunshots.

Drawing even closer, Volodyovski's soldiers caught their first sight of Swedes: Reiters in tall leather boots and black broad-brimmed hats. But there weren't many of them to be seen just then. Some of them were fighting groups of peasants armed with threshing flails and pitchforks, driving them away from the fenced yards of their little dwellings, chasing them into the cultivated vegetable fields beyond, and shooting them with pistols. Others drove sheep and cattle from the barns and byres, urging them on with the flat of their long, straight rapiers. Yet others, made almost invisible in a cloud of feathers, were draped with dozens of farmyard birds that dangled from their belts, some with their necks already wrung and some still flapping their wings in their final death throes. More than a dozen others held horses for at least twice or three times that many who were busy looting the huts and homes that hadn't yet been swept by the fires.

The road that sloped down into the village from a small hillock overgrown by birches, provided cover for the Laudani-ans in which to form their ranks, and gave them a clear view of the lurid scene below. What they saw was an almost classic picture of a village looted by an enemy. The crackling fires revealed every detail of the foreign soldiers, the clustered villag-ers jammed tightly together by the press of bodies, the screaming women dragged about by dismounted troopers, and the disor-dered clumps of men who were trying to defend themselves; and all of this seemed to jerk about in quick, violent motions, bringing to mind a village puppet show, but wrapped in the ever-present sound of shouts, curses and cries for help and mercy.

The conflagration spread so rapidly that it soon acquired the qualities of a firestorm. The leaping flames looked like a fiery mane shaken above the village and the roar of the fire drowned out all other sounds.

* * *

Pan Volodyovski ordered his men to slow down to an easy trot as they came to the gaping turnstile that marked the begin-ning of the little township. He could have charged straight in at a gallop and shattered the unprepared enemy at one blow. But he decided to 'taste' the Swedes, get a feel of their fighting mettle and a sense of their worth in a straightforward, cut-and-thrust cavalry encounter, so he did everything to be spotted in advance.

A few Swedish horsemen posted near the turnstile caught sight of the approaching Laudanians and one of them galloped to their officer, who stood with a drawn rapier in his hand before a large group of mounted troopers farther down the street. Volodyovski saw the runner saying something urgently, and pointing in the direction of the Lithuanians, while the officer twisted his head around and shaded his eyes against the blinding glare. He stared for a moment, nodded at his bugler, and a sharp, strident trumpet call cut through the deafening mass of human and animal bellowing and shouting.

And here the Polish knights could admire the discipline and training of the Swedish soldiers; the first few notes had barely sounded in the street when a crowd of Reiters poured out of the houses. Others threw down their loot and abandoned the cattle they were driving and all of them ran headlong for their horses.

In moments, or what seemed like one blink of an eye, they were all mounted, in formation, and Pan Volodyovski could only admire their spectacular efficiency and imposing military appearance. Each of them was a large, broad-backed man, dressed in a yellow leather coat and a polished breastplate, with a wide black leather baldric sloped across the shoulder, and a broad-brimmed hat cocked across the right eye with the left brim pinned up. They were all mounted on well-fed and well-curried horses as uniformly matched as the men themselves, and they stood in their ranks as still and steady as a wall, with their bared rapiers held firmly at the shoulder. None of them showed the slightest uneasiness or alarm as they watched the road both expectantly and calmly.

Their officer and bugler trotted a short distance towards the Lithuanian horsemen as if to ask who they were, probably assuming that the Laudanians were some Radzivill detachment which wouldn't interfere with what they were doing. The officer began to wave his hat and rapier and the trumpeter signaled for a parley.

"Fire a shot at them, one of you," Volodyovski called back to the ranks behind him. "Let them know what to expect from us."

A scatter gun boomed out, the load of flints and nails rattled harmlessly along the road, and the Swedish officer began to shout louder and wave his hat harder than before.

"He still doesn't get the point," Pan Michal observed. "Give him another one."

After the second discharge the Swedish officer seemed to understand that something was wrong and rode back to his men without any hurry, while they advanced towards him at a steady trot.

Meanwhile the leading ranks of the Laudanians were entering the village.

The Swedish officer barked an order and the stiff, upraised rapiers dropped at once and dangled on their wrist-straps, while each Reiter, moving with the speed and uniform precision of well-drilled regulars, drew a heavy pistol from his saddle holsters and rested it, cocked and with the barrel pointed upward, on his saddlehorn.

"Excellent soldiers," Volodyovski muttered. Then, with a quick glance back over his shoulder at his own men, he shouted: "Forward!"

The Laudanians bowed forward on the necks of their horses, spurred their animals into an instant gallop and charged into the village. The Reiters allowed them to get quite close before they fired a pistol volley straight into their faces, but only a few men dropped their reins and swayed back in their saddles; the rest came on, roaring like a windstorm, and crashed into the Swedes.

* * *

Light Lithuanian cavalry of those days, such as the Laudanians, still carried the long, wooden lances that derived from the age of chivalry, and which only the heavily armored winged *husaria* used in the Polish armies of the Commonwealth. But Pan Volodyovski, expecting a fight in cramped quarters among the burning buildings, ordered them left behind in the birch wood before the attack, so that the Swedish rapiers and Lithuanian sabers clashed immediately.

The weight of the charge didn't break the Swedes. It merely jarred them and threw them back a little, and left them fighting fiercely with their long, straight swords, while the Laudanians pushed on with grim determination, forcing them to give way a step at a time in the broad, fenced-in village street.

Dead men began to tumble thickly from their saddles on both sides and the press of men and horses tightened like a vise. The clash of swords and sabers drove the peasantry away from the street into fields and orchards. The scorching heat that welled out of the burning houses seemed to burn up the air and robbed everyone of breath, even though fenced, widespread patches of plum and apple groves lay between the roadway and these flaming dwellings.

The Swedes, forced back by the remorseless pressure of the Lithuanians, began a slow, dogged retreat, but maintained their order. Indeed, they couldn't have scattered if they wanted to, because the tall plank fencing turned the village street into a single channel that gripped and compressed everything within it. But escape seemed to be the last thing on their minds. Time and again they tried to hold fast against the pressure, dig in their heels and halt the Lithuanians, but they couldn't do it long enough to make any difference.

It was a strange battle, with both sides choked and squeezed within the narrow strip between the fenced-in orchards, that let only the lead ranks of each formation battle with the other, while the remainder shoved against the men ahead. But this merely focused the carnage on a narrow front and made it all the bloodier.

Pan Volodyovski, who asked Yan Skshetuski and the older colonels to keep an eye on things when the battle started, fought in the first rank like a simple soldier, getting his taste of Swedes and satisfying his curiosity about them. Time and again a black Swedish hat swept to the ground before him, a husked rapier flew into the air, and the stricken trooper tumbled off his horse with a short, shrill scream. One black hat after another loomed before his eyes, followed by yet another, and then a third and a fourth, but he kept moving forward like a grim, diminutive spirit of destruction. His merry little eyes narrowed and glowed like coals; his movements were as cold as ice; and the swift strokes of his saber were so slight, and seemingly so careless, as to be almost imperceptible. Death from his hand was all the more terrible because it took so little effort on his part.

There were moments when there wasn't anyone within reach before him. Then he turned both his face and saber to the left or right, his hand made a scarcely noticeable movement, and another Reiter slid out of his saddle, so that for all his small size he seemed superhuman. What came to mind to the men around him was the image of a harvester who vanishes from sight under the high, nodding crests of vegetation towering in a hemp field, and whose invisible passage is marked by the toppling of the plants cut down from below. Quite hidden from view among the taller Reiters, he was easily tracked by the devastation he caused in their ranks.

Pan Stanislav and the grim, one-legged Yozva Butrym advanced right behind him.

★   ★   ★

At last the Swedish ranks backed out of the fenced-in street into the broad church square, pushed out of their confining trap like a cork slapped out of a bottle. A quick, sharp order from their officer turned their narrow, tightly jammed and largely useless column into a wide formation thrown across the whole front of their enemies, so that all of them could come into action at one time, but the Laudanians didn't follow suit. Led by Pan Yan Skshetuski, they charged the Swedish battle line in a tight troop column, struck it at its thinned-out weakest point, broke through at once like a steel wedge driven into a log, and swept around one half of the shattered Swedes while Mirski and Stankevitch charged the other half with the Laudanian reserve and Kowalski's troopers.

Two battles blazed in place of one but neither lasted long. The left wing, split and broken by Skshetuski, never had the time to form another battle line and was the first to scatter. The right wing, which contained the Swedish officer, put up a fierce resistance but it was stretched too wide. It cracked soon after, broke and fell apart, and the battle turned into pursuit and slaughter. Kept in the killing ground by another circle of heavy oak fencing, and barred from escaping by strong gates at the far end of the churchyard which the parish servants closed and reinforced against them, the Swedes galloped helplessly back and forth, chased by the Lithuanians, or fought doggedly in small surrounded groups and in single duels, amid the clash of steel and the crack of pistols.

Here and there a Swede dodged one saber only to fall under another; or some other Reiter or Laudanian scrambled up from under a fallen mount only to find a sword blade hissing down on him from above; while a herd of panicked, wildly neighing horses ran blindly among them under empty saddles, savaging the men and other animals alike, and lashing out with their hooves at the struggling soldiers.

Pan Volodyovski searched for the Swedish officer even as he cut down one Reiter after another, then spotted him fighting against two Butryms and spurred to him at once.

"Step aside!" he shouted, charging up. "Get out of my way!"

The two soldiers sprang away at once and the little knight collided with the Swede so violently that both their horses sat back on their haunches.

The officer wanted to unhorse him with a single thrust, but Pan Volodyovski caught his rapier on the crosspiece of his dragoon saber, twisted it with one lightning movement of his hand, and the long blade whirled away in pieces. The officer stooped at once towards his holsters, but Volodyovski's saber hissed across his face before he could draw and cock a pistol, and he dropped his reins and fell forward across his horse's neck.

"Take him alive!" Volodyovski shouted to the Butryms who seized the wounded man, and held him swaying on his bloody saddle, while their terrible little colonel disappeared in pursuit of other Swedish riders.

But the hand-to-hand fighting had now turned against the Swedes everywhere, as the Laudanian gentry, who like all their kind took great pride in their swordsmanship, cut them down in dozens. More and more Reiters threw down their weapons or seized them by the blade and held out the hilts towards their enemies, and cries of '*Pardon!*' started to ring out across the killing ground. But Pan Michal had ordered that only a few were to be taken prisoner, so all those others who threw down their rapiers or wanted to surrender picked up their swords again and fought to the death with the grim ferocity of Europe's finest soldiers, taking as many of their enemies with them as they could.

Within another hour only their last few remnants were still able to defend themselves, and the infuriated peasants poured back into their village to catch the riderless horses, finish off the wounded, and to strip the dead.

So ended the first encounter between the Swedes and the Lithuanians.

★ ★ ★

Meanwhile Pan Zagloba, waiting in the birch grove beside the wagon that contained Kowalski, had to listen to the wretched young man's bitter complaints against himself.

"How could a kinsman do what you did to me, uncle?" Pan Roche demanded, trembling with indignation and despair. "You've doomed me altogether. It's not just that I'll get a bullet in the head as soon as I reach Keydany but I'll be shamed for all time as well. From now on if someone wants to call someone else a numbskull he'll say Roche Kowalski."

"And he won't find many who'd want to disagree," Pan Zagloba told him. "The best proof that you have only chaff between your ears is your surprise that I could make such a fool of you. Who did you think you were dealing with? I used to have the Khan of all the Tartars dancing as if he was a puppet on a string, so who are you to match your puny wits with mine? Did you think I'd let you take me and those other decent men to Birjhe, and feed us to the Swedes as if we were a sack of sausages? Us? The flower of the country's knighthood? The pride of the Commonwealth?"

"But I wasn't taking you there of my own free will!" the desperate dragoon tried to defend himself.

"Maybe not. But you were acting as a hangman's errand boy and that's a shameful thing for a gentleman to do. If you don't atone for that disgrace I'll turn my back on you and all the Kowalskis! Tfui! What's the matter with you, anyway? To be a traitor is worse than being a common dog-catcher, but to be a traitor's helper is the worst thing of all!"

"I served the Hetman..."

"And he serves the Devil! So what did that make you? You're a fool, Roche, accept that from the start, and don't get into arguments with people who use their heads for something other than wearing a hat. You might possibly turn into a human being if you do only what I tell you and cling to my coat-tails for dear life. Understand? And remember that there are many great men walking the earth today who achieved their positions by taking my advice."

★ ★ ★

A pistol volley put a temporary end to Pan Zagloba's sermon because the battle started just then in the village, and the shouts and clatter came clearly all the way to the little birch grove.

"Pan Michal is working hard over there," Zagloba remarked, cocking his ear to the sound of fighting. "He's not much to look at but he bites harder than a viper. They'll be knee-deep in that foreign chaff over there, you'll see, and I'd also rather be there than here and it's all your fault! Is that how you show your gratitude, eh? Is this the way that you repay a kinsman?"

"But what do I have to be grateful for?" Pan Roche asked, bewildered.

"For the fact that you're not plowing a traitor's fields, you ox, although that's the best thing you are suited for, seeing that you're both strong and stupid! Ay, but things are heating up over there, d'you hear? It must be the Swedes who are doing all that bellowing like a herd of cattle."

Here Pan Zagloba grew somewhat more thoughtful, because he wasn't quite as much at ease near a battlefield as he liked to seem, and stared sharply into Kowalski's eyes.

"And whom do you wish a victory?" he demanded.

"Our own men, of course."

"There you are! And what about the Swedes?"

"I'd rather be pounding on them too, if I had my choice. What's ours is ours and what's their is theirs."

"Good. Your conscience is awakening. So if that's how you feel about the Swedes how could you cart your own blood relative to them?"

"Because I had orders."

"But you don't have any orders now, do you?"

"That's true. I don't."

"Your only superior now is Pan Volodyovski, nobody else. Is that clear to you? He's your new commander."

"Seems like... he ought to be."

"So you've got to do what Pan Volodyovski tells you, am I right?"

"Seems like I do since there isn't anybody else..."

"So here is his order!" Pan Zagloba shouted. "He's ordering

you to forget about Radzivill from now on and serve your own country with the rest of us!"

"How's that again, uncle?" Pan Roche began to scratch his head once more.

"Orders!" yelled Zagloba.

"Yessir," said Kowalski. "An order is an order."

"That's better! So what are you going to do the next time we come across some Swedes? You're going to pound on them, am I right?"

"Seems like I'll have to," Pan Roche said and sighed as if a huge weight had rolled off his shoulders. "I've got to obey my commander's orders."

Pan Zagloba also drew a deep, satisfying breath because he had some plans of his own for Pan Roche Kowalski, and the two of them settled down to listen to the sounds of the battle which went on for another hour or more.

But Zagloba grew more fidgety and less at his ease by each passing minute.

"Could they be in trouble over there?" he worried. "Maybe the fight is going against them?"

"Ey, uncle," Pan Kowalski said. "You're an old soldier and you can say such things? If the Swedes were winning and smashing our people they'd be coming back this way, right past us, wouldn't they?"

"That's true. I see that even your wits aren't so dull that I can't find some use out of them."

Then they listened to the sound of a large body of mounted men nearing along the road.

"There, uncle," Pan Kowalski said. "You hear the hoofbeats out there on the highway? They're coming at a walk. They must've crushed the Swedes."

"Hmm. If only that's our men... I think I'd better ride up and take a look."

* * *

So saying Pan Zagloba let his saber dangle by its wrist strap, grasped a pistol, eased out of the birch grove and trotted out ahead. He didn't have far to go before he saw a dark mass of mounted men moving slowly on the road before him and heard the growl of voices in lively conversation. A small group of horsemen rode ahead of the others and Pan Zagloba's sharp ears picked up Volodyovski's welcome voice at once.

"Good men, fine soldiers," Pan Michal was saying, out of breath. "I don't know about their infantry, that's still to be tasted, but the cavalry is first rate."

Much relieved, Zagloba spurred forward.

"How are you all?" he cried. "I almost died of impatience back there! I was all set to charge down and help you! Nobody's wounded, I hope?"

"No, we're all fine, thank God," Pan Michal replied. "Although we lost a few good men, perhaps more than twenty."

"And the Swedes?"

"Dead as doornails, all but a handful of them."

"You must have had a better time down there, Michal, than a puppy in a duck pond!" Pan Zagloba cried. "And was it right to leave me back there on guard, with nothing to do? My mouth was watering at the thought of all that Swedish meat. I'd have eaten them raw!"

"You can have them roasted, if you like, because a few of them got singed in the fire."

"Let the dogs eat them if they've the stomach for it! And did you take many prisoners, eh?"

"We have the captain and half a dozen troopers."

"And what d'you have in mind for them?"

"I'd just as soon have them hanged, if it was up to me," the little knight replied. "Because they attacked a defenseless village, like a band of brigands. But Yan says that won't do."

"Hmm. I've an idea about that," Pan Zagloba said. "I've given it some thought since I had nothing better to do in that birch grove, and I think we ought to set them free and send them back to Birjhe as soon as we can."

"And why should we do that?"

But here Pan Zagloba showed another facet of his character to those who didn't know him, and impressed even more those who knew him well.

"You've seen me as a warrior," he said nodding wisely and putting on his most profound expression. "Now meet me as a statesman. We'll release the Swedes but we won't tell them who we are. On the contrary, let them think that we're Radzivill's soldiers and that we cut them down on the Hetman's orders just like we'll do to any other Swedes we meet along our way. We'll tell them that Radzivill merely pretended to go over to them, all the better to draw them into a trap, and let them pass the word to their commanders! They'll be scratching their heads about that for a long time to come and that damned traitor Radzivill will lose a lot of his credit with them."

"That's not a bad thought at all," Mirski said.

"Not bad?" Pan Zagloba laughed. "The more I look at it the surer I am that it's worth even more than your victory, gentlemen! And if it isn't, may I sprout a hairy tail like a horse and wear a horse blanket instead of my short-coat! It's far from Keydany to Birjhe, and even farther to Pontus de la Gardie in Estonia, and before they get it all explained among themselves they might come to blows. We'll set one dog against the other, turn the invaders against the traitor, and who'll profit most by that if not the Commonwealth?"

"By God," Stankevitch said. "This advice really is worth our victory."

"You have a chancellor's brain, my friend," Mirski told Zagloba and nodded with respect. "Because if that doesn't throw them into chaos and confusion at this stage of their game, then nothing will."

"Then that's what we'll do," Pan Michal said. "I'll let the Swedes go first thing tomorrow morning. But right now all I want to hear about is rest. Phew...! It was as hot as an oven on that road. And I'm so tired I can hardly lift a hand. That officer wouldn't be able to leave tonight anyway because his wound needs dressing."

"Only how are we going to give them all this information?" Pan Yan wondered. "Which of us speaks their language? Do you have any thoughts about that, father?"

"I do indeed," Zagloba said at once. "Kowalski tells me that he has two Prussians among his dragoons, a smart quickwitted pair who can jabber to the Swedes in German. The Swedes are sure to understand the language, having fought in Germany for so many years. As for Kowalski, by the way, he's ours body and soul now. He's a good lad and I expect a lot of useful service out of him."

"Good!" said Volodyovski. "Will one of you gentlemen see to all that for me? I'm so tired I can hardly talk."

"I'll do that for you," Pan Stanislav said.

"Good. Thank you. All our men need to catch a breath so we'll stay in this birch grove until morning. The peasants are bringing us hot food from the village but our main order of business for tonight is sleep! I tell you, gentlemen, my eyelids are so heavy I need to prop them open so that I can see you."

"Well, if that's so, I've more good news for you," Pan Zagloba said. "There's a fine haystack not far from the birch grove. Let's luxuriate in there for a few hours, rest our backs and stimulate the brain, and tomorrow we can be on our way. We won't be in these parts again, I expect, unless we come back with Pan Sapyeha against Radzivill."

Part Six

Chapter Thirty-three

WHAT STARTED THEN in Lithuania was a civil war which, along with the two invasions from the East and West and with the sharpening war in the Ukraine, filled the country's measure of misfortune to the brim.

The Grand Duchy's Polish-Lithuanian regulars, so few in number that they couldn't show effective resistance to either enemy, now split into two warring camps and fought against each other. One, especially the foreign mercenary contingents, stood by Radzivill. The vast majority of the rest denounced the Hetman as a traitor, renounced his authority, refused to obey him, and resisted the union with Sweden by force of arms. They had, however, neither unity among themselves, nor a joint plan of action, nor an overall commander. Such a leader could be the *Voyevode* of Vitebsk, the next ranking civil dignitary among the Lithuanians, but he was far too occupied with the defense of Bykhov—a long way southeast of insurgent Zmudya—and with the desperate fighting elsewhere in the country, to take immediate charge of the opposition.

Meanwhile the two invaders—the Swedes and the Russians—each looking at the entire country as their own possession, started to send threatening embassies to each other. The Commonwealth saw its own eventual salvation in these clashes between her invaders, but before they actually began to fight each other all of Lithuania stood in the grip of chaos. Radzivill was bitterly disappointed in his calculations, his situation was more perilous than he ever dreamed in his worst nightmares, and he was savagely determined to force his mutinous regiments back into obedience.

Pan Volodyovski had barely brought his men to Ponevyesh after the fight at Klevany, when he heard about the destruction of Mirski's and Stankevitch's regiments by the Hetman's soldiers. Part of the shattered units was forcibly absorbed by Radzivill's army and the rest was scattered to the four winds or stamped into the ground. Survivors wandered singly or in small groups through the woods and villages, looking for refuge from the Hetman's vengeance and pursuit, and ran to join Pan Michal whenever they were able.

These refugees added daily to his strength but the news they brought was even more important. And the most encouraging word came in those days from Podlasye, where the regular troops stationed in the area of Bialystok and Tykotzin mutinied against Radzivill. They had been posted there after the Russian destruction of Vilna to bar Hovansky's access to the Polish Crown territories further to the south. But hearing of the Hetman's treason they formed a confederation under Colonels Horotkevitch and Yakob Kmita, a distant cousin of Pan Andrei Kmita, who was now known and hated throughout the whole country as Radzivill's most loyal and dangerous henchman. His name had become a synonym for bitterness and horror among the rebel soldiers. It was repeated everywhere with fear and loathing. Survivors told that it was he who had crushed the Mirski and Stankevitch loyalists, executing the captured mutineers without mercy. According to the shocked, wretched refugees who flocked to the Laudanians, the Hetman trusted him more than any of his men, and had just sent him against Nevyarovski's regiment which refused to follow its colonel into treason.

*   *   *

Pan Volodyovski listened to these reports with a great deal of attention a few days after his victory at Klevany, then turned to the other officers who came to help him to decide what course to follow next.

"What would you say," he asked, "if we went to Podlasye and joined those Confederates rather than trying to go all the way to Bykhov and the *Voyevode* of Vitebsk?"

"You took the words right out of my mouth," Pan Zagloba said. "A man always feels better about everything when he's closer to home."

"There's also word that His Majesty is calling back some of Pan Pototzki's troops from the Ukraine," Yan Skshetuski added. "And if that should happen we'll find ourselves among our old comrades rather than rattling around here from one strange corner to another."

"And who's to command those Ukrainian regiments? Does anyone know?"

"People say it'll be Pan Tcharnyetzki," Volodyovski answered. "But that's no more reliable than guesswork at this time because it's too soon for accurate information to come all this way."

"Whatever the facts of the matter might be," Pan Zagloba said. "I advise getting through to Podlasye as fast as we can. We can stir up all of that local gentry, sweep up those mutinied Radzivill regiments, and bring them to the King. And that could even lead to some recognition."

"Let's do it, then!" Oskierka and Stankevitch agreed.

"It won't be easy," cautioned Volodyovski. "We'll have to slip between the Hetman's fingers to get to Podlasye. But it's worth a try. And if, by some stroke of luck, we get our hands on Kmita on the way, I've a couple of words to whisper in his ear that'll turn him green."

"He deserves it," Mirski said. "I don't wonder at some of the old Radzivill soldiers who served him all their lives. It isn't easy to break the habits of a lifetime and turn against the man you have always followed. But that lawless scoundrel serves him out of greed and the sheer joy he finds in his treason."

"So it's to be Podlasye for us, then?" Oskierka asked.

"Podlasye it is!" all the others chorused.

* * *

But getting past Keydany and the Hetman proved just as hazardous as Pan Volodyovski warned: it was like creeping past the lair of a hungry lion.

All the roads, woodland tracks, villages and townships were in Radzivill's hands. Just south of Keydany was Kmita with a corps of cavalry, infantry and cannon. The Hetman was already aware of the escape of the captive colonels, the mutiny of

Volodyovski's regiment and the Klevany massacre of the Swedes, and that last piece of news was literally almost the last stroke for the furious traitor. He was seized by such a frightful rage when he heard about it that he couldn't breathe, fell senseless to the floor, and almost choked to death.

He had good reason for rage and even for despair because that battle brought a storm of Swedish anger on his head. First of all it served as an instant signal for Zmudyan resistance. Small Swedish units were attacked and slaughtered everywhere by groups of local gentry and insurgent peasants. A fierce partisan warfare burst out throughout the land and the Swedes held Radzivill responsible for it all, especially since the Reiter officer and troopers set free in Klevany testified before the commandant in Birjhe that it was a Radzivill regiment that destroyed them, acting on his orders.

A week later the Prince received an angry demand for an explanation from the Swedish commandant at Birjhe, and ten days after that came a bitterly accusing letter from Pontus de la Gardie, the commander in chief of all Swedish forces in Estonia, Latvia, Lithuania and Courland.

'*Either Your Highness lacks the influence and power to control your country,*' wrote the enraged field marshal, '*in which case you had no right to sign agreements on its behalf, or you are out to destroy His Majesty's forces by treachery and cunning! If that's the case, then you have lost His Majesty's regard, and earned the retribution that is sure to come falling down upon you unless you show humility, do the proper penance, and erase your guilt by faithful and obedient service.*'

Radzivill dispatched messengers with instant explanations but the blow to his pride couldn't be erased. It became a burning, seeping wound that tormented him more profoundly than all his other disappointments.

'*How is it then?*' he had to ask himself. '*Can I really be as powerless as that?*'

... Ah! And again his asthma threatened to strangle him with fury.

"How can this be?" he raged.

Didn't his will count for anything any longer in that vast, thickly populated country which was so much greater than Charles Gustav's Sweden?

Wasn't he rich and powerful enough to buy all the Swedish

lords, if he wished to, for a mere fraction of everything he owned? Hadn't he challenged his own King, looked with scorn at other reigning monarchs, stunned the known world with his military victories, and walked in his own pride and glory as if it was the sun? And was he now to listen to the threats of a Swedish general and take lessons in humility from Charles Gustav's upstart brother-in-law? And who was that Swedish King himself if not an usurper whose crown, by rights of bloodline and inheritance, belonged to Yan Casimir anyway?

But the burning core of the Hetman's fury focused upon those who brought this terrible humiliation upon him, and he swore to crush Volodyovski and those colonels who were riding with him, and to wipe the Laudanians off the face of the earth. With this in mind he moved everything he had against them, surrounded them in much the same way that hunters throw a cordon around a wolf's lair in a forest, and drove them without a chance to catch their breaths.

★ ★ ★

In the meantime he got word that Kmita had destroyed Nevyarovski's rebels, either scattering or killing off its enlisted gentry and forcing the ordinary men-at-arms into his own units. He then ordered Kmita to send him a part of his forces so that the destruction of Volodyovski's rebels could be all the surer.

'*Those men,*' he wrote to Kmita, '*and especially Volodyovski and that other stray for whose lives you clamored so insistently, got away on the road to Birjhe and now they're causing us immeasurable damage.*'

He went on to say that he purposely sent them in the keeping of his most stupid officer, '*so that they wouldn't be able to turn him,*' but that the gambit failed either through the rebels' cunning or the officer's treason.

'*Now Volodyovski has a whole regiment behind him and deserters swell his ranks every day. He already slaughtered one hundred and twenty Swedes at Klevany, announcing that this was done according to Our orders, which has caused the greatest difficulties with Pontus de la Gardie.*

'*Our whole cause has been placed in jeopardy by these traitors,*' he wrote on. '*Which wouldn't have happened if you hadn't begged their lives from Us in Keydany, and if We'd had their heads lopped off their shoulders while We had them safely in Our hands.*'

He then ordered Kmita to send him all his cavalry, dispatch the guns and the infantry to Keydany '*in case those incorrigible scoundrels dare to move against it,*' and then to fetch Pan Tomasz and Olenka from Billevitche with no more delay and take them to the city.

'*This means as much to Us nowadays as it does to you, because whoever holds them controls all the Laudanians who might otherwise follow Volodyovski.*'

He finished by saying that he was sending Harasimovitch to his Podlasyan estates in Zabludov '*with instructions on how to deal with those confederates out there,*' and commending Kmita to God and to his own continuing affection.

Kmita was secretly delighted that Volodyovski, Zagloba and the other colonels managed to slip out of Swedish hands, and he wished them the same luck with Radzivill, but he did everything that the Hetman ordered. He sent him all his cavalry, garrisoned Keydany with the infantry, and even started to fortify the castle and the town with earthwalls and redoubts. At the same time he promised himself to go to Billevitche as soon as he'd finished.

"I won't use force," he told himself. "Except as a last resort. And I won't touch Olenka. It's not my will anyway, it's the Prince's order. She won't be glad to see me, I know that, but with God's mercy she'll discover in time that I serve Radzivill to save our country, not to injure it."

Comforting himself in this way he worked day and night to fortify Keydany which was to be his Olenka's residence, keeping her safe in those days of chaos and disaster.

★ ★ ★

Meanwhile Pan Volodyovski scurried to escape the Hetman who pursued him with all the relentless, single-minded dedication of his unforgiving and implacable nature.

But for all his great skills in this war of cunning and maneuver, things were getting rather tight for the little colonel because the Swedes moved large forces south of Birjhe, the eastern territories of the country were held by the Russians, and the road to and past Keydany was blocked by Radzivill.

Pan Zagloba was made most unhappy by this turn of events and he asked his little friend more and more frequently every day about their mutual chances.

"Will we be able to cut our way through, Michal? For God's sake, will we manage?"

"We won't fight our way through," the little knight replied. "That's out of the question. You know me. You know that I'll take on anybody, including the Devil. But the Hetman is too much for me. He's a great commander. You said yourself that he's a pike and we're a school of perches, didn't you? I'll do what I can to slip through his fingers but if it comes to an all-out battle then he'll beat us hollow."

"And then he'll have us well peppered with lead and feed us to his dogs," Pan Zagloba said. "Dear God, put me in any hands other than Radzivill's! Wouldn't it be better, then, to turn back and run to Pan Sapyeha?"

"It's too late for that now. We've not only the Hetman's troops barring the way but the Swedes as well."

"The Devil must have given me that damfool idea to lead the Skshetuskis to Radzivill!" the fat knight despaired.

"He doesn't have us yet."

★ ★ ★

Pan Michal remained optimistic, especially since everyone in the country—peasants as well as gentry—turned against Radzivill and warned him about every move that the Hetman made. He dodged and twisted as best he could, and he knew how to do it very well. He'd spent all his years, practically from childhood, in wars against the Tartars and the Cossacks in the Wild Lands and the open Steppe. He was famous in the old army of Yeremi Vishnovyetzki for his running fights with the Tartar *tchambuls*, for his sudden raids, his lightning turns and his unexpected sallies.

Now, locked in an area of a few square miles between Rogov and Upita on one side, and the Nevyesh River on the other, he weaved back and forth, avoiding an out-and-out confrontation with the Hetman, and snapping at the net that tightened about him.

He ran, backtracked, dodged and darted much like a canny old wolf chased by a pack of mastiffs, slipping when he could past the waiting hunters and flashing his fangs whenever the dogs came too close. But when Kmita's cavalry came up from the south, the Hetman plugged up the last of the bolt-holes, and arrived in person to make sure that the two ends of the net drew properly together.

The regiments of Ganhof and Myeleshko, with two additional cavalry detachments led by the Prince himself, formed the arc of a bow with the river as the bowstring and with Pan Michal and his Laudanians trapped within that space. True, the little knight had the only ford across the swampy river right in front of him, but on the other side waited two regiments of Scottish infantry, a two hundred man battalion of Radzivill Cossacks, and half-a-dozen field guns which commanded the crossing in such a way that not a single man could escape their fire.

Then the bow started tightening with the Hetman himself commanding the center of the arc.

Luckily for Pan Volodyovski a pitch-black night and a sudden rainstorm slowed down the advance. But by that time the trapped Laudanians were left with only a few furlongs of riverside meadow overgrown with reeds between Radzivill, the river, and the Scotsmen on the other side, and the terrible Prince was certain of his victory.

The Hetman's advance resumed just as soon as the first light of dawn gilded the tops of the reeds and broke on the dark water. The grim ranks marched forward like beaters in a bear-hunt, crushing the undergrowth and trampling every square foot of the shrinking refuge. Volodyovski's trap tightened with their every step. And finally the arc of the bow lay flat against the river and the Radzivill soldiers stared about, dumb with admiration and amazement.

Their quarry was gone.

"Did the earth swallow them up, or what?" the soldiers asked each other.

The reeds were beaten flat. They could conceal nothing. But there was no sign that Pan Volodyovski and some five hundred horsemen had ever been there.

Radzivill himself was dumbstruck with surprise but then a real hurricane of fury burst over the heads of the officers whose regiments guarded the crossing on the other side. Another terrible attack of asthma seized the Prince—so violent that his men feared for his life once more—but his rage overcame even this sudden seizure. He ordered the immediate execution of two officers who were entrusted with the watch on the river-bank, but Ganhof managed to get them a reprieve for at least as long as it took to find out how that sly little rebel managed to elude his hunters.

It soon became apparent that Pan Volodyovski made good use of the rain and he darkness to lead his regiment into the river, and then either wade or swim the men and the horses down-stream, well past the right flank of the Radzivill army. A few abandoned horses which had sunk belly-deep in the mud showed where he came ashore on the southern bank.

Other tracks suggested that he set off towards Keydany with all the speed he could get out of his men and horses, and the Hetman guessed at once that the little colonel wanted to reach Podlasye and the confederate mutineers of Yakob Kmita and Pan Horotkevitch.

But, he thought at once, wouldn't the uncanny little raider be tempted to loot the castle and fire the town while passing Keydany?

A sudden fear for his money gripped the worried Hetman. He'd sent his costliest possessions to Tikotzin, but most of his ready gold was still in Keydany. And what if Kmita hadn't garrisoned the palace as he was supposed to? Radzivill didn't doubt that the daring little colonel had quite enough imperti-nence and gall to reach into his residence itself, especially since having set off early in the night he had at least a six hours' start on any pursuit.

There was nothing else for Radzivill to do but ride as fast as possible to save his Keydany.

* * *

The furious Hetman left all his infantry behind and drove his cavalry south at a killing pace but when he reached his capital he found everything secure and in order.

Kmita was away but the result of his hard work was evident everywhere and the Hetman's high opinion of the young com-mander soared even higher at the sight of the freshly raised ramparts around the town and the field artillery emplaced in the redoubts. He inspected all these new defenses straight away and said to Ganhof in admiration later in the evening:

"That Kmita is a real find. He did all this on his own. He

didn't need my orders. And look how well he built those defenses. They'd hold a long time even against artillery. That young man will go far, I tell you, if he doesn't twist his neck in the meantime."

There was another man whose recollected image filled the Grand Hetman with a certain, grudging admiration, but it was respect mixed with rage and hatred since that man was Pan Volodyovski.

"I'd soon finish with the mutineers if I had two such servants," he said that night to Ganhof. "Kmita might even be the more daring of the two but he doesn't have the experience of Volodyovski. That little fellow comes from Yeremi's school, way across the Dnieper, and there have never been better soldiers than that."

"Does Your Highness wish to have him pursued?" Ganhof asked.

"What for?" The Prince shrugged. "He'd beat you and he'd escape from me."

After some time, however, his look of troubled, grim determination returned to his face.

"We'll have to go to Podlasye ourselves very soon," he said. "It's quiet enough around here now but it's time to finish with those others."

"Highness," Ganhof said. "Let us take just one step away from these territories and everyone alive will rise against the Swedes."

"What do you mean by everyone?"

"The gentry, Highness. The peasants. And it won't be just the Swedes they'll go after, either. The fate of all the Protestants in Zmudya is in jeopardy because the whole country blames us for the war, for going over to the enemy, and even for inviting the Swedes into Lithuania."

"I'm more concerned about Prince Boguslav," Radzivill said coldly. "I don't know if he'll be able to cope with those confederates in Podlasye."

"And I'm worried about Lithuania, Highness," Ganhof dared to say. "It's getting harder every day to enforce obedience. And not just to us, sire, but to His Swedish Majesty as well."

But the Prince-*Voyevode* didn't need to be told about that, and he began to pace through his apartment, snarling like a bear.

"If I could just get Horotkevitch and Yakob Kmita into my

hands somehow," he grated out. "They'll ruin me down there...
They'll raid my properties, burn and loot everything that isn't
nailed down, and they won't leave two scorched stones standing
on each other!"

"Perhaps we can ask Field Marshal de la Gardie to send a
Swedish army here for the time that we'll be in Podlasye,"
Ganhof offered, and immediately regretted the suggestion because the Hetman's face swelled with a sudden rush of blood and
his breath began to hiss and rattle in his chest.

"Ask Pontus... never!" he snarled. "Maybe the King himself.
But not Pontus! Ever! Why should I negotiate with servants
when I can talk directly to their master? If Charles Gustav
ordered him to send me a couple of thousand cavalry that'd be
another matter... But I won't ask Pontus! It's time to send
somebody to the King and start to make arrangements with
Charles Gustav in person."

Ganhof's thin, narrow face flushed in anticipation and his eyes
glittered with longing and ambition.

"If Your Highness ordered me to go," he began, but Radzivill
shrugged and waved the offer aside as if it weren't worth another
thought.

"You'd go. I know that. But whether you'd get there is
another matter. You're a German, and it's as much as a foreigner's life is worth these days to travel through these war-torn
territories. Moreover, who knows where Charles Gustav is
right now, or where he'll be in a month or even in two weeks?
Poznan? Krakow? Warsaw? He could be anywhere in Poland!
You'd have to track him through the entire country. And
besides, I can't send a foreign officer. It has to be one of our
own kind, and a wellborn and high-ranking man at that, so that
Charles Gustav can see for himself that I've not been deserted
by all the Lithuanians."

"An inexperienced man could do a lot of damage," Ganhof
suggested cautiously.

"Whoever I send won't have much to do except hand over
my letters and bring back the reply. As for explaining that it
wasn't I who ordered that massacre at Klevany, any fool can do
that."

Disappointed, Ganhof said nothing more, and the Prince
resumed his restless pacing up and down the chamber, while his

dark, furrowed brow mirrored the deep struggle that was going on inside him.

He hadn't had one moment of certainty and peace from the day he signed that treaty with Pontus de la Gardie, and each hour after that seemed more worrying and threatening. Pride and humiliation gnawed at him. He was seared by fleeting pangs of conscience. He was consumed by rage and disappointment at the opposition he faced in his own army as well as in the country.

Each night he faced the specters of an uncertain future. His growing doubts turned into a certainty of ruin that tore at him, banished the possibility of sleep, drained all his strength and undermined his health. His eyes peered suspiciously out of deep, dark-rimmed circles as if they were drowning in two wells of fear. He'd become drawn and thin. His huge body bowed towards the ground. His face, once flushed crimson with confidence and power, acquired an uncertain blue-grey tinge, and his thick hair and moustache became streaked with white almost by the hour.

Watching him carefully as he paced the room, Ganhof could tell that he was living within a soul-destroying agony and torment which might, eventually, break him altogether.

The German cavalry commander still hoped that the Prince might change his mind and send him on the mission to the King of Sweden, when a sudden look of horror and revelation flashed across Radzivill's staring face.

"Two regiments of cavalry to mount up at once!" he shouted. "I'll lead them myself!"

"An expedition, Highness?" Ganhof queried.

"Move!" the Prince ordered and Ganhof turned at a run towards the doors. "Pray God it's not too late."

Chapter Thirty-four

PAN ANDREI PUT OFF going to Billevitche as long as he could. But when he finished with the Keydany defenses, making both the town and castle safe from a surprise attack, he had no more excuses for delay in fetching the old constable and Olenka as the Prince had ordered.

He was in such low spirits as he took the road to the family seat of the Billevitches as if he was riding into a hopeless battle. He had a powerful premonition that the Billevitch patriarch wouldn't be pleased to see him, and he shuddered at the thought that the old noble might refuse to come, or that he'd put up some kind of armed resistance, in which case he'd have to seize him and Olenka and drag them to Keydany by force.

He was determined to convince them rather than compel them, ready to plead if that proved necessary, so he left his fifty dragoons at a wayside inn about half a furlong from the old man's village and almost two furlongs from the manor house, riding ahead with just his sergeant and a groom. This way, he thought, his visit might seem less like an armed incursion. The comfortable traveling carriage that he brought along was to arrive on its own shortly afterwards.

It was well into the afternoon when he reached the village. The sun had already dipped into the west. But the day remained bright and clear after a wet and stormy night, with a mere scattering of pinkish woolly clouds that left the western edges of the sky looking like a flock of sheep wending their way homeward.

Kmita rode through the village with his heart hammering in

431

his chest, and peering as uneasily all around him as a Tartar scout watching for an ambush, but no one paid the three riders any particular attention. Barefooted peasant children scampered out of their way while their elders bowed to the handsome officer all the way to the ground. Kmita rode on, passed the village, and finally saw the Billevitch manor with broad orchards spreading out behind it all the way to the low-lying distant meadows close to the horizon.

With his goal in sight, Kmita rode even slower, trying out the answers he might give to the expected questions and, in the meantime, letting his distracted eyes wander along the front of the structure before him. This was by no means a magnate's residence, but one glance was enough to show that whoever lived there was more than just an ordinary squire. The house was spacious, facing the main road and backed into the orchards, but it was made entirely out of wood. Its pine planks were so dark with age that the windows seemed quite white in contrast. Its tall overhanging roof showed four chimneys clustered in the center and a raised dovecote at each of the corners. A cloud of doves and pigeons swirled above the roof, either lifting upward with beating wings, or settling down on the blackened eves like fresh winter snow, or fluttering about the heavy wooden uprights that supported the overhang above the wide, deep porch, and formed a sharply angled peak above the main doors.

This peaked porch, with the Billevitch coats-of-arms painted in its arch, spoiled the building's symmetry since it stood closer to one side of the manor than the other, instead of in the center where it should have been. It was immediately apparent that the original manor must have been much smaller, but the addition was so dark with age that one couldn't say where the old building ended and the newer walls began. Two unusually long wings stretched from the main building, giving the structure the appearance of a massive horseshoe, and containing guest rooms used during rare family gatherings, the kitchens, the supply pantries, and the bathing rooms, along with a carriage house and stables for the riding horses that the owners liked to have close to hand, and quarters for the estate managers and servants, and a barrack room for the manor Cossacks.

A cluster of old linden trees stood in the middle of the cobbled courtyard with storks nesting in their upper branches, and with a captive bear perched on a wagon wheel among their gnarled roots. Two stone wells, with long wooden hoists poised over them, crouched at the sides of this wide enclosure; and a carved wooden Christ, flanked by a stand of spears, hung from a life-sized crucifix at the open gate, completing the picture of this wealthy, rural noble's residence and home. Edging from behind the right side of the manor, and partly hidden by their own linden groves, peered the thatched roofs of cow barns, byres, and sheepfolds, and the squat wooden silos used for storing winter grain and fodder.

★ ★ ★

Kmita rode through the hospitably opened gates, flung as wide by tradition as the open arms of a welcoming host, announced by the barking of a pack of hounds that lay about or wandered through the courtyard, while a pair of grooms ran out of one of the long wings of the manor to help him dismount and to hold his horse. At the same time he caught sight of a woman—Olenka, he was certain—who appeared in the main doors of the house.

His heart beat faster as he swung his legs off the saddle and jumped to the ground.

He threw his reins to the groom and moved towards the porch, with his sheathed saber carried in one hand and his cap clutched nervously in the other, while she shaded her eyes for a moment against the glare of the setting sun, and then whirled and vanished as suddenly as she appeared, as if alarmed by an unwelcome guest.

"A bad sign," Pan Andrei grunted, unhappy and ill at ease. "She's hiding from me."

He started feeling very badly then, all the worse since the setting sun and the peaceful manor with its rustic quietness started to give him hope. He knew how she felt about him now, she had made it clear, but even so he had a vague but persistent notion that he had come to the home of his future wife, a girl whom he loved, who'd maybe greet him with a flush of joy spreading through her cheeks and eyes that shined with pleasure at the sight of him.

Now this dream-bubble popped and disappeared. She fled just as soon as she recognized him, as if he was some kind of evil spirit, and the old constable came out in her place looking both anxious and annoyed.

"I've long wanted to pay my respects to Your Worship," Kmita bowed and said. "But it's hard to find the time in such unsettled days no matter how much I wished to do it."

"I'm grateful for your kindness," the old constable said with restrained courtesy. He was ill at ease, perhaps even worried, and stood for a while rubbing the top of his head as if he didn't know what else to do with his hand. Then he stepped aside to let his guest go first. "But come in... come in, won't you?"

Pan Andrei wanted to follow him into the house, as a sign of a young man's respect for his elder, so they stood bowing to each other on the porch until the absurdity of it all forced Kmita to lead the way inside. There he found two other guests, both of them local nobles and Billevitch neighbors, who bristled like a pair of mastiffs when they heard his name. Pan Andrei threw them both a sharp, unfriendly glance and then decided to behave as if they weren't there.

A long silence followed.

Kmita became impatient and started to chew on the ends of his mustache. The two gruff, middle-aged squires glared at him out of the corners of their eyes, and the old constable went on stroking the top of his head.

"Perhaps you'll take a glass of our poor country mead with us," the old man said at last, nodding towards a demijohn and glasses. "Please help yourself."

"I'll drink with you, sir," Kmita answered brusquely, making it clear that he wasn't about to drink with the others. But they knew better than to pick a quarrel in a neighbor's house, particularly with a well-connected roughneck whose reputation for ruthlessness and violence terrified all the countryside around them.

★ ★ ★

Meanwhile Pan Tomasz clapped his hands to summon a servant, and ordered a fresh goblet which he filled for Kmita.

"To your health, sir," he said and raised his own cup. "You're... ah... always welcome in my house."

"I wish that were really so," Kmita said sincerely. But the old constable sidestepped this chance to reassure him and took refuge in stilted politeness.

"A guest is a guest," he murmured, still stroking his topknot. Then, evidently thinking it his duty as a host to keep the conversation going, he asked: "And what's new in Keydany? How is the Hetman's health these days?"

"Not too good, sir. But it can hardly be otherwise in such times as these. The Prince has much to worry him nowadays."

"We can believe that!" one of the visiting local gentry said with a hint of sarcasm.

Kmita gave him another long cold look, ignored him, and turned again to speak to Pan Tomasz.

"His Illustrious Swedish Majesty promised us reinforcements, so the Prince expected to march at once to avenge the burning of Vilna. I expect you've heard that there's nothing left of that city now except ruin and ashes. The Russians burned and looted it for seventeen days."

"A terrible misfortune," Pan Tomasz sighed.

"Yes it is," Kmita stated firmly. "If it couldn't be avoided then at least it ought to be avenged and the enemy's own capital should be turned to ruins. And we wouldn't be far from that today if it wasn't for a pack of disobedient scoundrels who question His Highness' best intentions, accuse him of treason, and turn their swords against him instead of riding with him against the enemy. So it's not much of a surprise that the Prince's health is suffering, when he sees all those great plans for which God has picked him threatened by human envy, jealousy and malice. His oldest friends have disappointed him, those on whose trust and understanding he thought he could count, and now they're either turning their backs on him or joining his opponents."

"True," Pan Tomasz murmured.

"It's a cause of great pain for His Highness," Kmita added. "I heard him myself wondering why these good and valued friends of his don't come to Keydany to speak to him about it face to face."

"And whom does he have in mind in particular?" the constable asked.

"You sir, most of all. I know that the Prince has the highest

possible regard for you, yet he suspects that you too are turning
against him."

Pan Tomasz started stroking the top of his head even faster
and harder than before, and then, seeing that the conversation
was taking an unwanted turn, clapped his hands sharply to call
back the servant.

"Bring some lights!" he shouted. "What's the matter with
you? Can't you see that it's getting dark?"

"God knows that I had my own friendly courtesies in mind
when I came calling on you," Kmita told the fidgety old man.
"But I'm also here on the Prince's orders. He would have come
to Billevitche himself if public matters gave him enough time."

"Our roof is far too humble for that," Pan Tomasz said
uneasily.

"Oh, don't say that, sir," Kmita said at once. "Good neighbors always come calling on each other, it's a normal thing. It's
only that the Prince doesn't have one moment to himself these
days. But he sent me with his invitation for you and Panna
Aleksandra to come to Keydany—and to do it at once, today not
tomorrow—because he's not quite sure himself where he might
have to be in the next few days. So that's why I'm here, sir, to
take you to His Highness. I'm happy to find you both in such
good health, having caught sight of Panna Aleksandra earlier at
the door, although she vanished like a will o' the wisp when she
saw me coming."

"Yes," Pan Tomasz murmured and turned his face slightly into
the shadows. "I sent her out myself to see who'd come to call..."

"So now I'm anxious to hear your reply, sir," Kmita said.

                                   ★ ★ ★

Just then the servant lad brought in some lighted candles and
their bright glow revealed the worried frown on the old noble's
face.

"It's a real honor for me," he muttered. "But I... ah... can't
come right away. Not at a moment's notice. You see yourself
that I've guests in the house..."

"That shouldn't be a problem," Kmita said. "Those gentlemen will surely accommodate His Highness."

"We've tongues of our own," snapped one of the visitors.
"We can speak for ourselves."

"Not waiting for what someone else might decide for us," said the other sharply.

"There... you see, sir?" Kmita smiled broadly, pretending to take these threatening growls for polite agreement. "I knew straight off that these were civilized, obliging cavaliers who wouldn't stand in the Prince's way. But,"—and he sent the two nobles a cold, wolfish grin—"just to make sure they've no reason to feel slighted here, I'll invite them to Keydany too in His Highness' name!"

"We don't deserve such kindness!" both the visitors said grimly. "And we've other things to do anyway."

Kmita looked them both up and down with a particularly insolent and telling stare, and then spoke harshly into the air above their heads as if addressing yet another person: "When the Prince asks there is no refusing!"

The two nobles glared and jumped to their feet and the old constable turned suddenly crimson. "You're taking us by force, then?" he demanded.

"No, sir, not you!" Kmita answered quickly but his voice was as cold as ice and as sharp as steel. "Your two guest will come whether they want to go or not, because that's what I feel like having them do, but I don't want to use any pressure on you or Panna Aleksandra. I'm only asking that you oblige the Prince. I'm here on duty and I've orders to bring you to Keydany no matter what it takes. But I am asking you as courteously as I can, and I'll continue to plead with you as long as there is any hope that you will come of your own free will, and I swear that no harm will come to you in the Prince's hands. All he wants is to have a talk with you, and to have you stay in Keydany in these dangerous times when even the peasants are rising up in armed mobs everywhere. That's all there is to it! You'll be treated with all due respect as the Prince's special guest and friend, that much I can promise."

"I protest!" Pan Tomasz burst out angrily. "This goes against the statutes! This is a violation of my civil rights and I've the law behind me!"

"And our sabers too!" cried the visiting nobles.

★ ★ ★

But now Kmita began to laugh softly straight into their faces, and his eyebrows formed a bitter line above his cold grey eyes.

"You'd be advised keep those sabers out of sight," he hissed out with a terrible, thin smile. "Or I'll have you both propped up against a barn and shot!"

All their quick, angry courage drained out of the three shaken gentlemen at once, although the old constable shouted one more protest.

"This is an outrage! It tramples on our basic guarantees! It's an abridgement of the gentry's freedoms!"

"There won't be any outrage, sir, if you do as you're being asked," Kmita answered. "And your best proof of that is that I left my dragoons in the village and came up here alone, like a friend, to talk to you as one neighbor to another. Don't say 'No,' I beg you, because protests don't mean much these days and it's hard to take any notice of them. The Prince himself will make his excuses to you, and you can be quite sure that you'll be received respectfully as a good friend and neighbor."

Quite pale with suppressed anger of his own, but also anxious to placate the truculent old noble, Pan Andrei did his best to keep his voice steady.

"Please understand that I'd much rather face a firing squad a hundred times over than come here to fetch you if that weren't so. No harm will come to any Billevitch as long as I'm alive! Remember who I am, recall Pan Heracles and his testament, and then ask yourself if the Prince would have sent me here if his plans for you were anything but sincere."

"Then why does he resort to force? Why do I have to go under duress? How can I trust him when all of Lithuania talks about the terrible repressions that honest citizens live under in Keydany?"

Kmita allowed himself a sigh of relief because the old noble's words and tone suggested that his opposition was starting to weaken, and this relief found a quick echo in his own reply.

"My dear sir!" he answered in a gentler tone. "What's taken for force and pressure among neighbors is often the start of later gratitude. Even if—God forbid!—I were to have you roped and dragged off to Keydany by dragoons, it would still turn out for your own good in the long run. Just think sir: the mutineers plague the countryside with acts of lawlessness, the peasants are up in arms, Swedish troops are coming, and you believe that you can escape unscathed in all this commotion? You think that one or another of those hungry wolf packs won't raid you here, any time they feel a need to do it? That they won't rob you, burn your properties, and harm your own person? What is this manor house, some kind of a fortress? How can it protect you? So what is it that the Prince wants for you in Keydany if it isn't your own wellbeing and safety? And here in Billevitche we'll put a Hetman's garrison to watch over your property and possessions with as much care as if it was their own. And if you find one pitchfork missing from your inventory after you've come back, I'll let you put a lien on my entire fortune."

Still worried and unhappy, but having something else to think about as well, the old constable started pacing nervously up and down the chamber.

"Can I trust your words?" he asked at last.

"As if they were an oath!" Kmita said.

★ ★ ★

But in that moment Aleksandra came into the room. Kmita turned towards her and took an instinctive step in her direction; but her cold, shuttered face reminded him of what happened between them in Keydany and fixed him in place, so he merely bowed to her and waited in silence.

"We're to go to Keydany!" the old noble stopped his pacing in front of Olenka.

"Why?" she asked.

"Because the Prince invites us."

"Courteously!" Kmita threw in at once. "Like a neighbor!"

"Yes, most courteously," Pan Tomasz added with a certain bitterness. "But if we don't go of our own free will then this cavalier has orders to surround us with dragoons and take us by force."

"God forbid that this should ever happen!" Kmita cried.

"Didn't I tell you, uncle," Aleksandra said, "that we should run as far away from here as we could because they'd never leave us in peace? And now it's come true!"

"What can we do?" the old man cried out. "How can we avoid it? There is no cure for an act of outrage!"

"That's right," the young woman said. "But we must never go willingly to that despicable and ignoble house. Let these brigands take us by force, if that's what they want. We won't be the only victims of a traitor's vengeance and oppression. But let him know that we'd rather die than share his infamy."

And here she turned to Kmita with such contempt burning in her face that his heart constricted.

"So take us, Master Hangman," she said. "And drag us with you on a rope's end, because we won't go with you by any other means!"

Kmita's face turned crimson with a rush of blood; it looked for a moment as if he'd give way to a terrifying rage but he managed to hold himself in check.

"Ah, my lady," he said in a stifled voice. "There's no mercy for me in your eyes if you want to see me as a brigand, a traitor and a lawless scoundrel. So be it. Let God judge who's right, whether it's I who do my duty by my Hetman, or you who treat me like a mongrel dog. God gave you great beauty but no heart. You'd be glad to suffer if that caused greater pain for somebody else. But now you go too far, my lady. As God's my witness, you've carried this too far, and it won't do anyone any good!"

"The girl's right, by God!" shouted the old noble who felt a sudden surge of returning courage. "We won't go of our own free will! Take us with your dragoons!"

But Kmita paid no attention to him. He was far too deeply hurt and overwrought for that.

"You find your pleasure in human misery," he said to Olenka. "You call me a traitor, without giving me a chance to say one word in my own defense, or show you why I'm doing what I have to do. So be it, as said! I no longer care! But you'll go to Keydany one way or another, it's all one to me! You'll discover there what this is all about. You'll see if you've wronged me and which one of us was the other's torturer. I don't want anything else from you, because you've torn and clawed at my love for you until it finally cracked. But I will have that much! There's an ugliness crawling under that great beauty of yours like a snake under a flower, God blast you and damn you!"

"We won't go!" the old constable repeated with an even greater determination than before.

"That's right! We won't!" cried the other gentry and both of them reached down to their sabers.

* * *

But now Kmita's rage broke out into the open. He no longer cared about keeping it in bounds. His face lost all color, he was shuddering with anger, and his teeth were rattling as if he was in the grip of fever.

"Try it," he hissed at the constable's two guests. "Just try it! D'you hear the hoofbeats out in the yard? Well? Those are my dragoons! Say one more word, any one of you, about not going with me... Just one word!"

The clatter of many horsemen was now loud in the cobbled courtyard just outside the windows, and the three older nobles stared numbly at each other. It was clear to them all that there was nothing anyone could do.

"Lady!" Kmita ordered, quivering with fury. "You've five minutes to be in that carriage! Otherwise your uncle gets a bullet in the head!"

His rage, as everyone could see, had soared beyond any possibility of control.

"On your way!" he shouted.

But in that moment the outer doors creaked open, and some strange voice asked softly from beyond the threshold: "Where to, Master Kmita?"

Everyone stared in amazement and all eyes turned towards the doorway where a little man dressed in battle armor stood with a bare saber in his hand.

Kmita took one step backwards, as shaken as if he'd seen a ghost.

"Pan... Volodyovski!" he cried out.

"At your service," the little man said quietly and advanced to the center of the room, followed by Mirski, Zagloba, the two Skshetuskis, Stankevitch, Oskierka and Pan Roche Kowalski.

"Ha!" said Zagloba. "Looks like the tables are turned, aren't they. Like the old proverb says, the Cossack caught a Tartar but the Tartar has him by the head."

"Save us, gentlemen, whoever you are!" Pan Tomasz appealed. "Save a free citizen of the Commonwealth seized and imprisoned in spite of every law and all the privileges of his birth and station! The precious liberties of all the gentry are being threatened here!"

"You don't need to worry about that, sir," Pan Volodyovski said. "This officer's dragoons are already trussed up like geese at the market, and he's in far greater need of saving than anyone here."

"And what he needs the most is a priest," Pan Zagloba said.

"You don't have much luck with me," Volodyovski turned to Kmita. "This is the second time I've got in your way, but you don't have to look forward to a third. You didn't expect to see us here, did you?"

"No," Kmita said. "I didn't. I thought the Prince had you in his hands by now."

"Not quite. We've just slipped out of them, and this as you know, is the quickest way to Podlasye. But no matter. The first time you seized this lady I called you out to a sword fight, didn't I."

"That's right," Kmita said, and reached mechanically to the scar across his head.

"Now it's a different story. That time you were just a willful ruffian, which happens among the gentry. Now you're not fit to face a decent man."

"And why's that?" Kmita asked, indifferent with disdain, and stared straight into Volodyovski's eyes.

"Because you're a damned renegade and a traitor," Volodyovski answered. "Because you've been the hangman of good and loyal soldiers who stood by their country. And because it's by your doing, yours and your traitor master's, that all our people live under oppression! In short, get ready to die, because as God's in his Heaven, your minutes are numbered."

"By what right do you judge me and condemn me?" Kmita demanded coldly.

"My dear sir," Zagloba said gravely. "You'd do better to say your prayers than question our rights. If you've something to say in your defense then hurry up and say it because you won't find another living soul who'd speak on your behalf. I've heard that this young lady who is here among us begged your life from Pan Volodyovski once before, but I doubt if she'd speak for you again after everything you've done."

Everyone looked towards Aleksandra whose face, in that

moment, was as still as marble. She stood unmoving like a statue chiseled out of ice, her cold eyes fixed on the floor before her, and she neither stepped forward nor said a word.

"I don't ask that lady to intercede for me," Kmita said abruptly and Olenka didn't break her silence.

"Come in here!" Volodyovski shouted towards the door.

Heavy footsteps, along with the grim jingle of spurs, sounded in the hall, and six soldiers led by Yozva Butrym marched into the chamber.

"Take him out of here," Volodyovski ordered. "Lead him to the other side of the village, put him before a firing squad, and shoot him."

Yozva Butrym's huge hand grasped Kmita's coat collar and two other Laudanian fists fell into place beside it.

"Don't let them drag me like a dog!" Pan Andrei turned to Volodyovski. "I'll go on my own."

The little knight nodded to the soldiers who let go of their prisoner at once but surrounded him closely, and he walked out among them, calm now and saying nothing to anyone, while his lips moved in a silent prayer.

Olenka also left the room.

She slipped out, unnoticed, through the opposite door that led into the interior of the house. She walked blindly through one unlighted room then entered another—stretching her hands before her in the darkness—but suddenly everything spun before her eyes, there didn't seem to be enough air for her to breathe, and she fell unconscious to the floor.

Chapter Thirty-five

A DEEP SILENCE settled on the men gathered in the front room as if each of them was looking into his own heart and listening to his conscience. But Pan Tomasz expressed at last what all of them were feeling.

"Is there no way," he asked, "to show him any mercy?"

"I'm sorry for him," Zagloba admitted. "He went to his death like a real man."

"He had several dozen of my soldiers shot by a firing squad," Mirski said. "Not counting the ones he had killed in combat."

"The same with my people," said Stankevitch. "I hear he didn't leave one of Nevyarovski's men alive."

"He must have had orders from Radzivill to do it that way," Pan Zagloba said.

"Gentlemen," the old constable reminded. "Killing him here you're bringing Radzivill's vengeance on my head!"

"Then you must run for it," Pan Zagloba told him. "We're on our way to Podlasye where several good regiments have risen against the traitors, so you and your niece can come with us a part of the way. There's nothing else you can do to save yourself. You can take shelter in Byelovyezha if you like. One of Pan Skshetuski's relatives is the King's Forester there, and he'll keep you and your niece safe from any harm. No one will find you there, not even Radzivill."

"But he'll find all my property here."

"The Commonwealth will restore it to you," Pan Michal said. "Once Radzivill is beaten."

But Zagloba stirred suddenly and got to his feet. "I think I'll go and see if that poor wretch doesn't have a few orders in his pockets. Do you recall, Michal, what I found with our Roche Kowalski?"

"Good idea. Go. You've still time to reach him before he's been shot and the papers get too bloody to decipher. I had them take him beyond the village so that the execution volley wouldn't upset Panna Aleksandra. You know how sensitive women are about that kind of thing."

* * *

Zagloba left the room and in a few moments the clatter of his horse's hooves announced his departure from the manor. In the meantime Pan Volodyovski turned to the old landowner.

"Where is your kinswoman?" he asked.

"She's probably praying for that man's miserable soul, now that he's about to face his maker."

"God give him peace," Yan Skshetuski said. "I'd be the first to speak for him if he wasn't serving Radzivill of his own free will. But failing one's country is one thing, selling one's soul to a traitor is another."

"Quite right!" said Volodyovski.

"He's guilty and he deserves what is happening to him," Pan Stanislav nodded. "But I'd rather see Radzivill or Opalinski standing in his place. Oh, if only it was Opalinski!"

"There's no question about his guilt," Pan Oskierka said. "Not even this young woman, who was his fiancee, could find anything to say on his behalf. I noted her pain. She was really suffering, but she didn't breathe a word. Because how could anyone plead for such a traitor?"

"And she really loved him at one time," the old constable added. "I know it. Ah, but let me go and see how she's taking this. It's not an easy thing for a woman, you know."

"And get ready for the journey, won't you?" Pan Michal called after him. "We're here only to let our horses catch their breaths and then we're going on. Keydany is too close and Radzivill must have come back there by now."

"I'll do that," the old noble said and stepped from the chamber, but a mere moment later the knights heard him shouting for help and ran to see what happened. They burst out of the room, stumbling and shoving in the darkness of an unfamiliar house through a throng of servants, who ran every which way with lighted brands and lanterns. They pushed at last into a woman's bedroom where they almost ran into the old noble who was trying to lift Olenka off the floor.

Volodyovski leaped forward to help, they placed Olenka on a couch, and an old housekeeper came trotting up, jingling all her keys, and with a flask of smelling salts and restoratives in her hands.

"You men are useless here," she told the knights without any ceremony. "Go back into that other room and we women will manage here well enough."

* * *

The worried constable led his guests into the chamber they occupied before.

"I wish that none of this had happened," he said in a troubled and uncertain voice. "You gentlemen could've taken that wretch and disposed of him somewhere along the road, not here on my lands. You've doomed us. And how are we to get away from here now with the girl half dead like she is? The shock was just too great. She could get seriously ill bumping along the roads into the unknown."

"What's done is done. We can't undo what happened," Pan Michal said and shrugged in regret. "We'll have to put the lady in a carriage because she's no safer here than you. Radzivill's vengeance doesn't spare anyone."

"She looks like a strong young woman," Yan Skshetuski offered. "Perhaps she'll recover in a few more minutes."

"A comfortable traveling coach is harnessed and ready because Kmita brought it with him to take you to Keydany," Volodyovski said and turned to Pan Tomasz. "Go, sir, and tell Lady Olenka what's at stake because your escape can't be delayed by another moment. Let her do her best to get her strength together. We must leave right away. Radzivill's men can be here by sunrise."

"That's true!" the constable said and left the room again.

He was back in a short time with his grand-niece, who apparently not only recovered from her shock and her collapse, but was already fully dressed for the journey. Only her face retained its feverish flush and her eyes were unnaturally bright as if she'd been weeping.

"Let's leave this place, let's leave...!" she repeated entering the room.

Volodyovski went out into the hall to send some men for the coach, and in less than a quarter of an hour the cobblestones in front of the manor rumbled under heavy carriage wheels and the clattering of horseshoes.

"Let's start," Olenka urged in a feverish hurry.

"Let's go, let's get started!" the officers called out, when suddenly the doors flew open with a crash and Pan Zagloba burst into the room like a cannon ball.

"I stopped the execution!" he shouted from the threshold.

Olenka stood as still as if she'd turned to stone. Where only moments earlier she looked as if she were burning up with anxiety and fever, she now became as white as a piece of chalk. But if she was about to lose her strength again no one noticed it, because all eyes were fixed in varying degrees of astonishment on the wheezing and gasping Pan Zagloba, who struggled for breath in the middle of the room like a foundered whale.

"You stopped the execution?" asked the surprised Pan Volodyovski. "And why did you do that?"

"Why...? Ooof, let me catch my breath... I'll tell you why! Because if it wasn't for that very Kmita—that fine man, that decent human being—we'd be hung out for crowbait, every one of us, on the Keydany trees... We wanted to kill our own benefactor!"

"What? Why? How can that be?" all of them cried out together.

"How? Here... read this letter. That'll tell you how."

And here Zagloba handed Pan Volodyovski the letter that Radzivill wrote weeks before to Kmita, blaming him for Volodyovski's freedom and all the catastrophic events that derived from his intercession on the small knight's behalf. Pan Michal read the letter aloud so that everyone could hear it, pausing in surprise at almost every phrase, and exchanging puzzled glances with his amazed companions.

"And what do you say to that?" Zagloba repeated each time Pan Michal paused.

The letter ended with Radzivill's order to bring the old constable and Olenka to Keydany which might have been why Kmita brought it with him. He might have thought he'd need to show it to the constable, Pan Michal believed, to prove both his authority and good faith. But one thing was clear no matter why he had it: if it weren't for Kmita's intercession, both the Skshetuskis, Zagloba and Pan Volodyovski would have been murdered in Keydany right after that famous banquet when the Hetman announced his treaty with Pontus de la Gardie.

"Gentlemen!" Pan Zagloba said. "You command here, not I. But if you still order that man to be shot, I'll leave your company and never have anything to do with you again!"

"That's out of the question now!" Pan Michal assured him.

"How lucky you had the foresight, father, to read the letter on the spot," Yan Skshetuski said.

"They had to feed you larks' tongues when you were a baby!" Mirski cried, once more astonished by the quickness of Zagloba's mind.

"Ey? Hmm? What?" Pan Zagloba, who loved to have his virtues recognized, couldn't have been happier. "Anyone else would've brought that letter back here before looking at it, and in the meantime that fellow would've had his head stuffed with lead. But not me. Something nudged me as soon as the troopers brought me that paper they found in his pockets. Two of them had gone ahead with lanterns but I called them back. '*Throw a little light on this thing here,*' I told them. '*Let's see what it says.*' Well, I tell you, my head started spinning when I read it. It was as if someone cracked me across the skull with a fist. '*For God's sake,*' I said to Kmita. '*Why didn't you show this letter to us?*' And he says, proud as the Devil to the very end: '*Because I didn't feel like having you see it.*' So I grabbed hold of him and threw my arms around him. '*If it hadn't been for you,*' I told him, '*we'd all have been a heap of crows' droppings by now!.*' And then I had him marched back here again with no more nonsense about executions. I almost killed my horse getting back before him, so I could tell you how close we'd come to killing the man who saved us!"

"Who'll ever be able to understand this man?" observed Pan Stanislav. "It seems there's at least as much good as evil in him..."

★ ★ ★

But before Pan Stanislav finished what he started saying, the doors flew open once more and the soldiers marched in with the silent Kmita.

"You're free," Volodyovski said at once. "And none of us will raise a hand against you as long as we're alive. But why didn't you show us that letter straight away? We wouldn't have put you through all this."

Kmita said nothing and Pan Volodyovski nodded to the soldiers. "Stand aside," he snapped. "Let him go. Go out and mount up."

The soldiers fell back and Pan Andrei remained alone in the middle of the room. His face was calm, although he still looked as remote and indifferent as he had been when the Laudanians marched him out to his execution, and he stared at the assembled officers with haughtiness and disdain.

"You're free," Volodyovski said again. "Go where you want, even if it's back to Radzivill, although it hurts everyone here to see such a fine cavalier helping a traitor against his own country."

"Make sure you know exactly what you're doing when you set me free," Pan Andrei said coldly. "Because I'm telling you here and now that that's exactly where I'll go."

"Why don't you throw in your lot with us?" Pan Zagloba cried. "Let lightning hit that tyrant in Keydany! You'll be our friend and dear companion, and our Motherland will forgive your trespasses against her."

"That'll never happen!" Kmita said, and his voice rang with power and conviction. "God will judge in His own good time who serves our country better, whether its you who start up a civil war, or I who serve the only man who can save our unhappy Commonwealth. Go your way, and I'll go mine! This is no time for converting anybody but I'll tell you this much: it's you who sin against our Motherland. It's you who bar the way to her salvation. I won't call you traitors because I know you're all decent men, and you think you're doing the right thing, but here's the short of it: our country is drowning, Radzivill is stretching out his hand to save her, and you hack at that hand and slander everyone who stands by him and believes in him."

"By God!" Zagloba said. "If I didn't see with my own eyes how steady you were going to your death, I'd think that sheer fright has addled all your wits! To whom did you swear your loyalty as a noble, Radzivill or Yan Casimir? The Commonwealth or Sweden?"

Kmita shrugged.

"I knew it would do no good to talk to you," he said and turned to go. "Keep well."

"Wait just one minute," Zagloba raised his hand and pulled a sheet of paper from inside his coat. "Do you read German?"

"Yes I do," Kmita frowned, impatient. "What of it?"

"Wait, I said. This is a serious matter. Did Radzivill promise you in Keydany that he'd let us live?"

"Yes he did!" Kmita said, raising his head proudly. "You were to sit out the war in Birjhe with the Swedes."

"Then meet your Radzivill, who betrays his own people just as easily as he does his King and his country. This is his letter to the commandant of Birjhe which I took off the officer who commanded our convoy. Read it and see who it is you're serving!"

Kmita took Radzivill's letter and scanned it quickly while sweat broke out all along his forehead and his face flushed with shame and disappointment. At last he clenched his fist around the paper, crushed it as if it was something offensive and unclean, and threw it on the floor.

"Keep well," he said coldly. "I'd have preferred it if you killed me."

And then he turned and walked out of the room.

"There is a real problem with that man," Yan Skshetuski said, shaking his head with pity. "He can't be judged as harshly as we have been doing. It's obvious he believes in Radzivill as blindly as a Turk believes in his Mohammed, though God only knows what could have convinced him. I thought just as you all did that he serves that traitor out of some private ambitions for himself, and to line his own pockets like every other scoundrel, but that's not the case. This isn't a really evil man. He's just misled and terribly confused."

"Well!" Pan Zagloba said. "If he worshiped that Mohammed up to know then I've dug a real hole under that faith of his! Did you see how he jumped when he read that letter? You'd think he'd been stabbed. There's going to be a real fracas when he and his Hetman stand face to face again, because that cavalier is ready to beard the Devil, not merely Radzivill! I'll swear by God's love that nothing makes me happier than saving his life. No, not if you were to give me a whole herd of Turkish thoroughbreds!"

"It's true you saved his life," Pan Tomasz said. "No one can deny that. He'd be as dead as a doornail right now if you hadn't read that letter when you did."

"Let God take care of him," Volodyovski shrugged and turned to more immediate matters. "But we've more urgent problems to decide right now. What's the next thing to do?"

"Be on our way, what else?" Pan Zagloba said. "The horses have had enough of a breather I should think."

"That's it!" Mirski nodded. "The sooner the better! And you, sir,"—he turned to Pan Tomasz—"will you be coming with us?"

"I won't be able to stay here in peace, not for long, that's certain," the old noble said. "I have to go somewhere. But if you're leaving right away... well, then I have to tell you that it's not all that easy for me to gallop off at a moment's notice."

"Radzivill's men can be here by morning," the little knight reminded.

"True. But since no harm happened to that other fellow they won't murder me, or burn me out straight off, and a long journey like that takes some organizing. God only knows when I'll be back, and it's not like there's nothing to be left behind. This and that must be taken care of, the better things must be crated up and hidden, the baggage must be packed and the livestock and equipment sent off to the neighbors. I also have some buried gold I'd like to take along... Hmm, yes, I'd be ready to go by sunrise but not like this, sir. Not at the snap of a finger."

"Well, we can't wait, sir," Volodyovski told him. "We're running on borrowed time as it is and Radzivill's hounds can't be far behind us. But where do you think you might look for refuge?"

"In Byelovyezha, just as you advised. At least I'll be able to leave the girl there while I find a way to make myself useful. I'm not so old that my saber won't come handy to His Majesty and the Commonwealth."

"Then God keep you," said the little knight. "And may He let us meet again in better times."

"His blessings on you all for saving us here," the old noble said. "And we'll meet again. It's likely we'll run across each other on some battlefield."

"Good luck to you, then."

"And to you. God keep you."

They started to say their goodbyes and then each of the departing knights approached Aleksandra to bow to her and wish her happier days.

"You'll meet my wife in the forest, my lady," Yan Skshetuski told her. "And my three boys. Kiss them from me and stay well yourself."

"And give a thought, now and then, to a soldier who maybe didn't have a lot of luck with you, but who's always ready to do what he can to make your life easier," Volodyovski added.

She listened to them all, saying a few quiet words to each of them in turn, and then it was time for Pan Zagloba to give his good wishes.

"Accept an old man's kindest thoughts, little flower," he said. "Give Pani Skshetuska a good hug from me and kiss those little rascals! They're worth a million, each of them!"

Olenka didn't answer.

Instead she took his hand and pressed her warm, trembling lips against it in silence.

Chapter Thirty-six

LATER THAT NIGHT, barely two hours after Volodyovski's detachments rode out of Billevitche, the Hetman himself arrived at the head of a large body of cavalry, fearing that Kmita might have fallen into Volodyovski's hands. Discovering what happened, he swept up Pan Tomasz and Olenka and rode back to Keydany without even giving the horses time to rest.

He was immensely angered by what he heard from the old constable, who told the story in fulsome and painstaking detail wanting to divert the terrifying Hetman's attention from himself. For much the same reason he didn't dare to voice any objections to leaving for Keydany, congratulating himself in secret that the entire storm had blown away so easily. But Radzivill, who suspected the Billevitch patriarch of plotting against him, had too much on his mind just then to remember it.

The escape of Volodyovski threatened to change the entire *status quo* in Podlasye.

Horotkevitch and Yakob Kmita, who stood at the head of the mutineers' anti-Radzivill confederation throughout those territories, were good soldiers and experienced regimental leaders. But they lacked the one essential virtue needed to command Poles and Polish-Lithuanian gentry: they weren't known well enough, nor were they sufficiently admired and respected. In short they lacked *povaga*—which meant everything associated with stature, bearing, dignity and position—and which in turn robbed the entire confederation of authority. But among Volo-

453

dyovski's fugitives rode such men as Mirski, Stankevitch and Oskierka, not to mention the little knight himself, and all of them were famous throughout the army.

Prince Boguslav was also in Podlasye, resisting the confederates with his own household regiments and waiting for help from his uncle, the Brandenburg Elector. But the canny Prussian was taking his time, apparently waiting to see who would come out the winner, and in the meantime Boguslav's opponents grew stronger every day. The Hetman thought of marching down to Podlasye himself, and crushing the mutineers with one dreadful blow, but he had good reason to believe that all of Zmudya would rise to a man against him once he left that country, in which case his own *povaga* would shrink to nothing in the eyes of the Swedes.

He even started wondering if he should abandon Podlasye altogether for a time and summon Prince Boguslav to join him in Zmudya.

Time and need were both pressing. Radzivill was hearing dangerous news from the territories still held against the Russians by the *Voyevode* of Vitebsk. He'd done his best to draw him into his own plans, but Pawel Sapyeha didn't even reply to his letters. Instead, the Hetman heard, he was selling everything he owned, auctioning off his lands and livestock for cash-on-the-barrel, melting down his silverware into coins, and even pawning his carpets and wall-hangings to the Jews so that he could raise new regiments and equip fresh soldiers.

Yanush Radzivill couldn't believe these reports at first: they simply defied his comprehension. Himself tight-fisted and miserly by nature, and quite unable to part with his money for the common good, he couldn't understand how anyone was able to throw away his whole material substance as a wholehearted sacrificial offering to his country's cause.

But time proved these accounts correct.

Sapyeha grew in power every day.

He attracted all the fugitives, all the landed gentry, every patriotic soldier and each man who saw himself threatened by the influence and power of the Radzivills. Worse than that, he also won the loyalties of former Radzivill supporters, and—as if this were not enough—even of the Hetman's own kinsmen such as Prince Michael Casimir, the third most important and influential magnate among the Radzivills. Nothing depressed and enraged the brooding Hetman more than to hear that his cousin Michael deeded all the incomes from his estates to Sapyeha's army, even though most of them lay in the grip of Hovansky's Russians or Zoltarenko's Cossacks.

Everywhere he looked in those days, Radzivill saw disquieting visions. A network of cracks seemed to have burst across the huge structure that his own pride and ambition built in his imagination, and these disruptive fissures were spreading from the foundations themselves. The monument was tottering. It was to have been vast enough to house all of the Commonwealth, Radzivill remembered, but all too soon it proved not enough to contain one Zmudya.

Sometimes, the Hetman thought, he seemed to be wandering blindly in a circle, where each solution only flowed into another problem, and where every difficulty merely became another. Nor was there anything he could see that he could do about it. He could call on the Swedes, who were spreading across more of the country every day, to destroy Sapyeha. But that would be as good as confessing his own helplessness, and that he neither dared to demonstrate nor wanted to admit. Besides, his relationship with Pontus de la Gardie was badly damaged by that Klevany fracas, he knew bitterly, and what had once been a source of inner strength for him, giving him a sense of power beyond his own means, had turned into mutual dislike, ill-will and suspicion.

★   ★   ★

He hoped, setting off to help or rescue Kmita, that he might still be able to catch and crush Volodyovski, and when that calculation also proved to be an illusion he rode back to Keydany with storm clouds in his face.

He was surprised not to meet Kmita on the road that led to Billevitche, and it wasn't until the next day, when he reached Keydany, that he was told what happened. Kmita had come back alone, without his dragoons whom Volodyovski immediately enlisted in his own detachments; and he'd ignored the highway that wound through Plemburg and Eilau, and cut straight across the forests to get to Keydany.

But Kmita was the first man that Radzivill summoned to him after his return.

"Well," he said. "Things didn't quite work out for you, anymore than they did for me. The Constable of Rosyen already told me that you fell into the hands of that little demon."

"I did," Kmita said.

"But my letter saved you?"

"Which letter does Your Highness have in mind?" Pan Andrei asked coldly. "Because after they read to themselves the letter that they found on me, they read me another, the one that Your Highness wrote to the commandant in Birjhe!"

"Ah..."—and a blood-colored mist seemed to spread across Radzivill's gloomy face—"so you know about that?"

"I do!" All of Kmita's shame and disappointment was ringing in his voice. "How could Your Highness do such a thing to me? A common country squire would be ashamed to break his word! So what's to be expected from a Prince and Hetman?"

"Be silent!" said Radzivill.

"No I won't be silent! Because I had to swallow Your Highness' bad faith before those people! They tried to pull me over to their side and I said: '*No, I serve Radzivill. His is the road of reason, decency and virtue.*' So they showed me that other letter. '*Meet your Radzivill,*' they said. And I had to shut my mouth and choke on my shame."

Radzivill's lips started quivering with fury. He felt such an overwhelming craving to twist that irreverent and disrespectful head off its neck that his hands jerked up by reflex to clap for his guard and servants.

Anger blinded him.

Rage choked him.

His breath began to rattle in his throat and an asthmatic seizure clamped around his chest, saving Kmita from the consequences of his own explosion. The Prince leaped out of his chair like a man possessed and stood, beating his arms helplessly against the air, while he gasped for breath. His face seemed to turn black. His eyes were bulging redly. And his throat uttered thick, strangled sounds in which Pan Andrei recognized only a single phrase:

"I'm... choking."

The conflict of emotions that clashed in Pan Andrei was too confused for him to read just then, but he ran for help, got the court physicians, and the next fearful hour passed in their attempts to revive the unconscious Hetman. Kmita stood over him until his eyes flickered open and blinked in recognition.

Then he left the chamber.

In the corridor he came across Pan Kharlamp who had recovered from the wounds and bruises he received in that struggle against Oskierka's mutinied Hungarians.

"What's new, then?" the long-nosed captain asked.

"He's come to himself again," Kmita said, nodding towards the doors of the Prince's chamber.

"That's good. But someday he won't. It'll be a bad day for us, colonel, when that happens, because when the Prince dies we'll be the ones to pay for his actions. The only hope is in Volodyovski who might offer some protection to old comrades in arms. Which is why,"—and here Pan Kharlamp let his voice drop into a whisper—"I'm glad he got away up there on that river."

"Were things that tight for him, then?"

"Tight's not the word for it! Imagine, colonel, there were wolves in those thickets and they didn't get away, but he did! May God bless the man! Who knows if it won't come to catching hold of his coat-tails some day, because our chances are starting to look pretty poor around here. The gentry's getting awfully set against our Prince. They're saying they'd rather have a real enemy on their necks, like a Swede or a Tartar, than a renegade. That's what we've come to! And here the Prince has us hunting down and jailing more citizens each day... which, between you and me, goes against the law and our civil liberties as well..."

Troubled, Pan Kharlamp searched for an example, then remembered: "They brought in the Constable of Rosyen today."

"They did? Today?"

"That's right. Along with his grand-niece. A lady like a flowering almond tree! Let me congratulate you, colonel."

"And where are they quartered?"

"In the right wing, right here in the palace. They've been given very good apartments. The only thing they might have to complain about are the sentries tramping outside their doors. So when's the wedding, colonel?"

"I haven't ordered the band yet," Kmita snapped, putting the long-nosed captain at a distance.

* * *

Kmita left Kharlamp and went to his own quarters. After a sleepless night, the emotional ups and downs of recent events, and his latest confrontation with the Prince, he was so exhausted that he could hardly keep on his own two feet. Added to that was another torment. Just as a bruised and tired body translates every touch into a shard of pain, so his battered mind turned the most innocent questions into suffering. Kharlamp's well-meant query about the wedding, threw him into a bitter contemplation of Olenka's icy silence, and of her pale, tight-pressed lips when his captors were leading him to his execution. It didn't matter whether anything she said could have made a difference, or if Volodyovski would have listened to her appeals and pleading. The fact was she said nothing! Not a single word! And all of Kmita's pain, along with its bitterness and regret, sprung from that very silence, especially since she didn't hesitate to save him twice before.

Was the chasm between them so unbridgeable now, and were the last flickering embers of her love for him so totally extinguished, that she was unable to find an expression of even ordinary human pity and compassion for him? Had he fallen that low in her estimation? The more he thought about it the more cruel Olenka seemed to him, the more bitterness he felt towards her, and the more implacable she appeared.

'*What is it that I'm supposed to have done?*' he asked himself a hundred times over. '*Not even someone excommunicated by the Church and placed beyond the pale is treated with such harshness and contempt.*'

And even if there was something wrong now and then in all the harsh things he'd done while serving Radzivill, how did he deserve the treatment of an evildoer whose every act is designed to serve only himself?

'*I can say with my hand on the sacraments,*' the racked young man thought, '*that I've a clear conscience. That I don't serve for my own advancement, or for private gain, or even for money! I do it because I see the country's benefits flowing from that service. So why am I condemned without a trial and judgment?'*

"Good!" he snarled to himself, finding no other solution to his own self-torture. "Let it be like that if that's how it must be. I won't go begging for penance when I've committed no sin that has to be forgiven. I won't plead for mercy or for understanding!"

But the pain didn't lessen. On the contrary, every new thought merely added to the sum total of his embittering reflections. Back in his quarters, Pan Andrei threw himself on his bed and tried to find some refuge in sleep but even that eluded him in spite of his exhaustion.

At last he got back to his feet and started pacing up and down his room.

"What it is," he told himself aloud, "what this is all about, is that this girl simply has no heart."

And a moment later:

"That's something I didn't expect from you, my lady! May God pay you for it!"

* * *

An hour passed like that. Then another followed. He sat slumped heavily on his bed, nodding his dull, leaden head on the threshold between utter weariness and sleep. But before he could sink into that merciful oblivion, one of the Prince's courtiers summoned him to Radzivill.

The Prince had recovered and breathed a lot easier, but his ashen face showed how close he'd come to his own final judgment. He sat in a deep, leather-covered chair, with a court physician standing near him, but he sent the medic out of the room as soon as Kmita entered.

"I had one foot in the other world already," he told Pan Andrei. "And it was through you!"

"I said what I thought, Your Highness."

"Well. Don't do it again. Don't add to the burdens I'm obliged to carry. And remember that I forgave you where no one else would've been forgiven."

Kmita kept silent.

"If I ordered those men's deaths in Birjhe," Radzivill said slowly, "after I listened to your pleas for them here in Keydany,

it wasn't to deceive you. It was to spare you pain. I let it seem
as if I bowed to your wishes because I've a weakness for you.
But they had to die."

Kmita said nothing and the Prince went on.

"Do you think I do these things for nothing? Do you see me
as some sort of blood-thirsty executioner who slaughters his
own people for the joy of it? When you've lived a bit longer
you'll see that those who want to accomplish something in this
world can't give way to anybody's weakness, especially their
own, and that minor matters can't ever stand in the way of a
greater purpose...

"Those men," he resumed after a pause, "should have died
right here. No, don't interrupt! Look at what your intercession
caused! The spirit of resistance in the country has found a fresh
focus. A civil war is raging. Our friendship with the Swedes has
been undermined, and a bad example was given to others, so that
the rebellion is spreading like a plague. And if that's not enough
for you, there's even more! I had to go after them myself, and
then look like a fool in front of my whole army when they
slipped through my fingers. You almost lost your life. And now
they're free to break out into Podlasye where they will become
the heads of the rebellion...!

"Look and learn!" the Hetman urged, speaking with what
seemed like more regret than anger. "None of this would have
happened if they had died here. But you had only your own
loyalties in mind while you were begging for them. You didn't
think of what they represented in the total context. I sent them
to their deaths in Birjhe because I'm blessed with a greater
vision. I see beyond the obvious because I'm experienced in
politics and government, and because I know that once a man
trips over some small stone, and falls—especially if he was
moving swiftly at the time, with his eyes firmly on the goals
ahead—then getting back on his feet again can be difficult.
Indeed, it might even prove impossible...! Ah, God keep us
from all the harm that those men have done!"

"But how much can they do, sir?" Kmita asked. "Surely they
can't affect all of Your Highness' great plans, or spoil your
far-reaching undertakings."

"You think not? If they did nothing more than cause this

breach between Pontus and myself, it would be an inestimable damage. It's all been explained now, Pontus knows that they weren't acting on my orders, but there's still the matter of his letter to me. That I won't forgive him! He may be the brother-in-law of the King of Sweden, but I doubt that he could become one of mine. He might find a Radzivill threshold too high for him to climb...!"

"Your Highness should deal with the King himself, not with his underlings," Pan Andrei suggested.

"And that's just what I'll do!" The Hetman's face started to darken again with rage and his breathing shortened. "I'll feed some humble pie to that puny, spindly-legged little Swede, if only all my troubles don't gnaw me to death in the meantime. Ah, yes, it might come to that. Who can tell. I've certainly been spared nothing. Ah, it's hard to live like this, I tell you. Who'd believe that I'm the same man I was in the Cossack wars? That I'm the same Radzivill who triumphed at Loyov, Resitz, Mozyr, Turov, Kiev and Berestetchko? All of the Commonwealth stared in awe at me and Vishnovyetzki as if we were twin suns shining overhead! Everyone shook before Hmyelnitzki, and he trembled before me like a leaf! And the same regiments which I led to such astounding victories, in a time of universal calamity and disasters, now turn against me and call me a parricide... a traitor..."

"But surely that's not so!" Pan Andrei said impulsively. "Not everyone deserted Your Highness. You still have people who believe in you!"

"Kind of them," Radzivill hissed bitterly. "Most kind. They trust me until it proves inconvenient for them to trust me any longer. God grant that I don't get poisoned by this kindness. Each one of you stabs me in the back even though few of you realize what it is you're doing..."

"Your Highness should consider the motives, not the words," Kmita said.

"Thanks for the good advice. From now on I'll pay close attention to each squint and grimace I see on the face of every camp follower and hired man-at-arms. I'll go out of my way to win every piddling corporal's approval."

"Bitter words, Your Highness."

"And is life any sweeter? God made me for great things and

here I am, wasting my strength on a county war such as one settlement of the petty gentry fights against another! I wanted to pit myself against reigning monarchs, and I'm obliged to hunt for some little Pan Volodyovski in my own possessions! Instead of stunning the whole world with my power, I'm astonishing it with my impotence. Instead of avenging the ashes of Vilna by burning down the Kremlin, I have to thank you for putting up a few defenses around my Keydany...

"Ah...,"—and the Hetman's huge chest began to heave again as he gasped for air—"I need space... I need room to breathe... I'm strangling with my own inability to command events, not some lung disease. It's my helplessness that's killing me, do you understand? I need room, space, scope... and instead the walls are closing in on me..."

"I too thought that things would turn out differently," Pan Andrei murmured.

Radzivill took some time to regain and control his breathing but the words seeped out of him as if strained through a fissure in a cracking wall.

"Before I reach for any other crown, I have to wear this crown of thorns pressed into my head. I had Pastor Anders cast my horoscope. He tells me the conjunctions are unfavorable but that it'll pass. In the meantime I suffer. I can't sleep at night. Something stalks through my rooms in the dark. I see strange faces peering down at me from the shadows, and sometimes there's an icy chill everywhere around me. That means that Death is near me. I must get ready for new betrayals and desertions, because I know that there are many men around me whose loyalties have begun to shake..."

"No sir!" Kmita said. "There are none like that left, not any more. Whoever was going to desert you has already done it."

"Don't delude yourself. You know full well that all our remaining Poles and Lithuanians are looking for some way out of their commitment to me."

Pan Andrei recalled suddenly what he heard from Kharlamp and found that he had nothing more to say.

"But that's alright," Radzivill said. "It's hard to bear this burden. Hard and even frightening. But we'll survive this trial. Don't tell anyone what you heard from me today, you understand? It would terrify and panic too many shaky souls. It's a good thing I had that seizure earlier in the day because it won't repeat itself for a while, and I need all my strength for tonight's reception. I want to give a great banquet and show myself untroubled and at ease so that everyone around me may feel confident again."

Kmita remained silent.

"Yes," Radzivill resumed. "And you too must show a smiling face. Don't repeat what you heard here. That must stay between us. I said what I did only so that you'll stop adding to my torments. Anger carried me away as well and that's always dangerous. Make sure it doesn't happen again if you want to keep your own head on your shoulders, understand?"

Kmita nodded, still silent.

"Ah, but that's all over. That's all in the past. I've already forgiven your insolence," Radzivill said kindly. "Those little earthworks you've thrown around Keydany, by the way, are first rate. Peterson couldn't have done them any better... Go now and send Myeleshko to me. They've caught some deserters from his regiment today and I want them hanged. We must set a stern example to the others. And make sure to look your most cheerful tonight at the banquet! I want this to be a joyful night in Keydany, you hear? Something the people will talk about and remember!"

Chapter Thirty-seven

PAN TOMASZ BILLEVITCH had a most difficult time with Panna Aleksandra before he induced her to attend the banquet that Radzivill gave that night for his supporters. He had to beg the stubborn and fearless young woman, practically with tears in his eyes, and to convince her that his neck depended on her presence, since everyone—not just the military officers but all the private gentry living within the Hetman's reach—were ordered to be there or risk the Prince's anger. Since that was so, he argued, how could he and she, living quite literally at the mercy of that terrifying man, refuse to be present?

Not wanting to expose her great-uncle to danger, Aleksandra eventually agreed.

The gathering was a large one since many of the country nobles brought their wives and daughters, although most of the banqueters were army officers serving in the foreign, mercenary contingents, who had remained loyal to the Prince. Radzivill himself took great care to look as pleased and carefree as if he didn't have a worry on his mind. He meant his banquet to lift the spirits of his officers and supporters and, at the same time, to demonstrate that most of the country's gentry was firmly on his side, and that it was only a handful of undisciplined and unimportant troublemakers that opposed his union with the Swedes. He wished to show that the entire Zmudyan population was pleased with the new reality so he spared neither costs nor trouble to make the celebration both sumptuous and widely talked about. A hundred pitch barrels blazed at sunset along the

464

road to the castle gates and in the palace courtyard; the cannon thundered with salutes; and the massed soldiers had orders to utter enthusiastic cheers.

A long procession of coaches, carriages, charabancs and *britch-kas* wound into the courtyard throughout the afternoon and evening, bringing their loads of wealthy local landowners from whom Radzivill wanted to extract a loan, but there was also a swarm of such small country gentry that some of them didn't even own a horse. The broad square between the wings of the palace was soon packed with vehicles, horses and crowds of grooms, footmen, coachmen, postilions and lackeys.

A vast throng dressed in brocades, costly furs and velvets filled the so-called Golden Hall of the palace, and when the Prince finally appeared among his guests—glittering from head to foot with precious stones and jewels—the gathered officers shouted in one great voice: "Long live the Prince Hetman! Long live the *Voyevode* of Vilna!"

Radzivill stood before the gathering with a kindly smile on his usually dour and gloomy face which was now also ravaged by anxiety and illness, and his uneasy eyes darted among the nobles to see how many of them would echo his officers' ringing salutation. And when a dozen or so tremulous voices joined this acclamation he started bowing to them all and to thank his guests for their 'sincere and unanimous affections.'

"With your help, gentlemen," he said and then kept saying to anyone who listened. "With your support and faith, we'll take care of those who want to doom the country! God bless you! God bless you!"

And he moved through the vast, brilliantly lighted hall, stopping before men he recognized, or whose names he knew, and showering them with such greetings as 'my dear brother' and 'my dear neighbor' while many glum faces brightened here and there under the warm rays of a great magnate's friendliness and goodwill.

"It just can't be," said some who until then viewed his activities with doubt and suspicion, "that such a great lord would do anything that might hurt the country. So either he had no other choice about it or there's something hidden in all this which will benefit the Commonwealth in the long run."

"We already have less trouble with that other enemy who's none too anxious to challenge the Swedes over us," said others. "God grant that everything should change for the better soon."

But there were others, many others, who merely shook their heads and exchanged cold glances that said as clearly as if the words were spoken: "We're here because we have to be. It was either this or a bullet in the head."

Radzivill cocked his ears to whatever anyone was saying, listening with special eagerness to those who had more to gain from clinging to his coat-tails, who were less determined and easier to mold, and who spoke in especially loud voices so that he could hear them.

"It's better to change a King than doom the country," these flatterers were saying. "Let the Poles take care of their own problems and we'll handle ours."

"Who gave us the example, anyway, if not Vyelkopolska?"

"*Extrema necessitas extremis nititur rationibus!*" someone said.

"That's right!" The loud, eager sycophantic voices reached the Hetman's ears and poured over him like a soothing balm. "Extreme needs call for extreme measures."

"*Tentanda omnia!*"

"Let's trust our Prince and let him do our thinking. Let him rule Lithuania. Let him have the power."

"He's worthy of both. He's our best salvation. If he doesn't pull us out of this abyss then nobody will!"

"He's closer to us than Yan Casimir anyway. This is our own Lithuanian blood we're talking about here."

★　★　★

Radzivill didn't care that these words came from flatterers or cowards, weak men who'd be the first to desert him in any kind of danger, and people who bent like straws before every wind sniffing only for their own advantage. He couldn't hear enough of them. He gulped them down thirstily—indeed, he was intoxicated by them —and soothed both his ambition and his conscience by repeating the one overheard phrase that seemed to justify him best in his own eyes: "*Extrema necessitas extremis nititur rationibus!*"

But when he passed a cluster of nobles grouped around a loud, red-faced squire named Yushtitz, and heard him say: 'He's

closer to us than Yan Casimir,' then the last crease of care ebbed
out of his face. The mere comparison with the King flattered
his sense of his own importance while the completed phrase
opened up vistas of enormous glory and attainable ambitions.

He stopped at once, turned towards Pan Yushtitz, and joined
the group around him.

"You're quite right, dear brother," he said. "Because for
every quart of blood in Yan Casimir's body there's a mere pint
of ours, while I have nothing but Lithuanian blood flowing in
my veins. And if, up till now, the pint gave orders to the quart,
then it's up to you to change that around."

"And we're ready to drink to Your Highness' health by the
quart as well," Pan Yushtitz retorted, flushed with wine and
swaying on his feet.

"You've guessed my thoughts exactly!" Radzivill's voice had
become quite merry. "Enjoy yourselves, dear brothers! I wish
I could invite all of Lithuania here."

"She'd have to shrink a little more for that," said Pan
Zanetzki, a landowner from Dalnov, who was well-known for
his boldness and the sharpness of both his tongue and saber.

"And what do you mean by that?" The Prince eyed him
coldly.

"Only that Your Highness' heart is wider than Keydany," the
glib noble said.

But Radzivill had got the real point and his smile became
tight and forced while some of his pleasure ebbed.

★ ★ ★

Luckily for Pan Zanetzki, the master of the revels distracted
the Prince just then with the announcement that dinner could
now be served and the vast crowds surged towards the same
great chamber in which the union with Sweden was proclaimed.
The chamberlain seated everyone at the tables according to their
rank but it was clear at once, to Kmita as well as to Aleksandra,
that he was using the old seating plan. Otherwise, both he and
she were sure, Pan Andrei would not have found himself between Aleksandra and the Constable of Rosyen.

Both of them felt a tremor when they heard their names
called out together and both hesitated. Only a wish to avoid
avid glances and curious speculations drove them to sit down

beside each other without some sort of protest. Both were upset. Both felt uncomfortable and tried to pretend indifference as if each was seated beside a total stranger. But both of them realized at once that this was quite beyond their means; the usual conversation between accidental dinner partners was out of the question. Each of them knew instinctively that in that broad assembly of differing needs, cravings, longings and emotions, he could think only about her and she about him.

They also knew as surely as if a Last Judgment had ruled on the matter that neither of them could—or wanted—to open his or her heart to the other, and to say honestly and clearly what troubled them the most. They shared a past but they had no prospects of a common future. Old feelings lay in shreds. All they had in common was mutual disappointment with each other, anger and regret. Perhaps they would have been more at ease if that last binding link were finally broken as well, and if neither of them needed to give a thought to the other again, but only time could bring forgetfulness and it was still too soon for that for both of them.

Kmita felt so badly about this, and perhaps about being in that banquet hall as well, that the night became a real torment for him. Yet he knew he wouldn't change the chamberlain's seating arrangement if he could. His ear caught every rustle of her dress. He noted each of her movements while pretending that he noticed nothing. He felt her warmth pulsing at his side and, along with that, a sense of loss mixed with a strange, doomed joy he was unable to express.

After a while he noticed that she too was painfully aware of who sat beside her even though she took care to pretend indifference.

He was seized by an irrepressible need to look at her, and started peering sideways out of the corner of an eye until he caught sight of a clear white brow, eyes hidden under lowered dark lashes, and a pale face untouched by rouge in contrast with the other women. That face held something so magnetic for him, drawing him to her simply by existing, that he felt his heart turn over with pain and pity.

'*How can such bitter hatred live within such angelic beauty,*' he asked himself with sadness and regret. But his resentment was just as deep as his sense of loss so that soon he added: '*There's nothing for me with you. Let someone else take you.*'

And suddenly he knew that if some man took him at his word just then, and asked for her hand, he'd hurl himself upon him and slice him into ribbons. A frightful rage shook him at this thought. He subdued that fury and brought himself under full control only when he remembered that it was he who sat beside her at this table, not some future suitor; and that no one, at least at this juncture, made any formal moves in her direction.

'*I'll just look at her once more,*' he thought. '*And then I'll turn the other way.*'

He shot her one more sideways glance, but she did the same thing towards him in that very instant, and both of them looked down at the plates before them feeling as humiliated as if someone caught them in a sin.

★ ★ ★

Aleksandra was also struggling with her feelings. All recent events, everything Kmita said and did in Billevitche, as well as all she heard there from Zagloba and Skshetuski, showed her that he was not as much at fault as she thought. He was wrong, yes; he was terribly wrong but he wasn't evil and didn't deserve that profound contempt and that immutable condemnation she showed him before.

'*Didn't he save those other decent men from death?*' she had to ask herself.

And, once he fell into their hands, didn't he ignore that letter that might have mitigated a lot of his guilt, or at least saved him from a firing squad...? And what about the way he went to his execution? Without a word, with his head held high, and with a truly heroic indifference and contempt for death?

Brought up by an old soldier, Olenka held contempt for death among the highest virtues. She admired courage. She understood at last that Pan Andrei served the Prince in the best of faiths, believing that his road led to their country's good, so how could she think of him as Radzivill's partner in premeditated treason?

And yet, she knew, no one hurt him as deeply as she did with her accusations. She didn't spare him a single insult. She didn't hide or divert one fraction of her loathing. She didn't want to forgive him even in the moment of his death!

"Make good the harm you've done," she whispered to herself. "Everything is over between us, everything is finished, but let him know that you judged him too quickly and unfairly."

She owed that much to herself, she knew.

But she was just as proud and stubborn in her way as he was in his, so she decided that Kmita most likely no longer gave a hoot about what she thought of him, and an angry flush spread across her cheeks.

"If he doesn't care," she told herself, "then I don't have to care!"

Even so, her conscience wouldn't let her rest. Simple justice told her that injustice had to be made good whether the injured person wanted it or not. But pride, and that included all her disappointments, called for a different course.

'*Whether he's guilty or not, whether he plots with traitors or merely follows them blindly through error and confusion, it all adds up to the same thing in the end: he serves the enemy against his own country. What difference is it if he does it out of stubbornness and stupidity rather than from something far more sinister? He hurts the country either way. God might forgive him but people must condemn him and the name of 'traitor' will stay with him one way or the other. Yes, that's true! And even if he can't be blamed all that much, for whatever reason, what kind of a man is it who can't tell the difference between right and wrong and evil and good?*'

Here anger seized her once more and her cheeks flushed with new disappointment and disdain.

'*I won't say a word!*' she thought. '*Let him suffer. As long as I don't see any repentance in him, I've a right to treat him as he deserves.*'

And she glanced at him quickly as if to see whether some repentance wasn't already visible in his face. It was then that their eyes met and fell, and they sat beside each other as if each of them had done something shameful.

Pan Andrei's face may have been unrepentant but Aleksandra saw such pain and weariness etched across his features that her heart constricted.

He was as drained of color as if he were ill.

Pity replaced her anger.

Compassion filled her eyes with tears and she bowed lower across the table to hide her real feelings.

* * *

Meanwhile the banquet took a livelier turn as the cups and goblets were filled and drained, and refilled and drained again. The earlier low, uneasy muttering began to give way to more spirited conversations, and a better feeling settled among the banquet guests.

At last the Prince rose.

"Gentlemen," he said as if he needed anyone's permission: "I ask for the floor."

"The Prince wants to speak!" loud voices shouted from every side and corner of the hall. "His Highness is speaking!"

"The first toast,"—Radzivill raised his cup—"is to the health of His Most Illustrious Majesty, the King of Sweden, who aids us against our enemies and who won't relinquish control over the country until peace reigns among us once again. Rise, gentlemen, because this kind of toast must be drunk while standing."

All the men rose to their feet. The women remained seated. All the cups were drained but there were no cries or shouts or enthusiastic cheers, as Radzivill wanted or expected. Indeed, he saw that Pan Zanetzki was murmuring something to the men beside him—he was, apparently, jeering at Charles Gustav—and they bit down on their whiskers to keep themselves from bursting into laughter. But his second toast would bring a warmer response, he was sure.

"To my beloved guests!" Radzivill cried out. "To all my dear friends who came here from the far corners of the country to show their trust and faith in Our undertakings!"

"We thank you!" came the thunderous reply. "We thank Your Highness with all our hearts!"

"Long live our Prince!"

"*Vivat! Vivat* our Lithuanian Hector!"

"Long life to him! Long may he live, our Hetman and *Voyevode* of Vilna!"

And here Pan Yushtitz, who had drunk far more than his wits could cope with, staggered to his feet and shouted: "Long live Yanush the First! Grand Duke of Lithuania!"

Radzivill flushed as crimson as a flattered maiden, but he saw at once that the whole vast gathering sat in a stunned and amazed silence, not sure if they should laugh or cheer. So he added quickly: "Even that is in your power, gentlemen. But it's too soon, too soon my dear Squire Yushtitz, to wish me anything like that."

"Long live Yanush the First, Grand Duke of Lithuania!" Pan Yushtitz howled again with the pig-headed stubbornness of a drunken man.

"Yes!" And now Pan Zanetzki rose calmly, cup in hand. "Grand Duke of Lithuania, King of Poland, and Emperor of the Holy Roman Empire," he drawled out, unsmiling.

This time, however, the stunned silence lasted for only a moment, and then a vast wave of laughter swept across the chamber. Everywhere he looked Radzivill saw moist bulging eyes, mustaches that trembled in empurpled faces, open mouths that gasped for new breath, and bellies that couldn't stop shaking. The huge, guffawing laughter boomed against the walls and echoed among the arches overhead and then, as suddenly as it had burst out, it was gone.

A deep silence settled on the gathering again as the gentry caught sight of the fury in the Hetman's face.

"This is no time for jokes, Master Zanetzki," the Hetman grated out, barely able to control the terrifying rage that shook his whole body.

"Who's joking, Highness?" The noble pursed his lips as if he had nothing on his mind but a simple fact. "That's also an elective throne, isn't it? If, as a Polish noble, Your Highness can be elected King of Poland, why shouldn't you become Emperor of the Germans since you're a Prince-Elector of their Empire as well? You have just about as far or near to go with the one as you've with the other. And if there's someone here who doesn't wish you all these well-deserved distinctions, no matter how remote or unlikely they might be, let him stand up and say so! We'll soon cut him down!"

And here he turned his cold, contemptuous eyes on all the other banqueters around him.

"Stand up, anyone who doesn't wish the Imperial German crown for the *Voyevode* of Vilna!"

No one rose, of course.

Neither did anyone feel like laughing anymore because Pan Zanetzki's voice carried so much pointed insolence and malice that everyone started to worry about what might happen next.

★　★　★

But nothing happened. Not then, anyway. Only the last dribblets of pleasure and well-being seeped out of the assembly, and no amount of wine poured by the palace servants could restore the former gaiety.

The banquet guests looked depressed and worried. Radzivill's inflamed features had gone through all the angry colors of the spectrum, but he made a superhuman effort to restrain his fury even though the aim of his banquet was totally destroyed. Pan Zanetzki's ironic toasts stirred up a wave of cynical amusement in all of his guests, suggesting that he had just as little chance of becoming a Lithuanian Grand Duke as a German Emperor, and dwarfed him in the eyes of the more thoughtful gentry.

Everything he hoped to achieve that night turned into a foolish, vulgar joke. The idea of a Radzivill as a sovereign ruler, which was one of the reasons for this costly gathering, was now ridiculous. What's more, Radzivill felt a touch of real terror at the thought that this demonstration of how absurd he was in his deepest cravings, would undermine the faith and loyalty of those officers who had some inkling of his real plans.

Ganhof, he saw, drained one cup after another as if the wine was water and avoided Radzivill's questioning eyes.

Kmita drank nothing.

Instead he stared gloomily at the table as if pondering something and fighting a great inner battle with himself, and Radzivill shuddered at the thought that the unvarnished image of who he was, and what he really wanted, might come at any moment to that quick-tempered, ruthless and incalculable hothead, and illuminate the truth that cowered in the shadows.

And what would happen then?

What would become of his pretended patriotism and love for the Commonwealth when this universally feared officer—who was, without a doubt, the last strong link between the shaky remnants of the Hetman's Polish and Lithuanian regiments and

the Radzivill cause—awoke to the truth, broke that final chain,
and turned against the Radzivills even if it killed him?

Kmita had long become a burden on the Hetman's patience
and, if it wasn't for the strange run of circumstances that gave
him such importance, he'd have paid for his insolence a long
time ago. But the Prince was wrong to suspect him of doubts
or disloyal thinking at that moment, because all that filled Pan
Andrei's mind just then—all that he could think of—was Olenka
and the heart-numbing split between them.

He felt such love and passion for this girl who sat silently
beside him that the entire world dwindled into nothing. And
then, just as strongly, he blazed with such unmitigated hatred
that he'd have gladly killed her on the spot and himself as well.
His life, he knew, had become so tangled and confused on so
many levels, that his simple and straightforward nature didn't
know what to do about it.

He saw himself as some kind of wild and raging animal caught
in a net he didn't understand and from which he couldn't claw
his way to freedom.

The gloomy and uneasy mood of the gathering around him
drove him to the highest pitch of irritation. He didn't think that
he'd be able to stand that dull, grey atmosphere for another
moment.

Meanwhile the banquet turned gloomier by the minute so
that Radzivill's guests began to feel as if they were sitting under
a falling roof that was about to hurtle down upon their heads
with all of its leaden weight.

★ ★ ★

In the meantime a new guest came into the hall. The Prince
threw one look at him and called out: "That's Pan Suhanyetz
from Prince Boguslav! D'you have letters for me?"

"Indeed I do, Your Illustrious Highness," the new arrival
bowed deeply and said. "I've come straight from Podlasye."

"Let's have those letters! You gentlemen,"—and Radzivill
turned his eyes on his silent guests—"forgive me if I read them
in the middle of a celebration. But they might contain news that
I'd want to share with you at once."

Pan Suhanyetz turned over a packet of letters and found his
way to the banquet table, while the Prince began to crack the

seals on the first of the folded papers. Blood flooded into his face once more as he scanned the pages and rage glinted darkly in his eyes.

"Well, here's some news, my friends, that you ought to hear!" he burst out in fury. "Prince Boguslav writes me that those so-called confederates—those *patriots,* if you please, who preferred to mutiny against me than to march with us to avenge the ashes of Vilna—are now engaged in looting my Podlasyan holdings! There's a fine knighthood for you! It's more to their taste to make war on village women, it appears, than to defend their country! But I'll deal with them yet! You can be sure they'll be well rewarded!"

The second letter had an opposite effect. Radzivill barely broke the seal and glanced at the writing when his whole face lit up with triumph and joy.

"The Palatinate of Syeradz has surrendered to the Swedes!" he shouted. "The Syeradz nobles have followed the example of the Vyelkopolians and asked for Charles Gustav's protection!"

And then, shortly after:

"And here's the latest news! It couldn't be better! Yan Casimir has been beaten at Zarnov and Vidava...! His own army is deserting him while he retreats to Krakow with the Swedes hot on his heels...! Boguslav writes that Krakow is sure to fall!"

"Let's drink to that, gentlemen," Pan Zanetzki said in a strange, strained voice.

"Yes, let's drink! Let's celebrate!" the Hetman repeated, having missed the darkly threatening undertone in Zanetzki's voice.

A great joy shined in the Prince's face which, suddenly, looked many years younger. An aura of pride and power seemed to glow around him, bathing his whole body. His eyes gleamed with happiness, and his hands were trembling in anticipation as he ripped open the last of the letters, and then his whole being seemed suffused with light as if he were a sun.

"Warsaw has fallen!" he shouted with overwhelming joy. "Long life to Charles Gustav!"

★ ★ ★

It was only then that he became aware of the effect this news had on the gathered officers and nobles. None of them showed anything like his joy or shared his sense of exaltation and fulfillment. Everyone sat in silence, exchanging worried and uncertain glances. Some men frowned darkly. Others hid their faces in their hands as if plunged in grief. Not even his own courtiers, sycophants and flatterers dared to suggest pleasure at the thought of Swedes marching into Warsaw, of the inevitable fall of Krakow, or of the shameful image of entire provinces falling away from their rightful monarch one after another and surrendering to an enemy without a shot.

Even Radzivill knew that there was something monstrous in that satisfaction with which the commander-in-chief of one half of the Commonwealth's armed forces, and at the same time one of the country's highest civil dignitaries, announced her disasters.

"My dear friends," he moved at once to soothe that harsh and sickening impression. "I'd be the first among you to weep at this news if it meant harm to the Commonwealth. But it doesn't! All it means is that we're changing sovereigns. Instead of the unlucky Yan Casimir we'll have a great and fortunate warrior for our leader. I can already see all our enemies defeated and all our wars brought to a successful end."

"Your Highness is right as always," Pan Zanetzki said. "This is exactly what Radeyovski and Opalinski were saying at Uistye. Drink, gentlemen! Let's be happy! Down with Yan Casimir...!"

His chair fell over with a crash as he rose. He pushed himself away from the table with as much revulsion as if it was something ugly and unclean, and stalked out of the room.

"Bring us the best wines in the cellars!" shouted Radzivill.

* * *

The chamberlain ran to carry out his orders. The banquet hall buzzed with conversation like a great, stone beehive, as the first shock of the news wore away and the gentry started arguing about what it meant. Dozens of men surrounded Pan Suhanyetz, asking for details about the situation in Podlasye and its neighboring Mazovia which was already occupied by the Swedes. In the meantime aged, moss-covered casks were rolled into the room, a swarm of lackeys started knocking out the sealed wooden bungs, the wine started flowing, and moods and humors both underwent a gradual improvement.

More and more voices began to repeat: "It's happened. There is nothing we can do about it." Or: "Maybe it'll all turn out for the best. One has to make one's peace with things as they are."

"The Prince won't let anybody do us any harm!" others assured each other. "We're a lot better off with him than without him, others should be so lucky!"

"Long life to Yanush Radzivill, our *Voyevode*, Hetman and Prince!" others resumed shouting, and Pan Yushtitz, now so far gone in liquor that he no longer saw or heard anything around him, bellowed again: "Grand Duke of Lithuania!"

But no one laughed this time. Nor was there a return to that wondering silence of some moments earlier. Instead, several dozen hoarse but eager throats roared out: "We wish it! With all our hearts and souls we wish it! Long let him live and rule us!"

The magnate rose and towered over them with a face that flushed an almost royal purple, finally hearing what he wished to hear.

"I thank you, my dear friends," he said seriously and gravely.

The hall, in the meantime, had become so hot and stifling with massed candlelight, the fumes of liquor, and the acrid exhalations of human excitement, that its thick air was as suffocating as a Turkish bath. Olenka lost whatever color she had and beads of sweat appeared on her forehead.

"I'm feeling ill," she said to Pan Tomasz, leaning across Kmita. "I want us to go."

"How can we?" the old man whispered, throwing anxious glances at the triumphant Hetman. "What will he think? He'll hold it against us...!"

He was, as Kmita knew, a brave man on a battlefield and a stubborn defender of his rights and privileges, but Radzivill simply terrified him. What's more the Hetman chose this moment to cry out: "I'm happy today! Any man who doesn't drink with me tonight is my enemy!"

"Did you hear?" the old man asked.

"Uncle... I'm really ill," Olenka said in a pleading voice. "I really have to leave..."

"Then go on your own."

Aleksandra rose, trying to slip from the room without attracting anybody's notice, but all her strength was finally drained out of her, she barely managed to get to her feet, and she clutched desperately at the back of her chair.

But suddenly a strong arm went around her waist and held her, close to fainting, on her feet.

"I'll help you," Pan Andrei said.

And neither asking her permission nor caring about it, he lifted her up as if she were a child and carried her outside.

Chapter Thirty-eight

PAN ANDREI INSISTED on seeing the Prince as soon as the banquet ended but Radzivill couldn't spare the time that night. He was closeted behind locked doors with Pan Suhanyetz discussing confidential matters and couldn't be disturbed. But when Kmita returned shortly after daybreak he was admitted to Radzivill's rooms at once.

"Highness," he said as soon as he stood before the Hetman. "I come with a request."

"What can I do for you?" Radzivill asked.

"I can't live here any longer, sir," the distraught young man said. "Every day causes a greater torment. Perhaps Your Highness can think of some mission for me, something that would take me away from Keydany. I hear that some of the regiments are to march against Zoltarenko's Cossacks. Let me go with them."

"Zoltarenko, eh?" The Grand Hetman smiled. "He'd be glad to take another crack at us but he doesn't dare; we're under Swedish protection here. But neither can we go after him ourselves without Swedish help. Pontus de la Gardie is moving troops into the country but he's taking his time about it and we know why, don't we. He just doesn't trust me. But what's the matter? Aren't you happy here in Keydany at my side?"

"Your Highness has been kindness itself to me yet I'm so miserable here that I can't find the words for it. To tell the truth, sir, I thought it would all be different... I thought we'd be fighting day and night, living in smoke and fire. That's what God made me for. That's what I understand. But to sit around

479

day after day listening to discussions, either doing nothing or hunting our own people rather than an enemy, that's as good as death for me! I simply can't bear it any longer. As God's my witness, Highness, it's sheer torture for me."

"I know where this desperation comes from." The Prince nodded briefly. "A sour love affair, that's all. You'll laugh at that kind of torment when you're a bit older. But I saw last night that you and that girl weren't getting along any more."

"I've nothing to give her and she has nothing for me," the young man said and shrugged in resignation. "Whatever existed in the past is gone."

"Ah... And she was taken ill last night, was she?"

"Yes."

The Prince said nothing for a time.

"I told you once and I'll say it again." He shrugged with indifference. "If you want her, take her with or without consent. I'll order a wedding for you today, if you like. Oh, there'll be a few wails and tears but what of it? If she's still crying and complaining on the morning after then there's something wrong with you!"

"I asked Your Highness for a military mission, not a wedding," Kmita answered coldly.

"So you don't want her any longer?"

"No. I don't. And she wants to have nothing to do with me. All I ask is to be sent as far away as I can go and forget everything before I go mad. There is nothing for me to do in Keydany, and empty hands are worse than anything because that's when a man's troubles gnaw at him like gangrene. Please recall, Highness, how badly we all felt last night before the good news came. That's how it is for me all day long, every day, and there is nothing I can do about it! I think my head will crack with all that bitter thinking unless I throw myself into some kind of action! But where? How? God alone can understand these times, or this kind of war, but it is truly more than I can stand. If Your Highness doesn't give me something useful to do soon, I think I'll just go off, collect a band of raiders on the highways, and go to war on my own!"

"Against whom?" Radzivill asked quickly.

"Anybody! I'll go to Vilna and raid Hovansky like I did

before. Let me have my regiment, Your Highness, and the war will start taking a different turn."

"I need your men here," Radzivill said abruptly. "We haven't finished with our internal enemies."

"And that's another point!" Kmita cried. Radzivill was staring at him in a watchful, calculating manner but the young soldier was too desperate to notice. "I can't sit here on my hands, that's like a living death for me, but neither do I want to hunt through the countryside for some Pan Volodyovski, with whom I'd much rather be riding against a real enemy."

"I do have something for you..."

Radzivill paused. He studied the young man before him. His eyes became both piercing and remote.

"No, I won't give you your regiment or let you go to Vilna on your own," he said, shaking his head slowly. "Moreover, if you go anywhere without my permission that'll be the end of your service with me, understand?"

"But I'll be serving our country!" Kmita cried, distressed beyond reason.

"Whoever serves me, serves the country," Radzivill said firmly. "I've already convinced you of that, and don't forget your oath! But if you start acting like a partisan volunteer you'll automatically pass from under my military jurisdiction and you know what is waiting for you in the courts."

"Ah... What do courts mean nowadays." Kmita's shrug suggested more sorrow than indifference.

"Beyond Kaunas nothing, that's true. That country's in chaos. But here, where things are still comparatively peaceful, they function as before. You can ignore the summons if you like, but the judgment will fall on you anyway and the verdict will hold until quieter times. Whoever is once judged and condemned in the courts can expect to be reminded of it many years later, and the Laudanians will make sure that you're not forgotten."

But Kmita didn't respond to this half-veiled threat with the contemptuous shrug Radzivill expected, and the Hetman began to watch him with even sharper eyes.

"To tell you the truth, Highness, I'm ready to accept my punishment when it comes." Kmita's shrug showed quite another kind of resignation. "Maybe I was too ready to fight the

entire Commonwealth just to make my point, or wear my cloak
lined with summonses the way the late Pan Lashtch did it in the
Crown lands. But that's all over now. Perhaps my conscience
never troubled me before but now, for some reason, it's like a
poisoned wound. I don't want to find myself stumbling into
things that lie beyond a man's proper limitations. It's as if there
was some strange, new power that watches all my thoughts and
holds me back from all those old, mindless acts of violence."

"So you've developed scruples, have you?" Radzivill mused
quietly. "A bit late for it, isn't it? But no matter! I told you I
had a mission for you and it's a good and important one. Ganhof
is after me every day to give it to him but he just won't do. I
need a man with an important name, and a Polish one at that, to
show that not all of my wellborn, wealthy gentry has deserted
me. You fit that bill exactly, especially since you're the kind
who'd rather have others bowing to you than do the bowing
yourself, am I right about that?"

"You are, sir. As always. But what is this mission?"

"It's... a long journey."

"I'm ready to leave today!"

"And at your own expense," the Prince added quickly, "because I'm short of money. Some of my eastern lands now feed
Hovansky's Russians, our own mutineers are helping themselves
to my other incomes, and nothing comes in on time. I have to
pay my army these days out of my own pocket! True, I have the
Treasurer of Lithuania under lock and key, but he isn't likely to
give me any money even if he had some! I take whatever public
funds I can but there's not much of it to find, with or without
permission. As for the Swedes, money is the last thing they'd
give to anybody. Their hands shake with avarice whenever they
see a shilling."

"You don't have to explain all this at such length, Highness,"
Kmita said. "If I go it'll be at my expense. I always pay my
way."

"But you'll have to make a real showing over there! You
can't pinch your pennies!"

"I've never done that," Pan Andrei said proudly. "And I
never will."

"That's what I like about you!" Radzivill smiled broadly.
"Ganhof would be scratching at my purse at once but you're a

different sort. Listen, then, to what I have in mind. First you'll
go to Podlasye. It's a dangerous journey because those damned
confederates are raiding my possessions everywhere. It's up to
you how you slip around them. Your kinsman, that Yakob
Kmita, might let you get away, but watch for those others,
especially Volodyovski and his Laudanians."

"They had me once," Kmita both remembered and reminded.
"And nothing happened to me."

"Good. But keep out of their hands anyway. Look in on
Harasimovitch in Zabludov and tell him to squeeze as much
money as he can out of my estates, impose whatever public taxes
he can on everybody else, and send it all to me. But not here!
Tell him to send everything to Tilsit, in the Elector's Prussia,
where all my better furnishings are stored anyway. Let him
pawn everything he can with the Jews—goods, leases, inventory,
everything —and then give some thought to those confederates.
But that's not for you to be concerned about. I'll send him my
own instructions on how to deal with them. You just give him
my letters and then go on to Prince Boguslav in Tikotzin."

★ ★ ★

Here the Prince paused and began to struggle noisily for
breath because even shorter monologues exhausted him quite
quickly in those days, while Pan Andrei leaned eagerly towards
him, anxious to catch every word. The journey, full of unexpected adventures and dangers, promised to be exactly that cure
for his private anguish that he came to ask for.

"I can't understand Boguslav," the Hetman resumed as if
speaking only to himself. "Why is he staying in Podlasye? He
could destroy me and himself as well...! But pay attention now,
because even though I'll be writing to him about all this, it's
essential that you be able to support it with the spoken word and
explain everything that can't be put on paper. Yes, last night's
news was good... but it's not as good as I told the gentry nor as
I thought myself at the time..."

"You mean those letters were untrue, sir?" Kmita asked,
disturbed. "It was all some kind of subterfuge?"

"No, no! It's true the Swedes are winning everywhere.
They've taken Vyelkopolska, Mazovia and Warsaw. The Syeradz gentry surrendered their whole province to them.

They're chasing Yan Casimir to Krakow and they'll lay siege to it as surely as there's a God in heaven... But who can see the future?"

A wry look of anger and distaste spread slowly across Radzivill's gloomy features as if he was contemplating some new antagonist, or perhaps a rival for glory and power, whom he both hated, envied and despised.

"Krakow is going to be defended by Tcharnyetzki, I am told, and he's a good soldier, even though he's nothing more that a fresh-made castellan and so recently appointed to the senate that he hasn't had the time to warm his chair cushion. Wittemberg is an expert at besieging cities and Krakow hasn't even been fortified against him but strange things can happen! That strutting little castellan could hold out for a month or two, perhaps even longer. Such miracles have taken place before, as in the Siege of Zbarajh, for example. He could upset all our calculations if he clings to Krakow long enough."

"How could any one man do that?" Kmita was so convinced of Radzivill's power, wisdom, sincerity and honesty of purpose that even the famous name of Stefan Tcharnyetzki had no effect on him.

"Listen and learn,"said Radzivill. "Start understanding the art of politics on a broader scale. The Austrian Hapsburgs are likely to view the rising might of Sweden with a jaundiced eye and they could come out on Yan Casimir's side. The Tartars too are ready to get behind him, largely because they'd rather have a weak man on the throne of Poland, as they always have, and if they launch an all-out war against the Cossackry and Moscow then all those Polish regiments in the Ukraine will be free to fight against the Swedes! Yan Casimir looks like a ruined man today but tomorrow he can be something altogether different..."

Radzivill had to rest again and Pan Andrei found himself struggling with a wholly new set of contradictions, wondering why he—a Radzivill supporter allied with the Swedes—experienced such a surge of joy at the thought that Sweden's luck might turn.

"Suhanyetz told me how it was in those two battles at Vidava and Zarnov that Yan Casimir lost,"the Prince went on slowly. "It was a close-called thing. Our vanguard, that is to say Yan

Casimir's vanguard,"—he was quick to correct himself—"ground the Swedes into dust, by all accounts."

"But they won? In both places?"

"They did. But only when some of the Crown regular contingent mutinied because they weren't paid in more than a year, while the gentry of the General Levy agreed to take their places in the battle line but refused to fight. Even so, the Swedes showed that they aren't better soldiers than Tcharnyetzki's regulars, and one or two more victories could change everything in Poland. Let Yan Casimir get some gold from Vienna so he can pay his soldiers and he will have an obedient army. Hetman Pototzki doesn't have many troops in the Ukraine, but they're all well-trained, experienced professionals and as fierce as hornets. The Tartars will come with him because they love Tcharnyetzki. And to make matters worse, the Prince-Elector of Brandenburg is starting to have second thoughts."

"In what way, Highness?" Discovering matters he never thought about before, Kmita was suddenly anxious to learn everything.

"Boguslav and I both counted on the Brandenburgers to join us in our Swedish alliance right from the beginning," Radzivill said with a wry shrug and grimace, as if he should have known better than to trust his Prussian relative. But once again it seemed as if he was musing to himself, reviewing his choices, rather than saying anything to Kmita. "We know what the Elector thinks of his allegiance to the Commonwealth."

"So he won't join the Swedes, then?"

"Perhaps... Perhaps not. He's a careful, calculating man and he thinks only about his own advantage. He's keeping his ears down nowadays, sitting as still and quiet as a rabbit in the grass, sniffing the wind and waiting to see which way he ought to jump, and in the meantime he's forming alliances with the Baltic cities which stand heart and soul behind Yan Casimir. I'm dead certain there is some devious purpose to all that. Our uncle Friedrich wouldn't be himself if he kept his word. But he could be harboring some doubts about Charles Gustav's eventual success and that is likely to add to my problems."

The Hetman's labored breathing forced him into another long moment of silence, in which his own suspicions, doubts and disappointments crept across his face like reptiles driven from their muggy shadows into open sunlight.

"Oh, it'll all resolve itself in time," he resumed with a weary shrug. "But for the time being his anti-Swedish alliance with the Prussian cities is a fact! And if the Swedes slip just once in the south of Poland then everything they've taken will simply disappear! Vyelkopolska and Mazovia will rise up against them... the Prussians will follow... and then... and then..."

"Then what, Highness?" Kmita pressed, impatient and suddenly aware that some passing thought had simply terrified the Hetman.

"Then... not one Swede will escape from the Commonwealth alive," Radzivill grated out and went on to murmur: "And then our own prospects will fall just as low as they were high before."

But Kmita had enough confusion, contradictions and challenges on his troubled conscience, feeling as if his faith in his Hetman was about to snap and shatter him as well. He leaped up, his eyes alight with questions and excitement, and with a deep crimson flush spreading across his face.

"What is this, Highness?" he cried out. "What's going on here? Didn't Your Highness tell me himself that the Commonwealth is finished, and that only Swedish help and your own rule could save her? What am I to believe? What you told me then or what you're saying now? And if things really are as you say today, then why are we still standing with the Swedes? Why aren't we fighting them with everything we've got if the Commonwealth can be saved without them?"

Radzivill stared grimly at the trembling young man and then his own sunken eyes glittered with dangerous fires.

"You're being insolent!" he warned.

But Kmita was too distressed to care, as if his quick and volatile instincts were a wild horse snapping its ropes and traces and sweeping him away.

"We can talk later about what I am!" he cried out. "Now I want an answer from Your Highness!"

"This is my answer, then," Radzivill said slowly, stressing every word. "If... things turn out as I said they could... then we will fight the Swedes."

"I'm a fool!" Kmita cried and slapped his open palm against his own forehead.

"That I won't deny," Radzivill said coldly. "And I'll add that your impertinence is fast approaching the limits of my patience. Know this much more: I'm giving you this mission precisely so that you can assess the situation for me, do you understand?"

Kmita nodded, waiting.

"All I want is our country's good, nothing more," Radzivill breathed deeply. "What I just told you is merely speculation. It need never happen, and most likely, won't. But great affairs call for care and caution! If you want to save yourself from drowning you have to learn to swim, and if you're walking through a trackless forest you have to stop now and then and check your direction... is that finally clear?"

"As clear as sunshine, Highness."

"All right then. We can recant our commitment to the Swedes if that's what the country's good demands. But we won't be able to do that if Prince Boguslav stays in Podlasye much longer! I can't understand it! Has he lost his head? Sooner or later he'll have to choose one side or the other if he is down there and it would be the worst thing of all if he were to do so at this time!"

"I must be really stupid, Highness!" Kmita cried out again. "Because once more I can't understand your reasoning!"

"Podlasye lies next to Mazovia, am I right? And just south of the Elector's Prussia?"

"Yes, Highness!"

"So either the Swedes will occupy it all or the Prussians will reinforce it against the Swedes, do you follow me?"

"As if with a lantern!"

"So either way, if Boguslav is still sitting there, he'll have to make an open choice, is that also clear?"

"Yes, Highness. But why shouldn't he declare himself openly?"

"Because the longer he stays uncommitted the more important we are to both sides. Furthermore, if it comes to our turning on the Swedes, he'll be able to serve as my connection to Yan Casimir, which he would never be able to do once he declared himself firmly behind Charles Gustav. And because he won't be able to avoid declaring himself in Podlasye one way or the other, let him go north to Prussia, to our estates in Tilsit, and do his waiting there! The Elector is careful to stay in

Brandenburg these days so Boguslav will be the highest dignitary in Prussia. He can take command of the Prussians—and that means all those rich Hanseatic cities—raise a large new army and help me to expand my own, and put himself at the head of a powerful coalition that will have everybody knocking on our doors! That way our House will not merely survive but acquire new greatness... and that's all that matters."

"Your Highness said that it's our country's good that matters the most," Kmita interrupted.

"Don't seize on every careless word I utter!" Radzivill snapped, annoyed. "I've told you already that all these things are one! Prince Boguslav signed the Act of Union with the Swedes right here in Keydany but he's managed to make himself appear as my unwilling partner. And that's good. I want him, and you too, to spread the word that I forced him to it. That could help him make contact with those confederates; maybe invite their leaders to a conference and then seize them and carry them off to Prussia. We must do something about those people before they ruin our country altogether!"

"Is that all that I have to do?" Kmita asked with some disappointment.

"No! That's the least important part. After you've seen His Highness you'll go with my letters to Charles Gustav himself. I can't deal with Pontus de la Gardie since that Klevany massacre by Volodyovski. He keeps watching me as if I were some kind of criminal, and he's quite certain that I'll turn on the Swedes just as soon as they trip up somewhere and the Tartars throw themselves on Russia and the Cossacks."

"Judging by what Your Highness has just told me he is right to think so," Kmita said.

"Right or wrong I'm sick of it!" Radzivill burst out. "I don't want him peering into my hands to see what cards I'm playing, and besides, he's personally obnoxious to me. He's sure to be writing all kinds of things against me to the King, namely that I'm either too weak to matter or too untrustworthy to believe, and I want that stopped. If the King asks you about that Klevany business you can tell him the full unvarnished truth. You can even tell him that you begged me for the lives of those perpetrators whom I condemned to death before they caused that trouble. Your honesty will sound most convincing. Don't worry, the Swedes won't do you any harm. They might even like your devotion to your friends."

"I don't much care what they like," Kmita said abruptly. "I am not doing any of this to please them."

"Don't say anything directly against Pontus de la Gardie," the Hetman cautioned. "He's married to Charles Gustav's pet sister, after all. But if the King should ask you what people are saying around here about our falling out, you can say that the whole country is troubled by the fact that Count Pontus shows such small appreciation for their Hetman's loyalty to Sweden, and that the Prince himself—that is to say myself—is most upset about it. Then, if he asks if it's true that I've been deserted by all my regular soldiers, tell him it's a lie and cite yourself as the best example. You're a full colonel so use your rank and titles. Say that it was only Pan Gosyevski's clients and supporters who mutinied against me, but add that I've got him safely in my hands. Tell the King that if Count Pontus would only send me some artillery and a few regiments of heavy cavalry I'd scatter those confederates like chaff before the wind, and say that this is also something that everyone is saying."

"And is that all, Your Highness?"

"Yes. No." Again Radzivill seemed to have forgotten that he wasn't speaking only to himself. "Other than that, watch and note everything around you, keep an open ear to what is being said near and around the King, and keep me constantly informed through Prince Boguslav in Tilsit. You can use the Elector's courier service for that if you come across it. I hear you speak German?"

"Yes, I do. I had a Courlander for a comrade once, a man named Zendt whom the Laudanians murdered. He taught me a fair German. I've also been often up north, among the Estonians, and they all speak German so I've had some practice."

"Excellent," the Prince said.

* * *

One thing remained to be determined, the current whereabouts of the King of Sweden, but here Radzivill wasn't very helpful.

"You'll find him where you'll find him. He can be anywhere

during a campaign. If you have to look for him near Krakow
it'll be all the better because I've some other letters for delivery
in that part of Poland."

"So there is someone else for me to visit?"

"That's right. You must get to Pan Lubomirski—the Marshal
or Lord High Constable of the Crown, as he likes to be addressed—whom I'd dearly like to draw into my plans. He's one
of the most powerful magnates in southern and south-western
Poland, as proud and jealous of his prerogatives as anyone in the
country, and with vast influence throughout Malopolska. A
great deal could depend on him in those parts. If he went over
wholeheartedly to the Swedes then there'd be nothing more for
Yan Casimir to do in the Commonwealth, do you follow?"

"Yes."

Kmita frowned and nodded.

"Let Charles Gustav know that I'm sending you to Lubomirski," the Hetman went on, "to pull him over to the Swedish side.
That ought to make him more than grateful to me. But don't
boast about it. Just let it slip out in conversation, as if you were
saying more than you intended. God grant that Pan Lubomirski
takes his place beside us! Oh, he'll hesitate, I know that. But I
also know what drives him. His vanity will prod him to remain
the only great lord still loyal to Yan Casimir. But I expect that
my letters will tip him to our side because there is a very special
reason why he'd want to oblige me at this time."

"A reason, Highness?"

Pan Andrei listened, attentive as ever, although all this plotting and conniving was making him dizzy.

"Yes." Radzivill's shrug showed both indifference and disdain. "I'll tell you what it is so that you'll know how to pull
Lubomirski's strings. It's been a long time now since he started
trotting in circles around me, like a hunter trying to pin down
a reclusive bear, to sniff out from a distance just how I would
feel about giving my only daughter to his son in marriage. They
are still children but we could arrange it for the future, which is
something His Lordship is after far more anxiously than I because there isn't a greater heiress in the Commonwealth. If our
two fortunes were to come together there wouldn't be another
like it in the entire world! And what if Lubomirski should

suddenly conclude that his son, married to my daughter, could inherit a ducal throne here in Lithuania? I think he'd choke on his own anxiety, trying to arrange it... Wake that hope in him and he'll take the bait because his House and his own grandeur have always mattered more to him than the Commonwealth."

"What am I to tell him?"

"That which I mustn't write. God help you if you let it slip that you heard me speak of a crown for myself. Any kind of crown. It's far too soon for that. But say that all the gentry in Zmudya and Lithuania are talking about it, that the Swedes make loud mention of it, and that you heard it said near the King himself. Find out which of his courtiers has the marshal's ear and suggest to him that if Lubomirski declared for the Swedes he could expect his son, Heracles, to marry the Radzivill heiress. And if the Lubomirskis then supported me for the Grand Ducal throne here in Lithuania that too would come to Heracles in time. Then take it a step further. Let slip the idea that once young Lubomirski is Grand Duke of Lithuania then, in time, he must be called to the Polish throne as well, and so the two crowns would come together in both of our Houses."

"But,"—and again Pan Andrei felt a wave of distraction and confusion—"isn't that something that Your Highness has reserved for himself?"

"Yes. No." Radzivill made another irritated gesture. "What you tell Lubomirski's people isn't necessarily what is going to happen! But if they don't seize this opportunity with both hands then they're far smaller then they've a right to be for the power they hold."

Kmita shook his head, led into areas of deviousness and cunning that were far beyond him, and the Hetman continued in a loud, harsh voice:

"Whoever doesn't set his sights high enough, or whose vision if too puny to grasp a grand design, can content himself with a Marshal's staff or a Hetman's baton, or some piddling little castellancy! Let him bend his neck all his life as somebody's servant, earning his master's smile through the goodwill of court favorites and attendants, because that's all he's worth! God made me for another purpose and that's why I dare to reach for everything a man can achieve and go as far as a human being is able to do!"

*   *   *

And here the Prince stretched out both his hands as if he wished to clutch some royal diadem that only he could see, and his flushed, impassioned face glowed as redly as a flaming torch. But his emotions tightened in his throat, he gasped for air, and his breath thickened in another paroxysm of choking.

"Ah," he resumed after a time in short, broken phrases. "When the soul soars... as if to the sun... the sick body says its *memento mori*. Let it all happen as it may. I'd rather die a King then live as a servant."

"Should I get a surgeon?" Kmita asked.

"No need." Radzivill made a brief, dismissive gesture. "No need. I'm already better. Well... and that's just about all that I had to tell you. Be sure you keep your eyes and ears open. Watch and see what the Pototzkis have in mind to do. They too are powerful, faithful to the Vasas, and always stick together. And nobody can tell which way the Konyetzpolskis and Sobieskis might go... Watch and learn. Ah... the breathlessness is over... Have you understood everything I said?"

"I have. Everything is clear. If I commit any error it'll be my fault."

"Most of my letters are already written. There are only a few more to finish. When do you wish to start?"

"Today! As soon as possible!"

"And is there something else I can do for you?"

"Your Highness..." Kmita began and then cut it short, unable to go on.

"Speak out!" the Hetman said. "You've nothing to fear."

"I'd be grateful,"—Kmita was struggling for selfcontrol and calmness—"if the Constable of Rosyen... and his grand-niece... were protected here."

"You can count on that. But I see that you still love that girl, eh?"

"I don't know!" said Kmita. "Is there a way to tell? I love her for one hour and hate her for the next! Maybe the Devil can tell what it's all about but it's too much for the likes of me. Everything is finished for us, as I said, there's only this awful suffering... But, even so, I don't want another man to have her. Don't let that happen, Highness! Ah, forgive me, sir... I don't know what I'm saying any longer... It's time for me to leave and the quicker the better! Please forgive this babbling. I'll get my wits together again as soon as I'm through the gates."

"I understand the feeling. Love cools with time, but until it does jealousy burns like fire. But be at ease about it. I won't let anyone come near her and I don't intend to stir out of Keydany. It won't be long before this whole countryside is full of foreign soldiers and too dangerous for travel. The best thing I could do is send her to Taurogen, near Tilsit on the Prussian border, where my wife is staying. So put that worry from your mind, Andrei! Go now, get ready for your journey, and have dinner with me before you leave."

★ ★ ★

Kmita bowed and left and Radzivill began to breathe steadily and deeply. He was glad that Kmita would soon be out of mind as well as out of sight. His name and regiment remained at the Hetman's service but his volatile and incalculable person was best far away.

Kmita had long become a burden to him in Keydany, the Prince-Hetman knew. Gone, he could render very useful service, but the Hetman was far more certain of him out of sight and reach than closer to hand, where his quick-triggered temperament and unstable nature could set off an explosion at almost any time with incalculable consequences for them both. His leaving was like a guarantee of his loyalty and the Hetman's safety, and Radzivill could breathe with relief.

"Go, you wild Devil and serve me at a distance!" he muttered, and stared with cold dislike at the door which closed behind Pan Andrei.

Then he summoned a page and ordered him to invite Ganhof to the Prince's chambers.

"You'll take over Kmita's place at court and his military command as well," he told the German colonel. "You'll also command all my cavalry."

"And Kmita, Highness?"

"He's going away."

A swift gleam of pleasure ran across Ganhof's icy features.

The mission he had hoped for had gone to another. But he had a far higher rank instead.

He bowed in silence.

"I'll thank Your Highness through faithful and obedient service," he murmured. Then he stood and waited.

"Is there something else?" the Prince asked.

"Yes, Highness. A nobleman from Vilkomir arrived here today. He tells us that Pan Sapyeha is marching against Your Highness with an army."

Radzivill quivered slightly but brought himself at once back under control.

"You can go," he nodded to Ganhof.

Then he sat deep in thought.

Chapter Thirty-nine

IT RAINED FOR THE REST of that day. Pan Andrei was anxious to get started, before nightfall if possible, as soon as the weather cleared and, in the meantime, he set about preparing for the journey and picking his escort.

He wanted to go well attended; first for his own protection on the road, and then to add to his stature as the Prince-Hetman's envoy. He settled finally on six of his best troopers, old Orshan roughnecks who rode with him in those simpler days when he fought his lone guerrilla war against Hovansky's Russians, and who would follow him to the ends of the world if that's what he ordered. All of them were Ruthenian petty boyars or rough-and-ready Polish border gentry, and they were also the last of that powerful company of ruffians whom the Butryms exterminated in his raid on their settlement. Leading them was Sergeant Soroka, an old retainer of the Kmitas and a first-rate soldier, who had his own collection of court verdicts hanging over him, stemming from even more numerous transgressions.

After his noon meal in the Hetman's chambers, Pan Andrei took charge of Radzivill's letters and also the passes for Swedish commandants in the major cities. The Prince sent him off with a show of almost fatherly concern, saying his goodbyes with an quite extraordinary warmth and cautioning him to be both shrewd and careful.

In the meantime the sky began to clear above Keydany by evening. A pale Autumn sun appeared and slipped behind the low-lying, crimson clouds that stretched in long ragged strips towards the west. There was nothing left to delay the journey. Kmita was drinking his stirrup cups with Ganhof, Kharlamp and a few other officers at twilight in his quarters when Sergeant Soroka came in to ask when they would be starting.

"In an hour," said Kmita.

"The men and horses are ready, commandant," the old sergeant said. "We're waiting in the courtyard."

The sergeant left and the wine flowed faster although Kmita pretended to be drinking more than he did in fact. The wine did nothing for him; it neither raised his spirits nor improved his humor, although his companions were well on their way to intoxication.

"Remember me to Prince Boguslav, colonel," Ganhof urged him warmly. "He's a great cavalier. You won't find another like him in the Commonwealth. It'll be like you're in France when you get down there."

"Down where?"

"To his court. They speak a different language, they have different customs, and a man can learn more about courtly usage among his attendants than he'd do beside Kings."

"I remember Prince Boguslav at Berestetchko," Kharlamp reminisced. "He had a French dragoon regiment like none I've ever seen. The officers were all Frenchmen or Hollanders and the troopers were mostly from France. Each time they killed someone they said '*Pardonnez-moi.*' And if you were ever downwind of them you'd swear you were passing an apothecary's shop, there was such a strong smell of perfumes and pomades. The prince rode among them with a handkerchief draped on his rapier hilt, always smiling no matter how hot the fighting got, because that's the French fashion, don't you see, to laugh during bloodshed. Some of the older soldiers sneered at him a little, because he wore rouge and powder and because his eyebrows were darkened with charcoal. His dressers brought him fresh collars and laces after every charge so that he'd always look his best, and they curled his hair with hot irons into fancy ringlets. But there was nothing womanly about him in combat. He was the first into the thickest of the fighting. He also challenged Pan Kalinovski to a duel because of something Kalinovski said, and His Majesty himself had to mediate that quarrel."

"Yes, yes... you'll see some worthwhile sights," Ganhof said.

"You'll see the Swedish King himself, and he's the greatest warrior in the world after our own prince."

"And you might see Tcharnyetzki!" said Kharlamp, who was beginning to forget where he was and what he was saying. "People are talking more and more about him."

"Tcharnyetzki stands with Yan Casimir," Ganhof reminded grimly. "And that makes him our enemy."

"Strange things... strange things," Kharlamp mused, half asleep and nodding over his goblet. "If someone said a year ago that the Swedes were coming, we'd be getting ready to fight them, what? And now look what's happened..."

"The whole Commonwealth received them with open arms," Ganhof said. "Not just we alone."

"That's right," Kmita said, deep in thought and not really listening. "That's the truth."

"Except for Pan Sapyeha, Pan Gosyevski, Pan Tcharnyetzki and both the Crown Hetmans," Kharlamp threw in.

"It'd be better not to mention that," Ganhof warned uneasily. "The walls have long ears. Well, colonel,"— and he turned to the thoughtful, preoccupied Kmita—"come back to us in good health. There'll be important promotions waiting for you here..."

"And the Billevitch lady," Kharlamp added.

"You keep your long nose well away from the Billevitch lady, Mister!" Kmita snarled.

"Of course I will. Why not? I'm too old for anything like that. Hmm... the last time I fell in love... when was that? Must've been during the election of our Merciful Majesty, King Yan Casimir..."

"You'd better get your tongue used to a different name," Ganhof reminded sourly. "Our King is now Charles Gustav!"

"Ah, that's right! How did I forget? Alright then, so it was during the election of Yan Casimir, our former King and sovereign. I fell head over heels for a young lady in the household of Princess Grizelda, wife of the late Prince Yeremi Vishnovyetzki. A cunning little creature she was too. But every time I wanted to get closer to her Pan Volodyovski popped up in the way. I was supposed to fight him over her except that Bohun, that famous Cossack hero, claimed his first attentions. Pan Michal gutted him like a rabbit for the roasting spit, which is just what would've happened to me if I ever fought him, but in those days I'd have picked a fight with the Devil himself! Ha, hmm... that's how thing were in the good old days... I would've dried up like a twig over that little sweetheart, if it wasn't for a certain remedy I was told about..."

"You have a remedy?" Pan Andrei asked quickly.

"The best. I'd have died without it, there's no doubt about that. I couldn't eat or drink or sleep or anything until His Highness sent me away from Warsaw. I had to go all the way to Smolensk, and I shook all that affection out of me on the way! The first mile made the going easier and by the time I reached the Vilya River, up around Vilna way, she'd flown right out of my head, and I stayed a bachelor ever since. There's nothing like a long trip to cure an unhappy love affair."

"You're sure about that?" Kmita wished to know. "A long trip will do it?"

"As I live and breathe! Let Beelzebub carry off every pretty face in Poland and Lithuania! I don't need one of them anymore!"

"And you went off just like that, without a goodbye?"

"That's right! No goodbyes! I just threw a red ribbon behind me, which is something I heard from an old woman who had a lot of experience in matters of the heart."

"Your good health, colonel," Ganhof interrupted, drinking to Pan Andrei.

"And yours," Kmita said. "Thank you with all my heart."

"Drink it down! To the bottom!" all the others cried. "It's time for you to be on your way, colonel, and we too need to get back to our duties. May God keep you, sir, and bring you back safely!"

"And you keep well too!"

"Throw a red ribbon behind you," Kharlamp urged. "Or pour a bucketful of cold water on your first campfire after you've halted for the night. Remember, that's the surest way if you want to forget..."

"Stay with God, my friend!"

"And you... and you... It'll be a long time before we see each other again."

"It might be on some future battlefield," the normally expressionless and icy Ganhof added with some warmth. "Let's hope we'll be fighting side by side and not against each other."

"It couldn't be any other way!" Kmita said.

And the officers departed.

★ ★ ★

The clock in the palace tower clanged seven times, ringing out the hour; outside, the horses pawed the stone pavement slabs with their iron-shod hooves and, through the windows, Pan Andrei caught a glimpse of his men all buttoned-up and mounted and ready to ride out. But an odd, uneasy feeling of alarm settled on the troubled young soldier as he thought about this journey into the unknown.

"I'm going, I'm going away at last," he told himself as if not quite able to believe it.

Strange lands and crowds of even stranger faces passed before him in his imagination and, at the same time, a rare sense of worry weighed down on him suddenly as if he'd never given any thought to this longed-for journey.

"Time to mount up and go," he muttered, ill at ease and gnawed by an anxiety he didn't understand. "Let things come as they may... what will be will be."

But now that the horses were whinnying and snorting in the cobbled courtyard, and the hour of departure was finally upon him, he felt that this new, distant life that was opening up before him would be altogether different from anything he knew, and that all he understood and cared about—everything that had become a part of his being—would stay behind in this country, these surroundings and this familiar town. The old Kmita would also stay behind and the man who rode away would be someone new, just as strange and unknown to everyone he met as they would be to him. A wholly fresh life would start for him over there and God only knew if he had the energy and interest to make something of it.

Pan Andrei was as profoundly heartsick as if his mind and soul were drained of thought and feeling. Somehow—and he had no idea when or how it happened—he'd lost control of his life. He'd become a distraught observer of his own past and present, and that's why he felt helpless to do anything about his own future. He was bitterly unhappy where he was right now and doubted that anything would change for him anywhere else. If it did, he thought, it would probably just turn for the worse.

But time was passing.

It was time to go: time to slap his cap on his head and be on his way.

But how? Without even telling her goodbye?

Could he actually do this? She was so near and soon she'd be so far away. Was it possible to vanish without a word? '*So that's what we've come to,*' he thought bitterly. '*That's where our paths have brought us.*' But what was he to tell her? '*Everything's gone sour for us,*' he could say. '*So you go your way, milady, while I go mine, and let each of us forget the other existed.*'

But why bother saying it when it was a sad, regretful fact with or without speaking? He wasn't her fiance anymore. She was no longer his future wife. Nothing that anyone could say would repair the damage. Everything they once had together was gone, ripped to shreds and tossed away like garbage, and nothing would ever mend it or restore it. So why add to the unhappiness with fresh words? It was a waste of time.

'*I won't go to see her,*' he thought. '*Let it ride. It's all best forgotten.*'

But, on the other hand, they were still linked together by a dead man's will. He should tell her clearly and without any bitterness and ill-feeling: '*You don't want me, so feel free of any obligation to me. Let's both act as if there never was a last will and testament that bound us together. Let each of us look for new happiness elsewhere.*' That, he thought, was the least he could do for her and for himself as well.

But what if she merely shrugged and said: '*Why are you telling me something I already know? I've said this to you a long time ago!*'

"I won't go!" Kmita said again. "To Hell with it all!"

He jammed his cap on his head and went out into the corridor, heading for the courtyard. What he wanted then was to be on his horse and far beyond the gates as fast as he could do it.

* * *

But something happened to him in that long stone passage. It was as if a huge fist seized him by the hair and hurled him towards the palace wing that held the constable's apartments, so that he stopped thinking, gave up all the processes of argument and reason, and ran pell-mell with closed eyes, oblivious of direction, as if he were about to throw himself into deep, dark water.

Before he knew it he was at the Billevitches' door, with no idea how he got there in the first place, and he almost bowled over the old constable's serving lad who was coming out.

"Is the constable in his quarters?" he asked.

"His Worship is with the officers in the barracks," said the lad.

"And the lady?"

"The lady is here."

"Go in and tell her that Pan Kmita is leaving on a journey and wants to say goodbye."

The boy obeyed but before he could come out again Kmita pressed the door handle and entered without permission.

"I've come to say goodbye to you, milady," he said, "since I don't know if we'll see each other again." Then, irritated by his own formality, he turned on the servant. "What are you still doing here?"

The boy bowed and left.

"My lady," Kmita went on desperately, when the doors closed behind the lad. "I had it in mind to leave without a word but I just couldn't do it. God only knows when I'll be back, or even if I come back at all because misadventures are easy to come by on a trip like this. But it seems to me it's best not to risk His anger by parting with bitterness or resentment in our hearts."

She stared at him, both wide-eyed and startled, and he pressed on blindly, feeling as if his heart was about to crack wide open with regret.

"There's so much to say... ah, so much... but there just aren't enough words to say it, d'you know what I mean? We had no luck, that's all. God's will wasn't with us, and where that fails a man might as well try knocking down a wall with his head, for the good it'll do him. The best we can do is stop blaming each other. Let's just forget about that testament because, as I said, a man's will is useless when God wills otherwise. Let Him give you other happiness and peace. The main thing is for us to forgive each other."

He pushed on, too distraught to notice how pale she'd become.

"I don't know what's waiting for me out there where I'm going." His blunt, rushing words spilled out of him as if they had acquired a life of their own. "But I can't stand it here any longer. In this torment! This anger and resentment... A man rattles between his own four walls day after day and can't find an answer or a cure! There's nothing to do here except wrestle with my own thoughts until it seems like my head is going to explode, but all it leads to is just more pain and anger. I need this journey like a fish needs water, or like a bird needs air, or I'll go stark crazy."

"May God give you some peace and happiness as well!" Aleksandra answered.

She stared at him as if stunned by his announced departure, by his distraught appearance and his wild words as well. A startled and confused mixture of emotions passed across her face and it was clear that she too was struggling for control over her jumbled feelings.

"I... don't feel any bitterness towards you," she said at last.

But he was too carried away by his own sense of loss to notice her sudden agitation.

"I wish to God that none of this had happened!" he cried out. "Some kind of evil spirit pushed his way between us and spilled a sea of differences to keep us apart. There's just no way to wade through all that water or to swim across it. Ah, I don't know what this is all about! A man didn't get to do what he wanted, or go where he was heading, as if something pushed him into things beyond his control, and now we've both come to a place from which there's no returning. But if we can't go on the rest of the way together, than let's at least cry out '*God be with you*' and wish each other well...

"Anger and resentment are one thing," he went on. "But sorrow is another. I've got rid of the anger, I want you to know that, but the bitterness just won't let go of me and I don't know whom to blame for it. I don't blame you, that's certain. Thinking about it won't do any good, but it seems to me that it'll all go easier for us both if we talk it out. You think me a traitor and that torments me more than anything, because I swear to you on my soul's salvation, that I've never been a traitor and I never will be!"

"I no longer think that," Olenka replied.

"But how could you think it even for an hour?" His voice shook with bitterness no matter how he struggled to suppress it. "You knew me. You knew what I used to be before, always ready for some mindless folly, I admit. To cut-up someone in a fight or shoot him, or set fire to something, is bad enough in its own way, but to commit treason for profit or promotions? Never! God strike me dead right now if it ever even crossed my mind! You may not have thought things out deep enough to know how to save our country, so why did you condemn me? Why brand me a traitor?"

Again, the terrible struggle he was fighting with himself threatened to burst into sudden fury, but Kmita crushed it and beat it down with all that ruthless strength that she both feared and admired in him.

"God knows I don't hold that against you like I used to," he said finally. "You did what you did and let God judge it like He does everything in us all. All I'll say about it is that only Radzivill and the Swedes can save us, and that it's those who think and act otherwise who are wrecking and threatening the country. But this is no time for arguments or debates. I have to be leaving. I just want you to know that I didn't sell myself to anyone, that I'm not a traitor, that I'd rather die than ever become one, and that you were wrong to despise me and condemn me like you did! I swear this to you with the last words that'll pass between us, and I'm only saying it to let you know that I've forgiven you completely, just as I want you to forgive me in return!"

But his long, impassioned plea gave Aleksandra the time she needed to come to herself.

"What you are saying, that I was wrong to judge you, is quite right," she said, struggling to control the tremor in her voice. "That's my fault... I acted without thinking... and I ask you to forgive me for it..."

Her voice broke despite all her efforts, and tears gleamed in her stricken eyes; and he, in turn, brought to the highest pitch of his own emotions, shouted out: "Forgive you? Of course I forgive you! I'd forgive you my own death if that's what you ordered!"

"May God guide you," she said with as much sincerity and

longing as if offering a prayer. "And may He help you find the right road instead of the one you've taken."

"Enough!" Kmita cried out. "Enough! I don't want another quarrel starting up between us! Whether I'm right or wrong, don't talk about it anymore! Let everyone act according to his conscience and may God judge the rest. I'm glad I came here to see you before leaving..."

And here his own voice broke and grief began to choke him.

"Let me at least kiss your hand once more," he cried, over-whelmed with sorrow. "To say goodbye... That much is still mine, isn't it? I won't see you tomorrow. Or the day after. Or in a month. Who knows, maybe never. Ay, Olenka! Nothing makes any sense to me anymore... Are we really never to see each other again?"

The tears she had fought to hold back spilled out of her eyes and ran as thickly as a handful of pearls down her pale cheeks.

"Andrei!" she cried. "Abandon the traitors and everything can still be like it was...!"

"Quiet! Quiet! Enough!" Kmita stammered out in a cracked, stricken voice. "I can't. That can't happen. I wish I could die and end all this torment...! For God's sake, what has happened to us? How did we deserve it? God keep you, for the last time. Death will be a favor... Stop crying, will you? Stop or I'll go mad!"

Swept away by feelings that were quite beyond his abilities to master, he caught her in his arms even though she pushed with her hands against him, and started kissing her eyes, and then her mouth, and then he threw himself on his knees before her, and finally he leaped up like a madman, seized himself by the hair and ran out of the apartment, shouting: "The Devil himself won't help here, not some damned red ribbon!"

She saw him through the window as he jumped hurriedly on his horse, and the seven riders broke into a trot. The Scots at the gatehouse slapped their musket butts as they presented arms, and then the heavy gates clanged shut behind the riders, and she lost sight of them on the dark road winding among the trees.

Night fell soon after, as deep and vast as the distances between them.

Chapter Forty

BECAUSE THE OLD CITY of Kaunas, or Kovno as it was known to Poles, and all of the roads and countryside on the left bank of the Vilya River lay in the grip of the Russian enemy, Kmita couldn't take the great highway to Podlasye that ran straight from Kaunas to Grodno and then to Bialystok. Instead he headed south along a series of minor country roads that paralleled the course of the Nevyesh River as far as its junction with the mighty Nyemen, which he crossed into the Palatinate of Trotzk near the settlement of Vilki.

He didn't expect much to happen to him on this short and secure stretch of his greater journey, since all that country lay firmly in Radzivill's hands. All towns and sometimes even the bigger villages in these parts were garrisoned by his household cavalry, or by small troops of Swedes whom the Hetman pushed on purpose as close as he could to Zoltarenko's hordes, which crouched uneasily just across the Vilya, so that some incident might provoke a war between Sweden and Zoltarenko's allies in the Kremlin. Zoltarenko's Cossacks were more than willing to oblige him, but they were under strict orders from Moscow to avoid any provocations. Indeed, in the event that Radzivill and the Swedes should march out against them, they were to retreat eastward as quickly as they could.

For that reason all the country on the right bank of the Vilya was peaceful and untroubled. But since only the narrow river separated the Swedish or Radzivill sentries from the Cossack outposts, a single, accidental musket shot could unleash a terrible war at almost any moment, and the inhabitants looked for safer homes in anticipation. Thus if the countryside was quiet it was also empty; the small towns through which Pan Andrei passed were swept clean of people, the manors were shuttered, and the villages were totally abandoned.

The fields were also abandoned that year because no one bothered to cut and stack the hay, sure that it would all go up in flames anyway at almost any moment. The country folk hid in the woods along with all their livestock and possessions, while the gentry looked for refuge in Electoral Prussia which, so far, had escaped the hot breath of war. But the roads and woodland tracks, by contrast, were alive with homeless refugees, all the more numerous since countless fugitives from the left bank of the Vilya were also there in droves, escaping from Zoltarenko's savage and tyrannical oppression.

These vast crowds consisted almost wholly of dispossessed peasants, since those landowners who still hadn't managed to get across the river were either held as captives in the Ukraine, or had been sold and driven into slavery in Asia Minor, or lay dead on the thresholds of their looted homes. But this northwestern part of the Trotzk Palatinate which lay closest to the Prussian border, was a rich, bountiful land, yielding two crops a year out of its black soil, so that its people had something to hide and preserve. Each moment brought in sight fresh groups of peasantry, both refugee and local, with their wives, children and household goods trundling in rickety carts behind them, and with herds of cattle, sheep and horses driven ahead of them.

The nearing Winter seemed to hold no threats for these local fugitives, who preferred to wait for better times in mossy woodland clearings, huddled in makeshift shelters under ice and snow, than to face certain death, and a cruel one at that, in their abandoned homes. Riding close to these trudging crowds, or nearing the glow of their campfires at night, Pan Andrei heard hair-raising tales of Cossack and Russian savagery beyond the Vilya, in the neighborhood of Kaunas, and in the seized territories farther to the east. Zoltarenko and his Moscow allies murdered everyone who fell into their hands. Men, women, children, the young and the aged, went under the knife. And the savage enemy didn't simply kill them. They tortured them to death, burned their homes, cut down their orchards, and left only earth and water untouched in their wake, so that many of the fleeing fugitives were driven mad by terror and despair. At night, their frightful howls filled the woodland darkness.

Others—even though they were now safe across the Nyemen and the Vilya, and separated from Zoltarenko's hordes by miles of swamps and forests—lived nervously as if in the grip of fever, expecting an attack from moment to moment, and stretched their arms towards the passing Kmita and his Orshan riders, begging for protection.

Nor was there less despair among the old men, women and children of the gentry whose charabancs and wagons carried them towards whatever safety they might find in Prussia. Kmita comforted these homeless exiles as best as he could, telling them that the Swedes would soon cross the river and drive the eastern invaders back to where they came from, and then he heard hundreds of heartfelt and grateful affirmations of his own faith in Yanush Radzivill.

"God bless the Prince!" cried the wanderers everywhere around him. "God give him health and life! Bless him for bringing a civilized nation to our aid. We'll be safe once the Swedes are here. We'll be able to go back to our homes, back to our ruins and ashes..."

Everyone among this wretched flotsam spoke of Radzivill as their only hope. Any day now, they assured each other, he would cross the Vilya with his army and a Swedish one as well, and save them from destruction.

"He's our Lithuanian Gideon," they murmured as if in a prayer. "Our Samson... our deliverer!"

Everyone praised the Swedes for their discipline and for their good treatment of the local people, and Kmita, listening to these hymns of benediction, added his own trust and gratitude for the man he followed.

"That's the kind of man I'm serving," he told himself over and over. "He may be strange at times, hard to understand and even terrifying, but he has a greater mind than anybody else. He can see farther. He knows better what has to be done. I'll stifle my doubts and follow him blindly wherever he is going because he is the only salvation for the country."

And at such thoughts he felt as if a stone slab had fallen off his chest, and he breathed easier and felt both happier and more optimistic, and then Keydany seemed far less dreadful in his memory.

* * *

Indeed, each day's distance transformed his memory into longing because Keydany also meant Olenka.

He didn't throw any red ribbons behind him nor did he toss a bucketful of water on his first campfire. It wouldn't do any good, he was sure. Besides, he didn't want to.

'*If only she was here*,' he thought, listening to the voices of the fleeing people. '*She wouldn't be telling me to find a new way, or think that I'm lost like some blinded heretic who turns his back on the truth and blunders into falsehoods, if she could hear these cries and see those tears. But no matter! She'll realize sooner or later how wrong she was to doubt the Prince. She'll know it was her mind that was at sixes and sevens, not mine. And then... who knows... perhaps God will change things. Perhaps we'll see each other again some day.*'

And the longing to see her again grew in him along with the conviction that he was on the right path, not stumbling among errors, and he began to feel a sense of rare inner peace.

Doubts left him.

The tangled jumble of gnawing and distressing thoughts dropped away behind him.

He rode straight ahead, plunged in what seemed to be endless woods and thickets, feeling happiness returning almost by the hour. Not since those days of his private war against Hovansky's armies, before he came to Lubitch, did he feel so well, and the world seemed a much better place.

Kharlamp was right about one thing, he thought: the open road was the best cure for anxiety and worries. He had, he knew, nerves of steel and a body as strong as forged iron. His health and his vitality were unshaken and his spirits soared with each passing mile. The future promised action and adventure as never before, and he smiled eagerly in anticipation as he drove his men and himself almost without rest, stopping only for short roadside halts at night.

'*I'll be back*,' he thought, picturing Olenka as he saw her last: in his arms, trembling like a trapped bird, and with her sky-blue eyes wet with spilling tears.

At times the grim, threatening image of the Hetman passed

across his mind but even that gloomy giant seemed dearer with distance. Until now, he knew, be bent before Radzivill's will, swept up by the power of the Hetman's vision in much the same way that a raging whirlpool seizes and consumes even a resisting and resentful object; now he began to love him and wanted to follow him of his own volition.

Distance gave even greater stature to that towering magnate so that he began to seem more than merely human. At night, before he closed his eyes in sleep, Pan Andrei saw him seated on a throne taller than the pine trees, a crown on his head, a sword and scepter in his hands, and the whole of the Commonwealth spread out at his feet.

And in those last bright-lit moments by a dwindling campfire, before he slipped into his own dreamless rest, Pan Andrei stared humbly at that huge, lowering face and paid homage to his leader's greatness.

★ ★ ★

On the third day Kmita and his men turned away from the Nyemen River, soon left it far behind them, and entered an even more thickly wooded country. But here the enemy was closer, no longer held at bay by the Hetman's garrisons or scattered Swedish outposts.

The roads were still crowded with fugitives from the east and those of the local gentry who were either too old or too infirm for the weight of armor. They fled, almost without exception, northwest towards Prussia because there were no Swedish or Radzivill forces in this countryside to halt enemy raiding parties as on the Vilya River.

Sometimes those raiders were little more than brigands only loosely connected with Zoltarenko's Cossacks, whose sole aim was pillage, and whom the local gentry fought off with their own retainers. These armed marauders, often led by local criminals, kept clear of regular troops or even local levies, but they showed no mercy to smaller, undefended villages, isolated manors or travelers on the roads. The gentry crushed them on their own whenever they could, and dressed the wayside pines with their dangling corpses, but it was easy to come across large bands of these human vultures in the dark seclusion of the woods, so that Kmita's party had to keep a sharp eye on everything around them from this moment on.

But not much further along their way they entered quieter country around the large market town of Pilvishkye, where the streams of refugees dwindled to a trickle, and where the local people had stayed where they were. The townspeople told Pan Andrei that just a few days earlier a powerful *vataha* of Zoltarenko's Cossacks, numbering at least five hundred men or more, invaded the region, and would have burned the town and massacred the entire population as was their usual custom, '*if help hadn't come to us as if from the sky.*'

"We already gave our souls to God," related the freeholder of an inn where Pan Andrei took quarters for the night, "when the good saints sent some Lithuanian regiment our way. We thought at first it was a fresh band of enemies, and thought ourselves lost, but they turned out to be our men. They fell on those Zoltarenko killers out of nowhere and it was all over with the Cossacks in an hour, especially since we all ran out to help as well."

"What regiment was that?" Kmita was anxious to know what troops were in the area.

"God give them life! God keep them! We don't know who they were because they didn't say, and we didn't dare ask too many questions. They grazed their horses for an hour or two, took some hay and provisions, and went off again."

"But where did they come from and where were they heading?"

"They came from Kozlova Ruda, which is north of here, and they rode off to the south. Most of the people around here wanted to run for it to the woods, but then we thought that after such a lesson the enemy wouldn't come this way again in a hurry, so we stayed put, as Your Worship sees."

But Kmita was most interested to hear about that battle. "Who led that regiment?" he asked. "Did anybody say?"

"No, sir. But we saw their colonel because he talked to some of us in the market square. A young man he was, and trim and perky as a little button. Didn't look half the warrior that he is..."

"Volodyovski!" Kmita cried.

"Maybe he was Volodyovski, maybe not," the innkeeper said.

"But may God bless his hands! May he get to be a Hetman someday, that's all I've got to say."

Pan Andrei, however, had some fresh food for thought. It was clear to him that he was following the same track as Pan Volodyovski and his Laudanians, which was quite natural since both of them were making for Podlasye. But it occurred to him that if he hurried his own journey at its present pace he might inadvertently catch up with the little knight and fall into his hands again. With Radzivill's letters in their possession, the confederates would be privy to the Hetman's most secret intentions. In that event, Kmita's mission would be rendered useless, and God alone could tell what damage that would do to the Radzivill cause.

He decided to interrupt his journey. A few days' rest in the quiet county town would let Volodyovski's regiment gain a little distance.

"We'll stay here a few days," Pan Andrei told Soroka. "Tell the men to unsaddle and stable the horses and find good quarters for themselves."

"The horses need a breather, commandant," the sergeant agreed. "We've been pushing hard all the way from Keydany. And the men could use a bit of rest as well."

"Good. Get them settled in. And get our packs and saddle bags in as well."

"Very good, commandant," Sergeant Soroka said.

* * *

The following morning proved to Kmita that he'd acted not only shrewdly but wisely as well. He no sooner dressed for the day when the innkeeper came knocking at his door.

"I have news for Your Worship," he said.

"Good, I hope?"

"Neither good nor bad, only that we've important visitors in town. There's a monstrous big court just pulled up at the *Starosta's* house. There's a whole regiment of foot soldiers! And there's no counting all the horsemen and carriages and servants. People thought at first that the King had come."

"Which King?"

"Hmm. That's right." The innkeeper threw a cautious glance at the young officer before him, as if not sure which King he'd like better. "We've two Kings now, don't we... But it's neither one King nor the other, sir. It's the Prince-Equerry."

Kmita leaped to his feet.

"What Prince-Equerry? Boguslav?"

"The same, Your Worship. First cousin of the Prince-Palatine of Vilna."

Pan Andrei slapped his hands together in surprise and pleasure.

"Ha! Imagine us running into each other like that!" he exclaimed.

The innkeeper took this to mean that his guest was a good acquaintance of Prince Boguslav, so he bowed even lower than before and backed out of the door. Pan Andrei dressed himself all over again in his finest clothing and accouterments, and an hour later he was standing before the house where the Prince was quartered.

★   ★   ★

Prince Boguslav's arrival quite transformed the unassuming little town which teemed with his soldiers. The infantry was busy stacking their muskets in the market square. Cavalry horses jammed the narrow side streets, and dismounted troopers were taking quarters in all the nearby homes. Soldiers, courtiers and household retainers in a variety of brilliant uniforms and costumes strolled along the streets or grouped before the houses, and sumptuously dressed officers chatted with each other in German or French.

But no one, Pan Andrei noted as he made his way into the market square, spoke a word of Polish. He didn't catch sight of a single Polish soldier or one item of Commonwealth uniform and equipment. He was accustomed to the foreign mercenary contingents which made up a large portion of the Polish and Lithuanian armies of his day—and which now formed the bulk of the Radzivill forces—but the musketeers, dragoons and cuirassiers he now passed along his way, seemed outlandish to him rather than merely foreign. The Hetman's Scottish regiments and Ganhof's heavy Reiters were armed, uniformed and drilled in the German fashion, derived from the Swedish conquerors in the Thirty Years' War, but Prince Boguslav modeled his troops on French manuals and usage, so that they didn't even resemble the Scots, Swedes and German mercenaries that Kmita knew in the Hetman's service.

Plumes, gold lace and ribbons made each private seem like an officer, and a foppish one at that, but it was clear at a glance that they were splendid soldiers. Kmita found himself looking at them with pleasure, fascinated by their magnificent bearing and appearance, and their officers watched him with a sharp curiosity of their own. He knew that he was quite resplendent in his own rich clothing; and his six soldiers, marching in step behind him, made a brave show in the bright new uniforms he ordered them to pack before they left Keydany.

He announced himself to the guard commander at the door, then waited while the officer went inside. The forecourt of the *Starosta's* house was filled from wall to wall by Prince Boguslav's courtiers and attendants, also dressed in fanciful French costumes, and Kmita stared, fascinated by all the novelty around him, at pages in plumed *birettas*, lackeys in velvet doublets, and grooms, equerries and coachmen in long Swedish boots with tops as wide as cartwheels extending to the thigh. It seemed as if the Prince didn't intend to stop in the town for long, since the coaches were out in the open, and the grooms fed the horses in their traces out of metal sieves they held in their hands.

But Pan Andrei didn't have long to look at them. The guard commander hurried back to him with word that the Prince was anxious to see the Hetman's messenger, and led him inside. Once through the entrance hall, they passed into what must have been the *Starosta's* dining room, where several courtiers, heads slumped heavily on their chests, sat nodding in sleep, with their booted legs stretched out on chairs before them; and Kmita concluded that they must have traveled hard, starting out well before the dawn, and that their last rest stop was many hours earlier.

The officer led him to yet another door and bowed with a flourish. "You'll find the Prince in there," he told him in German.

Kmita pushed open the door, entered and halted on the threshold. He had seen Prince Boguslav before; they met a few times in passing, especially during the final battles of the war of the Hmyelnitzki Rebellion which the Radzivills had done so much to win for the Commonwealth, but he could never resist an onrush of curiosity that bordered upon wonder whenever he caught sight of that extraordinary magnate.

* * *

The Prince sat before a tall mirror positioned in a corner of the room, so absorbed in studying his freshly rouged and powdered face that he didn't notice that someone had come into the room behind him. Two valets knelt before him, buckling the silver clasps on the instep of his long traveling boots, while he combed the pale, evenly trimmed fringe of his golden wig slowly with his fingers, although the thick, luxuriant hair might have been his own.

He was, Kmita knew, thirty-five years old, although he looked at least ten years younger. Watching him, Pan Andrei wondered why he always made such a lasting and indelible impression that once seen he couldn't be forgotten. It was, in part, his reputation for unrelenting courage, won mainly in duels with a variety of famous foreign magnates; but for the most part it was his extraordinary physical appearance, almost a caricature of himself in its juxtapositions, which made him unforgettable for anyone who met him.

The Prince was tall and almost as powerfully built as his older cousin, but his head was so small in comparison with his deep chest and broad shoulders, that it seemed transplanted from another body. His face was also as small and delicate as a child's, but even here the proportions went astray, because all his other features were quite dwarfed by a pronounced, aquiline nose, and a pair of black, glowing eyes of such size and brilliance that they reduced the rest of his face to insignificance.

Around those piercing, hawk-like eyes and that predatory Roman nose, all his remaining features practically disappeared, especially since they were so incongruously framed by the thick, curled locks of golden-yellow hair that fell to his shoulders. His soft, pouting mouth seemed particularly childish under the delicate little mustache that barely shaded his long upper lip, while his pampered skin, tinted with rouge and whitened with cosmetic lotions, gave the illusion of an almost girlish frailty despite the haughty pride, steely self-assurance, and ruthlessness he projected.

But there was nothing frail or equivocal in the sum total of

these contradictions. Everything about him reminded an observer that this was the famous '*chercheur des noises*,' as he was
called at the court of France: a man whose sword leaped out of
its scabbard just as swiftly, and with an effect that was just as
deadly, as the quick challenges that sprung from his lips at the
slightest opportunity.

Nor was he famous only as a duelist. His reputation as a
fearless military commander made him a byword in France,
Germany and Holland, where he threw himself into the thickest
of the fighting against the peerless Spanish infantry, storming
batteries that others believed unassailable, and capturing artillery
and banners with his own hand at the head of the regiments of
the Prince of Orange.

It was, as Kmita knew, Boguslav who shattered veteran German brigades in the Rhineland, leading the musketeer guards-
men of the King of France, and it was also he who wounded the
Duc de Fremouille in a famous duel, although de Fremouille was
known throughout Europe as the finest swordsman among the
French grandees. He once struck the Marquis de Rieux in the
face before the whole French court during a ball at the Louvre
because that great lord made some mild remark that offended
him. Baron von Goetz, another notorious adventurer, swordsman and swashbuckler, begged him on his knees to spare his life
in yet another duel. He also fought and wounded a certain
Baron Grotte, a German mercenary of questionable lineage,
which brought a storm of recriminations on his head from his
cousin Yanush for lowering the respect due to the Radzivills
because the German baron wasn't his match in rank.

All of this added up to a complex mixture of girlish vanity,
quickness of mind and a sharp intelligence, precociousness and
a ruthless courage, which along with his equally famous, innumerable love affairs, made him the talk of all the courts of
Europe.

He lived almost exclusively abroad.

His visits to the Commonwealth were rare and —as he said
himself without bothering to hide it —just as short as he was able
to arrange them.

The land of his birth bored him, as he put it, unless it offered
him yet another war, or some dangerous new development in

his family's long feud with the Sapyehas of Vitebsk and Smolensk, or an especially dangerous animal to hunt in his Lithuanian forests. In that event the gamekeepers were ordered to find
him the most savage game alive—female bears with cubs—which
he faced alone, armed only with a spear.

That same sense of constant restlessness and craving for danger, along with a true passion and talent for intrigue practiced
for its own sake, seemed to direct his countless amatory conquests, so that he was, in the parlance of his times, the terror of
all husbands who had beautiful wives in all the foreign courts
where he spent his time.

Kmita supposed that this also might have been the reason why
Prince Boguslav was still a bachelor, although his high birth and
nearly inexhaustible private and family fortune made him one of
the most sought-after single men in Europe. The King and
Queen of France, the French-born Queen Marie-Louise of
Poland, and the Prince of Orange, all tried to find him a suitable
marital alliance but he preferred his freedom.

'I don't need a dowry,' he would say with cynical amusement.
'And I've never yet run short of all the other pleasures.'

★　★　★

This then was the sum and substance of Prince Boguslav
Radzivill: a mannered, cultivated sophisticate on one side and
a fearless warrior on the other, who defied ordinary categoriza-
tions as if he could create his own character at will.

Kmita, standing on the threshold of the Prince's chamber,
watched curiously as the young Radzivill fingered his fringe
thoughtfully into place, staring intently at the reflection of his
deceptively childlike and effeminate face. Finally, after Pan
Andrei cleared his throat loudly a few times, the Prince stirred
and lifted his head slightly as if suddenly aware that he was not
alone.

"Who's there?" he asked, still staring into his mirror. "The
courier from the Hetman?"

"From the Hetman, yes!" Kmita said quietly but with dignity.
"But I'm not a courier!"

The Prince turned his head and fixed a long, careful glance at
the richly dressed young man who stood somewhat haughtily

just inside the door, and then he pursed his lips in an apologetic grimace as if excusing his own carelessness.

"Forgive me, cavalier," he said courteously. "I see that I've misjudged your rank. Your face is familiar although I don't quite recall the name. Are you a member of the Prince-Hetman's court?"

"My name is Kmita," Pan Andrei said. "And I'm not a courtier. I command a regiment which I raised in the Hetman's service."

"Kmita!" the Prince called out with a sudden sharp curiosity of his own. "The same famous Kmita who raided Hovansky in the last campaign? And then did so well fighting his own war? I've heard a lot about you, my dear fellow!"

The close attentive look in the Prince's eyes suggested that whatever he heard about the young soldier pleased him and intrigued him in just the same way that he was always pleased and intrigued by himself.

"Sit down, cavalier," he invited cordially. "I'll be glad to get to know you better. And what's the news from Keydany nowadays?"

"Here is a letter from the Hetman to Your Highness," Kmita said.

The valets had now finished buckling the Prince's boots. They rose, bowed and left, and he broke the seal on the letter and began to read it quietly to himself. But his face soon betrayed boredom and impatience.

"Nothing new," he shrugged and threw the letter on his dressing table. "The Prince-Palatine suggests that I move to Prussia, either to Tilsit or Taurogen, which as you see I'm in the process of doing. *Ma fois!*" he swore mildly in French. "I don't understand my cousin. He writes that the Elector sits in Brandenburg because he can't get to Prussia through the Swedes, and at the same time he informs me that he's quite desperate for me to go there and call on him on my way. How am I to do what the Elector can't? At any rate, I couldn't stand Podlasye for a moment longer. I almost died of boredom. I've speared every bear I could find in the entire province, but the women stink of sheepskins over there and that's one smell that I simply cannot tolerate... But do you happen to speak French or German?"

"I understand German," Kmita said.

"Thank God for that! I'll speak in German, then, because your language chaps my lips."

Here the Prince pushed out his lower lip and started patting it gingerly with his fingers as if to see whether it was blistered or cracked already. Then he glanced again into the mirror and went on:

"I heard that some noble named Skshetuski had an amazingly beautiful wife near Lukov. Yes, I know it was far! But I sent some people after her anyway... As luck would have it she was not at home."

"Your Highness was lucky," Pan Andrei said coldly. "Because her husband is a noted man. He is the famous Yan Skshetuski who made his way through Hmyelnitzki's forces at the Siege of Zbarajh and saved the whole army."

"Did he, now." The Prince looked amused. "The husband was besieged in Zbarajh and I'd have laid siege to his wife in Tikotzin... Do you think she'd resist as fiercely?"

"Your Highness doesn't need a war council for that kind of siege," Pan Andrei said harshly. This side of Boguslav's character, he thought, was his least attractive. "My opinion is unnecessary here."

"True." The Prince shrugged. "It would've been a waste of time anyway, most likely. So... do you have any other letters?"

"Not for Your Highness. But I do need to find the King of Sweden. Would you happen to know where to look for him?"

"I've no idea. How would I? He's not in Tikotzin, that I guarantee, because if he ever poked his head into that provincial pest-hole he'd renounce the entire Commonwealth, crown and all. The Swedes hold Warsaw, as I already wrote to you people in Keydany, but he's not there either. He must be in or near Krakow unless he set out for Polish Prussia already. You can find out in Warsaw where to look for him."

Kmita bowed briefly, said nothing more, and waited while the Prince went on with his careless musing.

"In my opinion Charles Gustav has to give some thought to those Prussian cities. He simply can't leave them unoccupied behind him, threatening his routes of supply and communication. Ah, who'd imagine that while the whole Commonwealth is deserting its anointed sovereign, while all the gentry runs to join the Swedes, and while whole regions are surrendering without a shot one after another, it would be those East Prussian cities—German burghers and Protestants at that—who refuse to have anything to do with Sweden and are getting ready to resist? Imagine, they want to stay faithful to Yan Casimir and save the Commonwealth! I tell you, cavalier, starting this work, we thought they'd be the first to help us and the Swedes in carving up this meatloaf you call a Nobles' Republic... Unbelievable, what? It's a good thing the Elector is sharpening his teeth for those Prussian towns, so they won't be a problem much longer. He's already offered them help against the Swedes, but the Danzigers don't trust him, and quite rightly too."

"We already know this in Keydany," Kmita said.

"Yes. Well. Anyway," the Prince went on, laughing quietly in appreciation. "They've a good nose, those Germans. Because our dear uncle, the Elector, cares about the Commonwealth as much as I or the *Voyevode* of Vilna."

"Your Highness will forgive if I disagree," Kmita said at once. "Prince Yanush cares *only* about the Commonwealth! He's ready to spill his last drop of blood in her defense."

But now Boguslav burst into open laughter.

"You're young, cavalier!" he said, grinning with amusement. "So young! But no matter. All Uncle Friedrich Wilhelm has in mind is to help himself to your Prussian cities. That's why he's offering to aid them against Charles Gustav, don't you see? But once he has his own garrisons inside them he'd be ready to sit down to breakfast with the Swedes, Turks or the Devil the following morning. And if the Swedes should also cede him a part of Vyelkopolska he'll be glad to help them in carving up the rest of the country. The trouble is that the Swedes are also licking their chops for Prussia and that's why they're bickering with the Elector."

"I am amazed to hear what you're saying, Highness!" Kmita said.

But Prince Boguslav was too busy with his amused analysis of his uncle's motives to pay attention to anyone's amazement.

"I chewed my nails to the quick in that damned Podlasye!" he went on. "But what could I do? I had to stay put! The Prince-Hetman and I agreed that I wasn't to come out openly for the Swedes until the Prussian situation clarified itself.

Which makes good sense, of course.   It gives us room for maneuver, so to speak.   I even sent some secret messages to Yan Casimir, offering to call out a General Levy in Podlasye if only he'd send me the authority to do it.   The King might have done it, like the credulous fool he is, but the Queen must've smelled a rat and advised against it.   Ah, if it wasn't for that old harridan's interference, I'd be standing right now at the head of all the Podlasyan gentry.   And what is more, those confederates who are plundering the Hetman's possessions would have no choice but to place themselves under my command.   I'd have announced myself a Yan Casimir supporter, but in reality, having so much power in my hands, and with such a strong army at my beck and call, I'd be able to haggle a much better deal for us out of the Swedes.   But that French witch knows which way the wind is blowing.   She's the real King of Poland, not just a Queen, I tell you!   She has more shrewdness and perception in one finger than Yan Casimir has in his entire body!"

"The Prince-*Voyevode*," Kmita began again, but Boguslav made a quick, impatient gesture.

"The Prince-*Voyevode* gives late advice as always," he broke in, annoyed.   "He never fails to write do this or that when I've already done it.   Besides, he must be truly loosing his grip on affairs... Just listen to what he wants from me now!"

And here the Prince picked up the Hetman's letter and started reading out loud in an irritated voice, and Kmita—listening with a rising sense of disbelief and horror—felt an icy sweat bursting out on his forehead and the hair rising on his head.   The Hetman urged Boguslav to lure the confederates to Zabludov, drug them with the potent beers for which that region was famous through the country, and then have their throats cut in their sleep, with each peasant murdering the soldier quartered in his hut.

'*That's all they're worth and that's the quickest way to get rid of them*,' the Hetman concluded.   '*And once their leaders are out of the way the rest should scatter without further trouble.*'

Boguslav tossed away the letter with a gesture of annoyance and contempt.

"How am I to do this?"   His voice was both petulant and angry.   "Go to Prussia and, at the same time, organize a massacre in Zabludov?   Pretend that I am still a patriot and arrange the butchery of the very men who refuse to turn their backs on their King and country? Does this make sense? Does it hold together? *Ma fois*! The Hetman's mind is failing! I just came across a whole regiment of mutineers making for Podlasye. I'd have been happy to ride across their bellies, but how could I do that and still look like a Yan Casimir supporter? No, no, I must deny myself that kind of pleasure until I'm openly on the side of the Swedes, and our dear uncle has finally wormed his way into those Prussian cities... All I could do was parley with those rebels, as they did with me, and send them on their way."

★ ★ ★

Some time passed as Prince Boguslav leaned comfortably back in his armchair, folded his hands behind his head, and went on carelessly: "You've utter chaos in this pitiful Commonwealth of yours, my dear Master Kmita. There has never been anything like it in this world...!"

But then a quick new thought intruded on his musing. "Would you be going to Podlasye, then?" he asked.

"Surely," said Kmita. "I've letters of instruction for Harasimovitch in Zabludov."

"Well, if that isn't a coincidence!" the Prince said. "Harasimovitch is right here with me. He's taking some of the Hetman's belongings to Prussia, because we feared the confederates would get them... Wait, I'll have him sent for."

Boguslav clapped his hands, summoned one of his attendants, and dispatched him for the Radzivill official.

"What a lucky chance," he said. "It'll save you a few miles of travel, although it might have been useful for you to go to Podlasye. There's a relative of yours among the chiefs of the confederacy... You could have tried to draw him to our side."

"I wouldn't have time for that," said Kmita, "since I'm anxious to get to the Swedish King and Pan Lubomirski."

"Ah, so you've letters for the Marshal, too?"

"Yes, Highness.

"I can guess what that is all about. There was a time that His Lordship wanted to marry his boy to Yanush's daughter... Is the Hetman putting out a few feelers of his own?"

"That's just what it's about."

"They're children, both of them... and it's a delicate mission

too, because it's not the Hetman's place to be doing the asking..." Then the Prince narrowed his painted eyebrows and
jumped angrily out of his chair. "Besides, it won't come to
anything. It can't. Take it from me, the Hetman's daughter
isn't being raised for young Lubomirski. Yanush has to understand that his fortune must remain in Radzivill hands."

Pan Andrei watched Prince Boguslav with astonishment, as
the suddenly grim and glowering magnate started walking swiftly up and down the chamber. His pace quickened, until it
seemed that he was about to break into a run, and then he halted
abruptly before the young soldier.

"Give me your word that you'll tell the truth when I ask you
something," he demanded.

"Your Highness," Pan Andrei said coldly. "Only cowards feel
the need to lie and I'm not afraid of anybody here."

"Did the Hetman order you not to tell me about those
marriage plans with the Lubomirskis?"

"If he had I wouldn't have mentioned them."

"You could have been careless! Do I have your word?"

It was Kmita's turn to narrow his brows. "You do."

"Ah!" And Boguslav's strangely tightened face softened with
relief. "You've lifted a great weight off my heart, because—wouldn't you know it?—I started thinking that the
Prince was playing a double game with me as well..."

"I don't understand Your Highness' point of reference,"
Kmita said.

"I could have married the Duchesse de Rohan in France,"
Boguslav remarked. "Not to mention half a score of other
princesses. But I didn't. Can you imagine why?"

"No, I can't."

"Because there is an agreement between me and my cousin
Yanush. His girl and his fortune are both reserved for me! It's
a very private and quite secret matter... But,"—and Boguslav
shrugged with a sudden patronizing smile—"you're entitled to
know it, I expect, as a faithful servant of the Radzivills."

"I'm grateful for the confidence..." Kmita felt his own angry
pride leaping up in him, and his voice was both colder and
sharper than he had intended. "But Your Highness is mistaken
in one thing," he snapped. "I am no one's servant."

Boguslav's huge eyes opened even wider.

"Who are you, then?"

"I'm a Hetman's officer, not a court official. I hold a colonel's commission in the regular contingent. And besides, I'm related by blood to His Highness, the Prince-Hetman and *Voyevode* of Vilna."

"A relative? And how are you related?"

"Through the Kishkas. I am connected with the family of the Hetman's mother."

It was hard to say what was passing then through Prince Boguslav's mind. He gave Kmita a long, measuring glance down the length of his predatory nose, so lofty and speculating as to seem insulting, and the young man felt a hot flush spreading across his face. But suddenly the Prince gave a careless little shrug, a small wry smile fluttered across his lips, and he held out his hand.

"I'm sorry, *mon cousin*," he murmured pleasantly. "Congratulations on your high connections..."

And he turned to other matters, as if Kmita's links with his family were so peripheral and so unimportant that they couldn't have mattered less.

Chapter Forty-one

THE LAST FEW WORDS that Prince Boguslav spoke were said with such courtly elegance, but also with such elaborate indifference, that Pan Andrei felt them as painfully as a blow. His cheeks flushed even hotter, and his mouth snapped open to spill something biting in return, when the doors swung open and Harasimovitch sidled into the room.

"There's a letter for you," Prince Boguslav nodded at the obsequious estate manager, who stood bowing in the doorway like a creaky, animated puppet pulled up and down on invisible strings. "Read it out to us!"

Harasimovitch gave a fawning bow to the Prince and then another to Pan Andrei and opened the letter.

"Go on! Read it!" the Prince ordered.

"Of course, Highness! Immediately, Your Highness!" Harasimovitch whispered in his rustling voice. His thick, buttery smile looked as if it were pasted to his face, and then he bowed respectfully over the Hetman's letter.

"*The time has come for good servants to show their loyalty to their master,*" he began to read.

"I couldn't have said that better myself," the Prince interrupted.

"... Ah, *to their master,*" read Harasimovitch. "*As regards whatever moneys you can get your hands on in Zabludov, and whatever ready cash Pan Pshimski can gather in our estates in Orel...*"

"The confederates have chopped Pan Pshimski into mincemeat," the Prince interjected. "Which is why Pan Harasimovitch is running for dear life."

"*... In Orel,*" the steward continued with his oily, apologetic smile. "*Such as public taxes, debts and whatever rents can still be collected...*"

"The confederates have already collected them," the Prince threw in, laughing.

"*... You are to gather and forward to us at once,*" read the harassed official and then went on to list lands, villages and possessions to be leased or pawned, and expensive art, silverware and gold-plate to be shipped by the first available escorted wagon train.

"*I draw your attention to the great candelabrum in the church in Orel, the stud farm and the paintings in the manor there, and especially the cannon on the main porch of Our Orel residence...*"

"Late advice as always," the Prince said and yawned. "I have the cannon with me."

The guns, the Hetman wrote, were to be brought with or without their carriages '*but hauled in such a way that no one knows what is being carried or they might tempt an attack by the mutineers who are exerting such heavy pressure on Our counties there.*'

"Oh they're pressing," the Prince interrupted. "They are pressing hard. If they press any harder they'll squeeze all those properties as dry as a farmer's cheese."

"*... And who are moving on Zabludov,*" Harasimovitch struggled to go on with his respectful reading despite Boguslav's ironic interruptions, "*on their way to the King, and whom we can't fight because they are too many.*"

Yanush Radzivill's stewards were not to resist the confederates, the Grand Hetman ordered, but welcome them, drug them, get them drunk if possible, and either murder them at night in their beds or poison their liquor.

"*... Or, if that seems more convenient,*" Harasimovitch read, "*especially if Our own peasants aren't willing to help out, call in a few bands of local cut-throats, killers and marauders who would be glad to butcher them in their sleep just for the loot they'd find on their bodies.*"

"Nothing new, as I said," Prince Boguslav shrugged. "That's all taken care of. You can keep traveling with me, Master Harasimovitch."

"There's a *post scriptum,* Highness," the steward replied and suddenly his rustling voice grew shrill with fear as he continued reading. "*Be sure to bring everything from Our vintage cellars, because good wines are impossible to get here nowadays... But if you can't do that then sell them for quick cash!"*

And here the quaking Harasimovitch halted without any interruptions. He caught his head in both hands in terror and his small, calculating eyes shifted to Prince Boguslav in fearful supplication.

"Dear God!" he cried. "The wines are on the road half a day behind us! They're sure to fall into the hands of that rebel regiment that passed us! Oh Lord, what shall I do? That's a loss of at least a thousand gold pieces! I beg Your Highness to tell the Prince-Hetman that I loaded every vat and keg... but that they fell behind in the convoy...!"

The steward's despair would have been all the greater, Kmita thought remotely, if he knew the extent of Pan Zagloba's thirst and if he also knew that the old knight was riding with that rebel regiment he feared.

But in the meantime Boguslav started laughing. "Let them drink hearty," he said. "Read on!"

"Yes, Highness... well,"—and the sweating bailiff hid his quivering face behind the Hetman's letter—"*if, however, you have trouble finding a good buyer...*"

"We've found a whole regiment of them," Prince Boguslav had doubled up with laughter. "But Prince Yanush will have to give them credit, I'm afraid, because they don't pay cash."

"*... If you can't find a buyer,*" Harasimovitch read on in a mournful voice, "'*then bury the casks but do it so secretly that no more than one man, or two at most, could tell where to find them, and leave one or two poisoned barrels of the best and sweetest in plain sight both in Zabludov and Orel, so that at least the rebel leaders might drink from them and die... Serve me well in this, and secretly by God, and burn these instructions so that no one will ever know how We treated those loyalistic traitors, although if they don't find the barrels by themselves you might send them a few as a gift from some supposed Commonwealth supporter.*"

The fawning steward finished reading and started to peer slyly at the Prince as if anxious to guess his intentions, and Boguslav shrugged and yawned again.

"I see that my dear cousin gave a lot of thought to those confederates," he said at last. "Too bad that it's too late as always. It's not a bad idea. A week or two ago we might have tried it but he didn't think of it in time. But that is all we want from you just now, Master Harasimovitch. You can go."

Harasimovitch bowed again and left, and Prince Boguslav returned to his mirror.

★ ★ ★

Peering once more into the polished glass, he gave himself wholly to an intent inspection of his own appearance, turning his head slightly this way and that, stepping away from his image and then returning to it, shaking his flowing locks into place and shooting sideways glances at himself out of the corners of his narrowed eyes. Enthralled as he was with his own reflection, he paid no attention to Kmita, who sat as still as stone in the shadows, his back to the window.

A single glance tossed lightly at Pan Andrei would have told the Prince that some vast emotional upheaval had gripped the young envoy. Kmita was as pale as a sheet. Thick drops of sweat beaded his forehead and his clenched hands quivered in convulsive tremors. His body rose out of his chair, then dropped back down again like that of a man who fights a terrible battle with himself, and struggles to contain an outburst of either the most frightful anger or despair. He brought all his will-power, all his strength, and all the forces of his violent energy and nature to bear on the conflict and, at last, after what seemed to him like hours of remorseless combat, his features set into a rigid mask of icy self-control.

"Highness," he said calmly. "May I ask a favor?"

"Certainly, cavalier, or rather *cher cousin*," the Prince nodded kindly, still peering with total concentration into his dressing mirror.

"It's... a matter of information," Kmita's voice was steady. "As Your Highness may note from the confidence that the Prince-Hetman reposes in my loyalty, he sees no need to keep me in the dark about anything. He knows that I belong to him body and soul..."

"Which shows how intelligent you must be," the Prince interrupted.

"Yes... well,"—and Kmita did his best to sound like a callous traitor, indifferent to anything but his own advantage—"your

work is mine. As the Radzivill fortunes rise so will my own.
I'm ready for anything that the Hetman or Your Highness need.
But even though I'm right in the middle of these great affairs
there are a few things that I don't understand."

"No doubt," the Prince said carelessly to his own reflection.
"So how can I help you, cousin?"

"I need a lesson in statecraft, perhaps," Pan Andrei said softly.
"It would be a real waste, I think, not to take the opportunity
to learn from such statesmen as the Hetman and yourself. I'm
just not sure if Your Highness would deign to give me a sincere
answer..."

"That will depend on what you want to know." Boguslav was
still studying his face in the mirror. His voice rang with such
aloof indifference that it bordered on disdain. "And... on what
I feel like saying."

Kmita's eyes glinted dangerously but his voice remained calm,
tractable and controlled.

"Here is the thing," he said. "Prince Yanush explains everything he does in terms of the public good and the salvation of
the Commonwealth. You'd think that *Commonwealth* was his
favorite word...! Would Your Highness tell me, with all sincerity, if he really has only the country's good in mind? Or if that's
just a necessary, temporary pose?"

Intrigued, Boguslav threw a swift, sharp glance at Pan Andrei.

"And if I told you that it's just a pose," he said in a watchful
tone. "Would you keep on serving?"

Kmita shrugged. "Why not? As I said, my fortune will grow
beside those of Your Highnesses... I don't care how that happens
as long as it happens."

"You'll make something of yourself, my friend!" the Prince
said and nodded in approval. "Remember that I was the first to
see it in you... But why didn't Cousin Yanush ever talk to you
openly about it?"

"Maybe because he likes to keep things to himself," Kmita said
and shrugged. "Or maybe he didn't think he needed to say it."

"You've sharp wits, cavalier, because it's God's own truth that
he never likes to show his real colors. You couldn't have come
closer to the target! Why, would you believe that even when he
talks with me, he starts to color everything he says with his
love-of-country...! That's the way he's made! It's only when

I laugh into his face that he remembers what it's all about and gives up that nonsense."

"So it's all a pose?" Kmita asked.

* * *

The Prince turned the back of his chair towards the young soldier, straddled it as if he was sitting slumped on the back of a horse, rested his arms on the backrest, and sat in a long, contemplative silence as if weighing and considering something in his mind.

"Listen, Master Kmita," he said finally. "If we Radzivills were living in Spain, France or Sweden, where a King's son succeeds his father to the throne, and where monarchs rule by divine right responsible to nobody but God and their own fancy, then—putting aside such things as civil wars, the end of a dynasty, or some other extraordinary event—we'd probably serve our King and country loyally enough, contenting ourselves with the highest offices in the land, which are our due both by birth and fortune. But here, in this country, where a King's right to rule derives from the gentry which can elect anyone it pleases, we had to ask ourselves why it was a Vasa who sat on the throne and not a Radzivill...?

"Not that there's so much wrong with the Vasas," the Prince continued after another moment. "They are descended from hereditary monarchs. But who is to say that after the Vasas the gentry won't get the bright idea to give the Polish throne and the Lithuanian dukedom to Pan Harasimovitch? Who'll guarantee to us that we won't be serving some Master Myeleshko, or a Mister Pigfoot from Styville or some such place? Tfui! It could be anybody! And what about us? Are we, the Radzivills—hereditary princes of the German Empire!—to keep on kissing the royal hand of some clown from Pigstown? Tfui, in the name of all the Devils, cavalier! It's time to finish with all that, I tell you! Look at the German states and tell me how many of their ruling princes could just as well serve as overseers on our properties! We could buy them all for just one half of everything we own. And yet they have their places. They rule. They elect their Emperor and vote in the Imperial Council. They wear crowns and take precedence before us, although they could just as easily carry the tails of our cloaks behind us...

"It's time to end all that!" he spat out in disgust, his girlish features contorted with anger. "It's time for us to fulfill our destinies, which is what my late father contemplated a long time ago!"

Quite animated now, the Prince rose and started pacing through the chamber.

"It isn't going to be easy," he resumed in short, musing phrases. He was calmer now, oblivious of his audience, and speaking largely to enjoy the sound of his own voice, and the grasp of statecraft he displayed. "Nothing is ever easy if it is worth doing. Some of our own kin refuse to assist us. I know that Prince Michael-Casimir wrote to the *Voyevode* that we should be thinking about penitential hair-shirts rather than a crown. Well, let him wear it. Let him do his penance and cover himself with ashes and have the Jesuits flog him towards greater virtue. If all he wants to be is a minor princeling, with whatever puny Lithuanian title he's able to inherit, that's his choice and he's welcome to it. We'll do without him, but we will not stop what we have begun because now is the time to do it!"

Cold sunlight slanted through the window into his empty mirror. A tall Gdansk clock was ticking in the corner. He paced up and down, gripped by his own visions, and Kmita felt as if his entire world was turning upside down.

"This Commonwealth of yours is going to the dogs," the frightening, strangely contradictory figure drawled in explanation. "She's so helpless now that she can't defend herself against anybody. Every foreign mongrel trots in and out of her borders any time he pleases, like cattle pushing in through a rotten fence. What happened here with the Swedes hasn't happened anywhere else in the world! You and I, cavalier, can sing '*Te Deum laudamus*' at the sight of it but, in its own way, it's an abominable and unheard of thing..."

The small childlike head shook on its massive shoulders with incredulous amusement.

"Imagine. An invader, and well-known as a rapacious one at that, breaks into the country, and he not only encounters no resistance anywhere he goes, but every living soul deserts its rightful King and runs to a new one! Everyone! The great lords, the nobles, the gentry, the armies, the castles and the cities! Without shame, faith, or even a memory of their honor!

There hasn't been anything like it anywhere in history! Tfui, cavalier, tfui! Scum lives in this country. Human garbage with neither self-respect nor conscience! And you mean to tell me that this kind of nation has a right to live? Your gentry wanted Swedish protection, did they? They'll get it, oh they'll get! The Swedes are already using thumbscrews on the Vyelkopolian squires to get at their money, and that's how it will be everywhere here because that's how it has to be! This nation of yours is fit only for servitude and slavery, begging a humble living from its powerful neighbors. You don't deserve anything but extinction and contempt!"

All color had drained out of Kmita's face long before. He knew that he was holding onto his sanity with the last of his strength, stifling an outburst of uncontrollable fury that must result in madness, but the Prince was still paying no attention to him. His own words had quite carried him away. He was intoxicated with his own reasoning, his perspicacity and the clarity of his vision, to such an extent that he might have been quite alone in his room just then.

"There is a custom in this country, cavalier," he went on with cynical amusement, "that the relatives of a dying man jerk the pillows from under his head in his final moment so that he can stop suffering and die all the quicker. That's the service that I and the *Voyevode* of Vilna decided to render to the Commonwealth. But since there's a whole crowd of greedy heirs waiting to get their claws on the estate, we want our share, and a substantial one at that, well ahead of time. Why not? Aren't we blood kin to the corpse? Don't we deserve at least as much as those foreign grave robbers? But if that analogy doesn't make my point, let me tell it to you in another way. Think of the Commonwealth as a length of rich red cloth, with everyone around—the Swedes, Hmyelnitzki, Moscow, the Tartars, the Elector and God knows who else—pulling on it for all they are worth. Well, the Prince *Voyevode* and I told ourselves a long time ago that we must get enough of that cloth in our hands for a royal mantle, which is why we're not only letting it be torn apart by all our greedy neighbors, but we're pulling at it with all our strength ourselves. Let Hmyelnitzki keep the Ukraine for himself, let the Swedes and Brandenburgers haggle over Prussia

and the Vyelkopolian counties, let the Hungarians or whoever's
nearer help themselves to Krakow and southern Malopolska, but
Lithuania must go to Prince Yanush and, through his daughter,
to me!"

But Kmita had heard enough. He was finally standing on his
feet although his knees were trembling.

"Thank you, Your Highness," he said. "That's all I wished to
know."

"You're leaving?"

"Yes."

The Prince, at last, gave Kmita a careful look.

"What's the matter with you? You look like Lazarus crawling
from his grave."

"I'm tired, Highness. That's all. It's been a hard journey. I'll
be back to take my leave before I go on."

"Then you'd better hurry. I'm leaving myself in the afternoon."

"I'll be back no later than an hour."

Kmita bowed and left.

The Prince's courtiers came politely to their feet as he walked
through the antechamber, and he swayed past them like a
drunken man, blind and deaf to everything around him, and
neither seeing nor hearing anybody near him. But once he
stood in the fresh air of the threshold he paused, pressed his head
between both his hands, and whispered in horror:

"Jesus of Nazareth, King of the Jews... Jesus! Maria!
Joseph...!"

* * *

Walking as uncertainly as if he was about to fall, Kmita crossed
the courtyard to the outer gate where his men were waiting.

"Follow me!" he ordered.

Sergeant Soroka, who knew his young commander's every
mood as well as he knew himself, could tell at once that something extraordinary had happened.

"Watch your step," he hissed under his breath to the other
soldiers. "It's death to anyone who gets in his way when he
looks like that."

The soldiers hurried after him, careful not to say anything that
might draw attention to themselves, and Kmita staggered on as

if he was about to break into a run, jerking his arms wildly in the air, and mumbling half-choked phrases. Soroka heard: "Poisoners... oath-breakers... traitors! Criminal and traitor...! They're two of a kind...!"

Then Kmita spat out the names of his dead companions: Kokosinski, Kulvyetz, Ranitzki, Rekutz and the others. The names spilled out of his mouth like curses, as if they failed him when he needed them the most. Several times he mentioned Pan Volodyovski. Soroka watched and listened, surprised and alarmed, and muttered grimly to the six Orshan roughnecks who hurried beside him: "There's going to be some blood flowing here, lads, you mark my words."

At last they reached the inn. Kmita locked himself in his room and didn't give a sign of life for another hour. In the meantime his soldiers started packing their belongings and saddling their horses without waiting for their colonel's orders.

"It won't do any harm to be ready," Sergeant Soroka told them. "And I mean for anything."

"We're ready," the old raiders said, sniffing the air like wolves scenting prey.

A short while later they had proof of how well Soroka knew their colonel. Kmita appeared in the entryway, bareheaded, coatless and dressed in his shirt sleeves, and with a grim expression on his narrowed face.

"Saddle the horses!" he ordered.

"They're saddled, sir," they reported.

"Get the packhorses loaded up!"

"Everything's loaded, sir."

"A double gold-piece for each one of you!" shouted the young colonel who, despite the rage that boiled inside him, saw that these men were able to guess his wishes before he expressed them.

"We thank you, commandant!" they replied in chorus.

"I want two men to take the packhorses at once towards Dembova. Go slowly through the town. But once you're out, make full speed for the woods and don't stop till you're among the trees, understand?"

"Yessir! By your order, sir!"

"The rest of you load your scatter guns. And saddle two horses for me. Both are to be fully equipped and ready."

"I knew something was going to happen," the old sergeant muttered.

"And now Soroka, come with me!" Kmita shouted.

He set out briskly in his open, crumpled shirt and breeches, and headed for the well that stood in the middle of the yard, while Soroka followed watchfully.

"Douse me with water," he ordered, jerking his head at the bucket hanging by the well.

The sergeant knew how dangerous it was to question Kmita's orders in the best of times, and especially now when he seemed ready to explode. He seized the bucket with no more than one mental shrug, dipped it in the well, and hurled the contents into Kmita's face.

"More!" Pan Andrei shouted.

Soroka doused him with another bucketful, and then with another, throwing the water at his snorting colonel as if he was trying to put out a fire.

"Enough!" Kmita snarled at last. "Come with me. You can help me dress."

They headed back to the inn. At the outer gate they met two of their men riding out with a string of packhorses on long reins behind them.

"Slowly through the town!" Kmita reminded them. "And then run for the woods as if the air was on fire behind you!"

And he stepped inside.

★ ★ ★

He was out again in half an hour, dressed to ride in long rawhide boots and an elkskin coat cinched with a broad leather belt. He had a pistol thrust into the belt. His men also noted the edge of a chain-mail shirt peeping out from under his thick leather jerkin, as if he expected an armed clash at any moment, while his saber was hitched high on his hip, ready for a quick draw.

His face, as Soroka saw with one swift glance, was calm but set in cold, dangerous lines.

His men were armed and ready. He leaped into his saddle, tossed a gold-piece to the innkeeper, and clattered out into the street without another word. Soroka rode beside him. His three remaining soldiers fell in behind them leading a saddled spare mount just as he had ordered.

Soon, sooner than expected, they crossed the market square which was packed with Prince Boguslav's soldiers who were apparently getting ready to march out as well. The cavalrymen were tightening the girths on their saddles. The infantry was stripping their musket stacks, and horses were being hitched to wagons everywhere.

Kmita stirred then, as if coming awake after a long sleep.

"Listen, old man," he turned to Soroka. "The highway heads straight south out of the *Starosta's* house, doesn't it? We don't have to come back through the square to get out of town?"

"And which way are we heading, colonel?"

"To Dembova."

"Then it's just as you're saying, sir. The road goes right past the house. The square will be behind us and we just keep on going."

"Good!" Kmita grunted.

And, after a moment, Soroka heard him muttering softly under his breath: "Ay, if only those others were alive... We're few, damn few, for a thing like this..."

Meanwhile they passed the square and turned towards the *Starosta's* manor which lay about a furlong and a half farther along the road.

"Halt!" Kmita snapped at last.

The soldiers reined-in their horses and Kmita turned to face them.

"Are you ready to die?" he asked without warning.

"We're ready," the Orshans growled in chorus.

"We used to creep right down Hovansky's throat, didn't we? And he didn't eat us, right?"

"We remember!"

"A man has to take great chances nowadays," Pan Andrei observed coldly. "If we succeed with what we're about to do the King will make great lords out of all of you, you've my word on that." Then he paused and shrugged. "But if we fail you'll all go to the stake!"

"Why shouldn't it work out?" Soroka grunted, shrugged and grinned in his own turn, while a wolfish gleam appeared in his narrowed eyes.

"Sure it'll work!" growled the three Orshan troopers who were named Bilous, Zavratynski and Lubyenetz, eying their grim commander.

"But what is it that we're to do, colonel?" Soroka asked quietly.

"We have to seize and carry off the Prince," Kmita said.

He watched the soldiers to see how they'd react to what any ordinary man would dismiss as a madman's fancy. But they only stared stolidly back at him, saying nothing. No feeling showed in their harsh, weatherbeaten faces. Their eyes were fixed on him with unquestioning obedience, and only their heavy mustaches moved slowly up and down to betray that something extraordinary was taking place inside them, while their hard, ruthless features turned gradually as fierce and cruel as a roadside brigand's.

"It's a long way to any rewards," Kmita reminded them. "But the stake is near."

"There's not many of us," Zavratynski muttered.

"This is a lot tougher than that business with Hovansky," Lubyenetz added grimly.

"All the Prince's troops are in the market square," Kmita said. "All we have to contend with is a small halberdier guard, and about twenty courtiers who don't even have sabers close to hand and don't expect any kind of trouble. But you're quite right. This isn't like the things we did to harass Hovansky. To abduct a general from the middle of his entire army is an unheard of thing."

"If you're staking your head on this, commandant," Soroka shot back, "why shouldn't we stake ours?"

"Listen closely, then!" Kmita ordered. "If we don't get him by trickery and cunning then we won't get him at all. Listen now! This is how we'll do it. I'll go into his rooms and bring him outside. If the Prince mounts my horse then I'll mount the spare, and we'll all ride away at a trot. But after we've gone about a hundred paces I want two of you to grab him by the arms and ride like the Devil!"

"By your order, sir," said Soroka.

"But if we don't come out together," Kmita went on, "then listen for a pistol shot in the Prince's chamber. When you hear it, blast the guards with your scatter guns and hold my horse ready."

"We'll do it," Soroka said.

"Forward!" Kmita ordered.

★ ★ ★

They spurred forward once more and a quarter of an hour later they stood before the open gates of the *Starosta's* manor. Six halberdiers lounged in the gateway as before and four more stood in the entrance of the house itself. Coachmen and postilions bustled in the courtyard under the watchful eye of an imposing looking courtier who, like almost everyone else in sight, was a foreigner to judge by his wig and costume. Further along the yard, nearer to the coach house, grooms in Radzivill livery were busy harnessing matched teams of horses to two more light traveling carriages, backing the animals carefully into their traces, while a swarm of lackeys, hurried and watched over by a black-robed astrologer or court physician, loaded the carriages with baggage.

Kmita announced himself, as before, to the duty officer who led him to the Prince.

"How are you, cavalier?" Prince Boguslav seemed both amused and relieved to see him. "You left in such a rush that I thought my words woke some scruples in you. I almost didn't expect to see you again."

"How could I go without taking my leave of Your Highness?" Kmita said.

"All's well that ends well, eh? I didn't think the Prince-*Voyevode* would send someone of whom he wasn't sure on such a vital mission. In fact I'll make some use of you myself. I have a few letters of my own for you to deliver, including one to the King of Sweden. But why are you armed to the teeth as if you were riding into battle?"

"Because I'll soon be in confederate territory. Your Highness told me himself that a rebel regiment passed this way not long ago. I know who they are. They're a dangerous lot and they're led by a first-rate soldier."

"And who is that?"

"Pan Volodyovski. And he has other famous people with him, including Mirski, Oskierka, and that Yan Skshetuski whose wife Your Highness wanted to besiege in Tikotzin. All of them rebelled against the Hetman and that's a real pity because they are all fine and experienced soldiers. But what can one do? It seems there are still some stupid people in this Commonwealth who don't want to pull at that length of cloth along with the Cossacks and the Swedes."

"There's never a shortage of fools," the Prince said. "Especially in this country. But here are my letters! Besides which, I want you to tell his Swedish Majesty that I'm on his side just like my first cousin, only I have to pretend loyalty to Poland for a little longer."

"Who can avoid pretending?" Kmita answered. "Everyone pretends one thing or another, especially if he wants to accomplish something that'll matter."

"That's it exactly. Do well for us, cavalier, and I won't let Prince Yanush surpass me in rewarding you."

"Ah," Kmita said. "If that's the case, then I'd like to ask Your Highness for a favor in advance."

"I should've known it!" Boguslav answered laughing. "I imagine Prince Yanush didn't equip you too well for the journey, eh? He's as unwilling to dip his hand in his money bags as if he had snakes nesting in them."

"No, no, Highness, it's nothing like that," Pan Andrei assured him. "I took no money from the Hetman and I wouldn't ask for any from you. I pay my own way."

Prince Boguslav stared at the young soldier with genuine surprise. "You do, eh? Then the Kmitas must really be a rare breed... But what's it all about, then?"

"Here's the thing, Highness. Leaving Keydany, I took along a horse of even finer breed, so as to make a better showing among the Swedes. I'm not exaggerating when I say there's none better in the Hetman's stables. But now I'm sorry I did that. The journey might use him up and waste him, and that would be a crime. Or he might fall into the hands of the enemy —like that Pan Volodyovski, for example—who has a personal grudge against me, and who'd like nothing better than to rob me of something of great value. So I'd like to ask Your Highness to take him for safekeeping and use him until I return."

"You'd do better to sell him to me," Prince Boguslav said.

"That'd be like selling a friend, Your Highness. That horse saved my neck maybe a hundred times, because he has this great virtue that he fights in battle right along with his rider. He bites like a lion."

"Does he, now?" Prince Boguslav asked, showing immediate interest.

"And he does even more than that!" Kmita said. "If I could be sure that Your Highness wouldn't be offended, I'd bet a hundred gold-pieces that you don't have a horse like that yourself."

"Perhaps I'd take your bet if there was time to stage a race today. Alright, then, I'll keep him for you although I'd rather buy him. But where is this wonder?"

"Just outside the gate! But you are right, Highness, to call him a wonder. The Turkish Sultan isn't likely to have a horse like him. He's not from these parts. He's from Anatolia. But I think he'd be rare even there."

"Then let's go out and take a look at him."

"I'm at your service, Highness."

★ ★ ★

The Prince put on his plumed hat and they went outside to where Kmita's soldiers held two saddled thoroughbreds near the outer gate. One of the animals—black as a raven and with a white flash on his forehead and along his off-leg —was indeed a beauty.

"That's the one, eh?" the Prince said at once. "I don't know if he's as much of a wonder as you say he is, but he certainly looks magnificent."

"Walk him by!" Kmita ordered, and then changed his mind. "No! Hold it! I'll ride him past myself."

The horse looked even more beautiful under a skilled rider. His blood raced within him, his wide, protruding eyes glowed with life and courage, and the breeze lifted his rich, thick mane as Kmita wheeled to right and left before the gate, changed pace and stride with the pressure of his knees alone, and finally rode directly at the Prince until the animal's flared nostrils were a hand's breadth from the Prince's face.

"*Halt!*" he cried in German and the animal stood stock still as if rooted in the ground.

"Well?" Kmita asked.

"As they say," Prince Boguslav smiled. "The legs and eyes of a deer, the stride of a wolf, and the breast of a woman. And he obeys commands in German too?"

"I had a Courlander for a trainer," Kmita said. "And he drilled him in the German fashion."

"Better and better," mused the Prince. "And can he run?"

"A Tartar wouldn't be able to catch him. Your Highness will be able to outrun the wind!"

"He moves well. He must have been well trained."

"Is he trained?" Kmita laughed. "Your Highness won't believe this, but he can go at full gallop in a rank of other horses and he won't break formation by a nose even if you drop the reins. If Your Highness would deign to try him over a couple of furlongs, and if he sticks as much as half a head outside the rank, I'll give him to you for nothing!"

"That would be the greatest wonder of them all, if he kept ranks on free rein."

"It's not only a wonder but a great convenience," Kmita said. "I've done it on him many a time when it was useful to have a saber in one hand and a pistol in the other."

"And what if the rank wheels around?"

"Then he'll wheel right with it! Without breaking out by an inch or falling behind."

"That I don't believe," the Prince said. "No horse can do that. I saw in France the horses of the King's Musketeers, which are especially trained for ceremonial exercises, but even they can't turn like that without reins."

"This horse thinks like a man," Kmita said. "Why don't you try him, Highness?"

"Alright," the Prince said after a moment's thought. "Bring him here."

Kmita held the animal himself and the Prince leaped lightly into the saddle and started patting the horse's gleaming neck.

"It's a strange thing," he mused. "All horses get a little fly-blown in the Autumn but this one looks as if he'd just stepped out of running water. Which way shall we go?"

"Let's try a rank abreast towards the woods. The road is straight and wide in that direction and we won't run the risk of running into wagons as we would riding towards the town."

"Let it be the woods, then," the Prince agreed. "Two furlongs at the gallop?"

"That should do it, Highness. We'll form a rank with Your Highness in the middle and one of my men on each side. I'll come up behind. Now, if Your Highness would just drop the reins..."

"Done!" Prince Boguslav said. "Form ranks!"

Two of Kmita's soldiers drew up on each side of the Prince, the three horsemen faced the highway that led towards the woods and vanished among the trees, and Kmita, Soroka and the remaining soldier formed a second rank behind them.

"Forward at a gallop!" Prince Boguslav barked out a command. "Ride!"

* * *

The men spurred their horses, the animals leaped forward and only moments later they were in full gallop and flying like the wind.

A cloud of dust boiled up from under the hooves, hiding them almost at once from the curious eyes of the Prince's courtiers and attendants who had come out to watch, and who clustered excitedly by the gate. The well-trained animals hurtled forward with heaving flanks, running at full speed, and the Prince could note that after a furlong his mount kept in perfect line with the other horses, even though he rode with slack reins from the opening leap, his hands on his hips.

They ran through another furlong.

The woods neared them swiftly.

Kmita looked back and saw only a thick cloud of dust billowing behind them. There was no more than a dim, hazy outline of the receding house. He could see none of the Prince's courtiers and attendants.

"Take him!" he shouted suddenly in a terrifying voice.

Bilous and the gigantic Zavratynski seized the Prince at once, each grasping one of his arms with a fist like iron, and twisting it high behind his back; at the same time they spurred their animals into an even greater speed, while the horse on which the Prince was riding kept perfect pace between them.

Amazement, a flash of terror and then an utter fury swept through Boguslav's face. The wind struck him like a fist and robbed him of both breath and speech. He tried to twist free but the frantic movements merely added to the pain in his tortured shoulders.

"What is this, you scum?" he screamed out at last. "How dare you! Let me go! Don't you know who I am?"

But in that moment Kmita rode up behind him and pushed the barrel of a pistol between his shoulder blades.

"Don't struggle or you're dead!" he shouted.

"Traitor!" cried the Prince.

"And what are you?" asked Kmita.

And they galloped on.

Chapter Forty-two

THEY GALLOPED FOR a long time along the forest floor, riding at such breakneck speed that the pines seemed to fly past them in a pell-mell panic of their own.

The woodland miles vanished under them. They passed roadside taverns, the huts of the woodsmen, pitch makers' smoky clearings, and carters' drays plodding either singly or in groups towards the little market town they had left behind; these leaped up before them and vanished like a dream. The speed of their passage created a dizzying reality of its own. From time to time Prince Boguslav twisted in his saddle as if trying to wrench himself free again, but then his arms and shoulders pained him all the harder in the steel grasp of Kmita's men, while Pan Andrei pressed his pistol barrel to his back.

The Prince lost his hat.

The wind scoured his pampered skin and spilled the thick, lustrous coils of his wig into a tumbled, wind-whipped mass of pale golden threads, and they galloped on until coarse, white sheets of foam began to drip off the horses mouths and spatter the ground behind them.

At last they had to slow their pace to give both the animals and the men time to draw a breath. Pilvishkye was so far behind them now that all chance of pursuit was gone and they went on at a walk, shrouded in the white mist of the animals' weary exhalations.

The Prince made no sound since that first, furious cry of anger and amazement until his raging senses cooled enough for him to regain control over his emotions. Then he asked:

"Where are you taking me?"

"You'll know when we get there," Kmita said.

Boguslav said nothing for a while longer. Then he drawled out with another weary, aristocratic grimace as if he was bored: "Tell those common louts of yours to let go of my arms, cavalier, or they'll wrench them off. I'll show them mercy if they do that. They will simply hang. Otherwise they'll gasp out their last breath on the stake."

"They aren't common louts, they're boyars and gentry!" Kmita said. "As for your threats, it's hard to say who'll be dying first, they or you."

"Do you know whom you've raised your hands against?" the Prince asked, turning to the soldiers.

"We know," they both answered.

"In the name of all the demons in Hell!" the Prince roared, enraged. "Will you tell these damned people to let me go or not?"

"I'll have Your Highness' arms roped behind your back if that'll be easier," Kmita said.

"That'll twist them off altogether!"

"If you were anybody else I'd accept your word that you won't try to get away. But your kind can't be trusted!"

"I'll give you my word, alright! I'm not only going to escape at the first opportunity but I'll have you torn apart with wild horses when I get my hands on you again!"

"God will give each of us whatever He pleases," Kmita shrugged. "But I'd rather have an honest threat than a lying promise. Let go of his arms," he said to the soldiers. "Just keep a good grip on his reins. If he tries to break free kill him on the spot. And you, Highness, take a look back here. One twitch of my finger and there'll be a bullet in your skull. I won't miss because I never do. So sit quiet and still on your horse and don't try to bolt."

"I couldn't care less, cavalier, for you or your bullets," the Prince said, as indifferent as if Kmita was beneath his notice, and stretched his arms to let his blood flow freely through his veins again, while the two soldiers seized his horse's reins.

After another moment Boguslav spoke again.

"Ha, but I see you don't even dare to look me in the eye, Master Kmita. You'd rather skulk behind my back."

"Not at all!" Pan Andrei answered, spurred his horse forward, pushed Zavratynski aside, seized the reins he held, and stared straight into Prince Boguslav's face.

"Well, how's my horse?" he asked. "Did I lie about him?"

"He's good," the Prince said. "I'll be glad to buy him if you like."

"Thanks for nothing, Highness! He deserves better than to carry a traitor for the rest of his life."

"You're a fool, Kmita."

"I know. I trusted the Radzivills."

★ ★ ★

And again there was a long moment of silence which the Prince broke first as he did before.

"Tell me, Mister Kmita. Are you sure that you're quite sane? That your wits aren't scrambled? Have you asked yourself, you madman, what it is you've done? Whom you've tangled with? Whom you are abducting? Hasn't it occurred to you that you'd be better off if you hadn't been born? And that there isn't a man alive in Europe, not just here in Poland, who'd dare to do something of this kind?"

"Then there can't be much spirit in that Europe," Kmita shrugged again. "Because I not only took Your Highness but I'm holding you and I won't let go."

"He has to be stark raving mad!" the Prince cried out as if to himself.

"My dear Prince," Pan Andrei answered with that same calm, contemptuous indifference which had angered him so much before in Boguslav's tone. "You're in my hands so make your peace with that and don't waste your breath. No one will help you because your people saw you leaving with us of your own free will. No one saw it when my men caught you by the arms because there was a cloud of dust between us and your retainers, and even if they could catch a glimpse of something it was too far for your people to make out what happened. They'll wait for you for two hours at least. In the third hour they'll become impatient. In the fourth and fifth they'll start getting anxious. In the sixth hour they'll send somebody to find you and by that time we'll be beyond Mariampol."

"So what?"

"So this: there is no pursuit. And even if there was one your men wouldn't catch us because their horses are worn from the road and ours are fresh and rested. But if by some miracle, or rather by some foul demonic intercession, they should catch up with us, then even that wouldn't help you much because—as you see me here!—I'd crush Your Highness' skull before they set you free! Which is exactly what I'll do if there's no other way. So here's the situation: Radzivill has a whole court, an army, cannon and dragoons, and Kmita has six troopers, but for all that Kmita holds Radzivill by the scruff of his neck and that's all there's to it."

"And what comes next?" the Prince asked.

"Nothing! Or rather whatever strikes my fancy! We'll go where I please. Your Highness had better give your thanks to God that you're still alive, because if I hadn't had ten buckets of cold water thrown over my head you'd be in the next world already, which means that you'd be squirming in Hell because you're not only a heretic but a traitor."

"You'd dare to do that?"

"I don't wish to boast but Your Highness would have a hard time finding something that I wouldn't dare. As you can see best by what happened to you."

★   ★   ★

The Prince looked with greater care into the young man's coldly narrowed features.

"The Devil wrote it in your face that you're ready for anything," he said. "And you're right, I'm the best example. I'll even tell you that you've surprised me with your daring and that's no easy matter."

"Think what you like, Highness, it's all one to me." Kmita shrugged again. "I couldn't care less. Just thank God that you're still alive and let it go at that."

"No! On the contrary! *You* give thanks for that! Because if you spilled one drop of my blood... or if a single hair should fall from head... then the Radzivills would find you even if you hid under the earth. If you're counting on the fact that there is now a split in our family, and if you think that the Radzivills of Nesvyesh and Olysa wouldn't hound you until you're rotting in the ground, then think again! Radzivill blood must always be avenged, a terrible example must be made, or there'd be no way for any of us to live in this Commonwealth. Nor can you hide abroad! The German Emperor will give you up because I'm a prince of the empire. The Elector of Brandenburg is my uncle. The Prince of Orange is his brother-in-law. The French King and Queen and all their ministers are my friends. So where can you go? The Turks and the Tartars will sell you to us as surely as there's a God in Heaven, even if you should cost us half of our combined fortunes! There isn't a safe corner for you anywhere on earth. There are no forests deep or trackless enough for you to escape us. Nor are there any people anywhere through whom we can't reach you!"

"Strange, isn't it,"—Kmita shrugged again—"that Your Highness is so concerned about my health. Here you are, one of the most powerful men alive, and all it'll take is one squeeze on this trigger and you'll be gone for ever."

"That I don't deny." It was Boguslav's turn to shrug. "It's happened before that a great man died at the hands of a totally unimportant one. The Great Pompey was killed by a nameless lout, to name just one. French Kings have been murdered by people of a lower order. My own father died like that, to look no further for examples... The only question I suggest to you is: what comes next?"

"Why should I care?" Kmita's grim smile seemed like disdain itself. "I never gave much thought to what might come tomorrow. If I must tangle with all the Radzivills at once, I'll do it, and only God can tell who'll have a hotter time of it! I've had one sword or another hanging over my head for years but that never robbed me of a good night's sleep. And if one Radzivill isn't enough for me I'll help myself to a second or a third."

"As God is dear to me!" Prince Boguslav laughed. "I like you more and more! I'll say again that you must be the only man in Europe who'd dare to try something of this kind..."

"And I'll say again that this Europe must be a dull, lifeless sort of place," Kmita said. "Because there wasn't much to this adventure."

"Ha!"—and the Prince shook his head in wonder and amusement—"there isn't a speck of worry in that creature! Not a thought of what will happen to him! I like daring men and there are getting to be fewer of them all the time... Imagine, he abducts a Radzivill and holds him without a care in the world, as if he owned him... Where are you from, cavalier? Where do they breed men like you?"

"Orsha," Kmita said.

"Well, my Orshan cousin, I'm sorry the Radzivills have lost you because men like you could do a lot for us. Hmm... if it wasn't a matter that concerned me directly I'd do a lot to win you over again."

"It's too late for that!" Kmita said.

"That goes without saying!" said the Prince. "It's far too late for anything like that. But this much I'll promise you. I'll have you shot by a firing squad rather than impale you. You deserve a clean, soldier's death."

Boguslav went on nodding and shaking his head in genuine amazement. "Imagine it... to take me like that, right from the middle of all my men...!"

Pan Andrei said nothing and the Prince plunged into a long moment of thought of his own.

"Ah, to the Devil with it!" he cried out at last. "What difference would it make? If you release me at once I'll give up my vengeance! Just give me your word that you won't mention this to anyone and order your men to keep their mouths shut about it too!"

"Out of the question!" Kmita said.

"What are you after, then? Is it ransom?"

"No."

"Then why did you abduct me, in the Devil's name? I don't understand this!"

"It'd take a lot of telling... Your Highness will find out in good time."

"And what are we to do in the meantime if we can't talk about it? Admit it, cavalier! You snatched me in a moment of fury and desperation and now you've no idea what to do with me!"

"That's my business!" Kmita snapped. "And as to whether I know what I'm doing, we'll see soon enough!"

★   ★   ★

They rode in silence for some minutes longer and then impatience flickered across Prince Boguslav's face.

"You don't have much to say, Master Orshan," he snapped angrily. "But tell me at least this one thing. Were you on your way to Podlasye with a ready plan to raise your hand against me? Or did that mad thought flash into your head later, on the spur of the moment?"

"That I can answer frankly,"Pan Andrei said with a quick rush of feeling. "Because my mouth is burning to spill out the truth of why I've turned against you Radzivills. Nor will I ever come back into your service, not as long as there's one gasp of breath left in my body! The Prince-Palatine of Vilna misled me! He had me swear on the cross that I wouldn't leave him until death...!"

"You have a curious way of keeping your vows, I must say," Boguslav interrupted.

"That's right!" Violence surged through Pan Andrei's voice. "If I've lost my soul... if I'm damned for ever... it's your Radzivill doing! But I'm throwing myself on God's mercy. Let Him judge my motives! I'd rather burn in Hell for the rest of time then to serve you knowing that I'm serving traitors! I'd rather burn a hundred times than serve you one day longer because I'd be damned to eternal hellfire anyway if I'd stayed faithful to you...

"I've nothing to lose now," he went on, trembling with emotion. "But at least I'll be able to say on Judgment Day: I didn't know to what I was swearing, and when I realized that my oath meant treason to my country, and to everything it means to be a Pole, I broke that oath gladly! And now, Lord, judge me if you will!"

"Most moving. But let's get back to the matter at hand, shall we?"Boguslav said calmly.

But Pan Andrei couldn't speak just then. His tortured breath came in chaotic gasps and he trembled all over at the thought of his broken vow. He rode in silence, his face contorted as if he were in agonizing pain, and he stared at the ground like a man crushed by an absolute calamity.

"Let's get on with it, shall we?"Boguslav said again, totally unmoved. "But could we be a little less dramatic about it, hmm?"

Kmita shook himself as if wakening from a nightmare, and

continued in a cracked, wondering voice as if his own words puzzled and confused him:

"I believed the Hetman. I trusted him as if he were my own father. I can't forget that banquet when he told us for the first time that he had joined the Swedes! God, what I felt that night, what I went through! Perhaps that suffering will count for something at the final judgment... Others—good, decent men, every one of them—threw their command insignia at his feet, taking the side of our Motherland no matter what it cost them, but I didn't stir! I stood as still and silent as a rotten tree trunk... gnawed by shame, disgrace and humiliation because someone called me a traitor to my face... Ah, dear God, and who was it who said it! Ey, it's best not to think about it, Highness... not to recollect... or I'll go mad and blow your brains out right here on the spot! It's you, you damned traitors and betrayers who led me to all that!"

★ ★ ★

A frightful, terrifying hatred crept out of the depths of Kmita's soul and twisted in his face like some dreadful prehistoric creature that crawled out of its dank subterranean cave into open daylight. Death gleamed in his eyes. But Prince Boguslav eyed him with a calm, undisturbed and quite fearless interest, much as he'd watch a chained, mad dog baying at a distance.

"Do go on," he drawled. "I find this quite amusing, as such things go."

Kmita dropped the reins of Prince Boguslav's horse and took off his cap as if he wished to cool his inflamed head and let the breeze run across his face.

"Later that night," he said, "I went to see the Hetman. He had me brought to him under guard but I'd have come without that. I thought: '*I'll break with him and break my oath as well. I'll strangle him with my own two hands, set fire to the powder stores and blow up Keydany, and let things happen as they may thereafter!*' But he could read my mind. He knew what I was. He never doubted that I was ready for anything, mad fool that I was! I saw how he fingered those pistols in that case. *That's nothing*, I told myself. *Either he'll miss or he won't! Either way the torment will be over...*"

A small smile flickered briefly across Boguslav's lips and he nodded quietly as if he already knew the rest, but Kmita went on talking in his grim, desperate voice:

"But he began to work on me, to tell me things I'd never be able to imagine, to paint such glorious prospects before my blind, inexperienced eyes that he quite dazzled my ignorant, simple mind and I began to see him as a savior...! Ah,"—and the puzzled young soldier turned to Prince Boguslav as if his own words baffled and confounded him—"can Your Highness guess what happened next?"

"He convinced a credulous young fool, I expect."

"To such an extent that I threw myself at his feet!" Kmita cried. "I saw him as a father, the country's only savior! I pledged myself to him with my heart, soul and body... everything! As if he was the Devil! I'd have thrown myself off the castle tower if that would prove his honesty and his decency to others!"

"I thought that would happen," Boguslav observed.

"What I lost in that service... well, I won't talk about that. But I served him well. I kept my own regiment in line and ranked behind him, may it kill him yet! I destroyed others who rebelled against him. My arms are red to the elbows with the blood of brothers but I thought that even that horror was necessary for the country's good. My whole soul ached and boiled when I had all those splendid soldiers shot by firing squads or when he made me some promise that he didn't keep. But I always thought: '*I'm stupid. He is wise. This must be done because it is needed.*' It's only now when I heard about those poisonings that the marrow seemed to freeze in all my bones! '*How's that?*' I asked myself. '*Is this the way a Hetman makes war?*' You want to poison good soldiers or slaughter them in their sleep? Is that the Radzivill way? And I'm to carry orders of that kind?"

"You don't know much about political expediency, cavalier," the Prince interrupted.

"To Hell with all your politics!" Kmita shouted fiercely. "Leave them to some Machiavellian poisoner, not to a Polish noble whom God gifted with a finer blood than others but whom He also gave the duty to fight with a saber, not with an apothecary's concoctions, and to guard his honor!"

"Is it those letters, then, that offended you so much that you decided to turn against the Radzivills?"

"No, not the letters! I'd have handed them to some hangman or tossed them in a fire because I'm not an poisoner's errand boy. I'd have given up this mission but I'd have kept on serving. As you said, that's politics, and I'd have found some other way to follow the Hetman. Who knows what I'd have done if I could keep trusting and believing him! But then it occurred to me that you Radzivills might be plotting to poison our country in just the same way that you planned to murder those poor loyal soldiers..."

Boguslav nodded briefly once again as if a fleeting thought had proved itself correct, and Kmita went on, as if he were in the grip of some profound trance:

"God let me keep a tight grip on myself though my head was burning like a lighted fuse. He let me swallow all that rage and horror. He gave me the ability to try to draw the truth out of you. He made it possible for me to present myself to you as someone just as low and treacherous and greedy and corrupt as a Radzivill, and to trick you with your own high opinion of yourself."

"*You?*" Nothing could have outraged Prince Boguslav more than to be bested in those devious manipulative skills of a diplomat and courtier on which he prided himself the most. "You thought you'd outmaneuver *me?*"

"That's right! And God helped me. So that a simple, ignorant, untutored soldier could outfox such a devious and experienced statesman! So that Your Highness thought me as corrupt as you Radzivills and didn't hide any of your own rottenness. So that you exposed all your machinations as clearly as if you etched them into the palm of my hand! I tell you, my hair was standing up on end in horror but I listened and I kept listening until I heard it all..."

And here Pan Andrei's voice broke at last with pain, rage and utter indignation.

"Oh you damned traitors! Parricides! How is it that lightning hasn't struck you yet? Why doesn't the earth open up before you and swallow you alive? So you plot the destruction of the Commonwealth along with Hmyelnitzki, the Swedes, the Russians, the Brandenburg Elector, the Hungarians and the

Devil himself for all I know? You want to carve a royal mantle for yourselves out of her living flesh? You want to sell her off? Divide her? Tear your own mother apart like a pack of wolves? Is that your gratitude for all the goodness that she showered on you for two hundred years? For all those offices and positions and honors and distinctions? For all your lands and holdings? For those rich counties she gave you to administer? For all that wealth that foreign kings might envy? And you're prepared to ignore her tears and her suffering and pain as long as your own selfish purposes are served? Where is your conscience? Where's your faith and your decency? What kind of monsters spewed you out into this world?"

"A moment, cavalier!" Prince Boguslav interrupted coldly. "You have me in your hands. Kill me if you wish. But do me one favor, will you? Don't bore me to death."

And then they both grew quiet.

★ ★ ★

But Kmita's words pierced Boguslav's vanity, where he hurt the most. They showed with perfect clarity that a simple soldier did, indeed, outfox the sophisticated, world-wise strategist, and that he managed to draw the whole naked truth out of him. Boguslav knew that he'd committed an unparalleled blunder and that his carelessness had betrayed the most secret plans that he and the Hetman worked so hard to create between them.

The wound was deep. His pride boiled in fury. His self-esteem suffered a painful blow.

"Don't flatter yourself, Master Kmita, that you got the truth out of me by your wits alone," he snarled, no longer bothering to hide his rage. "I spoke openly because I assumed that the Prince-Palatine would send me a man I could trust!"

"He did send you a trustworthy man!" Kmita rejoined hotly. "But you've lost him now! From now on you'll have only worthless scoundrels and ruffians in your service!"

"If this abduction isn't the act of a scoundrel then let my rapier grow into my hand the next time I draw it!" Boguslav swore, enraged.

"That's just a legitimate subterfuge of war. I learned it in a hard school, you can believe that much. Your Highness wanted to know who I am and where I have come from? You know it now. I won't be going to our King empty-handed!

"And do you really think that Yan Casimir will let a single hair fall from my head?"

"That's not for me to say." Kmita shrugged. "That's up to your judges."

But suddenly Kmita pulled up his horse and reined the Prince's mount as well. The cavalcade halted on the forest track.

"Hey!" he said. "And what about the *Voyevode's* letter? D'you have it with you, Highness?"

"Even if I had it I wouldn't give it to you!" the Prince shot back swiftly. "The letter stayed behind in Pilvishkye."

"Search him!" Kmita cried.

The soldiers seized the Prince by the arms again and Soroka started rummaging in his pockets. After a short while he found the letter and handed it to Kmita.

"Well, here's one piece of evidence against you and your plots," Pan Andrei said. "The King of Poland will know your true colors, and the King of Sweden will see that even though you're serving him just now, the *Voyevode* of Vilna is ready to turn against him the first time the Swedes slip in their campaign of conquest. All your plots and treasons will be exposed for the world to see. And I've other letters too, don't I? To the King of Sweden, to Wittemberg and to Radeyovski... Yes, you are great and powerful, you Radzivills. But I wonder if you'll find enough room to breathe when both these Kings discover what you're up to and pay you back in kind."

The chilly glow of hatred glittered for a moment in Prince Boguslav's eyes but he contained his rage.

"Good, cavalier!" he said. "We know where we stand. It's life or death between us from now on, and we'll meet again! You can add a little to our difficulties and cause us some trouble but I'll tell you this much: no one in this country has ever dared to do what you have done... No one! You've signed a death warrant for yourself and everybody who is dear to you!"

"I have a saber for my own defense," Kmita said and shrugged. "And I've the means to protect those I love."

"Ah," Prince Boguslav said, nodding in relief. "You have me for a hostage."

And despite all his rage he breathed freely once more. He understood at once that Kmita wouldn't kill him no matter what happened. He was too valuable to his abductor at the moment.

It was a thought which could be exploited.

* * *

They spurred their horses into a trot again and, in half an hour, they came across two riders, each leading a pair of pack-horses. These were Kmita's troopers sent ahead from Pilvishkye before the abduction.

"Anything new?" Kmita asked them.

"Not much, commandant. Only our nags have gotten real tired, 'cause we came at a dead run all this way."

"We'll halt in a moment."

"There's some kind of hut just around the bend, Your Honor. It could be an inn."

"Ride ahead and take a look, Soroka," Kmita ordered. "And get some feed ready for the horses. We have to halt for a bit whether it's an inn or not."

"Very good, commandant!"

Soroka spurred his horse into a tired gallop and the others followed slowly, at a walk. They came to a broad clearing where one belt of woods ended and another started. Kmita flanked the Prince on one side, Lubyenetz on the other. Each grasped the reins of Boguslav's horse.

Meanwhile Prince Boguslav appeared to have regained his detachment. He no longer spoke or tried to draw Pan Andrei into conversation. He looked depressed, as if he'd lost a lot of his spirit, and as if the journey or the situation in which he found himself had quite exhausted and disheartened him, and it was only the occasional sideways glance he threw at either Kmita or Lubyenetz which showed that his cold, calculating mind was still at work, judging his chances of knocking down one of his captors or the other and breaking out to freedom.

* * *

Meanwhile they'd drawn near a low, ramshackle structure crouched at the tip of the new belt of woods, which turned out to be a smithy and a wheelwright's shop rather than a tavern. It was one of those roadside havens, plentiful in that part of the country, where travelers could replace lost horseshoes and have their wagon wheels repaired or reset.

The blacksmith's forge stood back from the road, separated by a small, littered yard from the unpaved highway. It had no fence. Sparse grass grew in dusty clumps among the trodden spaces which were heaped with disordered piles of broken axles and remnants of wagons.

There were no travelers there when Kmita's troop approached. Only Soroka's horse, tied to a hitching post, showed that someone had stopped in this forlorn place that day. The sergeant himself was standing on the ground, questioning the Tartar blacksmith and his two assistants.

"We won't fill our bellies at this rest stop, that's certain," the Prince observed with a narrow smile.

"We have food and liquor with us," Kmita said.

"We do? That's good." Boguslav seemed surprisingly content. "We need something to restore our strength."

They reined-in their horses.

Kmita leaped to the ground, shoved his pistol into his belt, handed his own horse's reins to Soroka, and held onto the bridle of the Prince's mount which Lubyenetz was grasping from the other side.

"Your Highness will dismount," he said.

"Why? I can eat and drink in the saddle," the Prince said and leaned forward over Kmita's head.

"Please get down at once!" Kmita shouted fiercely.

"No, *you* go down!" cried the Prince in a savage voice while, at the same time, his hand shot out with lightning speed for Pan Andrei's pistol. He pulled it clear, snapped back the hammer and cocked it instantly with his other hand, and fired it straight into Kmita's face.

"Jezus Maria!" Kmita cried and fell.

But before his body hit the ground, the Prince struck his horse with both spurs at once and hauled back so savagely on the reins that the animal leaped straight into the air, while his rider twisted in the saddle and plunged the steel pistol barrel between Lubyenetz's eyes with the full force of his weight behind it.

Lubyenetz uttered one short scream and fell out of his saddle, and before the others could grasp what had happened the Prince burst through them like a hurricane, charged into the highway and galloped at full speed back the way they'd come.

"After him! Get him!" the troopers howled in rage and the three men who were still on horseback spurred into the road behind him.

Soroka seized a musket he had left leaning against the smithy wall and took careful aim at the fugitive, or rather at his horse which seemed to skim the ground like an arrow speeding to its target.

He fired.

He jumped forward through the smoke to see the result, shading his eyes with his gnarled hand, then spat in disgust and shook his grizzled head.

"Missed him!" he snarled.

In that moment Prince Boguslav vanished beyond the bend in the road and his pursuers vanished right behind him.

Then the old sergeant turned to the blacksmith and his terrified helpers and shouted:

"Water!"

They ran to the well and Soroka knelt beside the motionless Pan Andrei. The young man's face was black with burned gunpowder and thick with drops of blood. His eyes were closed. The left side of his temple, along with his cheek, eye and mustache, was sooty and scorched. The sergeant felt gingerly all along his skull to see if the bone was crushed anywhere, then nodded in satisfaction.

"The head's still in one piece," he muttered.

But Kmita gave no sign of life and blood welled thickly out of his ruined face. The blacksmith's helpers ran up with a bucket full of cold well-water and a handful of clean rags, and Soroka set about washing the wound which showed eventually among the sooty blisters. The bullet had torn a deep furrow in Kmita's cheek and carried away the end of his left ear but the cheekbone seemed to be intact and the old sergeant drew a deep, thankful breath.

"He'll live!" he cried out joyfully. "He'll recover!"

And then a soft, surprising tear rolled down the fierce face of the old marauder.

In the meantime Trooper Bilous, one of the three soldiers

who had pursued the Prince, appeared at the bend of the road and galloped to the smithy.

"Well?" Soroka asked.

The soldier shrugged.

"Nothing!" he said.

"Are the others coming back behind you?"

"They won't be back at all."

"What are you saying, trooper?"

"Sergeant! That man's a wizard! He's magic, I tell you. Zavratynski got to him first because he had the best horse of the lot of us and because that man let him catch him! Right before our eyes he tore the saber out of Zavratynski's hand and ran him through like a practice dummy. Vitkovski was next in line and leaped up to help and he cut him down in a flash as if lightning struck him! I didn't wait my turn. Sergeant, that's not an ordinary man, I tell you. He may very well be on his way back here right now to finish off the rest of us!"

"We're wasting time, then!" Soroka cried out. "Let's get out of here!"

★   ★   ★

They set about roping together a stretcher for Kmita and tied it securely between two packhorses while Soroka posted two men, armed with muskets, on the road just in case the terrible Prince reappeared among them.

But Prince Boguslav, sure that Kmita was dead, made his way calmly back towards Pilvishkye.

It was already evening, and a chilly twilight started to settle around him on the road, when he encountered an entire regiment of armored cuirassiers sent after him by the anxious General Peterson.

The commanding officer caught sight of him and galloped towards him.

"Your Highness!" he cried with relief. "We didn't know what to think... We weren't sure...!"

But Prince interrupted him with a careless gesture. "It was nothing," he said. "I was merely trying out this horse I bought, in the company of that cavalier who sold it."

And, after a moment, he smiled and added:

"And I paid him well."

Part Seven

Chapter Forty-three

THE FAITHFUL SOROKA carried his young colonel through deep, trackless forests, with no idea where to go, what to do, or where to turn for help.

Kmita was not only wounded but deafened as well. From time to time Soroka dipped a rag in a pail of water hanging from his saddlebow and washed Pan Andrei's face. At other times he halted his small troop to fill his bucket from the crystalline forest pools and fresh-water springs that rustled everywhere in the undergrowth. But neither the cooling touch of water, nor the occasional halts, nor the lurching motion of his cradle woke the wounded man. He lay as if dead, wide-open eyes staring emptily into the space above him, so that the soldiers who knew less than their old sergeant about treating wounds began to worry if he was still alive.

"He lives," Soroka set their minds at rest. "Give him three days and he'll be in the saddle like the rest of us."

Again his words proved to be prophetic because an hour later Kmita's eyes flickered and stayed open and a single murmur seeped out of his parched lips.

"Water," he whispered.

Soroka lifted a tin cup to his colonel's mouth but Pan Andrei couldn't drink. The raw, gaping wound and the ballooning cheek hurt him too much when he tried to open his mouth. But he stayed conscious. His eyes stared blindly into the depths of the primeval forest as if he didn't know where he was or what had happened to him.

He asked no questions.

His mindless stare wandered through the woodland shadows, into the bright blue splashes of the sky that gleamed between the tree crowns, and at his watchful troopers. But it was the dull, glazed stare of a drunken man waking from a nightmare he didn't understand. He didn't say a word. Not even a moan of pain escaped his lips as Soroka changed the dressings on his swollen wounds. On the contrary, the cool spring water which the sergeant dabbed on his ruined face seemed to give him pleasure and a fleeting smile appeared in his eyes.

Soroka did his best to comfort him.

"Tomorrow, colonel," he said, "you'll be back among us. You'll be yourself again. God grant that we'll get away safely and then you'll be alright."

And once more he proved to have guessed correctly because shortly before nightfall Kmita's eyes flew open, he gazed about with much more awareness, and asked suddenly:

"What's that ringing noise?"

"What ringing, sir?" asked Soroka. "There isn't any ringing."

The sound, apparently, existed only in Pan Andrei's head because the evening was calm, clear and quiet. The setting sun slanted through the thickets, threading its golden rays into the forest darkness, and framing the auburn trunks of the pines around them.

There was no wind.

The air was soft and still. Only dead leaves floated gently to the ground and, here and there, small frightened animals rustled in the undergrowth, scampering into the depths of the forest as the riders passed.

The evening's chill, however, had no effect on Pan Andrei's fever because he muttered thickly into his own half-dreamed, half-conscious visions: "It's a fight to the death between us now, Your Highness. To the death."

Finally the sun vanished altogether and Soroka had to think about stopping for the night. But because they were now in the dark, marshy heart of a trackless forest, with the dank swamp mud sucking greedily at their horses' hooves, they pushed on in search of higher and drier ground.

An hour passed like that. Then another followed. There seemed to be no end to the oozing mudholes. But a bright, full moon climbed over the horizon and hung above the trees so that they could see what lay under them and glimmered before them. Riding ahead of the others now, Soroka peered carefully at the sodden ground, and suddenly reined-in his horse, slipped out of his saddle and began to examine the wet forest floor.

"Some horses passed this way," he grunted. "There's tracks in the mud."

"Who'd ride this way?" asked one of the soldiers who was carrying Kmita. "There's no trail out here."

"But there's hoofprints. See? And a lot of them. There among the pines! It's as clear as daylight."

"Cattle, d'you think?"

"No way. This isn't the season for forest pasturing. Them's hoofprints, alright. Somebody passes this way and not just one time either. So keep a sharp eye. It'd be good to find a woodsman's hut somewhere."

"So let's follow the tracks," one of the soldiers said. "They got to lead somewheres..."

"Alright. Let's go, then!"

* * *

Soroka jumped back on his horse and they set off again. The hoofprints stood out clearly in the peat bog and some of them, bathed in the silver moonlight, looked quite new. But the tired, plodding horses sunk knee-deep in the mire and, after a time, the troopers started worrying if they were following a false trail, set on purpose to mislead a lost traveler, that would lead them only into deeper marshes.

In a half hour, however, they smelled smoke and tar.

"Looks like there's a pitch maker's hut somewheres around here," Soroka told the others.

"There!" said a soldier. "See it? Sparks!"

They halted, peered ahead, and saw a ribbon of reddish, coiled smoke around which leaped the bright yellow sparks of a pitch maker's fire burning in a pit.

They moved forward again, drew nearer, and saw a large, low, thatch-roofed hut, a stone well, and a broad barnlike shed built out of coarse, rough-hewn logs as thick as whole tree trunks. Their road-weary horses neighed suddenly, smelling the well water, and a shrill neighing of several other horses answered them at once from under the shed. At the same time a dark, indistinct human form rose from the broken ground before them.

"How'd you do this time?" the shadowy man asked calmly, apparently taking them for some other riders. "Got a lot of horses?"

Seen more clearly now, the shaggy, unkempt shape was a typical forest pitch maker dressed in soiled sheepskins worn with the wool outside.

"Whose place is this, peasant?" Soroka demanded and the woodsman grew immediately alarmed.

"Wh-wh-who are you?" the man stammered, backing off, frightened and surprised. "Where d'you come from? H-how d'you get in here?"

"Relax!" Soroka told him. "Take it easy. We aren't bandits, if that's what you're thinking."

"Get out! Go on with you!" the pitch maker cried and leaped back a step to get out of their reach. "There's nothing for you here!"

"Shut your mouth!" snarled Soroka. "And stand still! Can't you see we've got a wounded man with us? Lead us to your living quarters while I'm still asking you politely!"

"Who are you, then?"

"What do you care? You just make sure I don't answer you with a bullet, peasant! Do as you are told! Take us to the house or we'll boil you in your own pitch!"

"I can't fight you off all alone," the man grunted coldly. "But there'll be more of us here soon. You'll leave your heads here."

"There'll be more of us too," Soroka lied back. "Lead us to your *izba*, you hear me?"

The pitch maker shrugged. "Come on then. It's your necks, not mine."

"And give us food and liquor. Whatever you've got. We're carrying a rich lord who'll pay you well when he's feeling better."

"If he lives long enough," the pitch maker growled.

★   ★   ★

Snapping and snarling threats at each other they came to the dwelling, a fair-sized one-room *izba*, with a fire glowing on the hearth, and the smell of boiled smoked meats rising from several iron cauldrons as if a supper were being prepared for quite a few men. Soroka saw at once that there were six cots, piled with heaps of sheepskins, ranged along the walls.

"Somebody lives here, alright," he muttered to the others. "And there's more than a few of them too. Keep a sharp eye. Reload your pieces with fresh ball and powder. Make sure that peasant doesn't bolt for it, you hear? Let our hosts sleep outside tonight because this place is ours."

"The masters won't be home tonight," the pitch maker answered.

"That's even better," Sergeant Soroka said. "We won't have to argue with them about sleeping quarters, right? And we'll be on our way tomorrow before they are back. Meanwhile, though, get that stew on the table because we are hungry. And don't spare the oats for our horses either."

"Where would I get oats, Your Worship?" the pitch maker asked. "This is a tar plant, not a livery stable."

"We heard horses in the shed, remember? And where there are horses there's oats, am I right? You don't feed them on your tar and pitch, do you?"

"They aren't my horses, master..."

"Who cares whose they are? They have to eat, just like ours, don't they? So jump to it, peasant! Move or you'll lose some skin!"

The woodsman shrugged, said nothing, and went outside with one of the soldiers to keep an eye on him.

★ ★ ★

Meanwhile Soroka and the others placed the sleeping Pan Andrei on one of the cots and set about their supper. Beside the smoked meats stewing on the fire, they found a large pot of *bigos* made of venison and cabbage, while Soroka rummaged in a cupboard and produced a bowl of hardboiled eggs and a good-sized stoneware crock of homebrewed *gojhalka*.

But he didn't take more than a nip of the liquor, and he wouldn't let his soldiers drink at all that night, because he thought it best to stay on the alert in these borrowed quarters. Those six cots and that barnful of neighing horses seemed highly suspicious. Experience told him that this was, most likely, a hideout for bandits, and a quick inspection of the large lean-to cupboard in which he found the liquor confirmed his suspicions. Its walls were lined with a variety of weapons, there was a dry, well-wrapped keg of gunpowder, and also the most tell-tale sign of all: a litter of assorted bric-a-brac that seemed to have been looted from the gentry's manors. Soroka knew that he could expect neither hospitality nor mercy in the event that his absent hosts made an early and unexpected appearance in their lair, and he decided to hold out against them either by force of arms or by some kind of improvised agreement.

He had no choice about that, he knew. Kmita's return to health required rest and care and, in their frightening situation, with the possibility of pursuit always in his mind, Soroka looked at this hidden, secret lair as a real Godsend.

"He won't find us here," he muttered to himself, thinking of Prince Boguslav. But he also told himself not to bet much on that possibility. He was a canny and experienced campaigner himself, having spent half his life as an armed retainer in the Kmitas' service, and any ordinary fears were quite foreign to him. But sweat burst out all over him at the thought of the terrifying Prince.

"Is he magic, or what?" he growled in his whiskers, peering into shadows. "How could he do us like he did? How could he put down the colonel with so little trouble?"

If there was ever one thing on which Soroka was always ready to stake his life, it was the fearlessness of his young commander and his apparently magic luck. He'd witnessed countless times of seemingly suicidal valor, when destruction would have overwhelmed any other warrior, from which Kmita emerged not only safe but triumphantly victorious. He took part in all of Kmita's famous raids against Hovansky. He followed him through all those violent years, in and out of war, full of other raids, assaults, ambushes, fights, battles and abductions, and he became convinced that his young master could do anything he set his heart upon, rising unscathed out of any firestorm, and able to overcome every difficulty.

"So what's gone wrong all of a sudden?" the troubled old campaigner wished to know.

As far as this hard-headed, blindly loyal old soldier was concerned, Kmita was magic in his own right: the embodiment of invincible power, unbreakable strength, and brilliant luck that went beyond mere human understanding; but now he seemed to have met his match. No! More than that, by God! He had met his master.

"How can that be?" Soroka worried, peering about in the twilight gloom of his providential refuge.

How could one man alone, unarmed and totally in Kmita's hands, tear himself so easily out of the clutches of his fierce abductor? And—more than that!—how could he overthrow Pan Kmita himself, massacre his soldiers, and terrify the rest of them to such an extent that they ran off in fear that he might return?

This was a wonder to surpass all wonders, Soroka was sure, and he racked his brain to discover how such a thing could happen, because he still found it impossible to imagine that any man alive could ride over Kmita as if he was nothing.

"What is this, then?" he muttered, shaken in his faith and just as superstitious as any other soldier. "Could our good luck be over?"

So even though in those other times he was ready to follow Kmita blindfolded into Hovansky's own tents, surrounded as they were by eighty thousand warriors, now he felt his hair standing up on his head in superstitious terror at the thought of that rouged and painted Prince, with his soft skin and his girlish features. He was terrified that in a day or two they'd have to leave the shelter of the forest, and show themselves again on the open highway, where they'd be at the mercy of the Prince's vengeance.

Fear of the Prince himself rather than just his vengeance drove the old sergeant off the beaten track to start with, and that was also why he wanted to stay hidden in this forest, lying low in this bandit hideout as long as he could, until Boguslav's men either lost track of him or got tired of hunting for him in strange and hostile country.

★ ★ ★

But there were other reasons why this refuge didn't seem quite safe enough for him. He wanted to know more about its owners. With this in mind he told the soldiers to keep watch by the door and windows, and snapped at the gloomy peasant to get a lantern and follow him outside.

"I got no lantern, master," the gruff woodsman said.

"So bring a burning brand. It's all one to me if you burn down the barn and the horses in it."

At this, a lantern appeared as if by magic. Soroka made the pitch maker walk ahead of him while he followed with a cocked pistol in his hand.

"Who lives in that dwelling?" he asked along the way.

"The masters live there."

"What are their names?"

"That I can't tell. Don't dare."

"Listen, peasant," the old sergeant sighed. "Seems to me like you're going to get a bullet in the neck."

"I'll tell you any name you like, sir," the plodding serf grunted in reply. "What'll be the difference? You won't know it from the right one anyway."

"Hmm. That's true enough. Forget about it then. But how many of these masters do you have?"

"There's the old master, two young masters, and two body servants."

"What? You mean these people are gentry?"

"Sure they are gentry. Why shouldn't they be gentry?"

"And they live way out here?"

"Sometimes here, sometimes God knows where."

"And where do those horses come from?"

"The masters bring them. God knows where they get them from."

"Tell the truth now. Don't they rob people on the highways?"

"Who knows what they do? All I know is they bring horses here. Who they take them from is none of my business."

"And what do they do with those horses?"

"I don't know. They'll take ten, maybe a dozen, whatever's in the barn, and drive them somewheres... I don' ask no questions. I know what they tell me, no more."

At last they reached the barn where Soroka could hear snorting horses and they went inside.

"Hold up that light!" said Soroka.

The peasant lifted the lantern to cast its pale light along a row of animals tied along one wall. Soroka peered carefully around, inspected the animals thoroughly like a man who knows what he is doing around horses, and smacked his lips with pleasure.

"Not bad," he muttered. "Not bad at all... The late Pan Zendt would've been real pleased. There're some fine Polish runners, I see a good pair of Russian palfreys... Hmm... That German colt is a real beauty... ah, and so's that mare. Huh! And what do you feed them?"

"To tell the truth, master," the peasant squirmed, obviously uneasy about the need to tell the truth. "I got a couple of clearings sown with oats back there in the marshes... Had them here since Spring."

"So your masters have been bringing horses here all year?"

"No, not till like Summer... But they sent a groom with orders to get things started way back there in Spring."

"So you belong to them, then?"

"I did. Till they went off to war."

"Which war?"

"How would I know, master? They went off somewheres, far from here I reckon. Maybe a year ago or more. They came back this Summer."

"So who do you belong to now?"

"I don't know," the serf said and shrugged. "These are the King's forests."

"So who settled you here?"

"The King's forester, I reckon. He's kin to the masters. Used to go after the horses with them too, till one time he went and never came back."

"And does anybody ever come to see your masters here?"

"Here? How could they? Nobody can find his way in here, not if he don't know how to go. There's just this one dry track through the swamps. It's a real wonder to me that you got here like you did, with nobody to guide you. Anybody who don't know the trail gets sucked down in the bog, most times."

Soroka was about to lie that these woods and swamps were quite familiar to him and that he knew his way around them very well, but he thought better of it and kept his mouth shut. Instead he asked:

"How big are these woods, then?"

But the peasant didn't understand the question. "What d'you mean, how big?"

"How far do they stretch?"

"Who can tell?" Such distances were clearly beyond the

peasant's comprehension. He probably hadn't stirred more than a dozen miles from where he was born. "They go where they go. One forest ends and another starts. God only knows where they stop. I ain't never been there."

"That's good!" said Soroka.

* * *

He sent the pitch maker back to the main dwelling and followed more slowly, deep in thought. What should he do? He liked clear-cut orders. Indecision was confusing to him, and so was making up his own mind about a course to follow. On the one hand, seizing the opportunity created by their owners' absence, he'd have liked to take the horses for himself and drive them off for resale at some local horse fair later along the way, or to keep as remounts. This four-legged loot was valuable indeed, and the fine horseflesh appealed to the old soldier.

'*To take is easy,*' he thought and scratched his head. '*But what do I do next?*'

"Swamps all around," he muttered. "Only one way out. And how do I find it?"

Accident served him once. Could he count on another stroke of luck? It didn't seem likely. Following the horse tracks would be worse then useless; Soroka was quite familiar with the ways of highwaymen and bandits who'd be sure to lay out a variety of false, confusing trails that would lead an uninformed or unwary traveler straight into a quagmire.

He pondered, muttering to himself, and then he slapped his forehead with his open palm.

"I'm a fool!" he grunted. "I'll rope that peasant by the neck to my saddle-horn and have him lead us out to the main highway!"

But that last word had acquired its own special meaning that made him shudder with immediate fear. "The highway, huh? And that Prince chasing after us down there...?"

'*Fifteen good horses I got to turn my back on,*' the old marauder thought with real regret. '*Our good luck's run out for sure, there's no two ways about it...*'

There was nothing for it, he decided, but to lie low in that bandits' lair, whether its owners agreed to it or not, until Pan Kmita was well enough to take charge again.

'Then it'll be up to the colonel to find a way out.'

★ ★ ★

Plunged in such thoughts he made his way back to the dwelling, pleased to see that even though his troopers recognized the lantern gleaming from far off in the darkness, they challenged him and the pitch maker none the less. He gave the password and they let him enter. Then he posted a sentry at the door, sent one man outside to watch beside their horses, told them to change posts at midnight, threw himself down on a cot next to Kmita's, and tried to get some sleep.

A soft night hush settled on the *izba*. He could hear the crickets chirping through the chinks in the cabin's walls and the rustling of the mice in the littered cupboard. The wounded man groaned and muttered in his fevered dreams and Soroka listened to his brief, disjointed exclamations.

"Majesty, forgive me... They're traitors... I have all their secrets... The Commonwealth is a length of cloth... I've got you, prince... Hold him...! Not that way, Majesty, it's a trap!"

Soroka rose on his cot, listening intently each time that Kmita shouted in his nightmare, while his wounded colonel dozed for a time, grew silent, then shouted again:

"Olenka! Don't be angry! Olenka!"

It was close to midnight before he quietened down altogether and began to sleep restfully and deeply. Soroka also slipped into an uneasy sleep but he was soon awakened by a diffident knocking on the door.

"What's up, then?" The watchful old soldier was immediately alert.

"The pitch maker's got away, sergeant," a frightened trooper mumbled.

"Goddamit all to Hell!" Soroka exploded. "Now we're sure to get a mob of cut-throats on our necks! Who was watching him?"

"... Bilous."

"I was out there watering the horses," Bilous tried to explain himself. "I had him draw the water from the well while I was holding them..."

"And what? Did he jump inside?"

"No, sarge, not into the well... But there's piles of lumber stacked around there, and there's a mess of stump holes, and that's what he dived into. I let the horses loose because I figured there's others here if ours ran off and scattered, and I went after him, but I lost him in the first hole he jumped in. The night's as dark as pitch, the son-of-a-bitch knows his way around here, and so he got away, plague take him!"

"May lightning strike him!" old Soroka cursed. "He'll bring a whole herd of devils down on us, he will! You can bet on that much...!"

Then he shrugged, accepting the inevitable, and found his refuge in military procedures.

"Nobody goes to bed! Everybody stays up and alert! That mob may be here anytime."

And giving an example, he squatted on the threshold with a musket grasped in his hard, gnarled fists. The soldiers found places for themselves beside and around him, chatting quietly and chanting an occasional low-voiced song, while they cocked their ears to the night sounds that drifted among the trees. But they heard neither hoofbeats nor the muffled snorts and whinnies of approaching horses.

Chapter Forty-four

THE NIGHT AROUND SOROKA and his men was clear and bright with moonlight. It was also alive with a variety of sounds. Dry branches crackled under invisible hooves and feet, leaves rustled in their fall. This was the rutting season and the buck deer made their fierce announcements across the wooded darkness. Their short, snarling bellows, full of warning, challenge, anger and determination, resounded everywhere, rising hoarsely out of the far-off depths of the wilderness and booming close at hand as well, so that the vast dark spaces around the watching soldiers seemed to stir with life no farther than a hundred paces beyond the cabin.

"When those others get here, whoever they are, they'll be making all these calls as well,"Bilous said. "To confuse us, like."

"They won't come tonight,"offered another soldier. "It'll be daylight before that peasant finds them."

"What do you say, sergeant, if we look around a bit come sunlight? If there's bandits here then there's got to be some buried treasure someplace. Like under the walls?"

"The best treasures are right there in the shed," Soroka said, nodding towards the barn that held the horses.

"We're taking them with us, right?"

"How will you get them out through all those swamps around us, you damned fool?"

"We got through coming in, didn't we?" the other trooper shrugged. "We'll get through going out."

"Oh no you won't! There's false trails laid out everywhere, laddie. It was a miracle we found the right one coming in but we'll never do it again without a guide. You should've kept a better eye on that serf, Bilous, he was our best chance."

"The highway's only a short stretch out there," Bilous gestured towards the east. "We'll just head that way till we get to it, that's all."

"And you think you'll be home free once you're on the highway?"

"Sure, father," Bilous said. "Why not?"

"Maybe you'll have a better chance here with a bandit's bullet than with the noose that's waiting for you there."

"How's that, father? What noose?"

"They're looking for us there," Soroka said. "Remember?"

"Who's looking for us?"

"The Prince," Soroka said.

He slumped back into his gloomy silence and the others also grew as still as if suddenly afraid.

"Oy," Bilous said at last. "It's bad here and it's no good there... Looks like no way out any way you turn."

"They've got us trapped like wolves with beaters on one side and shooters on the other," another trooper muttered. "A mob of cut-throats here and that Prince over there..."

"May a thunderbolt set fire to them all!" Bilous cursed in answer. "But I'd rather have bandits on my neck than deal with that Prince again! He's magical, I tell you! Zavratynski used to wrestle bears, remember? And he tore the saber out of his hand like he was a child. He must've thrown a spell on him, how else could he do it? I saw myself how he started changing when he went after Vitkovski. He grew bigger than a pinetree in one twinkling of an eye! Huh, I'd have gone for him myself if that hadn't happened."

"You're a fool to let him get away whatever happened to the other two," Soroka growled.

"What choice did I have, sergeant? The way I saw it, he had the fastest horse so he could show me a clean pair of heels any time he wanted. And if he wanted to do me like he did the others I wouldn't be able to hold him off. How could I? There's nothing a man can do against magic, everybody knows that. A wizard like that can change himself into anything. He can turn into a whirlwind, or he can just vanish..."

"That's true," Soroka nodded, deep in thought. "Come to

think of it, when I was taking aim at him it was like a mist came down around him... and I missed! It's easy enough to miss a shot on horseback, when the nag is restless under you and milling around. But on foot? And with the musket resting on a saddle? That hasn't happened to me in ten years."

"What more is there to say?" Bilous spread out the fingers of one hand and began to count. "Lubyenetz, Vitkovski, Zavra- tynski and our colonel too... Every one of them could take on four men if he had to, you've all seen them do it, and all of them went down before just one man who wasn't even armed when the trouble started! Nobody could do that without getting a hand from the Devil!"

"We'd better give our souls to God, then," growled another soldier. "The Devil can lead him here as well."

"He don't need the Devil. He's got a long reach of his own, a great lord like that..."

"Quiet now!" Soroka hissed. "There's something heavy rus- tling in those thickets there."

★ ★ ★

The troopers quietened down at once. They strained their ears into the surrounding darkness which was suddenly thick with footfalls crackling heavily in the undergrowth and tram- pling the dead leaves.

"Horses?" Soroka whispered.

But the sounds receded and, shortly afterwards, they heard another buck trumpeting his challenge.

"Na-a-ah... it's just a deer..."

"Calling a doe or frightening off a rival..."

"There's so much noise in them woods tonight it's like the Devil was getting himself married," another trooper muttered.

Then they let silence fall again.

The troopers' heads dipped and they began to doze. Only the sergeant struggled to stay wide awake, peering into the tree line and listening to the night sounds, but even his grizzled head started to nod and sway.

An hour or two passed like that.

The black wall of the pines before them became tinged with grey. The tree tops whitened against the lightening sky as if

splashed with a ladle full of molten silver. The strident calls died
out in the forest and a deep silence settled on the wilderness.

The blue-grey light of dawn gave way before the sunrise,
drawing thin threads of yellow, gold and scarlet into its somber
colors, and finally a bright new day exploded in the clearing. It
bathed the worn faces of the huddled soldiers who slept on the
stoop of the hut, when suddenly the doors behind them flew
wide on their hinges and Kmita appeared on the threshold at
their backs.

"Soroka!" he cried. "Come here!"

The soldiers bounded to their feet.

"God save us!" cried Soroka, amazed and delighted. "Your
Honor is up on his feet already?"

"And you're snoring here like a herd of oxen!" Kmita
snapped. "Anyone could creep up on you and cut off your heads
and that's the first thing you'd ever know about it!"

"We watched all night, colonel," the old sergeant tried to
justify himself. "We didn't doze off till it was close to daylight."

Kmita looked around the unfamiliar clearing.

"Where are we, then?"

"In a forest, colonel."

"I can see that much. But whose cabin is this?"

"That we don't know, colonel."

"Come in a for minute, will you?" Pan Andrei stepped back
into the hut, beckoning to Soroka, and the sergeant followed.
"Listen,"—and the weakened Kmita sank down upon a cot—"it
was the Prince who shot me, wasn't it?"

"That's right, sir."

"And what happened to him?"

"He got away."

Another long silence settled on the *izba*.

"That's bad," Kmita said at last. "Very bad! It would have
been better to kill him then let him escape."

"Well, we tried, colonel. But..."

"But what?"

Soroka rendered a quick account of everything that happened
at the smithy, and afterwards on the road, and Kmita listened
with surprising calmness although his eyes began to glow with
hatred.

"Then he's on top," he snarled at the end. "But we'll meet again. Why did you leave the highway?"

"I thought he'd be sending people after us."

"You were right. He's sure to have done that. There are too few of us now to tangle with Boguslav... too damned few! Besides he's going on to Prussia, and we can neither chase him all the way up there or get our hands on him in the Elector's country. We'll just have to wait..."

Soroka expelled a long breath of relief.

It seemed that Pan Kmita wasn't all that frightened of the Prince if he was talking about chasing him all the way to Prussia. This calm assurance, so typical of the ruthless young commander, spread quickly to the faithful old soldier, who was quite accustomed to think only what his young colonel was thinking and to feel nothing that his master didn't feel.

Pan Andrei, in the meantime, plunged into deep thought. Then, suddenly, he sat up as if startled and started searching for something in his clothes.

"Where are my letters?" he asked.

"What letters, commandant?"

"Those I was carrying! Where is my belt? That's where I had them folded."

"I took off Your Worship's belt myself so you could breathe easier. It's lying over there."

"Get it here, then!"

Soroka passed him the broad elkskin belt lined with laced pockets made of softer leather. Kmita picked at the knots with impatient fingers until all the papers in the pockets were lying in his hands.

"Those are the passes for Swedish garrison commanders!" he said anxiously. "But where are the letters?"

"What letters?" Soroka asked again.

"Dammit to Hell!" Anxiety started to give way to panic. "The Hetman's letters to the Swedish King, to Pan Lubomirski... and all those others I had here!"

"If they're not in the belt, Your Honor, they must've fallen out on the way."

"Mount up and find them!" Kmita shouted in a terrifying voice.

But before the astonished Soroka could run out of the hut to carry out the order, Pan Andrei spun around in a helpless circle as if all his strength had suddenly ebbed away. He fell against the cot, seized his head in both hands and began to murmur in a broken voice:

"... My letters... ay, my letters...!"

★ ★ ★

All his men leaped into their saddles and galloped away—except one whom Soroka left on guard outside—and Kmita was alone. His situation, as he thought about it, was hardly to be envied. Boguslav had escaped. The terrible and unavoidable vengeance of the Radzivills now hung above Pan Andrei like the sword of doom. It was a deadly threat not merely to himself but to everyone he cared about: in short, to Olenka. She was in Keydany, totally at the mercy of a man who didn't know the meaning of mercy or forgiveness. Kmita knew that Yanush Radzivill wouldn't hesitate to strike where he would hurt him worst, and that he'd wring the last shred of retribution out of the girl that he knew Kmita loved.

There seemed to be nothing the distraught young soldier could do to avert this terrifying prospect. The more he looked at his own unenviable position, the more threatening, dangerous and hopeless it appeared to him. After his attempt to carry-off Boguslav, the Radzivills would damn him as a traitor. The loyalists fighting for Yan Casimir, along with Pan Sapyeha's men and the confederates gathered in Podlasye, already thought him the worst traitor who ever sold his soul. Among all the many camps, factions, foreign armies and armed bands struggling with each other, and amid all the conflicts that gripped the Commonwealth that year, there wasn't one that didn't see itself as his worst enemy. Hovansky had already fixed a bounty on his head; the Radzivills would now do the same; and who could tell if the loyalists hadn't also done it?

"Ay, it's a Devil's own brew I've cooked for myself," Pan Andrei muttered. "And now I've got to drink it to the bitter dregs."

Seizing Prince Boguslav he thought he'd throw him under the feet of the confederates, convince them that he had broken with the Radzivills, and buy his way into their ranks where he'd be able to fight for his rightful King and defend his country.

Moreover Boguslav in his hands was a guarantee of Olenka's safety. But his defeat at Boguslav's hands, as well as the Prince's escape into freedom, robbed him not only of whatever comfort he'd derive from knowing that the girl was safe but also of all the proofs he needed to show his change of heart.

The road to the confederates' camps lay open before him, Kmita knew. There was a good chance that Pan Volodyovski and his friends might spare his life if he appeared among them. But would they believe him? Would they be able to trust him? Wouldn't they suspect him as a spy sent to undermine the loyalty of their soldiers?

He recalled how much loyalist blood was staining his hands and how he destroyed the mutinied Hungarians and dragoons in the Keydany courtyard. It was quite beyond him to count all those loyal regiments and detachments he crushed for the Radzivills, or all the captured officers he sent to the firing squads, or the luckless soldiers he cut down without remorse.

Just by fortifying Keydany like he did he had assured the Radzivills' supremacy in Zmudya, he thought with despair.

"How am I to go there, then?" he asked himself, thinking about Volodyovski and the Laudanians. "They'd rather have the plague among them than someone like me!"

'Coming in with Boguslav on a rope's end,' he thought. 'That would be one thing... That could work... That they could believe...'

"But to come with nothing other than words in my mouth and with hands full of empty air?"

If he still had those all-important letters he'd at least be able to trade them for Olenka's safety, even if they wouldn't be enough to assure his welcome among the confederates, but some evil spirit saw to it, he thought, that they'd be lost as well.

So what could he do?

★ ★ ★

When all of this stood stark and clear before his eyes, and when he grasped the full extent of his terrible position, he clutched his head again in both hands, as close to despairing as he had ever been.

"I'm a traitor for the Radzivills," he groaned. "A traitor for Olenka... A traitor for the confederates and for His Majesty as well. I've lost my good name, thrown away my honor, and destroyed both Olenka and myself!"

The wound in his face was burning like a fire but it was nothing to the conflagration that scorched his mind and soul. The thought of Boguslav's easy triumph over him filled him with self-contempt and a bitter shame; his own pride and manhood seemed to be lying soiled at his feet. What happened to him in Lubitch at Pan Volodyovski's hand was child's play compared to what the Prince did to his vision of himself.

'*Over there,*' he thought, '*in Lubitch, I fought an armed master swordsman and was fairly beaten. But here, on that forest highway, I was overcome by an unarmed prisoner whom I was holding in my hands!*'

The more he thought about what he had done in the Hetman's service, the more revulsion he felt for himself, and each bloody memory opened up new vistas of horror before him. Each recollection filled him with disgust, and the longer that he thought about those vivid, brutal scenes, the more frightful and contemptible they became. It was as if he'd never known before about those dark, hidden corridors of his soul and conscience where he could now see the whole ugliness of his infamy, along with all the pain he heaped on Olenka, and the awful dangers he brought upon her and their country.

"Did I really do all that?" he asked himself in astonishment and fear. "How could I...? How could any man do so much harm alone?"

And then his hair stood erect on his head in terror.

"It just can't be!" he cried. "This has to be a part of my fever! Dear Mother of God, it can't be! This couldn't have happened!"

But his conscience told him coldly that it could. That it did. And that he was guilty of it all.

An overwhelming grief seized him then and brought him stumbling to his feet.

'*Oh, if I'd only been able to see this from the start!*' he cried silently within him. '*If I'd just said: the Swedes attack my country, I'll attack the Swedes! Radzivill sets himself against the King, I'll go against Radzivill! How different, how much better everything would have been!*'

Now that it was too late, he knew exactly what he would have done: gather a troop of cut-throats and hardcases no better than himself. They'd have come running from the darkest corners of the world if he sent out the call and he'd be as happy fighting at their head as a Gypsy pickpocket at a country fair! He'd ambush and raid the Swedes like he harassed Hovansky. He'd fight them with a clean heart and a clear conscience, bathed in fame and glory, and then he'd be able to stand before Olenka with pride in his eyes.

'*I'm not a bandit any longer,*' he would say to her when the war was over. '*I am not an outlaw. I've fought for my country. So love me like I love you and let's forget everything else that came between us in some other time.*'

And what could he say to her today?

But pride wouldn't allow him to shoulder all the blame. Not yet. Not all at once. It was his pride that always drove him to his worst excesses and later created the excuses for them. Now it wouldn't allow him to admit the full extent of his crimes without an equal partner. It was the Radzivills who buried him in infamy and horror. They were the ones who led him to destruction. It was their fault that he lost both his love and his honor, he thought, and ground his teeth in rage, and swore an implacable hatred to them all.

"Let me have vengeance!" he howled, shaking his fists in the direction of the distant Zmudya, where Yanush Radzivill crouched over his own captive country like a wolf above his murdered prey, and suddenly he threw himself on his knees in the middle of the room.

"I vow destruction to them, Christ!" he shouted into the dark rafters. "I swear to hound them and torment them with fire and sword and with the law as well, as long as there's a single breath left somewhere in my body! So help me, King of Nazareth! Amen!"

And then he thought he heard a sudden whisper of some unknown voice deep inside himself: '*First defend your country. Think of your vengeance later!*'

Pan Andrei leaped to his feet again. His lips were parched. His eyes seemed on fire, burning with his fever. He walked rapidly back and forth across the little room, making wild gestures and talking loudly to himself, and finally he hurled himself down on his knees once more and began to pray.

"Show me the way, Lord!" he cried out. "Tell me what to do before I go mad!"

The answer—if it was an answer—came to him in the form of a distant musket shot which flew among the pines, gathering force and sound with every fresh echo, until it struck against the cabin like a thunderbolt.

Kmita leaped up, seized his saber, and ran across the threshold.

"What was that?" he shouted.

"A shot, colonel!"

The sentry pointed to the eastern edge of the clearing which was invisible under the thick carpet of tangled undergrowth and deadfall.

"Out that way, somewheres..."

"Where is Soroka?"

"He's gone to look for Your Honor's letters. Out there! Where the shot just came from!"

The rapid pounding of horse hooves broke in upon them in that instant, and a moment later Soroka and another soldier galloped into the clearing. They rode up to the cabin, jumped to the ground, and aimed their muskets from behind their horses at the dark woods beyond.

"What is it, sergeant?" Kmita asked at once.

"They're coming, sir."

"Who is?"

"The people who live here."

Chapter Forty-five

THERE WAS A DEEP stillness then in the forest clearing but the hush didn't last longer than a moment. It was soon broken by quick rustling sounds coming from the thickets as if wild boars were running through the undergrowth. The closer these noises came, however, the slower and more cautious they became until the silence was restored again.

"How many of them are there?" Kmita asked.

"There'll be about six," Soroka replied. "Maybe eight. I didn't get a chance to count them properly."

"That's fine then! We're more than enough for them."

"That's right, sir. We'll hold them off. But we ought to get one of them alive, scorch his sides a little, and have him show us the way out."

"There'll be time for that. Now stay alert. Keep watching."

Kmita barely spoke the word *alert* when a streamer of white smoke curled out of the bushes and a soft, whispering sound hissed through the nearby grass as if a flock of birds had soared into the air at some thirty paces.

"They've fired a load of hobnails out of a scatter gun," Kmita said and smiled. "If they don't have muskets they won't harm us much. They don't have the range."

Soroka, who held his musket across his horse's saddle with one hand, now made a trumpet out of his other fist and began to shout:

"Show your head one of you, out there in the bushes, eh? We'll soon have you rolling in the grass!"

The silence returned and then a fierce, angry voice echoed from the thicket.

"Who are you?"

"A better kind than you, that's certain!" Soroka replied.

"By what right did you seize our place?"

"A bandit wants to know about his rights! A hangman will teach you your rights, so why not go and ask one?"

"We'll smoke you out like badgers!"

"Come on then! Just watch out you don't choke on that smoke yourself!"

The voice in the thicket dwindled into nothing. The newcomers were apparently deciding what to do. In the meantime Soroka whispered to Pan Andrei:

"We'll have to lure one of them over here, colonel, and throw a rope around him. That way we'll have both a hostage and a guide."

"If one of them comes here he'll do it only with a guarantee that we'll let him go. We'd have to pledge his safety on our word of honor."

"It's alright to break your word with bandits," Soroka shrugged, watching the silent bushes.

"Maybe. But it's best not to make promises unless you mean to keep them," Kmita said and, in that instant, the harsh old voice bellowed again out of the undergrowth.

"What do you want with us?"

"Nothing!" Pan Andrei shouted back. "We'd have gone just the way we came, you misbegotten numbskull, if you knew something about hospitality and didn't start a conversation with a scatter gun!"

"You won't last till nightfall!" the hidden ruffian roared. "There'll be a hundred of us here by sunset!"

"And we'll have two hundred dragoons here by evening! The swamps won't save you either because we have people who know their way across them."

"Are you soldiers, then?"

"It's certain we're not bandits!"

"What's your regiment?"

"And what are you, a Hetman? I don't have to report to the likes of you!"

"Do what you want! The wolves will have a good time gnawing on your bones."

"And the crows with yours!"

"Say what you like, you're as good as dead! Why did you crawl into our house, anyway?"

"Why don't you come and see? You'll save wear and tear on your throat instead of yelling from the bushes. Come closer, then! Come on!"

"With a safe-conduct, then? On your word of honor?"

"Honor is for the gentry, not for horse thieves and highway robbers. You want to trust us, go ahead and trust us. If you don't, then don't."

"How about two of us? Can two come together?"

"Come ahead!"

★ ★ ★

After another long moment of hesitation two tall, broad-backed men rose out of the bushes about a hundred paces in front of the cabin and started walking carefully towards Kmita and his men. One, somewhat stooped and bowed, must have been carrying a good load of years on his shoulders. The other, who peered about with as much simple curiosity as suspicion, held himself freakishly erect and stalked with the powerful assurance of the young. He stretched his long neck towards the cabin like a sniffing dog. Both of them wore the short sheepskin coats typical of the petty gentry, worn with the wool inside an outer covering of black cloth, tall rawhide boots, and Eastern-style caps, padded with felt and pointed like stiff hoods, pulled down over their eyes.

"... What the Devil?" Kmita muttered, watching the nearing pair through hard, narrowed eyes, then turned to Soroka. "Don't we know these men?"

"Colonel!" the old sergeant cried out, grinning in amazement. "Maybe it's a miracle but these are our people!"

The others came to a distance of a dozen paces but they couldn't tell much about Kmita and his men because the soldiers stood hidden behind their horses. Nor could they tell much about Pan Andrei who stepped out towards them because three quarters of his face lay under bandages and dressings. But they halted at once at the sight of him and started peering at him with curious and mistrustful eyes.

"And where is your other son, Mister Kemlitch?" Pan Andrei asked quietly. "Still alive, I trust?"

A thunderbolt falling on his head couldn't have had a more startling effect on the older man.

"Who's that? How's that? What? Who's asking? What?" the old man said in a strange, frightened voice.

He stared wide-eyed and open-mouthed, standing as still as if he had sprouted roots. But his son, whose young eyes were a great deal sharper, suddenly swept his cap off his head and leaped to attention. "God's truth! *O Jezu!* That's the Colonel, father!"

"O Jesus! O Sweet Jesus!"

And both of them drew themselves stiffly to attention, assuming the position of soldiers before their commander, while fear and amazement crept out on their faces.

"Ha, you scalawags!" Pan Andrei said smiling. "So you greet me with a load of hobnails out of a scatter gun?"

But now the old man jumped as if he'd been stabbed, still dumbstruck with surprise but starting to get his wits together, and began to shout back towards the bushes: "Come here all of you! Come here!"

Several more men emerged from the thickets, with Kemlitch's other hulking son and the fugitive pitch maker among them, and started running towards the hut with arms at the ready, but the old man set their minds at ease.

"On your knees, scoundrels!" he roared. "On your knees! This is Pan Kmita! Which of you dimwits fired that shot? Get him over here!"

"You fired it yourself, father!" said the younger Kemlitch.

"You lie! You lie like a dog! Colonel, who could suppose that it was Your Honor here in our poor house? 'Struth, I still don't believe my eyes!"

"Believe them," Kmita said and thrust out his hand. "I'm not an illusion."

"*O Jezu!*" the old man quavered in reply. "Such a guest here in the forest! Who'd ever believe it? How are we to receive Your Worship without warning? If we'd just known you were coming, sir..."

And then he turned suddenly on his sons.

"Move, one of you!" he roared. "Idiots that you are! Run to the cellar and bring up some mead!"

"Give us the key, then, father," said one of the young men.

"The key? You want the cellar key?" the old man started rummaging in his belt, shooting distrustful glances at his glowering twin sons. "You want the padlock key, do you? Ah, but I know you, you greedy whelps! You'll drink more than you'll bring up! I'll go myself. You just run and shift the lumber off the cellar door and I'll do the fetching. Huh! D'you think I'd trust you with the key?"

"Ah, so you have a storm cellar under that woodpile, Kemlitch?" Pan Andrei asked.

"Have to, sir! Where else can I save anything from those two cut-throats of mine?" the old man answered, pointing at his sons. "They'd eat their own father out of house and home if they got the chance! Are you still here, rascals? Get those logs moved out of the way! Is this how you listen to the man who sired you?"

The two young men jumped to obey their father and ran to the tall woodpile behind the hut.

"I see you still don't see eye-to eye with your sons," Pan Andrei said laughing.

"Who can?" the old man complained. "They fight well, and they know how to take loot off the enemy, but when it comes to sharing with their father I've got to tear my portion right out of their throats! That's how much comfort they are to me, the ungrateful dogs, though they're as big as a pair of oxen! Ah, but come in, sir! Come into the cabin because it's getting chilly out here in the open. As God's my witness, what a guest! What an honor! We took more loot serving with Your Worship than we found the rest of this whole year... Aye, these are thin times for us now, as anyone can see. Nothing but poverty everywhere you look... The times are bad, oh yes, and they're getting worse every day, nor is there much joy and comfort in old age anymore. But come in, sir. Cross our humble threshold... 'Struth, who'd have expected Your Honor to show up here?"

★ ★ ★

Old Kemlitch spoke in a curiously rapid, whiny voice, while shooting restless glances everywhere around him, and Pan Andrei thought he knew what worried the huge, rawboned old man whose face was always twisted in complaint. Like both his sons he had thin, slanted eyes, bushy eyebrows and an unkempt mustache from under which protruded his own most distinctive feature: a long lower lip thrust so far out beyond the rest of his face that it curved up almost to his nostrils, giving him the look of a toothless crone.

This crumpled old face stood in strange contrast to his quick, nervous gestures, spritely way of moving, and the thickset body which suggested a great store of energy and strength. He moved as jerkily as if a spring was coiled in his body, twisting his head about as if it were mounted on a screw, so that he could see everything around him and trying to be aware of everything at once.

But he was even more jumpy than usual, as Pan Andrei noted. His manner towards his unexpected guest had become so humble and servile that he was practically cringing in a crouch. This could be due in part to a guilty conscience, Pan Andrei supposed. But he could also see some old respect that the old man would have for his former leader, a few threadbare shreds of military discipline, and perhaps even a gleam or two of frightened admiration.

The three Kemlitches had served under him in White Ruthenia, or Byelorusia as it was now known under Russian occupation, distinguishing themselves by their voracious appetite for loot as much as their courage. Kosma, the older of the twins, carried the banner in Kmita's band of raiders for a time but gave up the honor because it interfered with his pillaging. As savage in their cruelty as they were fierce in battle, the Kemlitches had another quality that set them apart in Kmita's band of ruffians and marauders; while the bulk of his irregulars drank up and gambled away everything they got into their hands, the whining old man and his two hulking sons squirreled it all away, hoarding their loot in secret forest hideouts all over the country. They were especially greedy when it came to horses which they took from friend and enemy alike and sold at various country manors and small towns.

Now, watching the old man who hustled about the room like someone who had a guilty secret on his mind, Pan Andrei recalled other things about him. The father fought as fiercely as the sons but, after each battle, he clawed the main part of their loot out of their hands, whining and complaining about them as he did it, damning their greed, moaning about their unfilial cruelty to him, and threatening to lay a father's curse upon them. Their lives were an eternal snarling quarrel but they defended each other so ferociously, glad to spill their own blood to protect another, that Kmita's other cut-throats kept away from them. Nobody liked them. They could be terrible fighting side by side. Nor did anyone dare to question them about their reputed hoards of carefully hidden treasure.

Horses, or their obsessive greed for them, put an end to their service under him, Pan Andrei supposed. The last time he saw them was when he dispatched them to his winter quarters with a herd of mustangs about a year before. Kmita assumed that they were ambushed and killed somewhere along the way although his other soldiers held a different view; they maintained that a whole herd of horses would have been too much of a temptation for that rapacious trio.

Now, seeing the Kemlitches alive and well, hearing horses neighing in the barn, and noting that the old man's joy at seeing him again was so oddly mixed with servility and fear, Pan Andrei supposed that his other men were right.

* * *

Once in the cabin, Pan Andrei sat down on a cot, put his fists on his hips in a judgmental manner, and fixed the old man with a piercing stare.

"Where are my horses, Kemlitch?" he demanded.

"Oh Jesus! Oh Sweet Jesus!" the old man moaned. "Zoltarenko took 'em! He beat us, wounded us, scattered us and chased us sixteen miles before we got away. We barely saved ourselves, Your Worship... O Holy Mother! We couldn't find Your Excellency and the regiment after that. We didn't draw breath till we got to these swamps and forests...!"

His slitted eyes shot glances everywhere but avoided Kmita's.

"They chased us, robbed us, took the horses from us...!" The old man was clearly groping towards a safer subject. "Ah, but thank God nothing bad happened to Your Worship, though I see you're wounded... Could I change your dressings, sir? Lay on some herbs to draw out the fever...? Ah, ah! What do you

suppose happened to my sons? You send them on a simple job
and they disappear! What are they doing in that woodpile, the
scoundrels? They're always ready to crack the door and get into
that mead, I know them! Always out for themselves, they are.
There's nothing here but misery and hunger anyway. We live
on mushrooms here, poor wanderers that we are, but we'll
surely find something to eat and drink for Your Honor..."

"So it was Zoltarenko's people who took my horses from you,
eh?" Pan Andrei remarked.

"Yes... Yes,"—old Kemlitch shot a quick glance at
Kmita—"Zoltarenko's men took them other horses... ah, what's
the use of talking any more about it? They also robbed us of our
chance to keep on serving under you, Your Worship, so that it's
hard to find a crust of bread for a man's old age... Ay, it's a hard
life unless Your Honor takes mercy on us, takes us to his heart,
and lets us back into his service again?"

"That could happen," said Kmita.

The Kemlitch twins, Kosma and Damian, stamped into the
room just then and stood by the door, not daring to sit in Pan
Kmita's presence. They were as thickset, large and burly as their
father but without half his nervous energy and slyness. Their
bulging, look-alike heads were covered with an unkempt thatch
of stiff, bristly hair which they were obviously used to cutting
for themselves. It lay every which way across their skulls, stuck
out in thick clumps around their ears, and formed fantastic
cowlicks on the tops of their heads.

"The cellar door is clear," Damian said.

"Good," said the old man. "I'll go and fetch the mead." Then
he looked pointedly at the clumsy giants. "And those other
horses were taken from us by Zoltarenko's people, understand?"

He glared at the twins, bowed to Pan Andrei, and hurried
from the hut.

Left alone with the two huge young oafs, Kmita thought that
they looked like two coarse, rough-hewn statues hacked out of
a tree trunk with a woodsman's axe.

"What do you do with yourselves these days?" he asked.

"We go after horses!" the twins said in chorus.

"Who do you take them from?"

"Anybody."

"But for the most part?"

"From Zoltarenko's people."

"That's good. There's nothing wrong with taking booty from the enemy. But if you also rob your own kind then you're a bunch of bandits, not gentry, understand? And what do you do with those horses?"

"Father sells them. In Prussia."

"And did you ever take anything from the Swedes? I know there are Swedish garrisons not too far from here. Do you raid them as well?"

"Sure we do."

"Hmm. Then you must ambush small foraging parties, or pull down single troopers! And what do you do when they defend themselves?"

"We pound 'em."

"Ah, you've been pounding them, have you? Then you've some unpaid bills with the Swedes as well as Zoltarenko. It wouldn't go so well with you if you fell into either set of hands, I imagine."

Kosma and Damian said nothing in reply. They kept their mouths shut tight and their eyes fixed on the floor before them. Like their father, they always looked at Pan Kmita with superstitious awe, fearing and admiring him not just for his ruthlessness and courage but for his high birth and position in Orsha as well. Only the murderous Ranitzki, related as he was to men of senatorial rank, enjoyed a similar respect from them in Kmita's old band.

"You've picked a dangerous way to make a living," Pan Andrei went on. "More fitting for ruffians than the gentry. I expect you also have a few old verdicts hanging around your necks? Hmm? Like from the old days?"

"Sure do!" the twins chorused.

"That's what I thought. Where are you from anyway?"

"We're from around here. We're local."

"And where did your father live before?"

"Near by. In Borovitchko."

"Did he own the village?"

"In part. With the Kopystinskis."

"And what happened to them?"

"We pounded 'em."

"Aha! And you had to run from the law which is how you wound up under my command." Kmita shook his head slowly while the two clumsy giants fidgeted by the door.

"You're in deep trouble, you Kemlitches," Pan Andrei sighed at last. "And you'll end up dangling on a tree limb, take my word for it. Some hangman will light your way into the next world, there is no doubt about it!"

★ ★ ★

The door of the *izba* creaked open just then and the old man came in carrying two glasses and a mossy jug.

"Go and cover up the cellar again!" he told his two sons and threw a quick, suspicious, anxious glance at them and at Pan Kmita too, as if worried what they might have told him in his absence.

The twins stumbled out in great haste and old Kemlitch set his jug and glasses on the table and filled one for Kmita. He didn't dare to drink with him without his permission. But Pan Andrei was unable to drink either, because his wound had swollen and pained him too badly.

"Looks like the mead won't help much," the old man said at last, "unless we pour it on the wound to burn out the poisons? But maybe Your Worship will let me take a look? I know as much about treating wounds as any barber-surgeon."

Kmita agreed and Kemlitch removed the dressings and started peering closely at the injury.

"Hmm. The skin's all gone," he muttered. "But that's nothing. The bullet went along the top of the bone, that's why it's all so swollen."

"And that's why it hurts," Kmita said.

"But it couldn't have happened more than two days ago! Holy Mother! Someone took a shot at Your Worship from real short quarters!"

"And how can you tell that?"

"'Cause the powder never got a chance to burn off properly and the grains sit here under the flesh like poppy seeds in a roll! That's going to stay with Your Worship from now on, but some bread and cobwebs ought to heal the rest. Ay, ay, but that was a real close shot! It's a wonder Your Honor's still alive!"

"My time hadn't come, I expect" Kmita shrugged and grimaced. "Go and knead some bread and cobwebs then, Master Kemlitch, because I've a few things to say to you and my jaws hurt too much for talking."

The old man peered suspiciously at his colonel, alarmed that this conversation might relate to the subject of the missing horses supposedly taken by Zoltarenko's Cossacks, and his heart stirred uneasily in his breast. But he started moving about with alacrity, soaked and kneaded the necessary bread, and since there was no shortage of cobwebs in the cabin, soon had a new dressing in place on Kmita's face.

"That's better," said Pan Andrei. "Sit down, Master Kemlitch."

"By the Colonel's order!" the old man snapped out smartly and lowered himself to the edge of the cot. He perched there, stretching his bristly grey head towards his old commander, and with both his eyes fixed anxiously on Kmita's.

But Kmita neither talked nor asked any questions. He rested his head in his hands and slid into thought. Then he rose and started pacing the cabin floor, halting now and then to peer down at Kemlitch with distracted eyes, as if weighing something in his mind. When at least half an hour of this had gone by, the old man shifted nervously on his perch and couldn't stop squirming.

Then suddenly Kmita was standing before him. "Where," he asked, "are the nearest regiments which mutinied against the Prince-*Voyevode* of Vilna?"

The old man blinked, uneasily. "Is that where Your Honor wants to go?"

"I didn't ask you to question me," Kmita said, "but to give me answers."

"People are saying hereabouts that there'll be one camped nearby very soon, the same that came down this way from Zmudya a short while ago."

"Who says this?"

"The soldiers were saying it themselves when the regiment came by here."

"Whose regiment was it, do you know? Who was leading them?"

"Pan Volodyovski."

"That's good," Kmita said. "Call Soroka here!"

The old man stepped outside and returned almost at once with the sergeant who thought it best to keep close in case he was needed.

"Did you find my letters?" Kmita asked.

"No sir."

"Ay!" Kmita made a sharp, irritated gesture. "That's bad. Very bad. You can go, Soroka. But I tell you, you men should be hanged for losing me those letters. Go on now, dismissed."

And after the old sergeant marched outside he turned to old Kemlitch. "Mister Kemlitch," he said. "Is there something around here to write on?"

"Bound to be," the old man replied.

"Two sheets of paper and some quills will do."

The old man vanished behind the door of the lean-to shed, which seemed to be a storehouse for a variety of objects, and stayed there a long time. Meanwhile Pan Kmita paced the room telling himself that not everything was lost.

"I doesn't matter whether I have those letters or not," he reassured himself. "The Hetman doesn't know they're lost and he'll be sick with worry that I'll publish them. So I've got him! Let's fight cunning with cunning. I'll threaten to send them all to the *Voyevode* of Vitebsk. That's the way to put the fear of God in that traitor."

Old Kemlitch broke in on his further musing with an announcement that he found three sheets of writing paper but neither ink nor quills.

"No quills? Such a wealth of birdlife in this forest and you have no quills? Couldn't you shoot something?"

"I've a dead hawk nailed over the barn door."

"Then get me a wing! Jump to it!"

Kemlitch shot off as quickly as he could, propelled by the feverish urgency in Pan Kmita's voice, and returned only a moment later clutching a hawk's wing. Kmita seized it, plucked out a long brown feather, and started to trim it with his pocket knife.

"It'll do!" He eyed it against the light. "But it's a lot easier putting a notch in a man's head than trimming a quill. And now we need some ink!"

He rolled up a sleeve, jabbed himself firmly in the arm and dipped the quill in blood.

"Off you go, Master Kemlitch," he waved the old man away. "You can leave me now."

Chapter Forty-six

THE OLD MAN LEFT and Pan Andrei began to write his letter to Yanush Radzivill which was to be both his declaration of war and his means of protecting the Billevitch captives.

'*I am giving up Your Highness' service,*' he wrote, dipping his quill again and again in his own blood, '*because I don't want to serve traitors any longer. And because I swore upon the Cross never to leave or desert Your Highness, I throw myself upon God's mercy for my absolution and forgiveness. But even if I'm damned for this broken oath, and burn in Hell for ever, I'd rather do so for an honest error than for treason to my King and Country, done with full knowledge of what I was doing. Your Highness misled me, so that I was like a mindless sword in Your hands, spilling the blood of brothers at Your orders, for which I summon You to God's Judgment which will determine where lay the roots of treason and whose intentions were innocent and honest.*

'*I expect that we shall meet again,*'—Pan Andrei stabbed the quill into his arm for fresh blood to write with—'*and then, even though You are powerful, and though You can inflict agony on the entire Commonwealth with Your venom, I'll see to it that Your fangs are drawn.*'

He went on to say that nothing would ever cause him to put aside his vengeance, that he'd pursue the Radzivills to his dying breath, and that they would never know 'the hour nor the day' of his retribution.

'*Even though You've all the power in Your hands, and all I have is just my saber in my fist, I will demand a settlement and extract a price.*

And Your Highness knows well enough that I need neither armies, nor artillery nor castles to make my anger felt.

'*The letters that I hold,*' he went on, '*will ruin Your Highness in the eyes of both the Polish and the Swedish Kings since they prove Your bad faith to them both and expose You clearly as a devious traitor who plots against each of them at the same time.*

'*Nor will Your lies, Your influence and Your connections serve you in this matter because Your seals and signatures cannot be denied,*' Pan Andrei continued. '*Your ruin lies in my hands. I can destroy You even if You were twice as powerful as You are. So this is what I tell Your Highness in advance: let one hair fall off the heads of those I love, and who are now living in Keydany, and all these documents and letters will go to Pan Sapyeha, while I shall also have them copied, printed and spread throughout the country.*

'*So You have a choice.*

'*After the war, when peace is restored in the Commonwealth, You will return the Billevitches to me—unharmed and well-treated—and I, in turn, will give You back Your letters. But if I should hear some bad news from Keydany then Pan Sapyeha will pass those letters to everyone concerned, including Pontus de la Gardie.*

'*Your Highness wants a crown,*' he wrote, '*but it seems to me that you won't have anything on which to wear one, once your head has fallen under either a Polish or a Swedish axe. So an exchange looks like Your better choice.*

'*Nothing will halt or divert my pursuit of vengeance later on,*' he continued. '*But that will be a private matter between You and me. What I am talking about now is Your exposure before the whole world, that will destroy You for ever in the public eye, and which I'm willing to forego for the sake of the Billevitches' safety and wellbeing.*

'*In closing,*' he wrote and then signed his name: '*I would commend Your Highness to God if it wasn't for the fact that You serve the Devil.*'

But then something else occurred to him and he penned a post script.

'*Forget about Your planned poisoning of the confederates, because there will be someone who is leaving the Devil's service and enlisting in the cause of justice, and who will warn them not to drink Your beers in Zabludov and Orel.*'

★ ★ ★

Here Pan Kmita jumped to his feet again and began to march up and down the *izba*. His whole face felt as if it were on fire, inflamed by the contents of his letter.

This was his challenge hurled at the mighty oligarchs of Northern Lithuania.

They had the might, the connections and the wealth to shake the entire country, but he sensed a sudden, inexplicable surge of an extraordinary power of his own, so that he felt ready to stand eye to eye with that entire relentless and all-powerful clan and pull it down in ruins.

And was this really possible? Was he strong enough for that? He was just one member of the fighting gentry, no better born or connected than any simple knight. Moreover, he would now become an outlaw once again, hounded by the law, without a friend to speak for him or anyone to back him. But, suddenly, he could see himself the equal of a magnate whose might and influence gave him royal powers.

So it was possible! He could do what he said! Even though he was hated and despised by everyone to such an extent that he was seen as a public enemy wherever he turned, he felt an immense strength pouring into his mind and body, and he could already see the fall and humiliation of both the Radzivills, and his own inevitable triumph over them.

But how was he to conduct this war? Where was he to look for allies? How was he to bring about his victory?

He didn't know, but it didn't even occur to him to wonder about it. He knew—indeed, he believed it with all his heart and soul—that what he was doing was the thing to do. That Right and Justice, and therefore God himself, were standing behind him. And this filled him with such faith, confidence and conviction, as to defy computation by a human being.

He felt lighter, freer.

Wholly new landscapes and horizons were opening before him. All that he had to do (he thought) was to leap into his saddle, and ride towards those joyful, beckoning vistas, and he would find everything he had lost: his honor, his good name, his self-respect, new fame and Olenka.

"Surely nothing will happen to her now," he told himself over and over as if in a fever. "Their own letters, or my threats about them, are sure to protect her. The Hetman will guard her now like the apple of his eye! As I would myself! That's the way to handle the Radzivills! They may think of me as just a puny insect in comparison with their power and resources but they'll think twice about risking my sting anyway..."

But then another thought presented itself: What if I were to write to her as well? The same messenger can pass her my letter in secret. Why don't I tell her that I've broken with the Radzivills and that I'm seeking a new and better service?

This idea found an immediate echo in his heart. He sat down again, dipped his quill in the seeping little wound he'd scratched into his arm, and began to write.

'*... Dearest Olenka! Know that I am no longer with the Radzivills, having finally seen through their machinations...*' And then he stopped.

He thought.

He shook his head.

"No!" he said firmly. "I won't write to her. Let my actions be my witnesses from now on. Not words."

And he ripped through the crumpled sheet of paper.

* * *

Finally he wrote his last, short letter to Pan Volodyovski, warning him and the confederates about the Hetman's intentions towards them.

'*The undersigned friend,*' he began, '*warns you and the other confederate commanders to be on your guard. The Hetman wrote to both Prince Boguslav and Pan Harasimovitch to have you poisoned or to have you murdered by peasants in your quarters. Neither of them could comply with this order since both are now on their way to Prussia, but other Radzivill administrators might have received a similar command so trust none of them. Accept nothing from them and post strong guards at night wherever you are.*

'*I know this for a fact,*' he continued, '*that the Hetman plans to march down on you directly. He is only waiting for a Swedish cavalry reinforcement, fifteen-hundred strong, which Pontus de la Gardie is to send to him shortly. So take great care, watch for the unexpected, and make sure that the Prince-Voyevode doesn't catch you all dispersed in your Winter quarters and destroy you one at a time as he plans to do.*

Your best move is to send word to Pan Sapyeha to join you with his forces and take overall command. Believe me, it's a sincere well-wisher who sends you this warning. In the meantime keep close together, quartering one regiment near another so that you can come quickly to each other's help. The Hetman is short of cavalry, having merely a few dragoons and Kmita's regiment which, by the way, is no longer as dependable as it may have been.

'*Kmita himself is away just now,*'— he added after another thought—'*sent off on some mission, although apparently the Prince no longer trusts him. Nor is he quite as much a traitor as most people think, being more misled than sinning of his own free will.*'

Finished, he paused.

How was he to sign this? His own name, he thought bitterly, could cause only distrust and revulsion.

'*I commend you all to God's love and keeping,*' Pan Andrei concluded, and signed it: '*Babinitch.*'

"If they believe,"—he mused aloud, pacing through the room—"that it's best for them to dodge the Hetman in scattered little groups, rather than face him together and united, then my real name will lead them to suspect that Radzivill wants them all together to smash them at one blow. They'll take this warning for just another piece of treachery. But the name of Babinitch will mean nothing to them. They may be moved to trust it."

The name derived from a small country town in the lost Orsha regions, a possession of the Kmitas since the founding of their family in times before history. And that's what he would call himself from then on, he thought.

* * *

This letter, at the end of which he'd slipped a few timid phrases in his own defense, brought him a sense of encouragement and relief. He felt that he could breathe easier now than before he wrote it. He was happier. His conscience felt lighter. It was as if he had just struck his first blow on behalf of Pan Volodyovski, his friends, and all those other loyalist commanders who chose to stand with their King and Country rather than Radzivill.

He sensed, moreover, that this was a beginning that would lead him just where he wished to go, wherever that might lie, like a thread cast into the wind that would unravel further in due time to mark an unknown trail. The situation in which he found himself was, indeed, a hard one; a weaker man might think it desperate, he thought. The road ahead of him was rocky and shrouded in shadows. And yet even in all this unremitting darkness he'd stumbled upon a path and conceived a course that might take him into the sunlight of an open highway.

But now that he'd done his best to safeguard Olenka, and the confederates would be able to avoid a surprise attack, Pan Andrei found another question for himself.

What was he to do?

He'd broken with the traitors. He burned all his bridges. He wanted to serve only his own country from that moment on, bringing her an offering of all his strength and effort, all his determination, and the sacrifice of his life itself if that was required.

'*But how to go about that? Where to make a start? What to do?*'

And again his mind was seized by a single notion: '*Go to the confederates!*'

But what if they refused to take him in? What if they branded him a traitor all over again without even giving him a chance to explain himself? And what if they met his open arms with sabers?

'*Or,*'—and this was much more searing to him than any other shame—'*what if they simply drive me off like a dog?*'

"I'd rather they killed me on the spot!" he shouted and felt as if his whole body were on fire with a new rush of shame. He saw his shattered reputation as if for the first time, tasting the public hatred and his own disgrace. Contempt for himself swept over him.

"Seems like it's easier for me to protect Olenka and the confederates than to restore my good name!" he cried out bitterly.

★ ★ ★

This, he knew, was the bottom of the pit to which he had sunk. His ruthless passions stirred to life again, his pride rebelled, and rage leaped up inside him as if a seething cauldron had boiled over in his soul.

"What is this?" he asked himself, bewildered by his inability to find a way out of his dilemma. "Can't I do to the Radzivills and the Swedes what I did so often to Hovansky? I'll get a band together, raid the Swedes, burn them out, destroy them! What's hard about that?"

This was the course his old, stiff-necked pride and arrogance seized upon at once. Huh, he snarled. So no one in the country could stop the Swedes or turn their invasion, wasn't that correct? Everyone bowed before them, didn't they? Everyone either submitted or despaired. But he, Kmita, would do what others couldn't. He and he alone would fight them and resist them until all of the Commonwealth, not just Lithuania, repeated his name with gratitude and awe.

"That's it!" he shouted, so eager to throw himself into that bloody work that he leaped up, ready to run outside and order his men and the Kemlitches to mount up and start out at once. "That's it!"

But something stopped him halfway to the door. He paused, confused, as if an unseen hand had pressed against his chest and pushed him back, away from the threshold. He stood dumbstruck in the middle of the room, thrown off-stride and staring in amazement.

"How is it, then?" he asked. "Won't that be enough to erase my crimes?"

And here began a dialogue, as sharp as a duel, between Pan Andrei and his awakened conscience.

Conscience asked: *'And what about the penance?'*

"What penance!" his pride wished to know.

'You need to do more than kill and destroy.'

"Such as what?" Kmita asked.

'Service,' his conscience said. *'Only hard, unrelenting, unrewarded service will bring you atonement.'* And Kmita knew at once that it would have to be some immeasurable service, as honest and as pure as a tear.

'What sort of service is it to rouse a gang of ruffians and rampage through the countryside like a hurricane? You call it service, but you're sniffing at it like a chained dog hungry for bloody bones. That's play for the likes of you, not service! That's joy-riding, not war! That's banditry, not the defense of your Motherland!'

"Hovansky..." he began in his own defense but his conscience brushed his protestations aside with contempt.

'Cut-throats who scavenge in the forests are also ready to ambush and

loot the Swedes. And whom else could you get for your guerrillas anyway? Where will you look for them if not on the highways? You'll harass the Swedes, yes, but you'll also claw and tear at your own people. You'll expose them to Swedish vengeance and merely bring a new storm falling on their heads. And for what? Just so you may substitute another wild joy-ride for penance and atonement?'

He heard this voice as clearly as if it belonged to some angry living entity that had appeared suddenly before him, and he could see the truth of everything it said, and yet he felt a sense of loss and disappointment that it wasn't all going to be as easy as he thought.

"What shall I do, then?" he asked himself at last and his knees began to tremble under him. "Who'll show me what to do? Who'll save me?"

Perhaps it was just fever and fatigue, or perhaps there was a deeper and more compelling reason, but his knees buckled altogether then, he sank to the floor, and then he found himself kneeling before a cot, his hands clasped for prayer.

He begged Christ to show him the compassion He showed to the crucified thief on Golgotha. His one wish, he said, was to wash himself clean of all his sins, begin a new life, and serve a righteous cause to the best of his ability, but he didn't know how.

"I'm stupid," he said. "I served those traitors out of sheer stupidity. And I'm too stupid now to see how best to serve my country. Have mercy! Enlighten me! Tell me what to do or I'll be totally destroyed...!"

His voice quavered then, and he began to beat his chest so savagely that the pounding echoed like a kettledrum throughout the little cabin.

"Have mercy on my sins!" he cried over and over. "Have mercy! Have mercy!"

He glimpsed a strange, fleeting thought, no more than a flicker, that he was about to see or hear a signal from Heaven, or to become a sudden witness to a prophecy, as he began to pray fervently to the Holy Mother.

He prayed for her intercession with her Son. He asked for her help. He begged for her guidance in his agony of doubt. He pleaded for a chance to serve her and defend her.

His tears fell thickly now and he bowed his head in silence

over his cot. Time passed as he knelt, saying nothing, as if awaiting some answer to his prayers. The room was still around him. Nothing stirred. The only sound intruded from outside: the hushed murmur of the nearby pine trees in the evening breeze.

Then gravel crunched under heavy boots right outside the window and two voices began a conversation.

"What do you think, then, sergeant? Where will we go from here?"

"How would I know?" asked Soroka sharply. "We'll go where we'll go. Maybe far! Maybe as far as our poor King who's groaning way out there under a Swedish hand."

"Is it true, though, that everybody has deserted him?"

"Maybe. But God hasn't deserted him."

When Kmita rose his face was calm and clear. He went straight to the door, opened it, stepped out and said to the soldiers who gathered outside:

"Saddle up. We're leaving."

Chapter Forty-seven

PAN ANDREI'S SOLDIERS SET ABOUT at once preparing for the journey. They were pleased to be leaving the dark seclusion of the silent forest and looked forward to the broils and commotions of the world outside, particularly since they were still afraid that Prince Boguslav would track them down somehow in their borrowed hideout. Meanwhile old Kemlitch followed Kmita back into the cabin, understanding that the young colonel had some questions for him.

"Your Excellency will be leaving, then?" he asked.

"I will. You'll lead me out. You know all the trails in this forest, don't you?"

"I do Your Honor. This is my home country. And where would Your Worship want to go?"

"To the King."

The old man took a step back in astonishment.

"Mother of Wisdom!" he cried out. "Which King does Your Honor have in mind?"

"You can bet it's not the Swedish one!"

Old Kemlitch not only failed to find much reassurance in this blunt announcement but started to make rapid signs of the cross along his chest and shoulders.

"Then Your Worship can't have heard what people are saying! I mean that the King had to look for a safe refuge all the way down in Silesia somewheres because he's been abandoned by everybody now. Even the Crown Hetmans went over to the Swedes and Krakow is under siege."

"Then we'll go all the way to Silesia if we have to."

"And how are you going to get through the Swedes, Your Worship? The country's full of them from here on out!"

"Who cares how? I'll do it and that's all there's to it!"

"But it'll take an awful lot of time..."

"Let it. I've time to spare. Though the sooner it all begins the better I'll like it."

★ ★ ★

Old Kemlitch stopped wondering at this point. His astonishment was over. He was too shrewd and cunning not to see at once that there had to be some special, secret reasons for Kmita's undertaking. But what could they be? Kmita's men, clearly under orders, didn't breathe a word about anything that happened before they came to the cabin in the forest. He had no idea what drove them off the highway nor why they were on it in the first place. The most likely possibility seemed to be that the *Voyevode* of Vilna was sending his trusted young henchman on some kind of mission to the Polish King. He was all the more certain about that because he assumed that Kmita was still the most faithful follower of the Lithuanian Hetman. He knew all about his services to Yanush Radzivill because the confederates quartered throughout Podlasye were full of tales about his cruelties and treasons.

'Hmm... *The Hetman's sending his right hand to the King,*' he thought and that opened up all kinds of glittering prospects to the greedy Kemlitch. '*That means he wants to make his peace with the King and turn on the Swedes. He must've got tired of taking their orders. That's what this must be all about, I reckon... Why else would he send the colonel on a trip like that?*'

But old Kemlitch didn't waste his time on empty speculations. He didn't care whom he served as long as it meant money, loot and horses, although he'd always rather follow someone he feared and respected. He smelled a profit for himself in this situation and his greedy old heart beat up rapidly. Whatever was going on here, it seemed clear to him that if he helped Pan Andrei he would be helping both the Hetman and the King, and sooner or later that meant a reward. Furthermore, the goodwill of two such potentates might come in very handy if he ever had to account for some of his old misdeeds.

Moreover, the shrewd and canny old man could smell a new

war in this kind of underhand peacemaking, and war meant loot and pillage for the taking. All of this appealed powerfully to the rapacious Kemlitch who was bound to Kmita in any event by some peculiar feelings of his own. He was as terrified of him as if the young man was a roaring fire and, at the same time, he looked at him with immense respect, and with that strange, bemused affection which the reckless Kmita inspired in all his savage followers.

"Something good is sure to come out of this for me," he muttered to himself, eying the young colonel. And then he made his own difficult but instant decision.

"Your Worship must go all across the Commonwealth to get to the King," he said. "The Swedish garrisons aren't any problem. They don't stick their noses much out of the towns. If Your Worship keeps to the woods and the open country they'll never even know that you're anywhere around. But those woods are yet another problem."

"And what's that?"

"Bandits, colonel. It's like whenever there's any unrest in the country, the woods fill up with armed bands of marauders and Your Worship doesn't have a lot of people with him."

"You can come with me, Kemlitch," Pan Andrei shrugged and said. "You and your sons and the rest of your men ought to make us strong enough for any marauders."

"Go with you, sir?" The old man's nature required him to whine, haggle and squeeze the last ounce of profit out of everything. "I will if that's your order. But I'm a poor man. How am I to leave the only roof I have over my head?"

"You'll profit by it one way or another," Kmita said. "I've no doubt about it. And it'll pay you to carry your heads out of here, you and both your sons, while you still have them firmly on your necks."

"May all the saints protect me!" the old man exclaimed. "What's Your Worship saying? Heads? Necks? Who'd want them? Why would anybody do us any harm? What have we done? We're innocent, don't bother nobody, don't get in any-body's way...!"

But Pan Andrei was running out of patience.

"Everyone around here knows about you cut-throats!" he thundered. "You shared a freehold with the Kopystinskis and you sabered them to death! Then you ran from the tribunals and took service with me! Then you stole my horse herd...!"

"As God's my witness!" the old man whined, squirming and protesting. "Speak for me, Holy Mother! Protect the innocent!"

"Silence! Wait till I'm finished! You stole my horse herd, and you ran back to your old haunts, and you started raiding the countryside like a gang of robbers, pillaging and stealing horses everywhere you can. Save your denials for the judge because I don't care what you've been doing here, and you know yourself that I know you inside out, you old vulture! Taking horses from the Swedes and Cossacks isn't a bad thing but it's a dangerous business. They'll skin you alive, both of them, if they ever get their hands on you, but that's their business, not mine."

"That's an honorable thing to do, colonel," the flustered old man struggled to defend his rotten reputation. "Taking horses from the enemy is a fitting thing."

"But you raid everybody! You loot your own kind! Don't lie about it because your sons already made a clean breast of it. I know all about it. And that's plain banditry and a disgrace to the gentry! Shame on you, you scoundrels! You should've been born peasants!"

And now the old marauder flushed an offended crimson.

"Your Worship maligns us," he muttered. "We know our place and we don't act like peasants. We don't steal any horses at night out of a stable. But it's a different thing to lift a little herd off the pastures or take it on the highway. That's proper in wartime! That's allowed the gentry! A stabled horse is a holy thing unless a man is a Gypsy or a peasant or maybe a Jew! We don't touch stabled horses. But war is war and that's another matter!"

"Not even if there were ten wars going on around here at the same time!" Kmita thundered at him. "Even then the only loot you're allowed to take is a battle trophy! But if you take it on the public highway then you're a common cut-throat!"

"God's a witness to our innocence," the glum old man complained.

"And sooner or later you'll be hanged on that innocence of yours," Pan Andrei observed. "But that's your problem and I couldn't care less about it, like I never have. I'm taking you back into my service, Kemlitch, you and both your sons. You'll go with me, clean your old slate by faithful and honorable service, and regain your good name. And I dare say you'll do a lot better for yourselves, too, in fighting for your country, than by stealing horses."

"We will!" Old Kemlitch stated with absolute conviction. "We'll go with you, sir, and we'll guide you safely past all the Swedes and bandits! To tell the truth, Your Worship, it's time for us to leave. People are getting awfully cruel to us in these parts. And why? What have we done to them? Why do they torment us? Only because we're so poor, that's why! That's the only reason... Perhaps the Good Lord will take mercy on us and help us in our misery..."

And here the old marauder's eyes glittered with sudden greed and he began to rub his hands together.

'*The whole country's going to be boiling from these secret doings,*' he thought happily. '*And only a fool won't find a way to make a nice penny out of it.*'

★ ★ ★

But Kmita's cold grey eyes shot him a piercing glance and the old man shuddered.

"God help you, though, if you ever try to trip me up," the young colonel warned him. "Nothing on earth will save you if you try to cheat me or betray me."

"That," the old man said bitterly, "we have never done. And may God abandon me for ever if such a thought even occurred to me."

"I believe you," Pan Andrei said after a short moment. "Even the worst cut-throat wouldn't stoop to treason."

"What are your orders, then, Your Honor?" old Kemlitch straightened-up and stood at attention.

"First there are two letters that need to be delivered right away. Do you have a smart man or two in your service?"

"Where are they to go?"

"One letter is for the Prince-*Voyevode*. But your man doesn't have to put it in his hands. It'll be enough to drop it off at the first Radzivill regiment he comes to."

"The pitch maker can do that," Kemlitch said. "He's shrewd, he keeps his mouth shut, and he's been around."

"Good. The second letter must go to Podlasye. Your man has to find the Laudanian Regiment and hand the letter to Colonel Volodyovski himself."

The old man blinked his cunning little eyes, computing all the permutations possible in secret dealings that included the confederates as well, and instinctively rubbed his hands together once again.

"You Excellency!" he suggested firmly. "If there's no hurry about that second letter maybe we could hand it to some traveler we'll find on the highway once we've left these woods. Everybody around here supports the confederates and they'd be pleased to take a trip among them. Meanwhile we'll have saved ourselves a man."

"Good idea," Kmita said at once. "That way the man who delivers the letter won't know who it's from. And how long will it take us to get out of the forest?"

"As long as Your Worship likes," Old Kemlitch shrugged and said. "We can come out tomorrow or we can come out a couple of weeks from now. These forests run twenty miles in every direction."

"Good. We'll talk about that later," the young colonel nodded. "Now bend an ear, Kemlitch. Listen well!"

"I'm listening, Your Honor."

"I've been proclaimed far and wide as a savage murderer, a killer who sold himself to the Hetman and the Swedes as well. If His Majesty the King knew my real identity he might distrust me and reject all my good intentions. God sees what's in my heart but the King will know only what he hears! Are you listening, Kemlitch?"

"I'm listening, Your Worship."

"Then mark this. From now on my name is Babinitch, not Kmita, understand? No one is to know who I really am. If one of you breathes a word about it it'll be the last word that you ever utter. If anyone we meet asks you where I'm from you're to say you don't know, that you joined up with me on the road, and that if they want to know anything more about me I'm the man to tell them."

"I understand, Your Worship."

"Pass the word to your sons and to your body servants, you

hear? They are to say my name is Babinitch even if they're being flayed alive! Your own neck will depend on that."

"Yessir! I'll do that right away, sir!" old Kemlitch assured him. "Only it might take a little time, Your Worship, for this idea to sink in with those two dolts of mine. A man needs a shovel to put a new thought in their heads. They're a real punishment for my old sins, the dimwits. But what can I do? That's God's will, God's judgment... Ah, but will Your Worship allow me to make a suggestion?"

"Say what's on your mind."

"Seems to me it'd be better not to tell either the servants or the soldiers where we're going..."

"Agreed," Kmita said.

"It's enough for them to know that you're Pan Babinitch, not Pan Kmita... The next thing is to conceal your rank, Your Honor."

"And why should I do that?"

"Because the Swedes give travel passes to the more important people and whoever doesn't have one has to answer questions."

"A good thought," Kmita nodded. "But I have all the necessary papers."

Surprise gleamed for a moment in the old man's calculating eyes. These were deep waters, and getting muddier by the moment, and all of it meant good pickings somewhere along the way.

"Can I say one more thing, Your Honor?" he asked after a while.

"As long as you stick to the point," Kmita nodded. "I like the way you're thinking."

"Passes are good to have handy in a tight spot. But if Your Worship is doing secret work, the kind that nobody ought to figure out or track down in a hurry, then it's best not to show them. I don't know if those passes are issued in the name of Kmita or Babinitch but, either way, papers blaze a trail. If anybody wants to go after Your Worship, or know which way you've gone, they'd be a place to start."

"Good thinking!" Kmita cried. "I'd rather keep those passes out of sight until we have to use them. Let's do our best to get through without them if we can."

"We can, Your Excellency. We can use disguises. We can go

as peasants or as petty gentry of the poorest kind. That way nobody'll pay any attention to us, and I've a lot of old canvas caps, sheepskins and the like lying around here. We can be taking a herd of horses for sale, like I've done often enough before, and go with them from one horse fair to another all the way to Lovitch. Or even as far as Warsaw if we've a mind to go there. As I said, Your Honor, I've done that before and I know all the roads. Like right now, Your Worship, there's a big horse fair in Sobota that a lot of people come to from real far away. In Sobota we'll find out about other markets and go on, the farther the better! The Swedes don't even notice grayback petty gentry because there's so much of it milling around at the country fairs. If some patrol commander wants to question us we'll sing him our story. And if there aren't too many of the sons of bitches, always providing we have God's blessings for it, we'll ride right over them and leave them to the crows!"

"What if they confiscate our horses on the way?" Pan Andrei wished to know. "Forced requisitions are a common thing in wartime."

"Buy them or confiscate them, it's one thing to us," old Kemlitch replied. "If they buy them, we'll be going to Sobota *for* horses, not to sell them. If they take them from us without paying for them, we'll be going to complain in their headquarters in Warsaw or even to Krakow!"

"You're a shrewd man, Kemlitch," Kmita said. "And I can see that you'll be useful to me. And even if the Swedes confiscate your horse herd you can be sure that you'll be paid for it."

"Thank you, Your Worship!" Kemlitch's grasping old hands were rubbing together as if they had a mind and will of their own. He grinned and bobbed his head. Everything was turning out exactly as he hoped.

"I had a mind to go to Elk in Prussia anyway," he said. "There's a good horse market there that I've used before. And that's on our way. From Elk we'll follow the frontier to the west and then turn south for Ostrolenka, Pultusk and even Warsaw. It's a straight clear road to Sobota after that."

"Where is this Sobota of yours, then?" Kmita asked.

What happened then was one of those misunderstandings, so common in that country where some small towns were named for days, months and seasons of the year, and where *Sobota*, or

Saturday in Polish, stood next to a township named *Piatek*, which meant Friday.

"*Where is this Saturday of yours,*" Kmita was asking in effect and Kemlitch answered:

"Right next door to Friday."

"Are you being funny?" Kmita shot him a dangerous look and the old man shuddered.

"How would I dare, Your Honor?" he cried out, crossing his arms on his chest in proof of innocence. "The small towns down around Lovitch all have odd names like that! Thursday is next to Friday and Wednesday is the next along the road."

"And it's a major market, is it? That one in Sobota?"

"Lovitch is bigger but at this time of the year Sobota is best. People come to it from all over and the herders drive their horses all the way from Prussia. It shouldn't be any worse there this year than most other times. It's quiet in those parts. The Swedes have a tight grip on all of that country and nobody causes any trouble even if he wants to."

"Good! Then I accept your plan," Kmita said. "We'll drive your herd to market. And just so that you don't lose anything by it I'll pay you for it at full price in advance."

"Thank you, Your Worship!"

"So get together some petty-gentry sheepskins, horse blankets, and plain straight swords such as the clodhoppers wear around here, and we'll set out at once! Just tell your sons what to call me from now on, remember? I'm not your colonel anymore. I'm just an ordinary horse trader, understand? And you have all been hired to give me a hand. Jump to it, Master Kemlitch, jump to it!"

Old Kemlitch did, indeed, take a great leap towards the door but Kmita's voice halted him in mid-stride.

"And remember that no one is to call me Commandant, or Excellency or even Your Worship! I'm just an ordinary Mister now and my name's Babinitch!"

★ ★ ★

Old Kemlitch left and an hour later everyone was dressed in the costumes of poor country gentry and mounted for the journey.

Pan Kmita, wearing a grey homespun kaftan of the cheapest

linen, and with a threadbare lambskin cap jammed down on his head, looked no different from any of that rootless, footloose impecunious swarm of landless petty gentry, only a step above the peasantry, who wandered about the countryside from one fair to another. Even his bandaged face added to this appearance, suggesting a sword fight after a tavern brawl.

The horsemen grouped around him wore the same kind of clothing, with long straight swords dangling from their belts in steel, unornamented scabbards, and with even longer rawhide whips and lariats grasped in their heavy hands.

His soldiers couldn't quite believe that they were looking at their fierce, young colonel, and they muttered softly to each other about his masquerade. They were even more puzzled why he changed his name. But the order that they were to treat him as if he was no better than themselves made them drop their jaws.

"I'll tell you one thing," old Soroka growled inside his whiskers. "T10hat 'Mister' just isn't going to get past my throat. Say what you like, let him kill me for it, but I'll give him his military honors like I've always done."

"An order is an order, sarge," Bilous replied. "But Jesus, hasn't the colonel changed?"

"I'll say," Soroka said.

What the soldiers couldn't know about was that Pan Andrei's heart and soul had changed as utterly as his outside shell, and that he'd truly become a new Babinitch rather than the old Kmita that all of them knew.

"Let's move out, then!" Babinitch shouted suddenly.

The whips cracked loudly in the forest stillness. The herdsmen surrounded their milling, neighing charges and bunched them together, and then they moved forward.

Part Eight

Chapter Forty-eight

RIDING ALONG THE FRONTIER between Prussia and the Palatinate of Trotzk, and making their way through trackless forests along trails known to the Kemlitches alone, they came at last into territories subject to the Elector, and turned towards Elk where they could get fresh news from the Polish-Lithuanian refugees who'd found shelter there.

Elk itself looked like a camp ground or like some rural dietine seething with political arguments and disputes. The displaced gentry packed the inns and taverns, guzzling the strong Prussian beer, and discussed every piece of news they happened to hear, so that Pan Andrei—or rather Pan Babinitch—didn't need to ask any questions. He discovered that the Prussian cities, which enjoyed a full autonomy under Polish rule, declared themselves on the side of King Yan Casimir and that they entered into an agreement with the Brandenburg Elector by which each side would defend the other if attacked by Swedes. The Elector was the nominal ruler of these territories but he ruled here only as a vassal of the Polish Crown, bound by Polish treaties with the great Baltic cities of the Hanseatic League, even though the independent merchant population of those towns was predominantly Protestant and German. The word among all the disputants was that the rich, commercial cities refused to accept the Elector's garrisons, offered as part of their agreement with him, because they feared that the cunning prince would seize them for himself once he had his own army within their walls, or that he'd join the Swedes against the Commonwealth in spite of all the assurances he made.

The gentry growled at this obstinacy of the Prussian burghers, and Pan Andrei had to bite his tongue to suppress the urge to tell them what he knew about the Radzivill machinations with the Brandenburgers. He itched to pound the truth into those smug, ignorant, know-it-all debaters, but he kept his mouth shut because it wouldn't have seemed right for an insignificant drover to take part in discussions of such a weighty nature, and also because it wasn't safe to say anything against the Elector in the small towns and countryside he controlled.

Pan Andrei's little troop moved on. They sold a few horses to keep up their disguise, and quickly replaced them with others they bought elsewhere, and then they followed the frontier southward towards Stutin which lay at the tip of the salient formed by the Duchy of Mazovia between the borders of Prussia and Podlasye. Stutin itself was out of bounds for Pan Andrei who discovered that it was occupied by Pan Volodyovski and his Laudanians. It seemed that he and the little colonel were both going in the same direction, following the same trails, and that Volodyovski must have stopped in Stutin to rest his men and horses. The border of Podlasye lay just beyond the town and Pan Volodyovski may have picked temporary quarters in Stutin, where the countryside was able to provide him with fodder and supplies, before moving into confederate country which was stripped practically to the bone after half a year of supporting the mutineer division.

Whatever his reasons for this halt, Pan Andrei didn't want to cross his path just then. He had nothing that might convince Volodyovski of his change of heart. His words, he thought, wouldn't be enough. With this in mind, he changed direction two miles short of Stutin, and turned his little cavalcade west towards Vonsosh in Mazovia. As for the letter to Volodyovski that he carried with him, he thought he'd send it on through some passing stranger at the earliest opportunity.

* * *

It was still afternoon when the supposed horse traders stopped for the night at a roadside inn. They were still a few hours' distance from the township of Vonsosh. The inn was empty except for its Prussian landlord. There were no other travelers staying there that day and Pan Andrei looked forward to a few hours of rest before riding deeper into Vonsosh County early the next morning.

But he, the three Kemlitches and Soroka barely sat down to supper when the rattle of heavy wheels and the clatter of horse-shoes on the cobblestones outside drew him to the door.

He went out to see who had come, thinking it could be a passing Swedish column, but saw instead a sumptuous traveling carriage followed by two well-loaded wagons covered with tarpaulins and surrounded by armed grooms and lackeys.

One glance was enough to show that the new arrival was a personage of considerable importance. His coach was drawn by four stout Prussian horses. A postilion mounted on one of the lead pair held two beautiful hunting dogs on ornamental leashes. The coach driver and a young page dressed in Hungarian costume perched on the high seat above the animals. The young lord himself sprawled alone in the comfortable carriage seat, wearing a rich, sleeveless traveling coat lined and trimmed with wolfskin, and held together by rows of gilded buttons. Two heavy wagons loaded with packed possessions, and surrounded by eight lackeys armed with musketoons and sabers, trundled behind him into the cobbled courtyard.

The new arrival was very young, as Pan Andrei could see at the first quick glance. He may have been in his early twenties. His red, pudgy face glowed with good living and self-satisfaction as he peered about for someone to come out to greet him once his coach had stopped, and he seemed quite put out when no one came running. His page jumped off the driver's seat and ran to offer his hand to his descending master who, in the meantime, raised a lordly hand and beckoned to Pan Andrei with his traveling glove.

"Come here a minute, friend!" he commanded, irritating Kmita who was not yet accustomed to the offhand, conde-scending treatment accorded by the highborn to the lesser gen-try. He frowned and went back to his supper while the young lord followed him into the inn, blinking and narrowing his eyes in the shadowed gloom.

"Why doesn't anyone come out when I arrive?" he demanded.

"Because the landlord's gone to his store-room and we're travelers just like you, sir," Kmita said.

"Thanks for the information," the pudgy lordling answered rather grandly. "And who are you?"

"A gentleman taking horses to the market."

"And your company? Are they also gentry?"

"They're neither rich nor highborn, if that's what you have in mind sir, but yes, they are gentry."

"Greetings in that case, gentlemen," the young man nodded loftily around the supper table. "And where are you heading?"

"We travel from one horse fair to another, wherever we can sell an animal or two."

"If you are spending the night here," the young magnate said, "then I'll take a look at your stock tomorrow. I might find something that I like. In the meantime let me join you at the table."

★ ★ ★

The lordly young man asked whether he might join them but he did so in a manner that implied he was doing everyone an honor. Amused, Kmita played the role.

"Please do, sir," he replied politely. "Although there isn't much of a supper to share since all we have before us is sausage and peas."

"I've better things than that in my traveling hampers," the lordling said proudly. "But I have a soldier's palate, so to speak. Peas and sausage are just fine with me provided there is something good to drink as well."

He spoke so slowly that he seemed to be weighing and considering every word and sentence, but his shrewd little eyes darted swiftly from one face to another as he lowered himself to the bench where Pan Andrei moved to make room for him. Shrewdness and calculation marked his every gesture despite his moonfaced pudginess and his flushed, well-fed cheeks which suggested a greedy, pleasure-loving nature.

"Don't inconvenience yourself," he said both kindly and disdainfully as Pan Andrei offered him room to sit. "Matters pertaining to personal dignity can be set aside while a man is traveling, and it won't bother me if you touch me with your elbow now and then as we share a bench. In other words a crown won't fall off my head, as the saying goes."

Pan Andrei, who was in the process of passing him the bowl of peas, would have undoubtedly smashed the heavy dish on the head of this puffed-up little personage if there wasn't something so ridiculous in that pompous posturing that it made him laugh. He grinned, suppressing his irritated impulse, and said in the form and accent of the lesser gentry:

"All sorts of crowns are falling nowadays. Our own King Yan Casimir, for example, who has the right to wear two crowns if he wanted, doesn't have even one unless you count the crown of thorns they've stuck on his head."

The unknown lordling threw Pan Kmita a swift, calculating glance and peered around rapidly to see if anyone else was sitting in the shadows. Then he sighed and wagged his finger in a warning gesture.

"It's best not to talk about such things these days unless one knows who one is talking with, but I must say you've got that pictured rather well. One crown and that a crown of thorns, eh? Very nicely phrased. You must have been in service in some important household to pick up such ideas. Your own condition, and rather a low one as such things are counted, hardly indicates an educated man."

"A traveling horse-peddler rubs a lot of elbows and hears this and that," Pan Andrei replied, still playing his amused role as a country bumpkin. "But I was never in anybody's service."

"Indeed? And where do you come from?"

"From a country hamlet." A picture of the Laudanians' clustered villages passed across Kmita's darkening eyes and he frowned to blink the image out of memory. "In the Trotzk palatinate," he added.

"A hamlet? Don't worry about it," the young man said grandly. "Gentry is gentry no matter how close to the soil. And what's the news from Lithuania, nowadays?"

"Same thing as ever. The place is full of traitors."

"Traitors, you say? And who are these traitors, if you please?"

"Those who abandoned our King and the Commonwealth, of course."

"Hmm." The young lordling peered shrewdly out of the

corner of an eye. "And how's the health of the Prince-*Voyevode* of Vilna?"

"He's ill, people say. Has trouble breathing."

"My God look after him... I've always thought him such a kind and openhanded man."

"He's openhanded to the Swedes, alright, since he opened all our gates before them."

"Ah..." the young man murmured. "So you are not one of his partisans, I see?"

★ ★ ★

Kmita realized with a sudden start that while he was amusing himself with the self-important youth, and saying more than his disguise allowed, he was being rather shrewdly questioned and he returned at once to his humbler role.

"Ah, what do I care," he shrugged and waved his hand. "Let smarter heads than mine think about all that. My main worry is to keep my horses away from Swedish requisition parties."

"Then you should have sold them as soon as you got them. Or you might try Podlasye. Those regiments down there which oppose the Hetman are always short of horses."

"I wouldn't know about that,"—Kmita shrugged—"not having been among them. Though some passing traveler gave me a letter to deliver to one of their colonels."

"Why would anybody do that when you're not going there?"

"Because he knew I'd be passing Stutin, I expect. It's not too hard to find someone to take it on from here."

"You're right," the young lordling said. "I'm going there myself."

"Ah," Kmita bowed, still acting like someone inferior to the rich young stranger. "So you are also escaping from the Swedes, Your Worship?"

"Why do you say *also*?" the young man asked with a cool, calculating stare and Pan Andrei cursed himself for his careless question. "You're not escaping from them, are you? No, you're not. In fact you're riding straight into their hands and you'll be selling them your horses too if they don't take them from you without paying for them."

"I said *also* in reference to the gentry I saw sheltering in Elk," Kmita explained quickly. "As for how I feel about the Swedes,

I think that if everybody was as helpful to them as I intend to be they wouldn't be here very long."

"And aren't you afraid to say such things aloud?"

"No I'm not," Kmita said. "First because I don't frighten easily. And second, because Stutin is only a stone's throw away and everybody there says what he pleases as loudly as he wants. I just hope we all stop talking about the Swedes and get to work on them real soon."

"I see that you're brighter than your place in life suggests," the young man said again. "But if you're that deadset against the Swedes why aren't you joining those soldiers who turned against the Hetman? Why are you riding away from them instead?"

"Because I've business elsewhere," Kmita said.

"But don't you think those poor, homeless fellows in Podlasye would also rather be doing something else? They'd have been well-off staying with their Hetman but they rebelled against him because they wanted to stay loyal to the Commonwealth. It'll come to war soon enough between them and the Swedes, you can be sure of that."

"God grant it," said Kmita.

"I dare say it would've already happened if the Swedes found their way into that corner of the country. But give them a little time! They'll get around to that soon enough! And then you'll have as much fighting as you want to see."

"That's what I think too," Kmita said. "I mean that the resistance will begin here before anywhere else."

"Well then, why don't you join the confederates? Don't they need strong hands that know how to hold a saber? Haven't enough good, loyal men showed you the way already? Some of the greatest knights in the Commonwealth have gathered among them and more come running every day. You're from a part of the country where the Swedes are still a novelty. But take it from those who've had a chance to know them that there's no living under them for anyone in Poland. Vyelkopolska placed itself under their protection but they're already looting the whole country and squeezing the gentry. Nor is it any better right here in Mazovia. General Steinbeck made a proclamation that anyone who sits peacefully at home and doesn't cause trouble will be treated kindly and that his property will be left alone. But that's not the way things work under the Swedes!

The general says one thing and the local commandants do another and no one can be sure that he and his possessions will survive the day."

"The gentry should've fought the Swedes before they made themselves at home in those possessions," Kmita said.

"Yes. Yes they should!"

The plump young lordling was now apparently satisfied that Kmita didn't care for the Swedes any more than he did and turned to contemplating the times before the war.

"It used to be that a man could take pleasure in what he owned," he mused. "We had what we had and we were free to use it and enjoy it any way we pleased. And now what's the story? Some greedy foreigner shows up without even as much as a by your leave, and sticks out his paw, and you've got to give him everything he wants. If you don't, they'll find some reason to drive you off your land or they'll just cut your head off without an excuse. There's hardly a man left in the occupied provinces who doesn't weep bitter tears today, remembering the good life he had under his former King, and all of them are groaning in oppression and looking to those confederates to save them."

"I see that Your Worship doesn't like the Swedes much better than I do," Kmita said, and the young stranger immediately threw a hurried glance all around the room, as if reminded that walls had ears sometimes.

"No I don't," he said cautiously. "I think I can trust you. You may be just a simple fellow but you've got the look of an honest man about you. So I'll tell you that my fondest wish for them is that they choke to death on everything they've stolen. There! I've said it! But even if you were some kind of a scoundrel and I couldn't trust you, I'd know how to look after myself. I have armed men outside, and a saber close to hand right here, and if you tried to tie me up and drag me to the Swedes I wouldn't let you do it."

"That's the last thing I'd think of," Pan Andrei assured him. "I like your spirit, sir, it's close to my own heart. And it's a fine, brave thing for you to leave your properties to the greed and malice of the enemy while you go off to serve our Motherland and our King. That's something else of which you can be proud."

But here the proud, flushed patriot started to giggle as glee-fully as a little girl.

"Leave my properties? Hee Hee! D'you think me a fool? My first rule is that what's mine is mine and ought to stay that way, because whatever God gives anyone is a holy thing. I kept as quiet as a field mouse until I had my harvest in. Now it's a different story! I sold it all at a good price in Prussia along with all my tools and livestock, and now there's nothing left to keep me at home! Let them take from me whatever they can find!"

"Even so, you left your lands and buildings. It's true the Swedes can't carry them away but they can strip them bare and burn what they can't carry."

* * *

Pan Andrei had forgotten his humble role during this conver-sation and slipped gradually into his old tone and manner, also forgetting that such commanding airs were out of place in a poor horse-peddler, but the little rural potentate didn't seem to no-tice.

"Let them!" He shook all over, giggling all the harder. "I don't own an acre! I lease the arable lands in this county from the Palatine of Mazovia and my contract has just run out for the year, hee hee! I didn't even pay him my rents for the last quarter! What's more I won't do it, because I hear the *Voyevode* is siding with the Swedes and I can use the ready cash just as much as he can."

Now it was Kmita's turn to laugh. "God love you, young sir. I see that you're not only a brave cavalier but a shrewd and clever one as well!"

"And isn't that the truth?" Pleased with himself, the plump young stranger grinned from ear to ear. "Shrewdness is the thing! But we weren't talking about shrewdness, were we. We were talking about those good men in Podlasye..."

And here the self-satisfied young man stopped shaking and giggling and returned to his superior airs.

"If you feel real love for our King and Country," he admon-ished Kmita, "why don't you enlist with the confederates? You'll please God, you will have a chance to fight for our Motherland, and you might also do quite well for yourself. You wouldn't be the first of the petty gentry to make something of himself in wartime. I know! I can see by the looks of you that you're a sharp and resolute sort of chap yourself, and if low birth doesn't get in your way you can rise to a fair fortune once God starts letting you get your hands on a little booty. The trick of it is not to waste a penny and hang onto everything that sticks to your fingers. Do that and you'll be surprised how fast your purse will grow! I don't know if you have a little plot of land somewhere or if you have nothing. But you could have it, and that's the point I'm making! A full purse will let you rent some property and, once you're renting, it isn't far to leasing or a freehold. With God's help you could be leasing an entire county in a year or two. And so, even if you started out in service, you could die a landed gentleman. You can even try for some county office as long as you work hard, keep your eyes open, and don't spend too many hours snoring in your quilts. That's the way! That's the way to do it! You know what people say, and it's a wise saying: God always rewards the man who gets up at sunrise."

★ ★ ★

But by this time Pan Andrei thought that he'd burst with laughter that he was barely able to control. He chewed on his mustache. He gnawed on his knuckles. His face shook and quivered and he hissed and twisted with the pain of his wound, but the impulse to laugh into the stranger's face sent him into fresh paroxysms of barely stifled choking.

Meanwhile the little lordling went on with his lofty, patronizing tone:

"They'll let you join them. Don't worry. They need good men, I know. And besides, you've quite caught my fancy and I'll take you into my own service if you like, which is a sure way to a quick advancement."

Here the round, redfaced youth looked proudly at Kmita, lifting a small, plump hand to twirl his little mustache, and Pan Andrei thought that his last moment of restraint had come.

"Would you like to be my sword-bearer?" the young man asked kindly. "You can carry my saber behind me and watch over the lackeys."

But this was the last stroke.

Kmita roared with laughter.

"What's so funny?" The young man was surprised, displeased, frowning and alarmed all at the same time. "You think I'm making jokes?"

"It's... just the... ah... prospect of that service," Pan Andrei gasped. "That's... ah... what makes me so happy, ha ha ha!"

But the young personage chose to be offended.

"I can see that you learned your manners from a fool," he snapped. "Take care, fellow, that you don't overstep your limits! Particularly since you don't know who you're talking to."

"That's just it, sir!" Pan Andrei managed to control his laughter. "Forgive me. But Your Worship never told me who you are."

"I am Zjendjan, the Freeholder of Vonsosh," the young man said proudly, but although Pan Andrei had met and admired the famous Yan Skshetuski, he had never heard the name of Pan Yan's former servant.

Chapter Forty-nine

MEANWHILE, even as Kmita opened his mouth to introduce himself with his *nom-de-guerre*, one of his soldiers pushed urgently into the room.

"Your Excel...!" he began then caught himself, frozen by Kmita's glare, and gave way to confusion.

"There's some people coming," he choked out at last.

"Along which road?" Kmita asked.

"From Stutin."

It was Pan Andrei's turn to look unsure but he recovered quickly.

"Stay alert, all of you," he ordered. "How many of them are there?"

"It'll be a troop of ten, I'd say."

"Have your weapons handy. Now move out!"

Then, when the soldier marched out of the room, he turned in explanation to the young freeholder.

"It could be the Swedes."

"Why should that worry you?" Pan Zjendjan asked quietly. He had been eying the odd young horse trader with rising curiosity for some time. "Aren't you going towards them anyway? You're bound to run into them sooner or later."

"I'd rather meet the Swedes than the marauders who swarm through the countryside in wartime," Kmita explained quickly. "If you're driving horses you must be always on your guard. They're a tempting prize."

"If it's true that Pan Volodyovski is camped in Stutin, as I've heard he might be, then it could be one of his patrols," Zjendjan said. "They'd want to make sure that the country round about here is quiet and safe before they go into winter quarters. After all, the Swedes are only a jump and a skip away."

Hearing this, Pan Andrei glanced around the taproom and found a seat in the darkest corner, where the long overhang of the fireplace threw a black shadow on the table top. In the meantime everyone heard horses snorting and clattering outside, and a moment later several armed men stamped into the tavern. Their leader was a huge, dour man, so much so as to seem like a grizzled giant, and his wooden leg rattled on the loose planks with which the room was floored.

Kmita glanced at him out of his dark corner and his heart missed a beat. He recognized Yozva Butrym.

"Where's the innkeeper?" the Laudanian demanded from the middle of the room.

"Here, sir!" The Prussian hurried forward. "How can I be of service?"

"Get feed for our horses!"

"We have none here," the innkeeper said and then pointed to Zjendjan and the supposed horse herders. "Unless these gentlemen can spare some of theirs."

"Whose people are you?" Zjendjan asked.

"And who wants to know?"

"I'm the *Starosta* of Vonsosh," the young man replied in his loftiest and most authoritative manner.

He was not, of course, a *Starosta* of anything, as Pan Andrei would discover in due time. He merely leased the arable lands and pastures of the shire. But since his own workers normally addressed him as 'My Lord Sheriff' he liked to use the title at important moments. Yozva Butrym, however, took him at face value, swept his cap off his head and said in a much humbler voice and with a gentler manner: "Greetings, my lord. It's so dark in here a man can't tell one man's standing from another's."

"Who are you people, then?" Zjendjan said again, lifting his nose proudly in the air and placing his plump fists on his hips in the posture of authority and interrogation.

"We're Laudanians, sir. From the former Billevitch Regiment which is now commanded by Pan Volodyovski."

"For God's sake!" Zjendjan cried out in delight. "So Pan Volodyovski is in Stutin, is he?"

"Yessir. Along with several other officers who escaped from Zmudya."

"Thanks be to God for that!" said the supposed *Starosta*. "And who are these other officers, then?"

"Well, we had Colonel Mirski," the Butrym explained. "But he died of a heart attack a while back. But there's Pan Oskierka, Pan Kowalski, the two Skshetuski cousins..."

"What?" Zjendjan cried out. "What Skshetuski cousins? Is one of them from Bujhetz?"

"That I wouldn't know, sir," Yozva said. "All I know is that he's that famous hero who saved the army at the Siege of Zbarajh."

"Dear God Almighty! That's my master!"

Here Zjendjan realized how strange it must sound to have a high shire official like a *Starosta*, second only in rank to a *Voyevode*, talking about a master, and he added at once: "My... ah... friend and kinsman, I had meant to say."

★ ★ ★

This was another fragment of Zjendjan's boyhood past that Kmita would know about much later, but the rich, lordly and self-assured young man wasn't straying too far from the truth. As a teen-aged lad in the long-lost provinces of Prince Yeremi Vishnovyetzki, he was a loyal and devoted servant of Pan Yan Skshetuski, rendered him some great services in the Cossack Wars along with Pan Zagloba and Pan Volodyovski, and stood with them as one of the godfathers of Yaremka, Pan Yan's first-born son.

But Pan Andrei had other things on his mind just then. The first glimpse of the dangerous, implacable Yozva Butrym brought back such violent memories, and threw him into such a gnawing rage, that he bit his lips and clutched at his saber. He knew that it was Yozva who caused the massacre of his former comrades. The peg-legged Butrym was his fiercest enemy among the Laudanians. The old, savage Kmita, Pan Andrei knew, would have him seized at once, roped to a horse's tail and dragged through the stones and brambles in the yard outside, but the new Babinitch crushed this murderous impulse. Indeed, he worried that if the Laudanians recognized him here all his good intentions would be placed in jeopardy.

He was determined to keep his identity a secret at all costs and to avoid recognition as long as he could. He edged into an even darker patch of shadow, cradled his head on his arms on the table top, and tried to look as if he was asleep.

But at the same time he managed to whisper to Soroka: "Go to the stables. Get the horses ready. We'll leave as soon as it starts getting dark."

Soroka rose and went out of the room.

Kmita kept still, pretending that he had dozed off, but a swarm of memories assailed him like a flock of birds. The sight of the Laudanians brought to mind the woods and trails of their peaceful country. It wrenched him with a longing for those peaceful hours in Vodokty, and he recalled with a sharp pang of pity and regret that short blissful moment in his past when he was truly happy, and which now seemed no more real to him than a wished-for dream.

When Yozva Butrym said that he and his men were part of the old Billevitch Regiment, Pan Andrei's heart started pounding like a drum. It seemed to leap and shudder in his chest, and to fill with sadness, as if Olenka's family name alone was enough to plunge him into sorrow. The darkening Autumn afternoon looked suddenly like that January evening when he appeared in Vodokty with the Winter blizzard and saw Olenka among her spinning maids. The dim fire glowing on the hearth seemed to be the same. His eyes were closed but he could picture her in all her quiet, bright beauty. He heard again everything they said to each other that night, and he recalled every moment that happened between them. He saw her now as his lost Guardian Angel who wanted to lead him in the paths of decency and goodness, shield him from his own harsh impulses and actions, and show him the straight, simple road of human kindness, compassion and respect.

'*If only I'd listened to her then,*' he thought in despair. '*If only I'd listened...*'

She'd known at once what to do and whose side to take. She knew instinctively who was in the right and who represented the forces of evil and where to look for both honesty and duty.

'*... She'd have taken me by the hand and led me along the right trail,*' he thought. '*If only I'd listened.*'

And at this thought he felt such a powerful surge of love for that luminous young woman that he was ready to spill all his blood if he could just fall at her feet once more. He was even ready to throw his arms in friendship around that grim, one-legged Laudanian bear who'd murdered his companions, and he wanted this only because the man came from the Lauda country, and mentioned the Billevitch name, and used to know Olenka.

★ ★ ★

But it was his own name, repeated several times by Yozva, that brought him out of his saddened reverie. The young lord from Vonsosh was questioning the Laudanian about his old acquaintances, and Yozva was telling him everything that happened in Keydany since that memorable announcement of the Hetman's treaty with the Swedes. He spoke about the mutiny in the army, about the imprisonment of the loyal colonels, about their exile to Birjhe under guard, and about their rescue. Kmita's name resounded through these tales with all the hatred due to cruelty and treason. Apparently the unforgiving Butrym didn't know that Volodyovski, Zagloba and the two Skshetuskis owed their lives to Kmita and this is how he told what happened in Billevitche.

"So our colonel caught that traitor in the Billevitch manor, like a fox in a trap. And right away they had him sent out to be shot. I led him to his death with real joy in my heart, I tell you. I was real pleased that God's hand finally reached that hell-hound. I shined a light in his eyes as we went along, to see if maybe he'd show some sign of repentance, but no way! Not him! He walked like he didn't care that he'd be standing before God's judgment in another minute. That's how far gone he was in his crimes. That's how hardened his soul had become. And when I advised him at least to make the sign of the cross, he told me to shut up and mind my own business."

Pan Zjendjan pursed his lips and shook his head in wonder, as if he couldn't believe such depths of human stubbornness and depravity, and Yozva continued:

"So we led him into the fields, put him against a pear tree, and I just got the firing squad lined up, when Pan Zagloba comes riding up and says we should search him first in case he had some papers. Well he did. We found some letter on him. '*Throw some light on this,*' Pan Zagloba says and gets down to reading but he'd no sooner started when he grasps his head and shouts *'Jesus and Mary! Get him back to the manor house at once!'* He jumped on his horse and galloped away and we led Kmita back the way we'd come, thinking that maybe they'd want to lay him across the coals to question him further. But that's not what happened! They let the traitor go! It's not my place to question my superiors, but I'd have shot him no matter what it said in that letter Pan Zagloba found."

"What did the letter say?"

"I don't know. The way I see it the Hetman had some other officers in his hands whom he'd have shot if something happened to Kmita. Or maybe our colonel took mercy on the Lady who, as I hear it, took so ill that they could barely get her breathing again."

"Why would she do that if he came to take her to Keydany?"

"I don't know. People says she still loves him. They were to be married. All I know, though it's not my place to say it, that it's a real bad thing to have him loose again. Satan himself would be ashamed to do what that man had done. He sent all of Lithuania into tears and mourning. His name is a curse. And God only knows how many widows and orphans he left crying behind him. Whoever kills him will earn God's blessings and the thanks of everybody in the country just as if he'd shot a mad dog."

Here their conversation turned to Pan Volodyovski, the two Skshetuskis and the confederate regiments quartered in Podlasye.

"Victuals are hard to get," Yozva Butrym said. "The Prince-*Voyevode's* estates have been sifted clean. The farmer gentry is mostly as poor as our own in Zmudya, living in hamlets like we do in the Lauda country, so that neither our animals nor our men have a lot to chew on. All the colonels decided to split the regiments into small formations, maybe a hundred men to every detachment, and spread them out with two or three miles between each of them throughout the countryside. But I don't know what good that'll do in Winter."

* * *

Kmita, who had been sitting quietly in his shadowed corner, listening without a word while his name featured so grimly in

Yozva Butrym's story, now stirred and was about to say that the Hetman would pluck the dispersed confederates like crayfish from a sack, when the doors creaked open and Soroka reappeared on the threshold.

The firelight fell straight into the sergeant's face and illuminated his harsh, wolflike features, and Yozva Butrym gave him a long, hard stare.

"Is that your man, Your Worship?" he turned to Zjendjan. "I know him from somewhere."

"No," Zjendjan said and waved his hand in the direction of the others sitting about the room. "He's one of that party of small country gentry that's taking horses to market."

"What market?" Yozva asked.

"The one in Sobota," old Kemlitch replied.

"And where's that?"

"Near Piatek."

Yozva apparently took that answer for an attempt at humor, just as Pan Andrei had done in the Kemlitch hideout, and his face hardened into an angry challenge.

"Give me a straight answer when I'm asking for it!" he snapped at old Kemlitch.

"Why should I?" the old marauder growled in turn. "What gives you the right to ask me any questions?"

"I've the right because it's my duty," Yozva snapped, scowling dangerously. "I've been sent out to see if there're any suspicious people hereabouts. Well, it looks like I found a few who don't want to tell me where they're going!"

Kmita became concerned that some kind of quarrel could erupt out of this exchange and decided that he had better intervene.

"Don't get so angry, Mister Soldier," he said from his dark corner. "Piatek and Sobota are two market towns, like a lot of others, where you find horse fairs at this time of year. If you don't believe us, ask His Worship the *Starosta* here who is sure to know them."

"Of course I do!" Zjendjan said to Yozva and the dour Butrym became mollified at once.

"Well... that's all right, then," he muttered. "But why do you have to take your horses all the way out there? You can get rid of them in Stutin. We need them. We've lost quite a few, one way or another. We picked some up in Pilvishkye but they're either spavined or down with saddle sores."

"Everybody goes where he'd rather be," Kmita said and shrugged. "And we know what's best for us."

"I don't know where it's best for you, Mister," Yozva grunted. "But it's better for us if you don't take information to the Swedes along with your horses."

"It's strange to me too," said the shrewd little leaseholder of Vonsosh. "These people curse the Swedes but they seem in a real hurry to get in among them."

Then he turned directly to Pan Andrei. "And you don't look to me much like a drover, Mister," he said. "I saw a ring on your finger that a magnate wouldn't be ashamed to wear on a feast day."

"If Your Worship likes it then buy it from me," Kmita said at once. "I paid two groats for it in Elk."

"Two groats? Then it must be glass but it's a good setting. Show it to me, Mister!"

"Come and take it, sir."

"What's the matter, you can't bring it over? I am to fetch it for myself?"

"Ah... It's just that I'm so tired, Your Worship," Kmita said.

"Ey, fellow, it seems as if you're suddenly anxious not to show your features!"

Hearing this, Yozva Butrym didn't say a word. He stepped up to the hearth, picked up a burning brand, and carried it high overhead to Kmita's dark corner where he shined the light straight into his face. Pan Andrei rose to his full height, knowing that his masquerade was as good as over, and the two of them stared for a moment into each other's eyes. Then, suddenly, the burning torch fell out of Yozva's hand, hurling a thousand sparks as it hit the floor.

"*Jezus Maria!*" the Laudanian shouted. "That's Kmita!"

"That's right!" said Pan Andrei, seeing that all further disguises were useless.

But Yozva started shouting for his soldiers who were still outside. "Come in here! On the double! Hold him!" And then he cried straight into Pan Andrei's face:

"Is that you, you hellhound? You traitor? You masquerading Devil? You slipped out of my hands once already and now you're creeping in disguise to the Swedes? I've got you now, you Judas! You murderer! I've got you!"

Yozva clutched Pan Andrei by the neck, Kmita seized him by the throat in his own turn, but now the two Kemlitch twins were also on their feet, their shaggy heads bumping against the ceiling.

"What do you say, Pa?" Kosma asked. "Do we pound 'em now?"

"Pound 'em!" the old man bellowed hauling out his saber.

★ ★ ★

The doors of the tavern burst open as Yozva Butrym's soldiers ran into the room with Kmita's troopers and the armed Kemlitch grooms hard upon their heels. Yozva clamped his left fist on the back of Pan Andrei's neck, making lightnings around him with the naked rapier he grasped in his right hand, and Kmita seized him with both hands by the throat. He didn't have the massive Butrym's strength but Yozva's eyes bulged out of his head as if he was being throttled in a vise. The Laudanian tried to smash Pan Andrei's head with the iron guard of his heavy long-sword but Kmita drew his own. The cast-iron boss on top of the hilt split the top of Yozva's head, his fingers opened on Pan Andrei's neck, and he staggered backwards under the force of the blow. Kmita gave him a propelling push to clear some space around himself and slashed him with all his strength across the face.

Yozva fell like a toppled oak and struck the floorboards with the back of his skull.

"Kill!" Kmita howled and leaped on another Butrym as if the smell of blood woke the ruthless ruffian and marauder who lay submerged within him.

But he had no need to encourage anyone to murder. The taproom was already seething like the contents of a boiling cauldron. The two young Kemlitches advanced shoulder to shoulder like twin battering rams. They slashed to right and left with their heavy sabers, sometimes butting their opponents like enraged, wild bulls, and hurling a man to the ground with each savage blow. Their father followed step for step behind them, squatting now and then all the way to the floor for a stronger thrust, peering out through his slanted eyes, and lunging with his sword-point between the shoulders of his sons like an archer shooting through a loophole.

Soroka, however, spread the most terrifying carnage of them all. This was his element. He was at home in tavern brawls and fighting at close quarters. He emptied both his pistols into the jam-packed crowd, grappled with his enemies so closely that they were unable to swing a sword against him, and pounded their heads and faces with the bone grips and steel barrels of his discharged weapons. Each blow crushed a nose, gouged an eye or shattered mouths and teeth. Kmita's remaining troopers and the Kemlitch grooms fought to support their masters.

The fighting rolled from one end of the tavern to the other. The Laudanians defended themselves fiercely. But their defeat was a foregone conclusion from the moment that Kmita sent Yozva crashing to the floor and then, bounding into the fight, cut down another Butrym. Nor were Zjendjan's lackeys of much help to them. They had come running in with their swords and carbines, but even though their master shouted '*Cut!*'and '*Shoot!*' in his loudest voice, they didn't know whom they should be shooting because the grey-clad Laudanian gentry wore no distinguishing uniforms and looked no different than the men they fought. Both sides took Zjendjan's wretched servants for fresh enemies, and each battered them as fiercely as the other.

Zjendjan himself kept out of the fighting. He searched for Kmita in the crowd to point him out for a pistol shot, but the terrifying killer appeared and disappeared before his eyes like an evil spirit, leaping out of the murky gloom as scarlet with fresh-spilled blood as if he were the Devil, and vanishing in the twilight.

* * *

Meanwhile the innkeeper managed to edge his way around the battle ground and hurled a bucketful of water into the fireplace.

The room plunged into darkness.

The tightly packed crowd could no longer tell friends from enemies. They hammered each other indiscriminately with their fists, pressed too close together to use any weapons, and finally the fighting spilled across the threshold through the broken doors.

The Vonsosh lackeys were the first to flee. Then came the stumbling, battered Laudanians with Kmita's men practically riding on their necks, and the fight changed into flight and pursuit among the ditches, bushes and the roadside nettles, and in the sheds and stables and among the wagons, while pistol shots cracked out and panicked horses screamed and reared in the cobbled courtyard.

Whatever else was left of this wayside battle resolved itself around Zjendjan's wagons where his lackeys were making their last stand. They had already fired their carbines from under the wagons at the Laudanians, mistaking them for their worst tormentors, and now they howled in terror from behind the wheels while old Kemlitch poked at them through the spokes with the end of his sword.

"Give up!" the old man bellowed, stabbing blindly underneath a cart.

"Stop! We surrender!" several voices shouted and swords and firearms began to fly into the yard from under the wagons.

The Kemlitch twins started pulling the disarmed Vonsosh grooms by the neck into the open, pounding them in the process with their hamlike fists, until the old man shouted: "To the wagons! Take what you can! Quickly! Quickly! To the wagons with you!"

The young ruffians didn't need to be told a third time to begin their looting. They ran as if their lives depended on swiftness to rip back the tarpaulins that covered Zjendjan's baggage.

The first few bundles were already flying through the air when Kmita's voice thundered a command to stop.

"Hold it!" he shouted and enforced his order with the flat of his bloodied sword. "Leave it alone! Back! Back! Stand aside!"

Kosma and Damian wasted no time in getting out of their angry colonel's way but the old man set up a plaintive wailing.

"Your Worship...?" the old man moaned as if he were wounded. "Can't we help ourselves to a little... Can't we?"

"Don't you dare touch a thing!" Kmita cried. "Now find me the *Starosta!*"

The twins took off as if they'd sprouted wings, their father behind them, and they were back with Zjendjan in their clutches only moments later. This time the pudgy lordling bowed to the ground at the sight of Kmita.

"Begging Your Excellency's pardon," he began. "I'm being treated quite unfairly here! I wasn't looking for a fight with anyone. I didn't take sides. And just because I'm going to visit some old friends in Stutin... well, anyone is allowed to do that..."

Kmita said nothing, breathing deeply and leaning on his rapier, so Zjendjan went on:

"I've done no harm to the Swedes or to the Prince-Hetman either. I was just on my way to see Pan Volodyovski who's an old friend of mine. We served together in Ruthenia in the Cossack Wars. Why should I look for trouble? I wasn't in Keydany! What happened there is none of my business! All I care about is my own skin and the safety of those few things that God bestowed on me. I didn't steal them. I earned them with hard work. What does all this other business have to do with me? Why don't you just let me go my own way, Your Worship?"

But Kmita just kept gasping, struggling to control his chaotic breathing, and looking at Zjendjan with distracted eyes.

"I humbly beg Your Worship!" the plump young lordling started up again. "Your Excellency saw that I didn't know those other men! I wasn't their friend! They attacked Your Worship and they got what was coming to them. But why should I suffer for it too? Why should I lose what's mine? How am I to blame? I'll ransom myself from Your Honor's soldiers, if that's what they want, although I'm a poor man and can't afford a lot. But I'll give them a silver dollar each just so they have something for their trouble. I'll give them two apiece! And Your Excellency also should accept a little something from me..."

"Cover up those carts!" Kmita shouted suddenly to the Vonsosh servants. And to Zjendjan he said: "And you, fellow, take all the wounded and go to the Devil!"

"I thank Your Honor humbly."

Old Kemlitch, however, had to try once more. His hooked lower lip, along with the stumps of his remaining teeth, protruded in a plaintive pout that would have looked more convincing on an injured child.

"Your Worship...!" he whined. "That's ours... Holy Mirror of Justice, that's ours..."

But Kmita's glare crushed him so completely that he stopped moaning, stooped even lower than his humble crouch, and seemed to shrink right into the ground.

Zjendjan's servants ran to repack the baggage and harness all their horses and Kmita turned again to the humbled Freeholder of Vonsosh.

"Take all the dead and wounded you can find," he said. "Deliver them to Pan Volodyovski and tell him from me that I'm not as bad an enemy of his as he thinks I am. I know it sounds strange after what just happened but I may even be a better friend of his than he can imagine. I didn't want to meet with him just now. The time isn't right. He might believe me sometime in the future but now I don't have anything to prove that I can be trusted. Maybe there'll be a time... I hope so... But listen! Be sure to tell him it was his men who attacked me and that I had no choice but to defend myself."

"That's no more than the truth," Zjendjan said.

"Wait! Tell Pan Volodyovski to keep his regiment together. Don't let it disperse. Radzivill was just waiting for some cavalry from Pontus before marching on them. He could be on his way already, for all that I know. Both he and Prince Boguslav are plotting with the Elector so it's dangerous to camp so near the Prussian border. But the main thing is for the confederates to band together or they'll die for nothing. The *Voyevode* of Vitebsk is trying to force his way into Podlasye, they could go out to meet him and help him if he needs it."

"I'll tell it all as faithfully if I was paid for it by the word," Zjendjan said.

"Though it is Kmita who's saying all this," Pan Andrei said. "Though it's Kmita who is warning them, let them join up with the other colonels and all stay together. They must unite for strength. I repeat, Radzivill is coming, and I'm not an enemy of Pan Volodyovski."

But Kmita was yet to encounter another facet of *Pan Starosta* Zjendjan, the one that helped to lift him from the status of a body servant to his new rank and riches.

"It might go better if I had some personal sign from Your Worship," the plump youth suggested. "Like maybe a ring..."

"Why do you need a sign?"

"Because Pan Volodyovski would be more likely to believe Your Worship's intentions. He'd think there had to be something to your warnings if you sent a sign."

"Take my ring, then," Kmita said. "Though he'll find enough of my signs on the heads of those men you'll be taking to him."

He slipped his costly family signet ring off his finger and handed it to Zjendjan who pocketed it at once.

"My humble thanks to Your Worship," he said.

★ ★ ★

An hour later found Zjendjan and his wagons on their way to Stutin. His grooms had not been all that badly battered. But his wagons carried three dead Laudanians, and the rest all wounded, along with Yozva Butrym who lay senseless with a slashed face and a broken head.

On the whole, the shrewd young man decided as he rode along, he hadn't done too badly. The ring, whose pure stone seemed to throw magical lights in the silver moonlight, was more than enough to pay for any damage. But the man who gave it was a real puzzle. Having done so much already to hurt the confederates and to help both Radzivill and the Swedes, he was apparently anxious to save them from total extinction.

"Because what he advises came straight from the heart," Zjendjan murmured to himself. "It's always better to stick in a bunch then stand all alone without a friend nearby to help out if needed. But why should he go out of his way to give a special warning? Maybe out of some private gratitude or affection for Pan Volodyovski, like for not shooting him that time in Billevitche. He must be really fond of the little colonel! But that won't please the *Voyevode* of Vilna, that's certain! Hmm... I don't understand that man... He serves Radzivill but wishes our side well. And he's on his way into Swedish territory too. He's a hard one to figure out, that's certain."

And after a while Zjendjan added, peering at his new ring against the evening light: "Generous, too, I'd say. But it's a bad idea to get in his way."

Old Kemlitch, plodding behind Kmita in just the opposite direction, racked his brains just as hard, and to a similarly unrewarding purpose, to unravel a mystery of his own.

The question was: '*Whom is Kmita serving?*'

"He's going to the King but he's beating up on the confederates who stand by the King," the gloomy old marauder was growling to himself. "What's going on here? Nor does he trust the Swedes 'cause he's hiding from them... Ay, what will become of us in the end?"

Unable to find any reasonable answers he turned to pour his outrage on his sons.

"Scoundrels!" he hissed. "You'll die without a father's blessing! Couldn't you at least turn out a few pockets among the dead?"

"We were scared, Pa!" Kosma and Damian chorused and the old man sighed with a glance at Kmita.

Only Soroka was pleased with everything that happened and he rode happily just behind his colonel.

"We got rid of our bad luck," he grunted, grinning from ear to ear under his huge mustache. "We're winning again! I wonder whom we'll be beating next?"

He was no more concerned about that than he was about where they were going or why. He was glad enough to leave that to his colonel.

Kmita, however, rode ahead in such a grim and forbidding mood that no one dared to come near him or ask him anything. The night couldn't have been darker than his clouded face.

He felt that he would rather rip open his own heart than hurt those men in whose ranks he wanted to serve. But what would have happened even if he'd surrendered to the Laudanians and let himself be taken to Pan Volodyovski? What would Volodyovski think when he was told that his men caught Kmita, making his way to Swedish territory in disguise, and with passes for Swedish commandants in his pockets?

"Old sins are hounding and tormenting me," Kmita told himself. "I'll run as far from them as I can, if God shows me the way..."

And he began to pray as fervently as he could so that at least he'd drown the voice of his accusing conscience.

'*More corpses behind you*, it told him bitterly. '*And not Swedish, either.*'

"Have mercy on me, Lord," Kmita prayed. "Forgive my trespasses and keep me from temptations. I'm going to my King. My service begins there."

Chapter Fifty

ZJENDJAN HADN'T PLANNED on spending the night at the inn
where he encountered Kmita. The distance from Vonsosh to
Stutin was a short one and all he wanted was to rest his horses,
especially those that hauled the heavy wagons, so that he didn't
waste any time when Kmita let him continue with his journey,
and an hour later he was entering the small Podlasyan town.

The night was well along when his coach and wagons rolled
into the market place of Stutin. He announced himself to the
pickets and set up camp in the town square because every home
and building was packed to overflowing with Pan Volodyovski's
soldiers. Stutin, in those days, had the name of a town but was
in fact nothing more than a sprawling village, having neither
walls nor a town hall and court house, nor the seminary and
college which would be built there in the times of King Yan III
Sobieski. Its buildings were mostly thatched peasant huts huddled about the square, the square itself was little more than a
muddy common, and the only reason why this country township
was listed as a city was because it was laid out like one, forming
a rectangle around its market place, rather than straggling along
a village street.

Zjendjan caught a few hours' sleep under his warm wolfskin
traveling cloak and made his way to Pan Volodyovski's quarters
the first thing in the morning. Not having seen him for years,
the little colonel greeted him with joy. He led him at once to
the house occupied by Pan Zagloba and the two Skshetuskis and
here the young 'Starosta' forgot all about his new-found dignity.
He burst into happy tears at the sight of his former master whom

he served faithfully for so many years, and in whose service he went through so many adventures before he made his fortune, and started kissing his hands with all his old simplicity and devotion.

"Ai master, master!" he repeated, as moved as a child. "That we should meet again at a time like this..."

"But you, I see, have always been Fortune's child," Pan Zagloba said. "And you've turned out just as I predicted. I prophesied you'd grow into a decent human being if only nobody hanged you in the meantime! What are you up to these days?"

"Hey, master," Zjendjan said at once. "What were they to hang me for when I didn't do anything to hang for? I only did what God and the law allowed. I gave my master loyal service. If I ever swindled anybody it was to serve our country, so that's an act of virtue. And if, now and then, I tricked some rebel to his own destruction—as with that witch, Horpyna, d'you remember, master?—that's not a sin either. And even if it was a sin it would be yours rather than mine because I learned all my sharp practices from you."

"Listen to him, will you?" Fond of the shrewd, confident young man, Pan Zagloba was pleased with him as well. "If you want me to howl in Hell for your sins then let me enjoy the fruits of your sinning! You're the only one who profited from those riches you plucked from the Cossacks. And that's why you'll squirm alone when the Devil melts you into tallow!"

"That's up to God's mercy, master," Zjendjan shot back at once. "But it isn't true that I used everything only for myself. Do you recall my telling you about that old lawsuit my folks had with our neighbors, the Yavorskis? Fifty years it went on because of that pear tree that stands on our property and drops its fruit on what used to be the Yavorskis' land. Well, I sued the last shirt off their backs and I made sure my parents lacked for nothing. They're living safe and happy in our old homestead in Zjendjany, and nobody aggravates them now that the Yavorskis are begging on the highways, and I do the best I can for myself nearby."

"So you don't live on your family lands any more?" Pan Yan asked.

"No sir. My old folks live there like they did before. I live
in Vonsosh now and I can't complain because God was kind to
me and let good things happen. But when I heard you gentlemen were in Stutin, there was no way I could stay at home. I
told myself that it was time to go to war again if there is to be
one, and so here I am!"

"Why don't you admit that it was the Swedes who chased you
out of Vonsosh?" Pan Zagloba prodded.

"Ey, you don't see too many Swedes in the Vonsosh country,"
Zjendjan shrugged. "And if they do send a scouting party in
there they come real careful because the peasants are deadset
against them."

"That's good news," said Pan Volodyovski. "I sent out a
patrol yesterday to check on the Swedes because I didn't know
if Stutin was safe from them. I expect it was my men who
brought you here?"

"Well, as it happens it was I who brought them," Zjendjan
stirred uneasily. "Because, to tell the truth, there isn't one of
them who'd be able to sit on a horse without help."

"What do you mean? What are you telling us? What happened?" Pan Volodyovski asked.

"Well, they got knocked about pretty badly," Zjendjan said in
his slow, matter-of-fact manner.

"Who did it to them?"

"Pan Kmita," Zjendjan said.

Pan Zagloba and the two Skshetuskis leaped to their feet and
started shouting questions one across the other.

"Kmita? Here? What brings him to these parts? Is the
Prince-Hetman himself here with his army? Hurry up! Tell us
everything that happened!"

★   ★   ★

Pan Volodyovski shot out of the room, apparently to see the
extent of the damage for himself, and Zjendjan said he'd wait
with his story until he returned.

"Why waste breath twice on the same tale?" he asked. "It's
Pan Volodyovski's affair anyway, since he's the troop commander, and a wise man saves the tear and wear on his tongue as long
as he can."

"Did you see Kmita with your own eyes?" Pan Zagloba asked.

"Sure I did. Like I see you, master."

"And did you talk with him?"

"How was I not to talk with him when we stopped at an inn, he and I, a stone's throw from here? He was there for the night and I pulled up just to rest my horses. We talked for an hour or more."

"What did you talk about?"

"What did we talk about? Swedes, mostly. I complained about them, and he did some complaining too..."

"He expressed dissatisfaction with the Swedes?" Pan Yan Skshetuski queried.

"He cursed them to the Devil even though he was on his way among them."

"Did he have a lot of troops with him?"

"Troops? He didn't have any troops. He was alone except for maybe a handful of servants. True, they were armed to the teeth and they had faces you'd expect to see on Herod's murderers, those who slaughtered the holy innocents. He passed himself off as one of the clodhopping gentry who drive horses to the local markets. They had a good little herd along with them too, but I didn't buy their story, not entirely. Pan Kmita has a way about him that you don't find among the horse drovers. And he had a real good ring on his finger, too... This one, as it happens!"

And here Zjendjan flashed the costly stone before his audience, and Pan Zagloba slapped his knee and wagged his head in wonder.

"And he wheedled it out of him, of course!" he exclaimed. "Zjendjan, my lad, I'd know you anywhere just by that alone!"

"Begging your pardon, sir," Zjendjan huffed a little. "But I didn't wheedle anything out of anybody. I am not a Gypsy. I may not own property of my own, leasing the lands I work until God lets me settle down in my own possessions, but I'm as good as any other noble. Pan Kmita gave me this ring as a sign of good faith, and so that you'd know he meant what he said, and I'll tell it all to you as soon as I can because, as it seems to me, it's a matter affecting our own skins."

"What do you mean by that?" Pan Zagloba was visibly puzzled and disturbed.

But in that moment Pan Volodyovski burst into the room

again. He was pale with anger. He hurled his cap on the table and shouted out: "This is past believing! Three men dead and the rest all wounded! Yozva Butrym is cut up so badly he can hardly breathe!"

"Yozva Butrym?" Even Pan Zagloba looked up in amazement. "How can that be? He's tougher than a bear!"

"Pan Kmita stretched him out himself right before my eyes," Zjendjan observed in his off-hand way.

"I've had enough of this Pan Kmita!" the little knight exploded. "That man leaves corpses behind him wherever he appears! He's worse than a plague! But this is the limit! We saved his neck just as he saved ours but now all debts are paid. We're starting a new account! Imagine, to attack my men like that and cut them up so badly... Ah, I'll make him pay for that the first time I see him!"

"The truth of the matter is that he didn't attack anybody," Zjendjan pointed out. "They did the attacking. He did his best to keep out of sight in the darkest corner he could find."

"And you!" Pan Volodyovski turned angrily on Zjendjan. "Instead of helping my people when they needed it, you're testifying for him!"

"I'm just saying what happened, that's all," Zjendjan defended himself earnestly. "As for helping out, my men did their best, only they couldn't do much in that scramble where nobody could tell who was on whose side. The fact that I got away from there with my skin in one piece, and all my goods intact, is only due to Pan Kmita's understanding and his good will for us. Because just listen, gentlemen, to what he said next."

★   ★   ★

Here Zjendjan gave a full account of everything that happened in the tavern, leaving no detail unsaid, and when he finished with what Kmita ordered him to tell a look of absolute amazement settled on all faces.

"He told you that himself?" Pan Zagloba asked.

"In person. I'm no enemy of the confederates and Pan Volodyovski, is what he said to me, though they may think different. It'll all come out in good time, but in the meanwhile let them stick close together, or as there's God in Heaven, the

Voyevode of Vilna will pluck them out one at a time like crayfish from a bucket."

"And did he say that the *Voyevode* is on his way already?" Pan Yan Skshetuski pressed.

"He said the Prince was just waiting for Swedish reinforcements and then he'll march straight down on Podlasye."

"What's one to think of all this, gentlemen?" Pan Volodyovski stared at his puzzled friends one after another.

"It's an astounding thing!" Pan Zagloba mused. "Either that man is turning on Radzivill or he's setting some trap of his own against us all. But what kind of trap could it be? He's advising us to stick close together and what harm can come to us from that?"

"We can starve," Pan Volodyovski said. "I've just had word that Colonels Zeromski, Kotovski and Lipnitzki plan to split their regiments into small detachments and scatter them through the entire Palatinate. They can't feed themselves when they're all together."

"And what'll happen if Radzivill really comes down upon us?" asked Stanislav Skshetuski. "Who'll be strong enough to oppose him then?"

No one could find a good answer because it was as clear as day to all these experienced officers that if the Grand Hetman of Lithuania caught the confederates scattered in winter quarters and dispersed throughout Podlasye he'd have no problem whatsoever in destroying them.

"An astounding thing!" Zagloba repeated. Then, after a moment's thought, he went on: "Kmita's already shown his good will for us once... Hmm, I could almost think that he's left Radzivill... But if that was so why would he try to sneak past us in disguise? And heading towards the Swedes?"

Then he turned to Zjendjan. "Didn't he tell you he was going towards Warsaw?" he asked.

"Yes he did!"

"Well, that's in Swedish hands," Pan Zagloba mused. "And so's the rest of the country around there."

"He'd have met up with them already," Zjendjan offered. "If he rode all night."

"Have you ever seen such a contradictory man?" Zagloba asked the others.

"There's no doubt that he's as full of good mixed with evil as wheat and chaff before they are threshed," Pan Yan Skshetuski said. "But I'll say straight out that there is nothing wrong with the advice he gives us. I don't know where he's going in disguise or why, and I'm not going to bother my head about it because there has to be more to it than we know. But I'll swear that his advice is sound, that he warns us sincerely, and that our only possible salvation is to do exactly as he said. Who knows if we're not about to owe our lives to him again."

"For God's sake!" Pan Volodyovski shouted out in protest. As the one who had just lost ten men at Kmita's hands, he wasn't likely to give him much credit. "How is Radzivill to get here through Zoltarenko's Cossacks and Hovansky's army? It's one thing for a single regiment like ours to slip by, and even we had to cut our way through them at Pilvishkye. And it's the same story with Kmita creeping past with just a few people... But the Prince will march with an entire corps! How is he going to get through without fighting them and starting a whole new war? That's the one thing about all this that makes no sense to me at all!"

* * *

Pan Michal was still speaking when the door creaked open and the duty orderly came into the room. "There's a man outside with a letter for the colonel," he reported.

"Bring it here at once!" Pan Volodyovski ordered, and when the orderly returned with the letter, he broke the seal, spread out a sheet of paper, and started to read aloud to the others.

"*Let me add a postscript to what I told the Freeholder of Vonsosh yesterday,*" he read. "*The Hetman has more than enough men to dispose of you but he's waiting for Swedish reinforcements so that he can march on you under Swedish banners. If the Muscovites tried to stop him they'd have to fight his Swedes and that would mean war with the King of Sweden. The situation with the Russians is a complex one, but they are shaking in their boots at the thought of taking on Charles Gustav, and none of them want to be responsible for starting a war that they're bound to lose. They've caught onto Radzivill's strategy of always pushing out the Swedes towards them so that they could kill one and get themselves trapped in a war with Sweden. That's why they're keeping so quiet nowadays, not sure what to do, since Lithuania is now a part of Sweden. That's also why they won't try to stop Radzivill when he moves against you. If he falls on you scattered as you plan, he'll crush you all like gravel underfoot. For God's sake get together as quickly as you can with all the other confederate commanders, and ask the Voyevode of Vitebsk to hurry towards you, especially since it's easier for him now to get through the Russians while they're standing around and wondering what to do. I wanted to warn you under another name, so you'd believe and trust me, but since it all came out anyway I'll just sign my own. You're as good as lost if you don't believe me and I'm also not what I used to be. With God's help you'll be hearing different tales about me."*

"You wanted to know how Radzivill will get through to us," Yan Skshetuski said. "Now you have the answer."

"That's true... It does make sense," the little knight agreed.

"True?" Pan Zagloba cried. "It couldn't be more true if you'd read it in the Gospels! None of us can doubt it! I was the first to guess the goodness in that man, and even though he carries more curses on his head than a dog has fleas, there'll be a day when we'll all bless his name, take my word for it! I can judge a man's worth at a glance. Do you remember how I took to him back there in Keydany? He also loves and admires all of us, as the great knights we are, and when he heard my name for the first time he just about strangled me out of admiration. Which is also why he helped me to liberate you as I did."

"Ey, but you'll never change, master," Zjendjan shook his head. "Why should Pan Kmita think more of you than of my old master or Pan Volodyovski?"

"You're a fool!" cried Zagloba. "He didn't waste much time seeing through you, did he? And the only reason he calls you a Freeholder rather than Dolt of Vonsosh is out of good manners!"

"So maybe he's also being polite about that admiration?" Zjendjan asked.

"Just look at how this calf shakes his horns at me!" Pan Zagloba cried. "You'll shake them a lot harder after you are married, my dear Freeholder, take my word for it!"

"That's all very well," Pan Volodyovski said. "But if he's sincerely on our side why did he try to slip past us like a wolf and chewed up our men?"

"Don't rack your brains about that, my dear Michal," Pan Zagloba told him, "because you've never been much of a strategist. You just do what we decide here and you'll do very well, because if your wits were half as sharp and quick as your saber you'd be the Crown Grand Hetman in place of Pan Revera Pototzki. But will you tell me why Kmita should've come here? So you'd mistrust him to his face as you mistrust his letter? It wouldn't take much to come to blows with such a fiery cavalier and what would happen then? But even if you did trust him and believe him, what about all the other colonels? What would your own Laudanians say and do? Wouldn't they try to chop him into mincemeat at the first chance they got?"

"You're quite right, father," Pan Yan observed gravely. "There was no way for him to come here."

But Pan Michal always clung to his preconceived ideas with just as much stubbornness, tenacity and determination as he showed in battle. "Then why is he going to meet the Swedes?" he demanded.

"How should I know?" Pan Zagloba bellowed. "The Devil himself wouldn't be able to guess what that firebrand will cook up next! That's not our affair. The thing for us to do is take his advice, believe in his warning, and carry our heads out of here while we still have them sitting on our shoulders."

"There's no point in even talking any more about it," Pan Stanislav said.

"We must send word at once to Zeromski, Kotovski, Lipnitzki and that other Kmita," said Pan Yan Skshetuski. "Write to them at once, Michal, but don't tell them where the warning came from. Otherwise they'll never take it seriously."

"We'll be the only ones to know whom to thank for this and we'll spread the word when the time is right!" Pan Zagloba shouted. "Let's go, Michal! Let's move!"

"And we ourselves will march to Bialystok," Pan Yan suggested, "having sent word to everyone to assemble there. Are we all agreed? Now let God just bring us the *Voyevode* of Vitebsk as soon as He can."

"The troops will have to send a delegation to him from Bialystok," Pan Zagloba went on excitedly. "With God's help we will face the Lithuanian Hetman on equal terms or stronger. It's not for us to lock horns with the likes of him but Pan Sapyeha is another story. What a good, decent man that is! There isn't another like him in the Commonwealth."

"D'you mean to say, sir, you know Pan Sapyeha too?" Pan Stanislav asked. "Is there anyone with whom you're not acquainted?"

"Do I know him? Ha! I knew him when he was a lad no taller than my saber and he was already as good as an angel!"

"People say that he not only sold off all his lands and jewels for the cause, but that he's even melting silver bridles into ready coin so that he can raise as big an army as he can against the enemy," Pan Volodyovski added.

"Thank God there's at least one like him in the Commonwealth," Pan Stanislav said. "Do you remember how we trusted in Radzivill too?"

"That's blasphemy!" Pan Zagloba roared. "The *Voyevode* of Vitebsk? We should distrust the *Voyevode* of Vitebsk? Long live the *Voyevode* of Vitebsk! And you, Michal, get to your dispatches. Let's leave this Stutin mud to the eels and ride at once to Bialystok where they've tastier fish. The Jews also bake some first-rate Sabbath *Chala* breads in those parts... Ha! So at last the war will start again! I must say I've missed it. We'll have Radzivill for an appetizer and then set about the Swedes! We've already shown them once what we can do! Write those dispatches, Michal! Time's wasting and there's *periculum in mora!*"

"And I'll go and alert the regiment," Pan Yan said, getting up to leave.

An hour later several dozen dispatch riders galloped out of Stutin, carrying the news of the Hetman's coming and the summons for assembly far into Podlasye, and the Laudanian Regiment followed shortly after. Their senior officers rode in front, making plans and discussing the great events that they had set in motion, while the troops that trotted at their backs were led by Roche Kowalski, newly appointed to be their lieutenant.

They headed for the towns of Osov and Gonetz which lay along their path towards Bialystok where they expected the other confederate regiments to gather. The war in Lithuania was about to blaze up again and take a better turn.

Chapter Fifty-one

PAN VOLODYOVSKI'S LETTERS alerting the confederates to Radzivill's march found a quick response in their widely scattered camps throughout Podlasye. Some of their colonels had already dispersed their formations across several districts. Others furloughed all but a handful of their enlisted gentry, keeping a mere dozen or so with the colors along with a few dozen grooms and men-at-arms. This was, in part, a means to avoid starvation in the Winter months, but it was also due to the fact that discipline was collapsing at an alarming rate among the rank and file mutineers, and if they hadn't been sent home on leave they might have deserted anyway. The sad truth was that once those regiments rose up against their rightful Hetman, and once these soldiers broke their oaths of obedience to their ultimate military authority, they were prone to question any order and to oppose their officers at the slightest pretext.

If the confederates had a single respected and admired leader, one who would march these regiments into instant battle against either of the Commonwealth's invaders, or even against Radzivill himself, their discipline would have lasted through all their privations. But in Podlasye—where all they had to do was take potshots at some of the smaller Radzivill castles, raid the Prince-Palatine's estates, and negotiate with Prince Boguslav—it cracked altogether, proving the old adage that disuse destroys a soldier.

Some of these furloughed or temporarily disbanded confederates and deserters began to molest the Palatinate's peaceful

654

country gentry. Others, especially from among the low ranking men-at-arms and the armed regimental servants, turned into highway brigands who terrorized and pillaged the countryside almost as ruthlessly as the oddly inactive Russian enemy would have done.

And yet these melting and disintegrating regiments that were the only Polish-Lithuanian troops which didn't side with one or the other of the two external enemies—and which were the last remaining hope of the Commonwealth and King Yan Casimir—had been practically ignored by both the invaders. The Swedes, flooding the country from the west and then heading southward, hadn't yet reached this secluded corner where Podlasye crouched between occupied Mazovia and northern Lithuania. The huge Russian armies of Hovansky, Trubetzkoy and Srebrnyi, supported by the raiding corps of Zoltarenko's Cossacks, stood hesitating in the eastern provinces they had occupied, as if rooted to the ground by their indecision.

In the embattled Ukrainian territories far to the southeast, the war against Hmyelnitzki's and Buturlin's Cossacks went on unabated and, only a few months earlier, a handful of Polish soldiers under Crown Hetman Pototzki suffered a defeat near the town of Grodek. But Lithuania was under the protection of the Swedes and—as Kmita pointed out in his letter to Pan Volodyovski—any further incursions into her territories would have brought all the wrath of that feared military nation upon the invader. Not even the ruthless and barbaric Hovansky wanted to take such risks, and so he left Podlasye and its rebel regiments to their own devices, while the leaderless confederates were too weak and scattered to threaten anyone or to try anything more significant than the pillaging of Radzivill estates.

Pan Volodyovski's letters seemed to shake the inactive rebel colonels out of their lethargy. If Yanush Radzivill was really on the move then the danger was pressing and immediate. The disintegrating regiments were brought together again. Leaves were canceled and the scattered troopers flowed back to the colors under the threat of punishment for desertion. Colonel Zeromski, being the most serious-minded and respected of the confederate commanders, and whose regiment was in the best

condition, was the first to head for Bialystok. Yakub Kmita
followed a week later, although all he could gather was a mere
hundred and twenty men. Kotovski's and Lipnitzki's troopers
straggled in singly or in small detachments, along with numbers
of local petty gentry and fresh volunteers from as far away as the
Lublin country. The wealthier gentry also began to make an
appearance, riding into the camp at Bialystok with armed
grooms and private men-at-arms, so that by the time that Pan
Volodyovski arrived with his Laudanians there were several
thousand men waiting for action and a leader they could trust
and follow.

All of this new martial activity was still somewhat disorderly
and confused, but nowhere near as chaotic as that Vyelkopolian
gathering that was supposed to stop the Swedes at Uistye,
because every one of these Podlasians, Lublinians and Lithuanians had some war experience, and there were few even among
the new volunteers who'd never smelled gunpowder other than
the eager, beardless youths tasting their first campaign. Each of
these members of the warrior gentry had fought Cossacks, Turks
or Tartars sometime in his life, and there were those among
them who remembered the former Swedish wars as well. But
standing head and shoulders above all of them, both in renown
and in the tales of his military exploits, was Pan Zagloba who
was never happier than in such lively gatherings of volunteers
and soldiers where no one discussed anything on a dry throat.

His stature soon soared above that of all the regimental
colonels and the crowds listened avidly to the tales told about
him by the Laudanians. His rescue of Volodyovski, Mirski,
Oskierka and the two Skshetuskis became a camp epic, while he
was also prone to giving himself full justice in his own accounts.

"I don't like to boast," he would say with becoming modesty,
"or babble lies about things that never happened, because pure
truth always is the main thing with me, as my nephew can
confirm for anyone who needs it."

At this point he would turn to Pan Roche Kowalski who'd
emerge from behind his back and roar in stentorian tones:
"Uncle doesn't lie!"

Then the huge ex-dragoon would flip an eye fiercely at the
listeners as if looking for an opportunity to back his words with
his hamlike fists. But no one ever called him on the challenge

and Pan Zagloba regaled the crowd with all his past successes. He told how he drove Hmyelnitzki to drink and distraction in the Cossack Wars; what he achieved at the Siege of Zbarajh; how the famous Prince Yeremi Vishnovyetzki relied on his counsel in everything that mattered, and how he entrusted him with leading all the sallies against the combined Cossack-Tartar armies.

"And after every sally," he would say, "when we wiped out five or ten thousand of that rebel rabble, Hmyel would batter his head against a wall and howl that nobody else could do that except that devil Zagloba! And when the war was over, and we sat down to draft the armistice at Zborov, the Tartar Khan himself pointed me out to his *murjahs* as one of the living wonders of the world and begged me for a picture he might send to the Turkish Sultan."

"That's the kind of men we need these days," his listeners told each other.

"If there were just a thousand like him in the Commonwealth," others said throughout the camp. "Nothing that happened to the country would've taken place."

"Let's thank God that we have at least one of his kind among us!"

And since the tales of Pan Zagloba's triumphs and achievements were told throughout the Commonwealth even without his help, the old knight basked in glory and renown wherever he appeared.

"He was the first to call Radzivill a traitor to his face!" the warrior gentry cried.

"And he pulled good men out of his claws! He struck the first blow!"

"And along the way he gave the Swedes such a beating at Klevany that not one of them escaped alive!"

"His was the first victory and with God's help it won't be the last one!"

* * *

The regimental colonels may have been a little less enthralled about Pan Zagloba but they showed him every sign of respect and consideration, asking his advice in every matter and showering him with praise both for his past valor and his present sagacity and wisdom.

As it happened, there was a vital problem to be resolved just then. Delegates from the gathered army had gone in search of the *Voyevode* of Vitebsk, inviting him to take command of the confederation, but since no one knew where exactly Pan Sapyeha was to be found just then these messengers seemed to have vanished into thin air. There was even news that some of them may have fallen into the hands of Zoltarenko's raiders who went on pillaging the country around Volkovysk without regard to the Russians' orders.

The gathered colonels knew by their own experience that they must elect a temporary generalissimo who would command them all until Pan Sapyeha's arrival, and each of them, excepting Pan Volodyovski, had himself in mind for that post of honor. But since the gathered troops declared that they wanted to take part in the election—and not through representatives but in a popular vote taken by them all—the encampment turned into a political convention where every candidate did his best to win and captivate supporters. Pan Michal, after consulting with his friends, decided to back Zeromski who was a highly-respected and honorable man, as well as a skilled and experienced soldier, and who appealed to the troops by his martial bearing and long senatorial beard. Zeromski, out of gratitude, backed Volody-ovski, but the other colonels didn't think that the youngest (and smallest) officer among them would have the stature necessary for such an important post, especially since he'd have to deal with the local citizenry as well as the army.

"Who's the oldest man among us, then?" they wanted to know.

"Uncle's the oldest!" Pan Roche Kowalski thundered in such a booming voice that every head in the gathering turned in his direction.

"It's a pity he doesn't have a regiment of his own," said Pan Yahovitch, who served as Zeromski's deputy commander.

"So what?" others began to shout at once. "Since when are we obliged to elect a colonel? Aren't we free to decide on anyone we want? If any noble can be elected to the throne why can't we pick our own generalissimo?"

Lipnitzki, who didn't like Zeromski and wanted to prevent his election at all costs, was quick to agree.

"That's right! It's a free vote and anyone can cast it for anyone he wishes! And it'll be all the better not to elect a regimental colonel so that no one else would feel either slighted or insulted!"

An extraordinary tumult and turmoil exploded then all across the camp. Crowds of soldiers started shouting: "To the polls! Let's vote!"

Others demanded: "Who's the most famous man among us? Who's a greater knight than Pan Zagloba? Who's a better soldier? We want Pan Zagloba! Long live Zagloba! *Vivat* Pan Zagloba, our generalissimo! *Vivat! Vivat! Vivat!*"

"Long life to him!" roared a thousand throats.

"We'll cut down anybody who opposes him!" howled the more restless, undisciplined and turbulent among the newer volunteers.

"No one's against him!" the crowds bellowed in reply. "We're all for him! Our vote is unanimous!"

"*Vivat!* Long live the conqueror of Gustaphus Adolphus! Long live the man who terrorized Hmyelnitzki!"

"He is the one who saved the captive colonels!"

"And who crushed the Swedes at Klevany!"

"*Vivat! Vivat!* Zagloba *dux!* Zagloba the leader! *Vivat! Vivat! Vivat!*"

And the huge swarming crowds of volunteers and soldiers hurled their bright caps into the air and started running through the camp in search of Pan Zagloba.

★ ★ ★

The new generalissimo was somewhat startled and taken very much aback by this unsought and unexpected honor, particularly since he wanted the post to go to Yan Skshetuski, and for the first few minutes he didn't know what to say or do. But when he realized that he was really the choice of all the army, and when he heard a mob of several thousand men crying out his name, he turned as crimson as a boiled beetroot and quite lost his breath.

"Look at him!" cried the joyful soldiers, seeing his confusion and crowding about him. "He's blushing like a maiden! His

modesty is even greater than his valor! May he live a long time
and lead us to victories!"

Meanwhile the regimental colonels also came running with
their congratulations, putting their best face on their disappointments, and some of them were actually quite pleased that this
new high rank didn't go to some rival of their own.

Pan Volodyovski said nothing, being quite as astonished by
this elevation as the new commander-in-chief was himself, and
only his pointed little whiskers twitched powerfully up and
down. But Zjendjan stared wide-eyed and open-mouthed, incredulous but respectful to the point of awe, as Pan Zagloba
gradually regained control over his amazement. He placed his
fists on his hips, his head jerked up proudly, and he began to
receive the homage of the gathering as his natural due.

Zeromski offered the congratulations of the colonels while
Trooper Zymirski, a gentleman-volunteer in Kotovski's Regiment, spoke on behalf of the rank and file, citing the classic
maxims of many ancient sages.

Zagloba listened with profound attention, nodding with the
aloof dignity of his rank, and when the speaker finally ran out of
quotations he struck an orator's stance of his own.

"Gentlemen!" he cried. "Even if someone wished to drown
true merit in the deepest ocean, or to bury it under the Carpa-
thian Mountains, it will emerge on its own and float to the
surface like oil on wine, so that it might cry out to everyone
who sees it: '*Here I am! Ready for my reward! Fearing neither the
light of day nor any human judgment!*' But since true virtue must
be set in modesty, just as a precious ring-stone is set in the purest
gold, therefore I ask you, gentlemen, standing here before you;
did I ever boast to you about my achievements? Didn't I try to
hide them from you and keep them to myself? Did I seek this
honor which you bestowed upon me? You've judged my merits
for yourselves but I am ready to deny them even now...!"

"No! No! Never!" a hundred voices shouted and Pan
Zagloba made a modest gesture. "There are worthier men than
I among you," he intoned and began to name all the gathered
colonels. "Even the ancient Romans never had such splendid
knights among them! Why did you choose me as your commander rather than one of them? It's not too late to change your

minds... Take this distinction off my shoulders, why don't you? Take it...! Give it to a better man!"

"Never! Never!" howled thousands of voices. "That'll never happen!"

"Never!" cried the colonels, delighted to be praised so handsomely before the whole army, and wanting to demonstrate their own new-found modesty.

"Well..." Pan Zagloba sighed at last, as if in resignation. "I see for myself that there's no other way. Let your will be done, then, gentlemen! I accept this burden! And I believe that with God's help you won't regret this trust that you show in me. Whatever fate has in mind for us, we'll face it together, and I swear to you that I'll stand by you for better or worse, just as you'll stand by me, and that we'll be sharing our glory even after death!"

Wild emotion seized everyone. Some men drew their sabers, offering them to Heaven. Others wept. Pan Zagloba's bald pate began to glisten with thick drops of sweat but his enthusiasm soared higher with each passing minute.

"We'll stand by our rightful King and our dear Motherland!" he shouted. "We'll live or die for them! Gentlemen! In all our history there have never been such calamities falling on our country. Traitors opened her gates and now there isn't one fistful of earth, other than this Palatinate, where some enemy isn't making himself at home. You are the country's only hope, and I am yours, and all eyes in the Commonwealth are turned on you and me! Let's show our Mother that she isn't crying out to us for nothing! As you ask for courage and faith from me, so I demand your discipline and obedience! And when we stand together, powerful and united, and when our example opens the eyes of those poor wretches who've been deceived by the enemy, then half the Commonwealth will run here to join us! Whoever has God in his heart will take his stand beside us, the powers of Heaven will aid us, and who'll be our equal then?"

Swept away to the heights of feeling, a thousand voices roared: "As God's in Heaven, that's how it'll be! That's what's going to happen! Listen to him! That's Solomon talking! Let's fight! To war! To war!"

And Pan Zagloba lifted both his arms towards the north and began to bellow:

"Come here, then, Radzivill! Come, my lord Hetman! My lord Heretic! Lucifer's *voyevode*! We're waiting for you united and together, not scattered and turned against each other! And it's not pacts and papers we hold in our fists but sabers and muskets! An army waits for you here, not a mob! And I'm waiting for you! Come out and fight Zagloba! Get all your devils to help you and come out!"

Here he stopped for breath, turned to face his army, and yelled so loudly that his voice boomed through the entire camp:

"As God's my witness, gentlemen! Prophetic visions are coming down upon me! All we need is unity and we'll crush those scoundrels, those foreign fancy-pants, those perfumed stocking-wearers and Swedish herring-eaters, and those other flea-bitten barbarians with their lousy sheepskins and nits in their beards who ride around in sleighs even in the Summer! We'll blow some pepper up their noses, you just wait and see! They'll run so hard they'll drop their drawers behind them! Fight them, whoever lives! Fight, whoever loves his God and country!"

Thousands of sabers leaped out of their scabbards at this flaming rhetoric and gleamed in the sunlight. Vast crowds surrounded Pan Zagloba, pushing and shoving and trampling anything that fell underfoot, and howling to high heavens: "Lead us! Lead us!"

"Tomorrow!" roared Zagloba, carried off by his own enthusiasm. "I'll lead you tomorrow! Get ready!"

* * *

The election took place in the morning and in the afternoon the regiments massed for inspection and review in the broad, green meadows. They stood in line next to each other, mustered in great order, with their colonels and standard-bearers at their head, while their commander-in-chief rode back and forth before them with a gilded *bulava* in his hand, a spray of heron feathers fixed to his sable cap, and with a horsetail standard carried over him.

"A natural-born Hetman, as I live and breathe!" the soldiers whispered to each other, feeling their hearts lift at the sight of this imposing figure, as he trotted among his regiments like a shepherd looking over his flock.

The regimental colonels rode out towards him to report, and he chatted briefly with each of them—praising one thing and correcting another—so that even those commanders who weren't too pleased at first at his election had to admit that their new leader knew his business well.

Only Pan Volodyovski twitched his whiskers with an odd, wondering look painted on his face when Pan Zagloba patted his shoulder in a kindly manner after the review and said to him in the hearing of all the other colonels:

"I'm pleased with you, Michal. Very pleased. Your regiment is in top shape, better than any other. Carry on like that and you can be sure that I'll keep you in mind."

"For God's sake," the little knight murmured to Skshetuski as they made their way to their quarters after the inspection. "Where does he get such poise? Could a real Hetman say anything different?"

Pan Zagloba immediately sent strong patrols in every direction, including some that were quite unnecessary, and when they returned the next day he listened carefully to their reports and then made his way to the quarters that Pan Volodyovski shared with the two Skshetuskis.

"I have to keep up a certain dignity and distance before the troops," he told them. "But when we're alone together we can be as easy with each other as before. Here I'm your friend, not your supreme commander. Your advice may also be quite useful even though I've a fine brain of my own, because I know that you're more experienced in military matters than most people in the Commonwealth."

They greeted him as warmly as ever and all of them were soon at ease with each other again. Only Zjendjan couldn't bring himself to be as familiar with the old knight as he used to be.

"What do you have in mind to do, father?" Yan Skshetuski asked.

"First of all I want discipline and order and I want to keep the troops busy all the time so that they don't fall apart like they did before. I heard you mumbling in your whiskers, Michal, when I sent those patrols to all points of the compass yesterday, but I had to do that to keep as many men as busy as I can. That's the first thing. The next question is: What do we need the most?

We've plenty of men and there'll be more coming. That Mazovian gentry that fled into Prussia will also make its way down here in due time. But no army in the world fights well on an empty belly. So I've been thinking to order the patrols to bring in everything that falls into their hands. Cattle, sheep, pigs, wheat, hay... everything they can find in this Palatinate and next door in Mazovia, where the Swedes haven't emptied all the larders yet."

"The local gentry will kick up a fuss," Skshetuski observed, "if they're robbed of their harvests and their livestock."

"Our troops are more important to me than the local gentry," the generalissimo replied. "Let them kick up whatever stink they want! Besides, we won't take anything for nothing because I'll order proper requisitions, with a signed receipt, and I prepared enough of them last night to buy or borrow half this territory! I've no money now but the Commonwealth will make good my exactions after the Swedes have been chased away. The gentry, indeed! They're far worse off when hungry soldiers plunder them at will. I've a mind to comb the woods as well because I hear there's a mass of peasants hiding in the forests along with all their goods. Let our men thank the Holy Ghost for their inspiration to name me their commander, because no one else would think of all these things or manage them this well."

"You have a senator's head, and that's for sure, Your Lordship," Zjendjan murmured humbly.

"Eh? Hmm? Don't I just?" Zagloba replied, pleased with the flattery and the new senatorial image of himself. "And you too, you rascal, know which end is up! Watch me appoint you a lieutenant just as soon as there's a vacancy."

"I thank you most humbly, Your Magnificence," the awed Zjendjan murmured.

"So that's my thinking!" Zagloba confided. "First we'll amass enough supplies to withstand a siege if we have to stand one. Then we'll create a regular walled camp. Let Radzivill come calling then, along with all his Swedes and devils! Call me a scoundrel if I don't turn this place into another Zbarajh!"

"As God's my witness!" cried Volodyovski. "That's not a bad idea! But where will we find the artillery we need?"

"Pan Kotovski has two howitzers, Yakub Kmita has a light

field mortar, and there are four carronades in Bialystok. Pan Stempalski, the local governor, told me they were meant for the castle in Tikotzin, which this area supports out of the yearly rents that Pan Vesolovski willed for national defense. He also says he has enough powder for four hundred rounds. We'll manage, gentlemen. We'll manage well enough just as long as you keep on supporting my ideas and remember the needs of the body too. And that body wouldn't mind something to drink just now since the sun is high enough for a cup or two."

* * *

Volodyovski ordered some cups and flagons and they continued to chat while sipping a fine vintage mead to take the chill out of the morning air.

"Ha!" Pan Zagloba said. "You thought you'd have a puppet general, didn't you. But nothing's going to be further from the truth! I didn't ask for this honor but since you gave it to me we'll have some discipline and order around here! I know what every position of authority is supposed to mean and you'll see that I'll grow into each one you give me. I'll make a second Zbarajh here, see if I don't. Radzivill and his Swedes will choke to death before they swallow me! I wouldn't mind if Hovansky tried to bite us either. I'd bury him so deep they won't know where to look for him on Judgment Day. Let the Russians come! They're not that far away! Let them try me! And let's have some more mead, Michal."

Pan Volodyovski refilled his cup which Pan Zagloba swallowed at one gulp. Then he furrowed his red face in thought as if trying to remember something.

"What was I saying?" he asked. "What did I want? Ah yes, more mead, Michal!"

Pan Michal filled his cup again and Pan Zagloba held forth on matters closest to his heart.

"They say the *Voyevode* of Vitebsk likes to take a cup now and then. And why shouldn't he? Every good man takes pleasure in his dram. Only traitors who need to hide their thoughts keep away from wine in case their dirty plots come floating up into the light. Radzivill drinks berry juice. Once he's in Hell he'll be drinking pitch, and may the Good Lord help me send him there as quick as I can! I've a feeling that Pan Sapyeha and I will get along very well together because we're as alike as a pair of boots or a horse's ears. Besides, he's a generalissimo, just like me, and I'll take care of things so well until he arrives that he'll find everything ready and waiting for him. There's a lot of weighty stuff resting in my hands these days, but what can I do? If nobody in the Commonwealth knows how to use his brains then it's up to old Zagloba to do all their thinking! The worst thing is that I don't have a chancellery."

"Why would you need a chancellery, father?" Yan Skshetuski asked.

"And why does the King have a chancellor? Why does an army have a military scribe? As it is, I'll have to send to some town to have a seal made for me."

"A seal...?" Zjendjan was staring at Pan Zagloba with the most profound respect imaginable.

"And what will you be sealing?" Volodyovski asked.

"What will I be sealing? Hmm, you can keep that sarcastic tone while we're alone, Michal, but I wouldn't advise it when we are out in public. The fact is I won't be sealing anything. My chancellor will do it, mark that well!"

Here Pan Zagloba gazed at his friends with such majestic dignity and power, that Zjendjan leaped to his feet as if it were sacrilege to sit in his presence, and Pan Stanislav muttered under his breath in Latin: "How honors change a man."

"So why do I need a chancellery?" Pan Zagloba resumed with a lofty gesture. "I'll tell you why. The way I see it, all these calamities that have fallen on our Motherland are due to just three things: loose living, greed for fleshly pleasures, and self-indulgence! More mead, Master Michal...!"

He drained another goblet.

"As I said, self-indulgence, which poisons everything around us like the plague. And one other thing, namely all these heretics we've been nurturing in our breasts, who've been getting braver and braver in their blasphemies against the Church and our Holy Patroness, the Virgin Queen of Heaven, so that She has good reason to be fed up with it all."

"That's quite right!" the knights chorused. "The Protestants were the first to join the enemy. And who knows if they didn't invite Charles Gustav here to start with?"

"As, *per exemplum*, the Grand Hetman of Lithuania!"

"There you have it!" Pan Zagloba nodded with all the gravity and profundity of Demosthenes. "But since this palatinate where I'm the generalissimo is also full of heretics, as in Tikotzin and other urban places, we'll seek God's blessing for our enterprise by issuing a decree whereby everyone who doesn't follow the true faith will have three days to convert and rejoin the Church. And those who fail to do so will have their properties confiscated to sustain the army."

The knights stared at each other in amazement. They knew that Pan Zagloba had quick wits and a fertile imagination but they didn't suspect the range of his thinking.

"And you ask where I'll find the money for my army?" the generalissimo gazed at them in triumph. "What about sequestrations? What about all the Radzivill possessions which will, at one stroke, pass to our treasury?"

"But will the law approve this?" Volodyovski asked.

"We live in such times that whoever has the sharper sword has the better laws," Pan Zagloba said. "And what law allows the Swedes and Russians to make themselves at home in the Commonwealth?"

"That's true!" Pan Michal nodded with conviction.

"And there's more!" Pan Zagloba cried, intoxicated with the brilliance of his own ideas. "The next decree will go to the Podlasian gentry, and to the gentry of the neighboring palatinates which are still free of enemy occupation, to take up arms as for a General Levy! Every landowner will have to bring his peasants so that we'll have enough infantry. I know that many people would be glad to join us but they keep waiting for some kind of document and some authority to follow. We'll give them all the papers and authority they need!"

"You really do have the brains of a Grand Chancellor of the Crown!" cried Pan Volodyovski.

"More mead, Master Michal! The third manifesto will go to Hovansky, telling him to go back where he came from and be quick about it, or we'll smoke him out of all his towns and castles. He's quiet enough these days in Lithuanian territory, and doesn't even try his hand at taking the regions that are still holding out against him, but Zoltarenko's Cossacks are another matter! They're pillaging far and wide, two or three thousand

at a time, and I've had enough of that! Let him hold them down
or we'll start taking them apart."

"We could start doing that anyway," Pan Yan said. "The
troops could use the training. Such exercise will sharpen our
newer volunteers and help the regulars keep their edge."

"I've been thinking about that, and I'm sending a column
towards Volkovysk today, but doing something is only as important as not omitting something else. So the fourth letter will go
to our good King, our dear elected monarch, to cheer him up in
his adversity. Let him know that there are still some loyal hearts
and sabers he can call on. Let him have this much consolation
in his foreign exile, our poor abandoned father... our beloved
master... our... our..."

And here Pan Zagloba, whose head was already spinning with
all the mead he'd drunk, choked, stumbled, lost the thread of
what he was saying, and began to hoot mournfully in pity over
the King's unhappy fate, while tears ran in streams down his
florid face. Pan Michal joined him in his piping tenor, Zjendjan
sniffed and sniffled, and the two Skshetuskis sat in grieving
silence, resting their bowed heads on their large, clenched fists.

But suddenly Pan Zagloba lost his temper.

"And what's the matter with that damned Elector? If he made
a pact with the Prussian cities let him declare against the Swedes!
Let him get off his fence! Let him do what every loyal vassal is
supposed to do, and that's to take the field in the defense of his
master and benefactor!"

"Who knows if he won't side with the Swedes in the long
run?" Pan Stanislaw asked.

"In the long run? Well, I have something here for his shorter
runs! The Prussian border isn't far from here and I've a few
thousand sharp sabers at my beck and call. He can pull the wool
over everybody's eyes as much as he wants but he won't get
away with trying to fool Zagloba! I swear to you, as you see me
here, that I'll invade that foxy weasel with fire and sword! So
we're short of supplies? Very well, we'll find them in Prussia!"

"Holy Mother of God!" Zjendjan cried, dazzled by these
prospects. "Your Excellency is ready to take on the crowned
heads of Europe!"

"I'll write to him at once!" Pan Zagloba threatened. "My dear
Elector, is what I'll say to him. Enough of your tricks! Enough

of all that two-faced monkey business! Come out against the Swedes or I'll come calling on you in your own backyard! And that's just what I'll do! Get me some ink, pens and paper, somebody! Zjendjan, you will be my envoy!"

"I will!" Zjendjan cried, delighted with his new appointment.

★ ★ ★

But before anyone could bring the writing implements, the gathered knights heard a roar of joy booming outside their windows and Pan Zagloba went out with his friends to see what was happening. Crowds of soldiers gathered in the meadows to greet the arrival of those four pieces of artillery that Pan Zagloba unearthed in Bialystok and which Pan Stempalski, the local governor, turned over to the new generalissimo with a long and complicated speech.

"For twenty years I've worked to sustain the Tikotzin Castle, as I'm bound to do," he went on. "But since it became the mainstay of our country's enemies in this province, I've been asking God and my conscience whether I should continue to arm it and support it..."

"You should not!" Pan Zagloba interrupted gravely.

"... Or whether I should turn over all those goods and weapons, bought out of this year's rents and properly entered in the ledgers, to Your Illustrious Person..."

"You should!" said Pan Zagloba.

"... And all I ask is that Your Illustrious Lordship should affirm in front of the whole army, and write me a receipt to that effect as well, that I didn't keep any of these goods for my own use but turned them over to the Commonwealth, as represented here by Your Esteemed Worship."

Pan Zagloba nodded his assent and got down at once to an inspection of Pan Stempalski's ledgers. These showed that beside his guns, the governor had three hundred German muskets and two hundred Russian pole-axes hidden in his attics, along with six thousand gold-pieces buried in the corn cribs.

"The money will go at once to pay the army," the generalissimo ordered. "As for the muskets and the halberds,"—and here he nodded towards Pan Oskierka—"I want you to take them, colonel, and form me an infantry battalion! We have a fair

number of former Radzivill infantrymen among us and you can
fill up the ranks with the best lads among the local millers."

Then he addressed everyone else in sight. "Gentlemen!" he
cried. "We have money and artillery! We will have infantry and
supplies! How's that for the start of my administration?"

"*Vivat!*" roared the army.

"And now, gentlemen, I want all your serving lads and
grooms to comb the nearby villages for every shovel, hoe and
pick they can find! We'll build a regular walled camp in this
place. A second Zbarajh! And whether you're a simple man-at-
arms or enlisted gentry I don't want one of you shirking your
turn with the shovels!"

With this the generalissimo made his way to his quarters,
followed by the joyful and excited shouts of his entire army.

"By God, Yan," Volodyovski muttered to Skshetuski. "That
man really has a great head on his shoulders. Things are beginning to look a lot better."

"I just hope that Radzivill doesn't come down on us right
away," Pan Stanislav offered. "He's the best field commandeer
in the Commonwealth. And while Pan Zagloba makes a good
quartermaster he doesn't have a chance of beating him in battle."

"That's true!" Pan Yan said. "We'll have to help him if it
comes to that. But Pan Sapyeha will join us as soon as he can
and that will be the end of Zagloba's generalship."

"And in the meantime we and he can do a lot of good," said
Volodyovski.

Chapter Fifty-two

AS IT HAPPENED, the troops did need a leader, even the kind they found in Pan Zagloba, because from the day of his election a far better order descended on the camp. Earthworks began to rise the next morning among the Bialystok rivulets and ponds. Pan Oskierka, who had served in some Western European armies and knew how to build field fortifications, directed the construction and, in just three days, an imposing wall—which did bear some resemblance to Zbarajh, since its flanks and rear were guarded by swampy pools—encircled the confederates' encampment.

The soldiers took heart at once, feeling that at long last they stood on solid ground. But their spirits soared even higher at the sight of the provisions brought into the camp by strong forage parties. Each day saw whole herds of cattle, sheep and pigs driven into the earthworks; every day welcomed convoys of grains and requisitioned fodder, some of it coming from as far as the Lukov country; and armed gentry of every kind found new confidence as they heard that there was now a legal government, an army and a generalissimo around whom to rally, and poured into the camp in ever greater numbers.

The local inhabitants grumbled that they found it hard to feed an entire division, but they had little choice. In the first place Pan Zagloba took what he needed without asking anyone's permission and, in the second place, it was better to give up half the crops and livestock to sustain the army, and enjoy the rest in peace, than to risk losing all of it to the swarms of footloose raiders and marauders who plagued the countryside in pure

Tartar fashion, and whom Pan Zagloba ordered tracked down and destroyed.

"If he turns out to be as good a general as he's a quartermaster," the soldiers told each other through the camp, "then the Commonwealth has yet to discover what a great man she has."

The Great Man himself, however, had few illusions about what would happen when Yanush Radzivill appeared at last before his walls.

He remembered all of Radzivill's former military triumphs and then the Hetman's image took on a monstrous shape in his imagination. "Ay, ay, who can face that kind of a dragon," he told himself when nobody could hear him. "I said he'd choke on me if he tried to gulp me down but I'll go down his throat as easily as a duckling down a pike's gullet."

And then he swore to avoid a battle with Radzivill as long as he could.

'*There'll be a siege,*' he thought. '*That always takes time. We can try a parley or two as well, and in the meantime Pan Sapyeha will manage to get here...*'

But just in case the *Voyevode* of Vitebsk didn't arrive in time, Pan Zagloba decided to take Yan Skshetuski's advice in everything, since he remembered how highly Prince Yeremi regarded that officer and his military talents.

"You, Michal," he told Pan Volodyovski, "were made for attacking and the rough and tumble of a fight on horseback. You can even be sent off with a fair sized column to harass the enemy because you'd fall on them like a wolf on a flock of sheep. But you wouldn't do so well commanding an army! No, no, my friend. You'll never operate a brain shop, because you don't have enough good sense in your own head to spare for sale to anybody else, but Yan has a real Hetman's head sitting on his shoulders. Only he could take my place here if something happened to me."

* * *

Meanwhile the news that reached the camp was different every day. Some reports already had Radzivill on the march through Prussia. Others had him beating Hovansky and occupying Grodno and marching south from there with a vast new army. There were men who insisted that it was Pan Sapyeha who'd beaten Hovansky with the help of Prince Michael Radzivill, but no one knew anything for sure. The only piece of real information that the patrols brought into the camp concerned a powerful detachment of Zoltarenko's Cossacks, some two thousand strong, that laid siege to Volkovysk and sent the countryside around it up in smoke.

Refugees from the stricken province soon confirmed that story, adding that the townsmen sent envoys to both Zoltarenko and Hovansky begging them for mercy. The Russian shrugged off the attackers as a loose band of ruffians who had nothing to do with him or his army, while the Cossack leader suggested that the besieged townsmen buy them off with tribute. But since the town was burned down to the ground only recently, and was pillaged several times in the past year as well, the burghers were too poor to purchase their safety.

The refugees begged his Lordship the Generalissimo to save them while the tribute negotiations were still going on, and he picked fifteen hundred of his finest men, with the Laudanian Regiment among them, and summoned Volodyovski.

"Alright then, Michal," he told the little colonel. "It's time for you to show what you can do. You'll go to Volkovysk and wipe out those cut-throats who threaten a defenseless town. It's not the first time you've gone to this kind of party, so I think you'll take it as a favor that I entrust you with it."

Then, turning to the other colonels, he said: "I have to stay here in the camp, of course, because the whole responsibility for everything is lying on my shoulders. And besides, it would undermine my dignity to go chasing after mere cut-throats. Let Radzivill show up here, let there be a pitched battle or a regular siege, and then we'll see who's the better man, the Hetman or the Generalissimo."

Volodyovski was pleased to go because life in country quarters bored him and he longed for action. The picked regiments also left the walled camp in high spirits, singing as they rode, and their supreme commander sent them off with considerable ceremony, sitting on horseback on the earthen rampart and blessing them with a crucifix.

Some people wondered why Pan Zagloba made such a great affair out of a mere punitive expedition but he recalled that other famous Hetmans, the immortal Zolkievski among them, had the habit of blessing the regiments they sent into battle. Besides, he liked to do everything with a ceremonial flourish because, as he put it, it made him look good in the soldiers' eyes.

But the departing troops had barely vanished in the morning mists when he started worrying.

"Listen Yan!" he turned to Skshetuski. "Maybe we ought to send a few more men to help Volodyovski?"

"Don't give it another thought, father," Pan Yan laughed. "Volodyovski does this kind of thing like wolfing down an omelet. Dear God, that's all he's been doing since he was a boy!"

"But what if he runs into a superior force? '*Nec Hercules contra plures*,' you know what they say... Even Hercules had his limitations."

"Don't you worry about Michal." Pan Yan smiled and shook his head. "He's too good a soldier to be caught like that. He'll check out everything thoroughly before he attacks, and if he's outnumbered too badly he'll snap up what he can and come back on his own, or send for reinforcements. You can go and take your nap in peace."

"Ha! I knew I could trust him!" the fat knight cried at once. "But, I tell you Yan, this Michal of ours must've slipped some kind of spell over me. I've a real weakness for that little fellow. I've never cared so much for anyone other than you and the late Pan Podbipyenta... That's what it's got to be, some kind of a spell."

★ ★ ★

But three days passed without a single word from the expedition. Provisions and volunteers poured into the camp but there was no sign of Pan Michal or his returning soldiers. Pan Zagloba's worry grew despite all of Skshetuski's assurances that there was no way for Volodyovski to come back from Volkovysk in so little time and he sent off another troop of Yakub Kmita's Light Horse to find out what happened.

But the troop left and vanished and two more days passed without a word.

Finally, on a grey, misty evening seven days after Pan Michal's departure, the camp servants who'd been sent towards the hamlet of Bobrovnik after new supplies, came back in a hurry with news that some kind of army was coming out of the woods beyond the settlement.

"That'll be Michal!" Zagloba shouted out with joy.

But the foragers disagreed. They hadn't gone to check on the new arrivals because they saw some regimental banners that didn't exist in Volodyovski's column. And besides, they said, it was a much stronger force than had left the camp.

"How big a force is it?" Zagloba wished to know.

But the lads couldn't tell him. Some said they'd counted three thousand men or more. Some said it was five thousand.

"I'll take twenty troopers and ride out to see," Lipnitzki volunteered and rode out at once.

An hour passed, and then another drew to an anxious close, and then the outposts came running in with word that an entire army was coming into sight and suddenly, for no apparent reason, a single vast shout echoed through the camp: "Radzivill is coming!"

This rumor swept like lightning through the regimental lines and shook the whole encampment. The soldiers ran to the walls. Some faces showed fear. The companies milled about in confusion and only Oskierka's new foot soldiers took their positions in good order. The newest volunteers gave way to signs of panic and wild rumors flew among their ranks.

"Radzivill wiped out Volodyovski and that troop of Kmita's!" some men cried. "There's not a man left alive among them!"

"And now Lipnitzki's vanished as if the earth had swallowed him up along with all his men! Where's the general? Where is our commander?"

The regimental colonels ran up to restore order, and since most of the soldiers were old hands with just a smattering of newly arrived volunteers among them, the troops were soon waiting smartly in their ranks, ready for anything that might happen next.

★ ★ ★

Meanwhile, Pan Zagloba lost much of his composure when he heard the cry "Radzivill is coming," but at first he couldn't believe that the dreaded hour had come on him at last. What, he asked himself, could have happened to Volodyovski? Could he have let himself be destroyed so completely that not a single witness survived to tell the story? And what about that second troop of Kmita's? What about Lipnitzki?

"It just can't be!" he muttered to himself, mopping the sweat that burst out thickly on his forehead. "Could that dragon, that man-eating monster, that Devil incarnate, get here already from Keydany? Has my final hour really struck at last? No, no, that just couldn't happen!"

But when the cries of "Radzivill! Radzivill!" started to echo loudly from every corner of the camp he could doubt no longer. He leaped to his feet and ran to Skshetuski's quarters.

"Yan! Help me out for God's sake!" he cried, bursting in. "Now is the time for you to take over!"

"Why? What's happened?" Pan Yan asked him calmly.

"What do you mean what's happened? Radzivill is coming! I'm placing the whole thing in your hands because Prince Yeremi used to say that you're a born commander! I'll keep an eye on things here and there, which is my proper function, but you take charge and tell me what to do!"

"It can't be Radzivill," Pan Yan said. "Which direction is this army coming from?"

"From the direction of Volkovysk. The word is that they've swallowed up Volodyovski and that other troop I sent after him."

"Do you think Volodyovski would let himself be swallowed at one gulp? You sound as if you didn't know him, father! You've seen him in action. That's Michal himself coming back, no one else."

"But the men are saying it's a much bigger force than his."

"God be praised then!" Pan Yan laughed. "That means that Pan Sapyeha has got here at last!"

"My God! D'you think so? But why didn't they send some word? Lipnitzki rode out to meet them..."

"There's your proof that this can't be Radzivill. Lipnitzki's men found out who it was, joined the column, and all of them are coming back together. Let's go out and greet them!"

"That's what I thought from the start!" Zagloba cried out. "Everybody else lost his head but I knew at once that it had to be the *Voyevode* of Vitebsk! That was my first thought! Let's go, Yan, let's go! Jump to it! Just imagine, all those others losing their heads like that... but not me!"

* * *

They hurried out and climbed up on the ramparts where the regiments were already waiting in firm ranks, and then they set out along the line of the entrenchments. Pan Zagloba strode boldly among his waiting soldiers, his face alight with the joy of battle, and then, remembering what Prince Yeremi said at the siege of Zbarajh, he stopped and shouted out so loudly that everyone could hear him:

"We've guests, gentlemen! Don't you lose heart, any of you, hear? If that's Radzivill then I'll soon send him packing back to his Keydany! I'll show him the way!"

"We'll show him!" roared the army.

"Light the beacons on the walls! We won't be skulking here in the shadows! Let them see us! We're ready for them! Come on, light the fires!"

The camp servants ran to obey and in fifteen minutes the entire encampment was ablaze with light so that the dark night sky reddened as if with a sunrise. The soldiers stared into the black space that spread in the direction of Bobrovnik, and some started calling out that they could hear the hoofbeats and the creaks and rattles of the approaching army.

Then musketry split the distant darkness and Pan Zagloba clutched the tail of Skshetuski's coat. "They've started shooting!" he said anxiously.

"In greeting," Pan Yan replied.

Joyful shouts followed the musket volleys and all doubts disappeared at once when a dozen riders galloped into the camp on foam-spattered horses, shouting: "Pan Sapyeha! The *Voyevode* of Vitebsk!"

The soldiers on the wall roared a joyous welcome, hurled their caps and helmets into the air, leaped off the parapets and poured down into the plain below; and then ran like a swelling river to meet their new leader, shouting and yelling so loudly in their joy that someone hearing them from a distance might have thought that a massacre was taking place among them.

Pan Zagloba, dressed for the occasion in all the symbols and badges of his office—wearing a heron's plume in his cap, hefting his gold *bulava*, and with a horsetail standard carried above his head—rode out to wait before the walls at the head of all his regimental colonels until the *Voyevode* of Vitebsk rode into the light, with Pan Volodyovski at his side and surrounded by his own officers and commanders.

The flames burning along the walls showed an average-looking man, already well-along in years, whose otherwise undistinguished features revealed a natural thoughtfulness and kindness. He wore his greying mustache clipped short above his lip which, along with his pointed little beard, made him look somewhat like a foreigner, but he dressed in the robes and costume of a Polish noble. Despite his well-earned reputation as a good and courageous soldier, he had the look of a statesman rather than a warrior so that, according to men who knew him well, '*Minerva took precedence over Mars*' in the *Voyevode's* face.

But there was something else in those quiet features, something beside the tell-tale marks of thoughtfulness and courage, which was far more rare in those times. This was a truly decent and sincere man, whose honesty, rising directly from his soul, glowed in his eyes like sunlight reflecting in clear water, so that everyone could tell at a glance that here was a truly caring human being, and a leader pledged to goodness, fairness and justice.

"We've been waiting for you as if you were our father!" cried the joyful soldiers.

"He's here!" others echoed with tears in their eyes. "He's come at last among us!"

"Long life to him! *Vivat! Vivat!*"

★ ★ ★

Pan Zagloba spurred his horse towards him, with the confederate colonels clustering eagerly about him, and the *Voyevode* bared his silvery head and started bowing quietly to the cheering soldiers with his lynx-fur cap.

"Illustrious *Voyevode!*" Zagloba launched into his ceremonial greeting. "Even if I possessed the eloquence of the ancient Romans—of Cicero himself or, reaching even farther back into antiquity, of that famous Demosthenes of Athens—I'd be unable to express the joy that floods all our hearts at the sight of your esteemed person among us at long last! All of the Commonwealth shares our joy in welcoming her wisest senator and her most faithful son, all the more fervently because your coming here is so unexpected...

"Here we stood, on these walls," Zagloba orated and raised his arms to heaven. "Prepared to fight rather than welcome anyone, straining our throats and ears for battle cries and the roar of cannon rather than shouts of greeting, and ready to spill our blood rather than tears of joy! But when good fortune told us with a hundred tongues that it's our Motherland's defender who is coming here, not a loathsome traitor... that it's the *Voyevode* of Vitebsk, not the false Grand Hetman of the Lithuanians... that it's Sapyeha, not Radzivill..."

But Pan Sapyeha appeared anxious to enter the camp because he made a quick, friendly gesture that combined his good-natured kindliness with the blunt directness of a highborn lord.

"Radzivill's coming too, don't worry," he broke in. "He'll be here day after tomorrow."

Pan Zagloba lost some of his poise again and stammered to a halt. This was, in part, because the interruption threw him off his stride, and partly because the news of Radzivill's nearness made him feel distinctly unwell. He stood as if dumbstruck for a moment before Pan Sapyeha, quite lost for words and feeling like a fool. But he recovered quickly, drew his *bulava* from behind his sash, and remembering how the King's commanders surrendered their authority to Prince Yeremi Vishnovyetzki before the siege of Zbarajh, said in a ceremonial tone:

"The army chose me for its leader but I place this symbol of my authority in worthier hands than mine. Let this be an example to younger generations of how to renounce even the most deserved distinctions for the public good."

The soldiers started cheering once again but Pan Sapyeha only smiled briefly, then nodded and said: "I just hope, my good friend, that Radzivill won't take your gesture as a sign of fear. He'd be pleased to think that you're surrendering your command just because he's coming."

"He knows me far too well for that," Zagloba replied. "I've already shown him what's what in Keydany and drew his other officers by my good example."

"Well, in that case lead the way," Pan Sapyeha said. "Volodyovski told me along the road that you're a rare provisioner and that there's something in your camp with which to break a fast. And we're all tired and hungry."

★   ★   ★

The *Voyevode* spurred his horse into the camp and the others followed amid songs and cheering.

Pan Zagloba, recalling what he'd heard about the Palatine's love of celebrations, decided to give a sumptuous banquet in honor of his coming, and he produced a feast of a kind that no one had seen in that camp before. Everyone ate and drank until long past midnight. Over the cups, Pan Michal related how the treacherous Zoltarenko sent help to his marauders, how vastly superior numbers surrounded him near Volkovysk so that matters started to look grave indeed, when the sudden arrival of Pan Sapyeha's army turned a desperate last stand into a splendid victory.

"We gave them such a beating to remember that they won't dare to stick their noses outside their camp again," he said with conviction.

Soon afterwards the talk at all the tables turned to Radzivill about whom Pan Sapyeha had the latest and most reliable news. Trusted informants kept him abreast of everything that happened in Keydany so that he even knew about Kmita's mission to the King of Sweden. The Hetman, he informed the others, had written to Charles Gustav begging him to join him in an attack on Podlasye from two sides.

"Now that's a real wonder, as far as I'm concerned!" Pan Zagloba cried. "Because if it weren't for that same Andrei Kmita we'd never have got together in one bunch and Radzivill could've gobbled us up one at a time like a bagful of fresh onion rolls."

"Volodyovski told me all about that," Pan Sapyeha said. "From which I gather that this man must have some personal affection for you. It's a pity he doesn't have it for his country too. But people who don't show much regard for anything greater than themselves, serve everyone badly, and they're always ready to betray their masters. As Kmita betrayed Radzivill in this case."

"But Your Lordship won't find any traitors among us," Zeromski assured him. "Each one of us is ready to give his life under your command."

"Yes, I know you're all good men and honest soldiers here," the Palatine said. "But I must say I never expected to find such a well ordered and provisioned army. For which, it appears, I have to thank the excellent Pan Zagloba."

The fat knight flushed with pleasure, because while it seemed to him that the *Voyevode* treated him well enough, showing a kindly interest in what he had to say, yet he failed to show the respect and recognition that the ex-generalissimo expected. He launched at once into a detailed exposition of how he had commanded, what he had done, what supplies he'd gathered, how he acquired his artillery and formed the infantry and, finally, what a voluminous correspondence he had been conducting.

"After my letter to him, the Prussian Elector has no choice but to declare himself openly for us or against us," he said with pride and great self-satisfaction.

But the *Voyevode* of Vitebsk was merry man who liked a good joke, or perhaps he had drunk enough to poke some sly fun at such an obvious target, so he stroked his mustache and smiled with amusement at the flushed Zagloba.

"You didn't write to the Holy Roman Emperor by any chance, did you?" he asked.

"No!" said the surprised Zagloba.

"Pity!" said the *Voyevode*. "We'd have had a correspondence between equals."

The colonels roared with laughter but Pan Zagloba showed at once that if His Lordship wanted to sharpen his wit on someone he'd need another whetstone.

"My lord," he said calmly. "I could write to the Prince-Elector because, as a gentleman of the Commonwealth, I'm an elector too and it wasn't all that long ago that I cast my vote for Yan Casimir."

"That was well said," the *Voyevode* said laughing.

"But it's not my place to correspond with such a potentate as the Emperor," Zagloba went on. "Or I'd risk turning myself into a Lithuanian joke."

"And what joke is that?"

"The one that says that Vitebsk cabbages are so good that

some people wear them on their shoulders in place of their heads."

The listening colonels grew cold with sudden fear but the *Voyevode* burst into helpless laughter.

"Look how he put me in my place!"he gasped out at last. "Let me hug you, brother! Next time I feel like shaving off my beard I'll borrow your tongue for a razor!"

The banquet lasted long into the night. It ended only when a few neighborhood gentry arrived from Tikotzin with word that Radzivill's advance guard was nearing that town.

Chapter Fifty-three

RADZIVILL WOULD HAVE ATTACKED Podlasye a long time before if it weren't for a number of important matters that kept him in Keydany.

First of all he waited for Swedish reinforcements which Pontus de la Gardie delayed for reasons of his own. Even though this Swedish commander in Estonia was linked by marriage with the King himself, neither his birth nor family nor standing —and that included his royal connection—could equal the standing and position of the Lithuanian magnate. True, Radzivill's treasury was short of gold just then but a mere half of his hereditary holdings and possessions could have turned all the Swedish generals into men of wealth beyond their every avaricious dream, so that when a twist of fate made Radzivill temporarily dependent on Pontus' goodwill, the Swedish marshal couldn't deny himself the satisfaction of keeping him waiting.

Radzivill didn't need the Swedes to crush the confederates. He had enough power of his own for that. But he wanted them at his side for the reasons that Kmita cited in his letter to Volodyovski. Hovansky's armies barred his access to Podlasye and any hostile act on the Russians' part would be a challenge to Charles Gustav if there Swedish soldiers under Radzivill's command. The Hetman prayed for such an outcome to his plans, and the quicker the better. He gnawed his nails with impatience while waiting for the Swedes to come from Estonia. Even a mere company of them would do. In the meantime he cursed Pontus and denounced him to his courtiers.

"He'd think himself honored if I'd written him a letter just a few years back," he snarled in his fury. "He'd pass it on to his descendants in his will! And now he's putting on the airs of my superior!"

To which a certain local squire known for his acid tongue and disrespectful manners said on one occasion: "As the proverb has it, Highness, if you lie down with dogs, you'll get up with fleas."

Radzivill flew into a rage and had the noble thrown into a dungeon. But he relented the next day, had the squire set free, and even gave him a gold clasp for his trouble because the squire was said to have some ready cash which the Hetman wished to borrow on a promissory note.

The squire took the clasp but didn't lend the money and Radzivill went on waiting and cursing the Swedes.

★ ★ ★

The Swedish reinforcements came at last, numbering eight hundred heavy cavalry, while Pontus sent another three hundred musketeers and a hundred Light Horse straight to Tikotzin wanting the castle in his own hands just in case. Hovansky's hordes parted before the Swedes just as Radzivill expected them to do, and the Swedish troops got to Tikotzin without any trouble because the confederates were still scattered through the countryside at that time, doing nothing more useful or significant than looting the Hetman's holdings.

Everyone expected Radzivill to march south at once but he still delayed because his spies reported the confusion among the mutineers, with each confederate colonel going his own way, and with serious differences flaring up between Kotovski, Lipnitzki and Yakob Kmita.

"We have to give them time to sharpen their nails and claw at each other," Radzivill told Ganhof, rubbing his hands in anticipation. "They'll tear each other to pieces without our assistance and we, in the meantime, will settle with Hovansky."

But suddenly the news from Podlasye took a different turn. The confederate colonels not only failed to come to blows but they banded together near Bialystok and the Prince-Hetman couldn't understand what happened to upset all his calculations. Then he heard of Zagloba as the confederates' new overall commander, of the walled camp and the provisioning of the mutineers' army, of cannon unearthed by the fat old knight whom he hated with an implacable passion anyway, of the confederates' growing strength and the floods of volunteers coming to swell their ranks, and he was seized by such a towering rage that even Ganhof, who was a fearless soldier, didn't dare to come near him for twenty-four hours.

★ ★ ★

At last the marching orders went out to his army and the entire division was ready in one day. The Prince would lead one full regiment of German infantry, two of Scots and one of Lithuanians. Pan Korf commanded the artillery and Ganhof took charge of all the cavalry.

Riding behind him were Kharlamp's dragoons and the newly arrived Swedish cuirassiers, the Light Horse of Nevyarovski and the Prince's own armored Household Cavalry. It was a strong force, all the more formidable since it consisted of experienced veterans. Radzivill hadn't had much more than that at his command when he won all those famous victories in the first war of the Cossack Rebellion that covered him with such immortal glory. With a force larger by only a few hundred men he crushed the Cossack atamans Polksyezitz and Nebaba; shattered the 60,000-man army of the famed Kshetchovski in the fields of Loyov, ravaged the Cossack strongholds of Mozyr and Turov, stormed into Kiev, and squeezed Hmyelnitzki so mercilessly in the Ukrainian Steppe that the Cossack warlord had to look for help in negotiations.

But the star of his fortunes seemed to be growing dim and the great war leader looked into a future full of premonitions. Nothing seemed clear to him. He could count on no one.

'So I'll march into Podlasye,' he mused in dour gloom. 'I'll shatter the confederates, have that loathed Zagloba skinned alive before my eyes, and what will it all mean? What will come next? How will my fortunes change?'

Would he then throw himself on Hovansky, avenge his own defeats suffered at Tzibihov and Shklov, and place new laurels of a conqueror on his head?

That's what he told everyone he would do but would he really be able to do it? More and more often he was hearing rumors that the Russian hordes were simply terrified of the

Swedes and would soon give up all their thoughts of conquest. They could even enter into an alliance with Yan Casimir. Sapyeha snapped at them where he could but he also kept up negotiations with them and so did Gosyevski. The Hetman's last chance to demonstrate his power and to assert his value on the greater European stage would vanish if the Russians gave up their invasion. And if Yan Casimir managed to win them over, and to throw these former enemies against the Swedes, he might be able to restore his own dimming fortunes and, at the same time, doom all of Radzivill's hopes, ruin his position, and undermine all his plans and visions.

True, the news that came to Radzivill from the former palatinates of Poland was uniformly good. The territories surrendered to Charles Gustav one after another. The Swedes ruled Vyelkopolska as if it was a native Swedish province. Radeyovski was the overlord of Warsaw. The lords of Malopolska, or Little Poland as it was also known, offered no resistance. Krakow was under siege and would shortly fall. King Yan Casimir, deserted by the magnates, the gentry and his army, had lost all confidence in his disloyal nation and fled to the German Emperor's Silesia, so that Charles Gustav himself found it difficult to understand how he had managed to crush that awesome power that had always been successful in its wars with Sweden.

But it was exactly this Swedish ease of conquest that seemed most threatening to the Lithuanian Hetman. He sensed that they'd become so dazzled by their own successes that they'd lose sight of him and his importance to them, particularly since he hadn't shown himself to be as powerful in his own Lithuania as everyone, including himself, had believed before.

'*So will they give me all of the old historic Lithuania?*' he asked himself in torment. '*Or even a scrap of the lost Byelorusian country?*'

Or would the Swedish King prefer to feed those eastern territories of the Commonwealth to her insatiable, eternally hungry neighbor so as to have his hands free in the rest of Poland?

* * *

These were the dark questions that tortured Radzivill night and day. Anxiety threatened to corrode his soul and undermine his spirit. He thought that Pontus de la Gardie wouldn't dare to treat him in such a lofty and high-handed manner if he didn't think Charles Gustav would approve.

"Or worse yet," the Hetman muttered grimly in the privacy of his guarded rooms. "What if Pontus is acting on the King's instructions?"

'They'll pay attention to me as long as I'm still standing at the head of several thousand men,' he thought, tearing at his hair. *'But what will happen when all the money's gone and my mercenary foreign regiments disappear as well? What will happen then?'*

No rents came to him from his vast possessions. Most of his huge land-holdings, scattered across all the territories of ancient Lithuania—as far as Kiev, Polesye, Podolia and beyond—lay in trampled ruins while Podlasye was drained dry by the confederates.

"Is this what all my work was for?" he asked himself time and time again. "Is this the road to the crown I wanted?"

He thought at times that he was falling into an abyss. Darkness lay around him. All he could see waiting for him at the bottom of the pit—the end result of all his work and plotting—was the name of *traitor*.

This terrified him, as did the thought of dying.

The skeletal image of Death stood almost every night at his bedside curtains, beckoning to him with her bony fingers, as if to say: *'Come with me. Into darkness. Across the unknown river...'*

He'd groan then in sudden terror, hating himself for his dreadful failure. Ah, if he was only standing at the height of his fame and power! If he could wear that crown he longed for so hungrily for just a single day—for no more than an hour!—he knew that he'd be able to face that awful, silent vision with an untroubled eye.

But the thought of dying to leave behind him no more than infamy and the contempt of his fellow-men seemed like a living Hell to this shaken magnate who knew himself to be as proud as Lucifer.

Alone, or in the company of only his astrologer whom he trusted more than any other courtier, he seized himself by the hair, crying out time and time again:

"I'm burning! I'm on fire! I'm burning...!"

★ ★ ★

These were the feelings, fears and anxieties under which the Prince-Palatine of Vilna prepared for his war on the confederates when, the day before the march was scheduled to begin at last, he was informed that Prince Boguslav had come from Taurogen.

The news revived him as if it were a miracle designed to raise the dead. Health flooded into him at once, even before he saw his handsome young cousin, because Boguslav represented everything he lacked and needed so badly: youth, confidence, strength and a blind faith in the future. The fading line of the Birjhan Radzivills was to find fresh roots in this extraordinary young magnate; it was for him and for no one else that Prince Yanush still plotted, planned and worked.

The Hetman wanted to rush out to meet him on the public highway as soon as he heard that he was on his way, but since court etiquette didn't permit a higher-ranking, older man to welcome his juniors on the doorstep, Prince Yanush sent a gilded coach after him with all of Nevyarovski's regiment as a ceremonial escort, and ordered his artillery to thunder its salutes off the castle walls and out of the defensive bastions that Kmita had built all around Keydany, as if to greet a monarch.

But once the rituals of greeting were done with, and the two cousins were alone, Prince Yanush seized Boguslav in his arms and started gasping in a shaken, emotion-laden voice: "My youth has come back! I have my health again!"

But Prince Boguslav threw him a cold, assessing glance and asked in a sharp, calculating voice: "What's wrong with Your Highness?"

"Let's drop the titles now that we're alone... What's wrong with me? Illness is gnawing at me as if I were a rotten old tree... But no matter! How's my wife and daughter?"

"They've left Taurogen. They've gone on to Tilsit. They're both well and little *Marie* is as lovely as a rosebud. She'll be a glorious bloom when she comes to flower. *Ma fois!* No woman in the world has a prettier leg and her hair hangs all the way to the ground."

"She seems that good to you, then? I'm glad. It's just as well that you've dropped in on me like this. God must've sent you here. I feel more alive right away! But what news do you bring me about public matters? What's the Elector up to?"

"You know already about his alliance with the Prussian cities?"

"Yes I do."

"Only they don't trust him much. Gdansk wouldn't accept his garrison. They've a good nose, those Germans."

"I know about that too. But haven't you been writing to him? What does he think about us?"

"About us?" Prince Boguslav repeated carelessly as if distracted by more important matters.

"Yes, *us*. What else?"

But Prince Boguslav started throwing quick, searching glances about the room, then jumped to his feet. Prince Yanush thought that he had misplaced something but he only ran up to a tall mirror in the corner, tilted it towards the light to get the best reflection, and began to poke and stroke his face with one probing finger.

"My skin's a little chapped," he murmured. "But it'll be fine tomorrow... What does the Elector think of us? Nothing. He wrote me that he won't forget about us."

"What d'you mean, *won't forget...*?"

"I have his letter with me, you can look at it for yourself. He writes that he'll keep us in mind no matter what happens. And I believe him too, because his own best interests oblige him to do it. The Elector cares about the Commonwealth about as much as I do about an old wig, and he'd be glad to toss her to the Swedes if he could only snatch East Prussia for himself. But he's starting to get worried about the growth of Swedish military power and he's looking for a good alliance for the times ahead. He knows he'll have one once you're sitting on the Lithuanian throne."

"If only that could happen! It's not for me that I want that throne!"

"We probably won't be able to haggle all of Lithuania for ourselves. Not at the beginning anyway. But we should be able to get a good slice of it, with Zmudya and Byelorusia for a start."

"And what about the Swedes?"

"The Swedes will be glad enough to have us form a barrier against the east."

"You're pouring pure balsam into me!" Prince Yanush cried.

"A balsam, is it? Aha! Talking about balsams... Some alchemist in Taurogen wanted to sell me a balsam that, he said, would make a man impervious to cold steel. All that you'd have to do, as he put it, is smear yourself with the stuff and it'll turn away a sword blade or a spear. Imagine that! I had him plastered with it right away and ordered a halberdier to thrust a lance at him, and what do you think happened? The lance went right through him!"

*   *   *

Here Prince Boguslav began to chuckle with amusement, showing his clean white teeth in a broadening grin. But the Hetman didn't have the time for light-hearted gossip, or for the trivial turn their conversation was taking, and moved again to more public matters.

"I sent some letters to the King of Sweden," he said. "And to several other dignitaries of ours. Wait, though... You must have got my letters from Kmita as well?"

"Yes. That's part of the reason I came down here just now. But tell me, what do you think of that Kmita of yours?"

"He's a madman, an impulsive hothead." The Prince-Palatine shrugged and showed a wry smile. "A dangerous man who can't stand to be told what to do. But he's one of those rare people who serve us in good faith."

"He's rare, alright," Prince Boguslav answered. "His good faith almost sent me into the next world."

"How's that, then?" Prince Yanush moved uneasily.

"Hmm. Wait a bit. The word is, dear brother, that you start choking just as soon as the bile moves in you. Promise me that you'll hear me out calmly and with patience and I'll tell you something about your Kmita you haven't heard before. Perhaps you don't know him as well as you think."

"Alright! I'll be patient! Just get to the point, will you?"

"It's a pure miracle that I got out of that devil's hands alive," Prince Boguslav said and started to relate everything that happened to him in Pilvishkye.

It was no lesser miracle that Prince Yanush didn't fall victim to an attack of asthma; instead it seemed as if he was about suffer an apoplectic stroke. His whole body quivered as if in a fever. He snapped and ground his teeth. He pressed his fingers against his bulging eyes. Then he began to shout in a hoarse, grating voice: "Very well...! But he forgot that his bitch is in my hands..."

"Get hold of yourself, for God's sake!"Prince Boguslav urged. "Keep listening! I dealt with him suitably enough, I think, and the only reason why I won't brag about it or note it in my diaries is that I'm ashamed to have let such a low-life boor trick me as he did. Imagine! Me, whom Mazarin himself called the most astute and skillful intriguer at the court of France! But back to the point... I thought at first I'd killed him back there on that road but now I've proof that he's licked himself back to health."

"Good! Then we'll find him! We'll get our hands on him if we have to dig him out of the earth itself! In the meantime I've a harder and more painful blow ready for him here than if I ordered him flayed alive."

"Wait, I said." Prince Boguslav made an impatient gesture. "Listen to me, will you? You won't strike any blows at him here or anywhere. You'll only strain your health. Listen to me a moment. On my way here I caught sight of some peasant on a piebald mare who seemed to be keeping close to my carriage on the road. It's that mare that made me notice him at all. I had him called over at last and asked what he was doing there. '*I'm going to Keydany*,' he said. '*What for?*' I asked. '*I've a letter here for the Prince-Voyevode*,' he tells me. I told him to hand it over to me, and since there are no secrets between us I read it. Here it is!"

Boguslav passed the letter that Kmita had written to the *Voyevode* in the forest hideout before setting out on his journey with the Kemlitches. The Hetman scanned it quickly, crushed it in his fist, and started to gasp, enraged:

"That's true! As God lives, it's true! He has my letters and there are things said there that'll not only make the Swedish King suspicious but that might actually turn him into my mortal enemy!"

Here he began to choke and the expected seizure gripped him by the chest. His mouth hung wide open. He gulped at the air as if he were drowning. His hands clawed at the clothing at his throat. Boguslav took one look at him and clapped for the servants.

"Look to your master," he told the frightened lackeys. "Tell

him to come to see me in my quarters when he can. In the
meantime I'll get a bit of rest."

And he left the chamber.

★   ★   ★

Two hours later Prince Yanush knocked on the door of
Boguslav's bedroom. His eyes were red with blood, their veins
raw and broken. His eyelids drooped. His swollen features had
a bluish tinge. Boguslav received him lying on his bed, his face
painted with a milky almond extract designed to soften the skin
and to give it a lustrous, youthful quality. He looked much
older without his full, curled wig, the rouge which normally
enlivened his cheeks, and the mascara with which he blackened
his pale eyebrows and lashes, but Prince Yanush hardly noticed
the difference.

"I've given some thought to those letters." He went straight
to the core of the matter. "Kmita can't publish them or he'd be
signing that girl's death warrant, and he knows it. But at the
same time it robs me of a chance for vengeance, and that gnaws
at me as if I had a mad dog in my chest."

"But we still must get those letters back!" Boguslav said
quickly.

"But how? *A quo modo?*"

"You have to send some clever man after him. Let the fellow
find him, become his friend, and—when he sees a chance —seize
the letters and put a knife in him. You'd have to offer a big
reward, of course."

"Who'd be willing to do that kind of thing?"

"If this was Paris or even Germany,"Boguslav said in a careless
voice, heavy with contempt, "I'd find you a hundred volunteers
in one day. But in this country even that commodity is in short
supply."

"It would have to be one of our own people. He'd be on his
guard with a foreigner."

"Leave it to me. I'll find someone in Prussia."

"If only I could get my hands on him alive! I'd pay him for
everything at once. I tell you, his insolence went beyond all
bounds. That's why I sent him off, to get him out of sight. He
used to drive me into an intolerable fury! He'd practically spit
in my face, like a cat, and tried to force his will on me every

chance he got. I was on the point of ordering him shot more than a hundred times but somehow I just couldn't do it."

"Is he really our kin?"

"His connection with the Kishkas is true enough, and with us through them."

"Be that as it may, he's a dangerous enemy and as hard to handle as a real demon."

"He doesn't know the meaning of fear. You could've sent him to Istanbul to kidnap the Sultan, or to rip Charles Gustav's beard out of his chin and bring it to Keydany! You can't imagine what he did here in the Russian war!"

"Yes, he has that look. And he swore vengeance on us until his last breath. It's lucky I taught him a lesson that we don't fall easily... Admit it, I treated him in pure Radzivill fashion, eh? If some French cavalier had something like that to boast about he'd be telling his lies all day long, except for the hours he'd need for sleep, food and amours... Because when they get together they tell so many lies that the sun stops shining out of shame."

"Yes, you did hit him hard. Though I'd rather that it hadn't happened."

"And I'd rather have you pick better henchmen for yourself, the kind who'd have more respect for Radzivill bones."

"Those letters!" the Hetman ground out between his teeth. "Those letters...!"

* * *

The two cousins sat without speaking for a time until Boguslav stirred and broke the silence.

"What's that girl like?" he asked.

"She's the Billevitch heiress."

"I didn't ask who she is but what she looks like. Is she pretty?"

"I don't pay much attention to that sort of thing but yes, since you ask, the Queen of Poland wouldn't be ashamed of that kind of beauty."

"The Queen of Poland? Marie-Louise? She may have been pretty as a child but now the dogs howl at the sight of her. If that's what your Billevitch hen is like you can keep her. But if she's really beautiful then send her to me in Taurogen and we'll think up some vengeance on Kmita between us, she and I."

Yanush thought deeply for a moment.

"No," he said at last. "Because you'll force her and then Kmita will publish those letters."

"Force her? Me?" Prince Boguslav laughed. "Far be it from me to boast, but I've had better conquests than one of your country wenches and I never had to force one of them... Except once, in Flanders. She was a stupid twit, a goldsmith's daughter... But then some Spanish pikemen came along and they got the blame."

"You don't know *this* girl. She comes from a good family. Good breeding too. And virtuous as a nun."

"A nun, eh?" Boguslav laughed again. "We've known a few nuns."

"And besides, she hates us. She's a real patriot, for all that she's a woman, and she thinks as clearly as a man. It was she who turned Kmita against us, I am sure, because she's Yan Casimir's most fervent supporter."

"Then we'll make him a few little supporters."

"That can't be or Kmita will publish the letters. I have to watch her like the apple of my eye, at least for the time being. Afterwards, when she no longer matters, I'll give her to you or your dragoons, whichever you like."

"I'll give you my word then, as a gentleman, that I won't take her by force, and I always keep my word when it's a private matter. Political promises are something else again. Besides, I'd be ashamed of myself if I couldn't succeed with her without using violence."

"You won't succeed anyway."

"Don't be so sure. The worst thing that can happen is that she'll slap my face and that's no dishonor coming from a woman. Look, you're going to Podlasye. What will you do with her? You can't take her with you. Nor can you leave her here because the Swedes are coming to Keydany and it's important that we always have her in our hands. We need her as a hostage. Wouldn't it make more sense for me to take her with me to Taurogen? And instead of sending an assassin after Kmita I'll send him an offer. '*Give us the letters*,' I'll say, '*and you can have your girl.*'

"That could work," Prince Yanush said after a thoughtful moment. "That's not a bad idea."

"And if I give her to him not quite in the condition that I got her from you that could be the beginning of our revenge on Kmita."

"But no force, eh? You gave your word?"

"I did. And I'll repeat, I'd be ashamed of myself..."

"Then you'll have to take her uncle, the Constable of Rosyen, who is here with her."

"I don't want her uncle. He's probably like all your local gentry who wear foot-cloths in their boots instead of socks or stockings and I can't stand that near me."

"She won't go alone."

"We'll see. Invite them both to dinner tonight so I can look her over and see if she's worth a taste, and I'll think of a way to interest her in a little journey. Only for God's sake don't tell her about Kmita's actions or it'll just confirm her in her loyalty to him. And don't contradict anything I say at the table no matter what it is. You'll see a few of my little tricks and you'll recall your own youthful years."

Prince Yanush shrugged and left the room with a dismissive gesture and Prince Boguslav clasped his hands behind his neck and started thinking about the various stratagems he had at his disposal. The evening, if nothing more, promised to be an amusing one.

Chapter Fifty-four

INVITED THAT NIGHT to the small, intimate supper with Yanush Radzivill, beside Olenka and her old great-uncle, were the chief Radzivill officers stationed in Keydany and a few of Prince Boguslav's courtiers.

He himself appeared in such magnificent costume that he literally dazzled almost every eye. His long, dark and carefully styled wig framed a face which, in its coloring, brought to mind creamy milk and roses. His thin, penciled mustache seemed like a silken fringe. His eyes glowed like softly veiled stars. He wore a black western-style doublet sewn out of vertical, alternating silk-and-velvet inserts and with the split sleeves buttoned between wrists and elbows. A broad white collar, made of priceless Flemish lace, lay on his chest and shoulders, matching the snowy lacework that spilled from his cuffs.

A golden chain dangled from his neck and, stretching diagonally from his right shoulder across the whole front of his doublet, hung a sword-belt of costly Holland leather which was so thickly encrusted with diamonds that it seemed like a single stream of light. The hilt and handle of his court *epee* was also glowing with a rich covering of diamonds while two more such jewels, each as large as a lustrous hazel nut, shined in the ribbons bunched along his shoetops. He carried a lace handkerchief in one hand while, with the other, he supported a plumed hat, hung in the European fashion of the day on the hilt of his sword, and whose unusually long black ostrich feathers practically swept the floor.

His whole person seemed as noble as it was beautiful and

696

everyone, including Prince Yanush, stared at him with awe and admiration.

Looking at his resplendent young cousin, the *Voyevode* was reminded of his own earlier years when he dazzled everyone at the court of France with his looks and riches. Those years were long gone but now it seemed to the Hetman that he had come alive anew in that splendid cavalier who bore the same name as his own.

Pleased, he touched Boguslav's chest with his index finger as he passed him.

"You're as radiant as the moon," he told him. "Is it the Billevitch girl for whom you've put on all this finery?"

"The moon can slip in anywhere," Boguslav answered with a touch of sly vanity in his voice.

Then he turned to talk to Ganhof, who was an almost incredibly ugly man, and whom he may have picked for a conversation partner because of the contrast between them. With his sallow, pockmarked face, hooked nose and ragged, upswept mustache, Ganhof looked like the embodiment of darkness. Standing beside him Boguslav seemed like the spirit of light.

★ ★ ★

Then the ladies entered: Olenka and Madame Korf, wife of the *Voyevode* of Wenden. Boguslav threw the girl one swift glance, bowed to Lady Korf, and was about to toss the young woman the customary kiss, when he took note of her grave features and her lofty bearing and changed his approach at once. He clutched his hat in his right hand, and moving quickly to stand before Olenka, bowed so deeply that he seemed to bend himself in half. His wig hung past his shoulders in twin folds, his court-sword dangled parallel to the ground, and he remained like that, still as a statue but moving his hat gently in the air before him, so that the long ostrich feathers swept the polished parquet at her feet. Not even the French Queen could have received a more courtly greeting, observers supposed, while Aleksandra, who knew that Prince Boguslav had come to Keydany, realized at once who he was and bowed to him in turn. She plucked at the edges of her dress with the tips of her fingers and sunk into a deep courtsey of her own.

Everyone murmured in appreciation of these courtly manners

which weren't all that common in Keydany at that time, because Prince Yanush's wife, as a Valachian heiress, found more delight in Eastern opulence than in fashionable Western-European usage, while her daughter, the Princess Maria, was still a young girl.

Boguslav looked up then, shook the folds of his wig back into place, and took a few quick, shuffling steps towards Aleksandra while, at the same time, tossing his hat to a page and extending his hand towards her.

"I don't believe my eyes," he murmured, leading her to the table. "Perhaps I am dreaming? But tell me, lovely Goddess, what miracle brings you to Keydany from Olympus?"

"Although I'm only a simple gentlewoman, not a Grecian Goddess," Olenka replied, "I'm not so simple that I'd take Your Highness' words for more than courtly flattery."

"No matter how courtly I might want to be, your mirror would tell you more than I could ever do."

"Perhaps it wouldn't tell me more," she said. "But it would tell the truth."

"I'd take you to one at once if there was one here. But, for the lack of a looking-glass, why don't you look at your reflection in my eyes? You'll see true admiration in them."

And Boguslav turned his face towards her, letting his large dark eyes rest on her like a warm, soft touch which, at the same time, seemed to pierce and burn. She flushed and moved away from him a little because she felt him pressing her hand to his side.

They reached the table. He seated himself next to her and it was clear at once that her beauty had made a really deep impression on him. He had expected a typical country squire's daughter, redfaced like a poppy, frisky as a doe and as shrill and giggly as a magpie; instead he found a cool, distinguished lady whose dark, serious brows showed a strong will and determination, whose eyes revealed dignity and high-minded reason, and whose whole face glowed with an untroubled childlike peacefulness. Moreover, her entire posture reflected such nobility, such grace and such a delicate aloofness that she'd attract serious and respectful attentions at any royal court.

Her beauty staggered him. He found it difficult to express it even to himself. Admiration struggled in him against simple lust. Oh yes, he wanted her. He wanted her badly. But her regal bearing imposed an unbreakable restraint on his carnal greed so that, despite himself, Boguslav thought that he had signaled his desire too soon.

'*I shouldn't have pressed her hand like that,*' the thought hissed swiftly through his mind. '*This one needs to be courted, not pursued.*'

Nevertheless, he was determined to win her and possess her and felt a savage joy at the thought that there'd come that moment when all this haughty innocence and that untouched beauty lay helpless before his will. Kmita's fierce face barred the way in his imagination but that only excited him the more. His blood started pounding in his veins like a goaded stallion's, and all his faculties leaped to sudden fervor, so that he seemed to radiate a hot, searing light as bright as his diamonds.

★   ★   ★

The conversation around the supper table became animated, turning into a chorus of flattery for Boguslav, to which he listened in a careless and distracted manner, showing a small, indulgent smile as if words of praise and admiration were something he heard every day.

The first topic was his military prowess. Then came accounts of his many duels. The names of princes, counts and barons who'd fallen at his hand spilled out as profusely as the lace that tumbled from his sleeves. From time to time he'd toss in another name with a careless smile. His listeners babbled with astonishment. Prince Yanush stroked his mustache with evident pleasure and, at last, Ganhof shook his grizzled head in open amazement.

"Even if my birth and standing weren't in the way," he said in admiration, "I'd hate to cause Your Highness' displeasure. I can't imagine how anyone in the world could be that foolhardy, knowing what you can do."

"What will you have, Ganhof?" the Prince shrugged as if in regret. "Some men have faces hammered out of steel and a stare as savage as a lynx so that people back away from them rather than provoke them... But that is something that God has denied me. My face, as anyone can see, wouldn't frighten even a helpless maiden."

"Just as a flaming torch doesn't alarm a moth," Madame Korf simpered, fluttering her lashes. "Until she burns in it."

Boguslav laughed, throwing back his head, and Madame Korf went on twittering inanely.

"You military gentlemen love to talk of duels. But we ladies would rather hear something of Your Highness' amatory conquests. The stories have reached us even here."

"Lies, all of them, my lady," Boguslav sighed smiling. "There's not a word of truth in any of it, believe me. You know how distance always swells a rumor... Yes, I admit, there have been some attempts to make a marriage for me... Her Majesty the Queen of France did take a kindly interest..."

"With the *Princesse de Rohan*, wasn't it?" Prince Yanush tossed in.

"And that other, de la Forse," Boguslav added, nodding. "But since not even a King can order true affection and we, God be thanked, don't need to look for a fortune among the French, there wasn't any wedding bread baked out of that sweet flour... They were both wellborn young ladies, true, and beautiful enough to dazzle the imagination, but we have lovelier flowers blooming right here in Lithuania. In fact I wouldn't have to leave this room to pick one."

He fixed his eyes on Olenka in a protracted stare but she pretended that she didn't hear him and started an animated conversation with the Constable of Rosyen who sat on her other side.

"Yes we do have some pretty girls among us," Madame Korf agreed. "But none of them can match Your Highness in high birth and fortune."

"You'll pardon me if I disagree, my lady," Boguslav said quickly. "First, because I don't believe that a Polish gentlewoman is inferior to the de Rohans or a de la Forse and, in the second place, because it's not unusual for the Radzivills to intermarry with our Polish gentry. It happens quite often! I assure you also that the girl who marries a Radzivill will take precedence over any foreign princess no matter what her origins might be."

"That's a truly human and down-to-earth lord," the old constable whispered to Olenka.

"That's how I always understood such matters," Boguslav

went on. "Although I'm sometimes ashamed of the Polish gentry when I compare it with the foreign nobles."

"In what way, Highness?" Madame Korf bridled and her small eyes glittered.

"Because what happened here could never happen there! It's an unheard of thing that everyone would abandon their anointed King as all the Polish lords appear to have done. Or that anyone would even think of raising his hand against his rightful monarch! A French noble could commit the most disgraceful acts but he would never turn against his master..."

The dinner guests began to glance uneasily at each other, and Prince Yanush glowered darkly out of an angered face, but Olenka fixed her sky-blue eyes on Boguslav with an expression of gratitude and wonder.

"Forgive me, Highness," Boguslav turned to Yanush who still hadn't managed to suppress his anger. "I know that you had no choice in what you did. All of Lithuania would have gone to a bloody grave if you had followed my advice. But, even so, respecting you as my elder and loving you like a brother, I'll never cease to argue Yan Casimir's case before you. We're among good friends here so I say openly what is in my heart. I love our King! I don't have enough tears to shed for that kind, God-fearing and decent master, who is doubly dear to me because I was the first among the Poles to rally to him when the French released him from imprisonment. I was practically a child then, which is why that memory lives stronger than any other, and I'd gladly spill all my blood to shield him from the heartless killers who plot against his life."

Yanush had grasped the point of Boguslav's game by then but he didn't bother to hide his displeasure because he thought the ploy too bold and risky for such a trivial goal.

"Good God!" he exclaimed. "What kind of plots are you talking about? Is someone threatening our ex-King's life? Who'd do such a thing? That's just too monstrous! That's never happened among Poles before!"

Boguslav hanged his head as if ashamed to even speak about it.

"No later than a month ago," he said sadly. "As I was on my way from Podlasye to my home in Prussia, a certain Polish noble came to see me... A wellborn man. Good family and lineage...

Not knowing my true feelings towards our dear master he must have assumed that I was the King's enemy, like so many others. Well, to cut it short, he made me an offer. He said he'd go to Silesia, seize Yan Casimir for a large reward, and turn him over, dead or alive, to the Swedes."

The dinner guests grew numb and still with horror.

"And when I turned him down with anger and disgust," Boguslav continued as if hardly able to relate such horrors, "this stone-hearted man, this monster without soul or conscience, said to me: Well, then I'll go to Radeyovski. He'll pay for Yan Casimir by the pound..."

"I'm no friend of the ex-King," Prince Yanush snapped hotly. "But if someone came to me with such a proposition I'd have him propped up against a wall with six musketeers before him."

"That was my first thought too," Boguslav explained. "But we were talking without witnesses and I didn't want to bring about any kind of misguided public outcry against 'Radzivill tyranny and lawlessness...!' So I just put him in his place by saying that Radeyovski, the King of Sweden or even Hmyelnitzki himself would have his head for such an offer... In short, I forced this criminal to drop his idea."

"A man like that shouldn't be left alive!" Pan Korf cried out. "He deserves the stake!"

Boguslav nodded and turned towards the Hetman.

"I think so too," he said. "And I hope that he won't die an ordinary death when he is tried and punished. Your Highness alone can bring him to justice because he falls under your jurisdiction as one of your colonels."

"Mine?" Yanush cried out. "Who is he? Speak up, Your Highness! What's his name?"

"His name is Kmita!" Boguslav said firmly.

"Kmita?" all the others echoed in fear and horror.

"Kmita," Boguslav nodded.

"That's a lie!" cried Olenka, rising from her chair with her entire body trembling in emotion and with an angry light burning in her eyes.

* * *

A deathly silence fell at once on the gathering. Some of the supper guests were still too stunned by Boguslav's terrible revelation. Others were frightened and amazed by Olenka's daring in throwing a lie into the young magnate's face. The old constable started babbling weakly, "*Olenka... Olenka...*" and Boguslav's face took on a stricken and regretful look.

"If he's a relative or fiance of yours," he said gently and with obvious pity, "then I'm truly sorry that I had to bring you such terrible news about him. But banish him from your heart, my lady. He's not worth your caring."

She stood a moment longer in pain, terror and revulsion, but gradually the hot flush of anger ebbed out of her face and it became as white, set and frozen as if all life had seeped from her body.

"Forgive me, Highness," she said at last and dropped back into her chair. "I shouldn't have doubted you... That man is capable... of anything."

"He was this lady's fiance," Prince Yanush explained, nodding around the table. "In fact I tried to make a match for them myself. He's a young, mindless fellow, a wild hothead if ever there was one, and he has more than one criminal verdict hanging over him. I tried to shield him from the law because he's a good soldier, needed in these times... But for a nobleman to stoop as low as this! I didn't expect this even from that ruffian!"

"He was an evil man," Ganhof threw in quickly. "I knew it all along!"

"And you didn't warn me?" Prince Yanush asked in a reproachful tone.

"I didn't want Your Highness to think I was speaking out of spite since he always took precedence here over me."

"*Horribile dictu et auditu,*" Pan Korf intoned in Latin. "It's just as awful to say it as it is to hear it."

"Gentlemen!" Boguslav cried out. "Let us drop this subject! If it is hard for you to hear about this dreadful thing, think what it must be doing to Panna Billevitchovna!"

"Your Highness need not be concerned about me," Olenka said coldly. "I can listen to it all from now on."

But the dinner was running to its close. The valets brought bowls of scented water so that the diners could wash their hands. Then Prince Yanush rose and offered his arm to Madame Korf while Boguslav did the same thing for Olenka.

"God has already punished the traitor," he told her. "Because whoever loses you loses his hopes of Heaven... It's been a mere two hours since I've met you, gracious lady, but I would rather see you in happiness and joy than in pain and sorrow."

"I thank Your Highness," Olenka said calmly.

★ ★ ★

After the ladies adjourned, the men returned to the table to continue drinking. Prince Boguslav drank mindlessly. He guzzled like a drover. He had every reason, he believed, to be delighted with himself while Prince Yanush chatted with the Constable of Rosyen.

"I'm leaving for Podlasye with the troops tomorrow," he told the old man. "Keydany will get a Swedish garrison. It's neither safe nor right for your girl to be here with all that foreign soldiery, so you'll both go with Prince Boguslav to Taurogen where she can find a place among my wife's women."

"Your Highness," the old constable replied. "God gave us our own four walls. Why should we travel to a foreign country? It's a great kindness on your part to think of us but I don't want to put any further strain on your goodwill. We'd rather go back where we belong."

The Prince couldn't explain to Pan Tomasz exactly why he had to have Olenka in his hands at whatever price. But some of his reasons could be told and he did so with all the abrupt, autocratic bluntness of a magnate.

"If you want to think of it as kindness, so much the better. But it's also a political necessity. You'll be my hostage there for the good behavior of all the Billevitches. I know very well what they think about me and that they're ready to stir up a rebellion against me once I'm gone from Zmudya. Pass them the word to sit still at home and don't start anything with the Swedes or you and your grand-niece will answer for it with your heads."

But this was too much for the proud old noble, no matter how cautious he preferred to be.

"There's not much point in claiming the protection of the statutes!" he cried out. "Your Highness has the power to do what he likes! As for me, I'd as soon sit in prison there as here, if that makes a difference!"

"Silence! That's enough!" the Prince said in a threatening tone.

"Yes, it *is* enough!" the old noble shouted. "God will see to it that these outrages come to a quick end and that we return to the rule of law. In short, save your threats, Your Illustrious Highness, because I don't fear them!"

But Boguslav had caught sight of the wrathful lightnings gathering in the Hetman's eyes and moved swiftly towards the two angry men.

"What's wrong?" he asked.

"I told the Hetman that I'd rather sit in the Taurogen dungeons than the ones he keeps here!" Pan Tomasz snapped back.

"Taurogen is no dungeon," Boguslav said quickly. "It's my home. You'll be as comfortable there, good sir, as if you were sitting by your own fireside. I know that the Hetman sees you as a hostage but for me you're only a welcome guest."

"I thank Your Highness," the old man replied.

"No, no, it's I who thank you. Let's have a drink together, you and I. Friendship, they say, is a frail plant which has to be watered or it'll wither at the roots."

Smiling, Boguslav led the constable to the refreshments table where they started clinking their goblets, toasting each other, and drinking to each other's health. An hour later the old man made his unsteady way back to his own quarters, muttering as he went.

"What a kind, thoughtful lord! Decent, good, compassionate... You wouldn't find a better or more honest man if you went looking for one with a lantern... Pure gold, I say, pure gold... I'd be glad to spill my blood for him..."

* * *

Meanwhile the two Radzivills were left alone together. Their own discussion wasn't over yet. Moreover, a package of letters had arrived from somewhere while they were at dinner and now they sent a page to get them from Ganhof.

"Of course there wasn't a word of truth in what you said?" Prince Yanush asked. "I mean about Kmita?"

"Of course there wasn't. You know that better than anyone. But admit it, wasn't Mazarin right in what he said about me? Eh? Who else could wreak such cruel vengeance on an enemy and, with the same stroke, make a breach in that beautiful little fortress? That's what intrigue is all about! Say it! Wouldn't my ploy do credit to the most subtle courtiers in the world? Ah, but what a pearl she is, that Billevitch snippet... What a rare beauty! I thought I'd jump out of my own skin!"

"Just remember what you promised me. We'll be lost if that fellow publishes those letters."

But Boguslav had warmer matters on his mind. "What eyes!" he cried. "What a regal glance! It's almost enough for me to treat her with respect. Where does that girl get that lofty dignity? That majestic bearing? One time, in Antwerp, I saw a tapestry picturing Diana setting her dogs on Acteon... She's a spitting image!"

"Remember those letters," Prince Yanush reminded. "Or it'll be us that the dogs go after."

"On the contrary! It's Kmita whom I'll turn into an Acteon and hound him to death. I've struck him down twice already and that's just a start."

* * *

Just then a page entered with a letter, putting an end to further conversation.

The *Voyevode* of Vilna took the sealed package in his hand and made the sign of the cross over it, which he always did as a safeguard against disquieting news. But instead of opening it at once, he started to turn it over in his hands, studying the seals. Then his face darkened.

"There's a Sapyeha crest on the seal!" he cried out. "This is from the *Voyevode* of Vitebsk!"

"So hurry up and open it!" Prince Boguslav said.

The Hetman ripped open the package and began to read, interrupting himself with angry exclamations.

"He's going to Podlasye! He wants to know if there's something he can do for me in Tikotzin! He is jeering at me! Ah, it's even worse than that! Listen to what else he says!"

"*Does Your Highness want a Civil War?*" the Hetman read aloud. "*Do you want to plunge yet another sword into our Mother's breast? Then come to Podlasye! I'm waiting for you, confident that God will punish your pride and ambition with my hand...*"

The Hetman cursed out loud, swelling up in fury, and continued reading.

"... *But if you've any mercy on our Motherland, if you've a shred of conscience left at your disposal, if you regret what you've already done and want to make amends, then call out the General Levy, arm the peasantry, and strike the Swedes while the unsuspecting Pontus still thinks himself secure. Hovansky won't get in your way because as I hear from Moscow, the Russians are sharpening their teeth for the Swedish holdings on our side of the Baltic, although they're still anxious to keep it a secret. But even if he does start something I'll hold him at bay while you attack the Swedes. And, if I can trust Your Highness' change of heart, I'll do all I can to help you in saving our country.*

"... *It's all up to you, Your Illustrious Highness,*"the letter went on. "*You still have time to change course and show the world that you accepted Charles Gustav's protection only to save Lithuania in her last extremity, and not, as has been evident heretofore, to satisfy your personal ambitions. May God inspire Your Highness to that end, which is what I pray for every day, even though you choose to view me as your enemy who acts against you out of jealousy and envy.*"

Then there was a postscript.

"*I hear that the Russians have given up their siege of Nesvyejh and that Prince Michael intends to join my forces just as soon as he repairs the damage. See how the decent members of your family behave, take them for your example, and remember that this may be your last opportunity.*"

"You heard all that?" Prince Yanush asked when he finished reading.

"I did. And what of it?"

"We'd have to renounce all our hopes, give up everything we want, and tear up our work with our own hands..."

"And start a quarrel with the powerful Charles Gustav," Boguslav said scornfully. "Go down on our knees to the exiled Yan Casimir to beg his forgiveness so that he might allow us to remain his servants... and plead with Pan Sapyeha to intercede for us. Is that what you want?"

The Hetman's features were suffused with blood. "Note how he writes to me. '*Change your ways and I'll forgive you.*' Like a superior to his underling!"

"He'd take a different tone if he had six thousand sabers hanging over his neck."

"Nevertheless...." And Prince Yanush began to ponder deeply.

"Nevertheless what?" Boguslav demanded.

"It might save the country to do what Sapyeha advises."

"And what will it do for the Radzivills?"

Yanush said nothing then. He let his head rest on his clasped fists, his arms on the table.

"So be it!" he cried out at last. "Let it happen if that's what has to happen!"

"What have you decided?"

"Tomorrow I set out for Podlasye and in a week I'll strike at Sapyeha."

"Spoken like a true Radzivill!" Prince Boguslav said and the two cousins grasped each other's hands.

Soon afterwards Boguslav went to bed. Yanush was left alone. He paced heavily up and down his chamber and then clapped his hands to summon a valet.

"Send my astrologer here," he said to the servant. "I want to see his latest calculations in an hour."

The lackey left and the Prince resumed his heavy pacing, reciting his Calvinist prayers as he moved. Then he began to sing a psalm, singing it softly and interrupting it from time to time for lack of breath, as he glanced now and then through the windows at the stars that glittered overhead.

The castle darkened as the lights went out one by one and soon only one other person, beside the Prince and his astrologer, still remained awake.

Olenka knelt in prayer in her room. Her head was bowed. Her hands were clasped before her face and her eyes were closed.

"Have mercy on us," she pleaded. "Have mercy."

And for the first time since Kmita left Keydany, she neither could nor wanted to say a prayer for him.

Part Nine

Chapter Fifty-five

ALTHOUGH PAN KMITA carried the Grand Hetman's letters of safe-conduct, which he could show the Swedish captains, commandants and administrators in all the districts through which he had to pass, he had no safe way of making use of them. He expected that Prince Boguslav would have dispatched mounted messengers just as soon as he returned to Pilvishkye, warning the Swedes everywhere to be on their lookout, and ordering them to seize and hold Andrei Kmita at all costs.

Changing his name and station would help, he knew, as would the wide circle that he and his supposed drovers inscribed around the towns of Lomza and Ostrolenka where Boguslav's warning might have come the soonest.

He set his course for Warsaw through Prasnitch and Pultusk, going the long way round through Vonsosh, Kolno and Myshinyetz, partly because the Kemlitches knew their way through the local forests and in part because they had their dealings with the region's Kurpian population from whom they could get help in case of some unexpected trouble.

The countryside along the border between Prussia and the old Palatine of Mazovia was, for the most part, occupied by the Swedes who, however, confined themselves to garrisoning the more important towns. They kept their distance from the vast, trackless wilderness in whose primeval shadows lived a well-armed, dour and suspicious folk who resented strangers and who never ventured out of their leafy fastness. The Kurpian forest-dwellers were still considered so primitive in those days that the Queen, the French-born Marie-Louise of Poland, had a chapel built in Myshinyetz just the year before, and invited Jesuits to take charge of it, so that they could bring both the Faith and a gentler way of life to the fierce inhabitants of the wilderness.

"The longer we don't come across the Swedes the better for us," old Kemlitch said as they rode along.

"Sooner or later we have to come upon them," Pan Andrei replied.

"Whoever comes on them near a bigger town doesn't have much to worry about," the old marauder lectured. "A town always has some kind of law in it, and some commandant who'll hear a complaint. I've been asking people about this and I know that the Swedish King won't allow any lawlessness or looting in these parts. But the smaller forage parties or patrols, operating out in the countryside where the commandants can't watch them, don't pay much attention to their orders and strip everybody of everything they can take."

So Kmita and his party made their way through the deep, silent woods, meeting no Swedes anywhere and halting for the night near scattered little settlements and homesteads. Although almost none of the Kurpic folk had ever seen a Swede, they told the strangest tales about them. Some said they were a particularly greedy tribe of people—as fierce and hungry as forest wolves in Winter—who came from across the sea, didn't understand human speech, didn't believe in Christ and had a special hatred for the Holy Mother and the saints. Others told about their odd appetite for cattle, skins, nuts, honey and dried mushrooms which they demanded on the threat of setting the woods on fire. Yet others claimed that, on the contrary, Swedes were werewolves hungry for human flesh and the flesh of young virgins in particular.

These threatening rumors spread throughout the wilderness like wildfire, seeping into the deepest and darkest corners of the virgin forests, so that the Kurpians started to band together, sniffing the wind for trouble that was sure to come. The pitch and potash makers, hop-pickers, woodsmen, lumberjacks, and the fisherfolk who set their seines along the overgrown banks of the Rosog River, along with all the bird-catchers, hunters, beekeepers and trappers, began to gather in the larger clearings, listening to the tales, passing news and comments, and planning how to ambush and destroy those strange enemies in the event that they ever set foot among their trees.

Kmita and his party often came across groups of these forest people, all of them dressed in homespun shirts, tanned leggings, and the furs of foxes, wolves and bears, who barred the way on the winding paths and in the hidden clearings.

"Who are you?" they'd demand. "Not Swedes?"

"No!" Pan Andrei assured them.

"Then God keep you."

Pan Andrei looked with great curiosity at these forest dwellers who lived in the perpetual darkness of the trees, seldom seeing sunlight. He was particularly struck by their height and bearing, the sharp challenge he read in all their eyes, and the brisk confidence with which they faced a stranger. They were, he had no doubt, like no peasants he had ever seen.

The Kemlitches, who knew them well, assured him that there weren't any finer sharpshooters in the Commonwealth. All of them, he noted, carried good German flintlocks which they got in Prussia in exchange for furs. Their marksmanship amazed him whenever he had them put on a show for him.

'If I ever have to get some partisans together,' he thought. 'This is where I'll come.'

* * *

In the forest settlement of Myshinyetz itself, Kmita found a large Kurpian gathering. More than a hundred marksmen stood watch over the chapel and the mission, fearing that the Godless Swedes would come there first, since the *Starosta* of Ostrolenka had a road cut into the forest so that the priests could have some access to the world beyond. The hop-pickers, who carried their produce as far as the famous breweries of Prasnitch, and thus had the reputation of world travelers, told him that Lomza, Ostrolenka and Prasnitch were crowded with Swedes who'd made themselves as much at home there as if it were Sweden. Kmita began to urge the Kurpians not to wait for the Swedes but to strike them first, and offered to lead them against Ostrolenka, but a pair of priests talked them out of it. To start a war before the rest of the country stirred itself to action would only bring a terrible vengeance on the forest people, the missionaries told

them. But it had been close. The fierce, hardy woodsmen
could hardly wait to start their own war.

Pan Andrei rode on, sorry about this lost opportunity. But he
was encouraged by the thought that neither the King nor the
Commonwealth would lack defenders here later on if the flames
of resistance started somewhere else. '*If that's how things are going
elsewhere,*' he thought. '*A start could be made almost any time.*'

His hot, impatient nature urged him to instant action but
logic called for patience. These forest folk won't beat the
Swedes all by themselves, he reasoned. I'll see a lot of country
before I am finished. I'll watch and listen and then I'll do
whatever the King orders.

And he kept on riding.

Once he was out of the depths of the wilderness and in the
thicker-settled country that bordered the forests, he noted an
extraordinary commotion in the villages. The roads and highways were packed with gentry traveling in their *britchkas*, charabancs, coaches and on horseback to swear allegiance to their new
masters in the larger towns. In exchange they got certificates
that were supposed to protect them and their properties. Meanwhile, in all the territorial capitals and county seats, Swedish
military governors issued sonorous decrees guaranteeing their
freedom of religion and all the old privileges of the Polish
gentry.

The country squires hurried with their pledges more out of
caution than commitment because refusal brought retribution in
the form of confiscations and open, ordinary pillage. The
Swedes were already torturing people suspected of ill-will towards them in Mazovia, as they had been doing in Vyelkopolska
from the start, by screwing their fingers into the firing mechanism of a flintlock musket. The air was rife with rumors that
suspicion was often thrown on purpose on the wealthier gentry
as an excuse for looting.

All this added up to general conviction that it was just too
dangerous to stay in the countryside and the landowners poured
into the cities, where sitting under the watchful eye of Swedish
commandants, they wouldn't be suspected of plots against the
Swedes.

★   ★   ★

Pan Andrei paid close attention to the gentry's mutterings and gossip even though not too many of them wanted to talk to him. His disguise as a horse-drover and country-fair peddler—which was the bottom rung of their social scale—made him their inferior. But he was quick to note everywhere he halted that not even close neighbors or friends who'd known each other all their lives spoke openly to each other about the Swedes.

True, everyone complained about the requisitions. Not even Swedes could take offense at that because every small town and village was ordered to supply great stores of grain, cattle, bread, salt and money which added up to far more than anyone could spare. Whoever failed to meet his quota, having paid all he could once or twice already, found his allotment tripled without appeal.

The gentry groaned, complained, sighed and even wept when they talked about this. But they didn't sound convincing even to themselves. All of them were skimping on everything they could, denying themselves every luxury to meet these exactions, and thinking that things used to be a lot different not so long ago. They looked for comfort in the hope that these draconic measures would end with the war. The Swedes themselves assured them that their new King would rule them with a father's kindness once he had the entire country under his control.

The truth, however—as Pan Andrei's sharp eyes and ears noted soon enough—was that these harassed and worried country squires were simply too ashamed to voice their worst complaints. They had abandoned their King and their country of their own free will. Just a few months earlier they heaped their curses on the kindly and benevolent Yan Casimir, calling him a tyrant and suspecting him of trying to impose an absolute monarchy upon them. They fought him tooth and nail in the Diets and the dietines, protesting every measure he proposed that might strengthen the government of the country, and they were so impatient for something new and exotic in their lives that they accepted an invader with practically no resistance.

Their complaints, under those circumstances, sounded weak and hollow. Hadn't Charles Gustav freed them from their 'tyrant?' Didn't they have the changes they had wanted? And weren't their new burdens piled on their shoulders by the choices they had made themselves?

None of them dared to say what they really thought about the new order, giving a glad ear to those who assured them that the raiding sweeps, requisitions, pillage and confiscations were merely temporary and that they'd end once Charles Gustav found himself comfortably settled on the Polish throne.

"Ey, it's a hard life for us now, brother," some squire would mutter to another in Pan Andrei's hearing. "But, even so, we ought to be glad to have such a ruler. He's a great warrior. He'll clip the Cossacks' wings, check the Turks, drive the Russians out of the country's borders... And then we'll thrive here along with the Swedes."

"And even if somebody wanted to go against the tide," the other replied. "What could he do against such a power? It'd be like trying to bury the sun with a garden hoe."

Sometimes they found refuge from their own consciences in the oaths they'd taken to their new allegiance.

Kmita raged in silence when he heard that kind of reasoning and once, in a country tavern, when some sanctimonious noble stated that he had no choice but to uphold whichever King he'd sworn to obey and follow, Pan Andrei couldn't contain himself any longer.

"Then you must have two mouths in your head!" he shouted. "One for the oaths you keep and one for those you break! Because you swore your loyalty to Yan Casimir as well!"

* * *

This happened near Prasnitch, with a swarm of local gentry sitting in the tavern, all of whom stirred uneasily when they heard Kmita's insult. Some of them looked in awe at this bold intruder who didn't mince his words. Others flushed in shame and stared at the floor. At last the oldest and most distinguished-looking one among them said that Yan Casimir himself absolved them of their pledges.

"Nobody here broke his oath to the former King. He freed us from it when he left the country without giving any thought to its defense."

"May God strike you dead!" Kmita shouted at him, no longer able to restrain himself. "And how many times did King Vladyslav Lokietek have to flee the country? And yet he came back, didn't he, because we were still a Godfearing people then and the nation didn't turn its back on him! It wasn't Yan Casimir who abandoned us but the traitors who first abandoned him, and who now snap and snarl at him to whitewash their own guilt in the eyes of God and living men alike!"

"You're a sight too free with your mouth, young fellow," the grave old noble said. "Who are you to teach us the fear of God? Where did you spring from, Mister? Take care the Swedes don't hear you!"

"I'll tell you where I'm from, since you want to know," Pan Andrei snapped back. "I make my home in Prussia under the Elector. But since I've some Polish blood in my veins I'm fond of this country and I'm ashamed of the stone-hearted people who live here these days."

A quick curiosity, much stronger than whatever shame or anger the gentry might have felt, appeared in their faces and they surrounded the supposed East Prussian with their eager questions.

"So you're from Prussia, are you? So what's happening there? What's the Elector doing? Is he thinking of rescuing us from our oppression here?"

"What oppression?" Kmita barked at them. "Aren't you pleased with your new masters, after all? As you've made your beds so you'll sleep in them, remember?"

"We're pleased because we don't have any other choice. They've got a sword hanging over us. But you can speak to us as if we weren't pleased."

"Give him a drink, somebody, to loosen his tongue!" one of them called out. "Speak boldly, young fellow. You won't find any traitors here."

"You're all traitors here! Lick-spittles! Gutless wonders! I won't drink with Swedish errand-boys and lackeys!" Pan Andrei shouted and slammed out of the tavern.

He left behind a stunned and shamefaced silence. But no one there seized a saber to avenge the insult. No one followed him outside. No one stirred.

★   ★   ★

He, in the meantime, set out straight for Prasnitch but a

Swedish patrol picked him up a few furlongs outside the town and led him to the local commandant.

There were only six Reiters and a corporal in that small detachment so that Soroka and the three Kemlitches started to stare at them greedily, licking their lips like wolves near a sheepfold, and then questioned Kmita with their eyes to see if he'd permit a little bloodletting.

Pan Andrei was sorely tempted, especially since the Vengyerka River flowed close by, its banks thickly overgrown with concealing rushes, but he restrained himself and let the Swedes take him to their commander. There he identified himself as a subject of the Brandenburg Elector and said that he was on his annual drive to the Sobota horse fair. The Kemlitches also showed some references they picked up in Elk where they had good connections, but the commandant—a German from East Prussia in his own right—didn't cause them any difficulties anyway. He only questioned them at length about their livestock and asked to see the horses they were driving.

"I'll take them off your hands," he said to Kmita once he had looked them over. "I'd requisition them for nothing if you were a local, but I'll pay *you* since you're a fellow Prussian. How much?"

Kmita was thrown off stride. A sale would remove his pretext for traveling farther and oblige him to head north again. He gave such an inflated price that it was clearly twice as much as the animals were worth but, to his surprise, the officer neither argued with him nor haggled for a bargain.

"Fine," he said. "Drive them into the shed and I'll get your money."

The Kemlitches grinned from ear to ear, pleased to make such an enormous profit, but Kmita was beside himself with rage and began to curse. He had no choice but to drive the horses where he was told to drive them or fall under suspicion.

Meanwhile the officer came back from his quarters with a piece of scribbled paper in his hand.

"What's that?" said Pan Andrei.

"Your money. Or as good as money. It's your sales receipt."

"And where do I get paid?"

"At General Headquarters."

"And where's that?"

"In Warsaw," the officer said with a malicious smile.

"How? What? Where?" old Kemlitch began to whine and wring his hands. "We only trade for money...! Ready cash...! Oh Holy Gates of Heaven...!"

But Kmita turned a fierce glare at him and cowed him into silence. "The commandant's word is good enough for me," he said. "We don't mind going on to Warsaw, do we? We can find some fine goods in the Armenian Quarter to sell at a profit back home in Prussia, right?"

And when the commandant left them, Kmita found a few words of comfort for the greedy old man as well.

"Quiet, you skinflint," he growled in his ear. "This receipt is better than a pass! We can travel as far as Krakow if we have to, complaining all the way that we can't get our money anywhere. It's easier to squeeze water from a stone than cash from a Swede, but that suits me right down to the ground. This numbskull thinks he made fools out of us, but he has no idea what a service he just rendered to us... As for the nags, I'll pay you out of my own pocket so that you don't feel swindled."

The old man heaved a vast sigh of relief and went on complaining for a while longer only out of habit. "They robbed us... ruined us! Turned us into beggars..."

But Pan Andrei was pleased with the way it had all turned out. In fact he was delighted. He now had every reasonable excuse to go wherever he wanted. He was quite sure that no one would pay him for the sale in Warsaw, or anywhere else, and that he'd be able to travel to the farthest corners of the country in search of his money, even as far as Krakow where Charles Gustav himself was besieging the ancient capital.

★ ★ ★

In the meantime Pan Andrei stopped for the night in Prasnitch. His own mounts needed rest. He also decided to change his status to something higher than a poor horse trader because, as he'd noted, nobody showed him much consideration in his low disguise. Furthermore, it was hard to hobnob with the wealthier gentry and pump them for news, and it was easier to get robbed or cheated, since no one—Swedes or his countrymen alike—would worry much about the protests of a poor man from some rustic hamlet who eked out a living at the horse fairs. It was also harder for him to discover what his own class of people felt and thought.

He kept his false name but dressed himself more suitably to his place in life and made his way to the taverns among the local gentry. But he found no reason to like what he saw and heard. His brother gentry drank to the health of the Swedish King, clinked goblets with ranking Swedes, and laughed at the jokes the officers made about Yan Casimir and Pan Tcharnyetzki in Krakow. Fear for their own skins had so corrupted all these country nobles that they turned themselves into fawning jesters to amuse invaders.

But even this abysmal fall into their mean-spirited wretchedness and debasement had, apparently, some limits here and there. The gentry allowed jeering jokes about themselves, the King, the Polish Hetmans and even Pan Tcharnyetzki, but not about their Faith; and when some Swedish captain said in that Prasnitch tavern that his Lutheran religion was as good or better than the Church of Rome, a youngish man named Grabkowski who sat next to him struck him in the head with an iron mace, dived into the crowd, and escaped in the ensuing chaos.

Troopers went running after him at once but then something happened to turn everyone's attention into other channels. Couriers ran up with news that Krakow had fallen, that Pan Tcharnyetzki was taken prisoner, and that the last resistance to Swedish rule was over.

The drinking gentry were dumbstruck for a moment. But the Swedes cheered, rejoicing. They ordered church bells rung in the Chapel of the Holy Spirit and in the church and convent of the Bernardines, which Lady Mostovska, wife of the Palatine of Mazovia, founded not long before.

Swedish infantry and Reiters trooped in battle order out of their quarters in the breweries and sheep-shearing sheds. Cannon and musketry thundered in salutes. Barrels of mead, beer and home-brewed *gojhalka* were rolled out into the square and a wild celebration spread into the night. The Swedes dragged the burghers' wives and daughters out of their homes to dance with them in the streets, and crowds of shaken gentry wandered about among these mobs of howling soldiery, drinking with the troopers, and trying to look pleased with the fall of Krakow and Pan Tcharnyetzki's capture.

Sickened by all this, Kmita took early refuge in his quarters at the edge of town but he couldn't sleep. Feverish doubts gnawed at him, asking whether he hadn't changed his course too late now that the whole western, northern and southwestern portion of the country lay in Swedish hands. It seemed to him that everything was lost and that the Commonwealth would never lift itself out of this defeat.

'*This is no longer just a lost campaign,*' he thought in shame and horror. '*The kind that might end with the loss of one territory or another. This is an absolute disaster in which the Commonwealth itself becomes a Swedish province. Moreover, we did this to ourselves! And I contributed to it more than anyone!*'

Such thoughts burned him like fire. His conscience gnawed at him. Sleep fled beyond his reach. He didn't know what he should do next. Go back? Stay where he was? Go on? And even if he tried to get a troop of partisans together to harass the Swedes, he'd be hunted down like a common footpad, not fought as a soldier.

'*Besides,*' he thought helplessly: '*Who'd join me? I'm in a strange province. Nobody knows me here*'

Fierce fighters used to flock to him in the Lithuanian country where his famous name guaranteed victories and riches. But here, even if someone had heard about Kmita, they'd think him a traitor and friend of the Swedes. And who had ever heard of any Babinitch?

'*Too late,*' he thought. '*It's all been for nothing. It's too late to try to reach the King. Nor is there any point in going to Podlasye either because as far as the confederates are concerned I am still a traitor. No point in going back to Lithuania because that's Radzivill country now and there is no one left alive there who could challenge him.*'

Neither could he stay where he was because there was nothing he could accomplish among the downcast, dispirited Mazovians.

'*The best thing for me would be just to die,*' he thought. '*Stop struggling. Give up the ghost so that I won't have to look at this dreadful world, and put an end to all my misery.*'

But what kind of afterlife could he expect in that other world, arriving to God's Judgment with all his crimes unpaid for, his soul stained with sins, and without having done anything to make amends? Kmita threw himself about on his bed as if his room were a torture chamber. He hadn't undergone such torments even when he lay wounded and defeated in the Kemlitch hideout. He knew himself to be strong, healthy, enterprising and craving action with all his heart and soul. But what could he do with all his avenues of choice shuttered tight against him? Even if he hammered a hole in the wall with his own head he wouldn't find an exit, he was sure! Nothing could save him. He could see no hope.

★ ★ ★

After a night of sleepless suffering he leaped off his bed at dawn, woke his men, and set off straight ahead wherever the road would take him. The highway led towards Warsaw but he didn't know why he was going there. In other times he might have fled to the Zaporohjan Sietch, to hide among the Cossacks in the Wildlands, but those times were gone. In fact Hmyelnitzki's Cossacks and Buturlin's Russians had just recently squeezed Pan Pototzki, the Polish Grand Hetman, to the wall at Grodek in Polish Ruthenia, carrying their fire and sword into the southeastern territories of the Commonwealth herself, and sending their plundering hordes as far west as Lublin.

Everywhere on the Pultusk highway Pan Andrei met detachments of Swedish cavalry escorting wagons loaded with provisions, wheat, baked breads and barrels of beer, along with herds of livestock driven in their wake. Clusters of peasants and small rural gentry, all of them uttering plaintive cries and some of them in tears, walked with the carts and cattle. It was a lucky man among them, Kmita was told, who'd find his way home with his unloaded dray; it was more likely for the Swedes to round up these wretches for forced labor on various castle walls, and the construction of storehouses and sheds for the loot they brought.

He also noted that the closer he got to Pultusk, and the deeper he found himself in occupied country, the fiercer and more ruthless was the Swedes' behavior towards their Polish subjects.

"Why is that?" he questioned some of the gentry he met on his way. "They're not that bad up in Lithuania."

"The nearer you'll come to Warsaw," one of them informed

him, "the more cruelty you'll see. They are much kinder when they first occupy some region and before they've secured themselves behind castle walls. That's when they promulgate their decrees against exploitation and pay some notice to their guarantees of fair play and justice. But wherever they feel safe already, or wherever they've garrisoned some fortress, there you find them playing another tune. That's when they break all their promises, show no consideration to anyone, rob and steal and pillage the whole countryside, loot churches and convents, and even lay their hands on the clergy and the nuns. All this that you see here is nothing, though, compared to what is happening in Vyelkopolska proper. There are no words in the language for what's going on there."

Here the noble launched into an account of cruelty and repression in Vyelkopolian territories, listing robbery, looting and acts of violence. He told about makeshift thumbscrews and the other tortures with which the avaricious enemy squeezed the last penny out of the peoples' coffers. He also told about the murder of Father Branetzki, the Provincial of Poznan, in his own cathedral.

"As for how they treat the common people," he said. "All your hair would stand on end if you heard about it. It'll be like that everywhere soon. It's God's judgment on us. The Last Trumpet can't be far away. Life is more terrible every day and there is no help anywhere in sight."

"I'm a stranger here," Kmita said. "And I don't know how people feel about things in these parts. But how can all you gentry put up with all this, being knights and quality?"

"And what are we supposed to resist with?" the noble replied. "Tell me, what? They've all the castles, fortresses, cannon, muskets and gunpowder while we can't even have a bird-gun in the house. We still had some hope while Pan Tcharnyetzki was fighting them in Krakow. But when he's in chains, and the King is in exile in Silesia, how can anyone think about resistance? Yes, we have hands but there is nothing in them. Nor is there anyone to lead us."

"Nor is there hope," Kmita's own dull and empty voice supplied a gloomy echo.

* * *

They rode in silence after that because they'd come within sight and hearing of a Swedish convoy surrounding yet another stream of drays and footsore petty gentry.

It was a strange sight, Kmita thought. The mustached, beefy Reiters sat on glossy horses that were as fat with oats as pampered prize bulls. Each of them rode in a cloud of goosedown and chicken feathers, with his right hand cocked proudly at the hip, heads high, hats canted in a fierce, swashbuckling manner, and with dozens of hens and geese dangling from their saddles. It was easy to guess, looking at the haughty stares that glared out of these cruel, warrior faces, how safe, how powerful, and how pleased with themselves they felt. Stumbling along beside them in the dust, with their heads hanging in hopelessness and despair, walked the cowed and browbeaten local petty gentry, some of them shoeless and all of them terrorized and fearful, whom the Swedes urged along with harsh shouts and horsewhips.

Kmita's lips quivered at this sight as if in a fever and he started hissing over and over to the noble with whom he was riding: "My hands itch, my hands itch, my hands itch!"

"Quiet, for God's sake!" the noble whispered. "Quiet! Or you'll bring disaster on yourself! And on me and my poor children too!"

But sometimes there was an even stranger sight encountered on these highways: large groups of singing, celebrating, drunken Polish gentry, with companies of armed servants trudging along in the dust behind them, riding beside the enemy foraging detachments and treated by the Swedes and Germans as if they were brothers.

"How's that, then?" Kmita asked. "They torment and oppress some gentry and make friends with others? Who are those people I see among the Reiters? They must be the worst kind of Judases and turncoats."

"Not only turncoats," the noble told him. "But heretics as well. They squeeze Catholics harder than the Swedes themselves. Their time has come, you see. They pillage, burn, loot, rob, abduct girls and wreak their vengeance on the rest of us with absolute immunity. It's easier to get a court judgment against a Swede than one of our own homemade heretics these days. Any local commandant will tell you, as soon as you've uttered a breath of complaint: '*I've no right to touch him. He's your man, not mine. Go to your own tribunals.'* And what kind of courts do we have these days when everything is controlled by the Swedes? Who'd execute a verdict? Where a Swede can't find his way alone a heretic will lead him, and there's no one like them for oppressing the clergy and the Church. That's how they pay their Motherland for years of safe refuge and the freedom to practice their blasphemous religions, when in just about every other country they'd be hounded and persecuted even to the stake..."

But here the noble cut himself short and peered uneasily at Kmita beside him. "Ah... but didn't you tell me you were from East Prussia? Maybe you're a Lutheran yourself?"

"God save me from anything like that," Pan Andrei replied. "Yes, I'm from Prussia but my family comes from Lithuania and we've been Catholics for centuries."

"Thank God for that. I got really worried for a moment there... But, speaking of Lithuania, they've a lot of dissidents of their own, including their chieftain, the all-powerful Radzivill himself, who proved a worse renegade than anyone. Only Radeyovski can match him as a traitor."

"May the devils drag his soul out of his throat before the New Year!" Kmita shouted fiercely.

"Amen to that," the noble said. "And the same to those bloody-handed servants, helpers and hangmen of his, about whom we've heard even here, and without whose wholehearted assistance he wouldn't have dared to turn against his country."

* * *

Kmita grew pale and didn't say a word. He didn't ask—indeed, he didn't dare—what hangmen and assistants the noble had in mind.

Riding at a slow, unhurried pace, they came to Pultusk late in the evening, and Kmita was summoned at once to the Bishop's palace which served as the area commandant's headquarters, to give an account of himself.

"I supply remounts to the armies of his Swedish Majesty," he told the Swedish colonel. "And I've receipts on which to collect in Warsaw."

The colonel, whose name was Izrael, chuckled under his flared Reiter mustache.

"Oh, then you should hurry," he said with an ironic grin. "You should waste no time collecting your money. Just make sure you bring a good, strong wagon to carry all that gold."

"Thanks for your kind advice," Pan Andrei said. "I know that Your Excellency is having a little joke at my expense. But I'll go after my dues anyway, even if I have to go to His Majesty himself!"

"Go, go," the Swede urged, grinning all the while. "Stick to your guns. Don't give up what's yours. You've quite a nice sum coming to you, ha ha!"

"There'll be a time when you pay me everything you owe," Kmita said departing.

Outside, he found himself in the middle of a celebration because the Swedes had ordered that the fall of Krakow was to be commemorated by a public holiday that was to last three days. He found out, however, that the news he'd heard in Prasnitch was exaggerated; the Swedish triumph wasn't quite as total as had been reported. The Castellan of Kiev wasn't a prisoner at all. He'd marched out of the city with full military honors, taking his troops and cannon, and it was generally supposed that he would join the exiled Yan Casimir in Silesia. It wasn't much of a comfort, Pan Andrei thought, but it was better than it could have been.

Pultusk housed a powerful Swedish force which Colonel Izrael was to march to the Prussian border to put some fear into the Elector, so that neither the town, nor its suburbs, nor the spacious castle could contain them all, and—for the first of many such occasions—Kmita saw mercenaries quartered in a church. Inside the magnificent Gothic cathedral, founded more than two hundred years before by Bishop Gizhitzki, lay a regiment of hired German infantry. The vast nave was aglow with light, as if for Resurrection Sunday, because great cooking fires burned all along the floor. Cauldrons smoked and steamed in the open flames. Crowds of foreign soldiers, consisting for the most part of veteran pillagers who had plundered all of Catholic Germany, milled around breached vats of beer with a carelessness suggesting that this wasn't the first time they bivouacked in a holy place. The walls echoed with shouts, cries, calls and the growling mutter of a thousand voices. Hoarse throats were singing coarse camp-songs and ditties among the shrill screams and giggles of unkempt, screeching women who flocked behind the armies in those times.

Kmita stood numb with horror in the open entrance. He saw coarse, mustached faces made crimson with liquor. He peered through the smoke at the scarlet fires, at the hired mercenaries who sprawled or sat everywhere around on the kegs and barrels; he watched them swigging beer under the high altar, throwing dice, and gambling with cards. He saw others clutching at the screeching, brightly costumed harlots. Yet others haggled over looted vestments and sacred vessels amid wild howls, screams of women's laughter, the clash of tankards and the clatter of musket butts and spears.

The harsh echoes booming in the arches overhead deafened him until his head was reeling. His eyes refused to accept what they saw. All the air went out of his lungs and he couldn't breathe. Hell, he thought, wouldn't have horrified him more.

At last he shook himself free of his stunned and disbelieving stupor, seized himself by the hair and ran back into the street, repeating over and over as if he'd lost the last of his senses:

"God help us...! God punish and avenge us...! God save us."

Chapter Fifty-six

WARSAW HAD BEEN in Swedish hands a long time when Kmita finally got there. Wittemberg, who was the city's governor and garrison commander, was at Krakow with Charles Gustav at that time so that Radeyovski ruled Warsaw in his place. No fewer than two thousand soldiers occupied the city, both in the walled Main Town as it was then called, and in the outer *jurisdictions* or wards that lay beyond the walls with their magnificent church and private buildings. The castle and the town itself had suffered little damage at the time of seizure because Pan Vessel, the *Starosta* of Makov who was Yan Casimir's military commander in the capital when the Swedes appeared at the gates, gave up the city without a fight and fled hurriedly along with his command, fearing the private vengeance of Radeyovski who was his personal enemy since long before the war.

But when Kmita started to look around with closer attention, he noted the tell-tale signs of predators on many of the buildings.

These were, as he soon discovered, the homes of those inhabitants who left the captive city, unwilling to live under Swedish rule, or who tried to defend it when the Swedes arrived before the ramparts. Of all the many magnates' palaces outside the town walls, only those kept their former splendor whose owners stood heart and soul behind the invaders. The Kazanovski Palace, protected by their kinsman Radeyovski, remained in all its rich and rare glory along with Radeyovski's own. So did the Warsaw residence of the Konyetzpolskis and the great mansion built by King Vladyslav IV which was known later as the

Kazimirovski Palace. But the homes of the great princely dignitaries of the Crown, such as the residences of the Denhoffs and the Ossolinskis, stood either half wrecked or totally stripped and looted, partly because their distinguished owners were also ranking prelates of the Church.

The Ossolinski Palace in Reformatzka Street was a vacant shell. German mercenaries peered out of its windows, and all those priceless furnishings which the late chancellor imported with such care from Italy and elsewhere—all those Dutch tapestries and wall-hangings of Florentine leather, those side tables and writing desks inlaid with mother-of-pearl, the paintings and the bronze and marble statuary, the rare Venetian and Gdansk clocks and the crystal mirrors—either lay piled in huge disordered mounds along the palace courtyard, guarded by sentries but open to the ravages of the weather, or were already packed and crated for shipment to Sweden in one or another of thirty giant barges that waited in the Vistula for the fruits of pillage.

The town, he observed as he wandered through its avenues, looked and sounded like a foreign city. The languages and voices heard along the streets were, for the most part, anything but Polish. At every step he took along the cobbled roadways he came across Swedish and German troopers, French mercenaries, and contingents of hired soldiery from Scotland and England. Wherever he looked he saw foreign uniforms and headgear; tall plumed hats; Spanish-style helmets upswept and pointed fore-and-aft and crowned with a curved, raised ridge; the crimson, yellow or scarlet leather coats of musketeers and pikemen; the steel cuirasses and half-armor of Reiters and dragoons; and officers who strolled in buckled shoes and stockings or long high-topped Swedish riding boots. No matter where he turned, his eyes fell on multicolored foreign finery, saw foreign uniforms and faces, and his ears heard foreign songs and music. Even the heavy, broad-backed Pomeranian horses seemed of a different shape than those to which he was accustomed.

Warsaw was also full of sallow-skinned, black-haired Armenian traders in brightly colored skullcaps who flocked to the city to buy up looted treasures. But the most astonishing sight of all were the vast numbers of Gypsies who came to Warsaw in the wake of the Swedish armies for no reason that anyone could explain. Their covered wagons clustered along the avenues that flanked the Uyazdovski Palace, and massed throughout the whole inner town, so that it seemed as if a new canvas city had sprouted overnight amid the tall stone buildings.

The inhabitants of the city practically disappeared in these multilingual crowds. Most of them were glad enough to keep out of sight, staying in the shuttered safety of their homes, or hurrying through the streets if they had any business that took them outside. Only in rare instances did the carriage of some Polish magnate, rumbling towards the castle through the Krakow Prospect (as the city's principal street was known) and surrounded by traditionally garbed *Hajduk* and *Pajuk* outriders or household regiments in Polish military dress, remind the observer that this was a Polish town and the capital of Poland.

Only on Sundays and on days of Holy Obligation, when church bells summoned the inhabitants to Mass, did large crowds of Varsovians appear in their streets and the city acquired some of its former character. But even then the church squares filled with ranks of foreign soldiers who came to gawk and stare at the women, pull at their skirts when they hurried past with downcast eyes, laugh and joke and bellow their crude barracks ditties when Mass was sung inside.

★ ★ ★

All this flitted past Pan Andrei's eyes like a troubling and surprising dream but he didn't stay in Warsaw very long. He knew no one there. There was no one with whom to share his feelings or exchange a thought. He had nothing in common with those crowds of visiting Polish gentry who occupied the hostelries built in Dluga Street by King Sigismond III, the first of the Vasas who came from Sweden to be King of Poland, and with whom the line of the Commonwealth's elected Vasa monarchs had begun. He did buttonhole one or another of these new arrivals to get the latest news, but they were all confirmed Swedish backers who came to Warsaw in anticipation of Charles Gustav's return, and who clutched at Radeyovski's coat-tails in hopes of getting some profitable official appointment or the grant of confiscated Church properties or loyalist estates. None of them was worth the effort of spitting in their faces which Kmita felt like doing every time he met one.

As to the city's merchant population, Kmita soon discovered that all of them were longing for the return of better times, regretting the loss of a mild and beneficent monarch and a peaceful, law-abiding country. The merchant guilds—with the goldsmiths, the butchers, the tanners, and the powerful shoe-makers in particular—were said to be massing and concealing weapons, looking forward to Yan Casimir's return, and losing neither hope nor their determination to expel the Swedes as soon as some source of help appeared elsewhere in the country.

Kmita could hardly believe his ears when he heard about this. He couldn't understand how the lower classes could show a greater love and devotion for their Motherland, and a deeper loyalty to their rightful King, than the high nobility and the landed gentry who should have acquired such sentiments at birth.

But that was just what he observed and noted. The great lords and gentry sided with the Swedes while the common people showed courage and resistance to such an extent that when the Swedes drove them to forced labor on the city's walls, wanting to strengthen their hold on Warsaw and the surrounding country, the landless peasantry and the ordinary townsfolk accepted public whippings, prison and even death rather than add to the invaders' power.

Nor were things any different once he left the city. Every town and township that lay along the southwest highway that Pan Andrei traveled, in the general direction of Krakow and Silesia, was jammed with foreign troops and retainers of great lords and the landed gentry, and crowded with landholders and magnates who served the invader.

Nothing was Polish there.

Nothing he saw contained even some pale, buried ember of national resistance. Everything was seized, conquered, occupied and brought so thoroughly under a foreign heel as if all of it had been Swedish for all time.

He met only Swedes as he traveled through province after province or those who sided with them. The Polish members of his own class were either open turncoats or men who'd reached such a level of hopelessness and despair, convinced beyond all argument that everything was lost, that they no longer cared about anything. No one showed any opposition to the new order. No one voiced a thought that might contain refusal. Everyone hurried without complaint to do what they were told, carrying out orders that in former times would have brought a storm of protests and violent resistance. Servility and fear had reached such a point that even those who were openly mistreated were loud in their praises of the Commonwealth's new Swedish protector.

Pan Andrei knew—indeed, he remembered—how it used to be only a short time before, when a landholder met the county deputies, charged with collecting civil and military imposts, with armed servants at his back and a loaded musket in his hands. Now the Swedes imposed whatever tax they pleased and the gentry gave it up as meekly as sheep surrender their wool to the shears. It happened often that the same tax was collected twice. Receipts were no protection. The taxpayer thought himself lucky if the collecting officer didn't dip the receipt in his wine and ordered him to eat it. '*Vivat Protector!*' the cheated squire bellowed and sent his servants scrambling up on the manor roof to see if another collector was coming.

Nor were the Swedish requisitions and exactions the worst of the oppression that fell on the country. The renegades and turncoats who served the Swedes for private gain or money found an unparalleled opportunity to settle old accounts and pay off old scores. They encroached on their neighbors' lands, moved property markers, and took woodlands and pastures with impunity since no one dared to say a word against them, especially if they were Protestant co-religionists of their Swedish masters. Moreover, fierce armed bands of looters and marauders sprung up throughout the country, banding together out of decent men driven to desperation, as well those for whom any breakdown in law and public order signaled the road to arson, robbery and pillage. These bandits threw themselves like wolves on the gentry and the peasantry alike, aided by wandering gangs of Swedish and German deserters and local criminals and ruffians of all kinds.

This then was the moral and physical landscape of his fallen homeland through which Pan Andrei traveled. The countryside glowed at night with the fires of pillage. The towns and cities groaned in the iron grip of foreign mercenary soldiers. No one talked of mending and rebuilding the Commonwealth now that the war appeared to be over, nor looked for or mentioned a means of salvation, nor thought about freedom.

No one, Pan Andrei realized in his own despair, retained even a shred of tattered hope.

★   ★   ★

But something different happened along the way. Pan Andrei's road took him through the county town of Sohatchev, near which a band of Swedish and German deserters had just attacked the country manor of old Pan Lushtchevski, the local *Starosta*. The besieged landowner was well into his seventies but he put up a fierce defense which was still going on when Kmita rode within sight and hearing.

All of his stifled anger and suppressed impatience, which had been swelling in him like an abscess ready to burst at the first opportunity, broke into the open. He let the three Kemlitches 'pound 'em,'—as they referred to their favorite pastime—and charged the marauders with all the savagery of his own frustrations. He cut them down to the last man, crushed them without mercy, and even had the few disarmed wretches who tried to surrender drowned in the manor fishpond.

The rescued *Starosta*, for whom Kmita's help must have seemed like a gift from Heaven, welcomed him as a savior and begged him to feel himself at home. Pan Andrei in turn, seeing before him a man of age and experience, a personage of stature rather than just an ordinary person, and perceiving him as a thoughtful, contemplative man of an older era, confessed all his hatred for the Swedes and started to question him about the future of the Commonwealth. He did so hoping to hear something that would soothe his troubled mind and conscience, or pour a healing balm into his tortured soul, but the old man had quite a different way of looking at everything that happened.

"My dear young sir," he said. "I don't know what I would have told you if you'd asked that question when the hair in my mustache was still red, and my mind was cluttered with material matters. But now my beard is white, seven decades are hanging above my neck, and I can see the future because I stand at the edge of the grave. And so I'll tell you that all of Europe wouldn't be able to break Sweden's power, not just we, no matter what we do to correct our faults nor how we change ourselves."

"How can that be, sir ?" Kmita cried. "Where did that thought come from? When did Sweden get to be so invincible? Isn't the Polish nation larger, richer? Can't we raise greater armies? Did our soldiers ever show themselves inferior to the Swedes?"

"There are ten times as many of us just among the gentry as all the people in Sweden," the *Starosta* said, nodding in agreement. "God gave us such bounties that my lands alone grow more wheat than the Swedish Kingdom. As to our valor, I rode at Kirkholm where three thousand of our *husaria* ground eighteen thousand Swedes, the pick of their army, into sand and gravel."

"Well then?" asked Kmita whose eyes lit up like stars at this recollection of the Kirkholm victory. "If that's so, what possible reasons can there be why we can't beat them today as we did before?"

"This is the first," the old man murmured in a tired, slow voice. "That we've grown smaller in our minds and spirit while they grew larger, so that they threw us down with our own hands, just as they conquered Germany with Germans. That is God's will and I repeat that there's no power on earth which would be able to stand up to them today."

"But what if our gentry comes back to its senses?" Kmita pressed. "What if it rallies to its rightful King and every man alive among us runs to arms? What would Your Excellency advise then and what will you do?"

"Then I'll go with the rest. I'll find my death. And I advise everyone to fall if they can because the times ahead are such that it's best not to look at them at all."

"They can't be any worse than these!" Kmita cried. "As I live and breathe, they can't be! That's impossible!"

"Look, my young friend," the *Starosta* said. "Before the Last Judgment and the end of the world there is to be an antichrist, and it is written that '*evil shall rise up to challenge goodness, Satan will walk the Earth, a false faith shall be preached among men, and people will turn their faces away from God.*' By God's own will evil shall prevail everywhere until Heaven's trumpeters signal the world's end..."

Here the *Starosta* leaned back in the armchair in which he was sitting, let his eyelids slip over his eyes, and went on in the low, mysterious voice of mystical inspiration.

"It's said '*there shall be signs,*' and there were. A hand and a sword have been seen on the sun, God have mercy on us! Evil triumphs over good, as it has been written, because the Swede and his henchmen are winning everywhere. The True Faith falters because the Lutherans have risen among us...

"People!" he cried out suddenly, swept up by his vision. "Can't you see that the Days of Wrath are coming? '*Dies irae, dies illa...*' Can't you hear the trumpets? I am old, I stand on the bank of the Styx looking for Charon and his boat... I can see...!"

The *Starosta's* quivering old voice dwindled into silence and Kmita began to stare at him with fear because his reasoning seemed to make good sense and his conclusions sounded so terribly accurate. He grew thoughtful. He knew himself to be unready for Judgment. Oh, so far from ready! But the old man wasn't looking at him; instead he stared blindly into the darkening, empty air before him.

"So how are the Swedes to be conquered," he resumed, "when it's clearly God's design that they should be triumphant? His will is clear, the prophecies have revealed it, the word has been given...

"Ah, it's to Tchenstohova that people should go these days," he murmured at last as if that small country town in the southwestern corner of the country, with it's ancient monastery and the miraculous painting of the Holy Virgin, were the last salvation. "To Tchenstohova..."

And he sunk into another silence.

The room in which they sat had begun to darken. The sun was setting, it edged into the chamber from a narrow angle, and the slanting light broke into rainbow hues through the mullioned window, forming pools of separate colors on the floor. Kmita felt more and more uneasy in that mysterious gloom, starting to believe that the world would end as soon as this strange light ebbed away and failed, and that the call to Judgment wasn't far away.

"What are these prophecies which you've mentioned, sir?" he asked at last because the silence seemed more frightening with each passing moment.

Instead of speaking to him, however, the Starosta turned towards the door of the adjoining room and called out: "Olenka! Olenka!"

"God almighty!" Kmita shouted out. "Whom is Your Excellency calling?"

He could believe in anything just then, and he was sure that his own Olenka was about to appear before him, carried here miraculously from Keydany, and every other thought or memory disappeared at once as he sat, unmoving and unable to breathe, with his eyes fixed anxiously on the door.

"Olenka! Olenka!" the old man called again.

The door opened. The tall, willowy, beautiful young woman who entered was not Pan Andrei's Aleksandra, although she did resemble Olenka Billevitch in the gravity of her face and the peace which glowed quietly in her features.

She was extremely pale. Perhaps she was ill. Or perhaps she was still feeling the effects of terror caused by the marauders. She walked with cast-down eyes, moving so softly and with such little effort that it seemed as if she were propelled by a gentle breeze rather than any will or agency of her own.

"This is my daughter," the *Starosta* said. "My sons are not at home. They're with Pan Tcharnyetzki, the castellan of Kiev, and serve our poor exiled King. Thank this brave cavalier for coming to our help,"—he turned to his daughter—"and then read us the prophecy of St. Brigid."

The girl bowed silently to Pan Andrei, left the room, and returned shortly with a few printed sheets of paper in her hands. Then, standing in that fading rainbow light, she began to read.

"*First I will show you Five Kings and the Lands they rule,*" she recited in a gentle and melodious voice. "*They are Gustav, son of Erik, a Brazen Ass since he abandoned the True Faith and embraced a false one. Having turned away from the Apostolic Church, he brought the Augsburg Confession into his own country, thus staining his name. See Ecclesiastes where it's said of Solomon that he defamed himself by worshiping false Gods...*"

"You hear?" the *Starosta* turned his eyes on Kmita, lifting one finger and holding the others ready.

"I hear."

"... *Erik, son of Gustav, known as a Wolf for his ravenous greed,*" the girl went on reading. "*For which he brought the Hatred of all Men and his own brother John upon himself. First, thinking John guilty of secret dealings with the Danes and Poles, he made War upon him and kept him captive for four years with his wife and children. Freed by a change of fortunes, John overthrew him, stripped him of his Crown, and lodged him in a Dungeon, to dwell there for ever in perpetual darkness...*"

"Note this," the Starosta said and raised another finger. "That's the second one."

"... *John, Erik's brother,*" the young woman continued. "*A soaring Eagle, three times triumphant over Erik, the Danes and the Russians. His son Sigismond, known in his new lands as Zygmunt, ascended to the Throne of Poland. Goodness dwells in his blood. Glory be to his issue.*"

"Do you follow?" the *Starosta* asked.

"May God grant many years to Yan Casimir," Kmita said.

"... *Charles, Prince of Sudermanland, comes next,*" the girl went on. "*A Ram is his sign because he led the Swedes into the paths of Evil as a ram leads his sheep. He is the one who railed against the Truth.*"

"That's the fourth one!" the old man interrupted.

"*The Fifth is Gustav Adolf,*" the young woman read. "*A Lamb is his sign, because he was slaughtered like a Paschal Offering, yet he was not unblemished. His Blood brought Mankind quarrels and tribulations.*"

"Yes, that's Gustaphus Adolphus," the *Starosta* said. "Christina isn't mentioned because only the male line is listed in St. Brigid's vision. Read the conclusion now, my dear, which has a direct bearing on our times."

"... *I'll show you the Sixth one, who'll trouble both the Land and Sea and sadden the righteous... In his hands lie the times of my Anger. If he Fails to gain his ends quickly, then my Judgment will be rendered on him, and he will leave his People in Trouble and Sorrow because it is written that he who sows Discord will reap Pain and Tears. Nor will*"

I visit these on just that one Kingdom but on other Cities because they summoned a hungry man among them and he'll devour their Riches. There will be no lack of Evil among them and Disharmony shall lead them. Those who rule shall be Stupid, while the Wise and Old shall not raise their heads. Virtue and Honor shall fall until there comes One who will beg me to turn away my Anger, and who shall not spare his Soul for the sake of Truth."

"There you have it all," the *Starosta* said.

"It's all so true a blind man could see it!"

"And that's why the Swedes can't be overthrown," answered the *Starosta*.

"*Until there comes one who won't spare his soul for the sake of Truth!*" Kmita cried, quoting from the prophecy which had just been read. "Saint Brigid's vision doesn't strip us of our hope! It's salvation that is waiting for us in the end, not judgment and damnation!"

"Sodom was to be saved if ten just men were found within her walls," the old man replied, "but no such men were there. Here also we won't find that one man who'd give his soul for the sake of truth, and the hour of judgment will come down upon us."

"That just can't be, Your Excellency!" Kmita cried out in answer. "That simply can't be!"

* * *

But before the *Starosta* could form his next reply, the door swung open and an elderly man, buckled into a breastplate and carrying a musket, stepped into the room.

"Is that Pan Shebryski?" the *Starosta* queried.

"Yes," said the new arrival. "I heard that Your Worship was having trouble with marauders, so I armed a few stable lads and here I am to help."

"Not a sparrow falls unless it's God's will," answered the old man. "This cavalier has already saved us. And where do you come from now?"

"Sohatchev."

"Is there any news?"

"Every time there's news it's worse than the time before." The elderly noble sighed and tugged at his whiskers. "And now there's a fresh calamity..."

"What happened?"

"The Palatinates of Krakow, Sandomir, Ruthenia, Lubelsk, Beltz, Volhynia and Kiev have placed themselves under Charles Gustav's protection. The treaty is already signed by the territorial envoys and Charles Gustav as well."

The *Starosta* began to nod his head and finally turned to Kmita. "Do you see?" he asked. "And do you still think that someone who'd risk his soul for the sake of truth can be found among us?"

Kmita started to tear at his hair. "Sheer desperation!" he shouted, shaken to his soul.

"Meanwhile," Pan Shebryski continued. "People say that what's left of the regular Crown Army is refusing to obey Hetman Pototzki's orders and demands to be taken to the Swedes. The Hetman isn't even sure of his own life among them so he must do what they want."

"*They who sow discord shall reap pain and tears,*" the *Starosta* said. "Whoever wants to do penance for his sins ought to do it now because the time has come."

But Kmita could no longer listen to either prophecies or news. What he wanted was to leap onto his horse as quickly as he could and to cool his burning head in the cold night air. He jumped to his feet and started to take his leave.

"Where are you off to in such a hurry?" the *Starosta* asked.

"To Tchenstohova, because I'm also a sinner."

"In that case I won't hold you back, though I'd be glad to have you for a guest. But that's a far more pressing matter because Judgment Day is near."

* * *

Kmita left the room. The young woman followed, wanting to pay her respects to a departing guest, since her father had trouble with his legs and couldn't see to it himself.

"Keep in good health, my lady," Kmita said to her at the door. "You don't know what a well-wisher you have in me."

"If you wish me well, sir," she said, "then do me a service. You're traveling to Tchenstohova... take this gold-piece and have Mass said at the chapel."

"In whose behalf?"

The seeress averted her eyes, sadness flowed into her face and a pale flush rose into her cheeks. "In behalf of Andrei," she said in a low, hoarse voice, as whispery as the rustling of dead leaves. "May God turn him into the paths of goodness and away from evil..."

Kmita took a step back, eyes wide with amazement, and quite unable to utter a word.

"By Christ's holy wounds," he said at last, his voice cracked and stammering with astonishment. "What kind of house is this? Where am I? There's nothing here but prophecies, auguries and divinations... Your ladyship's name is Olenka and you are buying a Mass for a sinful Andrei? This can't be just an ordinary coincidence... This is a sign, some kind of second-sight, it must be! Sweet Christ, it's more than my brain can cope with! It's... It's as if God himself were pointing out my way... Am I going mad?"

"What's wrong with you, sir?"

But he seized both her hands in his own and began to shake them violently.

"Keep prophesying! Tell me everything! If that Andrei turns away from evil, will his Olenka keep faith with him? Tell me! Answer me or I won't go without that!"

"What's wrong with you!"

"Will Olenka remain true to him?" Kmita said again and kept on saying it until tears flooded out of the young woman's eyes and poured down her face.

"To her last breath," she said among her sobs. "Until her last hour!"

She was still speaking when Kmita hurled himself on the ground before her. She drew back, startled by his violence. She wanted to escape him. But he seized her feet and covered them with kisses even as he stammered on and on:

"I'm also a sinful Andrei who wants to find the right way! I also have a beloved Olenka. May your Andrei, sweet lady, find his way to decency and goodness and may my Olenka keep her faith with me... You've restored my hope. You've poured a soothing balsam into my troubled soul... God bless you! God bless you!"

Then he leaped to his feet, jumped into his saddle and rode off.

Chapter Fifty-seven

THE WORDS of the *Starosta's* daughter made a great impression on Pan Kmita. They reawakened hope and he couldn't get them out of his head for three days. He thought about that strange experience all day while on horseback and most of the night when he tossed and twisted in his bed, and reached the same conclusion every time. *'This can't be just a simple accident. It has to be a sign from God... a prophecy... an omen.'* He had to believe that if he stayed on his good new path of service, patriotism and duty—which was exactly the road that Olenka had pointed out to him—then the girl would keep faith with him, keep loving him, and that eventually he would be able come back to her.

"Because if the *Starosta's* daughter stays true to her Andrei," he reasoned, "and he is still on the wrong road with no idea that he ought to change, then what about me who already wants to serve our country, our King and the cause of goodness? It's clear—it *has* to be —that there's some hope left for me as well."

On the other hand Pan Andrei also had many troubling doubts. He knew that his intentions were honest and sincere but hadn't he left them a bit late? Was there still some path of service left to him? Would he still be able to find an opportunity? The drowning Commonwealth seemed to sink deeper every day and it simply wasn't possible to avoid the terrible, inescapable conclusion that there was no longer any avenue of rescue for his fallen nation. There was nothing Kmita wanted more than to begin some kind of work in his country's service but he could see no willing hands anywhere around him. A live mosaic of strange new faces spread out before him as he traversed the miles, but looking at them, and listening to what they said, merely undermined whatever hope he had.

Some served the Swedes with all their hearts and souls. For them this was a time of drunken celebrations. They swilled their liquor, drowning their guilt and shame as if at a wake.

Others argued blindly about the mighty, unimaginable power that the Commonwealth would become in partnership with Sweden, ruled by the greatest warrior in the world, and these were the most dangerous since they honestly believed that all mankind would have to bow before such an irresistible alliance.

Another, and possibly the most numerous kind, were like the old *Starosta* of Sohatchev—all of them decent, honest and admirable people who had their country's best welfare at heart—who looked for signs and omens in the sky and everywhere around them, cited prophecies, saw God's will in everything that happened, resigned themselves to fate, and preached their inescapable conclusion that there was neither hope nor salvation possible in the world, that God's forgiveness was the only sensible thing to strive for, and that only madmen would continue struggling here on earth.

Finally there were those who either fled from their unbearable reality by hiding in the forests or took themselves abroad where they might keep living as they had before. This meant that the only kinds of people Kmita met on his laborious journey were the corrupt and morally depraved, the desperate or the fearful, or those who had drowned long ago in their own sense of doom. He met no one capable of either faith or hope.

★ ★ ★

Meanwhile, as he heard and noted wherever he went, the Swedish fortunes soared everywhere. Rumors that the drained and worn-out remnants of the Polish regular contingent in the east were swept by mutiny, that they banded together to threaten their Hetmans and demanded to be taken to Charles Gustav's camp, acquired greater substance every day. News that Pan Konyetzpolski, a hero of Zbarajh in the Cossack wars, surrendered his division to the Swedes and gave them his allegiance, reverberated through the entire country. He was soon followed by another Zbarajh hero, the almost legendary Marek

Sobieski, *Starosta* of Yavorov, and by Prince Dmitri Vishnovyetzki, a kinsman of the unforgettable Yeremi, whose name still stood for heroism and sacrifice in the name of duty.

Nor was there much to hope for from George Lubomirski, the immensely powerful and wealthy Lord of Malopolska, who was courted assiduously by both sides. So far he'd sided with Yan Casimir, largely because it flattered him to think that he was the last great magnate of the Commonwealth to keep his old allegiance, but that could change any day, depending on his whim. People who knew him well said that his patriotism didn't stand a chance against his enormous vanity, his craving for attention, and his obsession with his own importance, so that now when Charles Gustav seemed like such a clear-cut winner, he was having doubts. What still kept him on the side of the exiled King was his satisfying notion that he alone was holding the fate of the entire nation in his hands. But his vanity was demanding more. He was beginning to fret like a spoiled child, feeding his pride on the humiliation of another, and letting the unfortunate Yan Casimir know in no uncertain terms that he could either save him or cause his final ruin, whichever he pleased.

Meanwhile, the homeless King-wanderer waited with a handful of loyalists in Glogau and watched as one or another of them left him every day. Days of unending calamity and misfortune, as Pan Andrei knew, have that effect on the faint-of-heart, even if in the brave, early days of struggle they made honest commitments to hardship and endurance. Charles Gustav received them with open arms, showered them with promises and rewards, and did his best to induce the rest to follow their example.

Whole ranks of *Voyevodes*, castellans, and civil officials of both Lithuania and the Crown were in his camp already, along with swarms of gentry and whole brigades of the incomparable Polish cavalry who stared into his eyes like faithful hounds ready to do his bidding. His successes fed upon themselves. He conquered Poland and the Poles with their own resources.

Meanwhile the war blazed hotter than ever in the east where the last, small remnants of the Polish regular contingent shouted at their Hetman: '*Go and pledge your allegiance to the Swedes! Bow before Charles Gustav! We want to be with him!*' Five thousand

sabers glittered before his eyes to enforce the will of his rebellious army while the terrible Hmyelnitzki laid another siege to
Lvov, the Russians swept past the unbreachable walls of Zamost,
and the hordes of Moscow arrived at the gates of Lublin.

Nor was there any hope to be seen elsewhere. Lithuania was
now entirely in the hands of Sweden and Hovansky. Radzivill
threw himself into a bloody civil war in Podlasye. The Elector
was still hesitating, sniffing the wind and weighing his decision,
but he looked ready to give the final *coup de grace* to the dying
Commonwealth and, in the meantime, he strengthened his grip
on the Prussian cities.

Winter was on its way. Leaves rustled softly to the ground as
Pan Andrei passed along the tree-lined highways. Vast flocks of
ravens, crows and blackbirds swirled like a storm cloud above all
the towns and cities of the Commonwealth, and envoys hurried
from every corner of the country to wish the King of Sweden
success in his conquests.

Beyond Piotrkov, about half way between Warsaw and his
destination, Kmita began to meet Swedish troops which
crowded every highway that ran to the north. People said that
after taking Krakow and accepting the submission of the eastern
and southern provinces, Charles Gustav was planning to invade
the Prussians, and that he was sending his armies ahead to the
Prussian border while he waited for the last Polish troops, those
who were fighting Buturlin and Hmyelnitzki under Hetman
Pototzki and Pan Lantzkoronski, to come into his camp.

Pan Andrei met with no interference at this point in his
journey. No one barred his way because, in general, the gentry
no longer aroused suspicion. Large groups of them rode happily
along with the Swedes, while so many others were going to
Krakow to bow to their new master and get one thing or another
out of him, that the Swedes didn't bother to check documents
and passes. Besides, Charles Gustav was so busy wooing his new
subjects that his soldiers didn't dare to molest anybody so close
to his presence.

★ ★ ★

Kmita's last night before Tchenstohova passed in the small
market town of Krushin. But he no sooner unpacked at the inn
when other guests appeared.

First to arrive was a squadron of about a hundred Swedish cavalry led by several lieutenants and a thoughtful-looking senior officer. He was a tall, broad-shouldered, well-built man in his middle years, with a pair of shrewd, darting eyes peering from his face, whose imposing bearing suggested ruthlessness and authority. He carried himself with the assurance of a man who is conscious of his own dignity and position, and although he had the looks, uniform and manner of a foreigner, he addressed Pan Andrei in faultless Polish, questioning him closely about who he was and where he was going.

This time Pan Andrei called himself a gentleman from the countryside near Sohatchev because he thought the officer might think it suspicious to find one of the Elector's subjects that far to the south. But when he said that he was on his way to the Swedish King with a complaint about an unpaid bill the officer didn't think it strange at all.

"The higher the altar, the more effective the prayers," he said and shrugged. "You're quite right to go to the King himself. He has a thousand matters on his mind just now, but even so he never turns a petitioner away. As for you Polish gentry, he is so solicitous about you that even the Swedes are envious."

"Just as long as his moneybags are full," Kmita shrugged in turn.

"Charles Gustav is not your former Yan Casimir who had to borrow money even from the Jews because he'd give away everything he had to the first man who asked. Besides, there'll be lots of money in the treasury once we succeed in a certain enterprise we're planning."

"And what enterprise is that?"

"Sorry, cavalier. We don't know each other well enough for secrets. I'll just say that in a week or two His Majesty's treasury will be as full as that of the Sultan."

"Then he must have found an alchemist to make him some gold because there's no other way to get it in this country."

"In this country?" the officer laughed briefly. "All anyone needs is the daring to reach for it. And we've enough of that, as you see by the fact that we're the masters here."

"True, true," Kmita nodded. "And we're all glad to have you as our masters. Especially if you'll teach us how to make money out of woodchips."

"You had the means all along. But you'd have rather starved to death than take one coin from there."

Kmita gave the officer a cold, measuring glance. "That is because there are some places that even Tartars wouldn't dare to touch!"

"Your wits are a sight too sharp, cavalier," the officer replied. "You guess too much too quickly. But just keep in mind that it's not the Tartars you're going to for your money but the Swedes."

★ ★ ★

The arrival of another cavalcade interrupted further conversation. The officer, who apparently expected the newcomers, hurried outside while Kmita sidled up to the door to see who had arrived. He saw a closed traveling coach, surrounded by a troop of Reiters, rolling to a halt before the inn. The officer with whom he'd been talking ran up to the coach, opened its door, and bowed with a deep, respectful flourish to the unseen personage inside.

'*It must be somebody important*,' Kmita thought.

Meanwhile some of the earlier troopers brought flaming torches out of the hostelry into the darkened courtyard, and Pan Andrei caught sight of some stately foreign dignitary who stepped from the carriage. He wore a long, black traveling cloak richly lined with fox furs and a tall, plumed hat. The officer snatched a torch from a Reiter's hand, bowed again and said: "This way, Excellency."

Kmita retreated swiftly into the tavern parlor and the others entered almost on his heels.

"Excellency!" the officer said and bowed for the third time. "I am Veyhard, chief provisioning officer of His Swedish Majesty, sent to escort you to him."

"I'm pleased to meet such a distinguished officer," the black-garbed personage replied, matching him bow for bow.

"Does Your Excellency wish to stop here for any length of time? Or to continue your journey straight away? His Majesty is most anxious to see you as soon as possible."

"I had it in mind to hear Mass in Tchenstohova," the new arrival answered. "But I heard in Vyelun that His Majesty orders me to hurry so let's rest here for a little while and go on.

Meanwhile, will you send back my original escort and thank the captain who led it?"

"*Jawohl, Excellenz,*" the officer saluted and went out to carry out the order but Pan Andrei stopped him on the way.

"Who is that?" he asked.

"Baron Lisola, special envoy of the Holy Roman Emperor in Vienna, who is on his way to our King from the court of the Brandenburg Elector."

* * *

The officer went outside, returned, reported to the Baron that his orders had been carried out, and took his place at the table across from the Baron, who invited him to sit there with a lordly gesture.

"The wind is beginning to blow quite hard outside," said the Imperial envoy. "And the rain is thickening. We might have to stay here longer than we planned. Meanwhile let's talk a little before supper, shall we? What are people saying in these parts? We've heard that the eastern palatinates have made their submission to his Swedish Majesty."

"That's so, Excellency. His Majesty is only waiting for the remainder of the Polish army to submit, after which he'll march at once to Warsaw and Prussia."

"Is it so certain, then, that they will submit?"

"The army's representatives are already in Krakow. Besides, what choice do they have? If they don't acknowledge His Majesty's sovereignty, Hmyelnitzki will exterminate them all."

Baron Lisola bowed his head and nodded regretfully and gravely.

"Terrible times," he murmured. "Who had ever heard of such a thing."

Veyhard stirred uneasily. He and the Baron were talking in German, which Pan Andrei understood perfectly, and he strained his ears not to miss a word.

"Excellency!" Veyhard offered. "What happened here simply had to happen."

"Perhaps so. Still, it's hard not to have some sympathy for this magnificent Commonwealth which tumbled into ruin almost before our eyes. And whoever isn't Swedish must feel some compassion."

"I'm not a Swede," Veyhard said politely. "But if the Poles themselves don't regret their tragedy I see no reason to do their mourning for them."

"True!" Lisola looked up and eyed him carefully. "Your name isn't Swedish. What is your nationality, if you please?"

"I am a Czech."

"Ah...! A subject of His Imperial Majesty, then? We serve the same master, it appears."

"I'm in the service of the King of Sweden," Veyhard replied with a courteous bow.

"Far be it from me to say anything against that service," the Baron said smoothly. "But such allegiances tend to be short-lived. Meanwhile, your position as a subject of our gracious master remains intact no matter where you go or whom you are serving."

"That I don't deny."

"I'll tell you then, as one Imperial subject to another, that our master feels deeply about the ruin of this splendid Common-wealth and he regrets the fate of its unfortunate former King. Nor can he look with pleasure at those of his subjects who help in the destruction of a friendly power. What did the Poles ever do to you that you should show them such ill-will?"

"I could cite a long list, Excellency," Veyhard said. "But I don't want to put a strain on Your Grace's patience."

"Don't be concerned about my patience," the Baron said quietly. "It's part of my office to watch, listen and question informed persons. You seem like a thoughtful and perceptive man as well as a distinguished officer. Speak frankly and as fully as you wish, it won't weary me. And if you ever apply for service with our imperial master, which I urge you most warmly to consider, you'll find me a good friend who'll vouch for you, and offer your excuses, if anyone should question your present service here."

"In that case I'll say whatever's on my mind. I'm like many younger sons of the nobility, Your Grace, who are obliged to seek their fortunes in a foreign country. I came here because this nation shares common roots with my own and because they're always glad to employ foreigners."

"And didn't you like your welcome?"

"On the contrary, sir. They made me the administrator of all their salt deposits. I found a good livelihood, important friends, and access to the King himself. Now I serve the Swedes. But I'd protest most strongly if someone charged me with ingratitude."

"And why is that, if I may ask?"

"Here is why, Your Grace: Why should anyone expect more from me than from the Poles themselves? Where are they today? Where are all the senators, princes, magnates, gentry, the knighthood and the officers of this Kingdom if not among the Swedes? Shouldn't they be the first to know where their duties lie, what they ought to do, and what's good for their country? I have done only what they are all doing so how could one of them accuse me of being an ingrate? Why should I—a foreigner—show greater loyalty to the Polish King and the Commonwealth than they? Why should I deny myself that very service which they seek so avidly for themselves?"

Lisola said nothing in reply. He let his bowed head rest in the palm of his hand, his elbow on the table, and appeared to be sunk in profound meditation. He sat as still and silent as if he were listening to the thin whistling of the wind outside and to the tapping of the Autumn rain on the tavern windows.

"Continue, sir," he said after some moments. "I find what you are saying... most significant."

"I look for my fortune wherever I can find it," Veyhard went on. "And the fact that this nation is going through its death-throes shouldn't concern me more than it does its people. But even if I did worry about it, what good would it do? This nation *has* to die!"

"And why is that?"

"In the first place because that is what it wants and in the second place because it deserves it!"

"*Wants* to die? *Deserves* it?"

"Your Grace!" the Czech soldier-of-fortune cried out heatedly. "Is there a people in this world more disorderly, anarchic and self-absorbed than this one? Is there another country where everyone thinks only of himself? Who rules here? Not the King, because his subjects don't allow him to... Not Parliament, because they break it up at will...! Just look at them, sir! They don't have armies because they won't pay taxes; there is no respect for authority among them because they see discipline and obedience as an abridgment of their private freedoms; there is no justice because there is no way to enforce the verdicts and everyone tramples on court decrees with impunity if he feels himself strong enough to do it. They have neither faith nor loyalty because they've turned their backs on their rightful King; nor is there even any love for their own country among them since they turned it over to the Swedes. And for what? What did the Swedes have to give them in return? No more than a promise that they'll be allowed to live in their old, self-serving anarchy!

"Where else," the Czech continued with rising impatience and contempt, "could such things occur? What other people would help an invader conquer their own country? Who else would turn against his King for no better reason than that a stronger man happened to appear? Who else in the world shows such contempt for the public good and seeks only to press his own advantage? Tell me, Excellency, what do these people have that might cause others to respect them? I wish someone could cite me just one Polish virtue, be it thoughtfulness, diplomacy, sobriety, stability, endurance or quick-thinking. But that's the last thing to look for among them...!

"So tell me, Your Grace, what is there about this nation that is worth remembering? Good cavalry? Yes, that's about the sum of it... The Numidians and the ancient Gauls also had good horsemen and where are they now? They've vanished. They're gone without a trace just like this nation must vanish from the earth. Whoever wants to save them is wasting his time because they don't even want to save themselves! Only mindless fools, ungovernable madmen, corrupt evildoers and self-serving turn-coats inhabit this country!"

* * *

The Czech's concluding words were spoken with such passion that they seemed to brim over with hatred, which might have seemed strange in a foreigner who had found his livelihood in another country. But the Baron didn't show surprise. He was a worldly man, Pan Andrei supposed, one who understood human minds and actions, and who'd know that men whose natures were unable to repay generosity with kindness went out of their way to find fault with their benefactors so as to take the sting out of their own shortcomings.

Besides, he may have agreed with that harsh assessment. He offered no protest. Instead, he turned to Veyhard with an unexpected question.

"Do you happen to be a Catholic, Master Veyhard?" he asked suddenly.

Veyhard looked startled for a moment.

"Yes I am," he said.

"I heard in Vyelun that there are men around the King of Sweden who urge him to seize the Yasna Gora monastery... is that true?"

"Your Grace! The monastery lies close to the Silesian border. Yan Casimir could draw considerable support out of its resources. We have to forestall such a possibility hence the plans for an occupation... I was the first to turn His Majesty's attention to this matter which is why he was pleased to place it in my hands."

Here Veyhard remembered Kmita, cut short what he was saying, and approached Pan Andrei in the far corner of the room. "Do you speak German, cavalier?" he asked.

"Not a word," Kmita lied. "Not even if you pulled out all my teeth."

"Too bad. We would have liked to have you join our conversation." Then, turning to Lisola, he explained: "There's a traveling Polish noble here but he doesn't understand German. We can talk freely."

"There's nothing secret in what I have to say," Lisola replied. "I'm merely anxious, as a Catholic, that no harm comes to a holy place. And since I'm sure the Emperor shares these sentiments I'll beg His Swedish Majesty to spare it. I suggest that you delay your seizure of the place until a new decision can be made."

"My instructions are quite clear, Excellency. They are still secret and I mention them to Your Grace only because I want to remain the Emperor's loyal subject. But let me assure you that the sanctity of the holy place won't suffer any disrespect. After all, I'm a Catholic myself..."

"Of course you are." The Baron nodded in a soothing manner and smiled like a man who wants to draw the truth out of a less experienced source. "But you'll rattle the monks' treasure chest a bit, I expect, eh? That's possible, hmm?"

"Yes, that could happen," Veyhard said as if the notion was amusing to him. "The Holy Virgin has no need for the gold in the Prior's coffers. Let the monks pay for our protection like everyone else."

"And if they'd rather fight than pay?"

"Fight, Excellency?" The Czech laughed. "Who fights in this country? And even if they did want to defend themselves, how could they do it now? It's too late for that!"

"Yes. It *is* too late," Lisola repeated.

★   ★   ★

Their talk ended here. They set out as soon as they had eaten supper. Kmita was left alone. It was, he thought, the worst night he spent since leaving Keydany.

Listening to Veyhard he had to use all his strength to hold back from shouting "*Liar! You lie like a dog!*" and throwing himself on the man with his saber whirling in his fist. What kept him rooted in his place, however, was the sick realization that these bitter words contained a terrible, searing truth.

"What could I tell him?" he muttered to himself. "What arguments could I use other than a fist? He's right, damn his soul! And that imperial statesman agreed that it's all over now and that it's too late for struggling."

His pain was all the more piercing under these accusations because he knew that this '*too late*' had as much to do with his own hopes for happiness as with any real chance of saving his country.

"... Enough," he whispered. "That's enough."

He'd had more than enough of such tormenting thoughts. The strength of his convictions was starting to buckle. He heard nothing else through his weeks of travel than just such fatalistic acceptance of loss, defeat, hopelessness and surrender. In no place anywhere along his road—unless one counted that mad, brief moment in the *Starosta's* house—did he hear anything that might rekindle any kind of hope.

Going on, hurrying deeper into the country with no clear goal in mind, he pushed himself so hard night and day for no other reason than to escape his doubts and to find somebody, in some strange new region, who'd be able to offer him one consoling thought. But all he found wherever he appeared was only a greater sense of unavoidable calamity and more profound despair, and now, the Czech's harsh words filled that cup of gall beyond the brim.

They showed him something he had never really considered before: that it wasn't Swedes, Russians and Cossacks who'd murdered his country, but his countrymen themselves.

"... *Only fools, madmen, scoundrels, and self-serving turncoats inhabit this country,*" he repeated numbly after Veyhard. "*There aren't any others! They don't obey their King. They overthrow the Diets. They won't pay their taxes. They helped the enemy to conquer their own nation... They must be destroyed!*"

"Dear God!" he cried out then. "If I could call him a liar just once... in just one single instance! Are we really all evil and corrupt? Is our cavalry truly the only praiseworthy thing about us? Isn't there *one* virtue?"

Pan Andrei searched his soul for answers. He was so exhausted by the journey, by his anxieties, and by everything he had been through before, that his head was whirling. Chaotic visions tumbled through his mind. He felt that he was falling ill and giving way to a mortal weariness that would finally destroy him altogether.

His mind filled with a kaleidoscope of disembodied faces: people he knew well and those he'd barely met, old friends he knew from long before as well as strangers he barely remembered meeting on his journey. They were all arguing, endlessly debating as if at the diet, citing prophecies and maxims, and all of it had something to do with Olenka. She was waiting for Kmita to come to her rescue but Veyhard held him back, peered with disdain into his eyes, and chanted his grim '*too late... too late... what's Swedish is Swedish,*' while Boguslav Radzivill echoed him with laughter. Then suddenly all of them crowed out in concert: '*Too late! Too late! Too late!*' And then they seized Olenka and disappeared with her in some unfathomable darkness.

It seemed to Kmita then that Poland and Olenka were one and the same, and that he had doomed them both and handed them voluntarily to the Swedes.

This searing thought pierced the nightmare visions that surrounded him and shook him awake. He was seized by such an overwhelming grief that he lost all touch with reality, stared about with astonished and uncomprehending eyes, and then sat numb and listening to the wind which rattled in the chimney and hummed through all the cracks in the walls like a muted organ.

But the nightmare returned. Olenka and his country took on each other's forms again, blended with each other, and became one body which Veyhard dragged away repeating: '*It's too late! Too late!*'

★ ★ ★

At last the feverish night was over. Kmita hadn't slept. In moments of passing clarity he thought that he was in the grip of some malignant fever and stopped himself time and again from calling for Soroka to draw some blood out of his veins and ease the congestion. But then day came. Light showed in the windows. Kmita leaped up and went outside the inn.

This was still merely the first break of dawn but the day—a Sunday—promised to be clear. The night-clouds drew off to the west, forming long strips of receding darkness, but the eastern edges of the sky were aglow with sunlight. The last of the stars, glimpsed through the rising mist, gleamed whitely in the pale sky. Kmita woke his men, dressed carefully in his Sunday clothes, and they set off again.

Pan Andrei could barely keep himself erect in the saddle. He was heartsick and exhausted after a sleepless night. Not even that clear Autumn morning—so pale but also so cool, crisp and refreshing, with the mild bite of early frost hanging in the air—could dissipate the sadness that crushed the young man's heart. Whatever hope he'd had was now burned out to the last drop like oil in a darkened lamp.

What would this day bring him?

'*Nothing!*' he thought. '*Nothing.*'

The same grief and unsupportable anxiety were likely to return, adding to the grim weight of his desolation rather than helping to ease and lessen it.

He rode in silence, his eyes fixed on some point of light that glowed on the horizon. The horses snorted, announcing good weather. His men's sleepy voices rose here and there behind him, chanting the morning prayer.

Meanwhile the day grew brighter. The greyness of the sky gave way to a greenish golden hue, and that unknown, distant point of light glowed with such power that it dazzled the eyes.

The men stopped singing. All of them were staring in puzzlement at that light, and at last Soroka muttered: "What is that? Some kind of a wonder? That's the west out there, but you'd think it was another sunrise."

And the strange light did indeed seem like the spreading glow of yet another sunrise. The sharp, bright point became a burnished circle. The circle burst into a fiery globe so that it seemed as if a vast new star had been hung out there just above the earth, sending its bright beams into all the darkened space around it.

Kmita and his men stared at this spreading, pulsing glow as if it were some unearthly new manifestation, none of them knowing what it was they saw.

But then a peasant, on his way from the town where they had spent the night, trudged up in his cart. Turning towards him, Kmita saw that the countryman was holding his cap in his hands and that he was praying.

"Hey, peasant!" asked Pan Andrei. "What's that shining out there?"

"That's Yasna Gora," the countryman answered. "That's the holy place."

"Praise be to God and to the Holy Virgin!" Kmita cried out at once and snatched his cap off his head while all his men followed his example.

And then, after so many days of worry, doubt and fearful disappointment, Pan Andrei felt that something extraordinary was happening within him. It was as if the words Yasna Gora—the name of the nation's holiest shrine—were a magic potion that erased all sadness. A feeling of some strange, disquieting humility gripped the young knight, and along with that came a deep, rich joy of a kind he'd never experienced before. That church that glowed on its rocky mound in the first light of sunrise sent him a message of long-discarded hope; it restored that faith which he had sought so fruitlessly for so long; it armed him with that immeasurable strength on which he could rely. New life seemed to be flooding into him and to pound in his veins along with his blood. He drew a deep breath like a sick man rising from a fever and waking to a reality in which he could believe.

The church, meanwhile, glowed on as if it were drawing and absorbing all of the day's brightness. The land around it lay quietly and serenely at its foot, and it gazed down upon the countryside off its craggy mound as if it were its guardian and protector.

* * *

It was a long time before Pan Kmita could tear his eyes away from that healing light, wanting to fill himself with its soothing brightness, and all his men stared at it with a fearful fascination of their own. The sound of distant bells hung softly on the morning air.

"Dismount!" Kmita ordered.

All of them leaped out of their saddles, knelt in the road and began to pray. Pan Andrei recited the litany and his soldiers chorused the responses. In the meantime other carts and wagons had come up behind them. The peasant carters saw the group that knelt in prayer on the highway and hurried to join it so that soon a large chanting crowd had gathered behind them.

Pan Andrei rose along with all the others when the litany was over but he would continue on foot the rest of the way. He walked in the dust—calm, trusting and refreshed as never before—followed by his men who led their horses by the bridle-chains, singing an ancient hymn.

He walked as lightly as someone who'd been miraculously brought to life again and risen from the grave. It was, he felt, as if a pair of angels' wings unfolded at his shoulders. The church seemed to beckon, vanishing and reappearing at each bend of the road. It seemed to him that the whole world disappeared in darkness whenever the church sank from sight behind mists or hillocks and that all faces glowed with an unearthly radiance when it burst brightly into view once more.

They walked like that for a long time. The church, the contours of the monastery, and the fortified stone walls that surrounded them on their height of land, grew sharper by the hour. Each step they took seemed to infuse the structure with a vaster size and more imposing power. At last the distances narrowed to reveal the small town of Tchenstohova, and the rows of thatched huts and houses huddled at the foot of the sanctuary, so that they seemed like a scattering of birds' nests in its massive shadow.

It was, Pan Andrei recalled again, a Sunday. The road leading to the church filled up with wagons and people hurrying on foot as the sun climbed higher. Bells of all sizes called out to them from the tall spires and towers, summoning them to worship, and the air itself seemed suffused with richness at this sound. There was, Pan Kmita thought, some strange, unknown power dwelling in that sight and flowing out in the deep bronze booming of the bells; it was as if some profound majestic force were sending him its peaceful and untroubled message that all would be well. That strip of quiet, gently rolling land below Yasna Gora—so aptly named 'Bright Mountain' in Polish—was like no landscape he had seen anywhere else in the entire country.

Vast crowds of worshipers darkened the long slopes under the monastery walls. The foot of the hill was thick with wagons, carts, carriages and *britchkas*, and with the murmur of innumerable voices that blended with the snorts and neighing of the horses which each arriving pilgrim tethered at a gap-toothed little palisade. Further to the right, along the steep road that wound towards the church, lay rows of shops and stands that sold votive offerings, candles, scapulars and painted icons which reproduced the image of the miraculous Madonna inside. The thick human tide flowed upward steadily between them.

The gates stood wide open.

Everyone went in and out whenever they wished. There were almost no soldiers standing at the cannon on the walls. The monastery and the church seemed to be guarded by the holiness of the place itself. Or, Pan Andrei thought, perhaps the monks still trusted the assurances sent them by Charles Gustav who'd guaranteed their inviolability and safety.

Chapter Fifty-eight

THE DENSE HUMAN RIVER that flowed towards the church from the fortress gates was made up of every kind of man and woman, people of all ages and every condition—peasants, gentry, townsfolk from many different regions—who inched forward on their knees as they sang holy anthems and recited prayers.

The river moved so slowly, dammed now and then by the press of bodies, that it appeared to be scarcely moving. Religious banners arced above it like a rainbow. Every so often the hymns dwindled into silence and then the measured cadence of a litany rumbled as loud as thunder from one end of this creeping tide of pilgrims to the other. Between one anthem and the next, and between one prayer and another, the vast crowds prostrated themselves on the rocky road or beat their foreheads in the dust in silence, and then the air filled with the pleading voices of the beggars whose twisted and disfigured bodies formed the two banks of this penitential stream. Their plaintive howls rose in counterpoint to the ringing of the copper coins that showered into their tin and wooden bowls.

As this vast flowing mass drew closer to the church so their enthusiasm turned to exaltation. Arms and hands rose skyward. Eyes lifted. Faces paled with an onrush of emotion or flushed in concentration, absorbed in the prayers. Class differences disappeared. Wealth and position simply lost their meaning. Homespun peasant coats edged forward side by side with the traditional *kontush* garb of the landed gentry, and the buff and scarlet jerkins of the soldiers rubbed shoulders with the yellow gabardine of merchants.

Once at the open doors of the church itself, this dense stream thickened even further. The tight-pressed mass of creeping men and women became a bridge rather than a river, jammed together so closely that one could pass along their heads and shoulders without touching ground. Lungs worked for air, bodies struggled for space in which to breathe, but the spirit which moved, pushed and uplifted them gave them an iron will, strength and determination.

Everyone prayed.

No one thought about anything other than the nearing, miraculous experience they were about to witness.

Each of the pilgrims carried on his or her shoulders the total burden of the entire mass but no one fell or gave way to weakness. Pressed forward inch by inch by the thousands that pushed on behind them, they felt the strength of thousands welling up within them, and drove ahead with the combined power and endurance of the multitude, oblivious of anything around them, plunged into prayer and carried away by their exaltation.

* * *

Kmita, who crept with his men in the leading ranks, was among the first of the pilgrims to enter the church. The human current swept him into the Chapel of the Miracles where the whole gathering threw itself facedown on the flagstones, weeping in joy, embracing the smooth, cold flooring, and kissing the stone pavement.

Pan Andrei did the same and when, at last, he dared to lift his head, the feeling of unutterable bliss and happiness that swept over him, along with a sense of mortal fear and dread, came close to rendering him unconscious.

The chapel lay plunged in a reddish twilight, indifferent to the flames of innumerable candles that glowed before the altar.

Bright streams of multicolored light slanted into the sanctuary through the stained-glass windows, creating pools of violet, gold and scarlet that trembled along the walls, sliding along the planes and edges of the statuary, and drawing strange, dreamlike shapes out of the deeper darkness. Fragmented light gleamed mysteriously in the shadows, merging into the twilight with such imperceptible skeins and delineations, that all the differences between light and darkness seemed to disappear. All he could see were the golden halos that glowed above the candles, the smoke that twisted out of incense-burners into a purplish mist, and the white vestments of the officiating priest which had acquired the hues of a muted rainbow. All of this play of light on and against the darkness seemed only half-glimpsed, barely understood, sanctified and glorious, steeped in prayer, faith and adoration, unearthly and hidden behind mysteries.

A dull droning murmur like a sea came from the main nave of the church itself but here, in the Chapel of the Madonna which housed the holy image, there was a deep and all-pervading silence in which only the chanting voice of the Pauline priest, and the soft flute-like tones of a hidden organ, echoed among the arches.

The painting—the miraculous *Black Madonna*, so called throughout Christian Europe because antiquity had darkened the face painted many centuries earlier—was still concealed from view behind shrouding curtains, but everyone held his or her breath in anticipation. All that Pan Andrei could see around him were wide staring eyes fixed in that one direction, faces as still as if hammered out of stone and no longer caring about earthly matters, and hands pressed together in breathless adoration.

Then, suddenly, the thunderous blare of kettle-drums and trumpets sent a violent shudder rippling through the crowd and shattered the silence. The shrouds slid apart and a stream of light, as sharp and bright as diamonds, fell on the worshipers like a cloudburst nourishing parched soil.

Moans, shouts and sobbing burst across the chapel like one endless cry.

"*Salve Regina!*" roared the gathered gentry. "*Monstra te esse matrem!*"

"Holy Maiden! Golden Virgin! Queen of the Angels!" the peasants were shouting. "Save us! Help us! Console us! Have mercy upon us!"

A long time passed before the hush of worship replaced these pleading and exultant cries, the sobbing of the women, the tears of the unfortunate, and the wailing of the ill and crippled who begged for a healing miracle.

Pan Andrei thought that his soul would fly out of his body. He felt dwarfed and humbled and, at the same time, uplifted by something so immense and so immeasurable that all speculations about it were useless. Everything else dwindled into nothing beside the breadth and power of this reinforcement.

What did doubts matter, he asked himself mutely, next to this overwhelming trustfulness that filled his whole body? What were his fears and worries beside this vast infusion of confidence and hope? How could the might of Sweden match these unbreachable defenses? And, finally —if, indeed, there was an end to this blinding revelation—how could ordinary human evil and ill-will prevail against such a patron?

That was as much thinking as he was able to do. His mental processes dwindled, became unavailing. Thought vanished, replaced by pure feeling. He could no longer remember who and where he was nor how he had got there. He knelt transfixed, sure that he had died and that his freed spirit soared in that cloud of incense, carried beyond the walls by the music of the organ. His arms, so used to bloodshed and the heft of weapons, acquired a sudden, unburdened weightlessness and lifted in an ecstatic exultation of their own.

Then the Mass ended. Pan Andrei found himself in the main nave of the church, quite unaware of how he had come there. A priest was preaching the lesson for the day but Kmita didn't hear him, and didn't understand him, just as he neither heard nor understood anything else around him. He was, he knew, like a man freshly wakened out of sleep, who can't tell where the dream ends and reality begins.

But finally reality asserted itself. He heard words and voices and the first phrase which found an echo in his shaken mind was an admonition.

"This is the place where hearts and souls will become transformed because neither Swedish power nor the powers of darkness can prevail against the Light of the Truth."

"Amen!" Kmita murmured and he began to strike his chest in penance and contrition because it seemed to him that he had sinned by thinking that everything was lost and that no hope existed anywhere.

Outside, he stopped the first monk he saw and told him that he wanted to speak to the Prior on a matter concerning the monastery and the church.

* * *

Prior Kordetzki gave him an immediate hearing. He was a man well along in years and headed towards the evening of his life. His face was sunny and untroubled, framed in a thick black beard, and made remarkable by mild, sky-blue eyes of extraordinary clarity and peace. In his white Pauline habit, Kmita thought, he looked like a saint.

Pan Andrei kissed the sleeve of his robe and he, in turn, pressed Kmita's head between his hands in a gesture of fatherly affection and asked who he was and where he had come from.

"I come here from Zmudya," Pan Andrei said simply. "To serve Our Lady, our troubled Motherland, and our deserted King. I've sinned against them all which I'll confess in full, Reverend Father, as soon as you can hear me. Today wouldn't be too soon for me. I'm truly sorry for all I have done and I'm most anxious to make amends. I'll also tell you my real name, but only under the seal of the confessional, because it would prejudice everyone against me and hinder my best efforts to mend myself and to earn forgiveness. Here I'd prefer to be known as Babinitch, which is the name of one of my possessions taken by the Russians. In the meantime, father, I beg you to listen patiently to the news I've brought since it concerns the safety of this holy place."

"I'm glad you wish to live a better life," Prior Kordetzki said. "And I'll confess you before the night is over. Now tell me what you wish me to know."

"I've traveled a long time," Kmita said. "I've seen a lot of evil, and I've suffered a great deal of pain through it all... The enemy is powerful everywhere, the heretics are on the rise wherever you look, and even good Catholics are going over to the Swedes who've become so inflamed by this and all their other triumphs that now they plan to raise their sacrilegious hands against Yasna Gora."

"How do you come by this information?" Father Kordetzki asked.

"I spent last night in Krushin. There I met a Czech in Swedish service, an officer named Veyhard, and Baron Lisola, an emissary from the Emperor, who was on his way from the Elector's court to Charles Gustav in Krakow."

"Charles Gustav is no longer to be found in Krakow," the Prior said quietly, watching Pan Andrei with calm and curious eyes.

But Kmita's conscience was clear and he didn't doubt that he would be believed. He didn't glance away. He kept his own eyes fixed firmly on the Prior's.

"I don't know if he's there or not," he admitted. "But I do know that Lisola was on his way to see him and Veyhard was sent to meet him with an escort. They talked in German right in front of me, supposing that I couldn't understand them, so they held nothing back. But I speak German as well as I do Polish—it's a language that I've known since childhood—and I gathered from what they were saying that Veyhard plans to occupy the monastery and seize the church treasures and that he has Charles Gustav's approval for that undertaking."

"And you heard this with your own ears?"

"As I stand here before you, Reverend Father!"

"God's Will be done," the Prior said quietly.

Kmita felt a sudden surge of panic. He thought that the priest was referring to the orders of the King of Sweden as God's Will and that he wasn't thinking of offering any possible resistance.

"I saw a church in Swedish hands in Pultusk," he said, thrown off stride and shaken. "Beer barrels on the altars... soldiers gambling in the house of God... harlots with the soldiers..."

The priest's eyes remained fixed on Kmita's. "It's a strange thing you tell me," he said, nodding quietly. "Yet I see honesty and truth looking from your face..."

Kmita flushed with shame. "May I fall dead right here if I'm lying to you!"

"It's an important piece of information in any event," the Prior went on thoughtfully. "We must think more about it. You'll permit, cavalier, if I ask a few of the elders of our Order here? Along with some worthy gentry who advise us in these frightening times..."

"By all means!" Kmita cried. "I'll be glad to repeat it to them all over again."

★ ★ ★

Father Kordetzki left the room and returned within a quarter of an hour with four other priests. Soon afterwards a few landed gentry walked into the refectory. The Prior introduced the foremost as Pan Rozhitz-Zamoyski, the Constable of Syeradz, Pan Okelnitzki, a Crown office holder in Vyelun, and Pan Pyotr Tcharnyetzki, a young knight with a threatening martial face, whose tall, muscular body brought to mind the strength and hardiness of an oak. The Prior introduced Pan Babinitch from Zmudya and repeated Kmita's news in brief. They, in turn, took no trouble to hide their surprise and stared at Pan Andrei with open disbelief. But when none of them seemed anxious to make the first comment, Father Kordetzki took the floor again.

"May God restrain me from suspecting this cavalier of ill-will or of lying to us," he began. "But the news he brings us seems so unbelievable that I thought it best for us to discuss it further. With the best intentions, he could have been mistaken, or he misheard or misunderstood what he overheard, or he may have been misled on purpose by some heretics who'd like nothing better than to cause fear and confusion among us. I can't think of many who'd deny themselves the pleasure of disrupting our lives and interfering with our functions here."

"That seems quite likely to me," said Father Nyeskovski, who was the oldest and most venerable man at the gathering.

"We ought to find out first of all if this cavalier isn't a heretic himself," Pan Pyotr Tcharnyetzki said.

"I'm Catholic!" Kmita snapped. "Just like you!"

"We should consider what the Swedes might gain by such a thing," Pan Zamoyski offered. "And what it could lead to."

"It may be that God and His Holy Mother intend to blind the enemy on purpose," the Prior said quietly. "So that he'd go too far in his lawlessness and rapacity. Otherwise he'd never dare to raise his sword against this holy place. He didn't conquer this country by himself alone; our own people helped him. But no matter how low our nation has fallen, or how deeply steeped in sin it might be, there is a limit to every transgression which none of our people would ever go beyond. They turned their backs on their King and the Commonwealth but they never ceased to honor and worship their Patroness and Mother who has always been the true Queen of Poland."

He paused and nodded quietly in the silence with which the gathered priests and nobles drank in every word, then resumed in a voice laden with wisdom and perception:

"The enemy jeers at us and despises us, asking what's left of our former virtues. And I'll tell him this much: we've lost them all but one and that is our Faith and the honor we show to the Holy Mother, and that is the foundation on which we can reconstruct the rest. And I see this as clearly as the light of day, that if only one Swedish cannon ball ever scars these walls, then even our most hardened traitors will desert the Swedes, rise up against them and turn their swords upon them. Nor are the Swedes oblivious of this fact. They understand what is at stake here... Therefore, as I've said, if God hasn't blinded them by design, they'd never dare to strike at Yasna Gora. Because that day would be the end of their supremacy and the beginning of our reawakening."

Kmita listened to Prior Kordetzki's ringing and well-reasoned words as if they were an inspired revelation since they were such a clear-cut answer to the accusations he had heard from Veyhard.

"Why can't we believe, Venerable Father, that it's just as you said?" he asked, once he'd shaken himself free of his amazement. "And that God has blinded the enemy on purpose? Look at their arrogance, their greed for material wealth, the taxes with which they oppress everyone including the clergy, and it's quite clear that no sacrilege would be too much for them."

But instead of answering Pan Andrei directly, the Prior turned to the entire gathering.

"This cavalier tells us that he saw the Emperor's envoy going to the King of Sweden," he observed. "How can that be when the Pauline Fathers in Krakow write me that the King is no longer there and that he went straight back to Warsaw once Krakow had fallen?"

"That can't be right!" Kmita said. "And the best proof is that he has to wait for the surrender and submission of Hetman Pototzki..."

"The surrender is to be taken in his name by General Douglas," the Prior said calmly. "Or so I'm told in Krakow."

Kmita kept silent. He didn't know how to answer this and the priest went on:

"But let's assume that Charles Gustav didn't really want to see the Emperor's envoy at this time and that he made himself unavailable on purpose. He likes doing things like that, coming and going unexpectedly, and he's quite annoyed at the Emperor's attempts at mediation. I can believe that he went off to Warsaw pretending that he knew nothing about Lisola's coming. I'd be even less surprised that such a distinguished officer as Count Veyhard was sent to meet the envoy with an escort because they'd want to sugar-coat his unnecessary journey and sweeten his disappointment. But how can we believe that Count Veyhard would immediately reveal his plans to Baron Lisola, who is a Catholic and who is well known for his sympathies towards the Commonwealth and our exiled King?"

"That's quite impossible!" Father Nyeskovski said.

"I can't make head or tail of it either," added the Constable of Syeradz.

"Veyhard is a Catholic himself," threw in another priest. "And our benefactor."

"And this cavalier claims to have heard all this with his own ears?" Pan Pyotr Tcharnyetzki challenged, harsh with disbelief.

"Give some thought to this as well, gentlemen," the Prior continued. "That I have written guarantees from Charles Gustav himself by which the monastery and the church are to be always exempt from military intrusions and occupation."

"We must admit," Pan Zamoyski said seriously and gravely. "That this so-called information just doesn't hold together. The Swedes would lose, not gain, by taking Tchenstohova. The King is not in Krakow so Lisola couldn't have been going to visit him there. Veyhard couldn't have told him all his plans. Furthermore, Veyhard himself is a Catholic, not a heretic —a friend and benefactor of the monastery, not its enemy—and, finally, even if Satan did succeed in tempting him to attack this place, he'd never dare to do it against his King's orders and in the face of his King's personal guarantees."

Then he turned to Kmita.

"What are you telling us, then, cavalier?" he demanded. "And why, and to what purpose, are you trying to alarm these venerable fathers and the rest of us?"

★ ★ ★

Kmita stood before them like an accused felon before a court of justice. On the one hand he was terrified that if he couldn't win their trust and credibility the monastery and all that it contained, would become simple loot for the enemy; on the other hand he burned with shame because he knew that everything pointed against his story and that he could be taken for a liar. Anger clawed at him at this thought, his natural bent for rash and impulsive action came to life again, his injured pride leaped forward to defend itself, and the old, fierce, half-tamed and uncontrollable Kmita awoke in him once more.

He fought himself, bitterly and in silence, until he crushed his vanity and rage. He called on whatever patience he could find, telling himself over and over again that this was a penance for his crimes. And, finally, he mastered himself enough to say:

"I heard what I heard. I repeat, Veyhard is to seize the monastery. I don't know when but it can't be very far away. I've warned you..." And here his voice sharpened despite all his efforts. "The responsibility will be yours if you don't heed my warning!"

To which Pan Pyotr Tcharnyetzki uttered a warning of his own.

"Softly, cavalier, softly... Don't raise your voice here!" Then, turning to the gathering, the grim noble said: "Allow me, Reverend Fathers, to ask a few questions of this new arrival..."

"You've no right to insult me!" Kmita shouted.

"Nor do I care to," Pan Pyotr answered coldly. "But this concerns the monastery and the first city of the Holy Mother. That's why you must put aside whatever injury you're feeling or at least postpone it, because I'll satisfy your honor anytime, you can be sure of that. You've brought some news, we want to check it out, and that shouldn't come as a big surprise. But if you don't want to answer, we'll be right in thinking that you're afraid to risk making a mistake."

"Alright! Ask your questions!" Babinitch snarled through clamped teeth.

"That's more like it. So you say that you're from Zmudya, are you?"

"That's correct."

"And that you've come here so as not to serve the Swedes and that traitor Radzivill?"

"That's correct."

"Then why couldn't you do it there? Aren't there others who refuse to serve him? What about all those regiments that mutinied against him? How about Pan Sapyeha? Why didn't you join them?"

"That's my affair!"

"Ah... That's your affair," Tcharnyetzki said coldly and nodded with contempt. "Then maybe you can answer another kind of question?"

Pan Andrei's hands had begun to quiver. His eyes fixed themselves on a large brass bell standing on the table in front of him and then darted to the head of his interrogator. He was seized by a savage, nearly uncontrollable desire to snatch that heavy bell and bring it down on Pan Tcharnyetzki's skull. The former Kmita was starting to get the best of the new Babinitch.

But he mastered himself once again. "Ask it!" he snapped.

"If you're from Zmudya then you must know what is happening at the traitor's court. Give me the names of those other turncoats who helped him to destroy the country. Name me those colonels who stand with him in treason."

Kmita became as pale as a sheet. But he named half a dozen people.

Pan Tcharnyetzki heard him out, then said:

"I've a friend at His Majesty's court in Glogau. A gentleman-in-waiting named Tyzenhaus. He told me about yet another one, the worst hangman of the lot. Don't you know anything about that arch-scoundrel?"

"...No."

"How can that be? You don't know that Cain who spilled more of his brothers' blood then the rest of them together? You come from Zmudya and you never heard of Kmita?"

"Reverend Fathers!" Kmita shouted out, shaking as if in fever. "Let one of you question me and I'll bear it all... But don't let this piddling little noble torment me much further!"

"Let it rest, sir," Prior Kordetzki said quietly to Pan Pyotr.

"This cavalier is not our main concern just now." Then, turning to Kmita, he asked: "You didn't expect to be disbelieved by us here?"

"No more than I doubt that God is in his Heaven!"

"And what reward did you expect?"

But Pan Andrei didn't answer him directly. Instead, he plunged both his hands into a small leather sack that hung from his sash and hurled two glittering handfuls of pearls, emeralds, turquoises and other precious stones rattling across the table.

"There's your answer!" he cried in a cracked, gasping voice, hardly able to string a sentence together. "I didn't come here for your money...! Your rewards...! These pearls and other stones... they're booty ripped off the caps of the Russian Boyars... I've more and all of it's taken honorably in battle... Does it look as if I need rewarding...? I wanted to offer all this to Our Lady but only after a full confession, with a clean heart! Well, here they are anyway! Now you know about me! That's how much I need to be paid for my services, God blast you...!"

★ ★ ★

The gathered priests and nobles sat as still as carvings, quite stunned and dumbstruck by the sight of these incalculable treasures spilled out as easily before them as a bag of buckwheat. Each of them had to ask himself why this man came among them with his terrifying news if it wasn't for the sake of some reward. Why would he lie about such important matters if he didn't have to?

Pan Pyotr looked particularly hesitant and uncertain. It was, as everyone there knew, only human nature to be dazzled by the sight of another's man's wealth and power. The play of doubt on his wondering features showed that his suspicions were dwindling at this sight; how could he keep thinking that this great, rich lord, who could toss precious stones about as if they were gravel, wanted to frighten a few monks for the sake of profit?

So they sat in silence, staring at each other, and he stood above them and his scattered treasures as fierce as a young eagle, with his head held high, his face on fire with anger, and dangerous lights glittering in his eyes.

"Truth shines through your indignation, young sir," Prior

Kordetzki said to him at last. "But put away your jewels because Our Lady can't accept what's offered in anger, no matter how justified that might be. Besides, as I've said, we're not here to judge you. We're here to deliberate about your shocking and terrifying news. God alone can tell if there isn't some misunderstanding or misapprehension at play in this matter because, as you must see yourself, it doesn't hold together... How can we drive out the people who come here to worship, or take away from the honor they want to show Our Lady, and keep our gates locked night and day?"

"Keep them locked, for God's sake!" Kmita cried out wildly, twisting his fists in supplication so that his knuckles cracked. "In God's mercy, keep them locked!"

His voice was so full of terrifying truth and undisguised despair that all the others shuddered as if their danger was already upon them, and Pan Zamoyski said:

"We keep a watchful eye on the countryside as it is but we could take even greater care. And there's some repair work being done on the walls already..." Then, turning to the troubled priests, he added: "We could keep letting in the pilgrims during the day but it would do no harm to be on our guard, if for no other reason than because Charles Gustav *has* gone back to Warsaw and Wittemberg is ruling Krakow with an iron hand. He's always oppressed the clergy quite as much as he does ordinary people..."

"I'm still not convinced that we shall be attacked," Pan Pyotr Tcharnyetzki added. "But I see no harm in being extra careful."

"And I'll send a few brothers to Veyhard asking if the royal guarantees have lost all their meaning," Father Kordetzki said.

Weak with emotion, Kmita drew his first full breath of the day. "Thank God! Thank God!" he cried out.

"Young sir!" the Prior said to him. "May God repay your good intentions... If you have warned us in good cause then you'll have earned great merit, both as regards Our Lady and our country. But don't hold our doubts against us. We've heard alarming news before. Some people tell their frightening tales out of their hatred for the Church, so as to disrupt the worship of Our Holy Mother. Others do it out of greed, hoping to get something for themselves. Yet others spread fear and alarm just to make themselves important. There may have been some who were misled, as we suppose that you must have been misled, but there are others who foment fears on purpose...

"Satan is amazingly deadset against this place," he continued. "Nothing can please him more than to prevent as many people as he can from honoring Our Lady, because nothing drives him into greater fury than veneration of innocence and virtue... But now it's time for the evening prayer. Let us beg for Her intercession, place ourselves under Her protection, and then let us go and sleep in peace. Because where else can we find greater care and safety then under Her wing?"

The gathering ended then. Everyone went his way. The Prior himself took Pan Andrei to the confessional when the church emptied after evening prayers. The confession lasted a long time.

When it was over, Pan Andrei prostrated himself face down on the cold stone pavement, lying in silence until midnight with his arms spread out in the shape of the Holy Cross before the closed chapel doors.

At midnight he returned to the monk's cell in which he and his men were quartered, woke Soroka, and had him flog his naked back with a rawhide whip until blood ran in streams from his neck and shoulders.

Chapter Fifty-nine

NEXT MORNING, a puzzling new activity swept over Yasna Gora. The main gates stayed open, the worshipers and pilgrims entered as freely as before, and the services took their normal course. But all strangers were asked to leave the monastery grounds once worship was over.

The Prior himself toured the fortifications in the company of the Constable and Pan Pyotr Tcharnyetzki, inspecting the blind side of the ramparts and paying close attention to the buttresses which supported the walls both inside and out. Men were set to work on whatever repairs were found necessary, while the town blacksmiths received word to prepare a supply of pole-axes, siege-spears used in toppling scaling ladders, scythes set on end atop long thrusting poles, iron maces, and heavy, nail-studded logs. And because everyone knew that the monks possessed ample stores of that kind already, the whole town started talking about some new danger which fresh defensive measures confirmed by the hour.

Two hundred workmen were laboring on the walls by night-fall. The twelve heavy cannon which Pan Varshitzki, the castellan of Krakow, sent to Yasna Gora even before the Swedes laid siege to his city, were reset in new carriages and sighted in the proper manner. The monks and church servants trooped all day long out of the monastery cellars, carrying cannon balls and kegs of gunpowder and stacking them beside the guns. Stands of new muskets were broken out and issued to the garrison. Sentries climbed into the towers and stood guard along the angled bastions, keeping a close eye on everything that happened in the plain below, while trusted men were scattered throughout the villages and townships of the countryside to watch for anything unusual and give early warning.

The monastery larders didn't lack provisions but cartloads of new supplies began to flow at daybreak towards Yasna Gora, coming from the town, the neighboring church farms of Tchenstohovka or 'Little Tchenstohova,' and all the other villages belonging to the monastery.

The rumors of an impending attack on the holy place rolled through the countryside like thunder. Townsmen and peasants began to get together, planning what to do, although few of them could believe that any enemy would dare to threaten Yasna Gora. What most thought likely was that only the town of Tchenstohova would be occupied by Swedes but even that set angry minds aflame, especially when the more warlike among them reminded everyone that the Swedes were heretics to a man and that they'd miss no chance to offer insult to the Virgin Mary.

So while some people hesitated, doubted, and believed in turn, no one knew exactly what to do. Some wrung their hands in impotent despair, looking for signs of God's anger and expecting terrifying omens on earth and in the skies. Others sunk into a hopeless gloom. But others felt a frightful rage, more than an ordinary human being could experience, that seemed to set their heads on fire with fury. And as so often happens once sleepy and complacent minds are stirred and imaginations soar into flight, the rumors bred even wilder and more terrifying stories and feverish news spread everywhere with the speed of lightning.

It seemed to everyone whatever their feelings, that the whole neighboring countryside turned overnight into one vast, roiled and infuriated anthill, as if someone had thrust a giant stick among them or threw hot coals over their home lair.

* * *

Throughout the afternoon, groups of peasantry and townsmen came with their weeping wives and children to surround the monastery walls, holding them under a siege of their own and filling the air with their moans and prayers, until Father Kordetzki came out to them at sunset. "People," he asked as he walked among them. "What are you doing here?"

"We want to sign on to defend God's Mother!" the men cried

out, shaking gnarled fists that grasped scythes, pitchforks and other country weapons.

"We want to look at the Holy Maiden for the last time!" wailed the peasant women.

Father Kordetzki climbed to a slab of rock that angled out of the escarpment, looked down at the vast crowds that gathered below him and called on them to have trust and courage.

"The Gates of Hell shall never triumph over the Powers of Heaven," he said. "Calm yourselves and fill your hearts with faith. No heretic will set foot in this holy place. No Calvinist or Lutheran will ever practice his rituals in this house of goodness. I can't say if some ruthless, Godless enemy will dare to come this way. But I can tell you this much, that if he does come here, he'll leave broken, humbled and in shame. A far greater power than his will crush all his might, a far stronger goodness will destroy his evil, and all his good fortune will abandon him thereafter...

"Take heart!" he cried out. "This isn't the last time that you can look at our Holy Patroness! You'll see Her often in even greater glory and you will witness many more miracles in the years to come. Take courage, dry your tears, and confirm yourselves in your faith, because I say to you—and it's the Holy Spirit that is speaking through me—that no Swede will come within these walls. Mercy and grace live here, and darkness will never extinguish their light, just as this coming night will not prevent, God's sunlight from shining tomorrow!"

The sun set at just about that time. Darkness settled on the surrounding country and only the church still glowed in gold and scarlet in the last beams of daylight. Reassured and strengthened, the people knelt in worship all around the walls. The signal for the *Angelus* echoed from the towers and Prior Kordetzki began to sing the *Agnus Dei*, followed by the whole, vast multitude. The soldiers and gentry standing on the walls joined in, bells began to ring, and it seemed to everyone that the entire hill was alive with music like a huge organ playing to the four corners of the world.

The singing went on long into the night. Father Kordetzki blessed those who began to leave and said to all in parting: "Those of you men who have done some military service, know how to handle arms and feel courage in your hearts, come to the gates early tomorrow morning."

"I was a soldier one time!" many voices shouted. "I served in the infantry! I'll come!"

And the crowds slowly ebbed away.

* * *

The night passed without incident. The joyful cries that echoed along the walls next morning were: "Look... no Swedes!" Yet the artisans continued to deliver the ordered armaments and supplies all day.

An order also went out to the peddlers who kept the stands and souvenir shops along the slope, especially those who huddled against the eastern wall, to bring their trade goods into the monastery grounds, and the work on the walls continued as the day before. Special attention was given to the sally-ports, or narrow passages left in the fortifications, that would allow the defenders to raid the enemy without opening their gates. Pan Zamoyski ordered them loosely blocked with logs, quarried stone and bricks so that they could be opened from the inside when needed.

The supply wagons also rolled all day into Yasna Gora, along with several families of local gentry who were alarmed by the news of an imminent enemy arrival. The men sent out earlier to scout the countryside returned at noon with word that there were no Swedes anywhere near, except for those quartered some miles away in the market town of Krepitz, but the work on the walls went on as before.

Those of the local peasantry and townsmen who had seen some service in territorial infantry and provincial levies arrived to report for duty first thing in the morning. They were turned over to Pan Zygmunt Mosinski who had charge of the north-eastern tower. Pan Zamoyski drilled them all day, assigned their positions on the walls, showed them what to do, and sat in council with the Prior and the Pauline Fathers in the refectory.

Kmita looked at all these preparations with joy.

This was his element.

The drilling companies, the ready cannon in their embrassures, the stacks of muskets, spears and nail-studded logs made him feel alive. He felt all the lighter and happier because he had made a general confession as a dying man might do, cleansing himself of a lifetime of sins and wrong-doing and, to his surprise, received absolution. Father Kordetzki took into consideration his fervent desire to mend his ways and the fact that he had already stepped upon the right path.

Absolved, he was rid of an unsupportable burden which had just about brought him to his knees. His penance was hard. His back ran with blood every night under Soroka's lashes. He was ordered to rid himself of pride and practice humility and that was harder than bearing the pain of whipping because he still had no humility in his heart. On the contrary, now more than ever he was delighted with himself.

Father Kordetzki also ordered him to let his deeds affirm his wish to change but that was the easiest part of his heartfelt conversion because he wanted nothing else. All of his youthful spirit cried for deeds and action, by which he meant war and the slaughtering of Swedes without rest or mercy. He wanted to batter them all day long, from morning to nightfall, and what a marvelous opportunity he was about to get! The thought that he'd be fighting for his country and the King to whom he'd sworn his oath was exhilarating enough. But when he added the vision of himself as a defender of the Holy Mother, he felt a joy beyond anything to which he was entitled.

'*Where are those days when I stood bewildered at the crossroads?*' he asked himself with wonder. '*What happened to all those doubts and questions? They're gone! They've vanished! And did I really start to lose all hope?*'

Yet what was it that made him feel as if all his troubles were finally over?

'*These people,*' he thought peering all around him. '*These few white-robed monks—that handful of nobles and simple country folk—are getting ready to defend themselves! They'll fight to the death! They'll never surrender!*'

This was, he knew, the only corner of the Commonwealth where he could have found such a cause and such determination and he felt that he found it through more than any agency of his own.

'*A lucky star must have brought me here,*' he thought in gratitude and wonder.

He had no doubts about who would be victorious in this place. He was convinced that the whole might of Sweden wouldn't be enough to break through those walls and conquer those defenders. His heart was full of prayer, thanksgiving and joy.

★ ★ ★

He walked along the walls with a glowing face, watching everything that was going on, and pleased with all he saw. His trained, expert eyes told him that the preparations were in the hands of experienced people who'd know how to show their mettle when the fighting started. He couldn't get over the peacefulness and calmness of Prior Kordetzki whom he admired to the point of wide-eyed adulation. He was full of respect for the steadiness and seriousness of purpose shown by Pan Zamoyski. He was even willing to be friendly with Pan Pyotr for whom he still bore a certain grumbling grudge.

But that harsh, implacable young knight kept on looking at him with disfavor. Meeting him on the walls the day after the scouts returned from their survey of the surrounding country, he threw Kmita a cold, sideways glance, and said:

"The Swedes don't seem to be coming, cavalier. And if they don't show up then you'll be able to feed your reputation to the dogs."

"Let them eat hearty if that helps to protect this holy place!" Kmita said.

"But you'd rather not sniff the Swedes' gunpowder, eh? We know all about fair-weather heroes whose boots are lined with rabbit fur!"

Kmita let his eyes drop. He didn't want to argue.

"Why don't you give it up?" he asked. "What do I still owe you? I let myself forget your insults, why don't you forget about mine?"

"You called me a piddling little noble," Pan Pyotr answered sharply. "Where do you come from to say a thing like that? In what way is Babinitch better than Tcharnyetzki?"

"My dear sir," Kmita grinned and said as if he didn't have a care in the world. "If it wasn't for that humility I've been told to practice, and that whipping that cuts up my back after evening prayers, I'd soon call you a lot worse than that. Only I'm scared to fall back into my old sins, you see. As for who's better, Babinitch or Tcharnyetzki, we'll get a chance to see it when the Swedes show up."

"And what kind of rank d'you think you'll get here? Are you expecting to be one of the commanders?"

Kmita grew serious then. "First you thought I was after some kind of a profit," he said. "And now you're talking about taking charge. Let me say this much to you: I didn't come here looking for distinctions. I could have found promotions somewhere else, and a lot higher ones at that. I'll be a simple soldier here, that's all, even if I have to serve under you."

"Why *even*? What do you mean by *even*?"

"Because you're angry at me and you'd give me hell."

"Hmm. Well. Perhaps I misjudged you. I must say it speaks well of you that you'd as soon be an ordinary soldier, particularly since it's obvious you're a haughty character and eating humble pie isn't to your taste. Are you looking forward to the fighting?"

"As I said, we'll see that when the Swedes show up."

"And what if they don't?"

"Then... you know something?" Kmita laughed out loud and grinned from ear to ear. "We'll go looking for them!"

"That I like!" Pan Pyotr cried out. "That's my line of thinking! We could collect quite a decent little partisan formation... Silesia is close by and we'd find some good soldiers in no time at all. The senior commanders, like my uncle Stefan, had to take an oath of neutrality but plain soldiers weren't even asked and they'd come running like the wind if they knew there was something happening. We could raise a good force at the very first call!"

"And we'd set a good example for the rest of the country!" Kmita caught fire from his own enthusiasm. "I also have a real tough bunch of fighters with me... You should see them at work!"

"Well... well... I say," Pan Pyotr stammered out, his eyes alight with pleasure. "You're a damn good man, you know that? Come here, let me hug you, eh?"

And the two of them threw themselves into each other's arms.

Father Kordetzki was passing by just then. Seeing what was happening he began to bless them and they told him at once what they had decided. The Prior smiled quietly, nodded and went on.

"A sick man is coming back to health," he murmured to himself.

* * *

All the preparations were finished by nightfall and the monastery stood ready to defend itself. It was amply supplied, provisioned and armed to withstand even a lengthy siege. All that it lacked were walls of sufficient strength and a large, well-trained and experienced garrison.

Tchenstohova, or rather Yasna Gora itself, counted among the weaker and smaller fortresses of the Commonwealth, even though nature and military engineering made it strong enough to protect the monks from ordinary upheavals and disturbances and from minor enemy encroachments. As for a garrison, the Pauline Fathers could have had as many volunteers as they wanted, but they were careful to limit the number of defenders so that supplies might last.

There were, however, several men among them, especially among the hired German gunners, who were convinced that Tchenstohova wouldn't be able to defend itself. They thought that a fortress depended only on walls, guns and powder. They didn't know the power of uplifted hearts. Father Kordetzki dismissed them all but one, who passed for a real master at his trade, fearing that their doubts would undermine the faith and spirit of the others.

That same day, however, old Kemlitch and his sons knocked on Kmita's door, asked him to release them from his service and let them go their way.

"Dogs!" he shouted at them, enraged as he hadn't been in days. "You'd rather rob and loot out in the countryside than defend Our Lady? You'd give up such a chance for happiness of your own free will? Very well! I've paid you for your horses, and here is the rest!"

He took a purse out of a bureau drawer and threw it on the ground.

"Here's your pay!" he shouted. "Go and look for whatever you can steal outside the walls! Be bandits if you want to! Get out of my sight! You're not worthy to be here, you're not fit for the community of Christians, you're not good enough for the kind of death that waits for you among us! Get out! Get out at once!"

"Yes, yes, we're unworthy, we're unfit," the sly old man whined and groaned, spreading his arms in contrived haplessness and bowing to the ground. "We don't deserve to feast our eyes on all those Yasna Gora treasures... Dear Gates of Heaven! Star of the Morning! Refuge of the Damned! Yes, we're unfit, unworthy...!"

Here he stooped so low in faked humility that he seemed to bend himself in half while, at the same time, snatching up the purse with his gaunt, predatory claw.

"But we'll keep on serving even beyond the walls," he whined on, backing out of the chamber. "Yes, yes, Your Honor can always count on us... We'll send timely word about everything that happens over there... We'll go where we have to, do what must be done... Your Honor will have ready hands waiting for you whenever you need us..."

"Get out!" Kmita shouted.

They went on bowing and edging through the door, still terrified of Kmita and what they thought he might do to them, but with amazement and delight showing in their faces that he didn't cut their backs to ribbons, that he gave them gold, and that everything had turned out so well.

By nightfall they were gone, along with everyone else on whom the defenders wouldn't be able to depend to fight to the death. The fortress stood waiting.

Chapter Sixty

THE NIGHT WAS DARK and thick with a November drizzle. The morning would be the ninth day of November but Winter was already on its way and wet flakes of snow splashed out of the clouds along with the rain. The only sound that broke into the hushed and sodden silence on the battlements were the protracted cries of sentries that drifted from one watchtower to another, and the most frequent sight glimpsed by the huddled guards was Prior Kordetzki's white habit flitting through the darkness.

Kmita didn't sleep. He was on the walls with Pan Tcharnyetzki talking about past wars. He told about the war against Hovansky, careful to say nothing about his part in that campaign, while Pan Pyotr gave an account of skirmishes with the Swedes at Predbor, Zarnov and in the neighborhood of Krakow where he did well in some mounted clashes and couldn't help boasting a little about it.

"One did what one could. Every time I laid out some Swede I'd tie a knot in my saber straps. I've six already and with God's grace I'll have many more! That's why I wear my saber so high on my belt, you see? Pretty soon I'll have it in my armpit and the straps will be too short to use! But I'll have each knot studded with a turquoise and offer them after the war as a *votum* to our Holy Lady. And how about you? Do you have any Swedes on your conscience yet?"

"No," Kmita said, ashamed. "I smashed a band of them near Sohatchev but they were just marauding deserters..."

"How about the Russians? I expect you've notched enough of those?"

781

"Ah, there I'd find a few knots of my own!"

"It's harder with the Swedes because there're few among them who aren't magicians. The Finns taught them how to call up the Devil and now each of them has two or three demons jumping at his orders. Some have as many as seven, so it's hard to get at them in a fair fight... But the Devil won't be of much use to them here because Satan has no power within sight of any of the towers. Did you know about that?"

Kmita didn't answer. He started twisting his head about, listening through the chilly rustling of the rain, and then said suddenly:

"They're coming!"

"What? For God's sake...! Are you sure?"

"I hear cavalry."

"That's just the wind and the rain doing all that drumming."

"No, by Christ's wounds! That's no wind, those are hoof-beats! I've a good ear for that. There's a lot of cavalry coming... a lot, and they're close already! You'd hear them well enough if it wasn't for the wind blowing in our faces."

Then he leaped up, turned towards the towers, and started calling out: "Alarm! Alarm! Stand to arms! Alarm!"

* * *

Kmita's shout woke the sentries who were dozing nearby, chilled to the marrow in the freezing rain, but its last echoes were still in the air when the shrill, brassy voice of trumpets rose from the darkness below in a long, mournful and terrifying fanfare.

"What is this? Judgment Day?" the stunned men and women atop Yasna Gora asked themselves and each other fearfully, leaping to their feet.

Then everyone—monks, soldiers, gentry—spilled out of the buildings. The bell-ringers heaved on their ropes. All the bells clanged in alarm as if for a fire. Their ringing joined the protracted, gloomy clamor of the trumpets. Watchmen threw burning fuses into barrels of pitch that stood ready all along the walls and then cranked them up on pulleys to hang above the ramparts. A scarlet light flooded the foot of the rock and the defenders saw a troop of mounted trumpeters, their long brass horns still raised to their lips, and—stretching behind them as far as anyone could see—deep ranks of Swedish Reiters looming out of darkness under a grove of banners.

The trumpeters went on playing their shrill and frightening music for some time as if to terrify the monks altogether with this reminder of Swedish might and power. Then they were silent while a single horseman broke away from their ranks and rode to the gates waving a white flag.

"In the name of His Majesty!" he boomed out and then launched into a grim, measured recitation of titles, lands and peoples that constituted the awesome power that he represented: "The most illustrious King of the Swedes, Goths and Vandals! Grand Duke of Finland, Estonia and Karelia! Lord of Bremen, Verden, Stettin, Pomerania and Kasubia! Prince of Rugen and Ingria, Lord-Paramount of Vismarck and Bavaria, Count Palatine of the Rhineland, Cleves, Berg and Jutland...Open your gates!"

"Who sent you?" the Prior called down from the walls.

"Count Veyhard!"

"Let him in," Prior Kordetzki ordered.

The gate-guard opened a narrow sally-port set into the portals but not the gates themselves. The rider hesitated for a moment then climbed off his horse and stepped inside the walls. Peering about he saw a huddled little group of white Pauline habits and demanded: "Who's the Superior here?"

"I am," said Prior Kordetzki.

The herald handed him a package thick with dangling seals. "His Grace the Count is quartered at St. Barbara's down below," he announced abruptly. "He waits for your reply."

* * *

The Prior immediately asked the senior clergy and the leading gentry to join him in the *Definitorium* so that they might help him to decide the answer.

"You might as well come along too," Pan Pyotr said to Kmita.

"Alright," Pan Andrei said. He shrugged. "I'll go because I'm curious, but that's all. I didn't come here to fight for Our Lady by wagging my tongue... There's nothing for me to do in a council chamber."

But once the priests and gentry found seats for themselves around the refectory table, he paid close attention as Prior

Kordetzki broke the seals on the packaged letter, scanned it at a
glance and began to read aloud in a serious voice.

'*It is no secret to you, Honorable Fathers, how I have always favored
your Community, what goodwill I have always shown You, and with
what Sincerity and Devotion I have protected and supported the Sanctity of the Holy Place in former and less troubled times,*' Veyhard had
written.

'*... Bearing all this in mind, I wish to reaffirm my Friendship and
Regard for You and your Order, and my concern for the safety of its
Sacred Objects, asking that you place yourselves in my hands until safer
days. You may be certain that I don't come as an Enemy but as your
Wellwisher, seeking only to take your Monastery under my Protection
in these unsettled times when no one can be sure of what God's Will
may send his way from hour to hour. Do as I ask, oblige me in this
matter, and you will find the Means to continue in that Peace and
Safety which You desire so strongly.*'

Veyhard's words, as Pan Andrei could see, made a powerful
impression on many of the older clergy who would remember
his past kindnesses while he was still in the service of the
Commonwealth. He watched them uneasily, noting their trusting and eager expressions, as the Prior continued to read in the
same measured tones.

'*... I promise You,*'—Veyhard wrote—'*by all that is Holy, that all
your Sacred Objects will remain untouched, that no harm shall come to
your Possessions, that I myself shall furnish and provide the costs of
your Protection, and that I shall even add further to your goods and
means. Consider how much you will benefit by entrusting me with the
care of your Community and Church and place yourselves and your
Monastery in my hands, as I request and expect herewith.*

'*... And this is also something that You should remember,*' the
letter continued in a tone of warning. '*that if you decline my
Honest and Sincere offers, you may be held accountable by General
Mueller, my military superior, whose orders will be all the sterner
because, unlike myself, he is a Heretic and an Enemy of the Faith.*

'*... Should he come in my place,*' the letter concluded, '*You will
have to acquiesce in any event, surrender unconditionally to his demands, and regret the day when You rejected my caring and affectionate
Advice.*'

A thoughtful and uneasy silence fell on the gathering when

the reading ended and Pan Andrei could see that Veyhard's words had a profound effect. Recollections of his former goodwill worked side-by-side with fear of the unknown. Past kindnesses seemed to offer a shield against threatening choices, and many of the listening Brotherhood and gentry saw only what they wanted to see in his assurances: a peaceful means of averting fresh calamities and future disasters.

But no one spoke. All eyes rested on the silent Prior whose lips were moving in a voiceless prayer, and Kmita held his breath.

"Would a true friend come to us like this?" Father Kordetzki began to speak at last. "At night, in darkness, with armed thousands behind him, frightening God's resting servants with the cry of war horns? Why would he need an army at his back when, as our loyal friend and benefactor, he could expect only a joyful reception among us? What is the meaning of those regiments massed outside our walls if not a threat of armed violence done to our Holy Sanctuary if we don't give up our monastery to him as he asks...?

"He warns us," Father Kordetzki went on thoughtfully but firmly. "He reminds us of his General Mueller... But here is something else we have to remember: that these are enemies who never keep their word, honor their own safe-conducts or fulfill their guarantees to anyone. We ourselves have Charles Gustav's personal assurance, sent to us without any application on our part, which clearly states that the monastery will be exempt for all time from military seizure, but here they are tonight, standing in armed ranks below our walls and proclaiming the lie of all their promises with their dreadful trumpets!

"Dearest Brothers!" His strong, calm voice was grave with the seriousness of the moment as he turned to the assembled clergy. "Let each of you open his heart to Heaven so that the Holy Ghost might enlighten your deliberations, and then speak out and tell us what your minds and consciences dictate for the good of this community and this sacred ground."

But still no one spoke until Kmita's voice broke the heavy silence.

"I heard in Krushin," he said, "how Lisola asked him: '*But you'll rattle the monks' treasure chest, I expect?*' To which Veyhard answered: '*God's Mother doesn't need the silver in the Prior's coffers.'* Today that same Veyhard writes that he'll cover the costs of the occupation out of his own pocket and even add to the monastery's treasure... Judge his sincerity and honesty by that!"

Next to speak was Father Myeletzki, one of the older clergy gathered there and himself a soldier in his youth.

"We keep to vows of poverty here," he said. "Whatever earthly goods we have serve only to honor Our Lady. But even if we stripped Her altars to buy protection for this holy place, who'd guarantee that they'll keep their promise? That they won't raise their sacrilegious hands against Her ornaments and vestments? Or that they won't loot the votive offerings, chalices, and sacramental objects? Who can trust a liar?"

"We're duty-bound to consult our Provincial in any event," Father Dobrosh added. "We can't make such a far-reaching decision without him."

But doubt, fearfulness, the specter of a siege and bloodshed, and some anxiety for compromise and peaceful appeasement remained in many faces.

"War... if it comes to fighting and resistance... is not our profession," Father Tomitzki offered. "So let us hear the advice of the knights and soldiers who found shelter with us and who seek refuge with the Holy Mother."

At this all eyes turned on Pan Zamoyski as the senior among the gentry in terms of age, position and the dignity of office.

"It's your fates, Reverend Fathers, that are in question here, not ours" he said gravely. "So compare the power of the enemy with the resistance that you're able to offer, match your strength and resources against his, and act accordingly. We are merely your guests, how can we advise you? But since you ask what you ought to do I'll tell you this much: let's not think of yielding without resistance until there is no other course. Why? Because buying a doubtful peace with abject surrender to the first demands of an enemy who doesn't keep his word is not only shameful but ill-advised as well...

"We and our families came here among you to put ourselves under the protection of the Holy Maiden, trusting in Her mercy and casting our fates with yours come what may. Faith in God and His Holy Mother brought us to live here in your sanctuary in these desperate times and, if that's God's will, that same unshaken faith will let us die beside you without a murmur of complaint. Indeed, such a death would be a greater mercy than a life of slavery and shameful obedience...

"Who wouldn't rather die," he went on with a rising firmness, "than live to watch the profanation of our holiest shrine without the will and power to do anything about it? But is there someone here who can doubt that She who fills our hearts with the determination to rise in Her defense, won't come to help us against Godlessness and blasphemy?"

Here the Constable fell silent. The gathering sat in a long silence of its own, finding much in his simple and straightforward message that fortified their determination, while Kmita sprung up as impulsively as he used to do, seized the older man's hand and pressed it gratefully to his lips.

It was a moving and prophetic moment. Searching for almost anything that could be taken for a sign from Heaven, everyone saw it as a lucky omen. Kmita's enthusiasm leaped like a flame to the older men and the desire to defend the monastery hardened in their hearts. But then another, more unusual omen sounded beyond the refectory windows where the quavering old voice of a beggar woman, a lame crone named Konstancia, rose in an ancient hymn.

> *'In vain all your fierce Hussite rage and bluster,*
> *In vain the help of your Satanic master,*
> *In vain your fires and your swords so gory,*
> *Mine is the Glory.*
> *'Even if you come here in hordes as thick as flies,*
> *Even if your warriors ride dragons in the skies,*
> *Neither your swords nor terror shall avail,*
> *For I shall prevail. "*

"There," Father Kordetzki said, nodding quietly, "is a warning that God sends to us through the mouth of a humble beggar. Let us defend ourselves, Brothers, for I tell you that no besieged fortress in history had such reinforcements as we shall receive!"

"We'll give our lives gladly!" Pan Tcharnyetzki shouted. "Don't trust the oath-breakers!"

"Veyhard is a turncoat!"

"Don't listen to heretics or a Catholic who takes service with the Devil!" cried many other voices, drowning the half-hearted objections of those who still may have wanted to talk about submitting.

★ ★ ★

In the end, the gathering decided to be conciliatory but firm. They sent two priests to Veyhard with a declaration that the gates would stay closed and that the besieged community would defend itself which the King's exemptions allowed them to do. On the other hand, the two emissaries were to beg the Count to forget his plans or, at least, hold them in abeyance until the Paulines could obtain permission to comply from Father Theophilus Bronievski, their Order's Provincial, who was in Silesia at that time with King Yan Casimir.

Fathers Tomitzki and Benedykt Yaratchevski slipped out beyond the gates and the rest of their community waited anxiously in the refectory. No matter how determined they were to protect their heritage, they were also fearful.

War was new to them.

The thought that the hour of decision was upon them and that they'd soon have to choose between their duty and the rage of an implacable enemy terrified many of the peaceful priests. Their two envoys were back in less than half an hour. They were pale and shaken. Their heads hung low as if they had been brutally abused. They handed Veyhard's written answer to Father Kordetzki who read it out for everyone to hear. But it was only a cold, eight-point ultimatum for the immediate surrender of the monastery.

The Prior finished reading and gazed in silence into the still, worried faces of each of the monks and clergy who sat before him with castdown eyes and hands clasped in prayer. He seemed to peer into the depths of each man's heart and soul and then, after what seemed like an interminable time, he spoke out in a voice laden with the importance of the moment.

"In the name of the Father, the Son and the Holy Ghost!" he said. "In the name of the Immaculate and Holiest Mother of God! To the walls, dearest Brothers! To the walls!"

★ ★ ★

Soon afterwards a bright, glaring fire illuminated the lower slopes of the mound below Yasna Gora where Veyhard ordered the burning of several outbuildings that huddled around the wayside chapel of St. Barbara. The fire swept through the old, wooden buildings, leaping fiercely from one to another, until tall pillars of reddish smoke, licked by the flickering yellow tongues of fire, rose into the sky and a crimson lid hung over the entire countryside.

Seen clearly in that crimson glare, troops of mounted soldiers were on the move from one place to another, showing to some of the besieged their first glimpse of war. Cattle were driven from their barns, filling the air with their mournful bellowing. Flocks of sheep huddled together in panic and then pushed blindly into the fires so that soon the stench of burning flesh lifted to the ramparts.

New to the frightful ravages of their century's warfare, many among the priests and Brothers stared down in terror as the mounted Reiters galloped among the buildings, cutting and hacking at fleeing mobs of people and dragging screaming women by the hair. They were so near and so brightly lit that even individual words of the howling victims came clearly to the watchers on the walls.

Because the monastery cannon were still to fire a shot, the marauding Reiters leaped off their horses and approached the walls shouting threats and shaking their swords and carbines. Every so often some thick-necked lout in a yellow jerkin jumped up among the slabs of rock at the foot of the escarpment, folded his hands around his mouth, and bellowed curses at the defenders who listened to it all in silence as they stood at their guns with lighted fuses in hand.

Kmita was standing with Pan Pyotr Tcharnyetzki right across from the Chapel of St. Barbara, in the center of that violent half-circle of massacre and pillage, and saw everything as clearly as if each scene were etched in the palm of his hand. His face was flushed with eagerness and excitement. His eyes glowed like a pair of torches. His hands grasped a superb, handcrafted bow which he'd inherited from his father who, in turn, took it off a Turk at the battle of Khotim many years earlier. He listened to the threats and insults patiently enough until a huge armored Reiter started to shout his curses from the foot of the slope before him.

"In God's name!" he turned to Pan Tcharnyetzki. "He's

blaspheming against the Holy Mother... I understand German! It's awful... terrible... I can't stand to hear this!"

And he drew back the cord of the bow and aimed an arrow at the shouting Reiter but Pan Pyotr knocked the weapon aside.

"God will punish the blasphemy and the blasphemer," he said. "Meanwhile Prior Kordetzki has forbidden any of us to shoot unless they shoot first."

He had no sooner spoken when the cursing Reiter lifted his musketoon, pressed the butt into his shoulder, and fired. The lead ball fell short of the wall somewhere along the slope and Kmita shouted: "Is it alright now?"

"It is!" said Tcharnyetzki.

Kmita was immediately as calm as ice. The Reiter was peering at the walls, trying to see is he had scored a hit and shielding his eyes from the glare with one hand, and Pan Andrei drew back on the bowstring, flicked it with a finger until it made a warbling, birdlike sound, and leaned across the rampart crying out: "Here's your death!"

In that same instant the arrow hissed, the Reiter dropped his musket, his arms jerked up and out, his head tilted forward and he toppled over on his back. His body leaped and quivered for a moment like a fish taken out of water, his boots drummed spasmodically on the rocky soil, and then he was still.

"That's one!" Kmita said.

"Tie a knot in your saber strap," Pan Tcharnyetzki said.

"A bell rope won't be enough before I'm done!" Pan Andrei cried. "God willing!"

A second Reiter ran up to first, either to see what was wrong with him or to pick his pockets, but another arrow made its plaintive sound and the rummaging trooper fell facedown across the dead man's chest.

"That's two!" Kmita said.

* * *

In the meantime Veyhard's light horse artillery had begun to fire. He couldn't hope to do any serious damage to the fortress with cannon of such insignificant caliber, no more than he could take it with cavalry alone, but he wanted to give the monks a foretaste of heavier bombardments and to undermine their spirit.

Prior Kordetzki also appeared just then next to Pan Pyotr and

Kmita with Father Dobrosh walking close behind him. The aging Dobrosh was the monastery's peacetime artillerist, popping off salutes on holidays and feast days, and he was somewhat vain about his reputation as a master gunner. The Prior blessed the cannon on which Kmita and Pan Pyotr were leaning, nodded at Father Dobrosh, and the reverend cannoneer rolled up his sleeves and started fiddling with the aiming levers.

He sighted long and hard, aware that his reputation was at stake, aiming the gun at a gap between two burning buildings where an officer with a drawn sword in his hand sat his horse in a milling group of several dozen riders.

At last Father Dobrosh appeared satisfied. He laid a lighted fuse across the touch-hole. The gun heaved and roared and a thick, black cloud of smoke obscured everything before them until the fresh night breeze carried it away. The gap between the buildings was empty and clear except for a pile of dead men and horses.

The monks on the walls started to sing a hymn accompanied by the crash and crackle of collapsing buildings around the Chapel of St. Barbara. The night darkened and the shadows deepened as the gutted buildings fell inward on the flames and only a myriad sparks thrown up by the burned-out timbers swarmed upward like a mass of fireflies.

The trumpets sounded once more among Veyhard's horsemen but their strident calls grew dimmer in the distance. The fires dwindled. Darkness crept back to the foot of Yasna Gora. Horses still neighed shrilly in the plain but the sound grew weaker with every passing minute; Veyhard was retreating.

Father Kordetzki knelt on the wall and lifted both his arms to the crimson sky.

"Grant that he who comes next will leave as these have done," he prayed. "With shame in his heart and empty anger gnawing at his soul."

The night-clouds parted above him as he prayed, the pale glow of moonlight returned to the sky, and the silvery beams drifted down upon the silent towers, the walls, the kneeling prior and the smoldering ruins.

Part Ten

Part Ten

Chapter Sixty-one

PEACE RETURNED THE NEXT DAY to the slopes below Yasna Gora, giving the monks and priests a chance to work all the harder on their preparations.

Workmen finished the last repairs on curtain walls and bastions. The final loads of weaponry arrived at the fortress. Another company of peasants who had seen service in Furrow Infantry contingents came in from the hamlets of Zdebov, Krovodra, Elgota and Grabovka. They were quickly accepted and assigned to other companies of defenders.

Father Kordetzki seemed to be everywhere at once. He offered Mass, sat in council, led the religious community's devotions night and day, and toured the walls during intermissions to chat with the laboring peasantry and gentry. His pale, careworn face seemed wholly tuned to spiritual matters, suggesting an almost somnolent detachment; but the quiet, almost merry resignation and acceptance that glowed in his eyes, and the lips that moved constantly in a silent prayer, showed that he was fully aware of everything around him, that he never lost sight of the difficulties and the consequences, and that he offered himself as a sacrifice for everyone. His entire being was pointed towards God. The deep, unswerving currents of his faith nourished everyone around him, soothing doubts and healing troubled souls, so that all eyes glowed with confidence wherever his white habit appeared among them.

He was 'the good father.' The men of Yasna Gora called him 'our hope, our defender' and 'our consolation.' Gentry and peasantry alike kissed his hands and the edges of his robes as he passed among them, and he went on with his quiet, bright smile, leaving behind a feeling of joyfulness and trust.

Nor did he forget about earthly matters, seeking help wherever he could find it. The Pauline Fathers who entered his cell on monastery business found him either on his knees and praying or hunched across his writing table at work on one or another of the innumerable letters he sent everywhere.

He wrote to Wittemberg, the Swedish field marshal commanding in Krakow, begging him to have mercy on a holy shrine; he dispatched daily messages to Yan Casimir whose wanderings had taken him to Opole in Upper Silesia where he was making his last desperate efforts to save and reclaim his ungrateful nation; he wrote to Stefan Tcharnyetzki, the almost legendary Castellan of Kiev who sat uselessly in exile, bound to neutrality by the terms of his capitulation during the fall of Krakow, and fretting like a caged wolf in his enforced inactivity.

He even wrote appeals to Colonel Sadovski, a high-minded Czech Lutheran who served under Mueller, whose sense of honor and nobility of spirit moved him to intercede with his grim old general to abandon his plans against Yasna Gora.

★   ★   ★

But if the 'White Prior of Yasna Gora' represented the forces of Godliness and goodness in the southwestern Poland of his time, then Burchardt Mueller—who had raped and pillaged half of Germany in the Thirty Years' War—stood for rapacity, cruelty and bloodshed.

Two voices whispered in his ears in those days. Two trusted advisors influenced his thinking. Both of them were Czechs and subjects of the Holy Roman Emperor's Bohemia but as different in character and outlook as night is to daylight. The Catholic Veyhard, who was enraged by the setback he suffered at the monastery, urged him to march immediately on Tchenstohova, dismissing its defenses as a 'chicken coop,' and promising loot beyond the old raptor's wildest imagination.

"Few European monasteries and churches house a greater treasure," he assured the General.

The Lutheran Sadovski took a more reasoned view.

"General," he said to Mueller at a headquarters staff meeting. "You know how much time and blood even the weakest fortress can cost if the defenders are determined to fight to the end. After all, you've stormed and sacked so many German cities that all of Europe calls you the second Policertes..."

"So it should," Mueller growled. "But these monks won't fight."

"I think they will. The richer they are the harder they'll defend their treasures, particularly since Papist superstition all over this country holds that place to be unassailable. Recall what used to happen in the German wars when monks would show greater grit and determination in desperate situations than regular soldiers! The same thing is likely to happen in Tchenstohova, especially since the fortifications aren't as trivial as Count Veyhard makes them out to be. The monastery stands on solid rock so that siege-mining and sapping will be difficult. The walls are sure to have been reinforced by now. A rich place like that won't be short of cannon, provisions or powder. Add the fanaticism we can expect there and you have a very difficult operation."

"And you think they'll force me to withdraw?"

"No I don't. But I think we'll be tied up in that siege for a very long time, and that we'll need to send for heavier artillery than we have right now. In the meantime Your Excellency is expected to march against Prussia. We have to calculate the time we can spare against Tchenstohova, because if His Majesty should summon us to Prussia on more serious business, the monks won't fail to boast that it was they who forced you to give up the siege. Just think, sir, what that would do to Your Excellency's reputation. Who'd talk then about a second Policertes...?

"Moreover,"—and here Sadovski lowered his voice in caution as if afraid of being overheard—"a mere hint that we are planning to attack that monastery will have the worst possible effect in this country and may have incalculable consequences for us as well. You may not know this, General, because that's something no foreigner or non-Papist understands, but Tchenstohova has an immense importance for this nation.

"We must keep depending on that gentry which surrendered to us with so little trouble," he reasoned and reminded. "We have to keep counting on those great lords with their private armies and on those standing forces who came over to us along with their Hetmans... We'd hardly have accomplished half of what we did without their help. Half?"—he snorted with contempt—"What am I saying? It's their own hands that gave their country to us... But let one shot be fired at Tchenstohova and who can tell what'll happen everywhere else? There is no way to calculate the power of superstition. We may find that not a single Pole remains at our side and an entirely new war can burst out around us without any warning!"

Deep in his heart—or in what passed for a heart in that grim old looter—Mueller agreed with Sadovski's reasoning. He was all the more uneasy about Tchenstohova because he believed that all monks were magicians, in league with the Devil, and he feared black magic worse than any cannon. But he enjoyed a streak of grim perversity, particularly since he envied Sadovski's reputation for probity and honor, and he wouldn't leave well enough alone.

"You talk as if you were the Tchenstohova prior," he remarked with cruel and cynical amusement. "Or maybe as if the monks started their tribute with your pocketbook..."

Sadovski was a good, experienced soldier but a proud and impulsive man as well; he knew his own worth so he was quick to take offense.

"If that's what you think then that's the last word that Your Excellency will hear from me on this subject!" he snapped in swift anger.

Mueller, in turn, was irked by the haughty manner in which his subordinate dared to speak to him. "That's all I want to hear from you!" he barked.

"We'll see!" Sadovski shot back and marched out of the room.

With Sadovski's restraining influence removed, Veyhard pressed his case. He brought Mueller a letter he'd received in the meantime from Castellan Varshitzki, an old acquaintance from his days as a Commonwealth official, in which the former governor of Krakow asked that the monastery be left alone. But Veyhard found an entirely different meaning in those words.

"They're pleading," he told Mueller. "That means they know they can't defend themselves."

The next day Mueller's staff in Vyelun started to set in motion the march on Tchenstohova.

★ ★ ★

Meanwhile Winter began its own swift advance. A cold wind blew sharply across the plains. Mud hardened underfoot and, in the morning, the shallower pools of water stiffened under thin coverlets of ice. Father Kordetzki rubbed his reddened hands as he walked along the walls and said to anyone who heard him:

"God will use even the Winter frosts to help us, you'll see! It won't be easy for the enemy to dig in frozen ground for their batteries and emplacements, or to tunnel with their siege-works and approaches. You'll have warm rooms to rest in between spells of duty on the walls and they'll soon get sick of their siege in their freezing tents."

Nor was there any longer any doubt that the Swedes were coming. Mueller was so confident that the monastery would fall in a day or two that he made no secret of his expedition, so that the Pauline Brothers of the Vyelun convent heard of it almost as soon as the Swedes themselves, and Father Hyacinth Rudnitzki set out at once with a warning for the Yasna Gora fathers.

Not for a moment did the Vyelun Paulines think that the Yasnogorians would defend themselves. They merely wanted to send a timely word so that Prior Kordetzki might have all the facts and negotiate the best conditions he was able to obtain under the circumstances.

Nor did this final confirmation of their deepest fears have a good effect on the Yasna Gora brothers. The news undermined the spirits of many. Some lost heart altogether. But Father Kordetzki set their minds at rest, fortified their courage, lifted them from the depths of their despair, and melted their icy resignation with the hot fires of his own unquenchable faith in the triumph of goodness.

He promised days filled with miracles. He spoke of death itself as such a glorious and uplifting spiritual experience that their spirits rose to meet his own and they set about preparing for the assault in the same way that they celebrated the great religious observances of their Church: solemnly and with joy.

At the same time the Constable of Syeradz and Pan Pyotr Tcharnyetzki, who were appointed the lay garrison commanders, finished off their own preparations. They burned down all the stalls and shops that clustered against the walls and might have served as cover for the enemy. They didn't even spare the nearby buildings along the bottom of the slope so that a ring of fire surrounded the fortress throughout that last day. But when all these structures turned to scattered ashes, the monastery cannon looked out over empty spaces, free of all obstructions. Their black, iron mouths gaped across an open and uncluttered distance, as if impatient for the enemy and anxious to meet him with their fire and thunder.

That enemy, meanwhile, wasn't far away. The road from Vyelun to Tchenstohova was only a short one. The siege was to begin on November 18 and Mueller expected that it would be over in three or four days with no more effort on his part than a show of strength, perhaps a brief bombardment, and some negotiations. He led nine thousand Swedish veterans, mostly infantry, and nineteen heavy cannon. He also had three regiments of Polish irregular cavalry attached to his command but he knew that he couldn't expect much from them in this expedition. First, because cavalry was useless against a hilltop fortress and, in the second place, because the Poles showed every sign of coming against their will. Their colonels let him know in advance that they would take no part in any of the fighting, and that the only reason they came at all was to protect the shrine from the ravages of pillage once the walls were breached and the monastery had fallen.

That, at least, was the explanation the soldiers got from their own commanders. The real reason why they came was because they had to obey Mueller's orders. All Polish troops, regulars and volunteers alike, were now a part of the Swedish armies, marched to the beat of the Swedish drummer, and did what they were told.

★   ★   ★

Father Kordetzki, in the meantime, prepared the souls of his community's defenders.

All of the monastery's swollen population—clergy, gentry, refugees and peasant volunteers—attended Mass as if it were a celebration of the happiest feast day in the calendar, and if it weren't for the pallor on some tremulous faces it might have

been taken for a joyous Easter. The Prior himself offered the
solemn Mass and every bell was ringing from the towers. But
the observance didn't end with the services in the church because the whole community marched in procession afterwards
all around the walls.

Father Kordetzki carried the sacrament in a golden monstrance, supported on each side by the Constable and Pan Pyotr
Tcharnyetzki. Rows of young boys dressed in snowy surplices
headed the procession, carrying myrrh, amber and incense cen-
sers swinging on gold chains.

Walking in pairs before and behind the ceremonial canopy
held over the Prior, came the entire Brotherhood of the cloistered clergy, young and old, in the white habits of their Order,
and with their heads and eyes tilted towards the sky. Some were
bowed with age and their years of service so that they seemed
like crouched, pale mushrooms trembling in the rainy air. Others were novices, hardly out of boyhood, who had barely taken
their first step towards priesthood. The yellow flames of candles
in their hands were dancing in the wind, but they walked on,
singing and immersed in God, as if none of them could remember anything connected with this world.

Crowding behind them came the stern rural nobles with their
necks and heads shaved high into the temples; calm women
with tear-stained faces but with an infinite trust in God showing
through their tears; and the long-haired country folk dressed in
homespun coats whose simple faith resembled that of the early
Christians. The thin, piping voices of children and young lads
and girls added flutelike tones to the anthem that everyone was
singing, and no one doubted that God was listening to them,
that He accepted this outpouring of their anxious love, and that
He would accept them under His sheltering wings.

The wind died down. The air grew calm and still. The sky
cleared overhead and displayed its own azure canopy, and the
high, Autumn sun spilled its pale light all around the landscape
as if to warm and waken the grey, hardening soil.

The procession circled the entire wall but neither stopped nor
turned around nor scattered. Instead it went on. Golden lights
splintered off the monstrance and fell across the Prior's face so
that it also seemed fashioned out of precious metals and sending
out a radiance of its own. Father Kordetzki held his eyes half

closed. His lips wore a smile of transcendent sweetness, joy and exaltation. His spirit had left the earth and he seemed to be floating in a realm of eternal brightness, happiness and uninterruptable peace. Yet even there his ears were tuned to some vast inner voice which ordered him never to forget the tangible church behind him, the people, the fortress, and the hour of trial which was on its way, so that he stood still every now and then and lifted the sacrament overhead and blessed everything around him.

He blessed the people, the soldiers, and the banners that bloomed along the wall in a rainbow of insurgent colors; he blessed the ramparts and the rock on which they were standing and the land beyond them; he offered blessings to the smaller guns and to the heavy cannon, the lead and iron balls stacked beside the carronades, the powder kegs, and the grim, spiked weapons used in repelling an assault; he blessed the distant villages of the countryside below and the four cardinal points of the compass along the horizon—north, south, east and west—as if he wanted to extend God's might and mercy over all the earth.

It was then two o'clock in the afternoon. The procession was still winding around the parapets. The horizons lay under a pale blue mist so that it seemed as if the earth and sky had moved towards each other, that they were touching and becoming one, merging God's earthly realm with his celestial one. But something stirred in that distant haze, something began to move; dim shapes began to creep darkly into the sunlit plain and started to acquire form and definition, and a shrill, anxious cry broke out at the tail-end of the procession.

"The Swedes! The Swedes are coming!"

All other human sounds ceased at once as if every heart and tongue in that convocation had turned into stone. Only the bells kept ringing. And then Father Kordetzki's calm but carrying voice rose above the silence.

"Be joyful Brothers!" he cried out. "Lift your hearts to Heaven. The hour of miracles and triumphs is approaching!"

And a moment later:

"Grant us Your protection, our Mother and Queen!"

* * *

In the meantime, the dull, hazy cloud that stirred on the

horizon turned into a serpent which crawled ever closer. The mists paled behind it. Soon its thick, rippling coils were in plain sight, winding across the near distance, straightening out and twisting. It crept on and on, emerging into sunlight like a cold, textured river that flowed remorselessly out of some primeval, unimaginable source while the pale sun gleamed and darkened in turn on its armored scales.

The watchers on the walls were soon able to distinguish the various segments of the creeping monster—the quick, nervous horsemen flickering at its head; the grim, glistening body coiling and uncoiling. Regiments of infantry marched behind the horsemen, each locked into a rigid geometric matrix of battalion squares with a tall inner rectangle of pikes rising from its center.

Beyond them, still so far off that they seemed a part of the dark horizon, rolled the batteries of cannon, their thick, ungainly, black and yellow bodies throwing off gleams of threatening light, and their gaping, downturned jaws hunched over the soil. What seemed like an endless line of powder carts and ammunition drays bumped and shook behind them on the rough country track along with an even longer stream of siege and supply wagons.

It was a harsh, threatening sight, redolent of danger, and yet it had a sort of frightening and inspiring beauty as these regular, veteran formations marched past the Yasnogorians as if on parade. Perhaps the sight had been staged on purpose and these awesome ranks were meant to terrorize the defenders and cow their resistance.

The cavalry broke away, split into smaller units and detachments, scattered among the nearby villages after loot and forage, or approached the fortress. Small mounted troops began to trot around the defenses, looking over the fortifications, inspecting the surrounding ground and occupying whatever structures happened to be near. Single riders darted back and forth between the scouting parties and the deep ranks of infantry, reporting on possible positions and quarters.

The sharp click and rattle of the hoofbeats, the neighing of horses, the calls, cries and shouts of command, and the dull grinding clatter of the nearing cannon came clearly to the watchers on the walls who looked down in silent and wide-eyed amazement on this threatening, military display as if it were no more than a vast, entrancing puppet show put on expressly for their entertainment.

* * *

But the performance soon took its serious turn. The infantry regiments had marched up at last and started to maneuver around the defenses in search of positions. Meanwhile they sent several companies to storm the buildings of Little Tchensto-hovka, the huddle of farms that neighbored Yasna Gora, in which there were no armed men of any kind but where some local peasants had hidden behind closed shutters.

The Finland Regiment reached them first and charged the unarmed peasantry with a ferocity that stunned the watchers on the monastery wall. The troopers dragged the helpless farm-hands by the hair out of the barns and byres, slaughtered those who tried to defend themselves as mercilessly as if they were cattle, and drove the rest into the open plain where armored Reiters rode them down, trampled them, dispersed them, and chased them out of sight. A messenger from Mueller galloped up to the gates with a demand for an immediate surrender but the defenders who'd seen the savage soldiery at work in Tchen-stohovka replied with cannon fire.

Smoke wreathed the monastery as if it were a galleon ringed by pirates in a stormy sea, because now that all the local people had been driven from their homes and Swedish troops were taking quarters there, it was essential to demolish them with all possible speed. The guns bellowed, shattering the still air. The church and the other monastery buildings quivered with con-cussion and a thin, ringing sound came from the chapel win-dows. Incendiary shells arced overhead like comets trailing their fiery tails and hissed down on whatever shelters the Swedes occupied, splintering the ridgepoles, breaking through the roofs, and smashing through the walls where soon the smoke of fires lifted into the air.

The conflagration spread.

The astonished Swedes ran out of the collapsing buildings, the regiments retreated looking for new quarters, and soon whole brigades were wandering blindly across the plain unsure of where to stand. The cannoneers who'd barely unhitched their bumping carronades, ran to harness their milling teams again and to drag their guns to some place of safety. Signs of disorder started to appear.

Mueller stared, astonished. He had expected neither this kind of a reception at Yasna Gora nor such gunnery among its defenders.

Chapter Sixty-two

MEANWHILE NIGHT WAS NEARING and because Mueller needed several hours to bring his troops back under disciplined control he sent a trumpeter to the monastery asking the Prior for a brief ceasefire.

The Pauline Fathers agreed readily enough but not before their guns set fire to a vast brick warehouse, laden with provisions, in which the Swedish Westland Regiment found quarters for the night. The fire swept through the building with such speed, and the heated shot fell into it so accurately and so thickly, that the Westlanders abandoned their cartridges and muskets which also exploded in the conflagration, throwing their lighted wadding far into the descending darkness.

The Swedes didn't sleep that night. They set up their siege lines, raised artillery emplacements, shoveled revetments, and got their camp in order. But even though these were hardbitten professionals, inured to danger by years of war and innumerable battles, few of them looked forward to the coming day. The monastery's cannon inflicted such heavy casualties among them that the most experienced campaigners couldn't understand it, ascribing the setback to their own carelessness and the overconfidence of their commanders. But this poor beginning didn't bother them. Courage and endurance were their second nature. What made them so sluggish at their work that night was something far deeper.

"Why did we come here?" they muttered among themselves. What would the new day bring them? Conquest was their trade and they gloried in it. They had stormed and taken so many other cities which were much stronger and far more forbidding than this insignificant objective. Victory meant little to the *landsknechte* of their century without loot or glory and where was the chance of a spectacular distinction in overwhelming such a puny fortress?

Yes, there were said to be riches on that hilltop; in fact it was the thought of pillage after the assault that kept them all working through the night, but even that wasn't as much of a goad here as it had been everywhere else. Something of that strange, icy terror with which their allied Polish regiments rode with them towards Tchenstohova had slipped into their consciousness as well. But where the Poles trembled at the thought of sacrilege, the Swedes had no such rationale to explain their own uneasiness to themselves and so they looked for answers in the supernatural.

"Witchcraft," they whispered to each other. *"It has to be witchcraft."*

And since their general was clearly uneasy when it came to witchcraft they didn't see why they should feel differently about it.

They noticed that when Mueller rode up to the Chapel of St. Barbara, his horse shied violently under him, flattened his ears and whinnied in terror, and then threw himself suddenly back on his haunches and refused to move another step forward. What could that be but witchcraft?

The old general masked his feelings well enough, but he assigned that sector to the Prince of Hesse and took himself off to the opposite side of the monastery, along with the heaviest guns, where his men labored over massive earthworks. That was where the attack was to begin tomorrow.

★ ★ ★

Dawn came at last, a duel of the cannon started at first light, but this time it was the Swedish gunners who fired the first shots. Their goal wasn't to breach the walls for an all-out assault but to demoralize the garrison, bury the church and the monastery under a hail of iron, start fires, smash the defenders' cannon, inflict casualties and spread fear and panic.

The priests and Brothers responded with another religious procession since nothing lifted the spirits of the fighting men better than the sight of the holy sacrament carried calmly by the cloistered clergy. The monastery cannon matched the Swedes' barrage with flame for flame and thunder for thunder, with the gun crews working to the last of their strength and breath, until the rock seemed to be quivering under them and a thick canopy of smoke spread above the entire hilltop.

Who could have prepared people who had never stared into the scarlet eyes of war for that never-ending roar, the muzzle blasts that split the smoke like lightning, the terrifying whistle of grenades passing overhead, the iron clatter of solid shot leaping along the cobbled passageways, the dull thud of stone projectiles against the monastery walls, the high ringing sound of glass spilling out of cracked and shattered windows, the flash of bursting firebombs, the hiss of shrapnel, the crack and rattle of collapsing timbers, the chaos and destruction everywhere around them?

It must have seemed to the peaceful, contemplative Brothers working at the guns, and to the many others among the defenders who'd never heard a shot fired near them in anger, that they had tumbled into Hell.

Nor was there a single moment of rest or relief in all those terrifying hours. There was no air for the lungs choked with acrid smoke. All that came their way were fresh flocks of cannon balls swooping down upon them, and all they heard echoing hour after hour in their deafened ears were frantic voices shouting from every corner of the fortress, the church and the monastery buildings.

"Fire! Get some water here! Water!"

"There! On the roof! Get some axes up there!"

And on the battlements, where the soldiers caught their own kind of fire from the heat of battle, hoarse voices cried: "Get that muzzle higher! Crank it up! There... between those buildings...! *Shoot!*"

*　*　*

Near noon this work of destruction rose to such a pitch that it seemed as if nobody and nothing would emerge undamaged or alive; and that as soon as this veil of smoke had lifted, the Swedes would see only a mountain of spent cannon balls and grenades where the monastery had stood. Plaster and lime-dust, erupting in their own suffocating clouds from the pounded buildings, thickened that deep curtain and obscured everything. The world seemed to vanish in eternal darkness.

The priests brought out sacred relics to exorcise that blinding, sulfur-laden smoke so that their cannoneers could see where to shoot, and the chaotic roar changed from a constant, uninterrupted sound into a measured gasping, like the thick breath of an exhausted dragon. But suddenly music welled from the highest tower. An ancient hymn: '*Bogarodzica—She who gave birth to God.*' Trumpets crying out in perfect harmony spilled out their crystal notes and sent them flowing down everywhere at once, even as far as the Swedish gun posts; and soon human voices joined the horns and bugles; and the sacred words echoed among the iron roars, the hiss of shrapnel, the shouts, the grinding crashes, and the rattle of musketry all along the walls.

> "... *Mother of God, the Maiden,*
> *She whom God gave renown, Maria...!*"

Here several dozen firebombs exploded, one after another; rafters and roofing slates rained down on the singers; a cry of "*Water!*" crackled though the air, and the anthem soared as yet another swarm of explosive shells rained down on the buildings.

> "... *From Your Son, our Master*
> *There will come to us,*
> *He will send to us,*
> *Times of fruitfulness and plenty.*"

★ ★ ★

Kmita, who was at the cannon that faced Tchenstohova, fighting the battery that hurled the heaviest fire from Mueller's own position, pushed aside a less experienced gunner and got to work himself. The day was a cold one, sharp with a brisk November wind, but he was soon out of his furlined cloak and *zhjupan* undercoat, and laboring in his shirtsleeves.

Nothing around him bothered him; he was indifferent to the roar of cannon. He hardly noticed the damage everywhere. He didn't care about the swarming firebombs and grenades, paying no more heed to their flash and roar than he did to the air around him.

Watching him, and feeling their own hearts lifting at the sight of his calm, workmanlike concentration on the job at hand, the trembling Brothers who scurried around the carronade with ramming rods and sponges must have thought him a Salamander lizard at home in a bonfire. His brows were furrowed with total attention. His eyes glittered coldly. After each ear-splitting discharge of his gun he bent over the sighting mechanism—lifting, lowering, aiming and adjusting—wholly absorbed by range and corrections and thinking about nothing other than his deadly purpose, then he jumped back as Soroka stepped up with a smoldering fuse.

"Fire!" he'd shout as Soroka laid the fuse across the touchhole. The cannon bucked and roared, smoke blossomed out again, and Kmita ran to the edge of the parapet to see where his shot would fall.

"Dead as doornail!" he'd shout now and then and ran back to the smoking carronade.

He seemed to be able to see through the gunsmoke and the swirling dust cloud, and wherever he spotted plumed hats or Swedish helmets clustered among some buildings, he'd either crush them or scatter them with a well-aimed shot.

Sometimes he'd burst into a peal of laughter whenever he caused more than ordinary damage. He didn't spare a glance for the enemy projectiles that whirred near and over him like birds.

"One gun is down!" he shouted suddenly, peering into the distance after another shot. "They've only three working there now!"

He hardly drew a breath between noon and sunrise. His head was wet with sweat. His soaked shirt was steaming despite the chill. His face was black with soot and his eyes were shining like a pair of torches.

"It's plain to see you're not a newcomer to this work," Pan Tcharnyetzki told him. "What gunnery! Where did you learn so much?"

At three o'clock another gun fell silent in the Swedish battery, smashed by Kmita's shooting, and the rest were trundled out of their revetments and hauled to the rear.

"You've chased them off!" Pan Tcharnyetzki cried. "They can't hold that battery against you!"

Grinning in reply, Pan Andrei drew his first full breath of the day.

"Rest a bit," Pan Pyotr said. "You've earned it!"

"I'll do that. I could do with a bit of food as well," the young
soldier said and turned to Soroka. "Get me something to eat,
will you? Anything will do."

The old sergeant jumped to obey his order and was back in
no time at all with a handful of smoked fish and a quart of liquor.
Pan Kmita bent eagerly over his food, lifting his eyes now and
then to the passing bombs with no more interest than he'd show
to a flock of blackbirds. Mueller's main battery was silent now
outside Tchenstohova. This rain of shot and shells came from
the other side, carrying over the monastery and the church, to
fall inside the north wall and on the slope beyond it.

"I don't think much of their master gunners," Pan Andrei
shrugged and went on calmly with his dinner. "Their elevation
is all wrong. Look at that! Everything's going over the roofs
and coming down on us!"

* * *

Sitting beside him and listening to him as if he were uttering
the wisdom of the Gospels, was a young novice, barely seventeen years old, who had been carrying ammunition for Kmita's
carronade all day. War was a terrifying new experience for him,
every nerve jumped and quivered with fear in his body, and he
stared at Pan Andrei's matter-of-fact indifference with wide-
eyed admiration. Now, hearing his comment on the Swedish
gunners, he edged up towards him as if in search of shelter and
protection beside such a warrior, and asked in a trembling voice:

"But can they reach us from the other side?"

"Why not?" Pan Andrei answered. "Does that worry you so
much, little brother?"

"My lord," the trembling lad replied. "I thought that war
would be a terrible experience but I never imagined just how
terrible it could be."

"Not every bullet kills a man," Kmita shrugged.

"The worst are those firebombs, those... those grenades.
Have mercy, Holy Mother! Why do they burst like that, with
such an awful roar? And hurt people so horribly...?"

"Let me explain it to you, little father. Once you know how
something works, you see, it's never that frightening. Most
solid shot is just plain stone or iron. But a grenade is hollowed
out inside and packed full of powder..."

"Jezus of Nazareth!" cried the little novice.

"... And in one spot there is a little opening for a twist of cartridge paper, or sometimes a small wooden plug."

"A plug! Mother of God! A plug?"

"That's right. And in that plug is a combustible fuse, or wadding soaked in sulfur, which catches fire when the shot is thrown out of the cannon. Well, the way it should work is that the shell hits the target with the plug, knocks it inside, and touches off the powder. But it doesn't make much difference how the grenade lands because sooner or later the fuse burns down far enough anyway..."

And suddenly Kmita broke off, jerked his hand into the air and went on swiftly: "There, look! Look! Here's a good example!"

"Jesus Mary and Joseph!" the little Brother shouted at the sight of the grenade that came down towards them.

Meanwhile the bomb fell into the space behind the wall, and started bouncing on the cobblestones, whirring and whirling like a spinning-top with a thin wisp of bluish smoke trailing after it, until it rolled into a pile of wet sand that sloped all the way up to the parapet where the men were sitting. It landed there with the fuse up, but the sulfur plug went on burning in it because the smoke steadied and thickened at once.

"Hit the ground! Get down! Get down!" terrified voices lifted all around them but Kmita leaped up, slid down the sandpile to the trapped projectile, grasped the smoking plug with the speed of lightning, jerked it out, and holding it up in the air called out: "Get up! It's alright! It's like a toothless dog now! It can't hurt a fly!"

He laughed out loud and kicked the disarmed shell with disdain while everyone else sat frozen in amazement, unable to say a word at the sight of such courage and contempt for danger. At last Pan Pyotr Tcharnyetzki cried out:

"You madman! Don't you know you'd be turned into a handful of powder if that thing went off?"

But Pan Andrei was enjoying himself. His young white teeth glittered like a wolf's.

"And don't we need powder?" he asked, laughing as happily as a boy at play. "You'd be able to charge a cannon with me and I'd put a dent into a few Swedes even after death!"

The little monk pressed his hands together in mute admiration, staring at Kmita as if he'd just witnessed a miracle. But Prior Kordetzki, who happened to be passing by at that moment, had also seen his act of selfless heroism. He stooped over Kmita, pressed his head warmly to his chest and made a sign of the cross on his forehead.

"God bless you, my boy. Men like you won't surrender Yasna Gora," he murmured. "But I forbid you to take such risks! We need you alive!"

Then the Prior looked up and listened for a moment. "It sounds as if the shooting is dying down a little, don't you think? The enemy seems to have had enough for today, God be praised for it... Now take that shell to the Chapel, empty the powder out of it, and offer it to Our Lady. She'll be better pleased with that gift than with all those gems you wanted to give Her..."

"Reverend Father!" Kmita cried, moved almost to tears. "It's no great thing, believe me! I'd... I'd do anything for Her. Anything! Death... torture... I don't have the words. All I want is a chance to serve..."

Now tears did start shining in the young man's eyes and Father Kordetzki said quickly: "And take those tears to Her too before they dry away. Her mercy will flow down upon you, give you peace, soothe your troubles, and bring you safely to honor and respect."

He took Kmita's arm and led him to the church while Pan Pyotr Tcharnyetzki stared after them in silence for a time.

"I've seen a lot of brave men in my life," he said at last, shaking his head in wonder. "But that Lithuanian... I tell you, he's got to be the De..."

And here Pan Pyotr clamped a swift hand across his mouth so as not to name an unclean power in a holy place.

Chapter Sixty-three

THE ARTILLERY DUELS didn't get in the way of negotiations. The Pauline Fathers decided to make every use of them, wanting to deceive the enemy and to gain as much time as they could. Time, they calculated, was on their side. Sooner or later some help would come from somewhere even if it were no more than harsh Winter weather. On his part, Mueller never doubted that the priests and monks were putting up a struggle only to get the best possible conditions for themselves before giving up as the logic of their situation would force them to do.

At nightfall, then—right after that fierce bombardment—he sent the Polish Colonel Kuklinovski with a demand for the monastery's surrender. The Prior showed him Charles Gustav's promise of exemption from military seizure but Mueller had a later set of orders from the King. He'd been instructed to garrison the towns of Boleslav, Vyelun, Krepitz and Tchenstohova so he sent Kuklinovski back again.

"Tell those monks," he said, "that my new orders take precedence over their old guarantees of exemption. That ought to take the wind out of their sails."

But he was wrong.

Father Kordetzki agreed politely that the King's command had to be obeyed and that General Mueller was within his rights in seizing the town. But he pointed out that the order concerned Tchenstohova, not Yasna Gora, which had to be exempt since it wasn't specifically listed.

Hearing this answer, Mueller recognized that he was dealing

with shrewder minds and quicker wits than his, and with more skillful negotiators than he was himself. His last and best remaining argument were his guns.

The ceasefire, however, lasted through the night. The Swedes worked on the construction of far stronger siege lines, earthworks, embrassures, revetments and fortified artillery emplacements, while the Yasnogorians set about repairing the damage they sustained during the day's bombardment.

They were surprised to find that the widespread destruction they expected after that hail of iron was practically nonexistent. Here and there they came across holed roofs and smashed rafters; in some other places the paint and plaster had been knocked off the monastery walls; and that was just about the sum of it all. As for the men and women within those walls not one had been killed or even badly injured.

Touring the battlements that night, Father Kordetzki said smiling to the defenders: "Look at this! This enemy isn't as terrible as he was said to be. We sometimes have more damage here during pre-Lenten celebrations when the people get a bit too much to drink and forget themselves. God is protecting us, we are in His hand, and we'll see many other miracles if we just endure whatever comes our way."

* * *

Then came a Sunday, the Feast Day of the Annunciation. Nothing interfered with the solemn services because Mueller was waiting for the final reply to his demands which the monks promised to send in the afternoon. Meanwhile, recalling from the Scriptures how Israel put the fear of God in the Philistines by having the Arc of the Covenant carried through their camp, another procession walked the Sacrament around the fortress walls.

The Prior's letter reached Mueller by two o'clock in the afternoon but all it told him was a repetition of what he'd heard from Kuklinovski, namely that the town of Tchenstohova was one place while Yasna Gora was another, and that neither the church nor the monastery were obliged to accept Swedish occupation.

'*Which is why we beg Your Distinguished Excellency,*' wrote Father Kordetzki, '*to leave in peace both our Community and the*

*Church which is dedicated to the Glory of God and His Holy Mother,
so that the worship of His name may be uninterrupted here, and so that
we may continue to pray for the good health and successes of His
Illustrious Majesty. We, in the meantime, humbly commit ourselves to
the kind offices of Your Distinguished Excellency, confident that we may
rely on them in the future as we have before.'*

Present among others for the reading of this letter in Mueller's headquarters were Veyhard, Sadovski, the ruthless, one-
armed and fanatical Horn who had just been appointed
Governor of Krepitz, the brilliant French engineer de Fossis, and
the elegant German Prince of Hesse.

The Hessian prince was a somewhat haughty and high-handed
young man who may have been Mueller's subordinate in the
Swedish Army, but who never lost sight of his high birth and his
superior lineage and liked to put the old general in his place.
Now, hearing the Prior's letter, he turned to Mueller with a
malicious smile.

"They have confidence in your *kind offices*," he stressed the
ending of the Prior's message. "That's an allusion to the collection plate, ha ha! I'll ask you just one question, gentlemen: are
the monks better at their pleading or their shooting?"

"That's true!" Horn snarled. "We lost more men in these few
days here than in a good-sized battle."

"As for me," the Prince of Hesse continued, "I don't need
their money, I won't gain any glory in this piddling little siege,
and all I expect this Winter from those dilapidated peasant
hovels around here is a pair of frostbitten feet. What a pity we
didn't go to Prussia! It's a rich, cheerful country where each
new town is better than the one before."

Mueller, who struck hard and fast in battle but thought rather
slowly, grasped at last the full meaning of the Prior's letter.

"The monks jeer at us, gentlemen!" he snapped, red with
sudden anger.

"Perhaps not on purpose," the Prince of Hesse observed. "But
it amounts to the same thing."

"Very well! Then back to your positions! They didn't get
enough fire and steel from us yesterday!"

★ ★ ★

His orders passed quickly from one end of the Swedish lines

to the other and the earthworks erupted in fire and smoke. The monastery replied as energetically as before. Hollow, explosive firebombs trailed their fiery tails through the sky also as before, and so did canisters filled with hot coals and pitch-soaked, burning cotton, but this time the Swedish siege-guns were better emplaced and started to wreak heavier damage on the embattled defenders.

It seemed to the monks and soldiers laboring at the cannon that just as flocks of migrating cranes settled now and then to rest on the peaks of mountains, so these incendiary missiles swarmed about the lofty gables of the church and the wooden roofs of the surrounding buildings. Whoever wasn't needed on the battlements, or working at the guns, was up on the rooftops or carting waterbuckets. Some of them drew the water from the wells, others hauled it to the roofs on ropes, yet others fought the fires with water-soaked tarpaulins.

Some of the shells broke through the rafters and the roofing timbers, and burst in the storage and provision attics, so that a thick, greasy smoke and the reek of burning meats and grains spread quickly through the buildings, but even the attics had their crews of firefighters crouched over barrels of water. The heaviest shells, however, crashed right through the attics and the ceilings of the rooms below. The flaming bundles of firewood, coals and cotton that were pushed off the roofs formed massive bonfires at the foot of the walls and licked at the siding. The heat either cracked or blew out the windows; the women and children sheltering in the church choked with the smoke and the unbreathable hot air; and it began to look to everyone as if despite all their immense exertions the monastery would, sooner or later, fall victim to this rain of fire.

No sooner was one hailstorm of firebombs extinguished and their flames drowned or beaten down, and no sooner had the water drained off the battered roofs, than a fresh swarm of red-hot cannon balls, flaming rags, and canisters full of burning coals landed in their place. The whole area occupied by the monastery buildings lay under this deluge of fire so that it seemed as if the Heavens had opened up above it and an avalanche of thunderbolts was showering down upon it.

The monastery glowed like a giant ember but, to the anger and dismay of the Swedish gunners, it refused to burn. Flames roared above it but it didn't fall into a heap of rubble. Moreover it seemed to the astonished Swedes as if the tortured buildings had begun to sing, like the Children of Israel in their fiery Babylonian furnace, because once again the great religious anthem sounded from the tower along with peals of trumpets.

To the men crouched behind the battlements or laboring at the cannon this sound was like a soothing balm. They had every reason to believe that everything behind them was dying in the flames, and that nothing but a scorched heap of rubble would confront their eyes after this bombardment; but the music proved to them hour after hour that the monastery and the church were still standing in that firestorm, and that the fury of this man-made holocaust hadn't managed as yet to overcome the efforts of the defenders.

It became Father Kordetzki's custom in the days that followed to fill the air with music in their most threatening moments, both to lift up the hearts of the defenders and ease the terrors of the siege, and also as a means of keeping the dreadful shouts and curses of the enraged fighting men and soldiers from the ears of the children and the women.

★   ★   ★

But those choirs and trumpets had a profound effect on the Swedes as well. The troopers in the earthworks listened to these sounds first with admiration and then with growing superstitious fear.

"How is this," they muttered among themselves. "We've tossed enough fire and iron on that chicken coop to turn a real fortress into a heap of ashes and they're amusing themselves with a bit of music? What's going on here?"

"Witchcraft!" others answered.

"The shot bounces off the walls over there, have you noticed? The grenades roll off those roofs as if they were harmless loaves of bread...

"It's witchcraft, I tell you. Magic. Nothing good will happen to us here."

Even the officers were willing to assign some kind of mystical or unearthly meanings to those puzzling sounds. But others explained the music differently and Sadovski made sure that Mueller could hear him.

"They must be having a good time over there," he said pointedly. "Which means that we've been wasting our powder for nothing."

"Not to mention the fact that we're running short of it ourselves," added the Prince of Hesse.

"But *we* are led by the second Policertes," Sadovski replied in such a tone of voice that it was hard to judge whether he wanted to flatter Mueller or to sneer at him.

Mueller apparently took it for a jibe because he bit down angrily on his mustache and ordered a doubled rate of fire.

"We'll see if they still feel like singing in an hour!" he snapped.

But his angry urgency must have conveyed itself to the gunners because they carried out his orders in too great a hurry. The gun layers set the range too far, doubling on the charges, and their projectiles flew over the target. Some of them, soaring in thick, black flocks above the monastery and the church, reached the Swedish earthworks on the other side where they smashed gun carriages and platforms, shattered the revetments and inflicted casualties on the men.

Two hours passed like that but the solemn music went on and on, flowing unabated out of the church tower, and finally Mueller called for his looking-glass and stared for a long time at the hated structure.

"The bombardment isn't causing the church any harm at all!" the old warrior shouted in a raging fury, and hurled his spy-glass to the ground with such force that it shattered into half a dozen pieces. "That music will drive me mad!" he screamed out.

De Fossis, his chief of engineers, galloped up just then to the escarpment where Mueller and his staff were standing outside Tchenstohova.

"General," he said. "We can't tunnel here, not with the normal military equipment. There is solid rock right under the surface. We'll have to bring in some regular quarrymen and miners to make any headway on this job."

Mueller growled a curse. But his malediction still hung in the air when another officer galloped up to him, coming from the artillery positions directly before him.

"Our heaviest gun has been smashed," he reported. "Should I have another brought up from Elgota?"

Mueller said nothing. The fire from his batteries sounded weaker now. The music filled the air louder than before. He rode away without another word but he gave no orders to stop the bombardment. I'll wear them down to death, he thought. I'll give them no rest. They've a mere two hundred men fighting over there.

While he, of course, had thousands to take their turns on the firing line.

★ ★ ★

Night came at last, the cannon thundered as thickly as before but the monastery's counterfire proved even more effective than it was in daylight because the Swedish camp fires gave them clear targets.

It happened time and again that night that no sooner had some hungry troopers clustered around a fire and the soup kettle dangling over it, when a cannon ball flew out of the darkness and fell among them like a spirit of vengeance and destruction. The cook-fire would burst apart, scattering showers of sparks or hurling coals and embers high into the air, and the soldiers howled in terror and ran for their lives. By midnight hundreds of them were wandering aimlessly through the darkness—cold, hungry and demoralized by lack of sleep and by their own superstitious fear—or looking for some shelter beyond the range of the monastery's cannon.

But no such shelter was to be found that night. The monastery's cannonade swelled in range and volume as the hours passed, so that it proved impossible for the chilled, dispirited besiegers to light even a piece of kindling where they might warm themselves within sight of the surrounded fortress. It seemed as if the defenders wanted to hammer out a message of their own, letting their guns say on their behalf: '*You want to wear us down? Try it! We accept your challenge.*'

The tower clocks in Tchenstohova rang out the first hour after midnight, then the second hour. A thin, cold drizzle hung in the sodden air, forming a hazy and uneven mist which pierced the chilled men to the bone and thickened in the distance into fantastic shapes that looked like columns rising to the sky, or strange pediments and arches that glowed with a mysterious reddish light reflected from the fires.

Peering through these spectral corridors and gateways, the huddled Swedes caught menacing glimpses of the monastery which seemed to change shape right before their eyes. Sometimes it swelled or loomed taller in the darkness. At other moments it disappeared entirely. The night and the rainy mists created ghostly tunnels and arcades that stretched from their entrenchments all the way to the monastery walls which hurled death-bearing cannon balls towards them through those forbidding passageways. At times the air above this deadly structure glared as whitely as if it were illuminated by interior lightnings, and then the grim walls seemed as sheer as cliffsides, edged in colors of unearthly brightness, before they vanished as swiftly as they had appeared.

As superstitious as all soldiers of all times and places, the Swedes stared at this apparition with foreboding, nudging each other and muttering: "Did you see? This monastery comes and goes at will... There's nothing human about that place, I tell you..."

"I saw more than that," said another gunner. "We were sighting a cannon on it earlier in the day, the same one that blew up, when the whole fortress started jumping up and down like somebody up there was raising and lowering it on a rope... How's one supposed to aim at such a target? How is one to hit it?"

The gunner tossed down his swabbing brush in disgust, then added: "We won't get a thing out of this, believe me, no matter how long we keep waiting in this den of witches! None of us will get as much as a sniff of their money, you mark my words! Brrrr...! God, it's cold down here... Get a fire going in that pitch-barrel over there, will you? At least we'll get our hands warmed up a bit!"

One of the shivering troopers started to light the fire with a sulfur match, first getting a flame going on a twist of wadding and then dipping it slowly in the pitch.

"Put out that light!" an officer's voice rang out in the darkness.

But almost in that instant came the hissing rumble of an iron missile hurtling through the air, there was one sharp, broken cry that died on a half-note, and the brief gleam of light was swallowed up by darkness.

* * *

The night brought heavy losses to the Swedes. Uncounted numbers died by their cooking fires. In some positions they found themselves so badly shocked and scattered that panic overcame entire regiments before daylight could restore their shattered discipline and bring them back under command control. But the besieged defenders continued their merciless cannonade long after the sunrise as if to show that they needed neither rest nor relief from duty.

Dawn found them on the battlements. Their faces were drawn with fatigue, pale with strain and fogged with lack of sleep but there was a glare of fever in their eyes. Prior Kordetzki kept a night-long vigil in the Chapel of the Madonna, praying for Her help and intercession, and appeared on the walls at the first light of dawn to call out in every bastion, at the gates, and on each gun platform:

"God is creating another day for us, may His light be blessed! There is no damage to the church and not much in the other buildings! Master Mosinski!"—he stopped in mid-stride to speak to a tired noble at his post—"A firebomb rolled under your baby's cradle but went out causing no harm to anyone. Thank Our Good Lady and pay Her back in service!"

"Blessed be Her name for ever!" the soldier replied. "I serve as best I can!"

The Prior went on farther.

The sunrise was well along by the time he found himself beside Pan Pyotr and Kmita. He didn't notice Kmita because the young soldier had crawled to the other side of the wall to repair the supports of his cannon which had been shaken loose by a close hit from a Swedish siege-gun.

"Where is Babinitch?" the Prior asked at once. "Is he sleeping somewhere?"

"I should be sleeping on a night like that one?" Pan Andrei called back, clambering over the wall. "I'd have to have no conscience!" He laughed and jumped down inside the bastion. "It's better to keep watch in Our Lady's service."

"Better! Much, much better, you good and faithful servant!" replied Prior Kordetzki.

But Pan Andrei suddenly caught sight of a pale, anemic light flickering in the distance on the Swedish earthworks.

"There's a camp fire out there!" he shouted to his gun crew. "Get your sights on it! Higher! That's it! Shoot the sons of bitches!"

The gun heaved and roared. Kmita's eagerness put a bright, angelic smile on Father Kordetzki's face but he knew that earthly nourishment also had some meaning. The Prior hurried to the monastery kitchens to have some hot beer and barley soup, thickly seasoned with cubes of aged farmers' cheese, served to his work-worn soldiers, and half an hour later groups of priests, women and the innumerable old men who did odd jobs in and about the church scurried about the walls with steaming pots and kettles.

"We aren't mistreated in Our Lady's service!" the soldiers told each other, grinning with satisfaction, while sounds of greedy slurping echoed all along the walls. "The food's just fine, eh?"

"The Swedes have it a lot worse! They didn't get to cook much hot food last night, they'll get even less when this day is over."

"Serves them right, the dogs! They'll give themselves some rest during the day, that's for sure, so we'll get a bit of sleep ourselves... Their poor old guns must've got hoarse with all that coughing they did all last night."

* * *

But the monastery defenders were wrong. There was no rest for anyone that day. When his officers reported to Mueller that the night's cannonade brought no discernible results, other than further losses among their own men, the General ground his teeth and ordered them to keep firing as before.

"They have to get tired sometime," he told the Prince of Hesse.

"Perhaps. Meanwhile this is costing us great amounts of powder."

"It costs them something too, doesn't it?"

"They must have a great store of sulfur and nitrates up there. Nor will they lack charcoal if we succeed in burning down a few of their buildings. I rode up close to the walls last night and I heard a mill grinding away inside. It has to be a powder mill, nothing else."

But Mueller was just as stubborn as he was determined. "Keep up a double rate of fire until the sun goes down," he ordered. "We'll get some rest at nightfall. Meanwhile we'll see if they don't send out for a parlay before this day is over."

"Your Excellency knows that they sent emissaries to Wittemberg?"

"I know. And I'm going to send him a messenger myself in a day or two asking for the heaviest siege-guns in the arsenal. If we can't burn them out from the inside or scare them into reason we'll have to breach their walls and take them by storm."

"You expect then, Excellency, that the Field Marshal will approve this siege?"

"The Field Marshal knew all about it well ahead of time and didn't say a word," Mueller snapped abruptly. "If we succeed here, the Field Marshal will be pleased to take all the credit, as he always does, not to mention his share of the money. And if bad luck continues to plague me as it's done so far, the Field Marshal will use me for a scapegoat and His Majesty will accept his view of the matter. I know all about that. I've had to put up with a lot of the Field Marshal's ill temper and abuse, as if it was my fault that he's being eaten alive by the *mal francese*."

"There is no question about whom he'll blame," the Prince shrugged, indifferent. "Particularly if Sadovski's warnings turn out to be correct."

"What warnings? Sadovski pleads those monks' case as if he's been on their payroll from the start! What's he saying now?"

"That these shots will echo throughout this whole country from the Carpathians to the Baltic."

"Then let His Majesty have Veyhard skinned alive and send his hide to that monastery as a votive offering! This siege was his idea!"

But for all his furious rage and bluster, Mueller knew that his time was running out. The siege had to end. Yasna Gora couldn't be allowed to defy Swedish armies with impunity. Much more than just his own career was at stake.

"We've got to finish this!" he grunted, clawing at his hair.

"They've got to surrender! They've just got to! Something tells me they'll send us a negotiator tonight... So keep firing! Keep firing!"

Chapter Sixty-four

THE NEW DAY PASSED much like the one before, full of flames, smoke and thunder. It was just one of many of that kind that would dawn and set above Yasna Gora before the siege was over, and the defenders fought the fires and labored at their guns as doggedly as they would until the end. They soon discovered that half of them were enough for the job at hand so that the other half could find a little rest.

The constant roar no longer bothered them as much as in the beginning especially since the damage wasn't anywhere as bad as the thundering suggested. Those who had never before fired a shot in anger found sustenance in faith, but there were enough war-wise old campaigners in the little garrison, who went about their tasks with the cheerful calmness of experienced craftsmen, so that even the raw, untried villagers settled down to the hardships of the siege as if they'd never done anything else in their peaceful lives.

Soroka, who had spent most of his years in one war or another, won great respect among them because he paid no more attention to the terrifying roars than an old innkeeper does to the shouting of his drunken customers. They clustered about him at nightfall when the cannonading dwindled and listened avidly to his tales about the siege of Zbarajh. He hadn't been there himself but he knew all about it from soldiers who survived it and his stories were as colorful as they were inspiring.

"There were so many Cossacks, Turks and Tartars over there," he'd say, "that they had more cooks to boil their mutton stews for them than all the Swedes we've got against us here. But our people held out anyway. Moreover, evil spirits can't do a thing to anybody here, but over there it was only Fridays, Saturdays and Sundays that the Devils couldn't give a hand to those rebel cut-throats. The rest of the week they haunted our people every night. They even sent Death to our trenches so that she'd show herself to our lads and take the heart out of 'em in battle. I know this from one that saw her with his own two eyes."

"He saw her?" the awestruck peasants pressed eagerly around the old sergeant.

"With his own eyes! He was on his way to dig a well because they had no drinking water over there, and what was in the ponds was stinking with corpses. So he's going along, minding his own business, and there's this figure in a black sheet coming up towards him..."

"A black sheet? Not a white one?"

"Black. She wears black in wartime. It was getting dark just about then. So the soldier says: '*Halt! Who goes there?*' She doesn't say a word. So he tugs on the sheet, pulls it open and sees a skeleton. '*So what're you doing here, you old bag of bones?*' he asks. '*I'm Death,*' she says. '*And I'm coming for you in a week.*'

"The soldier figured that things were getting pretty bad for him," Soroka went on. "'*How come it's got to be a week?*' he asks. '*Can't you do it sooner?*' But she says no, she can't get to him for seven more days. '*Why not?*' he asks. '*Because that's my orders,*' she tells him. Well, thinks the soldier, if that's the way it has to be, then that's what'll happen. But why shouldn't he get a bit of his own back on Old Boney while she's under orders and can't do anything about it? So he grabs her, wraps her tight in that sheet of hers, and starts pounding her against the wall until all her bones were rattling in her head. '*Let me go! I'll make it two weeks!*' she begs him. '*Not enough,*' he tells her and starts pounding her against a pile of cannon balls. '*I'll give you three weeks! Four! Five! Ten!*' she hollers. '*I'll come for you after the siege, in a year, in two years, in fifteen!*' But he keeps on pounding her for all he's worth. '*I'll come in fifty years!*' she howls.

"The soldier gave that a bit of thought, seeing as he was already fifty at the time. '*A hundred years is long enough to live,*' he figured so he let her go. And he's alive and well to this day, and goes off to war as if it was a wedding, because what's he got to worry about, eh?"

"But if he'd took fright it'd be all over with him right away?"

"That's right," Soroka said gravely. "Worst thing you can do is be afraid of Death. That soldier not only saved himself but he did a lot of good for other people too. Because he gave Death such a beating, he banged her about so hard, that she took sick for three days and nobody in our camp got killed, even though they went out every night to raid the Cossacks in their own positions."

"How about us then, sergeant? Are we going to go after the Swedes some night?"

"That's for our better heads than ours to think about," Soroka replied.

★　★　★

Kmita was standing not too far way, close enough to hear, and when he heard the last question and the answer he slapped his own forehead. Then he took a long, hard look at the Swedish earthworks. Night had already fallen. It was dark as pitch. There had been no sound from the Swedes in more than an hour; their exhausted soldiers were sleeping around their guns. Far in the distance, at more than twice the range of the monastery's cannon, a few dozen fires glittered in the darkness but the batteries were as still and silent as the grave.

"That's the last thing they'd have on their minds," he whispered to himself. "They'd never suspect it!" And he went at once to Pan Pyotr Tcharnyetzki whom he found sitting on a gun carriage nearby, running a rosary through his fingers and knocking his heels together to warm his chilled feet.

"It's a cold night," he said at the sight of Kmita. "My head feels as if it weighed a ton after all that hammering. My ears won't stop ringing."

"Whose ears would after all that noise? But it looks as if we'll have a quiet night for a change. They're all snoring out there. We could creep up on them like hibernating bears. I doubt if muskets could wake them if we fired them right beside their ears."

"Aha!" Pan Tcharnyetzki raised his head and stared at Pan Andrei. "What's on your mind, then?"

"I keep thinking about Zbarajh and how the defenders used

to raid the enemy in his own positions. They inflicted some terrible casualties that way."

"I see you've blood on your mind at night like a wolf," Pan Pyotr said.

"Why not?" Kmita countered. "By God and his wounds, why don't we make a sally? We'll slaughter them like sheep, spike their guns... They don't expect a thing over there."

Pan Tcharnyetzki leaped to his feet. "They'll go mad tomorrow!" He clapped his hands together in excitement. "They probably think they've got us cowed, shaking in our boots and ready to surrender. Let's show them something else! As I love God, that's a fine idea! Why didn't I think of it? We'll just have to talk it over with Father Kordetzki and get his permission. He's in command here."

They found the Prior deep in consultation with the Constable of Syeradz in the *Definitorium*. Hearing their rapid footsteps, Father Kordetzki looked up, pushed aside his candle, and asked: "Who's that? Is there something new?"

"It's me, Tcharnyetzki," Pan Pyotr said. "And I've Babinitch with me. Neither of us can sleep, thinking about those Swedes over there. But that Babinitch is a real restless spirit, Father! He can't keep still for a moment, he's so full of energy and ideas. Now he wants to go across the walls and ask the Swedes if they plan to shoot at us tomorrow or if we're all going to have a little holiday."

"What's that?" Father Kordetzki couldn't keep the astonishment out of his voice. "Babinitch wants to leave the fortress?"

"In company! In company!" Pan Pyotr hurried to explain. "With me and a few dozen other men. It looks as if the Swedes are dead to the world in their gun positions. There's no sign of sentries or watch fires anywhere out there. They must be absolutely certain that we're too weak and tired to do them any harm."

"We'll spike their guns!" Pan Andrei urged warmly.

"Give me that Babinitch!" the Constable cried out. "Let me hug that man! So your sting is itching you, you horsefly, is it? You want to torment the enemy even after dark? That is a first rate gambit, a really sharp military idea, which can do us a great deal of good. God gave us just one Lithuanian, I tell you, but

He picked a good one! I approve this project and I'd be glad to go out myself!"

Father Kordetzki was worried about the plan at first because he didn't want to add to any new bloodshed especially if he wasn't there to share the risks. But giving it a closer look he decided that the Holy Mother might approve.

"Let me just pray a little," he said.

He knelt down before a small painting of the Madonna, prayed for a moment with closed eyes, raised head, and outspread arms, and then rose to his feet with a sunny smile etched across his face.

"Say a prayer yourselves," he urged. "And then go!"

★   ★   ★

A quarter of an hour later the four of them were standing on the battlements. The night was dark. The silent Swedish batteries seemed plunged in deep sleep.

"How many men do you want to take?" the Prior asked Kmita.

"I, Reverend Father?" Pan Andrei didn't bother to hide his surprise. "I'm not the leader here nor do I know the neighboring countryside as well as Pan Tcharnyetzki. I'll take my saber, that's all. Let Pan Pyotr take charge of the men and me along with them. All I ask is that my Soroka be allowed to go because there's no one like him at close quarters."

Pan Tcharnyetzki was pleased with this reply and so was the Prior who saw it as clear proof of true humility. Then they all got to work, picked their volunteers, ordered total silence and set the men to clearing the bricks, stones and logs out of a blocked sally-port. It took an hour's work to open the passage and then the raiders slipped through the narrow cleft onto the open hillside. They carried sabers, pistols and other firearms while the armed villagers among them hefted scythes that had been set with the broad blades upward into makeshift spears. It was a weapon to which they were the most accustomed.

Once they were through the wall they headed cautiously down the slope, making sure they made as little noise as possible. Now and then a scythe-blade clicked against another, or a stone grated under an accidental boot-heel, other than that they might have been wolves creeping towards a sheepfold. The moonless night concealed them. Tcharnyetzki led the way and Kmita closed their file, making sure that no one stumbled out of line and lost his way in the impenetrable darkness. Pan Andrei had suggested that they circle the Swedish earthwork, falling upon the unsuspecting sleepers from the rear, and then driving them towards a concealed detachment left crouched in ambush where the rocky slope leveled out into softer ground, and Pan Pyotr was quick to seize on that idea.

They left the ambush in charge of an experienced old soldier named Yanitch the Magyar and stepped out at a faster pace now that the sandy soil helped muffle their footsteps. Kmita joined Pan Tcharnyetzki at the head of the column. He marched with a drawn saber in his hand and whispered his last observations and instructions.

"The battery redan is probably set at some distance forward from the main camp, with open ground between them. If there are any sentry posts they'll be out in front of the embankment rather than on the other side... So we'll just make our way around them and hit them from where they'll least expect us."

"Good," Pan Pyotr answered. "Not one of them should get away alive."

"If someone challenges us as we're going in let me answer him," Pan Andrei continued. "I can rattle around in German as well as I speak Polish. They'll think it's someone from the general's headquarters."

"I just hope they don't have any guard posts on the camp side of the rampart," Pan Pyotr worried briefly.

"No problem if they do. It'll be too late. We'll just jump them and charge straight into the earthworks. Before they realize what's going on we'll be on their necks."

"It's time to make our turn," Pan Tcharnyetzki whispered. "Here is the flank of the fortification." Then, twisting his head towards the men behind them, he called out softly: "Turn to the right... turn right..."

The silent file began to make its turn. Moonlight flashed briefly behind the edges of a cloud and cast a quick white light on the open space behind the Swedish earthwork. There were no sentries anywhere in sight, as Kmita had supposed; the most cautious and farsighted commander would hardly expect an attack from the direction of his own main forces.

"Now,"Pan Tcharnyetzki hissed to the silent raiders gathering around him. "No sound from now on, understood?" And then he whispered into Kmita's ear: "Look, here are their tents, straight ahead."

"And lights burning in two of them... must be the commanders..."

"The front parapet is as sheer as a cliff,"Pan Pyotr murmured. "But the slope should be easier back here, don't you think?"

"Sure to be," Kmita whispered back, then pointed at some deep ruts in the frozen soil. "This is where they roll in the cannon and there ought to be some access ramps for the troops as well... Ah, here we go. Here's the start of the rear parados. Quietly, now. No talking, everybody. And keep your weapons muffled."

★　★　★

They had come to the battery ammunition park, as they saw at once; it was a broad, raised platform carefully engineered out of earth, stone and timbers behind the main bastion; and then they edged into the rows of powder carts, and the heavy drays used for hauling cannon balls, that were parked there with nobody near them. As they'd expected, the climb to the crew tents and the gun revetments on top of the rampart was an easy one. Pan Pyotr stopped them there, all weapons at the ready.

"As you see,"Kmita whispered to him. "Two of the tents are lit. Someone's still up, probably officers in conference. Why don't you hold the men here while I go ahead and see about those officers. When you hear my pistol shot, hit the rest."

He stepped out, no longer bothering to muffle his footsteps. The success of the raid was now a foregone conclusion. He passed several darkened, silent tents, his boots creaking boldly on the hard-packed soil while the crouching raiders held their breaths, but no one stirred in front of him.

No one challenged him.

He reached the lighted tent, raised the flap and stepped inside the broad pavilion with his pistol hanging loosely in one hand while his drawn saber dangled from its wrist-chain. He stopped in the entrance, dazzled for a moment by the candlelight that fell from a six-armed candelabrum on a portable field-table, and then his eyes fixed on three officers hunched over charts and plans.

"Who's there?" one of them asked, unalarmed and barely lifting his head from the sheets of paper he was studying.

"A soldier," Kmita said in German.

"What soldier?" Now all three officers looked up at him. The one who'd spoken first was de Fossis, the engineer who directed the main work of the siege. "From where?"

"From the monastery," said Kmita.

There was something so terrible in his voice that de Fossis leaped to his feet, pushed the blinding light aside, and peered sharply at the dark form that loomed in the entrance. Kmita stood as straight and still as an apparition. But his grim features, which brought to mind a dark bird of prey, signaled a sudden danger.

A line officer might have acted differently, but de Fossis was an engineer, a scientist rather than a soldier, and he must have thought that this was some deserter from the besieged fortress.

"What do you want here, then?" he asked uneasily.

"This!" Kmita said and fired his pistol straight into his chest.

A massed shout and the sudden crash of musketry split the air from one end of the earthwork to the other. De Fossis toppled like a pine struck by a thunderbolt; a second officer charged Kmita with a rapier, but Pan Andrei's saber struck him between the eyes with such force that the frontal plane of the skull split under the blow; the third officer threw himself on the ground and tried to claw his way outside under the stiff canvas, and Kmita reached him in one bound, trod on his back, and nailed him to the ground with his saber point.

Meanwhile the silent night outside turned into the screaming chaos of a Judgment Day. Wild yells of *"Kill!"* and *"Slaughter!"* became one with the terrified shouts for help and the mindless howling of panicked Swedish soldiers. Men tumbled from their tents, still dazed with sleep and driven half mad with a sudden, incomprehensible terror, and with no idea where to turn or where to look for safety. Some ran straight into the waiting Yasnogorians, bewildered, disoriented and confused about the direction from which the attack had come, and died under the sabers, scythes and axes before they caught their breath. Others hacked and stabbed their own comrades blindly in the darkness.

Yet others—barely covered with scraps of clothing snatched up on the run—stood hatless and unarmed with their hands raised high into the air or threw themselves face down on the ground and waited for death without offering resistance. A small group tried to fight and defend itself but a dark, panic-stricken mob of their own companions swept over them, hurled them down, and trampled them as it fled. The groans of the dying and the howls for mercy added to this terrible chorale of terror and confusion.

But a real frenzy swept over the assaulted victims when they realized at last where their unexpected killers came from in the first place: not from the side of the fortification that faced the monastery but, unbelievably, out of their own main camp! Someone screamed out that it was their allied Polish regiments that had turned on them and attacked them, and mobs of fleeing, terror-stricken musketeers and pikemen leaped off the sheer walls of their entrenchment and ran, as if for shelter, towards Yasna Gora. But soon fresh yells signaled another disaster as they stumbled into Yanitch's detachment which hunted and cut them down to the last man along the monastery slope.

Meanwhile the Yasnogorians had swept over the Swedish batteries. Men detailed in advance with iron spikes and mallets attacked the silent cannon and started hammering the spikes into the touch-holes while the rest went on with the slaughter. The peasant scythemen who wouldn't have been able to stand up to armed regulars in the open field now threw themselves in small groups against entire clusters.

The fearless Horn, who saved the day in many German battles, tried to rally the scattered cannoneers around him. He leaped up on the sloped angle of the battery revetment where everyone could see him, calling to his men and waving his rapier. The Swedes recognized him and crowded to his side but a swarm of attackers followed on their heels, friend and enemy being packed so tightly together that no one could tell one from the other.

"To me! To me!" Horn shouted. "Rally! Rally!"

But suddenly the hiss of a scythe sweeping through the air cut him short in mid-word. His gathering troopers broke and fled into the darkness. Kmita and Pan Tcharnyetzki with several dozen others threw themselves on the shattered fugitives and finished them all.

The bastion was taken.

The trumpets were already calling the troops to arms in the main Swedish camp, and the monastery's artillery shot off a salvo of firebombs to light the way back for the returning raiders. They hurried up the slope, panting and splashed with blood, like wolves running from pursuit by hunters after slaughtering a sheepfold. Pan Tcharnyetzki led them and Kmita closed the rear. In half an hour they joined up with Yanitch's detachment but the old Magyar wasn't there to greet them. His own men shot him by mistake when he chased too far into the darkness after some officer.

The raiders returned to the monastery amid the roar of cannon and in the red glare of the muzzle blasts. Father Kordetzki waited for them at the sally-port, counting each head as it appeared in the narrow cleft, but Yanitch was the only casualty of the night. Two men went out shortly afterwards to bring in his body because the Prior wished to honor him with a proper burial.

The night's silence, however, was broken beyond recall. The monastery walls spewed fire until dawn. The Swedish siege lines fell victim to uncontrollable disorder. Unable to tell in the chaos exactly what happened, assuming that a relieving army had come to aid the fortress and expecting powerful attacks from everywhere at once, the enemy fled from all their advanced positions. Entire regiments fell back, retreated without orders, and wandered about in desperate confusion until daylight, often taking their own men for enemies and opening fire on their own formations. Even as far to the rear as the main encampment, officers and soldiers grouped outside their tents on the point of panic, listening to garbled and terrifying rumors and waiting for that dreadful night to end.

Mueller, Sadovski, the Prince of Hesse, Veyhard and all the other senior officers made superhuman efforts to restore discipline and order to their demoralized regiments but to small avail. Their cannon shot off hundreds of firebombs to put an end to that confusing darkness but it would take the bright glare of daylight before their scattered forces calmed down and returned to their positions.

★ ★ ★

But at last the chaos-laden night came to its merciful end. Silence returned to Yasna Gora and to the Swedish earthworks. Daylight began to whiten the tops of the church spires, the monastery roofs regained the scarlet hues of their bricks and tiles, and light seeped back to the countryside below.

Mueller and his staff rode to the scene of the night's disaster. The old general knew that the monastery gunners would probably catch sight of him and his suite on that exposed bastion and might open fire but he ignored the danger. He had to see the damage for himself and count all his losses with his own eyes. His staff rode behind him, just as heartsick and horrified as he; their faces were as solemn as if they were following a funeral cortege.

They dismounted at the foot of the rear glacis and continued the rest of the way on foot, following more or less the path taken by the raiders. Evidence of the furious fighting lay everywhere around them: among the mute, spiked cannon in their ruined revetments, in the toppled shelters and torn canvas trampled underfoot and, lower down, amid the still lines of silent, empty tents and the stacks of corpses.

The piles of slaughtered men were particularly shocking; half naked, dressed in sodden rags, with blind staring eyes fixed on their own last moment of unutterable terror, they were clearly torn out of a deep sleep and killed before they realized that their sudden nightmare wasn't just a dream. Many of them were barefoot, few clutched a rapier in their lifeless hands, almost none wore helmets or any kind of headgear. Many were piled just inside their tents, having wakened barely enough to scramble off their cots and make for the exit; others littered the ground between the tents, killed as they tried to find refuge in the darkness.

There were so many dead piled upon each other in so many places that they resembled the aftermath of some cataclysmic, natural disaster. Some sort of deadly plague came to mind at first sight. But the deep wounds carved into their chests and faces, and the scorched features in which grains of gunpowder, fired at such close range that they didn't have the time to burn away, testified all too clearly that this was the work of human hands, not nature.

Mueller climbed higher. His cannon stood mutely in their embrassures, as useless as dead logs. The body of a cannoneer lay draped over one of them, cut almost in half by a terrible scythe-stroke, and staining the gun carriage and the ground beneath it with a pool of blood which had already started to congeal in that wintry air.

The general said nothing. He noted everything as carefully and as grimly as if he were performing a routine inspection and none of his officers dared to break his silence.

What could they say in any event?

How could they offer any consolation to their veteran commander who had sustained such a terrible defeat through his own underestimation of his enemy? A novice, fighting his first engagement, couldn't have shown greater miscalculation.

This was, they knew, not only a defeat but a disgrace as well. Because hadn't the general himself called that defiant third-rate fortress a chicken coop? Didn't he say that he'd crush it in his fingers like a clod of earth? Didn't he have nine thousand regulars under his command while over there, behind those puny walls, crouched a mere two hundred defenders?

And if that wasn't enough to humiliate him and ruin his reputation, wasn't he a soldier, an acknowledged master of his trade, while his opponents were a flock of monks?

For Mueller, the new day promised some harsh and difficult hours.

Meanwhile an infantry company had arrived and started carrying out the dead. Four of them bore a corpse on a sheet of canvas and halted before the General without a command.

Mueller glanced down and turned his eyes away.

"... De Fossis," he murmured.

The four pikemen had barely moved away when another stretcher party appeared in the near distance. This time Sadovski walked out to meet them and called back: "It's Horn they are carrying!"

The fearless Horn was still alive and he would suffer many days of torment. The peasant who had cut him down reached him with just the tip of his scythe, but the blow opened up his entire chest. Horn was still conscious. Catching sight of Mueller and the staff he smiled and tried to speak but his voice came out in a strangled hiss. Then pink froth bubbled out of his mouth, his red eyelids quivered and he slid into a silent darkness.

"Carry him to my tent!" Mueller ordered sharply. "Let my own surgeon look after him at once!" And then the officers heard him murmuring dully to himself: "Horn... Horn... I saw him last night in a dream... Ah, who can understand this? Who can explain such things?"

* * *

He fixed his eyes on the ground at his feet and stood deep in thought when suddenly Sadovski's frightened voice pulled him out of his gloomy introspection.

"General! General! Look, Your Excellency! There... Over there...! The monastery...!"

Mueller glanced up and then stared astonished. The morning was already bright with the full light of day. The last of the night's shadows were gone and only a few pale streamers of mist drifted above the ground. But the sky overhead was clear, pink with the last glows of sunrise, and promising sunny weather. A white layer of rising fog clung to the walls of Yasna Gora, as it did each morning, but rather than shrouding the entire church as it drifted upward, it seemed to lift it into the sky. Some quirk of nature or an optical illusion made it appear as if the church and its spire weren't merely protruding from the fog but soaring high above the rock and the mist itself, rising higher and higher as if they'd broken free of their foundations, and drifting free under the pinkish sky.

The shouts of nearby soldiers showed that they too had spotted the phenomenon.

"That's just the fog that's causing the illusion!" Mueller shouted.

"The fog is under the church, not over it," Sadovski observed.

"It's an amazing thing," said the Prince of Hesse. "But I'd swear this church is ten times taller than it was yesterday and that it's hanging in the air."

"It's rising! It's going up!" the soldiers were shouting all along the earthwall. "It's going to vanish...!"

Again, whatever the cause of the illusion, the banks of fog on which the church was seated started to boil upward, shooting straight up into the sky like a column of mysterious smoke, while the gleaming structure perched on its billowing summit seemed to lift and soar right along with it. Up and up it went, sweeping ever higher in its own white cocoon of mist that blazed with reflected sunlight, while at the same time it began to dwindle and dissolve in the wispy haze until, at last, it disappeared from sight.

Mueller's eyes showed amazement and superstitious fear as he turned to his officers. "I must say, gentlemen," he said. "That I've never seen anything quite like this before. It makes no natural sense. I don't understand it. Unless, of course, we're willing to talk about Papist witchcraft...?"

"I've heard the soldiers asking how are we to bombard this kind of a fortress?" Sadovski said and then went on to ask in his own right: "How indeed? I'm at a loss myself!"

"But what comes next, gentlemen?" the Prince of Hesse cried out. "Does anyone care to risk a wager? Is that church still in that fog up there or isn't it?"

★ ★ ★

They stood in a wondering and uneasy silence for several minutes longer.

"Even if there is a natural answer for this phenomenon," the Prince said at last. "I don't see it as a good sign for us. Just think gentlemen! In all the time we've been here, we haven't moved a single step forward!"

"Forward?" Sadovski shook his head. "I'd settle for standing still, never mind moving forward! The truth is that we've suffered one setback after another and last night's was the worst. The men are disheartened. They're losing their spirit and they're starting to drag their heels. You can't imagine what they're saying in the regiments. And there are other strange things that've started happening..."

"Such as what?" Mueller snapped.

"For quite some time none of our men have been able to go outside our lines alone or even in twos or threes. Those that do simply disappear. You'd think we had wolves circling Tchenstohova. I sent an ensign and three men to Vyelun not so long ago, to fetch me some warm clothing, and that's the last I've seen of them."

"It'll be even worse when Winter gets here,"added the Prince of Hesse. "Even now the nights are intolerably cold."

"The fog is thinning out!" Mueller interrupted.

A sharp wind started gusting across the plain and tugging at the mist. Something stirred dimly in the fog clustered about the hilltop, shapes hardened and acquired texture, and suddenly the air above Yasna Gora was clear, the hard-edged planes and angles of the monastery took their old form again, and everything stood where it did before. The fortress was as still and silent as if no one lived there.

"General," the Prince of Hesse said urgently. "You must try new negotiations. We have to bring this to an end!"

"And if the talks fail?" Mueller asked gloomily. "Will you advise that we drop the siege?"

The officers fell silent. Some time passed before Sadovski found his voice. "Your Excellency knows best what you should do," he murmured.

"Yes I do!" Mueller snarled, snatching at the remnants of his dignity. "And I'll tell you this much: I curse the day I came here,"—and here he aimed a poisonous glare at Veyhard—"along with the advisors who instigated this... this siege! But I won't leave this place, I tell you, not after everything that's happened, until I've turned it into a pile of rubble or die here myself!"

A grimace of distaste passed across the face of the Prince of Hesse. He seldom bothered to hide his disdain for Mueller whose coarse-grained violence set his teeth on edge. But those vainglorious words, spoken in that ruined battery beside those spiked guns—and in the silent presence of so many cruelly slaughtered soldiers—were particularly offensive. Crude boasts and empty posturing, he thought, wouldn't resurrect the dead.

"Your Excellency is in no position to make such promises," he drawled with contempt. "You'll lift the siege the moment His Majesty or Field Marshal Wittemberg order you to do so. And sometimes circumstances issue their own orders."

Mueller narrowed his bushy brows in fury and Veyhard took a quick step forward to ease the dangerous the tension.

"In the meantime let's try negotiations!"he urged desperately. "They'll have to surrender! They must!"

* * *

The cheerful sound of bells ringing out the signal for morning prayer in the church of Yasna Gora broke into whatever else he wanted to say. The General and his staff rode slowly towards Tchenstohova. But they were still some distance away from headquarters when a courier-officer galloped up on a foam-spattered horse.

"That must be from Field Marshal Wittemberg!" Mueller said.

Meanwhile the officer handed him a letter which he tore open with impatient fingers and scanned at a glance while a look of embarrassment and confusion spread across his features.

"No," he said uneasily. "It's a report from Poznan... Bad news, I'm afraid. The gentry is up in arms throughout Vyelk-opolska, the common people are joining the rebellion. They say they want to relieve Tchenstohova..."

"I said that these shots will echo from the Carpathians to the Baltic," Sadovski observed. "This nation can change at a moment's notice. You don't know the Poles yet but you'll get to know them soon enough."

"Good!" Mueller snarled. "So we'll get to know them. I'd rather have an open enemy than a treacherous ally, any day! They came over to us of their own free will and now they're taking arms against us, are they? Good, they'll get a taste of our arms as well!"

"And we'll get a bellyful of theirs," Sadovski barked back. "General, let's finish with this sorry business at once! Let's accept whatever terms the monks offer us! It's no longer just a question of taking a fortress but whether His Majesty can rule in this country!"

"The monks will give up," Veyhard clung to his single-minded notion with the desperate persistence of a drowning man. "Today, tomorrow... they have to!"

* * *

Meanwhile the monastery echoed with sounds of joy and celebration. Its whole population poured out of the church after the morning prayers. Those who hadn't taken part in the sally questioned those who did and the participants let fly all their imaginations, boasting shamelessly about their own achievements and the disaster they inflicted on the enemy.

Curiosity overcame all caution. The priests and the women

flocked to the walls to peer down at the site of the night's success. Their snowy habits and multicolored dresses turned the grim bastions into a glittering meadow. The women crowded around Pan Tcharnyetzki, calling him 'Our Savior! Our protector!' while he made half-hearted motions to defend himself, especially when they seized his hands and started to cover them with kisses.

"He's the one to thank!" he cried and pointed at Kmita. "His name may be Babinitch but he's no *Baba*, believe me! He won't let you kiss his hands because they're still bloody, but if some young woman wants to plant a nice one on his mouth he won't put up much of a fight, I'm sure!"

The younger girls did throw some curious and inviting glances at Pan Andrei, admiring his handsome face, his strong, straight-backed figure and his highborn bearing, but he offered them no encouragement. The girls reminded him too sharply of Olenka.

'*Hey there, my sweet one,*' he mused. '*If only you knew that I'm now a soldier of the Holy Mother, fighting Her battles against those enemies whom I served before at such terrible cost to both of us...*'

And he told himself that he would write to her as soon as the siege was over and have Soroka take the letter to her in Keydany.

"I've more than words and promises to offer her now," he murmured to himself. "I've some deeds to vouch for me as well. Let her know that it's all her doing and let her find some joy in the new life she gave me."

He was so moved by this thought that he didn't even notice the disappointed girls who moved away, saying to each other: "Yes, he's a handsome cavalier... But what's the use? It looks like all he cares about is war."

BALTIC SEA
SWEDISH POMERANIA
BRANDENBURG
HOLY ROMAN EMPIRE
HUNGARY
TRANSYLVANIA
COURLAND
ZMUDYA
ELECTORAL PRUSSIA
MAZOVIA
VYELKOPOLSKA
BYELOVYEZHA
POLESYE
KINGDOM OF POLAND
MALOPOLSKA
Ryga
Saulas
Upita
Memel
Rosyen
Taurogen
Keydany
Vilkomir
Tilsit
Kovno
Koenigsberg
Gdansk
Malbork
Elk
Grodno
Prostki
Njemen R.
Pila
Uistye
Poznan
Tiketain
Narev R.
Bialystok
Vistula R.
Warta R.
Vilkov
Kalish
Warsaw
Lukov
Brest
Varka
Syeradz
Bug R.
Lublin
Tchenstohova
Sandomir
Zamost
Opole
Krakow
San R.
Zhivyetz
Novy Targ
Lvov
Dniestr R.
Lubovla
N
S
E
W